Frankenstein;

or,

THE MODERN PROMETHEUS

Frankenstein;

or,

THE MODERN PROMETHEUS

MARY SHELLEY

Bounty
Books

Frankenstein was first published in Great Britain in 1818

This edition published in 2015 by Bounty Books,
a division of Octopus Publishing Group Ltd
Carmelite House
50 Victoria Embankment
London, EC4Y 0DZ
www.octopusbooks.co.uk

An Hachette UK Company
www.hachette.co.uk

Design and arrangement © Octopus Publishing Group Ltd 2015

ISBN: 978-0-7537-2971-7

A CIP catalogue record for this book is available from the
British Library

Printed and bound in the United Kingdom
10 9 8 7 6 5 4 3 2 1

PREFACE

The event on which this fiction is founded has been supposed, by Dr. Darwin, and some of the physiological writers of Germany, as not of impossible occurrence. I shall not be supposed as according the remotest degree of serious faith to such an imagination; yet, in assuming it as the basis of a work of fancy, I have not considered myself as merely weaving a series of supernatural terrors. The event on which the interest of the story depends is exempt from the disadvantages of a mere tale of spectres or enchantment. It was recommended by the novelty of the situations which it developes; and, however impossible as a physical fact, affords a point of view to the imagination for the delineating of human passions more comprehensive and commanding than any which the ordinary relations of existing events can yield.

I have thus endeavoured to preserve the truth of the elementary principles of human nature, while I have not scrupled to innovate upon their combinations. *The Iliad*, the tragic poetry of Greece – Shakspeare, in the *Tempest* and *Midsummer Night's Dream* – and most especially Milton, in *Paradise Lost*, conform to this rule; and the most humble novelist, who seeks to confer or receive amusement from his labours, may, without presumption, apply to prose fiction a licence, or rather a rule, from the adoption of which so many exquisite combinations of human feeling have resulted in the highest specimens of poetry.

The circumstance on which my story rests was suggested in casual conversation. It was commenced partly as a source of amusement, and partly as an expedient for exercising any untried resources of mind. Other motives were mingled with these as the work proceeded. I am by no means indifferent to the manner in which whatever moral tendencies exist in the sentiments or characters it contains shall affect the reader; yet my chief concern in this respect has been limited to the avoiding the enervating effects of the novels of the present day and to the exhibition of the amiableness of domestic affection, and the excellence of universal virtue. The opinions which naturally spring from the character and situation of the hero are by no means to be conceived as existing always in my own conviction; nor is any inference justly to be drawn from the following pages as prejudicing any philosophical doctrine of whatever kind.

It is a subject also of additional interest to the author that this story was begun in the majestic region where the scene is principally laid, and in society which cannot cease to be regretted. I passed the summer of 1816 in the environs of Geneva. The season was cold and rainy, and in the evenings we crowded around a blazing wood fire, and occasionally amused ourselves with some German stories of ghosts, which happened to fall into our hands. These tales excited in us a playful desire of imitation. Two other friends (a tale from the pen of one of whom would be far more acceptable to the public than anything I can ever hope to produce) and myself agreed to write each a story founded on some supernatural occurrence.

The weather, however, suddenly became serene; and my two friends left me on a journey among the Alps, and lost, in the magnificent scenes which they present, all memory of their ghostly visions. The following tale is the only one which has been completed.

MARLOW, September 1817.

Letter 1

St. Petersburgh, Dec. 11th, 17 –

You will rejoice to hear that no disaster has accompanied the commencement of an enterprise which you have regarded with such evil forebodings. I arrived here yesterday, and my first task is to assure my dear sister of my welfare and increasing confidence in the success of my undertaking.

I am already far north of London, and as I walk in the streets of Petersburgh, I feel a cold northern breeze play upon my cheeks, which braces my nerves and fills me with delight. Do you understand this feeling? This breeze, which has travelled from the regions towards which I am advancing, gives me a foretaste of those icy climes. Inspirited by this wind of promise, my daydreams become more fervent and vivid. I try in vain to be persuaded that the pole is the seat of frost and desolation; it ever presents itself to my imagination as the region of beauty and delight. There, Margaret, the sun is forever visible, its broad disk just skirting the horizon and diffusing a perpetual splendour. There – for with your leave, my sister, I will put some trust in preceding navigators – there snow and frost are banished; and, sailing over a calm sea, we may be wafted to a land surpassing in wonders and in beauty every region hitherto discovered on the habitable globe. Its productions and features may be without example, as the phenomena of the heavenly bodies undoubtedly are in those undiscovered solitudes. What may not be expected in a country of eternal light? I may there discover the wondrous power which attracts the needle and may regulate a thousand celestial observations that require only this voyage to render their seeming eccentricities consistent forever. I shall satiate my ardent curiosity with the sight of a part of the world never before visited, and may tread a land never before imprinted by the foot of man. These are my enticements, and they are sufficient to conquer all fear of danger or death and to induce me to commence this labourious voyage with the joy a child feels when he embarks in a little boat, with his holiday mates, on an expedition of discovery up his native river. But supposing all these

1

conjectures to be false, you cannot contest the inestimable benefit which I shall confer on all mankind, to the last generation, by discovering a passage near the pole to those countries, to reach which at present so many months are requisite; or by ascertaining the secret of the magnet, which, if at all possible, can only be effected by an undertaking such as mine.

These reflections have dispelled the agitation with which I began my letter, and I feel my heart glow with an enthusiasm which elevates me to heaven, for nothing contributes so much to tranquillize the mind as a steady purpose – a point on which the soul may fix its intellectual eye. This expedition has been the favourite dream of my early years. I have read with ardour the accounts of the various voyages which have been made in the prospect of arriving at the North Pacific Ocean through the seas which surround the pole. You may remember that a history of all the voyages made for purposes of discovery composed the whole of our good Uncle Thomas' library. My education was neglected, yet I was passionately fond of reading. These volumes were my study day and night, and my familiarity with them increased that regret which I had felt, as a child, on learning that my father's dying injunction had forbidden my uncle to allow me to embark in a seafaring life.

These visions faded when I perused, for the first time, those poets whose effusions entranced my soul and lifted it to heaven. I also became a poet and for one year lived in a paradise of my own creation; I imagined that I also might obtain a niche in the temple where the names of Homer and Shakespeare are consecrated. You are well acquainted with my failure and how heavily I bore the disappointment. But just at that time I inherited the fortune of my cousin, and my thoughts were turned into the channel of their earlier bent.

Six years have passed since I resolved on my present undertaking. I can, even now, remember the hour from which I dedicated myself to this great enterprise. I commenced by inuring my body to hardship. I accompanied the whale-fishers on several expeditions to the North Sea; I voluntarily endured cold, famine, thirst, and want of sleep; I often worked harder than the common sailors during the day and devoted my nights to the study of mathematics, the theory of medicine, and those branches of physical science from which a naval adventurer might derive the greatest practical advantage. Twice I actually hired myself as an under-mate in a

Greenland whaler, and acquitted myself to admiration. I must own I felt a little proud when my captain offered me the second dignity in the vessel and entreated me to remain with the greatest earnestness, so valuable did he consider my services.

And now, dear Margaret, do I not deserve to accomplish some great purpose? My life might have been passed in ease and luxury, but I preferred glory to every enticement that wealth placed in my path. Oh, that some encouraging voice would answer in the affirmative! My courage and my resolution is firm; but my hopes fluctuate, and my spirits are often depressed. I am about to proceed on a long and difficult voyage, the emergencies of which will demand all my fortitude: I am required not only to raise the spirits of others, but sometimes to sustain my own, when theirs are failing.

This is the most favourable period for travelling in Russia. They fly quickly over the snow in their sledges; the motion is pleasant, and, in my opinion, far more agreeable than that of an English stagecoach. The cold is not excessive, if you are wrapped in furs – a dress which I have already adopted, for there is a great difference between walking the deck and remaining seated motionless for hours, when no exercise prevents the blood from actually freezing in your veins. I have no ambition to lose my life on the post-road between St. Petersburgh and Archangel.

I shall depart for the latter town in a fortnight or three weeks; and my intention is to hire a ship there, which can easily be done by paying the insurance for the owner, and to engage as many sailors as I think necessary among those who are accustomed to the whale-fishing. I do not intend to sail until the month of June; and when shall I return? Ah, dear sister, how can I answer this question? If I succeed, many, many months, perhaps years, will pass before you and I may meet. If I fail, you will see me again soon, or never.

Farewell, my dear, excellent Margaret. Heaven shower down blessings on you, and save me, that I may again and again testify my gratitude for all your love and kindness.

Your affectionate brother,

R. Walton

Letter 2

TO MRS. SAVILLE, ENGLAND

Archangel, 28th March, 17 –

How slowly the time passes here, encompassed as I am by frost and snow! Yet a second step is taken towards my enterprise. I have hired a vessel and am occupied in collecting my sailors; those whom I have already engaged appear to be men on whom I can depend and are certainly possessed of dauntless courage.

But I have one want which I have never yet been able to satisfy, and the absence of the object of which I now feel as a most severe evil. I have no friend, Margaret: when I am glowing with the enthusiasm of success, there will be none to participate my joy; if I am assailed by disappointment, no one will endeavour to sustain me in dejection. I shall commit my thoughts to paper, it is true; but that is a poor medium for the communication of feeling. I desire the company of a man who could sympathize with me, whose eyes would reply to mine. You may deem me romantic, my dear sister, but I bitterly feel the want of a friend. I have no one near me, gentle yet courageous, possessed of a cultivated as well as of a capacious mind, whose tastes are like my own, to approve or amend my plans. How would such a friend repair the faults of your poor brother! I am too ardent in execution and too impatient of difficulties. But it is a still greater evil to me that I am self-educated: for the first fourteen years of my life I ran wild on a common and read nothing but our Uncle Thomas' books of voyages. At that age I became acquainted with the celebrated poets of our own country; but it was only when it had ceased to be in my power to derive its most important benefits from such a conviction that I perceived the necessity of becoming acquainted with more languages than that of my native country. Now I am twenty-eight and am in reality more illiterate than many schoolboys of fifteen. It is true that I have thought more and that my daydreams are more extended and magnificent, but they want (as the painters call it) 'keeping'; and I greatly need a friend who would have sense enough not to despise me as romantic, and affection enough for me to endeavour to regulate my mind.

Well, these are useless complaints; I shall certainly find no friend on the wide ocean, nor even here in Archangel, among merchants and seamen. Yet some feelings, unallied to the dross of human nature, beat even in these rugged bosoms. My lieutenant, for instance, is a man of wonderful courage and enterprise; he is madly desirous of glory, or rather, to word my phrase more characteristically, of advancement in his profession. He is an Englishman, and in the midst of national and professional prejudices, unsoftened by cultivation, retains some of the noblest endowments of humanity. I first became acquainted with him on board a whale vessel; finding that he was unemployed in this city, I easily engaged him to assist in my enterprise.

The master is a person of an excellent disposition and is remarkable in the ship for his gentleness and the mildness of his discipline. This circumstance, added to his well-known integrity and dauntless courage, made me very desirous to engage him. A youth passed in solitude, my best years spent under your gentle and feminine fosterage, has so refined the groundwork of my character that I cannot overcome an intense distaste to the usual brutality exercised on board ship: I have never believed it to be necessary, and when I heard of a mariner equally noted for his kindliness of heart and the respect and obedience paid to him by his crew, I felt myself peculiarly fortunate in being able to secure his services. I heard of him first in rather a romantic manner, from a lady who owes to him the happiness of her life. This, briefly, is his story. Some years ago he loved a young Russian lady of moderate fortune, and having amassed a considerable sum in prize-money, the father of the girl consented to the match. He saw his mistress once before the destined ceremony; but she was bathed in tears, and throwing herself at his feet, entreated him to spare her, confessing at the same time that she loved another, but that he was poor, and that her father would never consent to the union. My generous friend reassured the suppliant, and on being informed of the name of her lover, instantly abandoned his pursuit. He had already bought a farm with his money, on which he had designed to pass the remainder of his life; but he bestowed the whole on his rival, together with the remains of his prize-money to purchase stock, and then himself solicited the young woman's father to consent to her marriage with her lover. But the old man decidedly refused, thinking himself bound in honour to my friend, who, when he found the father inexorable, quitted his country, nor returned until he heard that his former mistress was married according to her inclinations. 'What a noble fellow!'

you will exclaim. He is so; but then he is wholly uneducated: he is as silent as a Turk, and a kind of ignorant carelessness attends him, which, while it renders his conduct the more astonishing, detracts from the interest and sympathy which otherwise he would command.

Yet do not suppose, because I complain a little or because I can conceive a consolation for my toils which I may never know, that I am wavering in my resolutions. Those are as fixed as fate, and my voyage is only now delayed until the weather shall permit my embarkation. The winter has been dreadfully severe, but the spring promises well, and it is considered as a remarkably early season, so that perhaps I may sail sooner than I expected. I shall do nothing rashly: you know me sufficiently to confide in my prudence and considerateness whenever the safety of others is committed to my care.

I cannot describe to you my sensations on the near prospect of my undertaking. It is impossible to communicate to you a conception of the trembling sensation, half pleasurable and half fearful, with which I am preparing to depart. I am going to unexplored regions, to 'the land of mist and snow,' but I shall kill no albatross; therefore do not be alarmed for my safety or if I should come back to you as worn and woeful as the 'Ancient Mariner.' You will smile at my allusion, but I will disclose a secret. I have often attributed my attachment to, my passionate enthusiasm for, the dangerous mysteries of ocean to that production of the most imaginative of modern poets. There is something at work in my soul which I do not understand. I am practically industrious – painstaking, a workman to execute with perseverance and labour – but besides this there is a love for the marvellous, a belief in the marvellous, intertwined in all my projects, which hurries me out of the common pathways of men, even to the wild sea and unvisited regions I am about to explore.

But to return to dearer considerations. Shall I meet you again, after having traversed immense seas, and returned by the most southern cape of Africa or America? I dare not expect such success, yet I cannot bear to look on the reverse of the picture. Continue for the present to write to me by every opportunity: I may receive your letters on some occasions when I need them most to support my spirits. I love you very tenderly. Remember me with affection, should you never hear from me again.

Your affectionate brother,
    Robert Walton

Letter 3

TO MRS. SAVILLE, ENGLAND

July 7th, 17 –

My dear Sister,

I write a few lines in haste to say that I am safe – and well advanced on my voyage. This letter will reach England by a merchantman now on its homeward voyage from Archangel; more fortunate than I, who may not see my native land, perhaps, for many years. I am, however, in good spirits: my men are bold and apparently firm of purpose, nor do the floating sheets of ice that continually pass us, indicating the dangers of the region towards which we are advancing, appear to dismay them. We have already reached a very high latitude; but it is the height of summer, and although not so warm as in England, the southern gales, which blow us speedily towards those shores which I so ardently desire to attain, breathe a degree of renovating warmth which I had not expected.

No incidents have hitherto befallen us that would make a figure in a letter. One or two stiff gales and the springing of a leak are accidents which experienced navigators scarcely remember to record, and I shall be well content if nothing worse happen to us during our voyage.

Adieu, my dear Margaret. Be assured that for my own sake, as well as yours, I will not rashly encounter danger. I will be cool, persevering, and prudent.

But success 'shall' crown my endeavours. Wherefore not? Thus far I have gone, tracing a secure way over the pathless seas, the very stars themselves being witnesses and testimonies of my triumph. Why not still proceed over the untamed yet obedient element? What can stop the determined heart and resolved will of man?

My swelling heart involuntarily pours itself out thus. But I must finish. Heaven bless my beloved sister!

R.W.

Letter 4

TO MRS. SAVILLE, ENGLAND

August 5th, 17 –

So strange an accident has happened to us that I cannot forbear recording it, although it is very probable that you will see me before these papers can come into your possession.

Last Monday (July 31st) we were nearly surrounded by ice, which closed in the ship on all sides, scarcely leaving her the sea-room in which she floated. Our situation was somewhat dangerous, especially as we were compassed round by a very thick fog. We accordingly lay to, hoping that some change would take place in the atmosphere and weather.

About two o'clock the mist cleared away, and we beheld, stretched out in every direction, vast and irregular plains of ice, which seemed to have no end. Some of my comrades groaned, and my own mind began to grow watchful with anxious thoughts, when a strange sight suddenly attracted our attention and diverted our solicitude from our own situation. We perceived a low carriage, fixed on a sledge and drawn by dogs, pass on towards the north, at the distance of half a mile; a being which had the shape of a man, but apparently of gigantic stature, sat in the sledge and guided the dogs. We watched the rapid progress of the traveller with our telescopes until he was lost among the distant inequalities of the ice.

This appearance excited our unqualified wonder. We were, as we believed, many hundred miles from any land; but this apparition seemed to denote that it was not, in reality, so distant as we had supposed. Shut in, however, by ice, it was impossible to follow his track, which we had observed with the greatest attention.

About two hours after this occurrence we heard the ground sea, and before night the ice broke and freed our ship. We, however, lay to until the morning, fearing to encounter in the dark those large loose masses which float about after the breaking up of the ice. I profited of this time to rest for a few hours.

In the morning, however, as soon as it was light, I went upon deck and found all the sailors busy on one side of the vessel, apparently talking to someone in the sea. It was, in fact, a sledge, like that we had seen before, which had drifted towards us in the night on a large fragment of ice. Only one dog remained alive; but there was a human being within it whom the sailors were persuading to enter the vessel. He was not, as the other traveller seemed to be, a savage inhabitant of some undiscovered island, but a European. When I appeared on deck the master said, 'Here is our captain, and he will not allow you to perish on the open sea.'

On perceiving me, the stranger addressed me in English, although with a foreign accent. 'Before I come on board your vessel,' said he, 'will you have the kindness to inform me whither you are bound?'

You may conceive my astonishment on hearing such a question addressed to me from a man on the brink of destruction and to whom I should have supposed that my vessel would have been a resource which he would not have exchanged for the most precious wealth the earth can afford. I replied, however, that we were on a voyage of discovery towards the northern pole.

Upon hearing this he appeared satisfied and consented to come on board. Good God! Margaret, if you had seen the man who thus capitulated for his safety, your surprise would have been boundless. His limbs were nearly frozen, and his body dreadfully emaciated by fatigue and suffering. I never saw a man in so wretched a condition. We attempted to carry him into the cabin, but as soon as he had quitted the fresh air he fainted. We accordingly brought him back to the deck and restored him to animation by rubbing him with brandy and forcing him to swallow a small quantity. As soon as he showed signs of life we wrapped him up in blankets and placed him near the chimney of the kitchen stove. By slow degrees he recovered and ate a little soup, which restored him wonderfully.

Two days passed in this manner before he was able to speak, and I often feared that his sufferings had deprived him of understanding. When he had in some measure recovered, I removed him to my own cabin and attended on him as much as my duty would permit. I never saw a more interesting creature: his eyes have generally an expression of wildness, and even madness, but there are moments when, if anyone performs an act of kindness towards him or does him the most trifling service, his whole countenance is lighted up, as it were, with a beam of benevolence and sweetness that I never saw equalled. But he is generally melancholy and despairing, and sometimes he gnashes his teeth, as if impatient of the weight of woes that oppresses him.

When my guest was a little recovered I had great trouble to keep off the men, who wished to ask him a thousand questions; but I would not allow him to be tormented by their idle curiosity, in a state of body and mind whose restoration evidently depended upon entire repose. Once, however, the lieutenant asked why he had come so far upon the ice in so strange a vehicle.

His countenance instantly assumed an aspect of the deepest gloom, and he replied, 'To seek one who fled from me.'

'And did the man whom you pursued travel in the same fashion?'

'Yes.'

'Then I fancy we have seen him, for the day before we picked you up we saw some dogs drawing a sledge, with a man in it, across the ice.'

This aroused the stranger's attention, and he asked a multitude of questions concerning the route which the demon, as he called him, had pursued. Soon after, when he was alone with me, he said, 'I have, doubtless, excited your curiosity, as well as that of these good people; but you are too considerate to make inquiries.'

'Certainly; it would indeed be very impertinent and inhuman of me to trouble you with any inquisitiveness of mine.'

'And yet you rescued me from a strange and perilous situation; you have benevolently restored me to life.'

Soon after this he inquired if I thought that the breaking up of the ice had destroyed the other sledge. I replied that I could not answer with any degree of certainty, for the ice had not broken until near midnight, and the traveller might have arrived at a place of safety before that time; but of this I could not judge.

From this time a new spirit of life animated the decaying frame of the stranger. He manifested the greatest eagerness to be upon deck to watch for the sledge which had before appeared; but I have persuaded him to remain in the cabin, for he is far too weak to sustain the rawness of the atmosphere. I have promised that someone should watch for him and give him instant notice if any new object should appear in sight.

Such is my journal of what relates to this strange occurrence up to the present day. The stranger has gradually improved in health but is very silent and appears uneasy when anyone except myself enters his cabin. Yet his manners are so conciliating and gentle that the sailors are all interested in him, although they have had very little communication with him. For my own part, I begin to love him as a brother, and his constant and deep grief fills me with sympathy and compassion. He must have been a noble creature in his better days, being even now in wreck so attractive and amiable.

I said in one of my letters, my dear Margaret, that I should find no friend on the wide ocean; yet I have found a man who, before his spirit had been broken by misery, I should have been happy to have possessed as the brother of my heart.

I shall continue my journal concerning the stranger at intervals, should I have any fresh incidents to record.

August 13th, 17 –

My affection for my guest increases every day. He excites at once my admiration and my pity to an astonishing degree. How can I see so noble a creature destroyed by misery without feeling the most poignant grief? He is so gentle, yet so wise; his mind is so cultivated, and when he speaks, although his words are culled with the choicest art, yet they flow with rapidity and unparalleled eloquence.

He is now much recovered from his illness and is continually on the deck, apparently watching for the sledge that preceded his own. Yet, although unhappy, he is not so utterly occupied by his own misery but that he interests himself deeply in the projects of others. He has frequently conversed with me on mine, which I have communicated to him without disguise. He entered attentively into all my arguments in favour of my eventual success and into every minute detail of the measures I had taken to secure it. I was easily led by the sympathy which he evinced to use the language of my heart, to give utterance to the burning ardour of my soul, and to say, with all the fervour that warmed me, how gladly I would sacrifice my fortune, my existence, my every hope, to the furtherance of my enterprise. One man's life or death were but a small price to pay for the acquirement of the knowledge which I sought, for the dominion I should acquire and transmit over the elemental foes of our race. As I spoke, a dark gloom spread over my listener's coun-tenance. At first I perceived that he tried to suppress his emotion; he placed his hands before his eyes, and my voice quivered and failed me as I beheld tears trickle fast from between his fingers; a groan burst from his heaving breast. I paused; at length he spoke, in broken accents: 'Unhappy man! Do you share my madness? Have you drunk also of the intoxicating draught? Hear me;

let me reveal my tale, and you will dash the cup from your lips!'

Such words, you may imagine, strongly excited my curiosity; but the paroxysm of grief that had seized the stranger overcame his weakened powers, and many hours of repose and tranquil conversation were necessary to restore his composure.

Having conquered the violence of his feelings, he appeared to despise himself for being the slave of passion; and quelling the dark tyranny of despair, he led me again to converse concerning myself personally. He asked me the history of my earlier years. The tale was quickly told, but it awakened various trains of reflection. I spoke of my desire of finding a friend, of my thirst for a more intimate sympathy with a fellow mind than had ever fallen to my lot, and expressed my conviction that a man could boast of little happiness who did not enjoy this blessing.

'I agree with you,' replied the stranger; 'we are unfashioned creatures, but half made up, if one wiser, better, dearer than ourselves – such a friend ought to be – do not lend his aid to perfectionate our weak and faulty natures. I once had a friend, the most noble of human creatures, and am entitled, therefore, to judge respecting friendship. You have hope, and the world before you, and have no cause for despair. But I – I have lost everything and cannot begin life anew.'

As he said this his countenance became expressive of a calm, settled grief that touched me to the heart. But he was silent and presently retired to his cabin.

Even broken in spirit as he is, no one can feel more deeply than he does the beauties of nature. The starry sky, the sea, and every sight afforded by these wonderful regions seem still to have the power of elevating his soul from earth. Such a man has a double existence: he may suffer misery and be overwhelmed by disappointments, yet when he has retired into himself, he will be like a celestial spirit that has a halo around him, within whose circle no grief or folly ventures.

Will you smile at the enthusiasm I express concerning this divine wanderer? You would not if you saw him. You have been tutored and refined by books and retirement from the world, and you are therefore somewhat fastidious; but this only renders you the more fit to appreciate the extraordinary merits of this wonderful man. Sometimes I have endeavoured to discover what quality it is which he possesses that elevates him so immeasurably above any other person I ever knew. I believe it to be an intuitive discernment, a quick but never-failing power of judgment, a penetration into the causes of things, unequalled for clearness and precision; add to this a facility of expression and a voice whose varied intonations are soul-subduing music.

August 19, 17 –

Yesterday the stranger said to me, 'You may easily perceive, Captain Walton, that I have suffered great and unparalleled misfortunes. I had determined at one time that the memory of these evils should die with me, but you have won me to alter my determination. You seek for knowledge and wisdom, as I once did; and I ardently hope that the gratification of your wishes may not be a serpent to sting you, as mine has been. I do not know that the relation of my disasters will be useful to you; yet, when I reflect that you are pursuing the same course, exposing yourself to the same dangers which have rendered me what I am, I imagine that you may deduce an apt moral from my tale, one that may direct you if you succeed in your undertaking and console you in case of failure. Prepare to hear of occurrences which are usually deemed marvellous. Were we among the tamer scenes of nature I might fear to encounter your unbelief, perhaps your ridicule; but many things will appear possible in these wild and mysterious regions which would provoke the laughter of those unacquainted with the ever-varied powers of nature; nor can I doubt but that my tale conveys in its series internal evidence of the truth of the events of which it is composed.'

You may easily imagine that I was much gratified by the offered communication, yet I could not endure that he should renew his grief by a recital of his misfortunes. I felt the greatest eagerness to hear the promised narrative, partly from curiosity and partly from a strong desire to ameliorate his fate if it were in my power. I expressed these feelings in my answer.

'I thank you,' he replied, 'for your sympathy, but it is useless; my fate is nearly fulfilled. I wait but for one event, and then I shall repose in peace. I understand your feeling,' continued he, perceiving that I wished to interrupt him; 'but you are mistaken, my friend, if thus you will allow me to name you; nothing can alter my destiny; listen to my history, and you will perceive how irrevocably it is determined.'

He then told me that he would commence his narrative the next day when I should be at leisure. This promise drew from me the warmest thanks. I have resolved every night, when I am not imperatively occupied by my duties, to record, as nearly as possible in his own words, what he has related during the day. If I should be engaged, I will at least make notes. This manuscript will doubtless afford you the greatest pleasure; but to me, who know him and who hear it from his own lips – with what interest and sympathy shall I read it in some future day! Even now, as I commence my task, his full-toned voice swells in my ears; his lustrous eyes dwell on me with all their melancholy sweetness; I see his thin hand raised in animation, while the lineaments of his face are irradiated by the soul within. Strange and harrowing must be his story, frightful the storm which embraced the gallant vessel on its course and wrecked it – thus!

CHAPTER I

I am by birth a Genevese, and my family is one of the most distinguished of that republic. My ancestors had been for many years counsellors and syndics, and my father had filled several public situations with honour and reputation. He was respected by all who knew him for his integrity and indefatigable attention to public business. He passed his younger days perpetually occupied by the affairs of his country; a variety of circumstances had prevented his marrying early, nor was it until the decline of life that he became a husband and the father of a family.

As the circumstances of his marriage illustrate his character, I cannot refrain from relating them. One of his most intimate friends was a merchant who, from a flourishing state, fell, through numerous mischances, into poverty. This man, whose name was Beaufort, was of a proud and unbending disposition and could not bear to live in poverty and oblivion in the same country where he had formerly been distinguished for his rank and magnificence. Having paid his debts, therefore, in the most honourable manner, he retreated with his daughter to the town of Lucerne, where he lived unknown and in wretchedness. My father loved Beaufort with the truest friendship and was deeply grieved by his retreat in these unfortunate circumstances. He bitterly deplored the false pride which led his friend to a conduct so little worthy of the affection that united them. He lost no time in endeavouring to seek him out, with the hope of persuading him to begin the world again through his credit and assistance.

Beaufort had taken effectual measures to conceal himself, and it was ten months before my father discovered his abode. Overjoyed at this discovery, he hastened to the house, which was situated in a mean street near the Reuss. But when he entered, misery and despair alone welcomed him. Beaufort had saved but a very small sum of money from the wreck of his fortunes, but it was sufficient to provide him with sustenance for some months, and in the meantime he hoped to procure some respectable employment in a merchant's house. The interval was, consequently, spent in inaction; his grief only became more deep and rankling when he had leisure for reflection, and at length it took so fast hold of his mind that at the end of three months he lay on a bed of sickness, incapable of any exertion.

His daughter attended him with the greatest tenderness, but she saw with despair that their little fund was rapidly decreasing and that there was no other prospect of support. But Caroline Beaufort possessed a mind of an uncommon mould, and her courage rose to support her in her adversity. She procured plain work; she plaited straw and by various means contrived to earn a pittance scarcely sufficient to support life.

Several months passed in this manner. Her father grew worse; her time was more entirely occupied in attending him; her means of subsistence decreased; and in the tenth month her father died in her arms, leaving her an orphan and a beggar. This last blow overcame her, and she knelt by Beaufort's coffin weeping bitterly, when my father entered the chamber. He came like a protecting spirit to the poor girl, who committed herself to his care; and after the interment of his friend he conducted her to Geneva and placed her under the protection of a relation. Two years after this event Caroline became his wife.

There was a considerable difference between the ages of my parents, but this circumstance seemed to unite them only closer in bonds of devoted affection. There was a sense of justice in my father's upright mind which rendered it necessary that he should approve highly to love strongly. Perhaps during former years he had suffered from the late-discovered unworthiness of one beloved and so was disposed to set a greater value on tried worth. There was a show of gratitude and worship in his attachment to my mother, differing wholly from the doting fondness of age, for it was inspired by reverence for her virtues and a desire to be the means of, in some degree, recompensing her for the sorrows she had endured, but which gave inexpressible grace to his behaviour to her. Everything was made to yield to her wishes and her convenience. He strove to shelter her, as a fair exotic is sheltered by the gardener, from every rougher wind and to surround her with all that could tend to excite pleasurable emotion in her soft and benevolent mind. Her health, and even the tranquillity of her hitherto constant spirit, had been shaken by what she had gone through. During the two years that had elapsed previous to their marriage my father had gradually relinquished all his public functions; and immediately after their union they sought the pleasant climate of Italy, and the change of scene and interest attendant on a tour through that land of wonders, as a restorative for her weakened frame.

From Italy they visited Germany and France. I, their eldest child, was born at Naples, and as an infant accompanied them in their rambles. I remained for several years their only child. Much as they were attached to each other, they seemed to draw inexhaustible stores of affection from a very mine of love to bestow them upon me. My mother's tender caresses and my father's smile of benevolent pleasure while regarding me are my first recollections. I was their plaything and their idol, and something better – their child, the innocent and helpless creature bestowed on them by heaven, whom to bring up to good, and whose future lot it was in their hands to direct to happiness or misery, according as they fulfilled their duties towards me. With this deep consciousness of what they owed towards the being to which they had given life, added to the active spirit of tenderness that animated both, it may be imagined that while during every hour of my infant life I received a lesson of patience, of charity, and of self-control, I was so guided by a silken cord that all seemed but one train of enjoyment to me.

For a long time I was their only care. My mother had much desired to have a daughter, but I continued their single offspring. When I was about five years old, while making an excursion beyond the frontiers of Italy, they passed a week on the shores of the Lake of Como. Their benevolent disposition often made them enter the cottages of the poor. This, to my mother, was more than a duty; it was a necessity, a passion – remembering what she had suffered, and how she had been relieved – for her to act in her turn the guardian angel to the afflicted. During one of their walks a poor cot in the foldings of a vale attracted their notice as being singularly disconsolate, while the number of half-clothed children gathered about it spoke of penury in its worst shape. One day, when my father had gone by himself to Milan, my mother, accompanied by me, visited this abode. She found a peasant and his wife, hard working, bent down by care and labour, distributing a scanty meal to five hungry babes. Among these there was one which attracted my mother far above all the rest. She appeared of a different stock. The four others were dark-eyed, hardy little vagrants; this child was thin and very fair. Her hair was the brightest living gold, and despite the poverty of her clothing, seemed to set a crown of distinction on her head. Her brow was clear and ample, her blue eyes cloudless, and her lips and the moulding of her face so expressive of sensibility and sweetness that none could behold her without looking on her as of a distinct species, a being heaven-sent, and bearing a celestial stamp in all her features.

The peasant woman, perceiving that my mother fixed eyes of wonder and admiration on this lovely girl, eagerly communicated her history. She was not her child, but the daughter of a Milanese nobleman. Her mother was a German and had died on giving her birth. The infant had been placed with these good people to nurse: they were better off then. They had not been long married, and their eldest child was but just born. The father of their charge was one of those Italians nursed in the memory of the antique glory of Italy – one among the 'schiavi ognor frementi', who exerted himself to obtain the liberty of his country. He became the victim of its weakness. Whether he had died or still lingered in the dungeons of Austria was not known. His property was confiscated; his child became an orphan and a beggar. She continued with her foster parents and bloomed in their rude abode, fairer than a garden rose among dark-leaved brambles.

When my father returned from Milan, he found playing with me in the hall of our villa a child fairer than pictured cherub – a creature who seemed to shed radiance from her looks and whose form and motions were lighter than the chamois of the hills. The apparition was soon explained. With his permission my mother prevailed on her rustic guardians to yield their charge to her. They were fond of the sweet orphan. Her presence had seemed a blessing to them, but it would be unfair to her to keep her in poverty and want when Providence afforded her such powerful protection. They consulted their village priest, and the result was that Elizabeth Lavenza became the inmate of my parents' house – my more than sister – the beautiful and adored companion of all my occupations and my pleasures.

Everyone loved Elizabeth. The passionate and almost reveren-tial attachment with which all regarded her became, while I shared it, my pride and my delight. On the evening previous to her being brought to my home, my mother had said playfully, 'I have a pretty present for my Victor – tomorrow he shall have it.' And when, on the morrow, she presented Elizabeth to me as her promised gift,

I, with childish seriousness, interpreted her words literally and looked upon Elizabeth as mine – mine to protect, love, and cherish. All praises bestowed on her I received as made to a possession of my own. We called each other familiarly by the name of cousin. No word, no expression could body forth the kind of relation in which she stood to me – my more than sister, since till death she was to be mine only.

CHAPTER II

We were brought up together; there was not quite a year difference in our ages. I need not say that we were strangers to any species of disunion or dispute. Harmony was the soul of our companionship, and the diversity and contrast that subsisted in our characters drew us nearer together. Elizabeth was of a calmer and more concentrated disposition; but, with all my ardour, I was capable of a more intense application and was more deeply smitten with the thirst for knowledge. She busied herself with following the aerial creations of the poets; and in the majestic and wondrous scenes which surrounded our Swiss home – the sublime shapes of the mountains, the changes of the seasons, tempest and calm, the silence of winter, and the life and turbulence of our Alpine summers – she found ample scope for admiration and delight. While my companion contemplated with a serious and satisfied spirit the magnificent appearances of things, I delighted in investigating their causes. The world was to me a secret which I desired to divine. Curiosity, earnest research to learn the hidden laws of nature, gladness akin to rapture, as they were unfolded to me, are among the earliest sensations I can remember.

On the birth of a second son, my junior by seven years, my parents gave up entirely their wandering life and fixed themselves in their native country. We possessed a house in Geneva, and a campagne on Belrive, the eastern shore of the lake, at the distance of rather more than a league from the city. We resided principally in the latter, and the lives of my parents were passed in considerable seclusion. It was my temper to avoid a crowd and to attach myself fervently to a few. I was indifferent, therefore, to my school-fellows in general; but I united myself in the bonds of the closest friendship to one among them. Henry Clerval was the son of a merchant of Geneva. He was a boy of singular talent and fancy. He loved enterprise, hardship, and even danger for its own sake. He was deeply read in books of chivalry and romance. He composed heroic songs and began to write many a tale of enchantment and knightly adventure. He tried to make us act plays and to enter into masquerades, in which the characters were drawn from the heroes of Roncesvalles, of the Round Table of King Arthur, and the chivalrous train who shed their blood to redeem the holy sepulchre from the hands of the infidels.

No human being could have passed a happier childhood than myself. My parents were possessed by the very spirit of kindness and indulgence. We felt that they were not the tyrants to rule our lot according to their caprice, but the agents and creators of all the many delights which we enjoyed. When I mingled with other families I distinctly discerned how peculiarly fortunate my lot was, and gratitude assisted the development of filial love.

My temper was sometimes violent, and my passions vehement; but by some law in my temperature they were turned not towards childish pursuits but to an eager desire to learn, and not to learn all things indiscriminately. I confess that neither the structure of languages, nor the code of governments, nor the politics of various states possessed attractions for me. It was the secrets of heaven and earth that I desired to learn; and whether it was the outward substance of things or the inner spirit of nature and the mysterious soul of man that occupied me, still my inquiries were directed to the metaphysical, or in its highest sense, the physical secrets of the world.

Meanwhile Clerval occupied himself, so to speak, with the moral relations of things. The busy stage of life, the virtues of heroes, and the actions of men were his theme; and his hope and his dream was to become one among those whose names are recorded in story as the gallant and adventurous benefactors of our species. The saintly soul of Elizabeth shone like a shrine-dedicated lamp in our peaceful home. Her sympathy was ours; her smile, her soft voice, the sweet glance of her celestial eyes, were ever there to bless and animate us. She was the living spirit of love to soften and attract; I might have become sullen in my study, through the ardour of my nature, but that she was there to subdue me to a semblance of her own gentleness. And Clerval – could aught ill entrench on the noble spirit of Clerval? Yet he might not have been so perfectly humane, so thoughtful in his generosity, so full of kindness and tenderness amidst his passion for adventurous exploit, had she not unfolded to him the real loveliness of beneficence and made the doing good the end and aim of his soaring ambition.

I feel exquisite pleasure in dwelling on the recollections of childhood, before misfortune had tainted my mind and changed its bright visions of extensive usefulness into gloomy and narrow reflections upon self. Besides, in drawing the picture of my early days, I also record those events which led, by insensible steps, to my after tale of misery, for when I would account to myself for the birth of that passion which afterward ruled my destiny I find it arise, like a mountain river, from ignoble and almost forgotten sources; but, swelling as it proceeded, it became the torrent which, in its course, has swept away all my hopes and joys. Natural philosophy is the genius that has regulated my fate; I desire, therefore, in this narration, to state those facts which led to my predilection for that science. When I was thirteen years of age we all went on a party of pleasure to the baths near Thonon; the inclemency of the weather obliged us to remain a day confined to the inn. In this house I chanced to find a volume of the works of Cornelius Agrippa. I opened it with apathy; the theory which he attempts to demonstrate and the wonderful facts which he relates soon changed this feeling into enthusiasm. A new light seemed to dawn upon my mind, and bounding with joy, I communicated my discovery to my father. My father looked carelessly at the title page of my book and said, 'Ah! Cornelius Agrippa! My dear Victor, do not waste your time upon this; it is sad trash.'

If, instead of this remark, my father had taken the pains to explain to me that the principles of Agrippa had been entirely exploded and that a modern system of science had been introduced which possessed much greater powers than the ancient, because the powers of the latter were chimerical, while those of the former were real and practical, under such circumstances I should certainly have thrown Agrippa aside and have contented my imagination, warmed as it was, by returning with greater ardour to my former studies. It is even possible that the train of my ideas would never have received the fatal impulse that led to my ruin. But the cursory glance my father had taken of my volume by no means assured me that he was acquainted with its contents, and I continued to read with the greatest avidity. When I returned home my first care was to procure the whole works of this author, and afterwards of Paracelsus and Albertus Magnus. I read and studied the wild fancies of these writers with delight; they appeared to me treasures known to few besides myself. I have described myself as always having been imbued with a fervent longing to penetrate the secrets of nature. In spite of the intense labour and wonderful discoveries of modern philosophers, I always came from my studies discontented and unsatisfied. Sir Isaac Newton is said to have avowed that he felt like a child picking up shells beside the great and unexplored ocean of truth. Those of his successors in each branch of natural philosophy with whom I was acquainted appeared even to my boy's apprehensions as tyros engaged in the same pursuit.

The untaught peasant beheld the elements around him and was acquainted with their practical uses. The most learned philosopher knew little more. He had partially unveiled the face of Nature, but her immortal lineaments were still a wonder and a mystery. He might dissect, anatomize, and give names; but, not to speak of a final cause, causes in their secondary and tertiary grades were utterly unknown to him. I had gazed upon the fortifications and impediments that seemed to keep human beings from entering the citadel of nature, and rashly and ignorantly I had repined.

But here were books, and here were men who had penetrated deeper and knew more. I took their word for all that they averred, and I became their disciple. It may appear strange that such should arise in the eighteenth century; but while I followed the routine of education in the schools of Geneva, I was, to a great degree, self-taught with regard to my favourite studies. My father was not scientific, and I was left to struggle with a child's blindness, added to a student's thirst for knowledge. Under the guidance of my new preceptors I entered with the greatest diligence into the search of the philosopher's stone and the elixir of life; but the latter soon obtained my undivided attention. Wealth was an inferior object, but what glory would attend the discovery if I could banish disease from the human frame and render man invulnerable to any but a violent death! Nor were these my only visions. The raising of ghosts or devils was a promise liberally accorded by my favourite authors, the fulfillment of which I most eagerly sought; and if my incantations were always unsuccessful, I attributed the failure rather to my own inexperience and mistake than to a want of skill or fidelity in my instructors. And thus for a time I was occupied by exploded systems, mingling, like an unadept, a thousand contradictory theories and floundering desperately in a very slough of multifarious knowledge, guided by an ardent imagination and childish reasoning, till an accident again changed the current of my ideas. When I was about fifteen years old we had retired to our house near Belrive, when we witnessed a most violent and terrible thunderstorm. It advanced from behind the mountains of Jura, and the thunder burst at once with frightful loudness from various quarters of the heavens. I remained, while the storm lasted, watching its progress with curiosity and delight. As I stood at the door, on a sudden I beheld a stream of fire issue from an old and beautiful oak which stood about twenty yards from our house; and so soon as the dazzling light vanished, the oak had disappeared, and nothing remained but a blasted stump. When we visited it the next morning, we found the tree shattered in a singular manner. It was not splintered by the shock, but entirely reduced to thin ribbons of wood. I never beheld anything so utterly destroyed.

Before this I was not unacquainted with the more obvious laws of electricity. On this occasion a man of great research in natural philosophy was with us, and excited by this catastrophe, he entered on the explanation of a theory which he had formed on the subject of electricity and galvanism, which was at once new and astonishing to me. All that he said threw greatly into the shade Cornelius Agrippa, Albertus Magnus, and Paracelsus, the lords of my imagination; but by some fatality the overthrow of these men disinclined me to pursue my accustomed studies. It seemed to me as if nothing would or could ever be known. All that had so long engaged my attention suddenly grew despicable. By one of those caprices of the mind which we are perhaps most subject to in early youth, I at once gave up my former occupations, set down natural history and all its progeny as a deformed and abortive creation, and entertained the greatest disdain for a would-be science which could never even step within the threshold of real knowledge. In this mood of mind I betook myself to the mathematics and the branches of study appertaining to that science as being built upon secure foundations, and so worthy of my consideration.

Thus strangely are our souls constructed, and by such slight ligaments are we bound to prosperity or ruin. When I look back, it seems to me as if this almost miraculous change of inclination and will was the immediate suggestion of the guardian angel of my life – the last effort made by the spirit of preservation to avert the storm that was even then hanging in the stars and ready to envelop me. Her victory was announced by an unusual tranquillity and gladness of soul which followed the relinquishing of my ancient and latterly tormenting studies. It was thus that I was to be taught to associate evil with their prosecution, happiness with their disregard.

It was a strong effort of the spirit of good, but it was ineffectual. Destiny was too potent, and her immutable laws had decreed my utter and terrible destruction.

CHAPTER III

When I had attained the age of seventeen my parents resolved that I should become a student at the university of Ingolstadt. I had hitherto attended the schools of Geneva, but my father thought it necessary for the completion of my education that I should be made acquainted with other customs than those of my native country. My departure was therefore fixed at an early date, but before the day resolved upon could arrive, the first misfortune of my life occurred – an omen, as it were, of my future misery. Elizabeth had caught the scarlet fever; her illness was severe, and she was in the greatest danger. During her illness many arguments had been urged to persuade my mother to refrain from attending upon her. She had at first yielded to our entreaties, but when she heard that the life of her favourite was menaced, she could no longer control her anxiety. She attended her sickbed; her watchful attentions triumphed over the malignity of the distemper – Elizabeth was saved, but the consequences of this imprudence were fatal to her preserver. On the third day my mother sickened; her fever was accompanied by the most alarming symptoms, and the looks of her medical attendants prognosticated the worst event. On her deathbed the fortitude and benignity of this best of women did not desert her. She joined the hands of Elizabeth and myself. 'My children,' she said, 'my firmest hopes of future happiness were placed on the prospect of your union. This expectation will now be the consolation of your father. Elizabeth, my love, you must supply my place to my younger children. Alas! I regret that I am taken from you; and, happy and beloved as I have been, is it not hard to quit you all? But these are not thoughts befitting me; I will endeavour to resign myself cheerfully to death and will indulge a hope of meeting you in another world.'

She died calmly, and her countenance expressed affection even in death. I need not describe the feelings of those whose dearest ties are rent by that most irreparable evil, the void that presents itself to the soul, and the despair that is exhibited on the countenance. It is so long before the mind can persuade itself that she whom we saw every day and whose very existence appeared a part of our own can have departed forever – that the brightness of a beloved eye can have been extinguished and the sound of a voice so familiar and dear to the ear can be hushed, never more to be heard. These are the reflections of the first days; but when the lapse of time proves the reality of the evil, then the actual bitterness of grief commences. Yet from whom has not that rude hand rent away some dear connection? And why should I describe a sorrow which all have felt, and must feel? The time at length arrives when grief is rather an indulgence than a necessity; and the smile that plays upon the lips, although it may be deemed a sacrilege, is not banished. My mother was dead, but we had still duties which we ought to perform; we must continue our course with the rest and learn to think ourselves fortunate whilst one remains whom the spoiler has not seized. My departure for Ingolstadt, which had been deferred by these events, was now again determined upon. I obtained from my father a respite of some weeks. It appeared to me sacrilege so soon to leave the repose, akin to death, of the house of mourning and to rush into the thick of life. I was new to sorrow, but it did not the less alarm me. I was unwilling to quit the sight of those that remained to me, and above all, I desired to see my sweet Elizabeth in some degree consoled.

She indeed veiled her grief and strove to act the comforter to us all. She looked steadily on life and assumed its duties with courage and zeal. She devoted herself to those whom she had been taught to call her uncle and cousins. Never was she so enchanting as at this time, when she recalled the sunshine of her smiles and spent them upon us. She forgot even her own regret in her endeavours to make us forget.

The day of my departure at length arrived. Clerval spent the last evening with us. He had endeavoured to persuade his father to permit him to accompany me and to become my fellow student, but in vain. His father was a narrow-minded trader and saw idleness and ruin in the aspirations and ambition of his son. Henry deeply felt the misfortune of being debarred from a liberal education. He said little, but when he spoke I read in his kindling eye and in his animated glance a restrained but firm resolve not to be chained to the miserable details of commerce.

We sat late. We could not tear ourselves away from each other nor persuade ourselves to say the word 'Farewell!' It was said, and we retired under the pretence of seeking repose, each fancying that the other was deceived; but when at morning's dawn I descended to the carriage which was to convey me away, they were all there – my father again to bless me, Clerval to press my hand once more, my Elizabeth to renew her entreaties that I would write often and to bestow the last feminine attentions on her playmate and friend.

I threw myself into the chaise that was to convey me away and indulged in the most melancholy reflections. I, who had ever been surrounded by amiable companions, continually engaged in endeavouring to bestow mutual pleasure – I was now alone. In the university whither I was going I must form my own friends and be my own protector. My life had hitherto been remarkably secluded and domestic, and this had given me invincible repugnance to new countenances. I loved my brothers, Elizabeth, and Clerval; these were 'old familiar faces,' but I believed myself totally unfitted for the company of strangers. Such were my reflections as I commenced my journey; but as I proceeded, my spirits and hopes rose. I ardently desired the acquisition of knowledge. I had often, when at home, thought it hard to remain during my youth cooped up in one place and had longed to enter the world and take my station among other human beings. Now my desires were complied with, and it would, indeed, have been folly to repent.

I had sufficient leisure for these and many other reflections during my journey to Ingolstadt, which was long and fatiguing. At length the high white steeple of the town met my eyes. I alighted and was conducted to my solitary apartment to spend the evening as I pleased.

The next morning I delivered my letters of introduction and paid a visit to some of the principal professors. Chance – or rather the evil influence, the Angel of Destruction, which asserted omnipotent sway over me from the moment I turned my reluctant steps from my father's door – led me first to M. Krempe, professor of natural philosophy. He was an uncouth man, but deeply imbued in the secrets of his science. He asked me several questions concerning my progress in the different branches of science appertaining to natural philosophy. I replied carelessly, and partly in contempt, mentioned the names of my alchemists as the principal authors I had studied. The professor stared. 'Have you,' he said, 'really spent your time in studying such nonsense?'

I replied in the affirmative. 'Every minute,' continued M. Krempe with warmth, 'every instant that you have wasted on those books is utterly and entirely lost. You have burdened your memory with exploded systems and useless names. Good God! In what desert land have you lived, where no one was kind enough to inform you that these fancies which you have so greedily imbibed are a thousand years old and as musty as they are ancient? I little expected, in this enlightened and scientific age, to find a disciple of Albertus Magnus and Paracelsus. My dear sir, you must begin your studies entirely anew.'

So saying, he stepped aside and wrote down a list of several books treating of natural philosophy which he desired me to procure, and dismissed me after mentioning that in the beginning of the following week he intended to commence a course of lectures upon natural philosophy in its general relations, and that M. Waldman, a fellow professor, would lecture upon chemistry the alternate days that he omitted.

I returned home not disappointed, for I have said that I had long considered those authors useless whom the professor reprobated; but I returned not at all the more inclined to recur to these studies in any shape. M. Krempe was a little squat man with a gruff voice and a repulsive countenance; the teacher, therefore, did not prepossess me in favour of his pursuits. In rather a too philosophical and connected a strain, perhaps, I have given an account of the conclusions I had come to concerning them in my early years. As a child I had not been content with the results promised by the modern professors of natural science. With a confusion of ideas only to be accounted for by my extreme youth and my want of a guide on such matters, I had retrod the steps of knowledge along the paths of time and exchanged the discoveries of recent inquirers for the dreams of forgotten alchemists. Besides, I had a contempt for the uses of modern natural philosophy. It was very different when the masters of the science sought immortality and power; such views, although futile, were grand; but now the scene was changed. The ambition of the inquirer seemed to limit itself to the annihilation of those visions on which my interest in science was chiefly founded. I was required to exchange chimeras of boundless grandeur for realities of little worth.

Such were my reflections during the first two or three days of my residence at Ingolstadt, which were chiefly spent in becoming acquainted with the localities and the principal residents in my new abode. But as the ensuing week commenced, I thought of the information which M. Krempe had given me concerning the lectures. And although I could not consent to go and hear that little conceited fellow deliver sentences out of a pulpit, I recollected what he had said of M. Waldman, whom I had never seen, as he had hitherto been out of town.

Partly from curiosity and partly from idleness, I went into the lecturing room, which M. Waldman entered shortly after. This professor was very unlike his colleague. He appeared about fifty years of age, but with an aspect expressive of the greatest benevolence; a few grey hairs covered his temples, but those at the back of his head were nearly black. His person was short but remarkably erect and his voice the sweetest I had ever heard. He began his lecture by a recapitulation of the history of chemistry and the various improvements made by different men of learning, pronouncing with fervour the names of the most distinguished discoverers. He then took a cursory view of the present state of the science and explained many of its elementary terms. After having made a few preparatory experiments, he concluded with a panegyric upon modern chemistry, the terms of which I shall never forget: 'The ancient teachers of this science,' said he, 'promised impossibilities and performed nothing. The modern masters promise very little; they know that metals cannot be transmuted and that the elixir of life is a chimera but these philosophers, whose hands seem only made to dabble in dirt, and their eyes to pore over the microscope or crucible, have indeed performed miracles. They penetrate into the recesses of nature and show how she works in her hiding-places. They ascend into the heavens; they have discovered how the blood circulates, and the nature of the air we breathe. They have acquired new and almost unlimited powers; they can command the thunders of heaven, mimic the earthquake, and even mock the invisible world with its own shadows.'

Such were the professor's words – rather let me say such the words of the fate – enounced to destroy me. As he went on I felt as if my soul were grappling with a palpable enemy; one by one the various keys were touched which formed the mechanism of my being; chord after chord was sounded, and soon my mind was filled with one thought, one conception, one purpose. So much has been done, exclaimed the soul of Frankenstein – more, far more, will I achieve; treading in the steps already marked, I will pioneer a new way, explore unknown powers, and unfold to the world the deepest mysteries of creation.

I closed not my eyes that night. My internal being was in a state of insurrection and turmoil; I felt that order would thence arise, but I had no power to produce it. By degrees, after the morning's dawn, sleep came. I awoke, and my yesternight's thoughts were as a dream. There only remained a resolution to return to my ancient studies and to devote myself to a science for which I believed myself to possess a natural talent. On the same day I paid M. Waldman a visit. His manners in private were even more mild and attractive than in public, for there was a certain dignity in his mien during his lecture which in his own house was replaced by the greatest affability and kindness. I gave him pretty nearly the same account of my former pursuits as I had given to his fellow professor. He heard with attention the little narration concerning my studies and smiled at the names of Cornelius Agrippa and Paracelsus, but without the contempt that M. Krempe had exhibited. He said that 'These were men to whose indefatigable zeal modern philosophers were indebted for most of the foundations of their knowledge. They had left to us, as an easier task, to give new names and arrange in connected classifications the facts which they in a great degree had been the instruments of bringing to light. The labours of men of genius, however erroneously directed, scarcely ever fail in ultimately turning to the solid advantage of mankind.' I listened to his statement, which was delivered without any presumption or affectation, and then added that his lecture had removed my prejudices against modern chemists; I expressed myself in measured terms, with the modesty and deference due from a youth to his instructor, without letting escape (inexperience in life would have made me ashamed) any of the enthusiasm which stimulated my intended labours. I requested his advice concerning the books I ought to procure.

'I am happy,' said M. Waldman, 'to have gained a disciple; and if your application equals your ability, I have no doubt of your success. Chemistry is that branch of natural philosophy in which the greatest improvements have been and may be made; it is on that account that I have made it my peculiar study; but at the same time, I have not neglected the other branches of science. A man would make but a very sorry chemist if he attended to that department of human knowledge alone. If your wish is to become really a man of science and not merely a petty experimentalist, I should advise you to apply to every branch of natural philosophy, including mathematics.' He then took me into his laboratory and explained to me the uses of his various machines, instructing me as to what I ought to procure and promising me the use of his own when I should have advanced far enough in the science not to derange their mechanism. He also gave me the list of books which I had requested, and I took my leave.

Thus ended a day memorable to me; it decided my future destiny.

CHAPTER IV

From this day natural philosophy, and particularly chemistry, in the most comprehensive sense of the term, became nearly my sole occupation. I read with ardour those works, so full of genius and discrimination, which modern inquirers have written on these subjects. I attended the lectures and cultivated the acquaintance of the men of science of the university, and I found even in M. Krempe a great deal of sound sense and real information, combined, it is true, with a repulsive physiognomy and manners, but not on that account the less valuable. In M. Waldman I found a true friend. His gentleness was never tinged by dogmatism, and his instructions were given with an air of frankness and good nature that banished every idea of pedantry. In a thousand ways he smoothed for me the path of knowledge and made the most abstruse inquiries clear and facile to my apprehension. My application was at first fluctuating and uncertain; it gained strength as I proceeded and soon became so ardent and eager that the stars often disappeared in the light of morning whilst I was yet engaged in my laboratory.

As I applied so closely, it may be easily conceived that my progress was rapid. My ardour was indeed the astonishment of the students, and my proficiency that of the masters. Professor Krempe often asked me, with a sly smile, how Cornelius Agrippa went on, whilst M. Waldman expressed the most heartfelt exultation in my progress. Two years passed in this manner, during which I paid no visit to Geneva, but was engaged, heart and soul, in the pursuit of some discoveries which I hoped to make. None but those who have experienced them can conceive of the enticements of science. In other studies you go as far as others have gone before you, and there is nothing more to know; but in a scientific pursuit there is continual food for discovery and wonder. A mind of moderate capacity which closely pursues one study must infallibly arrive at great proficiency in that study; and I, who continually sought the attainment of one object of pursuit and was solely wrapped up in this, improved so rapidly that at the end of two years I made some discoveries in the improvement of some chemical instruments, which procured me great esteem and admiration at the university.

When I had arrived at this point and had become as well acquainted with the theory and practice of natural philosophy as depended on the lessons of any of the professors at Ingolstadt, my residence there being no longer conducive to my improvements, I thought of returning to my friends and my native town, when an incident happened that protracted my stay.

One of the phenomena which had peculiarly attracted my attention was the structure of the human frame, and, indeed, any animal endued with life. Whence, I often asked myself, did the principle of life proceed? It was a bold question, and one which has ever been considered as a mystery; yet with how many things are we upon the brink of becoming acquainted, if cowardice or carelessness did not restrain our inquiries. I revolved these circumstances in my mind and determined thenceforth to apply myself more particularly to those branches of natural philosophy which relate to physiology. Unless I had been animated by an almost supernatural enthusiasm, my application to this study would have been irksome and almost intolerable. To examine the causes of life, we must first have recourse to death. I became acquainted with the science of anatomy, but this was not sufficient; I must also observe the natural decay and corruption of the human body. In my education my father had taken the greatest precautions that my mind should be impressed with no supernatural horrors. I do not ever remember to have trembled at a tale of superstition or to have feared the apparition of a spirit. Darkness had no effect upon my fancy, and a churchyard was to me merely the receptacle of bodies deprived of life, which, from being the seat of beauty and strength, had become food for the worm. Now I was led to examine the cause and progress of this decay and forced to spend days and nights in vaults and charnel-houses. My attention was fixed upon every object the most insupportable to the delicacy of the human feelings. I saw how the fine form of man was degraded and wasted; I beheld the corruption of death succeed to the blooming cheek of life; I saw how the worm inherited the wonders of the eye and brain. I paused, examining and analysing all the minutiae of causation, as exemplified in the change from life to death, and death to life, until from the midst of this darkness a sudden light broke in upon me – a light so brilliant and wondrous, yet so simple, that while I became dizzy with the immensity of the prospect which it illustrated, I was surprised that among so many men of genius who had directed their inquiries towards the same science, that I alone should be reserved to discover so astonishing a secret.

Remember, I am not recording the vision of a madman. The sun does not more certainly shine in the heavens than that which I now affirm is true. Some miracle might have produced it, yet the stages of the discovery were distinct and probable. After days and nights of incredible labour and fatigue, I succeeded in discovering the cause of generation and life; nay, more, I became myself capable of bestowing animation upon lifeless matter.

The astonishment which I had at first experienced on this discovery soon gave place to delight and rapture. After so much time spent in painful labour, to arrive at once at the summit of my desires was the most gratifying consummation of my toils. But this discovery was so great and overwhelming that all the steps by which I had been progressively led to it were obliterated, and I beheld only the result. What had been the study and desire of the wisest men since the creation of the world was now within my grasp. Not that, like a magic scene, it all opened upon me at once: the information I had obtained was of a nature rather to direct my endeavours so soon as I should point them towards the object of my search than to exhibit that object already accomplished. I was like the Arabian who had been buried with the dead and found a passage to life, aided only by one glimmering and seemingly ineffectual light.

I see by your eagerness and the wonder and hope which your eyes express, my friend, that you expect to be informed of the secret with which I am acquainted; that cannot be; listen patiently until the end of my story, and you will easily perceive why I am reserved upon that subject. I will not lead you on, unguarded and ardent as I then was, to your destruction and infallible misery. Learn from me, if not by my precepts, at least by my example, how dangerous is the acquirement of knowledge and how much happier that man is who believes his native town to be the world, than he who aspires to become greater than his nature will allow.

When I found so astonishing a power placed within my hands, I hesitated a long time concerning the manner in which I should employ it. Although I possessed the capacity of bestowing animation, yet to prepare a frame for the reception of it, with all its intricacies of fibres, muscles, and veins, still remained a work of inconceivable difficulty and labour. I doubted at first whether

I should attempt the creation of a being like myself, or one of simpler organization; but my imagination was too much exalted by my first success to permit me to doubt of my ability to give life to an animal as complete and wonderful as man. The materials at present within my command hardly appeared adequate to so arduous an undertaking, but I doubted not that I should ultimately succeed. I prepared myself for a multitude of reverses; my operations might be incessantly baffled, and at last my work be imperfect, yet when I considered the improvement which every day takes place in science and mechanics, I was encouraged to hope my present attempts would at least lay the foundations of future success. Nor could I consider the magnitude and complexity of my plan as any argument of its impracticability. It was with these feelings that I began the creation of a human being. As the minuteness of the parts formed a great hindrance to my speed, I resolved, contrary to my first intention, to make the being of a gigantic stature, that is to say, about eight feet in height, and proportionably large. After having formed this determination and having spent some months in successfully collecting and arranging my materials, I began.

No one can conceive the variety of feelings which bore me onwards, like a hurricane, in the first enthusiasm of success. Life and death appeared to me ideal bounds, which I should first break through, and pour a torrent of light into our dark world. A new species would bless me as its creator and source; many happy and excellent natures would owe their being to me. No father could claim the gratitude of his child so completely as I should deserve theirs. Pursuing these reflections, I thought that if I could bestow animation upon lifeless matter, I might in process of time (although I now found it impossible) renew life where death had apparently devoted the body to corruption.

These thoughts supported my spirits, while I pursued my undertaking with unremitting ardour. My cheek had grown pale with study, and my person had become emaciated with confinement. Sometimes, on the very brink of certainty, I failed; yet still I clung to the hope which the next day or the next hour might realize. One secret which I alone possessed was the hope to which I had dedicated myself; and the moon gazed on my midnight labours, while, with unrelaxed and breathless eagerness, I pursued nature to her hiding-places. Who shall conceive the horrors of my secret toil as I dabbled among the unhallowed damps of the grave or tortured the living animal to animate the lifeless clay? My limbs now tremble, and my eyes swim with the remembrance; but then a resistless and almost frantic impulse urged me forward; I seemed to have lost all soul or sensation but for this one pursuit. It was indeed but a passing trance, that only made me feel with renewed acuteness so soon as, the unnatural stimulus ceasing to operate, I had returned to my old habits. I collected bones from charnel-houses and disturbed, with profane fingers, the tremendous secrets of the human frame. In a solitary chamber, or rather cell, at the top of the house, and separated from all the other apartments by a gallery and staircase, I kept my workshop of filthy creation; my eyeballs were starting from their sockets in attending to the details of my employment. The dissecting room and the slaughter-house furnished many of my materials; and often did my human nature turn with loathing from my occupation, whilst, still urged on by an eagerness which perpetually increased, I brought my work near to a conclusion.

The summer months passed while I was thus engaged, heart and soul, in one pursuit. It was a most beautiful season; never did the fields bestow a more plentiful harvest or the vines yield a more luxuriant vintage, but my eyes were insensible to the charms of nature. And the same feelings which made me neglect the scenes around me caused me also to forget those friends who were so many miles absent, and whom I had not seen for so long a time. I knew my silence disquieted them, and I well remembered the words of my father: 'I know that while you are pleased with yourself you will think of us with affection, and we shall hear regularly from you. You must pardon me if I regard any interruption in your correspondence as a proof that your other duties are equally neglected.'

I knew well therefore what would be my father's feelings, but I could not tear my thoughts from my employment, loathsome in itself, but which had taken an irresistible hold of my imagination. I wished, as it were, to procrastinate all that related to my feelings of affection until the great object, which swallowed up every habit of my nature, should be completed.

I then thought that my father would be unjust if he ascribed my neglect to vice or faultiness on my part, but I am now convinced that he was justified in conceiving that I should not be altogether free from blame. A human being in perfection ought always to preserve a calm and peaceful mind and never to allow passion or a transitory desire to disturb his tranquillity. I do not think that the pursuit of knowledge is an exception to this rule. If the study to which you apply yourself has a tendency to weaken your affections and to destroy your taste for those simple pleasures in which no alloy can possibly mix, then that study is certainly unlawful, that is to say, not befitting the human mind. If this rule were always observed; if no man allowed any pursuit whatsoever to interfere with the tranquillity of his domestic affections, Greece had not been enslaved, Caesar would have spared his country, America would have been discovered more gradually, and the empires of Mexico and Peru had not been destroyed.

But I forget that I am moralizing in the most interesting part of my tale, and your looks remind me to proceed. My father made no reproach in his letters and only took notice of my science by inquiring into my occupations more particularly than before. Winter, spring, and summer passed away during my labours; but I did not watch the blossom or the expanding leaves – sights which before always yielded me supreme delight – so deeply was I engrossed in my occupation. The leaves of that year had withered before my work drew near to a close, and now every day showed me more plainly how well I had succeeded. But my enthusiasm was checked by my anxiety, and I appeared rather like one doomed by slavery to toil in the mines, or any other unwholesome trade than an artist occupied by his favourite employment. Every night I was oppressed by a slow fever, and I became nervous to a most painful degree; the fall of a leaf startled me, and I shunned my fellow creatures as if I had been guilty of a crime. Sometimes I grew alarmed at the wreck I perceived that I had become; the energy of my purpose alone sustained me: my labours would soon end, and I believed that exercise and amusement would then drive away incipient disease; and I promised myself both of these when my creation should be complete.

CHAPTER V

It was on a dreary night of November that I beheld the accomplishment of my toils. With an anxiety that almost amounted to agony, I collected the instruments of life around me, that I might infuse a spark of being into the lifeless thing that lay at my feet. It was already one in the morning; the rain pattered dismally against the panes, and my candle was nearly burnt out, when, by the glimmer of the half-extinguished light, I saw the dull yellow eye of the creature open; it breathed hard, and a convulsive motion agitated its limbs.

How can I describe my emotions at this catastrophe, or how delineate the wretch whom with such infinite pains and care I had endeavoured to form? His limbs were in proportion, and I had selected his features as beautiful. Beautiful! Great God! His yellow skin scarcely covered the work of muscles and arteries beneath; his hair was of a lustrous black, and flowing; his teeth of a pearly whiteness; but these luxuriances only formed a more horrid contrast with his watery eyes, that seemed almost of the same colour as the dun-white sockets in which they were set, his shrivelled complexion and straight black lips.

The different accidents of life are not so changeable as the feelings of human nature. I had worked hard for nearly two years, for the sole purpose of infusing life into an inanimate body. For this I had deprived myself of rest and health. I had desired it with an ardour that far exceeded moderation; but now that I had finished, the beauty of the dream vanished, and breathless horror and disgust filled my heart. Unable to endure the aspect of the being I had created, I rushed out of the room and continued a long time traversing my bed-chamber, unable to compose my mind to sleep. At length lassitude succeeded to the tumult I had before endured, and I threw myself on the bed in my clothes, endeavouring to seek a few moments of forgetfulness. But it was in vain; I slept, indeed, but I was disturbed by the wildest dreams. I thought I saw Elizabeth, in the bloom of health, walking in the streets of Ingolstadt. Delighted and surprised, I embraced her, but as I imprinted the first kiss on her lips, they became livid with the hue of death; her features appeared to change, and I thought that I held the corpse of my dead mother in my arms; a shroud enveloped her form, and I saw the grave-worms crawling in the folds of the flannel. I started from my sleep with horror; a cold dew covered my forehead, my teeth chattered, and every limb became convulsed; when, by the dim and yellow light of the moon, as it forced its way through the window shutters, I beheld the wretch – the miserable monster whom I had created. He held up the curtain of the bed; and his eyes, if eyes they may be called, were fixed on me. His jaws opened, and he muttered some inarticulate sounds, while a grin wrinkled his cheeks. He might have spoken, but I did not hear; one hand was stretched out, seemingly to detain me, but I escaped and rushed downstairs. I took refuge in the courtyard belonging to the house which I inhabited, where I remained during the rest of the night, walking up and down in the greatest agitation, listening attentively, catching and fearing each sound as if it were to announce the approach of the demoniacal corpse to which I had so miserably given life.

Oh! No mortal could support the horror of that countenance. A mummy again endued with animation could not be so hideous as that wretch. I had gazed on him while unfinished; he was ugly then, but when those muscles and joints were rendered capable of motion, it became a thing such as even Dante could not have conceived.

I passed the night wretchedly. Sometimes my pulse beat so quickly and hardly that I felt the palpitation of every artery; at others, I nearly sank to the ground through languor and extreme weakness. Mingled with this horror, I felt the bitterness of disappointment; dreams that had been my food and pleasant rest for so long a space were now become a hell to me; and the change was so rapid, the overthrow so complete!

Morning, dismal and wet, at length dawned and discovered to my sleepless and aching eyes the church of Ingolstadt, its white steeple and clock, which indicated the sixth hour. The porter opened the gates of the court, which had that night been my asylum, and I issued into the streets, pacing them with quick steps, as if I sought to avoid the wretch whom I feared every turning of the street would present to my view. I did not dare return to the apartment which I inhabited, but felt impelled to hurry on, although drenched by the rain which poured from a black and comfortless sky.

I continued walking in this manner for some time, endeavouring by bodily exercise to ease the load that weighed upon my mind.

I traversed the streets without any clear conception of where I was or what I was doing. My heart palpitated in the sickness of fear, and I hurried on with irregular steps, not daring to look about me:

> Like one who, on a lonely road,
> Doth walk in fear and dread,
> And, having once turned round, walks on,
> And turns no more his head;
> Because he knows a frightful fiend
> Doth close behind him tread.

Coleridge's *Ancient Mariner.*

Continuing thus, I came at length opposite to the inn at which the various diligences and carriages usually stopped. Here I paused, I knew not why; but I remained some minutes with my eyes fixed on a coach that was coming towards me from the other end of the street. As it drew nearer I observed that it was the Swiss diligence; it stopped just where I was standing, and on the door being opened, I perceived Henry Clerval, who, on seeing me, instantly sprung out. 'My dear Frankenstein,' exclaimed he, 'how glad I am to see you! How fortunate that you should be here at the very moment of my alighting!'

Nothing could equal my delight on seeing Clerval; his presence brought back to my thoughts my father, Elizabeth, and all those scenes of home so dear to my recollection. I grasped his hand, and in a moment forgot my horror and misfortune; I felt suddenly, and for the first time during many months, calm and serene joy. I welcomed my friend, therefore, in the most cordial manner, and we walked towards my college. Clerval continued talking for some time about our mutual friends and his own good fortune in being permitted to come to Ingolstadt. 'You may easily believe,' said he, 'how great was the difficulty to persuade my father that all necessary knowledge was not comprised in the noble art of bookkeeping; and, indeed, I believe I left him incredulous to the last, for his constant answer to my unwearied entreaties was the same as that of the Dutch schoolmaster in *The Vicar of Wakefield*: 'I have ten thousand florins a year without Greek, I eat heartily without Greek.' But his affection for me at length overcame his dislike of learning, and he has permitted me to undertake a voyage of discovery to the land of knowledge.'

'It gives me the greatest delight to see you; but tell me how you left my father, brothers, and Elizabeth.'

'Very well, and very happy, only a little uneasy that they hear from you so seldom. By the by, I mean to lecture you a little upon their account myself. But, my dear Frankenstein,' continued he, stopping short and gazing full in my face, 'I did not before remark how very ill you appear; so thin and pale; you look as if you had been watching for several nights.'

'You have guessed right; I have lately been so deeply engaged in one occupation that I have not allowed myself sufficient rest, as you see; but I hope, I sincerely hope, that all these employments are now at an end and that I am at length free.'

I trembled excessively; I could not endure to think of, and far less to allude to, the occurrences of the preceding night. I walked with a quick pace, and we soon arrived at my college. I then reflected, and the thought made me shiver, that the creature whom I had left in my apartment might still be there, alive and walking about. I dreaded to behold this monster, but I feared still more that Henry should see him. Entreating him, therefore, to remain a few minutes at the bottom of the stairs, I darted up towards my own room. My hand was already on the lock of the door before I recollected myself. I then paused, and a cold shivering came over me. I threw the door forcibly open, as children are accustomed to do when they expect a spectre to stand in waiting for them on the other side; but nothing appeared. I stepped fearfully in: the apartment was empty, and my bedroom was also freed from its hideous guest. I could hardly believe that so great a good fortune could have befallen me, but when I became assured that my enemy had indeed fled, I clapped my hands for joy and ran down to Clerval.

We ascended into my room, and the servant presently brought breakfast; but I was unable to contain myself. It was not joy only that possessed me; I felt my flesh tingle with excess of sensitiveness, and my pulse beat rapidly. I was unable to remain for a single instant in the same place; I jumped over the chairs, clapped my hands, and laughed aloud. Clerval at first attributed my unusual spirits to joy on his arrival, but when he observed me more attentively, he saw a wildness in my eyes for which he could not account, and my loud, unrestrained, heartless laughter frightened and astonished him.

'My dear Victor,' cried he, 'what, for God's sake, is the matter?

Do not laugh in that manner. How ill you are! What is the cause of all this?'

'Do not ask me,' cried I, putting my hands before my eyes, for I thought I saw the dreaded spectre glide into the room; "he' can tell. Oh, save me! Save me!' I imagined that the monster seized me; I struggled furiously and fell down in a fit.

Poor Clerval! What must have been his feelings? A meeting, which he anticipated with such joy, so strangely turned to bitterness. But I was not the witness of his grief, for I was lifeless and did not recover my senses for a long, long time.

This was the commencement of a nervous fever which confined me for several months. During all that time Henry was my only nurse. I afterwards learned that, knowing my father's advanced age and unfitness for so long a journey, and how wretched my sickness would make Elizabeth, he spared them this grief by concealing the extent of my disorder. He knew that I could not have a more kind and attentive nurse than himself; and, firm in the hope he felt of my recovery, he did not doubt that, instead of doing harm, he performed the kindest action that he could towards them.

But I was in reality very ill, and surely nothing but the unbounded and unremitting attentions of my friend could have restored me to life. The form of the monster on whom I had bestowed existence was forever before my eyes, and I raved incessantly concerning him. Doubtless my words surprised Henry; he at first believed them to be the wanderings of my disturbed imagination, but the pertinacity with which I continually recurred to the same subject persuaded him that my disorder indeed owed its origin to some uncommon and terrible event.

By very slow degrees, and with frequent relapses that alarmed and grieved my friend, I recovered. I remember the first time I became capable of observing outward objects with any kind of pleasure, I perceived that the fallen leaves had disappeared and that the young buds were shooting forth from the trees that shaded my window. It was a divine spring, and the season contributed greatly to my convalescence. I felt also sentiments of joy and affection revive in my bosom; my gloom disappeared, and in a short time I became as cheerful as before I was attacked by the fatal passion.

'Dearest Clerval,' exclaimed I, 'how kind, how very good you are to me. This whole winter, instead of being spent in study, as you promised yourself, has been consumed in my sick room. How shall

I ever repay you? I feel the greatest remorse for the disappointment of which I have been the occasion, but you will forgive me.'

'You will repay me entirely if you do not discompose yourself, but get well as fast as you can; and since you appear in such good spirits, I may speak to you on one subject, may I not?'

I trembled. One subject! What could it be? Could he allude to an object on whom I dared not even think?

'Compose yourself,' said Clerval, who observed my change of colour, 'I will not mention it if it agitates you; but your father and cousin would be very happy if they received a letter from you in your own handwriting. They hardly know how ill you have been and are uneasy at your long silence.'

'Is that all, my dear Henry? How could you suppose that my first thought would not fly towards those dear, dear friends whom I love and who are so deserving of my love?'

'If this is your present temper, my friend, you will perhaps be glad to see a letter that has been lying here some days for you; it is from your cousin, I believe.'

CHAPTER VI

Clerval then put the following letter into my hands. It was from my own Elizabeth:

My dearest Cousin,

You have been ill, very ill, and even the constant letters of dear kind Henry are not sufficient to reassure me on your account. You are forbidden to write – to hold a pen; yet one word from you, dear Victor, is necessary to calm our apprehensions. For a long time I have thought that each post would bring this line, and my persuasions have restrained my uncle from undertaking a journey to Ingolstadt. I have prevented his encountering the inconveniences and perhaps dangers of so long a journey, yet how often have I regretted not being able to perform it myself! I figure to myself that the task of attending on your sickbed has devolved on some mercenary old nurse, who could never guess your wishes nor minister to them with the care and affection of your poor cousin. Yet that is over now: Clerval writes that indeed you are getting better. I eagerly hope that you will confirm this intelligence soon in your own handwriting.

Get well – and return to us. You will find a happy, cheerful home and friends who love you dearly. Your father's health is vigorous, and he asks but to see you, but to be assured that you are well; and not a care will ever cloud his benevolent countenance. How pleased you would be to remark the improvement of our Ernest! He is now sixteen and full of activity and spirit. He is desirous to be a true Swiss and to enter into foreign service, but we cannot part with him, at least until his elder brother return to us. My uncle is not pleased with the idea of a military career in a distant country, but Ernest never had your powers of application. He looks upon study as an odious fetter; his time is spent in the open air, climbing the hills or rowing on the lake. I fear that he will become an idler unless we yield the point and permit him to enter on the profession which he has selected.

Little alteration, except the growth of our dear children, has taken place since you left us. The blue lake and snow-clad mountains – they never change; and I think our placid home and our contented hearts are regulated by the same immutable laws. My trifling occupations take up my time and amuse me, and I am rewarded for any exertions by seeing none but happy, kind faces around me. Since you left us, but one change has taken place in our little household. Do you remember on what occasion Justine Moritz entered our family? Probably you do not; I will relate her history, therefore, in a few words. Madame Moritz, her mother, was a widow with four children, of whom Justine was the third. This girl had always been the favourite of her father, but through a strange perversity, her mother could not endure her, and after the death of M. Moritz, treated her very ill. My aunt observed this, and when Justine was twelve years of age, prevailed on her mother to allow her to live at our house. The republican institutions of our country have produced simpler and happier manners than those which prevail in the great monarchies that surround it. Hence there is less distinction between the several classes of its inhabitants; and the lower orders, being neither so poor nor so despised, their manners are more refined and moral. A servant in Geneva does not mean the same thing as a servant in France and England. Justine, thus received in our family, learned the duties of a servant, a condition which, in our fortunate country, does not include the idea of ignorance and a sacrifice of the dignity of a human being.

Justine, you may remember, was a great favourite of yours; and I recollect you once remarked that if you were in an ill humour, one glance from Justine could dissipate it, for the same reason that Ariosto gives concerning the beauty of Angelica – she looked so frank-hearted and happy. My aunt conceived a great attachment for her, by which she was induced to give her an education superior to that which she had at first intended. This benefit was fully repaid; Justine was the most grateful little creature in the world: I do not mean that she made any professions; I never heard one pass her lips, but you could see by her eyes that she almost adored her protectress. Although her disposition was gay and in many respects inconsiderate, yet she paid the greatest attention to every gesture of my aunt. She thought her the model of all excellence and endeavoured to imitate her phraseology and manners, so that even now she often reminds me of her.

When my dearest aunt died every one was too much occupied in their own grief to notice poor Justine, who had attended her during her illness with the most anxious affection. Poor Justine was very ill; but other trials were reserved for her.

One by one, her brothers and sister died; and her mother, with the exception of her neglected daughter, was left childless. The conscience of the woman was troubled; she began to think that the deaths of her favourites was a judgment from heaven to chastise her partiality. She was a Roman Catholic; and I believe her confessor confirmed the idea which she had conceived. Accordingly, a few months after your departure for Ingolstadt,

Justine was called home by her repentant mother. Poor girl! She wept when she quitted our house; she was much altered since the death of my aunt; grief had given softness and a winning mildness to her manners which had before been remarkable for vivacity. Nor was her residence at her mother's house of a nature to restore her gaiety. The poor woman was very vacillating in her repentance. She sometimes begged Justine to forgive her unkindness but much oftener accused her of having caused the deaths of her brothers and sister. Perpetual fretting at length threw Madame Moritz into a decline, which at first increased her irritability, but she is now at peace for ever. She died on the first approach of cold weather, at the beginning of this last winter. Justine has returned to us, and I assure you I love her tenderly. She is very clever and gentle and extremely pretty; as I mentioned before, her mien and her expressions continually remind me of my dear aunt.

I must say also a few words to you, my dear cousin, of little darling William. I wish you could see him; he is very tall of his age, with sweet laughing blue eyes, dark eyelashes, and curling hair. When he smiles, two little dimples appear on each cheek, which are rosy with health. He has already had one or two little 'wives', but Louisa Biron is his favourite, a pretty little girl of five years of age.

Now, dear Victor, I dare say you wish to be indulged in a little gossip concerning the good people of Geneva. The pretty Miss Mansfield has already received the congratulatory visits on her approaching marriage with a young Englishman, John Melbourne, Esq. Her ugly sister, Manon, married M. Duvillard, the rich banker, last autumn. Your favourite school-fellow, Louis Manoir, has suffered several misfortunes since the departure of Clerval from Geneva. But he has already recovered his spirits, and is reported to be on the point of marrying a very lively, pretty Frenchwoman, Madame Tavernier. She is a widow, and much older than Manoir, but she is very much admired and a favourite with everybody.

I have written myself into better spirits, dear cousin; but my anxiety returns upon me as I conclude. Write, dearest Victor – one line – one word will be a blessing to us. Ten thousand thanks to Henry for his kindness, his affection, and his many letters; we are sincerely grateful. Adieu! My cousin, take care of yourself, and, I entreat you, write!

Elizabeth Lavenza
Geneva, March 18th, 17 –

'Dear, dear Elizabeth!' I exclaimed when I had read her letter. 'I will write instantly and relieve them from the anxiety they must feel.' I wrote, and this exertion greatly fatigued me; but my convalescence had commenced, and proceeded regularly. In another fortnight I was able to leave my chamber.

One of my first duties on my recovery was to introduce Clerval to the several professors of the university. In doing this, I underwent a kind of rough usage, ill befitting the wounds that my mind had sustained. Ever since the fatal night, the end of my labours, and the beginning of my misfortunes, I had conceived a violent antipathy even to the name of natural philosophy. When I was otherwise quite restored to health, the sight of a chemical instrument would renew all the agony of my nervous symptoms. Henry saw this, and had removed all my apparatus from my view. He had also changed my apartment, for he perceived that I had acquired a dislike for the room which had previously been my laboratory. But these cares of Clerval were made of no avail when I visited the professors. M. Waldman inflicted torture when he praised, with kindness and warmth, the astonishing progress I had made in the sciences. He soon perceived that I disliked the subject, but not guessing the real cause, he attributed my feelings to modesty and changed the subject from my improvement to the science itself, with a desire, as I evidently saw, of drawing me out. What could I do? He meant to please, and he tormented me. I felt as if he had placed carefully, one by one, in my view those instruments which were to be afterwards used in putting me to a slow and cruel death. I writhed under his words yet dared not exhibit the pain I felt. Clerval, whose eyes and feelings were always quick in discerning the sensations of others, declined the subject, alleging, in excuse, his total ignorance; and the conversation took a more general turn. I thanked my friend from my heart, but I did not speak. I saw plainly that he was surprised, but he never attempted to draw my secret from me; and although I loved him with a mixture of affection and reverence that knew no bounds, yet I could never persuade myself to confide to him that event which was so often present to my recollection but which I feared the detail to another would only impress more deeply.

M. Krempe was not equally docile; and in my condition at that time, of almost insupportable sensitiveness, his harsh, blunt encomiums gave me even more pain than the benevolent approbation of M. Waldman. 'D – n the fellow!' cried he. 'Why, M. Clerval,

48

I assure you he has outstripped us all. Ay, stare if you please; but it is nevertheless true. A youngster who, but a few years ago, believed in Cornelius Agrippa as firmly as in the Gospel, has now set himself at the head of the university; and if he is not soon pulled down, we shall all be out of countenance. Ay, ay,' continued he, observing my face expressive of suffering, 'M. Frankenstein is modest, an excellent quality in a young man. Young men should be diffident of themselves, you know, M. Clerval; I was myself when young; but that wears out in a very short time.'

M. Krempe had now commenced a eulogy on himself, which happily turned the conversation from a subject that was so annoying to me.

Clerval had never sympathized in my tastes for natural science, and his literary pursuits differed wholly from those which had occupied me. He came to the university with the design of making himself complete master of the Oriental languages, as thus he should open a field for the plan of life he had marked out for himself. Resolved to pursue no inglorious career, he turned his eyes towards the East as affording scope for his spirit of enterprise. The Persian, Arabic, and Sanskrit languages engaged his attention, and I was easily induced to enter on the same studies. Idleness had ever been irksome to me, and now that I wished to fly from reflection and hated my former studies, I felt great relief in being the fellow pupil with my friend, and found not only instruction but consolation in the works of the Orientalists. I did not, like him, attempt a critical knowledge of their dialects, for I did not contemplate making any other use of them than temporary amusement. I read merely to understand their meaning, and they well repaid my labours. Their melancholy is soothing, and their joy elevating, to a degree I never experienced in studying the authors of any other country. When you read their writings, life appears to consist in a warm sun and a garden of roses, in the smiles and frowns of a fair enemy, and the fire that consumes your own heart. How different from the manly and heroical poetry of Greece and Rome!

Summer passed away in these occupations, and my return to Geneva was fixed for the latter end of autumn; but being delayed by several accidents, winter and snow arrived, the roads were deemed impassable, and my journey was retarded until the ensuing spring. I felt this delay very bitterly, for I longed to see my native town and my beloved friends. My return had only been delayed so long from an unwillingness to leave Clerval in a strange place before he had become acquainted with any of its inhabitants. The winter, however, was spent cheerfully, and although the spring was uncommonly late, when it came its beauty compensated for its dilatoriness.

The month of May had already commenced, and I expected the letter daily which was to fix the date of my departure, when Henry proposed a pedestrian tour in the environs of Ingolstadt, that I might bid a personal farewell to the country I had so long inhabited. I acceded with pleasure to this proposition: I was fond of exercise, and Clerval had always been my favourite companion in the rambles of this nature that I had taken among the scenes of my native country.

We passed a fortnight in these perambulations; my health and spirits had long been restored, and they gained additional strength from the salubrious air I breathed, the natural incidents of our progress, and the conversation of my friend. Study had before secluded me from the intercourse of my fellow creatures and rendered me unsocial, but Clerval called forth the better feelings of my heart; he again taught me to love the aspect of nature and the cheerful faces of children. Excellent friend! How sincerely did you love me and endeavour to elevate my mind until it was on a level with your own! A selfish pursuit had cramped and narrowed me until your gentleness and affection warmed and opened my senses; I became the same happy creature who, a few years ago, loved and beloved by all, had no sorrow or care. When happy, inanimate nature had the power of bestowing on me the most delightful sensations. A serene sky and verdant fields filled me with ecstasy. The present season was indeed divine; the flowers of spring bloomed in the hedges, while those of summer were already in bud. I was undisturbed by thoughts which during the preceding year had pressed upon me, notwithstanding my endeavours to throw them off, with an invincible burden.

Henry rejoiced in my gaiety and sincerely sympathized in my feelings; he exerted himself to amuse me, while he expressed the sensations that filled his soul. The resources of his mind on this occasion were truly astonishing; his conversation was full of imagination, and very often, in imitation of the Persian and Arabic writers, he invented tales of wonderful fancy and passion. At other times he repeated my favourite poems or drew me out into arguments, which he supported with great ingenuity.

We returned to our college on a Sunday afternoon; the peasants were dancing, and everyone we met appeared gay and happy. My own spirits were high, and I bounded along with feelings of unbridled joy and hilarity.

CHAPTER VII

On my return, I found the following letter from my father: –

My dear Victor,

You have probably waited impatiently for a letter to fix the date of your return to us; and I was at first tempted to write only a few lines, merely mentioning the day on which I should expect you. But that would be a cruel kindness, and I dare not do it. What would be your surprise, my son, when you expected a happy and glad welcome, to behold, on the contrary, tears and wretchedness? And how, Victor, can I relate our misfortune? Absence cannot have rendered you callous to our joys and griefs; and how shall I inflict pain on my long absent son? I wish to prepare you for the woeful news, but I know it is impossible; even now your eye skims over the page to seek the words which are to convey to you the horrible tidings.

William is dead! – that sweet child, whose smiles delighted and warmed my heart, who was so gentle, yet so gay! Victor, he is murdered! I will not attempt to console you; but will simply relate the circumstances of the transaction.

Last Thursday (May 7th), I, my niece, and your two brothers, went to walk in Plainpalais. The evening was warm and serene, and we prolonged our walk farther than usual. It was already dusk before we thought of returning; and then we discovered that William and Ernest, who had gone on before, were not to be found. We accordingly rested on a seat until they should return. Presently Ernest came, and enquired if we had seen his brother; he said, that he had been playing with him, that William had run away to hide himself, and that he vainly sought for him, and afterwards waited for a long time, but that he did not return.

This account rather alarmed us, and we continued to search for him until night fell, when Elizabeth conjectured that he might have returned to the house. He was not there. We returned again, with torches; for I could not rest, when I thought that my sweet boy had lost himself, and was exposed to all the damps and dews of night; Elizabeth also suffered extreme anguish. About five in the morning I discovered my lovely boy, whom the night before I had seen blooming and active in health, stretched on the grass livid and motionless; the print of the murderer's finger was on his neck.

*He was conveyed home, and the anguish that was visible in my counte-
nance betrayed the secret to Elizabeth. She was very earnest to see the corpse.
At first I attempted to prevent her; but she persisted, and entering the room
where it lay, hastily examined the neck of the victim, and clasping her hands
exclaimed, 'O God! I have murdered my darling child!'*

*She fainted, and was restored with extreme difficulty. When she again
lived, it was only to weep and sigh. She told me, that that same evening
William had teased her to let him wear a very valuable miniature that
she possessed of your mother. This picture is gone, and was doubtless the
temptation which urged the murdered to the deed. We have no trace of him
at present, although our exertions to discover him are unremitted; but they
will not restore my beloved William!*

*Come, dearest Victor; you alone can console Elizabeth. She weeps contin-
ually, and accuses herself unjustly as the cause of his death; her words pierce
my heart. We are all unhappy; but will not that be an additional motive for
you, my son, to return and be our comforter? Your dear mother! Alas, Victor!
I now say, Thank God she did not live to witness the cruel, miserable death
of her youngest darling!*

*Come, Victor; not brooding thoughts of vengeance against the assassin,
but with feelings of peace and gentleness, that will heal, instead of festering,
the wounds of our minds. Enter the house of mourning, my friend, but with
kindness and affection for those who love you, and not with hatred for your
enemies.*

Your affectionate and afflicted father,

*Alphonse Frankenstein.
Geneva, May 12th, 17 – .*

Clerval, who had watched my countenance as I read this letter, was
surprised to observe the despair that succeeded the joy I at first
expressed on receiving new from my friends. I threw the letter on
the table, and covered my face with my hands.

'My dear Frankenstein,' exclaimed Henry, when he perceived
me weep with bitterness, 'are you always to be unhappy? My dear
friend, what has happened?'

I motioned him to take up the letter, while I walked up and
down the room in the extremest agitation. Tears also gushed from
the eyes of Clerval, as he read the account of my misfortune.

'I can offer you no consolation, my friend,' said he; 'your disaster is irreparable. What do you intend to do?'

'To go instantly to Geneva: come with me, Henry, to order the horses.'

During our walk, Clerval endeavoured to say a few words of consolation; he could only express his heartfelt sympathy. 'Poor William!' said he, dear lovely child, he now sleeps with his angel mother! Who that had seen him bright and joyous in his young beauty, but must weep over his untimely loss! To die so miserably; to feel the murderer's grasp! How much more a murderer that could destroy radiant innocence! Poor little fellow! one only consolation have we; his friends mourn and weep, but he is at rest. The pang is over, his sufferings are at an end for ever. A sod covers his gentle form, and he knows no pain. He can no longer be a subject for pity; we must reserve that for his miserable survivors.'

Clerval spoke thus as we hurried through the streets; the words impressed themselves on my mind and I remembered them afterwards in solitude. But now, as soon as the horses arrived, I hurried into a cabriolet, and bade farewell to my friend.

My journey was very melancholy. At first I wished to hurry on, for I longed to console and sympathise with my loved and sorrowing friends; but when I drew near my native town, I slackened my progress. I could hardly sustain the multitude of feelings that crowded into my mind. I passed through scenes familiar to my youth, but which I had not seen for nearly six years. How altered every thing might be during that time! One sudden and desolating change had taken place; but a thousand little circumstances might have by degrees worked other alterations, which, although they were done more tranquilly, might not be the less decisive. Fear overcame me; I dared no advance, dreading a thousand nameless evils that made me tremble, although I was unable to define them.

I remained two days at Lausanne, in this painful state of mind. I contemplated the lake: the waters were placid; all around was calm; and the snowy mountains, 'the palaces of nature,' were not changed. By degrees the calm and heavenly scene restored me, and I continued my journey towards Geneva.

The road ran by the side of the lake, which became narrower as I approached my native town. I discovered more distinctly the black sides of Jura, and the bright summit of Mont Blanc. I wept like a child. 'Dear mountains! my own beautiful lake! how do you welcome your wanderer? Your summits are clear; the sky and lake are blue and placid. Is this to prognosticate peace, or to mock at my unhappiness?'

I fear, my friend, that I shall render myself tedious by dwelling on these preliminary circumstances; but they were days of comparative happiness, and I think of them with pleasure. My country, my beloved country! who but a native can tell the delight I took in again beholding thy streams, thy mountains, and, more than all, thy lovely lake!

Yet, as I drew nearer home, grief and fear again overcame me. Night also closed around; and when I could hardly see the dark mountains, I felt still more gloomily. The picture appeared a vast and dim scene of evil, and I foresaw obscurely that I was destined to become the most wretched of human beings. Alas! I prophesied truly, and failed only in one single circumstance, that in all the misery I imagined and dreaded, I did not conceive the hundredth part of the anguish I was destined to endure.

It was completely dark when I arrived in the environs of Geneva; the gates of the town were already shut; and I was obliged to pass the night at Secheron, a village at the distance of half a league from the city. The sky was serene; and, as I was unable to rest, I resolved to visit the spot where my poor William had been murdered. As I could not pass through the town, I was obliged to cross the lake in a boat to arrive at Plainpalais. During this short voyage I saw the lightning playing on the summit of Mont Blanc in the most beautiful figures. The storm appeared to approach rapidly, and, on landing, I ascended a low hill, that I might observe its progress. It advanced; the heavens were clouded, and I soon felt the rain coming slowly in large drops, but its violence quickly increased.

I quitted my seat, and walked on, although the darkness and storm increased every minute, and the thunder burst with a terrific crash over my head. It was echoed from Saleve, the Juras, and the Alps of Savoy; vivid flashes of lightning dazzled my eyes, illuminating the lake, making it appear like a vast sheet of fire; then for an instant every thing seemed of a pitchy darkness, until the eye recovered itself from the preceding flash. The storm, as is often the case in Switzerland, appeared at once in various parts of the heavens. The most violent storm hung exactly north of the town, over the part of the lake which lies between the promontory of Belrive and the village of Copet. Another storm enlightened Jura with faint flashes; and another darkened and sometimes disclosed the Mole, a peaked mountain to the east of the lake.

While I watched the tempest, so beautiful yet terrific, I wandered on with a hasty step. This noble war in the sky elevated my spirits; I clasped my hands, and exclaimed aloud, 'William, dear angel! this is thy funeral, this thy dirge!' As I said these words, I perceived in the gloom a figure which stole from behind a clump of trees near me; I stood fixed, gazing intently: I could not be mistaken. A flash of lightning illuminated the object, and discovered its shape plainly to me; its gigantic stature, and the deformity of its aspect, more hideous than belongs to humanity, instantly informed me that it was the wretch, the filthy daemon, to whom I had given life. What did he there? Could he be (I shuddered at the conception) the murderer of my brother? No sooner did that idea cross my imagination, than I became convinced of its truth; my teeth chattered, and I was forced to lean against a tree for support. The figure passed me quickly, and I lost it in the gloom. Nothing in human shape could have destroyed the fair child. He was the murderer! I could not doubt it. The mere presence of the idea was an irresistible proof of the fact. I thought of pursuing the devil; but it would have been in vain, for another flash discovered him to me hanging among the rocks of the nearly perpendicular ascent of Mont Saleve, a hill that bounds Plainpalais on the south. He soon reached the summit, and disappeared.

I remained motionless. The thunder ceased; but the rain still continued, and the scene was enveloped in an impenetrable darkness. I resolved in my minds the events which I had until now sought to forget: the whole train of my progress toward the creation; the appearance of the works of my own hands at my bedside; its departure. Two years had now nearly elapsed since the night on which he first received life; and was this his first crime? Alas! I had turned loose into the world a depraved wretch, whose delight was in carnage and misery; had he not murdered my brother?

No one can conceive the anguish I suffered during the remainder of the night, which I spent, cold and wet, in the open air. But I did not feel the inconvenience of the weather; my imagination was busy in scenes of evil and despair. I considered the being whom I had cast among mankind, and endowed with the will and power to effect purposes of horror, such as the deed which he had now done, nearly in the light of my own vampire, my own spirit let loose from the grave, and forced to destroy all that was dear to me.

Day dawned; and I directed my steps towards the town. The gates were open, and I hastened to my father's house. My first thought was to discover what I knew of the murderer, and cause instant pursuit to be made. But I paused when I reflected on the story that I had to tell. A being whom I myself had formed, and endued with life, had met me at midnight among the precipices of an inaccessible mountain. I remembered also the nervous fever with which I had been seized just at the time that I dated my creation, and which would give an air of delirium to a tale otherwise so utterly improbable. I well knew that if any other had communicated such a relation to me, I should have looked upon it as the ravings of insanity. Besides, the strange nature of the animal would elude all pursuit, even if I were so far credited as to persuade my relatives to commence it. And then of what use would be pursuit? Who could arrest a creature capable of scaling the overhanging sides of Mont Saleve? These reflections determined me, and I resolved to remain silent.

It was about five in the morning when I entered my father's house. I told the servants not to disturb the family, and went into the library to attend their usual hour of rising.

Six years had elapsed, passed in a dream but for one indelible trace, and I stood in the same place where I had last embraced my father before my departure for Ingolstadt. Beloved and venerable parent! He still remained to me. I gazed on the picture of my mother, which stood over the mantel-piece. It was an historical subject, painted at my father's desire, and represented Caroline Beaufort in an agony of despair, kneeling by the coffin of her dead father. Her garb was rustic, and her cheek pale; but there was an air of dignity and beauty, that hardly permitted the sentiment of pity. Below this picture was a miniature of William; and my tears flowed when I looked upon it. While I was thus engaged, Ernest entered: he had heard me arrive, and hastened to welcome me: 'Welcome, my dearest Victor,' said he. 'Ah! I wish you had come three months ago, and then you would have found us all joyous and delighted. You come to us now to share a misery which nothing can alleviate; yet your presence will, I hope, revive our father, who seems sinking under his misfortune; and your persuasions will induce poor Elizabeth to cease her vain and tormenting self-accusations. – Poor William! he was our darling and our pride!'

Tears, unrestrained, fell from my brother's eyes; a sense of mortal agony crept over my frame. Before, I had only imagined the wretchedness of my desolated home; the reality came on me as a new, and a not less terrible, disaster. I tried to calm Ernest; I enquired more minutely concerning my father, and her I named my cousin.

'She most of all,' said Ernest, 'requires consolation; she accused herself of having caused the death of my brother, and that made her very wretched. But since the murderer has been discovered – '

'The murderer discovered! Good God! how can that be? who could attempt to pursue him? It is impossible; one might as well try to overtake the winds, or confine a mountain-stream with a straw. I saw him too; he was free last night!'

'I do not know what you mean,' replied my brother, in accents of wonder, 'but to us the discovery we have made completes our misery. No one would believe it at first; and even now Elizabeth will not be convinced, notwithstanding all the evidence. Indeed, who would credit that Justine Moritz, who was so amiable, and fond of all the family, could suddenly become so capable of so frightful, so appalling a crime?'

'Justine Moritz! Poor, poor girl, is she the accused? But it is wrongfully; every one knows that; no one believes it, surely, Ernest?'

'No one did at first; but several circumstances came out, that have almost forced conviction upon us; and her own behaviour has been so confused, as to add to the evidence of facts a weight that, I fear, leaves no hope for doubt. But she will be tried to-day, and you will then hear all.'

He then related that, the morning on which the murder of poor William had been discovered, Justine had been taken ill, and confined to her bed for several days. During this interval, one of the servants, happening to examine the apparel she had worn on the night of the murder, had discovered in her pocket the picture of my mother, which had been judged to be the temptation of the murderer. The servant instantly showed it to one of the others, who, without saying a word to any of the family, went to a magistrate; and, upon their deposition, Justine was apprehended. On being charged with the fact, the poor girl confirmed the suspicion in a great measure by her extreme confusion of manner. This was a strange tale, but it did not shake my faith; and I replied earnestly, 'You are all mistaken; I know the murderer. Justine, poor, good Justine, is innocent.'

At that instant my father entered. I saw unhappiness deeply impressed on his countenance, but he endeavoured to welcome me cheerfully; and, after we had exchanged our mournful greeting, would have introduced some other topic than that of our disaster, had not Ernest exclaimed, 'Good God, papa! Victor says that he knows who was the murderer of poor William.'

'We do also, unfortunately,' replied my father, 'for indeed I had rather have been for ever ignorant than have discovered so much depravity and ungratitude in one I valued so highly.'

'My dear father, you are mistaken; Justine is innocent.'

'If she is, God forbid that she should suffer as guilty. She is to be tried to-day, and I hope, I sincerely hope, that she will be acquitted.'

This speech calmed me. I was firmly convinced in my own mind that Justine, and indeed every human being, was guiltless of this murder. I had no fear, therefore, that any circumstantial evidence could be brought forward strong enough to convict her. My tale was not one to announce publicly; its astounding horror would be looked upon as madness by the vulgar. Did any one indeed exist, except I, the creator, who would believe, unless his senses convinced him, in the existence of the living monument of presumption and rash ignorance which I had let loose upon the world?

We were soon joined by Elizabeth. Time had altered her since I last beheld her; it had endowed her with loveliness surpassing the beauty of her childish years. There was the same candour, the same vivacity, but it was allied to an expression more full of sensibility and intellect. She welcomed me with the greatest affection. 'Your arrival, my dear cousin,' said she, 'fills me with hope. You perhaps will find some means to justify my poor guiltless Justine. Alas! who is safe, if she be convicted of crime? I rely on her innocence as certainly as I do upon my own. Our misfortune is doubly hard to us; we have not only lost that lovely darling boy, but this poor girl, whom I sincerely love, is to be torn away by even a worse fate. If she is condemned, I never shall know joy more. But she will not, I am sure she will not; and then I shall be happy again, even after the sad death of my little William.'

'She is innocent, my Elizabeth,' said I, 'and that shall be proved; fear nothing, but let your spirits be cheered by the assurance of her acquittal.'

'How kind and generous you are! every one else believes in her guilt, and that made me wretched, for I knew that it was impossible:

and to see every one else prejudiced in so deadly a manner rendered me hopeless and despairing.' She wept.

'Dearest niece,' said my father, 'dry your tears. If she is, as you believe, innocent, rely on the justice of our laws, and the activity with which I shall prevent the slightest shadow of partiality.'

CHAPTER VIII

We passed a few sad hours until eleven o'clock, when the trial was to commence. My father and the rest of the family being obliged to attend as witnesses, I accompanied them to the court. During the whole of this wretched mockery of justice I suffered living torture. It was to be decided whether the result of my curiosity and lawless devices would cause the death of two of my fellow beings: one a smiling babe full of innocence and joy, the other far more dreadfully murdered, with every aggravation of infamy that could make the murder memorable in horror. Justine also was a girl of merit and possessed qualities which promised to render her life happy; now all was to be obliterated in an ignominious grave, and I the cause! A thousand times rather would I have confessed myself guilty of the crime ascribed to Justine, but I was absent when it was committed, and such a declaration would have been considered as the ravings of a madman and would not have exculpated her who suffered through me.

The appearance of Justine was calm. She was dressed in mourning, and her countenance, always engaging, was rendered, by the solemnity of her feelings, exquisitely beautiful. Yet she appeared confident in innocence and did not tremble, although gazed on and execrated by thousands, for all the kindness which her beauty might otherwise have excited was obliterated in the minds of the spectators by the imagination of the enormity she was supposed to have committed. She was tranquil, yet her tranquillity was evidently constrained; and as her confusion had before been adduced as a proof of her guilt, she worked up her mind to an appearance of courage. When she entered the court she threw her eyes round it and quickly discovered where we were seated. A tear seemed to dim her eye when she saw us, but she quickly recovered herself, and a look of sorrowful affection seemed to attest her utter guiltlessness.

The trial began, and after the advocate against her had stated the charge, several witnesses were called. Several strange facts combined against her, which might have staggered anyone who had not such proof of her innocence as I had. She had been out the whole of the night on which the murder had been committed and towards morning had been perceived by a market-woman not far from the spot where the body of the murdered child had been afterwards found. The woman asked her what she did there, but she looked very strangely and only returned a confused and unintelligible answer. She returned to the house about eight o'clock, and when one inquired where she had passed the night, she replied that she had been looking for the child and demanded earnestly if anything had been heard concerning him. When shown the body, she fell into violent hysterics and kept her bed for several days. The picture was then produced which the servant had found in her pocket; and when Elizabeth, in a faltering voice, proved that it was the same which, an hour before the child had been missed, she had placed round his neck, a murmur of horror and indignation filled the court.

Justine was called on for her defence. As the trial had proceeded, her countenance had altered. Surprise, horror, and misery were strongly expressed. Sometimes she struggled with her tears, but when she was desired to plead, she collected her powers and spoke in an audible although variable voice.

'God knows,' she said, 'how entirely I am innocent. But I do not pretend that my protestations should acquit me; I rest my innocence on a plain and simple explanation of the facts which have been adduced against me, and I hope the character I have always borne will incline my judges to a favourable interpretation where any circumstance appears doubtful or suspicious.'

She then related that, by the permission of Elizabeth, she had passed the evening of the night on which the murder had been committed at the house of an aunt at Chene, a village situated at about a league from Geneva. On her return, at about nine o'clock, she met a man who asked her if she had seen anything of the child who was lost. She was alarmed by this account and passed several hours in looking for him, when the gates of Geneva were shut, and she was forced to remain several hours of the night in a barn belonging to a cottage, being unwilling to call up the inhabitants, to whom she was well known. Most of the night she spent here watching; towards morning she believed that she slept for a few minutes; some steps disturbed her, and she awoke. It was dawn, and she quitted her asylum, that she might again endeavour to find my brother. If she had gone near the spot where his body lay, it was without her knowledge. That she had been bewildered when questioned by the market-woman was not surprising, since she had passed a sleepless night and the fate of poor William was yet uncertain. Concerning the picture she could give no account.

'I know,' continued the unhappy victim, 'how heavily and fatally this one circumstance weighs against me, but I have no power of explaining it; and when I have expressed my utter ignorance, I am only left to conjecture concerning the probabilities by which it might have been placed in my pocket. But here also I am checked. I believe that I have no enemy on earth, and none surely would have been so wicked as to destroy me wantonly. Did the murderer place it there? I know of no opportunity afforded him for so doing; or, if I had, why should he have stolen the jewel, to part with it again so soon?

'I commit my cause to the justice of my judges, yet I see no room for hope. I beg permission to have a few witnesses examined concerning my character, and if their testimony shall not overweigh my supposed guilt, I must be condemned, although I would pledge my salvation on my innocence.'

Several witnesses were called who had known her for many years, and they spoke well of her; but fear and hatred of the crime of which they supposed her guilty rendered them timorous and unwilling to come forward. Elizabeth saw even this last resource, her excellent dispositions and irreproachable conduct, about to fail the accused, when, although violently agitated, she desired permission to address the court.

'I am,' said she, 'the cousin of the unhappy child who was murdered, or rather his sister, for I was educated by and have lived with his parents ever since and even long before his birth. It may therefore be judged indecent in me to come forward on this occasion, but when I see a fellow creature about to perish through the cowardice of her pretended friends, I wish to be allowed to speak, that I may say what I know of her character. I am well acquainted with the accused. I have lived in the same house with her, at one time for five and at another for nearly two years. During all that period she appeared to me the most amiable and benevolent of human creatures. She nursed Madame Frankenstein, my aunt, in her last illness, with the greatest affection and care and afterwards attended her own mother during a tedious illness, in a manner that excited the admiration of all who knew her, after which she again lived in my uncle's house, where she was beloved by all the family. She was warmly attached to the child who is now dead and acted towards him like a most affectionate mother. For my own part, I do not hesitate to say that, notwithstanding all the evidence produced against her, I believe and rely on her perfect innocence. She had no temptation for such an action; as to the bauble on which the chief proof rests, if she had earnestly desired it, I should have willingly given it to her, so much do I esteem and value her.'

A murmur of approbation followed Elizabeth's simple and powerful appeal, but it was excited by her generous interference, and not in favour of poor Justine, on whom the public indignation was turned with renewed violence, charging her with the blackest ingratitude. She herself wept as Elizabeth spoke, but she did not answer. My own agitation and anguish was extreme during the whole trial. I believed in her innocence; I knew it. Could the demon who had (I did not for a minute doubt) murdered my brother also in his hellish sport have betrayed the innocent to death and ignominy? I could not sustain the horror of my situation, and when I perceived that the popular voice and the countenances of the judges had already condemned my unhappy victim, I rushed out of the court in agony. The tortures of the accused did not equal mine; she was sustained by innocence, but the fangs of remorse tore my bosom and would not forgo their hold.

I passed a night of unmingled wretchedness. In the morning I went to the court; my lips and throat were parched. I dared not ask the fatal question, but I was known, and the officer guessed the cause of my visit. The ballots had been thrown; they were all black, and Justine was condemned.

I cannot pretend to describe what I then felt. I had before experienced sensations of horror, and I have endeavoured to bestow upon them adequate expressions, but words cannot convey an idea of the heart-sickening despair that I then endured. The person to whom I addressed myself added that Justine had already confessed her guilt. 'That evidence,' he observed, 'was hardly required in so glaring a case, but I am glad of it, and, indeed, none of our judges like to condemn a criminal upon circumstantial evidence, be it ever so decisive.'

This was strange and unexpected intelligence; what could it mean? Had my eyes deceived me? And was I really as mad as the whole world would believe me to be if I disclosed the object of my suspicions? I hastened to return home, and Elizabeth eagerly demanded the result.

'My cousin,' replied I, 'it is decided as you may have expected; all judges had rather that ten innocent should suffer than that one guilty should escape. But she has confessed.'

This was a dire blow to poor Elizabeth, who had relied with firmness upon Justine's innocence. 'Alas!' said she. 'How shall I ever again believe in human goodness? Justine, whom I loved and esteemed as my sister, how could she put on those smiles of innocence only to betray? Her mild eyes seemed incapable of any severity or guile, and yet she has committed a murder.'

Soon after we heard that the poor victim had expressed a desire to see my cousin. My father wished her not to go but said that he left it to her own judgment and feelings to decide. 'Yes,' said Elizabeth, 'I will go, although she is guilty; and you, Victor, shall accompany me; I cannot go alone.' The idea of this visit was torture to me, yet I could not refuse.

We entered the gloomy prison chamber and beheld Justine sitting on some straw at the farther end; her hands were manacled, and her head rested on her knees. She rose on seeing us enter; and when we were left alone with her, she threw herself at the feet of Elizabeth, weeping bitterly. My cousin wept also.

'Oh, Justine!' said she. 'Why did you rob me of my last consolation? I relied on your innocence, and although I was then very wretched, I was not so miserable as I am now.'

'And do you also believe that I am so very, very wicked? Do you also join with my enemies to crush me, to condemn me as a murderer?' Her voice was suffocated with sobs.

'Rise, my poor girl,' said Elizabeth; 'why do you kneel, if you are innocent? I am not one of your enemies, I believed you guiltless, notwithstanding every evidence, until I heard that you had yourself declared your guilt. That report, you say, is false; and be assured, dear Justine, that nothing can shake my confidence in you for a moment, but your own confession.'

'I did confess, but I confessed a lie. I confessed, that I might obtain absolution; but now that falsehood lies heavier at my heart than all my other sins. The God of heaven forgive me! Ever since I was condemned, my confessor has besieged me; he threatened and menaced, until I almost began to think that I was the monster that he said I was. He threatened excommunication and hell fire in my last moments if I continued obdurate. Dear lady, I had none to support me; all looked on me as a wretch doomed to ignominy and perdition. What could I do? In an evil hour I subscribed to a lie; and now only am I truly miserable.'

She paused, weeping, and then continued, 'I thought with horror, my sweet lady, that you should believe your Justine, whom your blessed aunt had so highly honoured, and whom you loved, was a creature capable of a crime which none but the devil himself could have perpetrated. Dear William! dearest blessed child! I soon shall see you again in heaven, where we shall all he happy; and that consoles me, going as I am to suffer ignominy and death.'

'Oh, Justine! Forgive me for having for one moment distrusted you. Why did you confess? But do not mourn, dear girl. Do not fear. I will proclaim, I will prove your innocence. I will melt the stony hearts of your enemies by my tears and prayers. You shall not die! You, my playfellow, my companion, my sister, perish on the scaffold! No! No! I never could survive so horrible a misfortune.'

Justine shook her head mournfully. 'I do not fear to die,' she said; 'that pang is past. God raises my weakness and gives me courage to endure the worst. I leave a sad and bitter world; and if you remember me and think of me as of one unjustly condemned, I am resigned to the fate awaiting me. Learn from me, dear lady, to submit in patience to the will of heaven!'

During this conversation I had retired to a corner of the prison room, where I could conceal the horrid anguish that possessed me. Despair! Who dared talk of that? The poor victim, who on the morrow was to pass the awful boundary between life and death, felt not, as I did, such deep and bitter agony. I gnashed my teeth and ground them together, uttering a groan that came from my inmost soul. Justine started. When she saw who it was, she approached me and said, 'Dear sir, you are very kind to visit me; you, I hope, do not believe that I am guilty?'

I could not answer. 'No, Justine,' said Elizabeth; 'he is more convinced of your innocence than I was, for even when he heard that you had confessed, he did not credit it.'

'I truly thank him. In these last moments I feel the sincerest gratitude towards those who think of me with kindness. How sweet is the affection of others to such a wretch as I am! It removes more than half my misfortune, and I feel as if I could die in peace now that my innocence is acknowledged by you, dear lady, and your cousin.'

Thus the poor sufferer tried to comfort others and herself. She indeed gained the resignation she desired. But I, the true murderer, felt the never-dying worm alive in my bosom, which allowed of no hope or consolation. Elizabeth also wept and was unhappy, but hers also was the misery of innocence, which, like a cloud that passes over the fair moon, for a while hides but cannot tarnish its brightness. Anguish and despair had penetrated into the core of my heart; I bore a hell within me which nothing could extinguish. We stayed several hours with Justine, and it was with great difficulty that Elizabeth could tear herself away. 'I wish,' cried she, 'that I were to die with you; I cannot live in this world of misery.'

Justine assumed an air of cheerfulness, while she with difficulty repressed her bitter tears. She embraced Elizabeth and said in a voice of half-suppressed emotion, 'Farewell, sweet lady, dearest Elizabeth, my beloved and only friend; may heaven, in its bounty, bless and preserve you; may this be the last misfortune that you will ever suffer! Live, and be happy, and make others so.'

And on the morrow Justine died. Elizabeth's heart-rending eloquence failed to move the judges from their settled conviction in the criminality of the saintly sufferer. My passionate and indignant appeals were lost upon them. And when I received their cold answers and heard the harsh, unfeeling reasoning of these men, my purposed avowal died away on my lips. Thus I might proclaim myself a madman, but not revoke the sentence passed upon my wretched victim. She perished on the scaffold as a murderess!

From the tortures of my own heart, I turned to contemplate the deep and voiceless grief of my Elizabeth. This also was my doing! And my father's woe, and the desolation of that late so smiling home all was the work of my thrice-accursed hands! Ye weep, unhappy ones, but these are not your last tears! Again shall you raise the funeral wail, and the sound of your lamentations shall again and again be heard! Frankenstein, your son, your kinsman, your early, much-loved friend; he who would spend each vital drop of blood for your sakes, who has no thought nor sense of joy except as it is mirrored also in your dear countenances, who would fill the air with blessings and spend his life in serving you – he bids you weep, to shed countless tears; happy beyond his hopes, if thus inexorable fate be satisfied, and if the destruction pause before the peace of the grave have succeeded to your sad torments!

Thus spoke my prophetic soul, as, torn by remorse, horror, and despair, I beheld those I loved spend vain sorrow upon the graves of William and Justine, the first hapless victims to my unhallowed arts.

CHAPTER IX

Nothing is more painful to the human mind than, after the feelings have been worked up by a quick succession of events, the dead calmness of inaction and certainty which follows and deprives the soul both of hope and fear. Justine died, she rested, and I was alive. The blood flowed freely in my veins, but a weight of despair and remorse pressed on my heart which nothing could remove. Sleep fled from my eyes; I wandered like an evil spirit, for I had committed deeds of mischief beyond description horrible, and more, much more (I persuaded myself) was yet behind. Yet my heart overflowed with kindness and the love of virtue. I had begun life with benevolent intentions and thirsted for the moment when I should put them in practice and make myself useful to my fellow beings. Now all was blasted; instead of that serenity of conscience which allowed me to look back upon the past with self-satisfaction, and from thence to gather promise of new hopes, I was seized by remorse and the sense of guilt, which hurried me away to a hell of intense tortures such as no language can describe.

This state of mind preyed upon my health, which had perhaps never entirely recovered from the first shock it had sustained. I shunned the face of man; all sound of joy or complacency was torture to me; solitude was my only consolation – deep, dark, deathlike solitude.

My father observed with pain the alteration perceptible in my disposition and habits and endeavoured by arguments deduced from the feelings of his serene conscience and guiltless life to inspire me with fortitude and awaken in me the courage to dispel the dark cloud which brooded over me. 'Do you think, Victor,' said he, 'that I do not suffer also? No one could love a child more than I loved your brother' – tears came into his eyes as he spoke – 'but is it not a duty to the survivors that we should refrain from augmenting their unhappiness by an appearance of immoderate grief? It is also a duty owed to yourself, for excessive sorrow prevents improvement or enjoyment, or even the discharge of daily usefulness, without which no man is fit for society.'

This advice, although good, was totally inapplicable to my

case; I should have been the first to hide my grief and console my friends if remorse had not mingled its bitterness, and terror its alarm, with my other sensations. Now I could only answer my father with a look of despair and endeavour to hide myself from his view.

About this time we retired to our house at Belrive. This change was particularly agreeable to me. The shutting of the gates regularly at ten o'clock and the impossibility of remaining on the lake after that hour had rendered our residence within the walls of Geneva very irksome to me. I was now free. Often, after the rest of the family had retired for the night, I took the boat and passed many hours upon the water. Sometimes, with my sails set, I was carried by the wind; and sometimes, after rowing into the middle of the lake, I left the boat to pursue its own course and gave way to my own miserable reflections. I was often tempted, when all was at peace around me, and I the only unquiet thing that wandered restless in a scene so beautiful and heavenly – if I except some bat, or the frogs, whose harsh and interrupted croaking was heard only when I approached the shore – often, I say, I was tempted to plunge into the silent lake, that the waters might close over me and my calamities forever. But I was restrained, when I thought of the heroic and suffering Elizabeth, whom I tenderly loved, and whose existence was bound up in mine. I thought also of my father and surviving brother; should I by my base desertion leave them exposed and unprotected to the malice of the fiend whom I had let loose among them?

At these moments I wept bitterly and wished that peace would revisit my mind only that I might afford them consolation and happiness. But that could not be. Remorse extinguished every hope. I had been the author of unalterable evils, and I lived in daily fear lest the monster whom I had created should perpetrate some new wickedness. I had an obscure feeling that all was not over and that he would still commit some signal crime, which by its enormity should almost efface the recollection of the past. There was always scope for fear so long as anything I loved remained behind. My abhorrence of this fiend cannot be conceived. When I thought of him I gnashed my teeth, my eyes became inflamed, and I ardently wished to extinguish that life which I had so thought-lessly bestowed. When I reflected on his crimes and malice, my hatred and revenge burst all bounds of moderation. I would have made a pilgrimage to the highest peak of the Andes, could I when there have precipitated him to their base. I wished to see him again, that I might wreak the utmost extent of abhorrence on his head and avenge the deaths of William and Justine. Our house was the house of mourning. My father's health was deeply shaken by the horror of the recent events. Elizabeth was sad and desponding; she no longer took delight in her ordinary occupations; all pleasure seemed to her sacrilege toward the dead; eternal woe and tears she then thought was the just tribute she should pay to innocence so blasted and destroyed. She was no longer that happy creature who in earlier youth wandered with me on the banks of the lake and talked with ecstasy of our future prospects. The first of those sorrows which are sent to wean us from the earth had visited her, and its dimming influence quenched her dearest smiles.

'When I reflect, my dear cousin,' said she, 'on the miserable death of Justine Moritz, I no longer see the world and its works as they before appeared to me. Before, I looked upon the accounts of vice and injustice that I read in books or heard from others as tales of ancient days or imaginary evils; at least they were remote and more familiar to reason than to the imagination; but now misery has come home, and men appear to me as monsters thirsting for each other's blood. Yet I am certainly unjust. Everybody believed that poor girl to be guilty; and if she could have committed the crime for which she suffered, assuredly she would have been the most depraved of human creatures. For the sake of a few jewels, to have murdered the son of her benefactor and friend, a child whom she had nursed from its birth, and appeared to love as if it had been her own! I could not consent to the death of any human being, but certainly I should have thought such a creature unfit to remain in the society of men. But she was innocent. I know, I feel she was innocent; you are of the same opinion, and that confirms me. Alas! Victor, when falsehood can look so like the truth, who can assure themselves of certain happiness? I feel as if I were walking on the edge of a precipice, towards which thousands are crowding and endeavouring to plunge me into the abyss. William and Justine were assassinated, and the murderer escapes; he walks about the world free, and perhaps respected. But even if I were condemned to suffer on the scaffold for the same crimes, I would not change places with such a wretch.'

I listened to this discourse with the extremest agony. I, not in deed, but in effect, was the true murderer. Elizabeth read my anguish in my countenance, and kindly taking my hand, said, 'My dearest friend, you must calm yourself. These events have affected me, God knows how deeply; but I am not so wretched as you are. There is an expression of despair, and sometimes of revenge, in your countenance that makes me tremble. Dear Victor, banish these dark passions. Remember the friends around you, who centre all their hopes in you. Have we lost the power of rendering you happy? Ah! While we love, while we are true to each other, here in this land of peace and beauty, your native country, we may reap every tranquil blessing – what can disturb our peace?'

And could not such words from her whom I fondly prized before every other gift of fortune suffice to chase away the fiend that lurked in my heart? Even as she spoke I drew near to her, as if in terror, lest at that very moment the destroyer had been near to rob me of her.

Thus not the tenderness of friendship, nor the beauty of earth, nor of heaven, could redeem my soul from woe; the very accents of love were ineffectual. I was encompassed by a cloud which no beneficial influence could penetrate. The wounded deer dragging its fainting limbs to some untrodden brake, there to gaze upon the arrow which had pierced it, and to die, was but a type of me.

Sometimes I could cope with the sullen despair that overwhelmed me, but sometimes the whirlwind passions of my soul drove me to seek, by bodily exercise and by change of place, some relief from my intolerable sensations. It was during an access of this kind that I suddenly left my home, and bending my steps towards the near Alpine valleys, sought in the magnificence, the eternity of such scenes, to forget myself and my ephemeral, because human, sorrows. My wanderings were directed towards the valley of Chamounix. I had visited it frequently during my boyhood. Six years had passed since then: I was a wreck, but nought had changed in those savage and enduring scenes.

I performed the first part of my journey on horseback. I afterwards hired a mule, as the more sure-footed and least liable to receive injury on these rugged roads. The weather was fine; it was about the middle of the month of August, nearly two months after the death of Justine, that miserable epoch from which I dated all my woe. The weight upon my spirit was sensibly lightened as I plunged yet deeper in the ravine of Arve. The immense mountains and precipices that overhung me on every side, the sound of the river raging among the rocks, and the dashing of the waterfalls around spoke of a power mighty as Omnipotence – and I ceased to fear or to bend before any being less almighty than that which had created and ruled the elements, here displayed in their most terrific guise. Still, as I ascended higher, the valley assumed a more magnificent and astonishing character. Ruined castles hanging on the precipices of piny mountains, the impetuous Arve, and cottages every here and there peeping forth from among the trees formed a scene of singular beauty. But it was augmented and rendered sublime by the mighty Alps, whose white and shining pyramids and domes towered above all, as belonging to another earth, the habitations of another race of beings.

I passed the bridge of Pelissier, where the ravine, which the river forms, opened before me, and I began to ascend the mountain that overhangs it. Soon after, I entered the valley of Chamounix. This valley is more wonderful and sublime, but not so beautiful and picturesque as that of Servox, through which I had just passed. The high and snowy mountains were its immediate boundaries, but I saw no more ruined castles and fertile fields. Immense glaciers approached the road; I heard the rumbling thunder of the falling avalanche and marked the smoke of its passage. Mont Blanc, the supreme and magnificent Mont Blanc, raised itself from the surrounding aiguilles, and its tremendous dome overlooked the valley.

A tingling long-lost sense of pleasure often came across me during this journey. Some turn in the road, some new object suddenly perceived and recognized, reminded me of days gone by, and were associated with the lighthearted gaiety of boyhood. The very winds whispered in soothing accents, and maternal Nature bade me weep no more. Then again the kindly influence ceased to act – I found myself fettered again to grief and indulging in all the misery of reflection. Then I spurred on my animal, striving so to forget the world, my fears, and more than all, myself – or, in a more desperate fashion, I alighted and threw myself on the grass, weighed down by horror and despair.

At length I arrived at the village of Chamounix. Exhaustion succeeded to the extreme fatigue both of body and of mind which I had endured. For a short space of time I remained at the window watching the pallid lightnings that played above Mont Blanc and listening to the rushing of the Arve, which pursued its noisy way beneath. The same lulling sounds acted as a lullaby to my too keen sensations; when I placed my head upon my pillow, sleep crept over me; I felt it as it came and blessed the giver of oblivion.

CHAPTER X

I spent the following day roaming through the valley. I stood beside the sources of the Arveiron, which take their rise in a glacier, that with slow pace is advancing down from the summit of the hills to barricade the valley. The abrupt sides of vast mountains were before me; the icy wall of the glacier overhung me; a few shattered pines were scattered around; and the solemn silence of this glorious presence-chamber of imperial nature was broken only by the brawling waves or the fall of some vast fragment, the thunder sound of the avalanche or the cracking, reverberated along the mountains, of the accumulated ice, which, through the silent working of immutable laws, was ever and anon rent and torn, as if it had been but a plaything in their hands. These sublime and magnificent scenes afforded me the greatest consolation that I was capable of receiving. They elevated me from all littleness of feeling, and although they did not remove my grief, they subdued and tranquillized it. In some degree, also, they diverted my mind from the thoughts over which it had brooded for the last month. I retired to rest at night; my slumbers, as it were, waited on and ministered to by the assemblance of grand shapes which I had contemplated during the day. They congregated round me; the unstained snowy mountaintop, the glittering pinnacle, the pine woods, and ragged bare ravine, the eagle, soaring amidst the clouds – they all gathered round me and bade me be at peace.

Where had they fled when the next morning I awoke? All of soul-inspiring fled with sleep, and dark melancholy clouded every thought. The rain was pouring in torrents, and thick mists hid the summits of the mountains, so that I even saw not the faces of those mighty friends. Still I would penetrate their misty veil and seek them in their cloudy retreats. What were rain and storm to me? My mule was brought to the door, and I resolved to ascend to the summit of Montanvert. I remembered the effect that the view of the tremendous and ever-moving glacier had produced upon my mind when I first saw it. It had then filled me with a sublime ecstasy that gave wings to the soul and allowed it to soar from the obscure world to light and joy. The sight of the awful and majestic in nature had indeed always the effect of solemnizing my mind and causing me to forget the passing cares of life. I determined to go without a guide, for I was well acquainted with the path, and the presence of another would destroy the solitary grandeur of the scene.

The ascent is precipitous, but the path is cut into continual and short windings, which enable you to surmount the perpendicularity of the mountain. It is a scene terrifically desolate. In a thousand spots the traces of the winter avalanche may be perceived, where trees lie broken and strewed on the ground, some entirely destroyed, others bent, leaning upon the jutting rocks of the mountain or transversely upon other trees. The path, as you ascend nigher, is intersected by ravines of snow, down which stones continually roll from above; one of them is particularly dangerous, as the slightest sound, such as even speaking in a loud voice, produces a concussion of air sufficient to draw destruction upon the head of the speaker. The pines are not tall or luxuriant, but they are sombre and add an air of severity to the scene. I looked on the valley beneath; vast mists were rising from the rivers which ran through it and curling in thick wreaths around the opposite mountains, whose summits were hid in the uniform clouds, while rain poured from the dark sky and added to the melancholy impression I received from the objects around me. Alas! Why does man boast of sensibilities superior to those apparent in the brute; it only renders them more necessary beings. If our impulses were confined to hunger, thirst, and desire, we might be nearly free; but now we are moved by every wind that blows and a chance word or scene that that word may convey to us.

> We rest; a dream has power to poison sleep.
> We rise; one wand'ring thought pollutes the day.
> We feel, conceive, or reason; laugh or weep,
> Embrace fond woe, or cast our cares away;
> It is the same: for, be it joy or sorrow,
> The path of its departure still is free.
> Man's yesterday may ne'er be like his morrow;
> Nought may endure but mutability!

It was nearly noon when I arrived at the top of the ascent. For some time I sat upon the rock that overlooks the sea of ice. A mist covered both that and the surrounding mountains. Presently a breeze dissipated the cloud, and I descended upon the glacier. The surface is very uneven, rising like the waves of a troubled sea, descending low, and interspersed by rifts that sink deep. The field of ice is almost a league in width, but I spent nearly two hours in crossing it. The opposite mountain is a bare perpendicular rock. From the side where I now stood Montanvert was exactly opposite, at the distance of a league; and above it rose Mont Blanc, in awful majesty. I remained in a recess of the rock, gazing on this wonderful and stupendous scene. The sea, or rather the vast river of ice, wound among its dependent mountains, whose aerial summits hung over its recesses. Their icy and glittering peaks shone in the sunlight over the clouds. My heart, which was before sorrowful, now swelled with something like joy; I exclaimed, 'Wandering spirits, if indeed ye wander, and do not rest in your narrow beds, allow me this faint happiness, or take me, as your companion, away from the joys of life.'

As I said this I suddenly beheld the figure of a man, at some distance, advancing towards me with superhuman speed. He bounded over the crevices in the ice, among which I had walked with caution; his stature, also, as he approached, seemed to exceed that of man. I was troubled; a mist came over my eyes, and I felt a faintness seize me, but I was quickly restored by the cold gale of the mountains. I perceived, as the shape came nearer (sight tremendous and abhorred!) that it was the wretch whom I had created. I trembled with rage and horror, resolving to wait his approach and then close with him in mortal combat. He approached; his countenance bespoke bitter anguish, combined with disdain and malignity, while its unearthly ugliness rendered it almost too horrible for human eyes. But I scarcely observed this; rage and hatred had at first deprived me of utterance, and I recovered only to overwhelm him with words expressive of furious detestation and contempt.

'Devil,' I exclaimed, 'do you dare approach me? And do not you fear the fierce vengeance of my arm wreaked on your miserable head? Begone, vile insect! Or rather, stay, that I may trample you to dust! And, oh! That I could, with the extinction of your miserable existence, restore those victims whom you have so diabolically murdered!'

'I expected this reception,' said the daemon. 'All men hate the wretched; how, then, must I be hated, who am miserable beyond all living things! Yet you, my creator, detest and spurn me, thy creature, to whom thou art bound by ties only dissoluble by the annihilation of one of us. You purpose to kill me. How dare you sport thus with life? Do your duty towards me, and I will do mine towards you and the rest of mankind. If you will comply with my conditions, I will leave them and you at peace; but if you refuse, I will glut the maw of death, until it be satiated with the blood of your remaining friends.'

'Abhorred monster! Fiend that thou art! The tortures of hell are too mild a vengeance for thy crimes. Wretched devil! You reproach me with your creation, come on, then, that I may extinguish the spark which I so negligently bestowed.'

My rage was without bounds; I sprang on him, impelled by all the feelings which can arm one being against the existence of another.

He easily eluded me and said –

'Be calm! I entreat you to hear me before you give vent to your hatred on my devoted head. Have I not suffered enough, that you seek to increase my misery? Life, although it may only be an accumulation of anguish, is dear to me, and I will defend it. Remember, thou hast made me more powerful than thyself; my height is superior to thine, my joints more supple. But I will not be tempted to set myself in opposition to thee. I am thy creature, and I will be even mild and docile to my natural lord and king if thou wilt also perform thy part, the which thou owest me. Oh, Frankenstein, be not equitable to every other and trample upon me alone, to whom thy justice, and even thy clemency and affection, is most due. Remember that I am thy creature; I ought to be thy Adam, but I am rather the fallen angel, whom thou drivest from joy for no misdeed. Everywhere I see bliss, from which I alone am irrevocably excluded. I was benevolent and good; misery made me a fiend. Make me happy, and I shall again be virtuous.'

'Begone! I will not hear you. There can be no community between you and me; we are enemies. Begone, or let us try our strength in a fight, in which one must fall.'

'How can I move thee? Will no entreaties cause thee to turn a favourable eye upon thy creature, who implores thy goodness and compassion? Believe me, Frankenstein, I was benevolent; my soul glowed with love and humanity; but am I not alone, miserably alone? You, my creator, abhor me; what hope can I gather from your fellow creatures, who owe me nothing? They spurn and hate me. The desert mountains and dreary glaciers are my refuge. I have wandered here many days; the caves of ice, which I only do not fear, are a dwelling to me, and the only one which man does not grudge.

These bleak skies I hail, for they are kinder to me than your fellow beings. If the multitude of mankind knew of my existence, they would do as you do, and arm themselves for my destruction. Shall I not then hate them who abhor me? I will keep no terms with my enemies. I am miserable, and they shall share my wretchedness. Yet it is in your power to recompense me, and deliver them from an evil which it only remains for you to make so great, that not only you and your family, but thousands of others, shall be swallowed up in the whirlwinds of its rage. Let your compassion be moved, and do not disdain me. Listen to my tale; when you have heard that, abandon or commiserate me, as you shall judge that I deserve. But hear me. The guilty are allowed, by human laws, bloody as they are, to speak in their own defence before they are condemned. Listen to me, Frankenstein. You accuse me of murder, and yet you would, with a satisfied conscience, destroy your own creature. Oh, praise the eternal justice of man! Yet I ask you not to spare me; listen to me, and then, if you can, and if you will, destroy the work of your hands.'

'Why do you call to my remembrance,' I rejoined, 'circumstances of which I shudder to reflect, that I have been the miserable origin and author? Cursed be the day, abhorred devil, in which you first saw light! Cursed (although I curse myself) be the hands that formed you! You have made me wretched beyond expression. You have left me no power to consider whether I am just to you or not. Begone! Relieve me from the sight of your detested form.'

'Thus I relieve thee, my creator,' he said, and placed his hated hands before my eyes, which I flung from me with violence; 'thus I take from thee a sight which you abhor. Still thou canst listen to me and grant me thy compassion. By the virtues that I once possessed, I demand this from you. Hear my tale; it is long and strange, and the temperature of this place is not fitting to your fine sensations; come to the hut upon the mountain. The sun is yet high in the heavens; before it descends to hide itself behind your snowy precipices and illuminate another world, you will have heard my story and can decide. On you it rests, whether I quit forever the neighbourhood of man and lead a harmless life, or become the scourge of your fellow creatures and the author of your own speedy ruin.'

As he said this he led the way across the ice; I followed. My heart was full, and I did not answer him, but as I proceeded, I weighed the various arguments that he had used and determined at least to listen to his tale. I was partly urged by curiosity, and compassion confirmed my resolution. I had hitherto supposed him to be the murderer of my brother, and I eagerly sought a confirmation or denial of this opinion. For the first time, also, I felt what the duties of a creator towards his creature were, and that I ought to render him happy before I complained of his wickedness. These motives urged me to comply with his demand. We crossed the ice, therefore, and ascended the opposite rock. The air was cold, and the rain again began to descend; we entered the hut, the fiend with an air of exultation, I with a heavy heart and depressed spirits. But I consented to listen, and seating myself by the fire which my odious companion had lighted, he thus began his tale.

CHAPTER XI

It is with considerable difficulty that I remember the original era of my being; all the events of that period appear confused and indistinct. A strange multiplicity of sensations seized me, and I saw, felt, heard, and smelt at the same time; and it was, indeed, a long time before I learned to distinguish between the operations of my various senses. By degrees, I remember, a stronger light pressed upon my nerves, so that I was obliged to shut my eyes. Darkness then came over me and troubled me, but hardly had I felt this when, by opening my eyes, as I now suppose, the light poured in upon me again. I walked and, I believe, descended, but I presently found a great alteration in my sensations. Before, dark and opaque bodies had surrounded me, impervious to my touch or sight; but I now found that I could wander on at liberty, with no obstacles which I could not either surmount or avoid. The light became more and more oppressive to me, and the heat wearying me as I walked, I sought a place where I could receive shade. This was the forest near Ingolstadt; and here I lay by the side of a brook resting from my fatigue, until I felt tormented by hunger and thirst. This roused me from my nearly dormant state, and I ate some berries which I found hanging on the trees or lying on the ground. I slaked my thirst at the brook, and then lying down, was overcome by sleep.

It was dark when I awoke; I felt cold also, and half frightened, as it were, instinctively, finding myself so desolate. Before I had quitted your apartment, on a sensation of cold, I had covered myself with some clothes, but these were insufficient to secure me from the dews of night. I was a poor, helpless, miserable wretch; I knew, and could distinguish, nothing; but feeling pain invade me on all sides, I sat down and wept.

Soon a gentle light stole over the heavens and gave me a sensation of pleasure. I started up and beheld a radiant form rise from among the trees. [The moon] I gazed with a kind of wonder. It moved slowly, but it enlightened my path, and I again went out in search of berries. I was still cold when under one of the trees I found a huge cloak, with which I covered myself, and sat down upon the ground. No distinct ideas occupied my mind; all was confused. I felt light, and hunger, and thirst, and darkness; innumerable sounds rang in my ears, and on all sides various scents saluted me; the only object that I could distinguish was the bright moon, and I fixed my eyes on that with pleasure.

Several changes of day and night passed, and the orb of night had greatly lessened, when I began to distinguish my sensations from each other. I gradually saw plainly the clear stream that supplied me with drink and the trees that shaded me with their foliage. I was delighted when I first discovered that a pleasant sound, which often saluted my ears, proceeded from the throats of the little winged animals who had often intercepted the light from my eyes. I began also to observe, with greater accuracy, the forms that surrounded me and to perceive the boundaries of the radiant roof of light which canopied me. Sometimes I tried to imitate the pleasant songs of the birds but was unable. Sometimes I wished to express my sensations in my own mode, but the uncouth and inarticulate sounds which broke from me frightened me into silence again.

The moon had disappeared from the night, and again, with a lessened form, showed itself, while I still remained in the forest. My sensations had by this time become distinct, and my mind received every day additional ideas. My eyes became accustomed to the light and to perceive objects in their right forms; I distinguished the insect from the herb, and by degrees, one herb from another. I found that the sparrow uttered none but harsh notes, whilst those of the blackbird and thrush were sweet and enticing.

One day, when I was oppressed by cold, I found a fire which had been left by some wandering beggars, and was overcome with delight at the warmth I experienced from it. In my joy I thrust my hand into the live embers, but quickly drew it out again with a cry of pain. How strange, I thought, that the same cause should produce such opposite effects! I examined the materials of the fire, and to my joy found it to be composed of wood. I quickly collected some branches, but they were wet and would not burn. I was pained at this and sat still watching the operation of the fire. The wet wood which I had placed near the heat dried and itself became inflamed. I reflected on this, and by touching the various branches, I discovered the cause and busied myself in collecting a great quantity of wood, that I might dry it and have a plentiful supply of fire. When night came on and brought sleep with it, I was in the greatest fear lest my fire should be extinguished. I covered it carefully with dry wood and leaves and placed wet branches upon it; and then, spreading my cloak, I lay on the ground and sank into sleep.

It was morning when I awoke, and my first care was to visit the fire. I uncovered it, and a gentle breeze quickly fanned it into a flame. I observed this also and contrived a fan of branches, which roused the embers when they were nearly extinguished. When night came again I found, with pleasure, that the fire gave light as well as heat and that the discovery of this element was useful to me in my food, for I found some of the offals that the travellers had left had been roasted, and tasted much more savoury than the berries I gathered from the trees. I tried, therefore, to dress my food in the same manner, placing it on the live embers. I found that the berries were spoiled by this operation, and the nuts and roots much improved.

Food, however, became scarce, and I often spent the whole day searching in vain for a few acorns to assuage the pangs of hunger. When I found this, I resolved to quit the place that I had hitherto inhabited, to seek for one where the few wants I experienced would be more easily satisfied. In this emigration I exceedingly lamented the loss of the fire which I had obtained through accident and knew not how to reproduce it. I gave several hours to the serious consideration of this difficulty, but I was obliged to relinquish all attempt to supply it, and wrapping myself up in my cloak, I struck across the wood towards the setting sun. I passed three days in these rambles and at length discovered the open country. A great fall of snow had taken place the night before, and the fields were of one uniform white; the appearance was disconsolate, and I found my feet chilled by the cold damp substance that covered the ground.

It was about seven in the morning, and I longed to obtain food and shelter; at length I perceived a small hut, on a rising ground, which had doubtless been built for the convenience of some shepherd. This was a new sight to me, and I examined the structure with great curiosity. Finding the door open, I entered. An old man sat in it, near a fire, over which he was preparing his breakfast. He turned on hearing a noise, and perceiving me, shrieked loudly, and quitting the hut, ran across the fields with a speed of which his debilitated form hardly appeared capable. His appearance, different from any I had ever before seen, and his flight somewhat surprised me. But I was enchanted by the appearance of the hut;

here the snow and rain could not penetrate; the ground was dry; and it presented to me then as exquisite and divine a retreat as Pandemonium appeared to the demons of hell after their sufferings in the lake of fire. I greedily devoured the remnants of the shepherd's breakfast, which consisted of bread, cheese, milk, and wine; the latter, however, I did not like. Then, overcome by fatigue, I lay down among some straw and fell asleep.

It was noon when I awoke, and allured by the warmth of the sun, which shone brightly on the white ground, I determined to recommence my travels; and, depositing the remains of the peasant's breakfast in a wallet I found, I proceeded across the fields for several hours, until at sunset I arrived at a village. How miraculous did this appear! the huts, the neater cottages, and stately houses engaged my admiration by turns. The vegetables in the gardens, the milk and cheese that I saw placed at the windows of some of the cottages, allured my appetite. One of the best of these I entered, but I had hardly placed my foot within the door before the children shrieked, and one of the women fainted. The whole village was roused; some fled, some attacked me, until, grievously bruised by stones and many other kinds of missile weapons, I escaped to the open country and fearfully took refuge in a low hovel, quite bare, and making a wretched appearance after the palaces I had beheld in the village. This hovel however, joined a cottage of a neat and pleasant appearance, but after my late dearly bought experience, I dared not enter it. My place of refuge was constructed of wood, but so low that I could with difficulty sit upright in it. No wood, however, was placed on the earth, which formed the floor, but it was dry; and although the wind entered it by innumerable chinks, I found it an agreeable asylum from the snow and rain.

Here, then, I retreated and lay down happy to have found a shelter, however miserable, from the inclemency of the season, and still more from the barbarity of man. As soon as morning dawned I crept from my kennel, that I might view the adjacent cottage and discover if I could remain in the habitation I had found. It was situated against the back of the cottage and surrounded on the sides which were exposed by a pig sty and a clear pool of water. One part was open, and by that I had crept in; but now I covered every crevice by which I might be perceived with stones and wood, yet in such a manner that I might move them on occasion to pass out; all the light I enjoyed came through the sty, and that was sufficient for me.

Having thus arranged my dwelling and carpeted it with clean straw, I retired, for I saw the figure of a man at a distance, and I remembered too well my treatment the night before to trust myself in his power. I had first, however, provided for my sustenance for that day by a loaf of coarse bread, which I purloined, and a cup with which I could drink more conveniently than from my hand of the pure water which flowed by my retreat. The floor was a little raised, so that it was kept perfectly dry, and by its vicinity to the chimney of the cottage it was tolerably warm.

Being thus provided, I resolved to reside in this hovel until something should occur which might alter my determination. It was indeed a paradise compared to the bleak forest, my former residence, the rain-dropping branches, and dank earth. I ate my breakfast with pleasure and was about to remove a plank to procure myself a little water when I heard a step, and looking through a small chink, I beheld a young creature, with a pail on her head, passing before my hovel. The girl was young and of gentle demeanour, unlike what I have since found cottagers and farmhouse servants to be. Yet she was meanly dressed, a coarse blue petticoat and a linen jacket being her only garb; her fair hair was plaited but not adorned: she looked patient yet sad. I lost sight of her, and in about a quarter of an hour she returned bearing the pail, which was now partly filled with milk. As she walked along, seemingly incommoded by the burden, a young man met her, whose countenance expressed a deeper despondence. Uttering a few sounds with an air of melancholy, he took the pail from her head and bore it to the cottage himself. She followed, and they disappeared. Presently I saw the young man again, with some tools in his hand, cross the field behind the cottage; and the girl was also busied, sometimes in the house and sometimes in the yard.

On examining my dwelling, I found that one of the windows of the cottage had formerly occupied a part of it, but the panes had been filled up with wood. In one of these was a small and almost imperceptible chink through which the eye could just penetrate. Through this crevice a small room was visible, whitewashed and clean but very bare of furniture. In one corner, near a small fire, sat an old man, leaning his head on his hands in a disconsolate attitude. The young girl was occupied in arranging the cottage; but presently she took something out of a drawer, which employed her hands, and she sat down beside the old man, who, taking up an instrument, began to play and to produce sounds sweeter than the voice of the thrush or the nightingale. It was a lovely sight, even to me, poor wretch who had never beheld aught beautiful before. The silver hair and benevolent countenance of the aged cottager won my reverence, while the gentle manners of the girl enticed my love. He played a sweet mournful air which I perceived drew tears from the eyes of his amiable companion, of which the old man took no notice, until she sobbed audibly; he then pronounced a few sounds, and the fair creature, leaving her work, knelt at his feet. He raised her and smiled with such kindness and affection that I felt sensations of a peculiar and overpowering nature; they were a mixture of pain and pleasure, such as I had never before experienced, either from hunger or cold, warmth or food; and I withdrew from the window, unable to bear these emotions.

Soon after this the young man returned, bearing on his shoulders a load of wood. The girl met him at the door, helped to relieve him of his burden, and taking some of the fuel into the cottage, placed it on the fire; then she and the youth went apart into a nook of the cottage, and he showed her a large loaf and a piece of cheese. She seemed pleased and went into the garden for some roots and plants, which she placed in water, and then upon the fire. She afterwards continued her work, whilst the young man went into the garden and appeared busily employed in digging and pulling up roots. After he had been employed thus about an hour, the young woman joined him and they entered the cottage together.

The old man had, in the meantime, been pensive, but on the appearance of his companions he assumed a more cheerful air, and they sat down to eat. The meal was quickly dispatched. The young woman was again occupied in arranging the cottage, the old man walked before the cottage in the sun for a few minutes, leaning on the arm of the youth. Nothing could exceed in beauty the contrast between these two excellent creatures. One was old, with silver hairs and a countenance beaming with benevolence and love; the younger was slight and graceful in his figure, and his features were moulded with the finest symmetry, yet his eyes and attitude expressed the utmost sadness and despondency. The old man returned to the cottage, and the youth, with tools different from those he had used in the morning, directed his steps across the fields.

Night quickly shut in, but to my extreme wonder, I found that the cottagers had a means of prolonging light by the use of tapers, and was delighted to find that the setting of the sun did not put an end to the pleasure I experienced in watching my human neighbours. In the evening the young girl and her companion were employed in various occupations which I did not understand; and the old man again took up the instrument which produced the divine sounds that had enchanted me in the morning. So soon as he had finished, the youth began, not to play, but to utter sounds that were monotonous, and neither resembling the harmony of the old man's instrument nor the songs of the birds; I since found that he read aloud, but at that time I knew nothing of the science of words or letters.

The family, after having been thus occupied for a short time, extinguished their lights and retired, as I conjectured, to rest.'

CHAPTER XII

I lay on my straw, but I could not sleep. I thought of the occurrences of the day. What chiefly struck me was the gentle manners of these people, and I longed to join them, but dared not. I remembered too well the treatment I had suffered the night before from the barbarous villagers, and resolved, whatever course of conduct I might hereafter think it right to pursue, that for the present I would remain quietly in my hovel, watching and endeavouring to discover the motives which influenced their actions.

The cottagers arose the next morning before the sun. The young woman arranged the cottage and prepared the food, and the youth departed after the first meal.

This day was passed in the same routine as that which preceded it. The young man was constantly employed out of doors, and the girl in various laborious occupations within. The old man, whom I soon perceived to be blind, employed his leisure hours on his instrument or in contemplation. Nothing could exceed the love and respect which the younger cottagers exhibited towards their venerable companion. They performed towards him every little office of affection and duty with gentleness, and he rewarded them by his benevolent smiles.

They were not entirely happy. The young man and his companion often went apart and appeared to weep. I saw no cause for their unhappiness, but I was deeply affected by it. If such lovely creatures were miserable, it was less strange that I, an imperfect and solitary being, should be wretched. Yet why were these gentle beings unhappy? They possessed a delightful house (for such it was in my eyes) and every luxury; they had a fire to warm them when chill and delicious viands when hungry; they were dressed in excellent clothes; and, still more, they enjoyed one another's company and speech, interchanging each day looks of affection and kindness. What did their tears imply? Did they really express pain? I was at first unable to solve these questions, but perpetual attention and time explained to me many appearances which were at first enigmatic.

A considerable period elapsed before I discovered one of the causes of the uneasiness of this amiable family: it was poverty, and they suffered that evil in a very distressing degree. Their nourishment consisted entirely of the vegetables of their garden and the milk of one cow, which gave very little during the winter, when its masters could scarcely procure food to support it. They often, I believe, suffered the pangs of hunger very poignantly, especially the two younger cottagers, for several times they placed food before the old man when they reserved none for themselves.

This trait of kindness moved me sensibly. I had been accustomed, during the night, to steal a part of their store for my own consumption, but when I found that in doing this I inflicted pain on the cottagers, I abstained and satisfied myself with berries, nuts, and roots which I gathered from a neighbouring wood.

I discovered also another means through which I was enabled to assist their labours. I found that the youth spent a great part of each day in collecting wood for the family fire, and during the night I often took his tools, the use of which I quickly discovered, and brought home firing sufficient for the consumption of several days.

I remember, the first time that I did this, the young woman, when she opened the door in the morning, appeared greatly astonished on seeing a great pile of wood on the outside. She uttered some words in a loud voice, and the youth joined her, who also expressed surprise. I observed, with pleasure, that he did not go to the forest that day, but spent it in repairing the cottage and cultivating the garden.

By degrees I made a discovery of still greater moment. I found that these people possessed a method of communicating their experience and feelings to one another by articulate sounds. I perceived that the words they spoke sometimes produced pleasure or pain, smiles or sadness, in the minds and countenances of the hearers. This was indeed a godlike science, and I ardently desired to become acquainted with it. But I was baffled in every attempt I made for this purpose. Their pronunciation was quick, and the words they uttered, not having any apparent connection with visible objects, I was unable to discover any clue by which I could unravel the mystery of their reference. By great application, however, and after having remained during the space of several revolutions of the moon in my hovel, I discovered the names that were given to some of the most familiar objects of discourse; I learned and applied the words, 'fire,' 'milk,' 'bread,' and 'wood.'

I learned also the names of the cottagers themselves. The youth and his companion had each of them several names, but the old man had only one, which was 'father.' The girl was called 'sister' or 'Agatha,' and the youth 'Felix,' 'brother,' or 'son.' I cannot describe the delight I felt when I learned the ideas appropriated to each of these sounds and was able to pronounce them. I distinguished several other words without being able as yet to understand or apply them, such as 'good,' 'dearest,' unhappy.

I spent the winter in this manner. The gentle manners and beauty of the cottagers greatly endeared them to me; when they were unhappy, I felt depressed; when they rejoiced, I sympathized in their joys. I saw few human beings besides them, and if any other happened to enter the cottage, their harsh manners and rude gait only enhanced to me the superior accomplishments of my friends. The old man, I could perceive, often endeavoured to encourage his children, as sometimes I found that he called them, to cast off their melancholy. He would talk in a cheerful accent, with an expression of goodness that bestowed pleasure even upon me. Agatha listened with respect, her eyes sometimes filled with tears, which she endeavoured to wipe away unperceived; but I generally found that her countenance and tone were more cheerful after having listened to the exhortations of her father. It was not thus with Felix. He was always the saddest of the group, and even to my unpractised senses, he appeared to have suffered more deeply than his friends. But if his countenance was more sorrowful, his voice was more cheerful than that of his sister, especially when he addressed the old man.

I could mention innumerable instances which, although slight, marked the dispositions of these amiable cottagers. In the midst of poverty and want, Felix carried with pleasure to his sister the first little white flower that peeped out from beneath the snowy ground. Early in the morning, before she had risen, he cleared away the snow that obstructed her path to the milk-house, drew water from the well, and brought the wood from the outhouse, where, to his perpetual astonishment, he found his store always replenished by an invisible hand. In the day, I believe, he worked sometimes for a neighbouring farmer, because he often went forth and did not return until dinner, yet brought no wood with him. At other times he worked in the garden, but as there was little to do in the frosty season, he read to the old man and Agatha.

This reading had puzzled me extremely at first, but by degrees I discovered that he uttered many of the same sounds when he read as when he talked. I conjectured, therefore, that he found on the paper signs for speech which he understood, and I ardently longed to comprehend these also; but how was that possible when I did not even understand the sounds for which they stood as signs? I improved, however, sensibly in this science, but not sufficiently to follow up any kind of conversation, although I applied my whole mind to the endeavour, for I easily perceived that, although I eagerly longed to discover myself to the cottagers, I ought not to make the attempt until I had first become master of their language, which knowledge might enable me to make them overlook the deformity of my figure, for with this also the contrast perpetually presented to my eyes had made me acquainted.

I had admired the perfect forms of my cottagers – their grace, beauty, and delicate complexions; but how was I terrified when I viewed myself in a transparent pool! At first I started back, unable to believe that it was indeed I who was reflected in the mirror; and when I became fully convinced that I was in reality the monster that I am, I was filled with the bitterest sensations of despondence and mortification. Alas! I did not yet entirely know the fatal effects of this miserable deformity.

As the sun became warmer and the light of day longer, the snow vanished, and I beheld the bare trees and the black earth. From this time Felix was more employed, and the heart-moving indications of impending famine disappeared. Their food, as I afterwards found, was coarse, but it was wholesome; and they procured a sufficiency of it. Several new kinds of plants sprang up in the garden, which they dressed; and these signs of comfort increased daily as the season advanced.

The old man, leaning on his son, walked each day at noon, when it did not rain, as I found it was called when the heavens poured forth its waters. This frequently took place, but a high wind quickly dried the earth, and the season became far more pleasant than it had been.

My mode of life in my hovel was uniform. During the morning I attended the motions of the cottagers, and when they were dispersed in various occupations, I slept; the remainder of the day was spent in observing my friends. When they had retired to rest, if there was any moon or the night was star-light, I went into the woods and collected my own food and fuel for the cottage. When I returned, as often as it was necessary, I cleared their path from the snow and performed those offices that I had seen done by Felix. I afterwards found that these labours, performed by an invisible hand, greatly astonished them; and once or twice I heard them, on these occasions, utter the words 'good spirit,' 'wonderful'; but I did not then understand the signification of these terms.

My thoughts now became more active, and I longed to discover the motives and feelings of these lovely creatures; I was inquisitive to know why Felix appeared so miserable and Agatha so sad. I thought (foolish wretch!) that it might be in my power to restore happiness to these deserving people. When I slept or was absent, the forms of the venerable blind father, the gentle Agatha, and the excellent Felix flitted before me. I looked upon them as superior beings who would be the arbiters of my future destiny. I formed in my imagination a thousand pictures of presenting myself to them, and their reception of me. I imagined that they would be disgusted, until, by my gentle demeanour and conciliating words, I should first win their favour and afterwards their love.

These thoughts exhilarated me and led me to apply with fresh ardour to the acquiring the art of language. My organs were indeed harsh, but supple; and although my voice was very unlike the soft music of their tones, yet I pronounced such words as I understood with tolerable ease. It was as the ass and the lap-dog; yet surely the gentle ass whose intentions were affectionate, although his manners were rude, deserved better treatment than blows and execration.

The pleasant showers and genial warmth of spring greatly altered the aspect of the earth. Men who before this change seemed to have been hid in caves dispersed themselves and were employed in various arts of cultivation. The birds sang in more cheerful notes, and the leaves began to bud forth on the trees. Happy, happy earth! Fit habitation for gods, which, so short a time before, was bleak, damp, and unwholesome. My spirits were elevated by the enchanting appearance of nature; the past was blotted from my memory, the present was tranquil, and the future gilded by bright rays of hope and anticipations of joy.'

CHAPTER XIII

I now hasten to the more moving part of my story. I shall relate events that impressed me with feelings which, from what I had been, have made me what I am.

Spring advanced rapidly; the weather became fine and the skies cloudless. It surprised me that what before was desert and gloomy should now bloom with the most beautiful flowers and verdure. My senses were gratified and refreshed by a thousand scents of delight and a thousand sights of beauty.

It was on one of these days, when my cottagers periodically rested from labour – the old man played on his guitar, and the children listened to him – that I observed the countenance of Felix was melancholy beyond expression; he sighed frequently, and once his father paused in his music, and I conjectured by his manner that he inquired the cause of his son's sorrow. Felix replied in a cheerful accent, and the old man was recommencing his music when someone tapped at the door.

It was a lady on horseback, accompanied by a country-man as a guide. The lady was dressed in a dark suit and covered with a thick black veil. Agatha asked a question, to which the stranger only replied by pronouncing, in a sweet accent, the name of Felix. Her voice was musical but unlike that of either of my friends. On hearing this word, Felix came up hastily to the lady, who, when she saw him, threw up her veil, and I beheld a countenance of angelic beauty and expression. Her hair of a shining raven black, and curiously braided; her eyes were dark, but gentle, although animated; her features of a regular proportion, and her complexion wondrously fair, each cheek tinged with a lovely pink.

Felix seemed ravished with delight when he saw her, every trait of sorrow vanished from his face, and it instantly expressed a degree of ecstatic joy, of which I could hardly have believed it capable; his eyes sparkled, as his cheek flushed with pleasure; and at that moment I thought him as beautiful as the stranger. She appeared affected by different feelings; wiping a few tears from her lovely eyes, she held out her hand to Felix, who kissed it rapturously and called her, as well as I could distinguish, his sweet Arabian. She did not appear to understand him, but smiled. He assisted her to dismount, and dismissing her guide, conducted her into the cottage. Some conversation took place between him and his father, and the young stranger knelt at the old man's feet and would have kissed his hand, but he raised her and embraced her affectionately.

I soon perceived that although the stranger uttered articulate sounds and appeared to have a language of her own, she was neither understood by nor herself understood the cottagers. They made many signs which I did not comprehend, but I saw that her presence diffused gladness through the cottage, dispelling their sorrow as the sun dissipates the morning mists. Felix seemed peculiarly happy and with smiles of delight welcomed his Arabian. Agatha, the ever-gentle Agatha, kissed the hands of the lovely stranger, and pointing to her brother, made signs which appeared to me to mean that he had been sorrowful until she came. Some hours passed thus, while they, by their countenances, expressed joy, the cause of which I did not comprehend. Presently I found, by the frequent recurrence of some sound which the stranger repeated after them, that she was endeavouring to learn their language; and the idea instantly occurred to me that I should make use of the same instructions to the same end. The stranger learned about twenty words at the first lesson; most of them, indeed, were those which I had before understood, but I profited by the others.

As night came on, Agatha and the Arabian retired early. When they separated Felix kissed the hand of the stranger and said, 'Good night sweet Safie.' He sat up much longer, conversing with his father, and by the frequent repetition of her name I conjectured that their lovely guest was the subject of their conversation. I ardently desired to understand them, and bent every faculty towards that purpose, but found it utterly impossible.

The next morning Felix went out to his work, and after the usual occupations of Agatha were finished, the Arabian sat at the feet of the old man, and taking his guitar, played some airs so entrancingly beautiful that they at once drew tears of sorrow and delight from my eyes. She sang, and her voice flowed in a rich cadence, swelling or dying away like a nightingale of the woods.

When she had finished, she gave the guitar to Agatha, who at first declined it. She played a simple air, and her voice accompanied it in sweet accents, but unlike the wondrous strain of the stranger. The old man appeared enraptured and said some words which Agatha endeavoured to explain to Safie, and by which he appeared to wish to express that she bestowed on him the greatest delight by her music.

The days now passed as peaceably as before, with the sole alteration that joy had taken place of sadness in the countenances of my friends. Safie was always gay and happy; she and I improved rapidly in the knowledge of language, so that in two months I began to comprehend most of the words uttered by my protectors.

In the meanwhile also the black ground was covered with herbage, and the green banks interspersed with innumerable flowers, sweet to the scent and the eyes, stars of pale radiance among the moonlight woods; the sun became warmer, the nights clear and balmy; and my nocturnal rambles were an extreme pleasure to me, although they were considerably shortened by the late setting and early rising of the sun, for I never ventured abroad during daylight, fearful of meeting with the same treatment I had formerly endured in the first village which I entered.

My days were spent in close attention, that I might more speedily master the language; and I may boast that I improved more rapidly than the Arabian, who understood very little and conversed in broken accents, whilst I comprehended and could imitate almost every word that was spoken.

While I improved in speech, I also learned the science of letters as it was taught to the stranger, and this opened before me a wide field for wonder and delight.

The book from which Felix instructed Safie was Volney's Ruins of Empires. I should not have understood the purport of this book had not Felix, in reading it, given very minute explanations. He had chosen this work, he said, because the declamatory style was framed in imitation of the Eastern authors. Through this work I obtained a cursory knowledge of history and a view of the several empires at present existing in the world; it gave me an insight into the manners, governments, and religions of the different nations of the earth. I heard of the slothful Asiatics, of the stupendous genius and mental activity of the Grecians, of the wars and wonderful virtue of the early Romans – of their subsequent degenerating – of the decline of that mighty empire, of chivalry, Christianity, and kings. I heard of the discovery of the American hemisphere and wept with Safie over the hapless fate of its original inhabitants.

These wonderful narrations inspired me with strange feelings.

Was man, indeed, at once so powerful, so virtuous and magnificent, yet so vicious and base? He appeared at one time a mere scion of the evil principle and at another as all that can be conceived of noble and godlike. To be a great and virtuous man appeared the highest honour that can befall a sensitive being; to be base and vicious, as many on record have been, appeared the lowest degradation, a condition more abject than that of the blind mole or harmless worm. For a long time I could not conceive how one man could go forth to murder his fellow, or even why there were laws and governments; but when I heard details of vice and bloodshed, my wonder ceased and I turned away with disgust and loathing.

Every conversation of the cottagers now opened new wonders to me. While I listened to the instructions which Felix bestowed upon the Arabian, the strange system of human society was explained to me. I heard of the division of property, of immense wealth and squalid poverty, of rank, descent, and noble blood.

The words induced me to turn towards myself. I learned that the possessions most esteemed by your fellow creatures were high and unsullied descent united with riches. A man might be respected with only one of these advantages, but without either he was considered, except in very rare instances, as a vagabond and a slave, doomed to waste his powers for the profits of the chosen few! And what was I? Of my creation and creator I was absolutely ignorant, but I knew that I possessed no money, no friends, no kind of property. I was, besides, endued with a figure hideously deformed and loathsome; I was not even of the same nature as man. I was more agile than they and could subsist upon coarser diet; I bore the extremes of heat and cold with less injury to my frame; my stature far exceeded theirs. When I looked around I saw and heard of none like me. Was I, then, a monster, a blot upon the earth, from which all men fled and whom all men disowned?

I cannot describe to you the agony that these reflections inflicted upon me; I tried to dispel them, but sorrow only increased with knowledge. Oh, that I had forever remained in my native wood, nor known nor felt beyond the sensations of hunger, thirst, and heat!

Of what a strange nature is knowledge! It clings to the mind when it has once seized on it like a lichen on the rock. I wished sometimes to shake off all thought and feeling, but I learned that there was but one means to overcome the sensation of pain, and that was death – a state which I feared yet did not understand. I admired virtue and good feelings and loved the gentle manners and amiable qualities of my cottagers, but I was shut out from intercourse with them, except through means which I obtained by stealth, when I was unseen and unknown, and which rather increased than satisfied the desire I had of becoming one among my fellows. The gentle words of Agatha and the animated smiles of the charming Arabian were not for me. The mild exhortations of the old man and the lively conversation of the loved Felix were not for me. Miserable, unhappy wretch!

Other lessons were impressed upon me even more deeply. I heard of the difference of sexes, and the birth and growth of children, how the father doted on the smiles of the infant, and the lively sallies of the older child, how all the life and cares of the mother were wrapped up in the precious charge, how the mind of youth expanded and gained knowledge, of brother, sister, and all the various relationships which bind one human being to another in mutual bonds.

But where were my friends and relations? No father had watched my infant days, no mother had blessed me with smiles and caresses; or if they had, all my past life was now a blot, a blind vacancy in which I distinguished nothing. From my earliest remembrance I had been as I then was in height and proportion. I had never yet seen a being resembling me or who claimed any intercourse with me. What was I? The question again recurred, to be answered only with groans.

I will soon explain to what these feelings tended, but allow me now to return to the cottagers, whose story excited in me such various feelings of indignation, delight, and wonder, but which all terminated in additional love and reverence for my protectors (for so I loved, in an innocent, half-painful self-deceit, to call them).'

CHAPTER XIV

Some time elapsed before I learned the history of my friends. It was one which could not fail to impress itself deeply on my mind, unfolding as it did a number of circumstances, each interesting and wonderful to one so utterly inexperienced as I was.

The name of the old man was De Lacey. He was descended from a good family in France, where he had lived for many years in affluence, respected by his superiors and beloved by his equals. His son was bred in the service of his country, and Agatha had ranked with ladies of the highest distinction. A few months before my arrival they had lived in a large and luxurious city called Paris, surrounded by friends and possessed of every enjoyment which virtue, refinement of intellect, or taste, accompanied by a moderate fortune, could afford.

The father of Safie had been the cause of their ruin. He was a Turkish merchant and had inhabited Paris for many years, when, for some reason which I could not learn, he became obnoxious to the government. He was seized and cast into prison the very day that Safie arrived from Constantinople to join him. He was tried and condemned to death. The injustice of his sentence was very flagrant; all Paris was indignant; and it was judged that his religion and wealth rather than the crime alleged against him had been the cause of his condemnation.

Felix had accidentally been present at the trial; his horror and indignation were uncontrollable when he heard the decision of the court. He made, at that moment, a solemn vow to deliver him and then looked around for the means. After many fruitless attempts to gain admittance to the prison, he found a strongly grated window in an unguarded part of the building, which lighted the dungeon of the unfortunate Muhammadan, who, loaded with chains, waited in despair the execution of the barbarous sentence. Felix visited the grate at night and made known to the prisoner his intentions in his favour. The Turk, amazed and delighted, endeavoured to kindle the zeal of his deliverer by promises of reward and wealth. Felix rejected his offers with contempt, yet when he saw the lovely Safie, who was allowed to visit her father and who by her gestures expressed her lively gratitude, the youth could not help owning to his own mind that the captive possessed a treasure which would fully reward his toil and hazard.

The Turk quickly perceived the impression that his daughter had made on the heart of Felix and endeavoured to secure him more entirely in his interests by the promise of her hand in marriage so soon as he should be conveyed to a place of safety. Felix was too delicate to accept this offer, yet he looked forward to the probability of the event as to the consummation of his happiness.

During the ensuing days, while the preparations were going forward for the escape of the merchant, the zeal of Felix was warmed by several letters that he received from this lovely girl, who found means to express her thoughts in the language of her lover by the aid of an old man, a servant of her father who understood French. She thanked him in the most ardent terms for his intended services towards her parent, and at the same time she gently deplored her own fate.

I have copies of these letters, for I found means, during my residence in the hovel, to procure the implements of writing; and the letters were often in the hands of Felix or Agatha. Before I depart I will give them to you; they will prove the truth of my tale; but at present, as the sun is already far declined, I shall only have time to repeat the substance of them to you.

Safie related that her mother was a Christian Arab, seized and made a slave by the Turks; recommended by her beauty, she had won the heart of the father of Safie, who married her. The young girl spoke in high and enthusiastic terms of her mother, who, born in freedom, spurned the bondage to which she was now reduced. She instructed her daughter in the tenets of her religion and taught her to aspire to higher powers of intellect and an independence of spirit forbidden to the female followers of Muhammad. This lady died, but her lessons were indelibly impressed on the mind of Safie, who sickened at the prospect of again returning to Asia and being immured within the walls of a harem, allowed only to occupy herself with infantile amusements, ill-suited to the temper of her soul, now accustomed to grand ideas and a noble emulation for virtue. The prospect of marrying a Christian and remaining in a country where women were allowed to take a rank in society was enchanting to her.

The day for the execution of the Turk was fixed, but on the

night previous to it he quitted his prison and before morning was distant many leagues from Paris. Felix had procured passports in the name of his father, sister, and himself. He had previously communicated his plan to the former, who aided the deceit by quitting his house, under the pretence of a journey and concealed himself, with his daughter, in an obscure part of Paris.

Felix conducted the fugitives through France to Lyons and across Mont Cenis to Leghorn, where the merchant had decided to wait a favourable opportunity of passing into some part of the Turkish dominions.

Safie resolved to remain with her father until the moment of his departure, before which time the Turk renewed his promise that she should be united to his deliverer; and Felix remained with them in expectation of that event; and in the meantime he enjoyed the society of the Arabian, who exhibited towards him the simplest and tenderest affection. They conversed with one another through the means of an interpreter, and sometimes with the interpretation of looks; and Safie sang to him the divine airs of her native country.

The Turk allowed this intimacy to take place and encouraged the hopes of the youthful lovers, while in his heart he had formed far other plans. He loathed the idea that his daughter should be united to a Christian, but he feared the resentment of Felix if he should appear lukewarm, for he knew that he was still in the power of his deliverer if he should choose to betray him to the Italian state which they inhabited. He revolved a thousand plans by which he should be enabled to prolong the deceit until it might be no longer necessary, and secretly to take his daughter with him when he departed. His plans were facilitated by the news which arrived from Paris.

The government of France were greatly enraged at the escape of their victim and spared no pains to detect and punish his deliverer. The plot of Felix was quickly discovered, and DeLacey and Agatha were thrown into prison. The news reached Felix and roused him from his dream of pleasure. His blind and aged father and his gentle sister lay in a noisome dungeon while he enjoyed the free air and the society of her whom he loved. This idea was torture to him. He quickly arranged with the Turk that if the latter should find a favourable opportunity for escape before Felix could return to Italy, Safie should remain as a boarder at a convent at Leghorn; and then, quitting the lovely Arabian, he hastened to Paris and delivered himself up to the vengeance of the law, hoping to free De Lacey and Agatha by this proceeding.

He did not succeed. They remained confined for five months before the trial took place, the result of which deprived them of their fortune and condemned them to a perpetual exile from their native country.

They found a miserable asylum in the cottage in Germany, where I discovered them. Felix soon learned that the treacherous Turk, for whom he and his family endured such unheard-of oppression, on discovering that his deliverer was thus reduced to poverty and ruin, became a traitor to good feeling and honour and had quitted Italy with his daughter, insultingly sending Felix a pittance of money to aid him, as he said, in some plan of future maintenance.

Such were the events that preyed on the heart of Felix and rendered him, when I first saw him, the most miserable of his family. He could have endured poverty, and while this distress had been the meed of his virtue, he gloried in it; but the ingratitude of the Turk and the loss of his beloved Safie were misfortunes more bitter and irreparable. The arrival of the Arabian now infused new life into his soul.

When the news reached Leghorn that Felix was deprived of his wealth and rank, the merchant commanded his daughter to think no more of her lover, but to prepare to return to her native country. The generous nature of Safie was outraged by this command; she attempted to expostulate with her father, but he left her angrily, reiterating his tyrannical mandate.

A few days after, the Turk entered his daughter's apartment and told her hastily that he had reason to believe that his residence at Leghorn had been divulged and that he should speedily be delivered up to the French government; he had consequently hired a vessel to convey him to Constantinople, for which city he should sail in a few hours. He intended to leave his daughter under the care of a confidential servant, to follow at her leisure with the greater part of his property, which had not yet arrived at Leghorn.

When alone, Safie resolved in her own mind the plan of conduct that it would become her to pursue in this emergency. A residence in Turkey was abhorrent to her; her religion and her feelings were alike averse to it. By some papers of her father which fell into her hands she heard of the exile of her lover and learnt the name of the spot where he then resided. She hesitated some time, but at length she formed her determination. Taking with her some jewels that belonged to her and a sum of money, she quitted Italy with an attendant, a native of Leghorn, but who understood the common language of Turkey, and departed for Germany.

She arrived in safety at a town about twenty leagues from the cottage of De Lacey, when her attendant fell dangerously ill. Safie nursed her with the most devoted affection, but the poor girl died, and the Arabian was left alone, unacquainted with the language of the country and utterly ignorant of the customs of the world. She fell, however, into good hands. The Italian had mentioned the name of the spot for which they were bound, and after her death the woman of the house in which they had lived took care that Safie should arrive in safety at the cottage of her lover.'

CHAPTER XV

Such was the history of my beloved cottagers. It impressed me deeply. I learned, from the views of social life which it developed, to admire their virtues and to deprecate the vices of mankind.

As yet I looked upon crime as a distant evil, benevolence and generosity were ever present before me, inciting within me a desire to become an actor in the busy scene where so many admirable qualities were called forth and displayed. But in giving an account of the progress of my intellect, I must not omit a circumstance which occurred in the beginning of the month of August of the same year.

One night during my accustomed visit to the neighbouring wood where I collected my own food and brought home firing for my protectors, I found on the ground a leathern portmanteau containing several articles of dress and some books. I eagerly seized the prize and returned with it to my hovel. Fortunately the books were written in the language, the elements of which I had acquired at the cottage; they consisted of Paradise Lost, a volume of Plutarch's Lives, and the Sorrows of Werter. The possession of these treasures gave me extreme delight; I now continually studied and exercised my mind upon these histories, whilst my friends were employed in their ordinary occupations.

I can hardly describe to you the effect of these books. They produced in me an infinity of new images and feelings, that sometimes raised me to ecstasy, but more frequently sunk me into the lowest dejection. In the Sorrows of Werter, besides the interest of its simple and affecting story, so many opinions are canvassed and so many lights thrown upon what had hitherto been to me obscure subjects that I found in it a never-ending source of speculation and astonishment. The gentle and domestic manners it described, combined with lofty sentiments and feelings, which had for their object something out of self, accorded well with my experience among my protectors and with the wants which were forever alive in my own bosom. But I thought Werter himself a more divine being than I had ever beheld or imagined; his character contained no pretension, but it sank deep. The disquisitions upon death and suicide were calculated to fill me with wonder. I did not pretend to enter into the merits of the case, yet I inclined towards the opinions of the hero, whose extinction I wept, without precisely understanding it.

As I read, however, I applied much personally to my own feelings and condition. I found myself similar yet at the same time strangely unlike to the beings concerning whom I read and to whose conversation I was a listener. I sympathized with and partly understood them, but I was unformed in mind; I was dependent on none and related to none. 'The path of my departure was free,' and there was none to lament my annihilation. My person was hideous and my stature gigantic. What did this mean? Who was I? What was I? Whence did I come? What was my destination? These questions continually recurred, but I was unable to solve them.

The volume of Plutarch's Lives which I possessed contained the histories of the first founders of the ancient republics. This book had a far different effect upon me from the Sorrows of Werter. I learned from Werter's imaginations despondency and gloom, but Plutarch taught me high thoughts; he elevated me above the wretched sphere of my own reflections, to admire and love the heroes of past ages. Many things I read surpassed my understanding and experience. I had a very confused knowledge of kingdoms, wide extents of country, mighty rivers, and boundless seas. But I was perfectly unacquainted with towns and large assemblages of men. The cottage of my protectors had been the only school in which I had studied human nature, but this book developed new and mightier scenes of action. I read of men concerned in public affairs, governing or massacring their species. I felt the greatest ardour for virtue rise within me, and abhorrence for vice, as far as I understood the signification of those terms, relative as they were, as I applied them, to pleasure and pain alone. Induced by these feelings, I was of course led to admire peaceable lawgivers, Numa, Solon, and Lycurgus, in preference to Romulus and Theseus. The patriarchal lives of my protectors caused these impressions to take a firm hold on my mind; perhaps, if my first introduction to humanity had been made by a young soldier, burning for glory and slaughter, I should have been imbued with different sensations.

But Paradise Lost excited different and far deeper emotions. I read it, as I had read the other volumes which had fallen into my hands, as a true history. It moved every feeling of wonder and awe that the picture of an omnipotent God warring with his creatures was capable of exciting. I often referred the several situations, as their similarity struck me, to my own. Like Adam, I was apparently united by no link to any other being in existence; but his state was far different from mine in every other respect. He had come forth from the hands of God a perfect creature, happy and prosperous, guarded by the especial care of his Creator; he was allowed to converse with and acquire knowledge from beings of a superior nature, but I was wretched, helpless, and alone. Many times I considered Satan as the fitter emblem of my condition, for often, like him, when I viewed the bliss of my protectors, the bitter gall of envy rose within me.

Another circumstance strengthened and confirmed these feelings. Soon after my arrival in the hovel I discovered some papers in the pocket of the dress which I had taken from your laboratory. At first I had neglected them, but now that I was able to decipher the characters in which they were written, I began to study them with diligence. It was your journal of the four months that preceded my creation. You minutely described in these papers every step you took in the progress of your work; this history was mingled with accounts of domestic occurrences. You doubtless recollect these papers. Here they are. Everything is related in them which bears reference to my accursed origin; the whole detail of that series of disgusting circumstances which produced it is set in view; the minutest description of my odious and loathsome person is given, in language which painted your own horrors and rendered mine indelible. I sickened as I read. 'Hateful day when I received life!' I exclaimed in agony. 'Accursed creator! Why did you form a monster so hideous that even you turned from me in disgust? God, in pity, made man beautiful and alluring, after his own image; but my form is a filthy type of yours, more horrid even from the very resemblance. Satan had his companions, fellow devils, to admire and encourage him, but I am solitary and abhorred.'

These were the reflections of my hours of despondency and solitude; but when I contemplated the virtues of the cottagers, their amiable and benevolent dispositions, I persuaded myself that when they should become acquainted with my admiration of their virtues they would compassionate me and overlook my personal deformity. Could they turn from their door one, however monstrous, who solicited their compassion and friendship? I resolved, at least, not to despair, but in every way to fit myself for an interview with them which would decide my fate. I postponed this attempt for some months longer, for the importance attached to its success inspired me with a dread lest I should fail. Besides, I found that my understanding improved so much with every day's experience that I was unwilling to commence this undertaking until a few more months should have added to my sagacity.

Several changes, in the meantime, took place in the cottage. The presence of Safie diffused happiness among its inhabitants, and I also found that a greater degree of plenty reigned there. Felix and Agatha spent more time in amusement and conversation, and were assisted in their labours by servants. They did not appear rich, but they were contented and happy; their feelings were serene and peaceful, while mine became every day more tumultuous. Increase of knowledge only discovered to me more clearly what a wretched outcast I was. I cherished hope, it is true, but it vanished when I beheld my person reflected in water or my shadow in the moonshine, even as that frail image and that inconstant shade.

I endeavoured to crush these fears and to fortify myself for the trial which in a few months I resolved to undergo; and sometimes I allowed my thoughts, unchecked by reason, to ramble in the fields of Paradise, and dared to fancy amiable and lovely creatures sympathizing with my feelings and cheering my gloom; their angelic countenances breathed smiles of consolation. But it was all a dream; no Eve soothed my sorrows nor shared my thoughts; I was alone. I remembered Adam's supplication to his Creator. But where was mine? He had abandoned me, and in the bitterness of my heart I cursed him.

Autumn passed thus. I saw, with surprise and grief, the leaves decay and fall, and nature again assume the barren and bleak appearance it had worn when I first beheld the woods and the lovely moon. Yet I did not heed the bleakness of the weather; I was better fitted by my conformation for the endurance of cold than heat. But my chief delights were the sight of the flowers, the birds, and all the gay apparel of summer; when those deserted me, I turned with more attention towards the cottagers. Their happiness was not decreased by the absence of summer. They loved and sympathized with one another; and their joys, depending on each other, were not interrupted by the casualties that took place around them. The more I saw of them, the greater became my desire to claim their protection and kindness; my heart yearned to be known and loved by these amiable creatures; to see their sweet looks directed towards me with affection was the utmost limit of my ambition. I dared not think that they would turn them from me with disdain and horror. The poor that stopped at their door were never driven away. I asked, it is true, for greater treasures than a little food or rest: I required kindness and sympathy; but I did not believe myself utterly unworthy of it.

The winter advanced, and an entire revolution of the seasons had taken place since I awoke into life. My attention at this time was solely directed towards my plan of introducing myself into the cottage of my protectors. I revolved many projects, but that on which I finally fixed was to enter the dwelling when the blind old man should be alone. I had sagacity enough to discover that the unnatural hideousness of my person was the chief object of horror with those who had formerly beheld me. My voice, although harsh, had nothing terrible in it; I thought, therefore, that if in the absence of his children I could gain the good will and mediation of the old De Lacey, I might by his means be tolerated by my younger protectors.

One day, when the sun shone on the red leaves that strewed the ground and diffused cheerfulness, although it denied warmth, Safie, Agatha, and Felix departed on a long country walk, and the old man, at his own desire, was left alone in the cottage. When his children had departed, he took up his guitar and played several mournful but sweet airs, more sweet and mournful than I had ever heard him play before. At first his countenance was illuminated with pleasure, but as he continued, thoughtfulness and sadness succeeded; at length, laying aside the instrument, he sat absorbed in reflection.

My heart beat quick; this was the hour and moment of trial, which would decide my hopes or realize my fears. The servants were gone to a neighbouring fair. All was silent in and around the cottage; it was an excellent opportunity; yet, when I proceeded to execute my plan, my limbs failed me and I sank to the ground. Again I rose, and exerting all the firmness of which I was master, removed the planks which I had placed before my hovel to conceal my retreat. The fresh air revived me, and with renewed determination I approached the door of their cottage.

I knocked. 'Who is there?' said the old man. 'Come in.'

I entered. 'Pardon this intrusion,' said I; 'I am a traveller in want of a little rest; you would greatly oblige me if you would allow me to remain a few minutes before the fire.'

'Enter,' said De Lacey, 'and I will try in what manner I can to relieve your wants; but, unfortunately, my children are from home, and as I am blind, I am afraid I shall find it difficult to procure food for you."

'Do not trouble yourself, my kind host; I have food; it is warmth and rest only that I need.'

I sat down, and a silence ensued. I knew that every minute was precious to me, yet I remained irresolute in what manner to commence the interview, when the old man addressed me. 'By your language, stranger, I suppose you are my countryman; are you French?'

'No; but I was educated by a French family and understand that language only. I am now going to claim the protection of some friends, whom I sincerely love, and of whose favour I have some hopes.'

'Are they Germans?'

'No, they are French. But let us change the subject. I am an unfortunate and deserted creature, I look around and I have no relation or friend upon earth. These amiable people to whom I go have never seen me and know little of me. I am full of fears, for if I fail there, I am an outcast in the world forever.'

'Do not despair. To be friendless is indeed to be unfortunate, but the hearts of men, when unprejudiced by any obvious self-interest, are full of brotherly love and charity. Rely, therefore, on your hopes; and if these friends are good and amiable, do not despair.'

'They are kind – they are the most excellent creatures in the world; but, unfortunately, they are prejudiced against me. I have good dispositions; my life has been hitherto harmless and in some degree beneficial; but a fatal prejudice clouds their eyes, and where they ought to see a feeling and kind friend, they behold only a detestable monster.'

'That is indeed unfortunate; but if you are really blameless, cannot you undeceive them?'

'I am about to undertake that task; and it is on that account that I feel so many overwhelming terrors. I tenderly love these friends; I have, unknown to them, been for many months in the habits of daily kindness towards them; but they believe that I wish to injure them, and it is that prejudice which I wish to overcome.'

"Where do these friends reside?'

"Near this spot.'

'The old man paused and then continued, 'If you will unreservedly confide to me the particulars of your tale, I perhaps may be of use in undeceiving them. I am blind and cannot judge of your countenance, but there is something in your words which persuades me that you are sincere. I am poor and an exile, but it will afford me true pleasure to be in any way serviceable to a human creature.'

'Excellent man! I thank you and accept your generous offer. You raise me from the dust by this kindness; and I trust that, by your aid, I shall not be driven from the society and sympathy of your fellow creatures.'

'Heaven forbid! Even if you were really criminal, for that can only drive you to desperation, and not instigate you to virtue. I also am unfortunate; I and my family have been condemned, although innocent; judge, therefore, if I do not feel for your misfortunes.'

'How can I thank you, my best and only benefactor? From your lips first have I heard the voice of kindness directed towards me; I shall be forever grateful; and your present humanity assures me of success with those friends whom I am on the point of meeting.'

"May I know the names and residence of those friends?' 'I paused. This, I thought, was the moment of decision, which was to rob me of or bestow happiness on me forever. I struggled vainly for firmness sufficient to answer him, but the effort destroyed all my remaining strength; I sank on the chair and sobbed aloud. At that moment I heard the steps of my younger protectors. I had not a moment to lose, but seizing the hand of the old man, I cried, 'Now is the time! Save and protect me! You and your family are the friends whom I seek. Do not you desert me in the hour of trial!'

'Great God!' exclaimed the old man. 'Who are you?'

At that instant the cottage door was opened, and Felix, Safie, and Agatha entered. Who can describe their horror and consternation on beholding me? Agatha fainted, and Safie, unable to attend to her friend, rushed out of the cottage. Felix darted forward, and with supernatural force tore me from his father, to whose knees I clung, in a transport of fury, he dashed me to the ground and struck me violently with a stick. I could have torn him limb from limb, as the lion rends the antelope. But my heart sank within me as with bitter sickness, and I refrained. I saw him on the point of repeating his blow, when, overcome by pain and anguish, I quitted the cottage, and in the general tumult escaped unperceived to my hovel.'

CHAPTER XVI

Cursed, cursed creator! Why did I live? Why, in that instant, did I not extinguish the spark of existence which you had so wantonly bestowed? I know not; despair had not yet taken possession of me; my feelings were those of rage and revenge. I could with pleasure have destroyed the cottage and its inhabitants and have glutted myself with their shrieks and misery.

When night came I quitted my retreat and wandered in the wood; and now, no longer restrained by the fear of discovery, I gave vent to my anguish in fearful howlings. I was like a wild beast that had broken the toils, destroying the objects that obstructed me and ranging through the wood with a staglike swiftness. Oh! What a miserable night I passed! The cold stars shone in mockery, and the bare trees waved their branches above me; now and then the sweet voice of a bird burst forth amidst the universal stillness. All, save I, were at rest or in enjoyment; I, like the arch-fiend, bore a hell within me, and finding myself unsympathized with, wished to tear up the trees, spread havoc and destruction around me, and then to have sat down and enjoyed the ruin.

But this was a luxury of sensation that could not endure; I became fatigued with excess of bodily exertion and sank on the damp grass in the sick impotence of despair. There was none among the myriads of men that existed who would pity or assist me; and should I feel kindness towards my enemies? No; from that moment I declared everlasting war against the species, and more than all, against him who had formed me and sent me forth to this insupportable misery.

The sun rose; I heard the voices of men and knew that it was impossible to return to my retreat during that day. Accordingly I hid myself in some thick underwood, determining to devote the ensuing hours to reflection on my situation.

The pleasant sunshine and the pure air of day restored me to some degree of tranquillity; and when I considered what had passed at the cottage, I could not help believing that I had been too hasty in my conclusions. I had certainly acted imprudently. It was apparent that my conversation had interested the father in my behalf, and I was a fool in having exposed my person to the horror of his children. I ought to have familiarized the old De Lacey to me, and by degrees to have discovered myself to the rest of his family, when they should have been prepared for my approach. But I did not believe my errors to be irretrievable, and after much consideration I resolved to return to the cottage, seek the old man, and by my representations win him to my party.

These thoughts calmed me, and in the afternoon I sank into a profound sleep; but the fever of my blood did not allow me to be visited by peaceful dreams. The horrible scene of the preceding day was forever acting before my eyes; the females were flying and the enraged Felix tearing me from his father's feet. I awoke exhausted, and finding that it was already night, I crept forth from my hiding-place, and went in search of food.

When my hunger was appeased, I directed my steps towards the well-known path that conducted to the cottage. All there was at peace. I crept into my hovel and remained in silent expectation of the accustomed hour when the family arose. That hour passed, the sun mounted high in the heavens, but the cottagers did not appear. I trembled violently, apprehending some dreadful misfortune. The inside of the cottage was dark, and I heard no motion; I cannot describe the agony of this suspense.

Presently two countrymen passed by, but pausing near the cottage, they entered into conversation, using violent gesticulations; but I did not understand what they said, as they spoke the language of the country, which differed from that of my protectors. Soon after, however, Felix approached with another man; I was surprised, as I knew that he had not quitted the cottage that morning, and waited anxiously to discover from his discourse the meaning of these unusual appearances.

'Do you consider,' said his companion to him, 'that you will be obliged to pay three months' rent and to lose the produce of your garden? I do not wish to take any unfair advantage, and I beg therefore that you will take some days to consider of your determination.'

'It is utterly useless,' replied Felix; 'we can never again inhabit your cottage. The life of my father is in the greatest danger, owing to the dreadful circumstance that I have related. My wife and my sister will never recover from their horror. I entreat you not to reason with me any more. Take possession of your tenement and let me fly from this place.'

Felix trembled violently as he said this. He and his companion entered the cottage, in which they remained for a few minutes, and then departed. I never saw any of the family of De Lacey more.

I continued for the remainder of the day in my hovel in a state of utter and stupid despair. My protectors had departed and had broken the only link that held me to the world. For the first time the feelings of revenge and hatred filled my bosom, and I did not strive to control them, but allowing myself to be borne away by the stream, I bent my mind towards injury and death. When I thought of my friends, of the mild voice of De Lacey, the gentle eyes of Agatha, and the exquisite beauty of the Arabian, these thoughts vanished and a gush of tears somewhat soothed me. But again when I reflected that they had spurned and deserted me, anger returned, a rage of anger, and unable to injure anything human, I turned my fury towards inanimate objects. As night advanced I placed a variety of combustibles around the cottage, and after having destroyed every vestige of cultivation in the garden, I waited with forced impatience until the moon had sunk to commence my operations.

As the night advanced, a fierce wind arose from the woods and quickly dispersed the clouds that had loitered in the heavens; the blast tore along like a mighty avalanche and produced a kind of insanity in my spirits that burst all bounds of reason and reflection. I lighted the dry branch of a tree and danced with fury around the devoted cottage, my eyes still fixed on the western horizon, the edge of which the moon nearly touched. A part of its orb was at length hid, and I waved my brand; it sank, and with a loud scream I fired the straw, and heath, and bushes, which I had collected. The wind fanned the fire, and the cottage was quickly enveloped by the flames, which clung to it and licked it with their forked and destroying tongues.

As soon as I was convinced that no assistance could save any part of the habitation, I quitted the scene and sought for refuge in the woods.

And now, with the world before me, whither should I bend my steps? I resolved to fly far from the scene of my misfortunes; but to me, hated and despised, every country must be equally horrible. At length the thought of you crossed my mind. I learned from your papers that you were my father, my creator; and to whom could I apply with more fitness than to him who had given me life? Among the lessons that Felix had bestowed upon Safie, geography had not been omitted; I had learned from these the relative situations of the different countries of the earth. You had mentioned Geneva as the name of your native town, and towards this place I resolved to proceed.

But how was I to direct myself? I knew that I must travel in a southwesterly direction to reach my destination, but the sun was my only guide. I did not know the names of the towns that I was to pass through, nor could I ask information from a single human being; but I did not despair. From you only could I hope for succour, although towards you I felt no sentiment but that of hatred. Unfeeling, heartless creator! You had endowed me with perceptions and passions and then cast me abroad an object for the scorn and horror of mankind. But on you only had I any claim for pity and redress, and from you I determined to seek that justice which I vainly attempted to gain from any other being that wore the human form.

My travels were long and the sufferings I endured intense. It was late in autumn when I quitted the district where I had so long resided. I travelled only at night, fearful of encountering the visage of a human being. Nature decayed around me, and the sun became heatless; rain and snow poured around me; mighty rivers were frozen; the surface of the earth was hard and chill, and bare, and I found no shelter. Oh, earth! How often did I imprecate curses on the cause of my being! The mildness of my nature had fled, and all within me was turned to gall and bitterness. The nearer I approached to your habitation, the more deeply did I feel the spirit of revenge enkindled in my heart. Snow fell, and the waters were hardened, but I rested not. A few incidents now and then directed me, and I possessed a map of the country; but I often wandered wide from my path. The agony of my feelings allowed me no respite; no incident occurred from which my rage and misery could not extract its food; but a circumstance that happened when I arrived on the confines of Switzerland, when the sun had recovered its warmth and the earth again began to look green, confirmed in an especial manner the bitterness and horror of my feelings.

I generally rested during the day and travelled only when I was secured by night from the view of man. One morning, however, finding that my path lay through a deep wood, I ventured to continue my journey after the sun had risen; the day, which was one of the first of spring, cheered even me by the loveliness of its sunshine and the balminess of the air. I felt emotions of gentleness and pleasure, that had long appeared dead, revive within me. Half surprised by the novelty of these sensations, I allowed myself to be borne away by them, and forgetting my solitude and deformity, dared to be happy. Soft tears again bedewed my cheeks, and I even raised my humid eyes with thankfulness towards the blessed sun, which bestowed such joy upon me.

I continued to wind among the paths of the wood, until I came to its boundary, which was skirted by a deep and rapid river, into which many of the trees bent their branches, now budding with the fresh spring. Here I paused, not exactly knowing what path to pursue, when I heard the sound of voices, that induced me to conceal myself under the shade of a cypress. I was scarcely hid when a young girl came running towards the spot where I was concealed, laughing, as if she ran from someone in sport. She continued her course along the precipitous sides of the river, when suddenly her foot slipped, and she fell into the rapid stream. I rushed from my hiding-place and with extreme labour, from the force of the current, saved her and dragged her to shore. She was senseless, and I endeavoured by every means in my power to restore animation, when I was suddenly interrupted by the approach of a rustic, who was probably the person from whom she had playfully fled. On seeing me, he darted towards me, and tearing the girl from my arms, hastened towards the deeper parts of the wood. I followed speedily, I hardly knew why; but when the man saw me draw near, he aimed a gun, which he carried, at my body and fired. I sank to the ground, and my injurer, with increased swiftness, escaped into the wood.

This was then the reward of my benevolence! I had saved a human being from destruction, and as a recompense I now writhed under the miserable pain of a wound which shattered the flesh and bone. The feelings of kindness and gentleness which I had entertained but a few moments before gave place to hellish rage and gnashing of teeth. Inflamed by pain, I vowed eternal hatred and vengeance to all mankind. But the agony of my wound overcame me; my pulses paused, and I fainted.

For some weeks I led a miserable life in the woods, endeavouring to cure the wound which I had received. The ball had entered my shoulder, and I knew not whether it had remained there or passed through; at any rate I had no means of extracting it. My sufferings were augmented also by the oppressive sense of the injustice and ingratitude of their infliction. My daily vows rose for revenge – a deep and deadly revenge, such as would alone compensate for the outrages and anguish I had endured.

After some weeks my wound healed, and I continued my journey. The labours I endured were no longer to be alleviated by the bright sun or gentle breezes of spring; all joy was but a mockery which insulted my desolate state and made me feel more painfully that I was not made for the enjoyment of pleasure.

But my toils now drew near a close, and in two months from this time I reached the environs of Geneva.

It was evening when I arrived, and I retired to a hiding-place among the fields that surround it to meditate in what manner I should apply to you. I was oppressed by fatigue and hunger and far too unhappy to enjoy the gentle breezes of evening or the prospect of the sun setting behind the stupendous mountains of Jura.

At this time a slight sleep relieved me from the pain of reflection, which was disturbed by the approach of a beautiful child, who came running into the recess I had chosen, with all the sportiveness of infancy. Suddenly, as I gazed on him, an idea seized me that this little creature was unprejudiced and had lived too short a time to have imbibed a horror of deformity. If, therefore, I could seize him and educate him as my companion and friend, I should not be so desolate in this peopled earth.

Urged by this impulse, I seized on the boy as he passed and drew him towards me. As soon as he beheld my form, he placed his hands before his eyes and uttered a shrill scream; I drew his hand forcibly from his face and said, 'Child, what is the meaning of this? I do not intend to hurt you; listen to me.'

He struggled violently. 'Let me go,' he cried; 'monster! Ugly wretch! You wish to eat me and tear me to pieces. You are an ogre. Let me go, or I will tell my papa.'

'Boy, you will never see your father again; you must come with me.'

'Hideous monster! Let me go. My papa is a Syndic – he is M. Frankenstein – he will punish you. You dare not keep me.'

"Frankenstein! you belong then to my enemy – to him towards whom I have sworn eternal revenge; you shall be my first victim.'

The child still struggled and loaded me with epithets which carried despair to my heart; I grasped his throat to silence him, and in a moment he lay dead at my feet.

I gazed on my victim, and my heart swelled with exultation and hellish triumph; clapping my hands, I exclaimed, 'I too can create desolation; my enemy is not invulnerable; this death will carry despair to him, and a thousand other miseries shall torment and destroy him.'

As I fixed my eyes on the child, I saw something glittering on his breast. I took it; it was a portrait of a most lovely woman. In spite of my malignity, it softened and attracted me. For a few moments I gazed with delight on her dark eyes, fringed by deep lashes, and her lovely lips; but presently my rage returned; I remembered that I was forever deprived of the delights that such beautiful creatures could bestow and that she whose resemblance I contemplated would, in regarding me, have changed that air of divine benignity to one expressive of disgust and affright.

Can you wonder that such thoughts transported me with rage? I only wonder that at that moment, instead of venting my sensations in exclamations and agony, I did not rush among mankind and perish in the attempt to destroy them.

While I was overcome by these feelings, I left the spot where I had committed the murder, and seeking a more secluded hiding-place, I entered a barn which had appeared to me to be empty. A woman was sleeping on some straw; she was young, not indeed so beautiful as her whose portrait I held, but of an agreeable aspect and blooming in the loveliness of youth and health. Here, I thought, is one of those whose joy-imparting smiles are bestowed on all but me. And then I bent over her and whispered, 'Awake, fairest, thy lover is near – he who would give his life but to obtain one look of affection from thine eyes; my beloved, awake!'

The sleeper stirred; a thrill of terror ran through me. Should she indeed awake, and see me, and curse me, and denounce the murderer? Thus would she assuredly act if her darkened eyes opened and she beheld me. The thought was madness; it stirred the fiend within me – not I, but she, shall suffer; the murder I have committed because I am forever robbed of all that she could give me, she shall atone. The crime had its source in her; be hers the punishment! Thanks to the lessons of Felix and the sanguinary laws of man, I had learned now to work mischief. I bent over her and placed the portrait securely in one of the folds of her dress. She moved again, and I fled.

For some days I haunted the spot where these scenes had taken place, sometimes wishing to see you, sometimes resolved to quit the world and its miseries forever. At length I wandered towards these mountains, and have ranged through their immense recesses, consumed by a burning passion which you alone can gratify. We may not part until you have promised to comply with my requisition. I am alone and miserable; man will not associate with me; but one as deformed and horrible as myself would not deny herself to me. My companion must be of the same species and have the same defects. This being you must create.'

CHAPTER XVII

He being finished speaking and fixed his looks upon me in the expectation of a reply. But I was bewildered, perplexed, and unable to arrange my ideas sufficiently to understand the full extent of his proposition. He continued,

You must create a female for me with whom I can live in the interchange of those sympathies necessary for my being. This you alone can do, and I demand it of you as a right which you must not refuse to concede.'

The latter part of his tale had kindled anew in me the anger that had died away while he narrated his peaceful life among the cottagers, and as he said this I could no longer suppress the rage that burned within me.

'I do refuse it,' I replied; 'and no torture shall ever extort a consent from me. You may render me the most miserable of men, but you shall never make me base in my own eyes. Shall I create another like yourself, whose joint wickedness might desolate the world. Begone! I have answered you; you may torture me, but I will never consent.'

'You are in the wrong,' replied the fiend; 'and instead of threatening, I am content to reason with you. I am malicious because I am miserable. Am I not shunned and hated by all mankind? You, my creator, would tear me to pieces and triumph; remember that, and tell me why I should pity man more than he pities me? You would not call it murder if you could precipitate me into one of those ice-rifts and destroy my frame, the work of your own hands. Shall I respect man when he condemns me? Let him live with me in the interchange of kindness, and instead of injury I would bestow every benefit upon him with tears of gratitude at his acceptance. But that cannot be; the human senses are insurmountable barriers to our union. Yet mine shall not be the submission of abject slavery. I will revenge my injuries; if I cannot inspire love, I will cause fear, and chiefly towards you my archenemy, because my creator, do I swear inextinguishable hatred. Have a care; I will work at your destruction, nor finish until I desolate your heart, so that you shall curse the hour of your birth.'

A fiendish rage animated him as he said this; his face was wrinkled into contortions too horrible for human eyes to behold; but presently he calmed himself and proceeded:

'I intended to reason. This passion is detrimental to me, for you do not reflect that you are the cause of its excess. If any being felt emotions of benevolence towards me, I should return them a hundred and a hundredfold; for that one creature's sake I would make peace with the whole kind! But I now indulge in dreams of bliss that cannot be realized. What I ask of you is reasonable and moderate; I demand a creature of another sex, but as hideous as myself; the gratification is small, but it is all that I can receive, and it shall content me. It is true, we shall be monsters, cut off from all the world; but on that account we shall be more attached to one another. Our lives will not be happy, but they will be harmless and free from the misery I now feel. Oh! My creator, make me happy; let me feel gratitude towards you for one benefit! Let me see that I excite the sympathy of some existing thing; do not deny me my request!'

I was moved. I shuddered when I thought of the possible consequences of my consent, but I felt that there was some justice in his argument. His tale and the feelings he now expressed proved him to be a creature of fine sensations, and did I not as his maker owe him all the portion of happiness that it was in my power to bestow? He saw my change of feeling and continued,

'If you consent, neither you nor any other human being shall ever see us again; I will go to the vast wilds of South America. My food is not that of man; I do not destroy the lamb and the kid to glut my appetite; acorns and berries afford me sufficient nourishment. My companion will be of the same nature as myself and will be content with the same fare. We shall make our bed of dried leaves; the sun will shine on us as on man and will ripen our food. The picture I present to you is peaceful and human, and you must feel that you could deny it only in the wantonness of power and cruelty. Pitiless as you have been towards me, I now see compassion in your eyes; let me seize the favourable moment and persuade you to promise what I so ardently desire.'

'You propose,' replied I, 'to fly from the habitations of man, to dwell in those wilds where the beasts of the field will be your only companions. How can you, who long for the love and sympathy of man, persevere in this exile? You will return and again seek their kindness, and you will meet with their detestation; your evil passions will be renewed, and you will then have a companion to aid you in the task of destruction. This may not be; cease to argue the point, for I cannot consent.'

'How inconstant are your feelings! But a moment ago you were moved by my representations, and why do you again harden yourself to my complaints? I swear to you, by the earth which I inhabit, and by you that made me, that with the companion you bestow I will quit the neighbourhood of man and dwell, as it may chance, in the most savage of places. My evil passions will have fled, for I shall meet with sympathy! My life will flow quietly away, and in my dying moments I shall not curse my maker.'

His words had a strange effect upon me. I compassionated him and sometimes felt a wish to console him, but when I looked upon him, when I saw the filthy mass that moved and talked, my heart sickened and my feelings were altered to those of horror and hatred. I tried to stifle these sensations; I thought that as I could not sympathize with him, I had no right to withhold from him the small portion of happiness which was yet in my power to bestow.

'You swear,' I said, 'to be harmless; but have you not already shown a degree of malice that should reasonably make me distrust you? May not even this be a feint that will increase your triumph by affording a wider scope for your revenge?'

'How is this? I must not be trifled with, and I demand an answer. If I have no ties and no affections, hatred and vice must be my portion; the love of another will destroy the cause of my crimes, and I shall become a thing of whose existence everyone will be ignorant. My vices are the children of a forced solitude that I abhor, and my virtues will necessarily arise when I live in communion with an equal. I shall feel the affections of a sensitive being and became linked to the chain of existence and events from which I am now excluded.'

I paused some time to reflect on all he had related and the various arguments which he had employed. I thought of the promise of virtues which he had displayed on the opening of his existence and the subsequent blight of all kindly feeling by the loathing and scorn which his protectors had manifested towards him. His power and threats were not omitted in my calculations; a creature who could exist in the ice caves of the glaciers and hide himself from pursuit among the ridges of inaccessible precipices was a being possessing faculties it would be vain to cope with. After a long pause of reflection I concluded that the justice due both to him and my fellow creatures demanded of me that I should comply with his request. Turning to him, therefore, I said,

'I consent to your demand, on your solemn oath to quit Europe forever, and every other place in the neighbourhood of man, as soon as I shall deliver into your hands a female who will accompany you in your exile.'

'I swear,' he cried, 'by the sun, and by the blue sky of heaven, and by the fire of love that burns my heart, that if you grant my prayer, while they exist you shall never behold me again. Depart to your home and commence your labours; I shall watch their progress with unutterable anxiety; and fear not but that when you are ready I shall appear.'

Saying this, he suddenly quitted me, fearful, perhaps, of any change in my sentiments. I saw him descend the mountain with greater speed than the flight of an eagle, and quickly lost among the undulations of the sea of ice.

His tale had occupied the whole day, and the sun was upon the verge of the horizon when he departed. I knew that I ought to hasten my descent towards the valley, as I should soon be encompassed in darkness; but my heart was heavy, and my steps slow. The labour of winding among the little paths of the mountain and fixing my feet firmly as I advanced perplexed me, occupied as I was by the emotions which the occurrences of the day had produced. Night was far advanced when I came to the halfway resting-place and seated myself beside the fountain. The stars shone at intervals as the clouds passed from over them; the dark pines rose before me, and every here and there a broken tree lay on the ground; it was a scene of wonderful solemnity and stirred strange thoughts within me. I wept bitterly, and clasping my hands in agony, I exclaimed, 'Oh! Stars and clouds and winds, ye are all about to mock me; if ye really pity me, crush sensation and memory; let me become as nought; but if not, depart, depart, and leave me in darkness.'

These were wild and miserable thoughts, but I cannot describe to you how the eternal twinkling of the stars weighed upon me and how I listened to every blast of wind as if it were a dull ugly siroc on its way to consume me.

Morning dawned before I arrived at the village of Chamounix; I took no rest, but returned immediately to Geneva. Even in my own heart I could give no expression to my sensations – they weighed on me with a mountain's weight and their excess destroyed my agony beneath them. Thus I returned home, and entering the house, presented myself to the family. My haggard and wild appearance awoke intense alarm, but I answered no question, scarcely did I speak. I felt as if I were placed under a ban – as if I had no right to claim their sympathies – as if never more might I enjoy companionship with them. Yet even thus I loved them to adoration; and to save them, I resolved to dedicate myself to my most abhorred task. The prospect of such an occupation made every other circumstance of existence pass before me like a dream, and that thought only had to me the reality of life.

CHAPTER XVIII

Day after day, week after week, passed away on my return to Geneva; and I could not collect the courage to recommence my work. I feared the vengeance of the disappointed fiend, yet I was unable to overcome my repugnance to the task which was enjoined me. I found that I could not compose a female without again devoting several months to profound study and laborious disquisition. I had heard of some discoveries having been made by an English philosopher, the knowledge of which was material to my success, and I sometimes thought of obtaining my father's consent to visit England for this purpose; but I clung to every pretence of delay and shrank from taking the first step in an undertaking whose immediate necessity began to appear less absolute to me. A change indeed had taken place in me; my health, which had hitherto declined, was now much restored; and my spirits, when unchecked by the memory of my unhappy promise, rose proportionably. My father saw this change with pleasure, and he turned his thoughts towards the best method of eradicating the remains of my melancholy, which every now and then would return by fits, and with a devouring blackness overcast the approaching sunshine. At these moments I took refuge in the most perfect solitude. I passed whole days on the lake alone in a little boat, watching the clouds and listening to the rippling of the waves, silent and listless. But the fresh air and bright sun seldom failed to restore me to some degree of composure, and on my return I met the salutations of my friends with a readier smile and a more cheerful heart.

It was after my return from one of these rambles that my father, calling me aside, thus addressed me,

'I am happy to remark, my dear son, that you have resumed your former pleasures and seem to be returning to yourself. And yet you are still unhappy and still avoid our society. For some time I was lost in conjecture as to the cause of this, but yesterday an idea struck me, and if it is well founded, I conjure you to avow it. Reserve on such a point would be not only useless, but draw down treble misery on us all.'

I trembled violently at his exordium, and my father continued –

'I confess, my son, that I have always looked forward to your marriage with our dear Elizabeth as the tie of our domestic comfort and the stay of my declining years. You were attached to each other from your earliest infancy; you studied together, and appeared, in dispositions and tastes, entirely suited to one another. But so blind is the experience of man that what I conceived to be the best assistants to my plan may have entirely destroyed it. You, perhaps, regard her as your sister, without any wish that she might become your wife. Nay, you may have met with another whom you may love; and considering yourself as bound in honour to Elizabeth, this struggle may occasion the poignant misery which you appear to feel.'

'My dear father, reassure yourself. I love my cousin tenderly and sincerely. I never saw any woman who excited, as Elizabeth does, my warmest admiration and affection. My future hopes and prospects are entirely bound up in the expectation of our union.'

'The expression of your sentiments of this subject, my dear Victor, gives me more pleasure than I have for some time experienced. If you feel thus, we shall assuredly be happy, however present events may cast a gloom over us. But it is this gloom which appears to have taken so strong a hold of your mind that I wish to dissipate. Tell me, therefore, whether you object to an immediate solemnization of the marriage. We have been unfortunate, and recent events have drawn us from that everyday tranquillity befitting my years and infirmities. You are younger; yet I do not suppose, possessed as you are of a competent fortune, that an early marriage would at all interfere with any future plans of honour and utility that you may have formed. Do not suppose, however, that I wish to dictate happiness to you or that a delay on your part would cause me any serious uneasiness. Interpret my words with candour and answer me, I conjure you, with confidence and sincerity.'

I listened to my father in silence and remained for some time incapable of offering any reply. I revolved rapidly in my mind a multitude of thoughts and endeavoured to arrive at some conclusion. Alas! To me the idea of an immediate union with my Elizabeth was one of horror and dismay. I was bound by a solemn promise which I had not yet fulfilled and dared not break, or if I did, what manifold miseries might not impend over me and my devoted family! Could I enter into a festival with this deadly weight yet hanging round my neck and bowing me to the ground? I must perform my engagement and let the monster depart with his mate before I allowed myself to enjoy the delight of a union from which I expected peace.

I remembered also the necessity imposed upon me of either journeying to England or entering into a long correspondence with those philosophers of that country whose knowledge and discoveries were of indispensable use to me in my present undertaking. The latter method of obtaining the desired intelligence was dilatory and unsatisfactory; besides, I had an insurmountable aversion to the idea of engaging myself in my loathsome task in my father's house while in habits of familiar intercourse with those I loved. I knew that a thousand fearful accidents might occur, the slightest of which would disclose a tale to thrill all connected with me with horror. I was aware also that I should often lose all self-command, all capacity of hiding the harrowing sensations that would possess me during the progress of my unearthly occupation. I must absent myself from all I loved while thus employed. Once commenced, it would quickly be achieved, and I might be restored to my family in peace and happiness. My promise fulfilled, the monster would depart forever. Or (so my fond fancy imaged) some accident might meanwhile occur to destroy him and put an end to my slavery forever.

These feelings dictated my answer to my father. I expressed a wish to visit England, but concealing the true reasons of this request, I clothed my desires under a guise which excited no suspicion, while I urged my desire with an earnestness that easily induced my father to comply. After so long a period of an absorbing melancholy that resembled madness in its intensity and effects, he was glad to find that I was capable of taking pleasure in the idea of such a journey, and he hoped that change of scene and varied amusement would, before my return, have restored me entirely to myself.

The duration of my absence was left to my own choice; a few months, or at most a year, was the period contemplated. One paternal kind precaution he had taken to ensure my having a companion. Without previously communicating with me, he had, in concert with Elizabeth, arranged that Clerval should join me at Strasbourg. This interfered with the solitude I coveted for the prosecution of my task; yet at the commencement of my journey the presence of my friend could in no way be an impediment, and truly I rejoiced that thus I should be saved many hours of lonely, maddening reflection. Nay, Henry might stand between me and the intrusion of my foe. If I were alone, would he not at times force his abhorred presence on me to remind me of my task or to contemplate its progress?

To England, therefore, I was bound, and it was understood that my union with Elizabeth should take place immediately on my return. My father's age rendered him extremely averse to delay. For myself, there was one reward I promised myself from my detested toils – one consolation for my unparalleled sufferings; it was the prospect of that day when, enfranchised from my miserable slavery, I might claim Elizabeth and forget the past in my union with her.

I now made arrangements for my journey, but one feeling haunted me which filled me with fear and agitation. During my absence I should leave my friends unconscious of the existence of their enemy and unprotected from his attacks, exasperated as he might be by my departure. But he had promised to follow me wherever I might go, and would he not accompany me to England? This imagination was dreadful in itself, but soothing inasmuch as it supposed the safety of my friends. I was agonized with the idea of the possibility that the reverse of this might happen. But through the whole period during which I was the slave of my creature I allowed myself to be governed by the impulses of the moment; and my present sensations strongly intimated that the fiend would follow me and exempt my family from the danger of his machinations.

It was in the latter end of September that I again quitted my native country. My journey had been my own suggestion, and Elizabeth therefore acquiesced, but she was filled with disquiet at the idea of my suffering, away from her, the inroads of misery and grief. It had been her care which provided me a companion in Clerval – and yet a man is blind to a thousand minute circumstances which call forth a woman's sedulous attention. She longed to bid me hasten my return; a thousand conflicting emotions rendered her mute as she bade me a tearful, silent farewell.

I threw myself into the carriage that was to convey me away, hardly knowing whither I was going, and careless of what was passing around. I remembered only, and it was with a bitter anguish that I reflected on it, to order that my chemical instruments should be packed to go with me. Filled with dreary imaginations, I passed through many beautiful and majestic scenes, but my eyes were fixed and unobserving. I could only think of the bourne of my travels and the work which was to occupy me whilst they endured.

After some days spent in listless indolence, during which I

traversed many leagues, I arrived at Strasbourg, where I waited two days for Clerval. He came. Alas, how great was the contrast between us! He was alive to every new scene, joyful when he saw the beauties of the setting sun, and more happy when he beheld it rise and recommence a new day. He pointed out to me the shifting colours of the landscape and the appearances of the sky. 'This is what it is to live,' he cried; 'how I enjoy existence! But you, my dear Frankenstein, wherefore are you desponding and sorrowful!' In truth, I was occupied by gloomy thoughts and neither saw the descent of the evening star nor the golden sunrise reflected in the Rhine. And you, my friend, would be far more amused with the journal of Clerval, who observed the scenery with an eye of feeling and delight, than in listening to my reflections. I, a miserable wretch, haunted by a curse that shut up every avenue to enjoyment.

We had agreed to descend the Rhine in a boat from Strasbourg to Rotterdam, whence we might take shipping for London. During this voyage we passed many willowy islands and saw several beautiful towns. We stayed a day at Mannheim, and on the fifth from our departure from Strasbourg, arrived at Mainz. The course of the Rhine below Mainz becomes much more picturesque. The river descends rapidly and winds between hills, not high, but steep, and of beautiful forms. We saw many ruined castles standing on the edges of precipices, surrounded by black woods, high and inaccessible. This part of the Rhine, indeed, presents a singularly variegated landscape. In one spot you view rugged hills, ruined castles overlooking tremendous precipices, with the dark Rhine rushing beneath; and on the sudden turn of a promontory, flourishing vineyards with green sloping banks and a meandering river and populous towns occupy the scene.

We travelled at the time of the vintage and heard the song of the labourers as we glided down the stream. Even I, depressed in mind, and my spirits continually agitated by gloomy feelings, even I was pleased. I lay at the bottom of the boat, and as I gazed on the cloudless blue sky, I seemed to drink in a tranquillity to which I had long been a stranger. And if these were my sensations, who can describe those of Henry? He felt as if he had been transported to fairy-land and enjoyed a happiness seldom tasted by man. 'I have seen,' he said, 'the most beautiful scenes of my own country; I have visited the lakes of Lucerne and Uri, where the snowy mountains descend almost perpendicularly to the water, casting black and impenetrable shades, which would cause a gloomy and mournful appearance were it not for the most verdant islands that relieve the eye by their gay appearance; I have seen this lake agitated by a tempest, when the wind tore up whirlwinds of water and gave you an idea of what the water-spout must be on the great ocean; and the waves dash with fury the base of the mountain, where the priest and his mistress were overwhelmed by an avalanche and where their dying voices are still said to be heard amid the pauses of the nightly wind; I have seen the mountains of La Valais, and the Pays de Vaud; but this country, Victor, pleases me more than all those wonders. The mountains of Switzerland are more majestic and strange, but there is a charm in the banks of this divine river that I never before saw equalled. Look at that castle which overhangs yon precipice; and that also on the island, almost concealed amongst the foliage of those lovely trees; and now that group of labourers coming from among their vines; and that village half hid in the recess of the mountain. Oh, surely the spirit that inhabits and guards this place has a soul more in harmony with man than those who pile the glacier or retire to the inaccessible peaks of the mountains of our own country.' Clerval! Beloved friend! Even now it delights me to record your words and to dwell on the praise of which you are so eminently deserving. He was a being formed in the 'very poetry of nature.' His wild and enthusiastic imagination was chastened by the sensibility of his heart. His soul overflowed with ardent affections, and his friendship was of that devoted and wondrous nature that the world-minded teach us to look for only in the imagination. But even human sympathies were not sufficient to satisfy his eager mind. The scenery of external nature, which others regard only with admiration, he loved with ardour:

>...The sounding cataract
>Haunted him like a passion: the tall rock,
>The mountain, and the deep and gloomy wood,
>Their colours and their forms, were then to him
>An appetite; a feeling, and a love,
>That had no need of a remoter charm,
>By thought supplied, or any interest
>Unborrow'd from the eye.

Wordsworth's *Tintern Abbey.*

And where does he now exist? Is this gentle and lovely being lost forever? Has this mind, so replete with ideas, imaginations fanciful and magnificent, which formed a world, whose existence depended on the life of its creator; has this mind perished? Does it now only exist in my memory? No, it is not thus; your form so divinely wrought, and beaming with beauty, has decayed, but your spirit still visits and consoles your unhappy friend.

Pardon this gush of sorrow; these ineffectual words are but a slight tribute to the unexampled worth of Henry, but they soothe my heart, overflowing with the anguish which his remembrance creates. I will proceed with my tale.

Beyond Cologne we descended to the plains of Holland; and we resolved to post the remainder of our way, for the wind was contrary and the stream of the river was too gentle to aid us. Our journey here lost the interest arising from beautiful scenery, but we arrived in a few days at Rotterdam, whence we proceeded by sea to England. It was on a clear morning, in the latter days of December, that I first saw the white cliffs of Britain. The banks of the Thames presented a new scene; they were flat but fertile, and almost every town was marked by the remembrance of some story. We saw Tilbury Fort and remembered the Spanish Armada, Gravesend, Woolwich, and Greenwich – places which I had heard of even in my country.

At length we saw the numerous steeples of London, St. Paul's towering above all, and the Tower famed in English history.

CHAPTER XIX

London was our present point of rest; we determined to remain several months in this wonderful and celebrated city. Clerval desired the intercourse of the men of genius and talent who flourished at this time, but this was with me a secondary object; I was principally occupied with the means of obtaining the information necessary for the completion of my promise and quickly availed myself of the letters of introduction that I had brought with me, addressed to the most distinguished natural philosophers.

If this journey had taken place during my days of study and happiness, it would have afforded me inexpressible pleasure. But a blight had come over my existence, and I only visited these people for the sake of the information they might give me on the subject in which my interest was so terribly profound. Company was irksome to me; when alone, I could fill my mind with the sights of heaven and earth; the voice of Henry soothed me, and I could thus cheat myself into a transitory peace. But busy, uninteresting, joyous faces brought back despair to my heart. I saw an insurmountable barrier placed between me and my fellow men; this barrier was sealed with the blood of William and Justine, and to reflect on the events connected with those names filled my soul with anguish.

But in Clerval I saw the image of my former self; he was inquisitive and anxious to gain experience and instruction. The difference of manners which he observed was to him an inexhaustible source of instruction and amusement. He was also pursuing an object he had long had in view. His design was to visit India, in the belief that he had in his knowledge of its various languages, and in the views he had taken of its society, the means of materially assisting the progress of European colonization and trade. In Britain only could he further the execution of his plan. He was forever busy, and the only check to his enjoyments was my sorrowful and dejected mind. I tried to conceal this as much as possible, that I might not debar him from the pleasures natural to one who was entering on a new scene of life, undisturbed by any care or bitter recollection. I often refused to accompany him, alleging another engagement, that I might remain alone. I now also began to collect the materials necessary for my new creation, and this was to me like the torture of single drops of water continually falling on the head. Every thought that was devoted to it was an extreme anguish, and every word that I spoke in allusion to it caused my lips to quiver, and my heart to palpitate.

After passing some months in London, we received a letter from a person in Scotland who had formerly been our visitor at Geneva. He mentioned the beauties of his native country and asked us if those were not sufficient allurements to induce us to prolong our journey as far north as Perth, where he resided. Clerval eagerly desired to accept this invitation, and I, although I abhorred society, wished to view again mountains and streams and all the wondrous works with which Nature adorns her chosen dwelling-places. We had arrived in England at the beginning of October, and it was now February. We accordingly determined to commence our journey towards the north at the expiration of another month. In this expedition we did not intend to follow the great road to Edinburgh, but to visit Windsor, Oxford, Matlock, and the Cumberland lakes, resolving to arrive at the completion of this tour about the end of July. I packed up my chemical instruments and the materials I had collected, resolving to finish my labours in some obscure nook in the northern highlands of Scotland.

We quitted London on the 27th of March and remained a few days at Windsor, rambling in its beautiful forest. This was a new scene to us mountaineers; the majestic oaks, the quantity of game, and the herds of stately deer were all novelties to us.

From thence we proceeded to Oxford. As we entered this city our minds were filled with the remembrance of the events that had been transacted there more than a century and a half before. It was here that Charles I had collected his forces. This city had remained faithful to him, after the whole nation had forsaken his cause to join the standard of Parliament and liberty. The memory of that unfortunate king and his companions, the amiable Falkland, the insolent Goring, his queen, and son, gave a peculiar interest to every part of the city which they might be supposed to have inhabited. The spirit of elder days found a dwelling here, and we delighted to trace its footsteps. If these feelings had not found an imaginary gratification, the appearance of the city had yet in itself sufficient beauty to obtain our admiration. The colleges are ancient and picturesque; the streets are almost magnificent; and the lovely

Isis, which flows beside it through meadows of exquisite verdure, is spread forth into a placid expanse of waters, which reflects its majestic assemblage of towers, and spires, and domes, embosomed among aged trees.

I enjoyed this scene, and yet my enjoyment was embittered both by the memory of the past and the anticipation of the future. I was formed for peaceful happiness. During my youthful days discontent never visited my mind, and if I was ever overcome by ennui, the sight of what is beautiful in nature or the study of what is excellent and sublime in the productions of man could always interest my heart and communicate elasticity to my spirits. But I am a blasted tree; the bolt has entered my soul; and I felt then that I should survive to exhibit what I shall soon cease to be – a miserable spectacle of wrecked humanity, pitiable to others and intolerable to myself.

We passed a considerable period at Oxford, rambling among its environs and endeavouring to identify every spot which might relate to the most animating epoch of English history. Our little voyages of discovery were often prolonged by the successive objects that presented themselves. We visited the tomb of the illustrious Hampden and the field on which that patriot fell. For a moment my soul was elevated from its debasing and miserable fears to contemplate the divine ideas of liberty and self sacrifice of which these sights were the monuments and the remembrancers. For an instant I dared to shake off my chains and look around me with a free and lofty spirit, but the iron had eaten into my flesh, and I sank again, trembling and hopeless, into my miserable self.

We left Oxford with regret and proceeded to Matlock, which was our next place of rest. The country in the neighbourhood of this village resembled, to a greater degree, the scenery of Switzerland; but everything is on a lower scale, and the green hills want the crown of distant white Alps which always attend on the piny mountains of my native country. We visited the wondrous cave and the little cabinets of natural history, where the curiosities are disposed in the same manner as in the collections at Servox and Chamounix. The latter name made me tremble when pronounced by Henry, and I hastened to quit Matlock, with which that terrible scene was thus associated.

From Derby, still journeying northwards, we passed two months in Cumberland and Westmorland. I could now almost fancy myself among the Swiss mountains. The little patches of snow which yet lingered on the northern sides of the mountains, the lakes, and the dashing of the rocky streams were all familiar and dear sights to me. Here also we made some acquaintances, who almost contrived to cheat me into happiness. The delight of Clerval was proportionably greater than mine; his mind expanded in the company of men of talent, and he found in his own nature greater capacities and resources than he could have imagined himself to have possessed while he associated with his inferiors. 'I could pass my life here,' said he to me; 'and among these mountains I should scarcely regret Switzerland and the Rhine.'

But he found that a traveller's life is one that includes much pain amidst its enjoyments. His feelings are forever on the stretch; and when he begins to sink into repose, he finds himself obliged to quit that on which he rests in pleasure for something new, which again engages his attention, and which also he forsakes for other novelties.

We had scarcely visited the various lakes of Cumberland and Westmorland and conceived an affection for some of the inhabitants when the period of our appointment with our Scotch friend approached, and we left them to travel on. For my own part I was not sorry. I had now neglected my promise for some time, and I feared the effects of the daemon's disappointment. He might remain in Switzerland and wreak his vengeance on my relatives. This idea pursued me and tormented me at every moment from which I might otherwise have snatched repose and peace. I waited for my letters with feverish impatience; if they were delayed I was miserable and overcome by a thousand fears; and when they arrived and I saw the superscription of Elizabeth or my father, I hardly dared to read and ascertain my fate. Sometimes I thought that the fiend followed me and might expedite my remissness by murdering my companion. When these thoughts possessed me, I would not quit Henry for a moment, but followed him as his shadow, to protect him from the fancied rage of his destroyer. I felt as if I had committed some great crime, the consciousness of which haunted me. I was guiltless, but I had indeed drawn down a horrible curse upon my head, as mortal as that of crime.

I visited Edinburgh with languid eyes and mind; and yet that city might have interested the most unfortunate being. Clerval did not like it so well as Oxford, for the antiquity of the latter city was more pleasing to him. But the beauty and regularity of the new town of Edinburgh, its romantic castle and its environs, the most delightful in the world, Arthur's Seat, St. Bernard's Well, and the Pentland Hills compensated him for the change and filled him with cheerfulness and admiration. But I was impatient to arrive at the termination of my journey.

We left Edinburgh in a week, passing through Coupar, St. Andrew's, and along the banks of the Tay, to Perth, where our friend expected us. But I was in no mood to laugh and talk with strangers or enter into their feelings or plans with the good humour expected from a guest; and accordingly I told Clerval that I wished to make the tour of Scotland alone. 'Do you,' said I, 'enjoy yourself, and let this be our rendezvous. I may be absent a month or two; but do not interfere with my motions, I entreat you; leave me to peace and solitude for a short time; and when I return, I hope it will be with a lighter heart, more congenial to your own temper.

Henry wished to dissuade me, but seeing me bent on this plan, ceased to remonstrate. He entreated me to write often. 'I had rather be with you,' he said, 'in your solitary rambles, than with these Scotch people, whom I do not know; hasten, then, my dear friend, to return, that I may again feel myself somewhat at home, which I cannot do in your absence.'

Having parted from my friend, I determined to visit some remote spot of Scotland and finish my work in solitude. I did not doubt but that the monster followed me and would discover himself to me when I should have finished, that he might receive his companion. With this resolution I traversed the northern highlands and fixed on one of the remotest of the Orkneys as the scene of my labours. It was a place fitted for such a work, being hardly more than a rock whose high sides were continually beaten upon by the waves. The soil was barren, scarcely affording pasture for a few miserable cows, and oatmeal for its inhabitants, which consisted of five persons, whose gaunt and scraggy limbs gave tokens of their miserable fare. Vegetables and bread, when they indulged in such luxuries, and even fresh water, was to be procured from the mainland, which was about five miles distant.

On the whole island there were but three miserable huts, and one of these was vacant when I arrived. This I hired. It contained but two rooms, and these exhibited all the squalidness of the most miserable penury. The thatch had fallen in, the walls were unplastered, and the door was off its hinges. I ordered it to be repaired, bought some furniture, and took possession, an incident which would doubtless have occasioned some surprise had not all the senses of the cottagers been benumbed by want and squalid poverty. As it was, I lived ungazed at and unmolested, hardly thanked for the pittance of food and clothes which I gave, so much does suffering blunt even the coarsest sensations of men.

In this retreat I devoted the morning to labour; but in the evening, when the weather permitted, I walked on the stony beach of the sea to listen to the waves as they roared and dashed at my feet. It was a monotonous yet ever-changing scene. I thought of Switzerland; it was far different from this desolate and appalling landscape. Its hills are covered with vines, and its cottages are scattered thickly in the plains. Its fair lakes reflect a blue and gentle sky, and when troubled by the winds, their tumult is but as the play of a lively infant when compared to the roarings of the giant ocean.

In this manner I distributed my occupations when I first arrived, but as I proceeded in my labour, it became every day more horrible and irksome to me. Sometimes I could not prevail on myself to enter my laboratory for several days, and at other times I toiled day and night in order to complete my work. It was, indeed, a filthy process in which I was engaged. During my first experiment, a kind of enthusiastic frenzy had blinded me to the horror of my employment; my mind was intently fixed on the consummation of my labour, and my eyes were shut to the horror of my proceedings. But now I went to it in cold blood, and my heart often sickened at the work of my hands.

Thus situated, employed in the most detestable occupation, immersed in a solitude where nothing could for an instant call my attention from the actual scene in which I was engaged, my spirits became unequal; I grew restless and nervous. Every moment I feared to meet my persecutor. Sometimes I sat with my eyes fixed on the ground, fearing to raise them lest they should encounter the object which I so much dreaded to behold. I feared to wander from the sight of my fellow creatures lest when alone he should come to claim his companion.

In the mean time I worked on, and my labour was already considerably advanced. I looked towards its completion with a tremulous and eager hope, which I dared not trust myself to question but which was intermixed with obscure forebodings of evil that made my heart sicken in my bosom.

CHAPTER XX

I sat one evening in my laboratory; the sun had set, and the moon was just rising from the sea; I had not sufficient light for my employment, and I remained idle, in a pause of consideration of whether I should leave my labour for the night or hasten its conclusion by an unremitting attention to it. As I sat, a train of reflection occurred to me which led me to consider the effects of what I was now doing. Three years before, I was engaged in the same manner and had created a fiend whose unparalleled barbarity had desolated my heart and filled it forever with the bitterest remorse. I was now about to form another being of whose dispositions I was alike ignorant; she might become ten thousand times more malignant than her mate and delight, for its own sake, in murder and wretchedness. He had sworn to quit the neighbourhood of man and hide himself in deserts, but she had not; and she, who in all probability was to become a thinking and reasoning animal, might refuse to comply with a compact made before her creation. They might even hate each other; the creature who already lived loathed his own deformity, and might he not conceive a greater abhorrence for it when it came before his eyes in the female form? She also might turn with disgust from him to the superior beauty of man; she might quit him, and he be again alone, exasperated by the fresh provocation of being deserted by one of his own species.

Even if they were to leave Europe and inhabit the deserts of the new world, yet one of the first results of those sympathies for which the daemon thirsted would be children, and a race of devils would be propagated upon the earth who might make the very existence of the species of man a condition precarious and full of terror. Had I right, for my own benefit, to inflict this curse upon everlasting generations? I had before been moved by the sophisms of the being I had created; I had been struck senseless by his fiendish threats; but now, for the first time, the wickedness of my promise burst upon me; I shuddered to think that future ages might curse me as their pest, whose selfishness had not hesitated to buy its own peace at the price, perhaps, of the existence of the whole human race.

I trembled and my heart failed within me, when, on looking

up, I saw by the light of the moon the daemon at the casement. A ghastly grin wrinkled his lips as he gazed on me, where I sat fulfilling the task which he had allotted to me. Yes, he had followed me in my travels; he had loitered in forests, hid himself in caves, or taken refuge in wide and desert heaths; and he now came to mark my progress and claim the fulfillment of my promise.

As I looked on him, his countenance expressed the utmost extent of malice and treachery. I thought with a sensation of madness on my promise of creating another like to him, and trembling with passion, tore to pieces the thing on which I was engaged. The wretch saw me destroy the creature on whose future existence he depended for happiness, and with a howl of devilish despair and revenge, withdrew.

I left the room, and locking the door, made a solemn vow in my own heart never to resume my labours; and then, with trembling steps, I sought my own apartment. I was alone; none were near me to dissipate the gloom and relieve me from the sickening oppression of the most terrible reveries.

Several hours passed, and I remained near my window gazing on the sea; it was almost motionless, for the winds were hushed, and all nature reposed under the eye of the quiet moon. A few fishing vessels alone specked the water, and now and then the gentle breeze wafted the sound of voices as the fishermen called to one another. I felt the silence, although I was hardly conscious of its extreme profundity, until my ear was suddenly arrested by the paddling of oars near the shore, and a person landed close to my house.

In a few minutes after, I heard the creaking of my door, as if some one endeavoured to open it softly. I trembled from head to foot; I felt a presentiment of who it was and wished to rouse one of the peasants who dwelt in a cottage not far from mine; but I was overcome by the sensation of helplessness, so often felt in frightful dreams, when you in vain endeavour to fly from an impending danger, and was rooted to the spot.

Presently I heard the sound of footsteps along the passage; the door opened, and the wretch whom I dreaded appeared. Shutting the door, he approached me and said in a smothered voice, 'You have destroyed the work which you began; what is it that you intend? Do you dare to break your promise? I have endured toil and misery; I left Switzerland with you; I crept along the shores of the Rhine, among its willow islands and over the summits of its hills.

I have dwelt many months in the heaths of England and among the deserts of Scotland. I have endured incalculable fatigue, and cold, and hunger; do you dare destroy my hopes?'

'Begone! I do break my promise; never will I create another like yourself, equal in deformity and wickedness.'

'Slave, I before reasoned with you, but you have proved yourself unworthy of my condescension. Remember that I have power; you believe yourself miserable, but I can make you so wretched that the light of day will be hateful to you. You are my creator, but I am your master; obey!'

'The hour of my irresolution is past, and the period of your power is arrived. Your threats cannot move me to do an act of wickedness; but they confirm me in a determination of not creating you a companion in vice. Shall I, in cool blood, set loose upon the earth a daemon whose delight is in death and wretchedness? Begone! I am firm, and your words will only exasperate my rage.'

The monster saw my determination in my face and gnashed his teeth in the impotence of anger. 'Shall each man,' cried he, 'find a wife for his bosom, and each beast have his mate, and I be alone? I had feelings of affection, and they were requited by detestation and scorn. Man! You may hate, but beware! Your hours will pass in dread and misery, and soon the bolt will fall which must ravish from you your happiness forever. Are you to be happy while I grovel in the intensity of my wretchedness? You can blast my other passions, but revenge remains – revenge, henceforth dearer than light or food! I may die, but first you, my tyrant and tormentor, shall curse the sun that gazes on your misery. Beware, for I am fearless and therefore powerful. I will watch with the wiliness of a snake, that I may sting with its venom. Man, you shall repent of the injuries you inflict.'

'Devil, cease; and do not poison the air with these sounds of malice. I have declared my resolution to you, and I am no coward to bend beneath words. Leave me; I am inexorable.'

'It is well. I go; but remember, I shall be with you on your wedding-night.'

I started forward and exclaimed, 'Villain! Before you sign my death warrant, be sure that you are yourself safe.'

I would have seized him, but he eluded me and quitted the house with precipitation. In a few moments I saw him in his boat, which shot across the waters with an arrowy swiftness and was soon lost amidst the waves.

All was again silent, but his words rang in my ears. I burned with rage to pursue the murderer of my peace and precipitate him into the ocean. I walked up and down my room hastily and perturbed, while my imagination conjured up a thousand images to torment and sting me. Why had I not followed him and closed with him in mortal strife? But I had suffered him to depart, and he had directed his course towards the mainland. I shuddered to think who might be the next victim sacrificed to his insatiate revenge. And then I thought again of his words – 'I will be with you on your wedding-night.' That, then, was the period fixed for the fulfillment of my destiny. In that hour I should die and at once satisfy and extinguish his malice. The prospect did not move me to fear; yet when I thought of my beloved Elizabeth, of her tears and endless sorrow, when she should find her lover so barbarously snatched from her, tears, the first I had shed for many months, streamed from my eyes, and I resolved not to fall before my enemy without a bitter struggle.

The night passed away, and the sun rose from the ocean; my feelings became calmer, if it may be called calmness when the violence of rage sinks into the depths of despair. I left the house, the horrid scene of the last night's contention, and walked on the beach of the sea, which I almost regarded as an insuperable barrier between me and my fellow creatures; nay, a wish that such should prove the fact stole across me. I desired that I might pass my life on that barren rock, wearily, it is true, but uninterrupted by any sudden shock of misery. If I returned, it was to be sacrificed or to see those whom I most loved die under the grasp of a daemon whom I had myself created.

I walked about the isle like a restless spectre, separated from all it loved and miserable in the separation. When it became noon, and the sun rose higher, I lay down on the grass and was overpowered by a deep sleep. I had been awake the whole of the preceding night, my nerves were agitated, and my eyes inflamed by watching and misery. The sleep into which I now sank refreshed me; and when I awoke, I again felt as if I belonged to a race of human beings like myself, and I began to reflect upon what had passed with greater composure; yet still the words of the fiend rang in my ears like a death-knell; they appeared like a dream, yet distinct and oppressive as a reality.

The sun had far descended, and I still sat on the shore,

satisfying my appetite, which had become ravenous, with an oaten cake, when I saw a fishing-boat land close to me, and one of the men brought me a packet; it contained letters from Geneva, and one from Clerval entreating me to join him. He said that he was wearing away his time fruitlessly where he was, that letters from the friends he had formed in London desired his return to complete the negotiation they had entered into for his Indian enterprise. He could not any longer delay his departure; but as his journey to London might be followed, even sooner than he now conjectured, by his longer voyage, he entreated me to bestow as much of my society on him as I could spare. He besought me, therefore, to leave my solitary isle and to meet him at Perth, that we might proceed southwards together. This letter in a degree recalled me to life, and I determined to quit my island at the expiration of two days.

Yet, before I departed, there was a task to perform, on which I shuddered to reflect; I must pack up my chemical instruments, and for that purpose I must enter the room which had been the scene of my odious work, and I must handle those utensils the sight of which was sickening to me. The next morning, at daybreak, I summoned sufficient courage and unlocked the door of my laboratory. The remains of the half-finished creature, whom I had destroyed, lay scattered on the floor, and I almost felt as if I had mangled the living flesh of a human being. I paused to collect myself and then entered the chamber. With trembling hand I conveyed the instruments out of the room, but I reflected that I ought not to leave the relics of my work to excite the horror and suspicion of the peasants; and I accordingly put them into a basket, with a great quantity of stones, and laying them up, determined to throw them into the sea that very night; and in the meantime I sat upon the beach, employed in cleaning and arranging my chemical apparatus.

Nothing could be more complete than the alteration that had taken place in my feelings since the night of the appearance of the daemon. I had before regarded my promise with a gloomy despair as a thing that, with whatever consequences, must be fulfilled; but I now felt as if a film had been taken from before my eyes and that I for the first time saw clearly. The idea of renewing my labours did not for one instant occur to me; the threat I had heard weighed on my thoughts, but I did not reflect that a voluntary act of mine could avert it. I had resolved in my own mind that to create another like the fiend I had first made would be an act of the basest and most atrocious selfishness, and I banished from my mind every thought that could lead to a different conclusion.

Between two and three in the morning the moon rose; and I then, putting my basket aboard a little skiff, sailed out about four miles from the shore. The scene was perfectly solitary; a few boats were returning towards land, but I sailed away from them. I felt as if I was about the commission of a dreadful crime and avoided with shuddering anxiety any encounter with my fellow creatures. At one time the moon, which had before been clear, was suddenly overspread by a thick cloud, and I took advantage of the moment of darkness and cast my basket into the sea; I listened to the gurgling sound as it sank and then sailed away from the spot. The sky became clouded, but the air was pure, although chilled by the northeast breeze that was then rising. But it refreshed me and filled me with such agreeable sensations that I resolved to prolong my stay on the water, and fixing the rudder in a direct position, stretched myself at the bottom of the boat. Clouds hid the moon, everything was obscure, and I heard only the sound of the boat as its keel cut through the waves; the murmur lulled me, and in a short time I slept soundly.

I do not know how long I remained in this situation, but when I awoke I found that the sun had already mounted considerably. The wind was high, and the waves continually threatened the safety of my little skiff. I found that the wind was northeast and must have driven me far from the coast from which I had embarked. I endeavoured to change my course but quickly found that if I again made the attempt the boat would be instantly filled with water. Thus situated, my only resource was to drive before the wind. I confess that I felt a few sensations of terror. I had no compass with me and was so slenderly acquainted with the geography of this part of the world that the sun was of little benefit to me. I might be driven into the wide Atlantic and feel all the tortures of starvation or be swallowed up in the immeasurable waters that roared and buffeted around me. I had already been out many hours and felt the torment of a burning thirst, a prelude to my other sufferings. I looked on the heavens, which were covered by clouds that flew before the wind, only to be replaced by others; I looked upon the sea; it was to be my grave. 'Fiend,' I exclaimed, 'your task is already fulfilled!' I thought of Elizabeth, of my father, and of Clerval – all left behind, on whom the monster might satisfy his sanguinary and merciless passions. This idea plunged me into a reverie so despairing and frightful that even now, when the scene is on the point of closing before me forever, I shudder to reflect on it.

Some hours passed thus; but by degrees, as the sun declined towards the horizon, the wind died away into a gentle breeze and the sea became free from breakers. But these gave place to a heavy swell; I felt sick and hardly able to hold the rudder, when suddenly I saw a line of high land towards the south.

Almost spent, as I was, by fatigue and the dreadful suspense I endured for several hours, this sudden certainty of life rushed like a flood of warm joy to my heart, and tears gushed from my eyes.

How mutable are our feelings, and how strange is that clinging love we have of life even in the excess of misery! I constructed another sail with a part of my dress and eagerly steered my course towards the land. It had a wild and rocky appearance, but as I approached nearer I easily perceived the traces of cultivation. I saw vessels near the shore and found myself suddenly transported back to the neighbourhood of civilized man. I carefully traced the windings of the land and hailed a steeple which I at length saw issuing from behind a small promontory. As I was in a state of extreme debility, I resolved to sail directly towards the town, as a place where I could most easily procure nourishment. Fortunately I had money with me. As I turned the promontory I perceived a small neat town and a good harbour, which I entered, my heart bounding with joy at my unexpected escape.

As I was occupied in fixing the boat and arranging the sails, several people crowded towards the spot. They seemed much surprised at my appearance, but instead of offering me any assistance, whispered together with gestures that at any other time might have produced in me a slight sensation of alarm. As it was, I merely remarked that they spoke English, and I therefore addressed them in that language. 'My good friends,' said I, 'will you be so kind as to tell me the name of this town and inform me where I am?'

'You will know that soon enough,' replied a man with a hoarse voice. 'Maybe you are come to a place that will not prove much to your taste, but you will not be consulted as to your quarters, I promise you.'

I was exceedingly surprised on receiving so rude an answer

from a stranger, and I was also disconcerted on perceiving the frowning and angry countenances of his companions. 'Why do you answer me so roughly?' I replied. 'Surely it is not the custom of Englishmen to receive strangers so inhospitably.'

'I do not know,' said the man, 'what the custom of the English may be, but it is the custom of the Irish to hate villains.'

While this strange dialogue continued, I perceived the crowd rapidly increase. Their faces expressed a mixture of curiosity and anger, which annoyed and in some degree alarmed me. I inquired the way to the inn, but no one replied. I then moved forward, and a murmuring sound arose from the crowd as they followed and surrounded me, when an ill-looking man approaching tapped me on the shoulder and said, 'Come, sir, you must follow me to Mr. Kirwin's to give an account of yourself.'

'Who is Mr. Kirwin? Why am I to give an account of myself? Is not this a free country?'

'Ay, sir, free enough for honest folks. Mr. Kirwin is a magistrate, and you are to give an account of the death of a gentleman who was found murdered here last night.'

This answer startled me, but I presently recovered myself. I was innocent; that could easily be proved; accordingly I followed my conductor in silence and was led to one of the best houses in the town. I was ready to sink from fatigue and hunger, but being surrounded by a crowd, I thought it politic to rouse all my strength, that no physical debility might be construed into apprehension or conscious guilt. Little did I then expect the calamity that was in a few moments to overwhelm me and extinguish in horror and despair all fear of ignominy or death.

I must pause here, for it requires all my fortitude to recall the memory of the frightful events which I am about to relate, in proper detail, to my recollection.

CHAPTER XXI

I was soon introduced into the presence of the magistrate, an old benevolent man with calm and mild manners. He looked upon me, however, with some degree of severity, and then, turning towards my conductors, he asked who appeared as witnesses on this occasion.

About half a dozen men came forward; and, one being selected by the magistrate, he deposed that he had been out fishing the night before with his son and brother-in-law, Daniel Nugent, when, about ten o'clock, they observed a strong northerly blast rising, and they accordingly put in for port. It was a very dark night, as the moon had not yet risen; they did not land at the harbour, but, as they had been accustomed, at a creek about two miles below. He walked on first, carrying a part of the fishing tackle, and his companions followed him at some distance. As he was proceeding along the sands, he struck his foot against something and fell at his length on the ground. His companions came up to assist him, and by the light of their lantern they found that he had fallen on the body of a man, who was to all appearance dead. Their first supposition was that it was the corpse of some person who had been drowned and was thrown on shore by the waves, but on examination they found that the clothes were not wet and even that the body was not then cold. They instantly carried it to the cottage of an old woman near the spot and endeavoured, but in vain, to restore it to life. It appeared to be a handsome young man, about five and twenty years of age. He had apparently been strangled, for there was no sign of any violence except the black mark of fingers on his neck.

The first part of this deposition did not in the least interest me, but when the mark of the fingers was mentioned I remembered the murder of my brother and felt myself extremely agitated; my limbs trembled, and a mist came over my eyes, which obliged me to lean on a chair for support. The magistrate observed me with a keen eye and of course drew an unfavourable augury from my manner.

The son confirmed his father's account, but when Daniel Nugent was called he swore positively that just before the fall of his companion, he saw a boat, with a single man in it, at a short distance from the shore; and as far as he could judge by the light of a few stars, it was the same boat in which I had just landed.

A woman deposed that she lived near the beach and was standing at the door of her cottage, waiting for the return of the fishermen, about an hour before she heard of the discovery of the body, when she saw a boat with only one man in it push off from that part of the shore where the corpse was afterwards found.

Another woman confirmed the account of the fishermen having brought the body into her house; it was not cold. They put it into a bed and rubbed it, and Daniel went to the town for an apothecary, but life was quite gone.

Several other men were examined concerning my landing, and they agreed that, with the strong north wind that had arisen during the night, it was very probable that I had beaten about for many hours and had been obliged to return nearly to the same spot from which I had departed. Besides, they observed that it appeared that I had brought the body from another place, and it was likely that as I did not appear to know the shore, I might have put into the harbour ignorant of the distance of the town of – from the place where I had deposited the corpse.

Mr. Kirwin, on hearing this evidence, desired that I should be taken into the room where the body lay for interment, that it might be observed what effect the sight of it would produce upon me. This idea was probably suggested by the extreme agitation I had exhibited when the mode of the murder had been described. I was accordingly conducted, by the magistrate and several other persons, to the inn. I could not help being struck by the strange coincidences that had taken place during this eventful night; but, knowing that I had been conversing with several persons in the island I had inhabited about the time that the body had been found, I was perfectly tranquil as to the consequences of the affair.

I entered the room where the corpse lay and was led up to the coffin. How can I describe my sensations on beholding it? I feel yet parched with horror, nor can I reflect on that terrible moment without shuddering and agony. The examination, the presence of the magistrate and witnesses, passed like a dream from my memory when I saw the lifeless form of Henry Clerval stretched before me. I gasped for breath, and throwing myself on the body, I exclaimed, 'Have my murderous machinations deprived you also, my dearest Henry, of life? Two I have already destroyed; other victims await their destiny; but you, Clerval, my friend, my benefactor – '

The human frame could no longer support the agonies that I endured, and I was carried out of the room in strong convulsions.

A fever succeeded to this. I lay for two months on the point of death; my ravings, as I afterwards heard, were frightful; I called myself the murderer of William, of Justine, and of Clerval. Sometimes I entreated my attendants to assist me in the destruction of the fiend by whom I was tormented; and at others I felt the fingers of the monster already grasping my neck, and screamed aloud with agony and terror. Fortunately, as I spoke my native language, Mr. Kirwin alone understood me; but my gestures and bitter cries were sufficient to affright the other witnesses.

Why did I not die? More miserable than man ever was before, why did I not sink into forgetfulness and rest? Death snatches away many blooming children, the only hopes of their doting parents; how many brides and youthful lovers have been one day in the bloom of health and hope, and the next a prey for worms and the decay of the tomb! Of what materials was I made that I could thus resist so many shocks, which, like the turning of the wheel, continually renewed the torture?

But I was doomed to live and in two months found myself as awaking from a dream, in a prison, stretched on a wretched bed, surrounded by jailers, turnkeys, bolts, and all the miserable apparatus of a dungeon. It was morning, I remember, when I thus awoke to understanding; I had forgotten the particulars of what had happened and only felt as if some great misfortune had suddenly overwhelmed me; but when I looked around and saw the barred windows and the squalidness of the room in which I was, all flashed across my memory and I groaned bitterly.

This sound disturbed an old woman who was sleeping in a chair beside me. She was a hired nurse, the wife of one of the turnkeys, and her countenance expressed all those bad qualities which often characterize that class. The lines of her face were hard and rude, like that of persons accustomed to see without sympathizing in sights of misery. Her tone expressed her entire indifference; she addressed me in English, and the voice struck me as one that I had heard during my sufferings. 'Are you better now, sir?' said she.

I replied in the same language, with a feeble voice, 'I believe I am; but if it be all true, if indeed I did not dream, I am sorry that I am still alive to feel this misery and horror.'

'For that matter,' replied the old woman, 'if you mean about the gentleman you murdered, I believe that it were better for you if you were dead, for I fancy it will go hard with you! However, that's none of my business; I am sent to nurse you and get you well; I do my duty with a safe conscience; it were well if everybody did the same.'

I turned with loathing from the woman who could utter so unfeeling a speech to a person just saved, on the very edge of death; but I felt languid and unable to reflect on all that had passed. The whole series of my life appeared to me as a dream; I sometimes doubted if indeed it were all true, for it never presented itself to my mind with the force of reality.

As the images that floated before me became more distinct, I grew feverish; a darkness pressed around me; no one was near me who soothed me with the gentle voice of love; no dear hand supported me. The physician came and prescribed medicines, and the old woman prepared them for me; but utter carelessness was visible in the first, and the expression of brutality was strongly marked in the visage of the second. Who could be interested in the fate of a murderer but the hangman who would gain his fee?

These were my first reflections, but I soon learned that Mr. Kirwin had shown me extreme kindness. He had caused the best room in the prison to be prepared for me (wretched indeed was the best); and it was he who had provided a physician and a nurse. It is true, he seldom came to see me, for although he ardently desired to relieve the sufferings of every human creature, he did not wish to be present at the agonies and miserable ravings of a murderer. He came, therefore, sometimes to see that I was not neglected, but his visits were short and with long intervals.

One day, while I was gradually recovering, I was seated in a chair, my eyes half open and my cheeks livid like those in death. I was overcome by gloom and misery and often reflected I had better seek death than desire to remain in a world which to me was replete with wretchedness. At one time I considered whether I should not declare myself guilty and suffer the penalty of the law, less innocent than poor Justine had been. Such were my thoughts when the door of my apartment was opened and Mr. Kirwin entered. His countenance expressed sympathy and compassion; he drew a chair close to mine and addressed me in French, 'I fear that this place is very shocking to you; can I do anything to make you more comfortable?'

'I thank you, but all that you mention is nothing to me; on the whole earth there is no comfort which I am capable of receiving.'

'I know that the sympathy of a stranger can be but of little relief to one borne down as you are by so strange a misfortune. But you will, I hope, soon quit this melancholy abode, for doubtless evidence can easily be brought to free you from the criminal charge.'

'That is my least concern; I am, by a course of strange events, become the most miserable of mortals. Persecuted and tortured as I am and have been, can death be any evil to me?'

'Nothing indeed could be more unfortunate and agonizing than the strange chances that have lately occurred. You were thrown, by some surprising accident, on this shore, renowned for its hospitality, seized immediately, and charged with murder. The first sight that was presented to your eyes was the body of your friend, murdered in so unaccountable a manner and placed, as it were, by some fiend across your path.'

As Mr. Kirwin said this, notwithstanding the agitation I endured on this retrospect of my sufferings, I also felt considerable surprise at the knowledge he seemed to possess concerning me. I suppose some astonishment was exhibited in my countenance, for Mr. Kirwin hastened to say, 'Immediately upon your being taken ill, all the papers that were on your person were brought me, and I examined them that I might discover some trace by which I could send to your relations an account of your misfortune and illness. I found several letters, and, among others, one which I discovered from its commencement to be from your father. I instantly wrote to Geneva; nearly two months have elapsed since the departure of my letter. But you are ill; even now you tremble; you are unfit for agitation of any kind.'

'This suspense is a thousand times worse than the most horrible event; tell me what new scene of death has been acted, and whose murder I am now to lament?'

'Your family is perfectly well,' said Mr. Kirwin with gentleness; 'and someone, a friend, is come to visit you.'

I know not by what chain of thought the idea presented itself, but it instantly darted into my mind that the murderer had come to mock at my misery and taunt me with the death of Clerval, as a new incitement for me to comply with his hellish desires. I put my hand before my eyes, and cried out in agony, 'Oh! Take him away! I cannot see him; for God's sake, do not let him enter!'

Mr. Kirwin regarded me with a troubled countenance. He could not help regarding my exclamation as a presumption of my guilt and said in rather a severe tone, 'I should have thought, young man, that the presence of your father would have been welcome instead of inspiring such violent repugnance.'

'My father!' cried I, while every feature and every muscle was relaxed from anguish to pleasure. 'Is my father indeed come? How kind, how very kind! But where is he, why does he not hasten to me?'

My change of manner surprised and pleased the magistrate; perhaps he thought that my former exclamation was a momentary return of delirium, and now he instantly resumed his former benevolence. He rose and quitted the room with my nurse, and in a moment my father entered it.

Nothing, at this moment, could have given me greater pleasure than the arrival of my father. I stretched out my hand to him and cried, 'Are you, then, safe – and Elizabeth – and Ernest?'

My father calmed me with assurances of their welfare and endeavoured, by dwelling on these subjects so interesting to my heart, to raise my desponding spirits; but he soon felt that a prison cannot be the abode of cheerfulness. 'What a place is this that you inhabit, my son!' said he, looking mournfully at the barred windows and wretched appearance of the room. 'You travelled to seek happiness, but a fatality seems to pursue you. And poor Clerval – '

The name of my unfortunate and murdered friend was an agitation too great to be endured in my weak state; I shed tears.

'Alas! Yes, my father,' replied I; 'some destiny of the most horrible kind hangs over me, and I must live to fulfil it, or surely I should have died on the coffin of Henry.'

We were not allowed to converse for any length of time, for the precarious state of my health rendered every precaution necessary that could ensure tranquillity. Mr. Kirwin came in and insisted that my strength should not be exhausted by too much exertion. But the appearance of my father was to me like that of my good angel, and I gradually recovered my health.

As my sickness quitted me, I was absorbed by a gloomy and black melancholy that nothing could dissipate. The image of Clerval was forever before me, ghastly and murdered. More than once the agitation into which these reflections threw me made my friends dread a dangerous relapse. Alas! Why did they preserve so miserable and detested a life? It was surely that I might fulfil my destiny, which is now drawing to a close. Soon, oh, very soon, will death extinguish these throbbings and relieve me from the mighty weight of anguish that bears me to the dust; and, in executing the award of justice, I shall also sink to rest. Then the appearance of death was distant, although the wish was ever present to my thoughts; and I often sat for hours motionless and speechless, wishing for some mighty revolution that might bury me and my destroyer in its ruins.

The season of the assizes approached. I had already been three months in prison, and although I was still weak and in continual danger of a relapse, I was obliged to travel nearly a hundred miles to the country town where the court was held. Mr. Kirwin charged himself with every care of collecting witnesses and arranging my defence. I was spared the disgrace of appearing publicly as a criminal, as the case was not brought before the court that decides on life and death. The grand jury rejected the bill, on its being proved that I was on the Orkney Islands at the hour the body of my friend was found; and a fortnight after my removal I was liberated from prison.

My father was enraptured on finding me freed from the vexations of a criminal charge, that I was again allowed to breathe the fresh atmosphere and permitted to return to my native country. I did not participate in these feelings, for to me the walls of a dungeon or a palace were alike hateful. The cup of life was poisoned forever, and although the sun shone upon me, as upon the happy and gay of heart, I saw around me nothing but a dense and frightful darkness, penetrated by no light but the glimmer of two eyes that glared upon me. Sometimes they were the expressive eyes of Henry, languishing in death, the dark orbs nearly covered by the lids and the long black lashes that fringed them; sometimes it was the watery, clouded eyes of the monster, as I first saw them in my chamber at Ingolstadt.

My father tried to awaken in me the feelings of affection. He talked of Geneva, which I should soon visit, of Elizabeth and Ernest; but these words only drew deep groans from me. Sometimes, indeed, I felt a wish for happiness and thought with melancholy delight of my beloved cousin or longed, with a devouring 'maladie du pays', to see once more the blue lake and rapid Rhone, that had been so dear to me in early childhood; but my general state of feeling was a torpor in which a prison was as welcome a residence as the divinest scene in nature; and these fits were seldom inter-rupted but by paroxysms of anguish and despair. At these moments I often endeavoured to put an end to the existence I loathed, and it required unceasing attendance and vigilance to restrain me from committing some dreadful act of violence.

Yet one duty remained to me, the recollection of which finally triumphed over my selfish despair. It was necessary that I should return without delay to Geneva, there to watch over the lives of those I so fondly loved and to lie in wait for the murderer, that if any chance led me to the place of his concealment, or if he dared again to blast me by his presence, I might, with unfailing aim, put an end to the existence of the monstrous image which I had endued with the mockery of a soul still more monstrous. My father still desired to delay our departure, fearful that I could not sustain the fatigues of a journey, for I was a shattered wreck – the shadow of a human being. My strength was gone. I was a mere skeleton, and fever night and day preyed upon my wasted frame.

Still, as I urged our leaving Ireland with such inquietude and impatience, my father thought it best to yield. We took our passage on board a vessel bound for Havre-de-Grace and sailed with a fair wind from the Irish shores. It was midnight. I lay on the deck looking at the stars and listening to the dashing of the waves. I hailed the darkness that shut Ireland from my sight, and my pulse beat with a feverish joy when I reflected that I should soon see Geneva. The past appeared to me in the light of a frightful dream; yet the vessel in which I was, the wind that blew me from the detested shore of Ireland, and the sea which surrounded me told me too forcibly that I was deceived by no vision and that Clerval, my friend and dearest companion, had fallen a victim to me and the monster of my creation. I repassed, in my memory, my whole life – my quiet happiness while residing with my family in Geneva, the death of my mother, and my departure for Ingolstadt. I remembered, shuddering, the mad enthusiasm that hurried me on to the creation of my hideous enemy, and I called to mind the night in which he first lived. I was unable to pursue the train of thought; a thousand feelings pressed upon me, and I wept bitterly.

Ever since my recovery from the fever I had been in the custom of taking every night a small quantity of laudanum, for it was by means of this drug only that I was enabled to gain the rest necessary for the preservation of life. Oppressed by the recollection of my various misfortunes, I now swallowed double my usual quantity and soon slept profoundly. But sleep did not afford me respite from thought and misery; my dreams presented a thousand objects that scared me. Towards morning I was possessed by a kind of nightmare; I felt the fiend's grasp in my neck and could not free myself from it; groans and cries rang in my ears. My father, who was watching over me, perceiving my restlessness, awoke me; the dashing waves were around, the cloudy sky above, the fiend was not here: a sense of security, a feeling that a truce was established between the present hour and the irresistible, disastrous future imparted to me a kind of calm forgetfulness, of which the human mind is by its structure peculiarly susceptible.

CHAPTER XXII

The voyage came to an end. We landed, and proceeded to Paris. I soon found that I had overtaxed my strength and that I must repose before I could continue my journey. My father's care and attentions were indefatigable, but he did not know the origin of my sufferings and sought erroneous methods to remedy the incurable ill. He wished me to seek amusement in society. I abhorred the face of man. Oh, not abhorred! They were my brethren, my fellow beings, and I felt attracted even to the most repulsive among them, as to creatures of an angelic nature and celestial mechanism. But I felt that I had no right to share their intercourse. I had unchained an enemy among them whose joy it was to shed their blood and to revel in their groans. How they would, each and all, abhor me and hunt me from the world did they know my unhallowed acts and the crimes which had their source in me!

My father yielded at length to my desire to avoid society and strove by various arguments to banish my despair. Sometimes he thought that I felt deeply the degradation of being obliged to answer a charge of murder, and he endeavoured to prove to me the futility of pride.

'Alas! My father,' said I, 'how little do you know me. Human beings, their feelings and passions, would indeed be degraded if such a wretch as I felt pride. Justine, poor unhappy Justine, was as innocent as I, and she suffered the same charge; she died for it; and I am the cause of this – I murdered her. William, Justine, and Henry – they all died by my hands.'

My father had often, during my imprisonment, heard me make the same assertion; when I thus accused myself, he sometimes seemed to desire an explanation, and at others he appeared to consider it as the offspring of delirium, and that, during my illness, some idea of this kind had presented itself to my imagination, the remembrance of which I preserved in my convalescence. I avoided explanation and maintained a continual silence concerning the wretch I had created. I had a persuasion that I should be supposed mad, and this in itself would forever have chained my tongue. But, besides, I could not bring myself to disclose a secret which would fill my hearer with consternation and make fear and unnatural horror the inmates of his breast. I checked, therefore, my impatient thirst for sympathy and was silent when I would have given the world to have confided the fatal secret. Yet, still, words like those I have recorded would burst uncontrollably from me. I could offer no explanation of them, but their truth in part relieved the burden of my mysterious woe.

Upon this occasion my father said, with an expression of unbounded wonder, 'My dearest Victor, what infatuation is this? My dear son, I entreat you never to make such an assertion again.'

'I am not mad,' I cried energetically; 'the sun and the heavens, who have viewed my operations, can bear witness of my truth. I am the assassin of those most innocent victims; they died by my machinations. A thousand times would I have shed my own blood, drop by drop, to have saved their lives; but I could not, my father, indeed I could not sacrifice the whole human race.'

The conclusion of this speech convinced my father that my ideas were deranged, and he instantly changed the subject of our conversation and endeavoured to alter the course of my thoughts. He wished as much as possible to obliterate the memory of the scenes that had taken place in Ireland and never alluded to them or suffered me to speak of my misfortunes.

As time passed away I became more calm; misery had her dwelling in my heart, but I no longer talked in the same incoherent manner of my own crimes; sufficient for me was the consciousness of them. By the utmost self-violence I curbed the imperious voice of wretchedness, which sometimes desired to declare itself to the whole world, and my manners were calmer and more composed than they had ever been since my journey to the sea of ice.

A few days before we left Paris on our way to Switzerland I received the following letter from Elizabeth:

My dear Friend,

It gave me the greatest pleasure to receive a letter from my uncle dated at Paris; you are no longer at a formidable distance, and I may hope to see you in less than a fortnight. My poor cousin, how much you must have suffered! I expect to see you looking even more ill than when you quitted Geneva. This winter has been passed most miserably, tortured as I have been by anxious suspense; yet I hope to see peace in your countenance and to find that your heart is not totally void of comfort and tranquillity.

Yet I fear that the same feelings now exist that made you so miserable a year ago, even perhaps augmented by time. I would not disturb you at this period, when so many misfortunes weigh upon you, but a conversation that I had with my uncle previous to his departure renders some explanation necessary before we meet.

Explanation! You may possibly say, What can Elizabeth have to explain? If you really say this, my questions are answered and all my doubts satisfied. But you are distant from me, and it is possible that you may dread and yet be pleased with this explanation; and in a probability of this being the case, I dare not any longer postpone writing what, during your absence, I have often wished to express to you but have never had the courage to begin.

You well know, Victor, that our union had been the favourite plan of your parents ever since our infancy. We were told this when young, and taught to look forward to it as an event that would certainly take place. We were affectionate playfellows during childhood, and, I believe, dear and valued friends to one another as we grew older. But as brother and sister often entertain a lively affection towards each other without desiring a more intimate union, may not such also be our case? Tell me, dearest Victor. Answer me, I conjure you by our mutual happiness, with simple truth – Do you not love another?

You have travelled; you have spent several years of your life at Ingolstadt; and I confess to you, my friend, that when I saw you last autumn so unhappy, flying to solitude from the society of every creature, I could not help supposing that you might regret our connection and believe yourself bound in honour to fulfil the wishes of your parents, although they opposed themselves to your inclinations. But this is false reasoning. I confess to you, my friend, that I love you and that in my airy dreams of futurity you have been my constant friend and companion. But it is your happiness I desire as well as my own when I declare to you that our marriage would render me eternally miserable unless it were the dictate of your own free choice. Even now I weep to think that, borne down as you are by the cruellest misfortunes, you may stifle, by the word 'honour,' all hope of that love and happiness which would alone restore you to yourself. I, who have so disinterested an affection for you, may increase your miseries tenfold by being an obstacle to your wishes. Ah! Victor, be assured that your cousin and playmate has too sincere a love for you not to be made miserable by this supposition. Be happy, my friend; and if you obey me in this one request, remain satisfied that nothing on earth will have the power to interrupt my tranquillity.

Do not let this letter disturb you; do not answer tomorrow, or the next day, *or even until you come, if it will give you pain. My uncle will send me news of your health, and if I see but one smile on your lips when we meet, occasioned by this or any other exertion of mine, I shall need no other happiness.*

Elizabeth Lavenza
Geneva, May 18th, 17 –

This letter revived in my memory what I had before forgotten, the threat of the fiend – 'I will be with you on your wedding-night!' Such was my sentence, and on that night would the daemon employ every art to destroy me and tear me from the glimpse of happiness which promised partly to console my sufferings. On that night he had determined to consummate his crimes by my death. Well, be it so; a deadly struggle would then assuredly take place, in which if he were victorious I should be at peace and his power over me be at an end. If he were vanquished, I should be a free man. Alas! What freedom? Such as the peasant enjoys when his family have been massacred before his eyes, his cottage burnt, his lands laid waste, and he is turned adrift, homeless, penniless, and alone, but free. Such would be my liberty except that in my Elizabeth I possessed a treasure, alas, balanced by those horrors of remorse and guilt which would pursue me until death.

Sweet and beloved Elizabeth! I read and reread her letter, and some softened feelings stole into my heart and dared to whisper paradisiacal dreams of love and joy; but the apple was already eaten, and the angel's arm bared to drive me from all hope. Yet I would die to make her happy. If the monster executed his threat, death was inevitable; yet, again, I considered whether my marriage would hasten my fate. My destruction might indeed arrive a few months sooner, but if my torturer should suspect that I postponed it, influenced by his menaces, he would surely find other and perhaps more dreadful means of revenge. He had vowed 'to be with me on my wedding-night', yet he did not consider that threat as binding him to peace in the meantime, for as if to show me that he was not yet satiated with blood, he had murdered Clerval immediately after the enunciation of his threats. I resolved, therefore, that if my immediate union with my cousin would conduce either to hers or my father's happiness, my adversary's designs against my life should not retard it a single hour.

In this state of mind I wrote to Elizabeth. My letter was calm and affectionate. 'I fear, my beloved girl,' I said, 'little happiness remains for us on earth; yet all that I may one day enjoy is centred in you. Chase away your idle fears; to you alone do I consecrate my life and my endeavours for contentment. I have one secret, Elizabeth, a dreadful one; when revealed to you, it will chill your frame with horror, and then, far from being surprised at my misery, you will only wonder that I survive what I have endured. I will confide this tale of misery and terror to you the day after our marriage shall take place, for, my sweet cousin, there must be perfect confidence between us. But until then, I conjure you, do not mention or allude to it. This I most earnestly entreat, and I know you will comply.'

In about a week after the arrival of Elizabeth's letter we returned to Geneva. The sweet girl welcomed me with warm affection, yet tears were in her eyes as she beheld my emaciated frame and feverish cheeks. I saw a change in her also. She was thinner and had lost much of that heavenly vivacity that had before charmed me; but her gentleness and soft looks of compassion made her a more fit companion for one blasted and miserable as I was.

The tranquillity which I now enjoyed did not endure. Memory brought madness with it, and when I thought of what had passed, a real insanity possessed me; sometimes I was furious and burnt with rage, sometimes low and despondent. I neither spoke nor looked at anyone, but sat motionless, bewildered by the multitude of miseries that overcame me.

Elizabeth alone had the power to draw me from these fits; her gentle voice would soothe me when transported by passion and inspire me with human feelings when sunk in torpor. She wept with me and for me. When reason returned, she would remonstrate and endeavour to inspire me with resignation. Ah! It is well for the unfortunate to be resigned, but for the guilty there is no peace. The agonies of remorse poison the luxury there is otherwise sometimes found in indulging the excess of grief.

Soon after my arrival my father spoke of my immediate marriage with Elizabeth. I remained silent.

'Have you, then, some other attachment?'

'None on earth. I love Elizabeth and look forward to our union with delight. Let the day therefore be fixed; and on it I will consecrate myself, in life or death, to the happiness of my cousin.'

'My dear Victor, do not speak thus. Heavy misfortunes have

befallen us, but let us only cling closer to what remains and transfer our love for those whom we have lost to those who yet live. Our circle will be small but bound close by the ties of affection and mutual misfortune. And when time shall have softened your despair, new and dear objects of care will be born to replace those of whom we have been so cruelly deprived.'

Such were the lessons of my father. But to me the remembrance of the threat returned; nor can you wonder that, omnipotent as the fiend had yet been in his deeds of blood, I should almost regard him as invincible, and that when he had pronounced the words 'I shall be with you on your wedding-night,' I should regard the threatened fate as unavoidable. But death was no evil to me if the loss of Elizabeth were balanced with it, and I therefore, with a contented and even cheerful countenance, agreed with my father that if my cousin would consent, the ceremony should take place in ten days, and thus put, as I imagined, the seal to my fate.

Great God! If for one instant I had thought what might be the hellish intention of my fiendish adversary, I would rather have banished myself forever from my native country and wandered a friendless outcast over the earth than have consented to this miserable marriage. But, as if possessed of magic powers, the monster had blinded me to his real intentions; and when I thought that I had prepared only my own death, I hastened that of a far dearer victim.

As the period fixed for our marriage drew nearer, whether from cowardice or a prophetic feeling, I felt my heart sink within me. But I concealed my feelings by an appearance of hilarity that brought smiles and joy to the countenance of my father, but hardly deceived the everwatchful and nicer eye of Elizabeth. She looked forward to our union with placid contentment, not unmingled with a little fear, which past misfortunes had impressed, that what now appeared certain and tangible happiness might soon dissipate into an airy dream and leave no trace but deep and everlasting regret.

Preparations were made for the event, congratulatory visits were received, and all wore a smiling appearance. I shut up, as well as I could, in my own heart the anxiety that preyed there and entered with seeming earnestness into the plans of my father, although they might only serve as the decorations of my tragedy. Through my father's exertions a part of the inheritance of Elizabeth had been restored to her by the Austrian government. A small possession

on the shores of Como belonged to her. It was agreed that, immediately after our union, we should proceed to Villa Lavenza and
spend our first days of happiness beside the beautiful lake near
which it stood.

In the meantime I took every precaution to defend my person
in case the fiend should openly attack me. I carried pistols and a
dagger constantly about me and was ever on the watch to prevent
artifice, and by these means gained a greater degree of tranquillity. Indeed, as the period approached, the threat appeared more
as a delusion, not to be regarded as worthy to disturb my peace,
while the happiness I hoped for in my marriage wore a greater
appearance of certainty as the day fixed for its solemnization drew
nearer and I heard it continually spoken of as an occurrence which
no accident could possibly prevent.

Elizabeth seemed happy; my tranquil demeanour contributed
greatly to calm her mind. But on the day that was to fulfil my wishes
and my destiny, she was melancholy, and a presentiment of evil
pervaded her; and perhaps also she thought of the dreadful secret
which I had promised to reveal to her on the following day. My
father was in the meantime overjoyed and in the bustle of preparation only recognized in the melancholy of his niece the diffidence
of a bride.

After the ceremony was performed a large party assembled
at my father's, but it was agreed that Elizabeth and I should
commence our journey by water, sleeping that night at Evian and
continuing our voyage on the following day. The day was fair, the
wind favourable; all smiled on our nuptial embarkation.

Those were the last moments of my life during which I enjoyed
the feeling of happiness. We passed rapidly along; the sun was hot,
but we were sheltered from its rays by a kind of canopy while we
enjoyed the beauty of the scene, sometimes on one side of the lake,
where we saw Mont Saleve, the pleasant banks of Montalegre, and
at a distance, surmounting all, the beautiful Mont Blanc and the
assemblage of snowy mountains that in vain endeavour to emulate
her; sometimes coasting the opposite banks, we saw the mighty Jura
opposing its dark side to the ambition that would quit its native
country, and an almost insurmountable barrier to the invader who
should wish to enslave it.

I took the hand of Elizabeth. 'You are sorrowful, my love. Ah!
If you knew what I have suffered and what I may yet endure, you

would endeavour to let me taste the quiet and freedom from despair that this one day at least permits me to enjoy.'

'Be happy, my dear Victor,' replied Elizabeth; 'there is, I hope, nothing to distress you; and be assured that if a lively joy is not painted in my face, my heart is contented. Something whispers to me not to depend too much on the prospect that is opened before us, but I will not listen to such a sinister voice. Observe how fast we move along and how the clouds, which sometimes obscure and sometimes rise above the dome of Mont Blanc, render this scene of beauty still more interesting. Look also at the innumerable fish that are swimming in the clear waters, where we can distinguish every pebble that lies at the bottom. What a divine day! How happy and serene all nature appears!'

Thus Elizabeth endeavoured to divert her thoughts and mine from all reflection upon melancholy subjects. But her temper was fluctuating; joy for a few instants shone in her eyes, but it continually gave place to distraction and reverie.

The sun sank lower in the heavens; we passed the river Drance and observed its path through the chasms of the higher and the glens of the lower hills. The Alps here come closer to the lake, and we approached the amphitheatre of mountains which forms its eastern boundary. The spire of Evian shone under the woods that surrounded it and the range of mountain above mountain by which it was overhung.

The wind, which had hitherto carried us along with amazing rapidity, sank at sunset to a light breeze; the soft air just ruffled the water and caused a pleasant motion among the trees as we approached the shore, from which it wafted the most delightful scent of flowers and hay. The sun sank beneath the horizon as we landed, and as I touched the shore I felt those cares and fears revive which soon were to clasp me and cling to me forever.

CHAPTER XXIII

It was eight o'clock when we landed; we walked for a short time on the shore, enjoying the transitory light, and then retired to the inn and contemplated the lovely scene of waters, woods, and mountains, obscured in darkness, yet still displaying their black outlines.

The wind, which had fallen in the south, now rose with great violence in the west. The moon had reached her summit in the heavens and was beginning to descend; the clouds swept across it swifter than the flight of the vulture and dimmed her rays, while the lake reflected the scene of the busy heavens, rendered still busier by the restless waves that were beginning to rise. Suddenly a heavy storm of rain descended.

I had been calm during the day, but so soon as night obscured the shapes of objects, a thousand fears arose in my mind. I was anxious and watchful, while my right hand grasped a pistol which was hidden in my bosom; every sound terrified me, but I resolved that I would sell my life dearly and not shrink from the conflict until my own life or that of my adversary was extinguished.

Elizabeth observed my agitation for some time in timid and fearful silence, but there was something in my glance which communicated terror to her, and trembling, she asked, 'What is it that agitates you, my dear Victor? What is it you fear?'

'Oh! Peace, peace, my love,' replied I; 'this night, and all will be safe; but this night is dreadful, very dreadful.'

I passed an hour in this state of mind, when suddenly I reflected how fearful the combat which I momentarily expected would be to my wife, and I earnestly entreated her to retire, resolving not to join her until I had obtained some knowledge as to the situation of my enemy.

She left me, and I continued some time walking up and down the passages of the house and inspecting every corner that might afford a retreat to my adversary. But I discovered no trace of him and was beginning to conjecture that some fortunate chance had intervened to prevent the execution of his menaces when suddenly I heard a shrill and dreadful scream. It came from the room into

161

which Elizabeth had retired. As I heard it, the whole truth rushed into my mind, my arms dropped, the motion of every muscle and fibre was suspended; I could feel the blood trickling in my veins and tingling in the extremities of my limbs. This state lasted but for an instant; the scream was repeated, and I rushed into the room.

Great God! Why did I not then expire! Why am I here to relate the destruction of the best hope and the purest creature on earth? She was there, lifeless and inanimate, thrown across the bed, her head hanging down and her pale and distorted features half covered by her hair. Everywhere I turn I see the same figure – her bloodless arms and relaxed form flung by the murderer on its bridal bier. Could I behold this and live? Alas! Life is obstinate and clings closest where it is most hated. For a moment only did I lose recollection; I fell senseless on the ground.

When I recovered I found myself surrounded by the people of the inn; their countenances expressed a breathless terror, but the horror of others appeared only as a mockery, a shadow of the feelings that oppressed me. I escaped from them to the room where lay the body of Elizabeth, my love, my wife, so lately living, so dear, so worthy. She had been moved from the posture in which I had first beheld her, and now, as she lay, her head upon her arm and a handkerchief thrown across her face and neck, I might have supposed her asleep. I rushed towards her and embraced her with ardour, but the deadly languor and coldness of the limbs told me that what I now held in my arms had ceased to be the Elizabeth whom I had loved and cherished. The murderous mark of the fiend's grasp was on her neck, and the breath had ceased to issue from her lips.

While I still hung over her in the agony of despair, I happened to look up. The windows of the room had before been darkened, and I felt a kind of panic on seeing the pale yellow light of the moon illuminate the chamber. The shutters had been thrown back, and with a sensation of horror not to be described, I saw at the open window a figure the most hideous and abhorred. A grin was on the face of the monster; he seemed to jeer, as with his fiendish finger he pointed towards the corpse of my wife. I rushed towards the window, and drawing a pistol from my bosom, fired; but he eluded me, leaped from his station, and running with the swiftness of lightning, plunged into the lake.

The report of the pistol brought a crowd into the room. I

pointed to the spot where he had disappeared, and we followed the track with boats; nets were cast, but in vain. After passing several hours, we returned hopeless, most of my companions believing it to have been a form conjured up by my fancy. After having landed, they proceeded to search the country, parties going in different directions among the woods and vines.

I attempted to accompany them and proceeded a short distance from the house, but my head whirled round, my steps were like those of a drunken man, I fell at last in a state of utter exhaustion; a film covered my eyes, and my skin was parched with the heat of fever. In this state I was carried back and placed on a bed, hardly conscious of what had happened; my eyes wandered round the room as if to seek something that I had lost.

After an interval I arose, and as if by instinct, crawled into the room where the corpse of my beloved lay. There were women weeping around; I hung over it and joined my sad tears to theirs; all this time no distinct idea presented itself to my mind, but my thoughts rambled to various subjects, reflecting confusedly on my misfortunes and their cause. I was bewildered, in a cloud of wonder and horror. The death of William, the execution of Justine, the murder of Clerval, and lastly of my wife; even at that moment I knew not that my only remaining friends were safe from the malignity of the fiend; my father even now might be writhing under his grasp, and Ernest might be dead at his feet. This idea made me shudder and recalled me to action. I started up and resolved to return to Geneva with all possible speed.

There were no horses to be procured, and I must return by the lake; but the wind was unfavourable, and the rain fell in torrents. However, it was hardly morning, and I might reasonably hope to arrive by night. I hired men to row and took an oar myself, for I had always experienced relief from mental torment in bodily exercise. But the overflowing misery I now felt, and the excess of agitation that I endured rendered me incapable of any exertion. I threw down the oar, and leaning my head upon my hands, gave way to every gloomy idea that arose. If I looked up, I saw scenes which were familiar to me in my happier time and which I had contemplated but the day before in the company of her who was now but a shadow and a recollection. Tears streamed from my eyes. The rain had ceased for a moment, and I saw the fish play in the waters as they had done a few hours before; they had then been observed by

Elizabeth. Nothing is so painful to the human mind as a great and sudden change. The sun might shine or the clouds might lower, but nothing could appear to me as it had done the day before. A fiend had snatched from me every hope of future happiness; no creature had ever been so miserable as I was; so frightful an event is single in the history of man.

But why should I dwell upon the incidents that followed this last overwhelming event? Mine has been a tale of horrors; I have reached their acme, and what I must now relate can but be tedious to you. Know that, one by one, my friends were snatched away; I was left desolate. My own strength is exhausted, and I must tell, in a few words, what remains of my hideous narration.

I arrived at Geneva. My father and Ernest yet lived, but the former sunk under the tidings that I bore. I see him now, excellent and venerable old man! His eyes wandered in vacancy, for they had lost their charm and their delight – his Elizabeth, his more than daughter, whom he doted on with all that affection which a man feels, who in the decline of life, having few affections, clings more earnestly to those that remain. Cursed, cursed be the fiend that brought misery on his grey hairs and doomed him to waste in wretchedness! He could not live under the horrors that were accumulated around him; the springs of existence suddenly gave way; he was unable to rise from his bed, and in a few days he died in my arms.

What then became of me? I know not; I lost sensation, and chains and darkness were the only objects that pressed upon me. Sometimes, indeed, I dreamt that I wandered in flowery meadows and pleasant vales with the friends of my youth, but I awoke and found myself in a dungeon. Melancholy followed, but by degrees I gained a clear conception of my miseries and situation and was then released from my prison. For they had called me mad, and during many months, as I understood, a solitary cell had been my habitation.

Liberty, however, had been a useless gift to me, had I not, as I awakened to reason, at the same time awakened to revenge. As the memory of past misfortunes pressed upon me, I began to reflect on their cause – the monster whom I had created, the miserable daemon whom I had sent abroad into the world for my destruction. I was possessed by a maddening rage when I thought of him, and desired and ardently prayed that I might have him within my grasp to wreak a great and signal revenge on his cursed head.

Nor did my hate long confine itself to useless wishes; I began to reflect on the best means of securing him; and for this purpose, about a month after my release, I repaired to a criminal judge in the town and told him that I had an accusation to make, that I knew the destroyer of my family, and that I required him to exert his whole authority for the apprehension of the murderer.

The magistrate listened to me with attention and kindness. 'Be assured, sir,' said he, 'no pains or exertions on my part shall be spared to discover the villain.'

'I thank you,' replied I; 'listen, therefore, to the deposition that I have to make. It is indeed a tale so strange that I should fear you would not credit it were there not something in truth which, however wonderful, forces conviction. The story is too connected to be mistaken for a dream, and I have no motive for falsehood.' My manner as I thus addressed him was impressive but calm; I had formed in my own heart a resolution to pursue my destroyer to death, and this purpose quieted my agony and for an interval reconciled me to life. I now related my history briefly but with firmness and precision, marking the dates with accuracy and never deviating into invective or exclamation.

The magistrate appeared at first perfectly incredulous, but as I continued he became more attentive and interested; I saw him sometimes shudder with horror; at others a lively surprise, unmingled with disbelief, was painted on his countenance.

When I had concluded my narration I said, 'This is the being whom I accuse and for whose seizure and punishment I call upon you to exert your whole power. It is your duty as a magistrate, and I believe and hope that your feelings as a man will not revolt from the execution of those functions on this occasion.'

This address caused a considerable change in the physiognomy of my own auditor. He had heard my story with that half kind of belief that is given to a tale of spirits and supernatural events; but when he was called upon to act officially in consequence, the whole tide of his incredulity returned. He, however, answered mildly, 'I would willingly afford you every aid in your pursuit, but the creature of whom you speak appears to have powers which would put all my exertions to defiance. Who can follow an animal which can traverse the sea of ice and inhabit caves and dens where no man would venture to intrude? Besides, some months have elapsed since the commission of his crimes, and no one can conjecture to what place he has wandered or what region he may now inhabit.'

'I do not doubt that he hovers near the spot which I inhabit, and if he has indeed taken refuge in the Alps, he may be hunted like the chamois and destroyed as a beast of prey. But I perceive your thoughts; you do not credit my narrative and do not intend to pursue my enemy with the punishment which is his desert.'

As I spoke, rage sparkled in my eyes; the magistrate was intimidated. 'You are mistaken,' said he. 'I will exert myself, and if it is in my power to seize the monster, be assured that he shall suffer punishment proportionate to his crimes. But I fear, from what you have yourself described to be his properties, that this will prove impracticable; and thus, while every proper measure is pursued, you should make up your mind to disappointment.'

'That cannot be; but all that I can say will be of little avail. My revenge is of no moment to you; yet, while I allow it to be a vice, I confess that it is the devouring and only passion of my soul. My rage is unspeakable when I reflect that the murderer, whom I have turned loose upon society, still exists. You refuse my just demand; I have but one resource, and I devote myself, either in my life or death, to his destruction.'

I trembled with excess of agitation as I said this; there was a frenzy in my manner, and something, I doubt not, of that haughty fierceness which the martyrs of old are said to have possessed. But to a Genevan magistrate, whose mind was occupied by far other ideas than those of devotion and heroism, this elevation of mind had much the appearance of madness. He endeavoured to soothe me as a nurse does a child and reverted to my tale as the effects of delirium.

'Man,' I cried, 'how ignorant art thou in thy pride of wisdom! Cease; you know not what it is you say.'

I broke from the house angry and disturbed and retired to meditate on some other mode of action.

CHAPTER XXIV

My present situation was one in which all voluntary thought was swallowed up and lost. I was hurried away by fury; revenge alone endowed me with strength and composure; it moulded my feelings and allowed me to be calculating and calm at periods when otherwise delirium or death would have been my portion.

My first resolution was to quit Geneva forever; my country, which, when I was happy and beloved, was dear to me, now, in my adversity, became hateful. I provided myself with a sum of money, together with a few jewels which had belonged to my mother, and departed.

And now my wanderings began which are to cease but with life. I have traversed a vast portion of the earth and have endured all the hardships which travellers in deserts and barbarous countries are wont to meet. How I have lived I hardly know; many times have I stretched my failing limbs upon the sandy plain and prayed for death. But revenge kept me alive; I dared not die and leave my adversary in being.

When I quitted Geneva my first labour was to gain some clue by which I might trace the steps of my fiendish enemy. But my plan was unsettled, and I wandered many hours round the confines of the town, uncertain what path I should pursue. As night approached I found myself at the entrance of the cemetery where William, Elizabeth, and my father reposed. I entered it and approached the tomb which marked their graves. Everything was silent except the leaves of the trees, which were gently agitated by the wind; the night was nearly dark, and the scene would have been solemn and affecting even to an uninterested observer. The spirits of the departed seemed to flit around and to cast a shadow, which was felt but not seen, around the head of the mourner.

The deep grief which this scene had at first excited quickly gave way to rage and despair. They were dead, and I lived; their murderer also lived, and to destroy him I must drag out my weary existence. I knelt on the grass and kissed the earth and with quivering lips exclaimed, 'By the sacred earth on which I kneel, by the shades that wander near me, by the deep and eternal grief that I feel, I swear; and by thee, O Night, and the spirits that preside over thee, to pursue the daemon who caused this misery, until he or I shall perish in mortal conflict. For this purpose I will preserve my life; to execute this dear revenge will I again behold the sun and tread the green herbage of earth, which otherwise should vanish from my eyes forever. And I call on you, spirits of the dead, and on you, wandering ministers of vengeance, to aid and conduct me in my work. Let the cursed and hellish monster drink deep of agony; let him feel the despair that now torments me.'

I had begun my adjuration with solemnity and an awe which almost assured me that the shades of my murdered friends heard and approved my devotion, but the furies possessed me as I concluded, and rage choked my utterance.

I was answered through the stillness of night by a loud and fiendish laugh. It rang on my ears long and heavily; the mountains re-echoed it, and I felt as if all hell surrounded me with mockery and laughter. Surely in that moment I should have been possessed by frenzy and have destroyed my miserable existence but that my vow was heard and that I was reserved for vengeance. The laughter died away, when a well-known and abhorred voice, apparently close to my ear, addressed me in an audible whisper, 'I am satisfied, miserable wretch! You have determined to live, and I am satisfied.'

I darted towards the spot from which the sound proceeded, but the devil eluded my grasp. Suddenly the broad disk of the moon arose and shone full upon his ghastly and distorted shape as he fled with more than mortal speed.

I pursued him, and for many months this has been my task. Guided by a slight clue, I followed the windings of the Rhone, but vainly. The blue Mediterranean appeared, and by a strange chance, I saw the fiend enter by night and hide himself in a vessel bound for the Black Sea. I took my passage in the same ship, but he escaped, I know not how.

Amidst the wilds of Tartary and Russia, although he still evaded me, I have ever followed in his track. Sometimes the peasants, scared by this horrid apparition, informed me of his path; sometimes he himself, who feared that if I lost all trace of him I should despair and die, left some mark to guide me. The snows descended on my head, and I saw the print of his huge step on the white plain. To you first entering on life, to whom care is new and agony unknown, how can you understand what I have felt and still feel? Cold, want, and fatigue were the least pains which I was destined to endure; I was cursed by some devil and carried about with me my eternal hell; yet still a spirit of good followed and directed my steps and when I most murmured would suddenly extricate me from seemingly insurmountable difficulties. Sometimes, when nature, overcome by hunger, sank under the exhaustion, a repast was prepared for me in the desert that restored and inspirited me. The fare was, indeed, coarse, such as the peasants of the country ate, but I will not doubt that it was set there by the spirits that I had invoked to aid me. Often, when all was dry, the heavens cloudless, and I was parched by thirst, a slight cloud would bedim the sky, shed the few drops that revived me, and vanish.

I followed, when I could, the courses of the rivers; but the daemon generally avoided these, as it was here that the population of the country chiefly collected. In other places human beings were seldom seen, and I generally subsisted on the wild animals that crossed my path. I had money with me and gained the friendship of the villagers by distributing it; or I brought with me some food that I had killed, which, after taking a small part, I always presented to those who had provided me with fire and utensils for cooking.

My life, as it passed thus, was indeed hateful to me, and it was during sleep alone that I could taste joy. O blessed sleep! Often, when most miserable, I sank to repose, and my dreams lulled me even to rapture. The spirits that guarded me had provided these moments, or rather hours, of happiness that I might retain strength to fulfil my pilgrimage. Deprived of this respite, I should have sunk under my hardships. During the day I was sustained and inspirited by the hope of night, for in sleep I saw my friends, my wife, and my beloved country; again I saw the benevolent countenance of my father, heard the silver tones of my Elizabeth's voice, and beheld Clerval enjoying health and youth. Often, when wearied by a toilsome march, I persuaded myself that I was dreaming until night should come and that I should then enjoy reality in the arms of my dearest friends. What agonizing fondness did I feel for them! How did I cling to their dear forms, as sometimes they haunted even my waking hours, and persuade myself that they still lived! At such moments vengeance, that burned within me, died in my heart, and I pursued my path towards the destruction of the daemon more as a task enjoined by heaven, as the mechanical impulse of some power of which I was unconscious, than as the ardent desire of my soul.

What his feelings were whom I pursued I cannot know. Sometimes, indeed, he left marks in writing on the barks of the trees or cut in stone that guided me and instigated my fury. 'My reign is not yet over' – these words were legible in one of these inscriptions – 'you live, and my power is complete. Follow me; I seek the everlasting ices of the north, where you will feel the misery of cold and frost, to which I am impassive. You will find near this place, if you follow not too tardily, a dead hare; eat and be refreshed. Come on, my enemy; we have yet to wrestle for our lives, but many hard and miserable hours must you endure until that period shall arrive.'

Scoffing devil! Again do I vow vengeance; again do I devote thee, miserable fiend, to torture and death. Never will I give up my search until he or I perish; and then with what ecstasy shall I join my Elizabeth and my departed friends, who even now prepare for me the reward of my tedious toil and horrible pilgrimage!

As I still pursued my journey to the northward, the snows thickened and the cold increased in a degree almost too severe to support. The peasants were shut up in their hovels, and only a few of the most hardy ventured forth to seize the animals whom starvation had forced from their hiding-places to seek for prey. The rivers were covered with ice, and no fish could be procured; and thus I was cut off from my chief article of maintenance.

The triumph of my enemy increased with the difficulty of my labours. One inscription that he left was in these words: 'Prepare! Your toils only begin; wrap yourself in furs and provide food, for we shall soon enter upon a journey where your sufferings will satisfy my everlasting hatred.'

My courage and perseverance were invigorated by these scoffing words; I resolved not to fail in my purpose, and calling on heaven to support me, I continued with unabated fervour to traverse immense deserts, until the ocean appeared at a distance and formed the utmost boundary of the horizon. Oh! How unlike it was to the blue seasons of the south! Covered with ice, it was only to be distinguished from land by its superior wildness and ruggedness. The Greeks wept for joy when they beheld the Mediterranean from the hills of Asia, and hailed with rapture the boundary of their toils. I did not weep, but I knelt down and with a full heart thanked my guiding spirit for conducting me in safety to the place where I hoped, notwithstanding my adversary's gibe, to meet and grapple with him.

Some weeks before this period I had procured a sledge and dogs and thus traversed the snows with inconceivable speed. I know not whether the fiend possessed the same advantages, but I found that, as before I had daily lost ground in the pursuit, I now gained on him, so much so that when I first saw the ocean he was but one day's journey in advance, and I hoped to intercept him before he should reach the beach. With new courage, therefore, I pressed on, and in two days arrived at a wretched hamlet on the seashore. I inquired of the inhabitants concerning the fiend and gained accurate information. A gigantic monster, they said, had arrived the night before, armed with a gun and many pistols, putting to flight the inhabitants of a solitary cottage through fear of his terrific appearance. He had carried off their store of winter food, and placing it in a sledge, to draw which he had seized on a numerous drove of trained dogs, he had harnessed them, and the same night, to the joy of the horror-struck villagers, had pursued his journey across the sea in a direction that led to no land; and they conjectured that he must speedily be destroyed by the breaking of the ice or frozen by the eternal frosts.

On hearing this information I suffered a temporary access of despair. He had escaped me, and I must commence a destructive and almost endless journey across the mountainous ices of the ocean, amidst cold that few of the inhabitants could long endure and which I, the native of a genial and sunny climate, could not hope to survive. Yet at the idea that the fiend should live and be triumphant, my rage and vengeance returned, and like a mighty tide, overwhelmed every other feeling. After a slight repose, during which the spirits of the dead hovered round and instigated me to toil and revenge, I prepared for my journey.

I exchanged my land-sledge for one fashioned for the inequalities of the frozen ocean, and purchasing a plentiful stock of provisions, I departed from land.

I cannot guess how many days have passed since then, but I have endured misery which nothing but the eternal sentiment of a just retribution burning within my heart could have enabled me to support. Immense and rugged mountains of ice often barred up my passage, and I often heard the thunder of the ground sea, which threatened my destruction. But again the frost came and made the paths of the sea secure.

By the quantity of provision which I had consumed, I should

guess that I had passed three weeks in this journey; and the continual protraction of hope, returning back upon the heart, often wrung bitter drops of despondency and grief from my eyes. Despair had indeed almost secured her prey, and I should soon have sunk beneath this misery. Once, after the poor animals that conveyed me had with incredible toil gained the summit of a sloping ice mountain, and one, sinking under his fatigue, died, I viewed the expanse before me with anguish, when suddenly my eye caught a dark speck upon the dusky plain. I strained my sight to discover what it could be and uttered a wild cry of ecstasy when I distinguished a sledge and the distorted proportions of a well-known form within. Oh! With what a burning gush did hope revisit my heart! Warm tears filled my eyes, which I hastily wiped away, that they might not intercept the view I had of the daemon; but still my sight was dimmed by the burning drops, until, giving way to the emotions that oppressed me, I wept aloud.

But this was not the time for delay; I disencumbered the dogs of their dead companion, gave them a plentiful portion of food, and after an hour's rest, which was absolutely necessary, and yet which was bitterly irksome to me, I continued my route. The sledge was still visible, nor did I again lose sight of it except at the moments when for a short time some ice-rock concealed it with its intervening crags. I indeed perceptibly gained on it, and when, after nearly two days' journey, I beheld my enemy at no more than a mile distant, my heart bounded within me.

But now, when I appeared almost within grasp of my foe, my hopes were suddenly extinguished, and I lost all trace of him more utterly than I had ever done before. A ground sea was heard; the thunder of its progress, as the waters rolled and swelled beneath me, became every moment more ominous and terrific. I pressed on, but in vain. The wind arose; the sea roared; and, as with the mighty shock of an earthquake, it split and cracked with a tremendous and overwhelming sound. The work was soon finished; in a few minutes a tumultuous sea rolled between me and my enemy, and I was left drifting on a scattered piece of ice that was continually lessening and thus preparing for me a hideous death.

In this manner many appalling hours passed; several of my dogs died, and I myself was about to sink under the accumulation of distress when I saw your vessel riding at anchor and holding forth to me hopes of succour and life. I had no conception that vessels ever came so far north and was astounded at the sight. I quickly destroyed part of my sledge to construct oars, and by these means was enabled, with infinite fatigue, to move my ice raft in the direction of your ship. I had determined, if you were going southwards, still to trust myself to the mercy of the seas rather than abandon my purpose. I hoped to induce you to grant me a boat with which I could pursue my enemy. But your direction was northwards. You took me on board when my vigour was exhausted, and I should soon have sunk under my multiplied hardships into a death which I still dread, for my task is unfulfilled.

Oh! When will my guiding spirit, in conducting me to the daemon, allow me the rest I so much desire; or must I die, and he yet live? If I do, swear to me, Walton, that he shall not escape, that you will seek him and satisfy my vengeance in his death. And do I dare to ask of you to undertake my pilgrimage, to endure the hardships that I have undergone? No; I am not so selfish. Yet, when I am dead, if he should appear, if the ministers of vengeance should conduct him to you, swear that he shall not live – swear that he shall not triumph over my accumulated woes and survive to add to the list of his dark crimes. He is eloquent and persuasive, and once his words had even power over my heart; but trust him not. His soul is as hellish as his form, full of treachery and fiendlike malice. Hear him not; call on the names of William, Justine, Clerval, Elizabeth, my father, and of the wretched Victor, and thrust your sword into his heart. I will hover near and direct the steel aright.

August 26th, 17 –

You have read this strange and terrific story, Margaret; and do you not feel your blood congeal with horror, like that which even now curdles mine? Sometimes, seized with sudden agony, he could not continue his tale; at others, his voice broken, yet piercing, uttered with difficulty the words so replete with anguish. His fine and lovely eyes were now lighted up with indignation, now subdued to downcast sorrow and quenched in infinite wretchedness. Sometimes he commanded his countenance and tones and related the most horrible incidents with a tranquil voice, suppressing every mark of agitation; then, like a volcano bursting forth, his face would suddenly change to an expression of the wildest rage as he shrieked out imprecations on his persecutor.

His tale is connected and told with an appearance of the simplest truth, yet I own to you that the letters of Felix and Safie, which he showed me, and the apparition of the monster seen from our ship, brought to me a greater conviction of the truth of his narrative than his asseverations, however earnest and connected. Such a monster has, then, really existence! I cannot doubt it, yet I am lost in surprise and admiration. Sometimes I endeavoured to gain from Frankenstein the particulars of his creature's formation, but on this point he was impenetrable.

'Are you mad, my friend?' said he. 'Or whither does your senseless curiosity lead you? Would you also create for yourself and the world a demoniacal enemy? Peace, peace! Learn my miseries and do not seek to increase your own.'

Frankenstein discovered that I made notes concerning his history; he asked to see them and then himself corrected and augmented them in many places, but principally in giving the life and spirit to the conversations he held with his enemy. 'Since you have preserved my narration,' said he, 'I would not that a mutilated one should go down to posterity.'

Thus has a week passed away, while I have listened to the strangest tale that ever imagination formed. My thoughts and every feeling of my soul have been drunk up by the interest for my guest which this tale and his own elevated and gentle manners have created. I wish to soothe him, yet can I counsel one so infinitely miserable, so destitute of every hope of consolation, to live? Oh, no! The only joy that he can now know will be when he composes his shattered spirit to peace and death. Yet he enjoys one comfort, the offspring of solitude and delirium; he believes that when in dreams he holds converse with his friends and derives from that communion consolation for his miseries or excitements to his vengeance, that they are not the creations of his fancy, but the beings themselves who visit him from the regions of a remote world. This faith gives a solemnity to his reveries that render them to me almost as imposing and interesting as truth.

Our conversations are not always confined to his own history and misfortunes. On every point of general literature he displays unbounded knowledge and a quick and piercing apprehension. His eloquence is forcible and touching; nor can I hear him, when he relates a pathetic incident or endeavours to move the passions of pity or love, without tears. What a glorious creature must he have been in the days of his prosperity, when he is thus noble and godlike in ruin! He seems to feel his own worth and the greatness of his fall.

'When younger,' said he, 'I believed myself destined for some great enterprise. My feelings are profound, but I possessed a coolness of judgment that fitted me for illustrious achievements. This sentiment of the worth of my nature supported me when others would have been oppressed, for I deemed it criminal to throw away in useless grief those talents that might be useful to my fellow creatures. When I reflected on the work I had completed, no less a one than the creation of a sensitive and rational animal, I could not rank myself with the herd of common projectors. But this thought, which supported me in the commencement of my career, now serves only to plunge me lower in the dust. All my speculations and hopes are as nothing, and like the archangel who aspired to omnipotence, I am chained in an eternal hell. My imagination was vivid, yet my powers of analysis and application were intense; by the union of these qualities I conceived the idea and executed the creation of a man. Even now I cannot recollect without passion my reveries while the work was incomplete. I trod heaven in my thoughts, now exulting in my powers, now burning with the idea of their effects. From my infancy I was imbued with high hopes and a lofty ambition; but how am I sunk! Oh! My friend, if you had known me as I once was, you would not recognize me in this state of degradation. Despondency rarely visited my heart; a high destiny seemed to bear me on, until I fell, never, never again to rise.'

Must I then lose this admirable being? I have longed for a friend; I have sought one who would sympathize with and love me. Behold, on these desert seas I have found such a one, but I fear I have gained him only to know his value and lose him. I would reconcile him to life, but he repulses the idea.

'I thank you, Walton,' he said, 'for your kind intentions towards so miserable a wretch; but when you speak of new ties and fresh affections, think you that any can replace those who are gone? Can any man be to me as Clerval was, or any woman another Elizabeth? Even where the affections are not strongly moved by any superior excellence, the companions of our childhood always possess a certain power over our minds which hardly any later friend can obtain. They know our infantine dispositions, which, however they may be afterwards modified, are never eradicated; and they can judge of our actions with more certain conclusions as to the integrity of our motives. A sister or a brother can never, unless indeed such symptoms have been shown early, suspect the other of fraud or false dealing, when another friend, however strongly he may be attached, may, in spite of himself, be contemplated with suspicion. But I enjoyed friends, dear not only through habit and association, but from their own merits; and wherever I am, the soothing voice of my Elizabeth and the conversation of Clerval will be ever whispered in my ear. They are dead, and but one feeling in such a solitude can persuade me to preserve my life. If I were engaged in any high undertaking or design, fraught with extensive utility to my fellow creatures, then could I live to fulfil it. But such is not my destiny; I must pursue and destroy the being to whom I gave existence; then my lot on earth will be fulfilled and I may die.'

My beloved Sister, September 2nd

I write to you, encompassed by peril and ignorant whether I am ever doomed to see again dear England and the dearer friends that inhabit it. I am surrounded by mountains of ice which admit of no escape and threaten every moment to crush my vessel. The brave fellows whom I have persuaded to be my companions look towards me for aid, but I have none to bestow. There is something terribly appalling in our situation, yet my courage and hopes do not desert me. Yet it is terrible to reflect that the lives of all these men are endangered through me. If we are lost, my mad schemes are the cause.

And what, Margaret, will be the state of your mind? You will not hear of my destruction, and you will anxiously await my return. Years will pass, and you will have visitings of despair and yet be tortured by hope. Oh! My beloved sister, the sickening failing of your heart-felt expectations is, in prospect, more terrible to me than my own death. But you have a husband and lovely children; you may be happy. Heaven bless you and make you so!

My unfortunate guest regards me with the tenderest compassion. He endeavours to fill me with hope and talks as if life were a possession which he valued. He reminds me how often the same accidents have happened to other navigators who have attempted this sea, and in spite of myself, he fills me with cheerful auguries. Even the sailors feel the power of his eloquence; when he speaks, they no longer despair; he rouses their energies, and while they hear his voice they believe these vast mountains of ice are mole-hills which will vanish before the resolutions of man. These feelings are transitory; each day of expectation delayed fills them with fear, and I almost dread a mutiny caused by this despair.

September 5th

A scene has just passed of such uncommon interest that, although it is highly probable that these papers may never reach you, yet I cannot forbear recording it.

We are still surrounded by mountains of ice, still in imminent danger of being crushed in their conflict. The cold is excessive, and many of my unfortunate comrades have already found a grave amidst this scene of desolation. Frankenstein has daily declined in health; a feverish fire still glimmers in his eyes, but he is exhausted, and when suddenly roused to any exertion, he speedily sinks again into apparent lifelessness.

I mentioned in my last letter the fears I entertained of a mutiny. This morning, as I sat watching the wan countenance of my friend – his eyes half closed and his limbs hanging listlessly – I was roused by half a dozen of the sailors, who demanded admission into the cabin. They entered, and their leader addressed me. He told me that he and his companions had been chosen by the other sailors to come in deputation to me to make me a requisition which, in justice, I could not refuse. We were immured in ice and should probably never escape, but they feared that if, as was possible, the ice should dissipate and a free passage be opened, I should be rash enough to continue my voyage and lead them into fresh dangers, after they might happily have surmounted this. They insisted, therefore, that I should engage with a solemn promise that if the vessel should be freed I would instantly direct my course southwards.

This speech troubled me. I had not despaired, nor had I yet conceived the idea of returning if set free. Yet could I, in justice, or even in possibility, refuse this demand? I hesitated before I answered, when Frankenstein, who had at first been silent, and indeed appeared hardly to have force enough to attend, now roused himself; his eyes sparkled, and his cheeks flushed with momentary vigour. Turning towards the men, he said, 'What do you mean? What do you demand of your captain? Are you, then, so easily turned from your design? Did you not call this a glorious expedition? And wherefore was it glorious? Not because the way was smooth and placid as a southern sea, but because it was full of dangers and terror, because at every new incident your fortitude was to be called forth and your courage exhibited, because danger and death surrounded it, and these you were to brave and overcome. For this was it a glorious, for this was it an honourable undertaking. You were hereafter to be hailed as the benefactors of your species, your names adored as belonging to brave men who encountered death for honour and the benefit of mankind. And now, behold, with the first imagination of danger, or, if you will, the first mighty and terrific trial of your courage, you shrink away and are content to be handed down as men who had not strength enough to endure cold and peril; and so, poor souls, they were chilly and returned to their warm firesides. Why, that requires not this preparation; ye need not have come thus far and dragged your captain to the shame of a defeat merely to prove yourselves cowards. Oh! Be men, or be more than men. Be steady to your purposes and firm as a rock. This ice is not made of such stuff as your hearts may be; it is mutable and cannot withstand you if you say that it shall not. Do not return to your families with the stigma of disgrace marked on your brows. Return as heroes who have fought and conquered and who know not what it is to turn their backs on the foe.'

He spoke this with a voice so modulated to the different feelings expressed in his speech, with an eye so full of lofty design and heroism, that can you wonder that these men were moved? They looked at one another and were unable to reply. I spoke; I told them to retire and consider of what had been said, that I would not lead them farther north if they strenuously desired the contrary, but that I hoped that, with reflection, their courage would return.

They retired and I turned towards my friend, but he was sunk in languor and almost deprived of life.

How all this will terminate, I know not, but I had rather die than return shamefully, my purpose unfulfilled. Yet I fear such will be my fate; the men, unsupported by ideas of glory and honour, can never willingly continue to endure their present hardships.

September 7th

The die is cast; I have consented to return if we are not destroyed. Thus are my hopes blasted by cowardice and indecision; I come back ignorant and disappointed. It requires more philosophy than I possess to bear this injustice with patience.

September 12th

It is past; I am returning to England. I have lost my hopes of utility and glory; I have lost my friend. But I will endeavour to detail these bitter circumstances to you, my dear sister; and while I am wafted towards England and towards you, I will not despond.

September 9th, the ice began to move, and roarings like thunder were heard at a distance as the islands split and cracked in every direction. We were in the most imminent peril, but as we could only remain passive, my chief attention was occupied by my unfortunate guest whose illness increased in such a degree that he was entirely confined to his bed. The ice cracked behind us and was driven with force towards the north; a breeze sprang from the west, and on the 11th the passage towards the south became perfectly free. When the sailors saw this and that their return to their native country was apparently assured, a shout of tumultuous joy broke from them, loud and long-continued. Frankenstein, who was dozing, awoke and asked the cause of the tumult. 'They shout,' I said, 'because they will soon return to England.'

'Do you, then, really return?'

'Alas! Yes; I cannot withstand their demands. I cannot lead them unwillingly to danger, and I must return.'

'Do so, if you will; but I will not. You may give up your purpose, but mine is assigned to me by heaven, and I dare not. I am weak, but surely the spirits who assist my vengeance will endow me with sufficient strength.' Saying this, he endeavoured to spring from the bed, but the exertion was too great for him; he fell back and fainted.

It was long before he was restored, and I often thought that life was entirely extinct. At length he opened his eyes; he breathed with difficulty and was unable to speak. The surgeon gave him a composing draught and ordered us to leave him undisturbed. In the meantime he told me that my friend had certainly not many hours to live.

His sentence was pronounced, and I could only grieve and be patient. I sat by his bed, watching him; his eyes were closed, and I thought he slept; but presently he called to me in a feeble voice, and bidding me come near, said, 'Alas! The strength I relied on is gone; I feel that I shall soon die, and he, my enemy and persecutor, may still be in being. Think not, Walton, that in the last moments of my existence I feel that burning hatred and ardent desire of revenge I once expressed; but I feel myself justified in desiring the death of my adversary. During these last days I have been occupied in examining my past conduct; nor do I find it blamable. In a fit of enthusiastic madness I created a rational creature and was bound towards him to assure, as far as was in my power, his happiness and well-being. This was my duty, but there was another still paramount to that. My duties towards the beings of my own species had greater claims to my attention because they included a greater proportion of happiness or misery. Urged by this view, I refused, and I did right in refusing, to create a companion for the first creature. He showed unparalleled malignity and selfishness in evil; he destroyed my friends; he devoted to destruction beings who possessed exquisite sensations, happiness, and wisdom; nor do I know where this thirst for vengeance may end. Miserable himself that he may render no other wretched, he ought to die. The task of his destruction was mine, but I have failed. When actuated by selfish and vicious motives, I asked you to undertake my unfinished work, and I renew this request now, when I am only induced by reason and virtue.

Yet I cannot ask you to renounce your country and friends to fulfil this task; and now that you are returning to England, you will have little chance of meeting with him. But the consideration of these points, and the well balancing of what you may esteem your duties, I leave to you; my judgment and ideas are already disturbed by the near approach of death. I dare not ask you to do what I think right, for I may still be misled by passion.

'That he should live to be an instrument of mischief disturbs me; in other respects, this hour, when I momentarily expect my release, is the only happy one which I have enjoyed for several years. The forms of the beloved dead flit before me, and I hasten to their arms. Farewell, Walton! Seek happiness in tranquillity and avoid ambition, even if it be only the apparently innocent one of distinguishing yourself in science and discoveries. Yet why do I say this? I have myself been blasted in these hopes, yet another may succeed.'

His voice became fainter as he spoke, and at length, exhausted by his effort, he sank into silence. About half an hour afterwards he attempted again to speak but was unable; he pressed my hand feebly, and his eyes closed forever, while the irradiation of a gentle smile passed away from his lips.

Margaret, what comment can I make on the untimely extinction of this glorious spirit? What can I say that will enable you to understand the depth of my sorrow? All that I should express would be inadequate and feeble. My tears flow; my mind is overshadowed by a cloud of disappointment. But I journey towards England, and I may there find consolation.

I am interrupted. What do these sounds portend? It is midnight; the breeze blows fairly, and the watch on deck scarcely stir. Again there is a sound as of a human voice, but hoarser; it comes from the cabin where the remains of Frankenstein still lie. I must arise and examine. Good night, my sister.

Great God! what a scene has just taken place! I am yet dizzy with the remembrance of it. I hardly know whether I shall have the power to detail it; yet the tale which I have recorded would be incomplete without this final and wonderful catastrophe.

I entered the cabin where lay the remains of my ill-fated and admirable friend. Over him hung a form which I cannot find words to describe – gigantic in stature, yet uncouth and distorted in its proportions. As he hung over the coffin, his face was concealed by long locks of ragged hair; but one vast hand was extended, in colour and apparent texture like that of a mummy. When he heard the sound of my approach, he ceased to utter exclamations of grief and horror and sprung towards the window. Never did I behold a vision so horrible as his face, of such loathsome yet appalling hideousness. I shut my eyes involuntarily and endeavoured to recollect what were my duties with regard to this destroyer. I called on him to stay.

He paused, looking on me with wonder, and again turning towards the lifeless form of his creator, he seemed to forget my presence, and every feature and gesture seemed instigated by the wildest rage of some uncontrollable passion.

'That is also my victim!' he exclaimed. 'In his murder my crimes are consummated; the miserable series of my being is wound to its close! Oh, Frankenstein! Generous and self-devoted being! What does it avail that I now ask thee to pardon me? I, who irretrievably destroyed thee by destroying all thou lovedst. Alas! He is cold, he cannot answer me.'

His voice seemed suffocated, and my first impulses, which had suggested to me the duty of obeying the dying request of my friend in destroying his enemy, were now suspended by a mixture of curiosity and compassion. I approached this tremendous being; I dared not again raise my eyes to his face, there was something so scaring and unearthly in his ugliness. I attempted to speak, but the words died away on my lips. The monster continued to utter wild and incoherent self-reproaches. At length I gathered resolution to address him in a pause of the tempest of his passion. 'Your repentance,' I said, 'is now superfluous. If you had listened to the voice of conscience and heeded the stings of remorse before you had urged your diabolical vengeance to this extremity, Frankenstein would yet have lived.'

'And do you dream?' said the daemon. 'Do you think that I was then dead to agony and remorse? He,' he continued, pointing to the corpse, 'he suffered not in the consummation of the deed. Oh! Not the ten-thousandth portion of the anguish that was mine during the lingering detail of its execution. A frightful selfishness hurried me on, while my heart was poisoned with remorse. Think you that the groans of Clerval were music to my ears? My heart was fashioned to be susceptible of love and sympathy, and when wrenched by misery to vice and hatred, it did not endure the violence of the change without torture such as you cannot even imagine.

'After the murder of Clerval I returned to Switzerland, heart-broken and overcome. I pitied Frankenstein; my pity amounted to horror; I abhorred myself. But when I discovered that he, the author at once of my existence and of its unspeakable torments, dared to hope for happiness, that while he accumulated wretchedness and despair upon me he sought his own enjoyment in feelings and passions from the indulgence of which I was forever barred, then impotent envy and bitter indignation filled me with an insatiable thirst for vengeance. I recollected my threat and resolved that it should be accomplished. I knew that I was preparing for myself a deadly torture, but I was the slave, not the master, of an impulse which I detested yet could not disobey. Yet when she died! Nay, then I was not miserable. I had cast off all feeling, subdued all anguish, to riot in the excess of my despair. Evil thenceforth became my good. Urged thus far, I had no choice but to adapt my nature to an element which I had willingly chosen. The completion of my demoniacal design became an insatiable passion. And now it is ended; there is my last victim!'

I was at first touched by the expressions of his misery; yet, when I called to mind what Frankenstein had said of his powers of eloquence and persuasion, and when I again cast my eyes on the lifeless form of my friend, indignation was rekindled within me. 'Wretch!' I said. 'It is well that you come here to whine over the desolation that you have made. You throw a torch into a pile of buildings, and when they are consumed, you sit among the ruins and lament the fall. Hypocritical fiend! If he whom you mourn still lived, still would he be the object, again would he become the prey, of your accursed vengeance. It is not pity that you feel; you lament only because the victim of your malignity is withdrawn from your power.'

'Oh, it is not thus – not thus,' interrupted the being. 'Yet such must be the impression conveyed to you by what appears to be the purport of my actions. Yet I seek not a fellow feeling in my misery. No sympathy may I ever find. When I first sought it, it was the love of virtue, the feelings of happiness and affection with which my whole being overflowed, that I wished to be participated. But now that virtue has become to me a shadow, and that happiness and affection are turned into bitter and loathing despair, in what should I seek for sympathy? I am content to suffer alone while my sufferings shall endure; when I die, I am well satisfied that abhorrence and opprobrium should load my memory. Once my fancy was soothed with dreams of virtue, of fame, and of enjoyment. Once I falsely hoped to meet with beings who, pardoning my outward form, would love me for the excellent qualities which I was capable of unfolding. I was nourished with high thoughts of honour and devotion. But now crime has degraded me beneath the meanest animal. No guilt, no mischief, no malignity, no misery, can be found comparable to mine. When I run over the frightful catalogue of my sins, I cannot believe that I am the same creature whose thoughts were once filled with sublime and transcendent visions of the beauty and the majesty of goodness. But it is even so; the fallen angel becomes a malignant devil. Yet even that enemy of God and man had friends and associates in his desolation; I am alone.

You, who call Frankenstein your friend, seem to have a knowledge of my crimes and his misfortunes. But in the detail which he gave you of them he could not sum up the hours and months of misery which I endured wasting in impotent passions. For while I destroyed his hopes, I did not satisfy my own desires. They were forever ardent and craving; still I desired love and fellowship, and I was still spurned. Was there no injustice in this? Am I to be thought the only criminal, when all humankind sinned against me? Why do you not hate Felix, who drove his friend from his door with contumely? Why do you not execrate the rustic who sought to destroy the saviour of his child? Nay, these are virtuous and immaculate beings! I, the miserable and the abandoned, am an abortion, to be spurned at, and kicked, and trampled on. Even now my blood boils at the recollection of this injustice.

But it is true that I am a wretch. I have murdered the lovely and the helpless; I have strangled the innocent as they slept and grasped to death his throat who never injured me or any other living thing. I have devoted my creator, the select specimen of all that is worthy of love and admiration among men, to misery; I have pursued him even to that irremediable ruin. There he lies, white and cold in death. You hate me, but your abhorrence cannot equal that with which I regard myself. I look on the hands which executed the deed; I think on the heart in which the imagination of it was conceived and long for the moment when these hands will meet my eyes, when that imagination will haunt my thoughts no more.

Fear not that I shall be the instrument of future mischief. My work is nearly complete. Neither yours nor any man's death is needed to consummate the series of my being and accomplish that which must be done, but it requires my own. Do not think that I shall be slow to perform this sacrifice. I shall quit your vessel on the ice raft which brought me thither and shall seek the most northern extremity of the globe; I shall collect my funeral pile and consume to ashes this miserable frame, that its remains may afford no light to any curious and unhallowed wretch who would create such another as I have been. I shall die. I shall no longer feel the agonies which now consume me or be the prey of feelings unsatisfied, yet unquenched. He is dead who called me into being; and when I shall be no more, the very remembrance of us both will speedily vanish. I shall no longer see the sun or stars or feel the winds play on my cheeks. Light, feeling, and sense will pass away; and in this condition must I find my happiness. Some years ago, when the images which this world affords first opened upon me, when I felt the cheering warmth of summer and heard the rustling of the leaves and the warbling of the birds, and these were all to me, I should have wept to die; now it is my only consolation. Polluted by crimes and torn by the bitterest remorse, where can I find rest but in death?

Farewell! I leave you, and in you the last of humankind whom these eyes will ever behold. Farewell, Frankenstein! If thou wert yet alive and yet cherished a desire of revenge against me, it would be better satiated in my life than in my destruction. But it was not so; thou didst seek my extinction, that I might not cause greater wretchedness; and if yet, in some mode unknown to me, thou hadst not ceased to think and feel, thou wouldst not desire against me a vengeance greater than that which I feel. Blasted as thou wert, my agony was still superior to thine, for the bitter sting of remorse will not cease to rankle in my wounds until death shall close them forever.

'But soon,' he cried with sad and solemn enthusiasm, 'I shall die, and what I now feel be no longer felt. Soon these burning miseries will be extinct. I shall ascend my funeral pile triumphantly and exult in the agony of the torturing flames. The light of that conflagration will fade away; my ashes will be swept into the sea by the winds. My spirit will sleep in peace, or if it thinks, it will not surely think thus. Farewell.'

He sprang from the cabin window as he said this, upon the ice raft which lay close to the vessel. He was soon borne away by the waves and lost in darkness and distance.

THE END

Anne Tyler was born in Minneapolis, Mi[...] grew up in Raleigh, North Carolina, and [...] Southerner. She graduated at nineteen f[...] where she twice won the Anne Flexner [...] writing and became a member of Phi [...] done graduate work in Russian studies at Columbia U[...] and worked for a year as the Russian bibliographer at the Duke University Library.

Of her first novel *If Morning Ever Comes, The New York Times* said, 'Anne Tyler's touch is deft, her perceptions keen, her ear for speech phenomenal, her people triumphantly alive . . . only a rarely talented novelist could have written this fine book.' *Dinner at the Homesick Restaurant*, for which she is best known, was hailed by *The Times* as gripping and wise, sardonic and affectionate . . . a most rewarding book'. *The Accidental Tourist* won the National Book Critics Circle award for the most distinguished work of fiction in 1985.

nnesota, in 1941, but
considers herself a
rom Duke University,
Award for creative
Beta Kappa. She has
University

Anne Tyler

Searching for Caleb

Pavanne

Pan Books
London, Sydney and Auckland

First published in Great Britain 1976 by
Chatto & Windus Ltd
First published in paperback in Great Britain 1979 by
Hamlyn Paperbacks
This Pavanne edition first published 1988 by
Pan Books Ltd, Cavaye Place, London SW10 9PG
9 8 7 6 5 4 3 2 1
© Anne Tyler Modarressi
ISBN 0 330 30155 1
Printed and bound in Great Britain by
Richard Clay Ltd, Bungay, Suffolk

1

THE FORTUNE TELLER and her grandfather went to New York City on an Amtrak train, racketing along with their identical, peaky white faces set due north. The grandfather had left his hearing aid at home on the bureau. He wore a black suit, pearl-gray suspenders, and a very old-fashioned, expensive-looking pinstriped collarless shirt. No matter what happened he kept his deep-socketed eyes fixed upon the seat in front of him, he continued sliding a thumb over the news clipping he held in his hand. Either the train had turned his deafness absolute or else he had something very serious on his mind, it was hard to tell which. In any case, he would not answer the few things the fortune teller said to him.

Past his downy white head, outside the scummy window, factories and warehouses streamed along. Occasionally a left-over forest would coast into view and then out again—twisted bare trees, trunks ripped by lightning, logs covered with vines, tangled raspy bushes and beer cans, whisky bottles, rusted carburetors, sewing machines, and armchairs. Then some town or other would take over. Men wearing several layers of jackets struggled with crates and barrels on loading docks, their breaths trailing out of their mouths in white tatters. It was January, and cold enough to make the brick buildings appear to darken and condense.

The fortune teller, who was not a gypsy or even Spanish but a lanky, weedy blond woman in a Breton hat and a faded shift, took a *National Geographic* from a straw bag on the floor and started reading it from back to front. She flicked the pages after barely a glance, rapidly swinging one crossed foot. Halfway through the magazine she bent to rummage through the bag again. She felt her grandfather slide his eyes over to see what she was keeping there. Tarot cards? A crystal ball? Some other tool of her mysterious, disreputable profession? But all she showed was a spill of multicolored kerchief and then a box of Luden's cough drops, which she took out and offered him. He refused. She put one in her mouth, giving him a sudden smile that completely upturned every one of her pale, straight features. Her grandfather absorbed it but forgot to smile back. He returned to his view of the seat ahead, a button-on antimacassar with an old lady's netted hat just beyond.

In his hand, stroked by his puckered thumb, the newspaper clipping first rustled and then wilted and drooped, but the fortune teller knew it by heart anyway.

TABOR

Suddenly on December 18, 1972, Paul Jeffrey, Sr., of New York City, formerly of Baltimore. Beloved husband of Deborah Palmer Tabor. Father of Paul J. Tabor, Jr., of Chicago and Theresa T. Hanes of Springline, Massachusetts. Also survived by five grandchildren and seven great-grandchildren.

Services will be held Thursday at the . . .

"My throat is dry, Justine," her grandfather said.
"I'll get you a soda."

"What?"

"A *soda*."

He drew back, offended. No telling what he thought she had said. Justine patted his hand and told him, "Never mind, Grandfather. I'll just be gone a minute."

She left, sidling between shopping bags and weekend cases along the narrow aisle, holding tight to her saucer-like hat. Three cars up, she paid for two root beers and a sack of Cheez Doodles. She returned walking carefully, opening doors with her elbows and frowning at the plastic cups, which were filled to the brim. Just inside her own car, the Cheez Doodles fell and a man in a business suit had to pick them up for her. "Oh! Thank you!" she said, and smiled at him, her cheeks grown suddenly pink. At first glance she could be taken for a young girl, but then people saw the fine lines beginning to show in her skin, and the faded blue of her eyes and the veined, parched, forty-year-old hands with the scratched wedding band looking three sizes too large below one knobby knuckle. She had a ramshackle way of walking and a sharp, merry voice. "*Root* beer, Grandfather!" she sang out. If he didn't hear her, all the rest of the car did.

She put a cup in his hand, and he took a sip. "Ah yes," he said. He liked herby things, root beer and horehound drops and sassafras tea. But when she tore open the cellophane bag and presented him with a Cheez Doodle—a fat orange worm that left crystals on his fingertips—he frowned at it from beneath a tangle of white eyebrows. He had once been a judge. He still gave the impression of judging everything that came his way. "What *is* this," he said, but that was a verdict, not a question.

"It's a Cheez Doodle, Grandfather, try it and see."

"What's that you say?"

She held out the bag, showing him the lettering on the side. First he replaced the Cheez Doodle and then he wiped his fingers on a handkerchief he took from his pocket. Then he went back to drinking root beer and studying the clipping, which he had laid flat on one narrow, triangular knee. "Theresa," he said. "I never cared for that name."

Justine nodded, chewing.

"I don't like *difficult* names. I don't like foreignness."

"Perhaps they're Catholic," Justine said.

"How's that?"

"Perhaps they're Catholic."

"I didn't quite hear."

"*Catholic!*"

Faces spun around.

"Don't be ridiculous," her grandfather said. "Paul Tabor went to the same church I did, he was in my brother's Sunday school class. The two of them graduated from the Salter Academy together. Then this—dissatisfaction set in. This, this *newness*. I can't tell you how many times I've seen it come to pass. A young man goes to a distant city instead of staying close to home, he gets a job, switches friends, widens his circle of acquaintances. Marries a girl from a family no one knows, lives in a house of unusual architecture, names his children foreign names that never were in his family in any preceding generation. He takes to traveling, buys winter homes and summer homes and vacation cottages in godforsaken states like Florida where none of us has ever been. Meanwhile his parents die and all his people just seem to vanish, there's no one you can ask any more, 'Now, what is Paul up to these days?' Then he dies himself, most likely in a very large city where there's nobody to notice, only his wife and his barber and his tailor and maybe not even the last two, and what's it for? What's it all about? Now in Paul's case I just couldn't say for certain, of course. He was my brother's friend, not mine. However I will hazard a guess: he had no *stamina*. He couldn't endure, he wouldn't stay around to fight it out or live it down or sit it through, whatever was required. He hadn't the patience. He wanted something new, something different, he couldn't quite name it. He thought things would be better somewhere else. Anywhere else. And what did it get him? Watch, next time I'm in Baltimore I'll tell the family, 'Paul Tabor died.' 'Paul *who?*' they'll say. 'Paul Tabor, it was in the Baltimore *Sun*. Don't you read it any more? Don't you know?' Well, of course they do read it and would catch any familiar name in a flash but not Paul Tabor's. Forgotten, all forgotten. He discarded us, now he's dead and forgotten. Hear what I say, Justine. Do you hear?"

Justine smiled at him. "I hear," she said.

She had moved away from Baltimore herself. She and her husband and daughter now lived in Semple, Virginia; in another place last year and another the year before that. (Her husband was a restless man.) Next week they were moving to Caro Mill, Maryland. Was it Caro Mill? Caro Mills? Sometimes all these places would run together in her mind. She would mentally locate friends in towns those friends had never set foot in, she would await a visit from a client whom she had left two years ago without a forwarding address. She would ransack the telephone book for a doctor or a dentist or a plumber who was actually three hundred miles away and three or four or fourteen years in the past. Her grandfather didn't guess that, probably. Or care. He had scarcely bothered to learn the towns' names in the first place. Although he lived with Justine and made all those moves with her he called it visiting; he considered himself a citizen still of Baltimore, his birthplace. All other towns were ephemeral, no-account; he shuffled through them absent-mindedly like a man passing a string of shanties on the way to his own sturdy house. When he arrived in Baltimore (for Thanksgiving or Christmas or the Fourth of July) he would heave a sigh and lower the sharp narrow shoulders that he held, at all other times, so tightly hunched. The brackets around his mouth would relax somewhat. He would set his old leather suitcase down with finality, as if it held all his earthly goods and not just a shirt and a change of underwear and a scruffy toothbrush. "There's no place in the world like Baltimore, Maryland," he would say.

He said it now.

This morning they had passed through the Baltimore railroad station, even stopping a moment to let other, luckier passengers alight. The thought of having come so near must have made him melancholy. He looked down at his clipping now and shook his head, maybe even regretting this trip, which had been entirely his own idea. But when Justine said, "Are you tired,

Grandfather?"—thinning her voice to that special, carrying tone he would be certain to hear—he only looked at her blankly. It seemed that his mind was on Paul Tabor again.

"They don't say a word about where they buried him," he said.

"Oh well, I imagine—"

"If you died in New York City, where would you be buried?"

"I'm sure they have—"

"No doubt they ship you someplace else," he said. He turned his face to the window. Without his hearing aid he gave an impression of rudeness. He interrupted people and changed the subject willfully and spoke in a particularly loud, flat voice, although normally he was so well-mannered that he caused others to feel awkward. "I never made the acquaintance of Paul's wife," he said, while Justine was still considering cemeteries. "I don't recollect even hearing when he got married. But then he was younger than I of course and moved in different circles. Or perhaps he married late in life. Now if I had known the wife I would have gone up for the funeral, then asked my questions afterwards. But as it is, I hesitated to barge in upon a family affair and immediately put my case. It would look so—it would seem so self-serving. Do you think I did right to wait?"

He had asked her this before. He didn't listen for the answer.

"By now she will be calmer," he said. "Not so likely to break down at any mention of his name."

He folded the clipping suddenly, as if he had decided something. He creased it with one broad yellow thumbnail.

"Justine," he said.

"Hmm?"

"Am I going to be successful?"

She stopped swirling the ice in her cup and looked at him. "Oh," she said. "Why—I'm certain you are. Certainly, Grandfather. Maybe not *this* time, maybe not right away, but—"

"Truly. Tell me."

"Certainly you will."

He was looking too closely into her face. Possibly he hadn't heard her. She set her voice to the proper tone and said, "I'm sure that—"

"Justine, how much do you know?"

"What?"

"This telling fortunes. This bunk. This—*piffle*," said her grandfather, and he brushed something violently off his sleeve. "I hate the very thought of it."

"You've told me all that, Grandfather."

"It's not respectable. Your aunts go into a state whenever we speak of it. You know what people call you? 'The fortune teller.' Like 'the cleaner,' 'the greengrocer.' 'How's that grand-daughter of yours, Judge Peck, the fortune teller. How's she doing?' Ah, it turns my stomach."

Justine picked up her magazine and opened to a page, any page.

"But, Justine," her grandfather said, "I ask you this. Is there anything to it at all?"

Her eyes snagged on a line of print.

"Do you really have some inkling of the future?"

She shut the magazine. He locked her in a fierce, steady frown; his intensity made everything around him seem pale.

"I want to know if I will find my brother," he said.

Yet immediately afterward he turned away, watching the train's descent into the blackness beneath Manhattan. And Justine repacked her straw bag and brushed cheese crumbs off her lap and put her coat on, her expression calm and cheerful. Neither one of them appeared to be waiting for anything more to be said.

Because they were trying to save money, they took the subway from Penn Station. Justine loved subways. She enjoyed standing on them, gripping a warm, oily metal pole, feet planted slightly apart and knees dipping with the roll of the train as they careened through the darkness. But her grandfather distrusted them, and once they were off the shuttle and onto the IRT, he made her sit down. He continually rotated his face, scanning the car for enemies. Silent young people returned his stare. "I don't know, Justine, I don't know what's happening. I don't like this city at all any more," her grandfather said. But Justine was enjoying herself too much to answer. She watched each station as they drew into it, the murky light and bathroom-tile walls and those mysterious, grimy men who sat on benches, one or two at every stop, watching trains come and go without ever boarding one. Then when they were moving again she drank in the sensation of speed. *Getting* somewhere. She loved going fast in any kind of vehicle. She particularly liked the rickety sound of these tracks, on which something unexpected might happen at any moment. She hoped the wheels would howl in that eerie way they had while heading through the deepest stretch of darkness. Once the lights went out and when they came on again her face was surprised and joyous, open-mouthed; everybody noticed. Her grandfather touched her wrist.

"Are you watching for the proper station?" he asked.

"Oh yes."

Although she hadn't been.

Clutched in her hand was Mrs. Tabor's address, which she had copied from a telephone book. She had suggested calling ahead from Penn Station, but her grandfather refused. He was too impatient, or he wanted to hold onto his hopes just a little bit longer, or he was afraid of being turned away. Also he might have been anxious to reach Mrs. Tabor's bathroom. He preferred not to use any public facilities.

When they were above ground again—Justine taking gulps of the ashy, foreign air, the old man limp with relief—they walked a block and a half west and entered a gray building with a revolving door. "Look," her grandfather said. "Wood for the door and polished handles. Marble floor. I like old buildings. I like places like this." And he nodded to a lady just stepping out of the elevator—the first person in all New York whose existence he had recognized. He was disappointed, however, that the elevator was self-service. "*Once* upon a time they would have had a boy to do this," he said, watching Justine jab a button. The elevator toiled upward, creaking and sighing. Its walls were fine oak but on one panel there was a concentration of four-letter words that the old man covered immediately, stepping square in front of them without appearing to notice and then staring upward. Justine smiled at him. He pursed his lips and studied an inspection certificate.

On the eighth floor, at the end of a long dark hall, they pressed another button. Bolts slithered and locks rattled, as if connected somehow to the button. The door opened three inches and a rouged, seamed face peered out from behind a police chain. "Yes?" she asked.

"Mrs. Tabor?" said Justine.

Puffy eyes took her in from top to toe, her streaky ribbons of hair and her brown coat with the uneven hemline. "What is this," Mrs. Tabor said, "are you selling something? I don't need a thing and I already have religion."

So the grandfather had to step up and take over. There was no mistaking the elegance of his bow, or the way he raised one hand to his head even though he wore no hat. He presented her with his card. Not his business card, oh no, but his calling card, cream-colored, aged yellow around the edges. He slipped it beneath the police chain into her jeweled hand. "Daniel Peck," he said, as if she could not read, and she looked up into his face while one finger tested the engraving. "Peck," she said.

"I knew your husband. Paul? Back in Baltimore."

"Why didn't you *say* so?" she asked, and she unhooked the chain and stood back to let them in. They entered a room that Justine might have grown up in, all wine-colored and velvety, giving off a scent of dust although every piece of furniture gleamed. Mrs. Tabor's white hair was precisely finger-waved, webby with beauty parlor hairspray. She wore black wool and ropes and ropes of pearls. Her focus was on the old man and she barely looked at Justine even when he remembered to introduce her. "Of course you do know about his passing, Mr. Peck," she said.

"I beg your pardon?"

"You'll have to speak up," said Justine. "He left his hearing aid at home."

"You know he *passed*, Mr. Peck."

"Oh. Passed. Oh yes. Yes, naturally, I read it in the paper. You see we hadn't heard of Paul for many many years, we—" He followed, absently, to the couch where she led him. He sat down beside Justine, pinching the creases in his trousers. "We had no idea where he might be until that death notice, Mrs. Tabor. Why, I've made several trips to New York in my life and never even knew he was here! Never guessed! We could have talked over old times together."

"Oh, it's sad how people lose track," said Mrs. Tabor.

"Well, I wanted to offer my condolences. Our family thought highly of Paul and my brother Caleb in particular was very close to him."

"Why, thank you, Mr. Peck. It was painless, I'm happy to say, sudden and painless, just the way he would have wished it. All the more shock to *me*, therefore, but—"

"What was that?"

"*Thank* you."

"My brother's name was Caleb Peck."

"What a fine old-fashioned name," said Mrs. Tabor.

The old man looked at her for a minute, perhaps wondering whether it was worthwhile asking her to repeat herself. Then he sighed and shook his head. "I don't suppose you knew him, did you?" he said.

"Why, not that I remember, no. I don't believe so. Because of Paul's work we moved about so, you see. It was difficult to—"

"What? What?"

"*No*, Grandfather," Justine said, and laid one hand on top of his. He looked at her dimly for a moment, as if he didn't recognize her.

"I assumed he might have kept in touch with Paul," he told Mrs. Tabor. "Written, or sent Christmas cards. Or visited, even. You know they were very close. Perhaps he stopped to see you on his way to someplace else."

"We never had many visitors, Mr. Peck."

"Pardon?"

He looked at Justine. Justine shook her head.

"Or possibly Paul just mentioned his *name* on some occasion," he said.

"Possibly, yes, but—"

"Yes?"

He snatched his hand from Justine's and sat forward. "When would that have been?" he asked.

"But—no, Mr. Peck, I can't say I remember it. I'm sorry."

"Look here," he said. He searched a pocket and came up with something—a small brown photograph framed in gold. He leaned over to jab it in her face. "Don't you know him? Doesn't he look familiar in any way? Take your time. Don't be in a hurry to say no."

Mrs. Tabor seemed a little startled by the picture, but it took her only a second to make up her mind. "I'm sorry," she said. Then she looked at Justine. "I don't understand. Is this important in some way?"

"Well—" said Justine.

"We've lost track of Caleb too, you see," her grandfather said. He shoved the photograph back in his pocket. He turned down the corners of his mouth in a bitter smile. "You must think we're very careless people."

Mrs. Tabor did not smile back.

"However it was no more our fault in this case than in Paul's; he left us."

"Oh, what a pity," Mrs. Tabor said.

"Our family is very close knit, a *fine* family, we have always stuck together, but I don't know, periodically some . . . *explorer* sets out on his own." He scowled suddenly at Justine. "The last time I saw Caleb was in nineteen twelve. I have never heard of him since."

"Nineteen twelve!" Mrs. Tabor said. She sank back in her chair. Wheels seemed to be clicking in her head. When she spoke next her voice had become softer and sadder. "Mr. Peck, I'm so very sorry that I can't help you. I *wish* I could. Might I offer you some tea?"

"How's that?" he said.

"*Tea*, Grandfather."

"Tea. Oh. Well . . ."

This time when he looked at Justine he was handing the rest of the visit to her, and she straightened and clutched her carry-all. "Thank you, but I don't think so," she said. Phrases her mother had taught her thirty years ago came wisping back to her. "It's kind of you to . . . but we really must be . . . however, I wonder if my grandfather might freshen up first? He just got off the train and he . . ."

"Surely," said Mrs. Tabor. "Mr. Peck, may I show you the way?"

She beckoned to him and he rose without question, either guessing at where she was leading him or no longer caring. He followed her through a polished door that swept open with a hushing sound across the carpet. He went down a short hall with his hands by his sides, like a child being sent to his room. When she pointed him toward another door he stepped through it and vanished, not looking around. Mrs. Tabor returned to the living room with careful, outward-turned steps.

"That poor, poor man," she said.

Justine would not answer.

"And will you be in New York long?"

"Just till we find a train home again."

Mrs. Tabor stopped patting her pearls. "You mean you only came for this?"

"Oh, we're used to it, we do it often," Justine said.

"Often! You go looking for his *brother* often?"

"Whenever we have some kind of lead," said Justine. "Some name or letter or something. We've been at this several years now. Grandfather takes it very seriously."

"He'll never find him, of course," said Mrs. Tabor.

Justine was silent.

"Will he?"

"Maybe he will."

"But—nineteen *twelve!* I mean—"

"Our family tends to live a long time," Justine said.

"But even so! And of course, dear," she said, leaning forward suddenly, "it must be hard on *you.*"

"Oh no."

"All that wandering around? I'd lose my mind. And he can't be so easy to travel with, his handicap and all. It must be a terrible burden for you."

"I love him very much," said Justine.

"Oh, well yes. Naturally!"

But the mention of love had turned Mrs. Tabor breathless, and she seemed delighted to hear the bathroom door clicking open. "Well, now!" she said, turning to Justine's grandfather.

He came into the room searching all his pockets, a sign he was preparing to leave a place. Justine rose and hoisted her straw bag. "Thank you, Mrs. Tabor," she said. "I'm sorry about your husband. I hope we haven't put you to any trouble."

"No, no."

The grandfather ducked his head in the doorway. "If you should recollect at some later date . . ." he said.

"I'll let you know."

"I wrote my Baltimore number on my calling card. Justine has no phone. If you should chance to think of something, anything at all . . ."

"Will do, Mr. Peck," she said, suddenly jaunty.

"You do?"

"What?"

"She *will* do, Grandfather," Justine said, and led him into the hall. But he did not hear and was still turned to Mrs. Tabor, puzzled and unhappy, when the door swung shut and the locks began tumbling into place again.

In the railroad station they sat on a wooden bench, waiting for the next train home. Justine ate a sack of Fritos, a Baby Ruth, and two hot dogs; her grandfather would not take anything. Neither of them liked Cokes and they could not find any root beer so they drank warm, bleachy New York water begged from a concession stand. Justine finished the last of her cough drops. She had to go buy more, paying too much for them at a vending machine. When she came back she found that her grandfather had fallen asleep with his head tipped back and his mouth open, his empty hands curled at his sides. She moved some sailor's unattended seabag over next to him and adjusted his head to rest upon it. Then she opened her carry-all and took out magazines, scarves, a coin purse, road maps and unmailed letters and a snaggle-toothed comb and a clutch of candy wrappers, until at the very bottom she came upon a deck of playing cards wrapped in a square of old, old silk. She unwrapped them and laid them out on the bench one by one, choosing places for them as surely and delicately as a cat chooses where to set its paws. When she had formed a cross she sat still for a moment, holding the remaining cards in her left hand. Then her grandfather stirred and she gathered the cards quickly and without a sound. They were back in their silk before he was fully awake again, and Justine was sitting motionless on the bench with her hands folded neatly over her straw bag.

2

ON MOVING DAY they were up at five, not because there was any rush but because the house was so uncomfortable now with everything packed, the walls bare and the furniture gone, no place to sleep but mattresses laid upon newspapers. All night long one person or another had been coughing or rearranging blankets or padding across the moonlit floor to the bathroom. People fell out of dreams and into them again, jerking awake and then spiraling back to sleep. The hollow walls creaked almost as steadily as the ticking of a clock.

Then Justine rose and stalked around the mattress, working a cramp out of one long, narrow foot. And Duncan opened his eyes to watch her fling on her bathrobe, all flurry and rustling and sleight-of-hand. Darkness swirled around her, but that was only chenille. "What time is it?" he asked. "Is it morning yet?"

"I don't know," she said.

Neither of them wore watches. On them, watches broke or lost themselves or speeded up to keep some lawless schedule of their own so you could almost see the minute hand racing around the dial.

Duncan sat up and felt for his clothing, while Justine sailed through the living room. Her gritty bare feet whispered on the floor and her bathrobe sash galloped behind. "Coming through! Excuse me! Coming through!" Her daughter's bedclothes stirred and rumpled. In the kitchen, Justine switched on the light and went to the sink to make tap-water coffee. The room gave off an icy chill. Everything was bare, scraped and smudged by the past—four bald spots on the linoleum where the table had once stood, and dimples where Duncan had tipped back in his chair, scorches and chips on the countertop, the uncurtained window filmed with cooking grease, the rickety wooden shelves empty but still bearing rings of molasses and catsup. Justine made the coffee in paper cups and stirred it with a screwdriver. When she had set the cups on the counter she turned to find her grandfather teetering in the doorway. Noise could not wake him, but light could. He wore withered silk pajamas and held his snaptop pocket watch open in his hand. "It's five ten a.m.," he said.

"Good morning, Grandfather."

"Yesterday you slept till noon. *Regularity* is what we want to aim for here."

"Would you like some coffee?"

But he hadn't heard. He pursed his lips and snapped the watch shut and went back to his bedroom for his clothes.

Now throughout the house came the sounds of people dressing, doors opening and closing, teeth being brushed. Nobody spoke. They were struggling free of their dreams still—all but Justine, who hummed a polka as she darted around the kitchen. In her flimsy robe, flushed with heat when anyone else would be shivering, she gave an impression of energy burning and wasting. She moved very fast and accomplished very little. She opened drawers for no reason and slammed them shut, pulled down the yellowed windowshade and let it snap up again. Then she called, "Duncan? Meg? Am I the only one *doing* anything?"

Duncan came in with his oldest clothes on: a white shirt worn soft and translucent and a shrunken pair of dungarees. His arms and legs gawked out like a growing boy's. He had a boy's face still, the expression trustful and the corners of his mouth pulled upward. With his hair and skin a single color and his long-boned, awkward body he might have been Justine's brother, except that he seemed to be continually turning over some mysterious private thought that set him apart. Also he moved differently; he was slower and more deliberate. Justine ran circles around him with his cup of coffee until he stopped her and took it from her hands.

"I could be dressed and gone by now, the rest of you would still be lolling in bed," she told him.

He swallowed a mouthful of coffee, looked down into the cup and raised his eyebrows.

Justine went back through the living room, where Meg's mattress lay empty with her blanket already folded in a neat, flat square. She knocked on the bathroom door. "Meg? Meggie? Is that you? We're not going to *wait* all day for you."

Water ran on and on.

"If you set up housekeeping there the way you did yesterday we'll leave you, we'll walk right out and leave you, hear?"

She tapped the door once more and returned to the kitchen. "Meg is crying again," she told Duncan.

"How can you tell?"

"She's shut up in the bathroom running the faucet. If today's like yesterday, what are we going to do?" she asked, but she was already trailing off, heading toward her bedroom with her mind switched to something else, and Duncan didn't bother answering.

In the bedroom, Justine dressed and then gathered up heaps of cast-off clothing, a coffee cup and a half-empty bottle of bourbon and a *Scientific American*. She tried to fold her blanket as neatly as Meg's. Then she straightened and looked around her. The room swooped with shadows from the swinging light-bulb. Without furniture it showed itself for what it was: a paper box with sagging walls. In every corner were empty matchbooks, safety pins, dustballs, Kleenexes, but she was not a careful housekeeper and she left them for whoever came after.

When she returned to the kitchen her grandfather and Duncan were standing side by side drinking their coffee like medicine. Her grandfather wore his deerskin slippers; otherwise, he was ready to leave. No one was going to accuse him of holding things up. "One of the trials I expect to see in hell," he said, "is paper cups, where your thumbnail is forever tempted to scrape off a strip of wax. And plastic spoons, and pulpy paper plates."

"That's for sure," Duncan told him.

"What say?"

"Where's your *hearing* aid?" Justine asked.

"Not so very well," said her grandfather. He held one hand out level, palm down. "I'm experiencing some discomfort in my fingers and both knees, I believe because of the cold. I was cold all night. I haven't been so cold since the blizzard of eighty-eight. Why are there not enough blankets, all of a sudden?"

Duncan flashed Justine a wide, quick smile, which she returned with the corners tucked in. There were not enough blankets because she had used most of them yesterday to pad the furniture, shielding claw feet and bureau tops and peeling veneer from the splintery walls of the U-Haul truck, although Duncan had told her, several times, that it might be best to save the blankets out. This was still January, the nights were cold. What was her hurry? But Justine was *always* in a hurry. "I want to get things done, I want to get going," she had said. Duncan gave up. There had been no system to their previous moves either; it seemed pointless to start now.

Meg came into the kitchen and claimed her coffee without looking to left or right—a neat, pretty girl in a shirtwaist dress, with short hair held in place by a sterling silver barrette. She was scrubbed and shining, buttoned, combed, smelling of toothpaste, but her eyes were pink. "Oh, honey!" Justine cried, but Meg ducked out from between her hands. She was seventeen years old. This move was the worst thing that had ever happened to her. Justine said, "Would you like some bread? It's all we've got out."

"No, thank you, Mama."

"I thought we'd have breakfast when we get to what's-its-name, if it's not too long to wait."

"I'm not hungry anyway."

She said nothing to her father. It was plain what she thought: If it weren't for Duncan they would never have to move at all. He had gone and grown tired of another business and chosen yet another town to drag them off to, seemingly picked it out of a hat, or might as well have.

"Your father will be driving the truck all alone," Justine said, "since last time it made Grandfather sick. Would you like to ride with him?" She never would let a quarrel wind on its natural way. She knew it herself, she had no tact or subtlety. She always had to be interfering. "Why not go, he could use the company."

But Meg's tears were back and she wouldn't speak, even to say no. She bent her head. The two short wings of her hair swung forward to hide her cheeks. And Duncan, of course, was off on some tangent of his own. His mind had started up again; he was finally awake. His mind was an intricate, multigeared machine, or perhaps some little animal with skittery paws. "I am fascinated by randomness," he said. "Do you realize that there is no possible permutation of four fingers that could be called absolutely random?"

"Duncan, it's time to roll the mattresses," Justine said.

"Mattresses. Yes."

"Would you?"

"Hold up your hand," Duncan told the grandfather, leading him through the living room. "Then take away two fingers. The first and third elements, say, of a four-element . . ."

"Last night," said Meg, "Mrs. Benning asked me again if I would like to stay with her."

"Oh, Meg."

"She said, '*Why* won't your mother allow it? Just till the school year is over,' she said. She said, 'You know we'd love to have you. Does she think you'd be imposing? Would it help if I talked to her one more time?' "

"You'll be leaving us soon enough as it is," said Justine, stacking empty paper cups.

"At least we should consider my schooling," Meg said. "This is my senior year. I won't learn a thing, moving around the way we do."

"Teaching you to adapt is the best education we could give you," Justine told her.

"Adapt! What about logarithms?"

"Now I can't keep on and on about this, I want you to find the cat. I think she knows it's moving day. She's hiding."

"So would I," said Meg, "if I could think of a place." And she slid off the counter and left, calling the cat in her soft, sensible voice that was never raised even when she argued. Justine stood motionless beside the sink. When she heard footsteps she spun around but it was only her grandfather.

"Justine? There are neighbors here to see you off," he told her. He sniffed through his long, pinched nose. People who were not related to him ought to keep to themselves, he always said. He watched narrowly while Justine rushed through the house, hunting her keys and struggling into her coat and jamming her hat on her head. "Check your room, Grandfather," she called. "Turn off the lights. Will you help Meg find the cat? Tell her we're just about to leave."

"Knees?"

"And don't forget your hearing aid."

"They don't get better *that* fast, the cold has sunk into the sockets," her grandfather said. "Ask me again tomorrow. Thank you very much."

Justine kissed his cheekbone, a polished white blade. She flew through the living room and out the front door, into the chalky dawn. Cold air yanked at her breath. Frozen grass crunched under her feet. Over by the U-Haul truck, Mr. Ambrose was helping Duncan load the last of the mattresses. Mrs. Ambrose stood to one side, along with the Printzes and Mrs. Benning and Della Carpenter and her retarded daughter. And a few feet away was a newsboy Justine had never seen before, a canvas sack slung from one shoulder. Except for the newsboy they all wore bathrobes, or coats thrown over pajamas. She had known them for nearly a year and there were still these new things to be learned: Alice Printz favored fluffy slippers the size of small sheep and Mrs. Benning, so practical in the daytime, wore a nightgown made of layers and layers of see-through pink or blue or gray—it was hard to tell which in this light. They stood hugging themselves against the cold, and the Carpenter girl's teeth were chattering. "Justine, I never!" Alice Printz was saying. "You thought you could slip out from under us. But we won't let you go that easy, here we are at crack of dawn waiting to see you off."

"Oh, I *hate* goodbyes!" said Justine. She went down the row hugging each one, even the newsboy, whom she might after all know without realizing it. Then a light came on over the Franks' front door, three houses down, and Justine went to tell June Frank goodbye. All but the newsboy came along with her. June appeared on her cinderblock steps carrying a begonia in a plastic pot. "I had this growing for you ever since I knew you would be moving," she said, "and if you had run off in the night the way you're doing and not give me a chance to say goodbye it would have broke my heart in two." June rolled her hair up on orange juice cans. Justine had never known that before either. And she said not to thank her for the plant or its growth would be stunted. "Is that right?" said Justine, her attention sidetracked. She held up the pot and thought a minute. "Now why, I wonder?"

"*I* don't know why, I only know what my mother used to say to me," June said. "Justine, honey, I won't come any further, but you tell the others goodbye for me too. Tell that pretty little Meg and your sweet old grandfather, tell that handsome husband, hear? And I'm going to write you a letter. If my sister decides to get married again I have to write you first and ask you what the cards say. I wouldn't think of letting her go ahead without it. Can you manage such a thing long distance?"

"I'll surely try," said Justine. "Well, I won't say thank you for the plant then but I promise to take good care of it. Goodbye then, June."

"Goodbye, old honey," June said, and she grew sad all at once and came down the steps to lay her cheek softly against Justine's while the others looked on, suddenly still, tilting their heads and smiling.

Meanwhile Meg had settled in the rear of the battered Ford with an enormous gray tweed cat in her lap. The cat crouched and glared and Meg cried, causing a mist of tears to glaze the squat little house with its yellowed foundations, its tattered shrubs, the porch pillars rotting from the bottom up. In the front seat, her great-grandfather placed his hearing aid in his ear, adjusted a button, and winced. Duncan slammed the tailgate on the last of the mattresses and climbed into the truck cab. He turned on the headlights, coloring the gray and white scene in front of him—Justine being passed from hand to hand down a row of neighbors in their nightclothes. "Ho, Justine," he called softly. Of course she couldn't hear. He had to beep the horn. Then everybody jumped and screeched and a window lit up half a block down, but Justine only gave him a wave and headed for the car, unsurprised, because wasn't he always having to honk for her? She was late for everything, though she started out the earliest and the fastest and the most impatient. She was always leaving places the same way, calling scraps of goodbyes and then running, flying, bearing some shaking plant or parcel or covered dish, out of breath and laughing at herself, clutching her hat to her head as she sped along.

At nine o'clock in the morning, Red Emma Borden was wiping the counter in the Caro Mill Diner when these four unfamiliar people walked in—a man and wife, a teenaged daughter and a very ancient gentleman. Red Emma was about to have a cigarette (she'd been on her feet since four) and she wasn't eager to wait on anyone else. Still, it was nice to see some new faces. She had been born and raised and married and widowed in this town and she was sick of everybody in it. So she puffed up her orange curls, tugged her uniform down, and reached for the order pad. Meanwhile the strangers were trying to find acceptable seats, which was not all that easy to do. Two of the counter stools were broken, just topless aluminum pedestals, and another would tip you off as soon as you tried to perch upon it. They had to cluster at one end down near the exhaust fan. Even then, the old gentleman had a long tail of cotton batting dangling out from under him. But none of them made any complaint; they just folded their arms and waited for her behind four pairs of blue, blue eyes. "Well, now," said Red Emma, slapping down cracked plastic menu cards. "What you going to have?"

She addressed the woman first—a skin-and-bones lady wearing a hat. But it was the husband who answered. "Speedy here will have everything in the kitchen," he said.

"Speedy! I barely *inched* along," the woman said.

"I thought you had entered the Indy five hundred. And your seat belt flopping out the door, after I took all that time installing it for you—"

"I will take coffee and three fried eggs," the woman told Red Emma. "Sunny side up. And hotcakes, link sausages, and orange juice. And something salty, a sack of potato chips. Grandfather? Meg?"

Red Emma feared she would be cooking all morning, but it turned out the others just wanted coffee. They had the dazed, rumpled look of people who had been traveling. Only the woman seemed to care to talk. "My name is Justine," she said, "and this is my husband, Duncan. Our Grandfather Peck and our daughter Meg. Do you have the keys?"

"How's that?"

"We were told to stop here and pick up the keys for Mr. Parkinson's house."

"Oh yes," said Red Emma. She would never have supposed that these were the people for Ned Parkinson's house—a tacky little place next to the electric shop. Particularly not the old gentleman. "Well, he did say somebody might be by," she said. "Have you took a good look at it yet?"

"Duncan has. He chose it," said Justine. "You haven't told us *your* name."

"Why, I'm Red Emma Borden."

"Do you work here all the time?"

"Mornings I do."

"Because I like to eat in diners. I expect we'll run into you often."

"Maybe so," said Red Emma, breaking eggs onto the grill. "But if you come after noon it'll be my late husband's cousin, *Black* Emma Borden. They call her that because she's the one with black hair, only she's been dyeing it for years now." She poured coffee into thick white cups. "You say your husband chose the house?" she asked Justine.

"He always does."

Red Emma flung him a glance. A fine-looking, straw-colored man. His conscience did not appear to be bothering him. "Look, honey," she told Justine. She set the coffeepot down and leaned over the counter. "How come you would let your husband choose where you live? Does *he* understand kitchens? Does he check for closet space and woodwork that doesn't crumble to bits the first time you try to scrub it down?"

Justine laughed. "I doubt it," she said.

Red Emma had once sent her husband to a used car lot to buy a family automobile and he had come home with a little teeny red creature meant for racing, set low to the ground, slit eyes for windows. It ate up every cent they had saved. She had never forgiven him. So now she felt personally involved, and she glared at this Duncan. He sat there as calm as you please building a pyramid out of sugar cubes. The grandfather was reading someone's discarded newspaper, holding it three feet away from him as old people tend to do and scowling and working his mouth around. Only the daughter seemed to understand. A *nice* girl, so trim and quiet. She wore a coat that was shabby but good quality, and she kept her eyes fixed on a catsup bottle as if something had shamed her. *She* knew what Red Emma was getting at.

"There's other places," Red Emma said. "The Butters are letting, oh, a *big* place go, over by the schoolhouse."

"Now on the average," Duncan said, and Red Emma turned, thinking he was speaking to her, "on the average a single one of the blocks in Cheops's pyramid weighed two and a half tons." No, it was the grandfather he meant that for, but the grandfather only looked up, irritated, maybe not even hearing, and turned a page of his paper. Duncan spun toward Meg, on his left. "It is accepted that wheels as such were not used in the construction," he told her. "Nor any but the most primitive surveying tools, so far as we know. Nevertheless, the greatest error to be found is only a little over five degrees on the east wall, and the others are almost perfect. And have you thought about the angle of the slant?"

Meg looked back at him, expressionless.

"It's my belief they built it from the top down," he said. He laughed.

Red Emma thought he must be crazy.

She flipped the hotcakes, loaded Justine's plate, and set it in front of her. "The Butters' house is a *two*-story affair," she said. "They also have a sleeping porch."

"Oh, I believe Mr. Parkinson's place is going to be just fine," said Justine. "Besides, it's near where Duncan's going to work. This way he can come home for lunch."

"Now where's he going to work?" Red Emma asked.

"At the Blue Bottle Antique Shop."

Oh, Lord. She should have known. That gilt-lettered place, run by a fat man nobody knew. Who needed antiques in Caro Mill? Only tourists, passing through on their way to the Eastern Shore, and most of them were in too much of a hurry to stop. But Red Emma still clung to a shred of hope (she liked to see people *manage*, somehow) and she said, "Well now, I suppose he could improve on what that Mr.—I don't recall his name. I suppose if he knows about antiques, and so on—"

"Oh, Duncan knows about everything," said Justine.

It didn't sound good, not at all.

"He hasn't worked with antiques before but he did build some furniture once, a few jobs back—"

Yes.

"The man who owns the Blue Bottle is Duncan's mother's sister's brother-in-law. He wants to ease off a little, get somebody else to manage the store for him now that he's getting older."

"We've used up all my mother's *blood* relations," Duncan said cheerfully. He was correcting the pitch of one pyramid wall. The truth that was coming out did not appear to embarrass him. "The last job was with my uncle, he owns a health food store. But no one in the family has a fix-it shop, and fixing is what I really do. I can fix anything. Do you need some repair work here?"

"No indeed," Red Emma told him firmly.

And she turned back to Justine, ready to offer her sympathy, but Justine was munching potato chips with a merry look in her eye. Her hat was a little crooked. Could she possibly be a drinker? Red Emma sighed and went to clean the grill. "Of course," she said, "I don't mean to say anything against Ned Parkinson's house. Why, in lots of ways it's just fine. I'm sure you'll all be happy there."

"I'm sure we will be," Justine said.

"And certainly your husband can handle any plumbing and electrical problems that might arise," Red Emma said, wickedly sweet, because she did not for a moment think he could.

But Duncan said, "Certainly," and started plunking his sugar cubes one by one back into the bowl.

Red Emma wiped the grill with a sour dish rag. She felt tired and wished they would go. But then Justine said, "You want to hear something? This coming year will be the best our family's ever had. It's going to be exceptional."

"Now, how do you know that?"

"It's nineteen seventy-three, isn't it? And three is our number! Look: both Duncan and I were born in nineteen thirty-three. We were married in nineteen fifty-three and Meg was born on the third day of the third month in nineteen fifty-five. Isn't that something?"

"Oh, Mama," Meg said, and ducked her head over her coffee.

"Meg's afraid that people will think I'm eccentric," said Justine. "But after all, it's not as if I believed in *numerology* or anything. Just lucky numbers. What's your lucky number, Red Emma?"

"Eight," said Red Emma.

"Ah. See there? Eight is forceful and good at organizing. You would succeed at any business or career, just anything."

"I would?"

Red Emma looked down at her billowing white nylon front, the flowered handkerchief prinked to her bosom with a cameo brooch.

"Now, Meg doesn't have a lucky number. I'm worried that nothing will ever happen to her."

"*Mama.*"

"Meg was due to be born in May and I wondered how that could happen. Unless she arrived on the third, of course. But see? She was premature, she came in March after all."

"I always ask for eight at the Basket of Cheer lottery," said Red Emma. "And I've won it twice, too. Forty dollars' worth of fine-quality liquor."

"Of course. Now, who's the fortune teller in this town?"

"Fortune teller?"

The grandfather rattled and crackled his paper.

"Don't tell me you don't have one," said Justine.

"Not to my knowledge we don't."

"Well, you know where I'll be living. Come when I'm settled and I'll tell your fortune free."

"You tell fortunes."

"I do church fairs, bazaars, club meetings, teas—anybody's, any time. People can knock on my door in the dead of night if they have some urgent problem and I will get up in my bathrobe to give them a reading. I don't mind at all. I like it, in fact. I have insomnia."

"But—you mean you tell fortunes *seriously?*" Red Emma asked.

"How else would I tell them?"

Red Emma looked at Duncan. He looked back, unsmiling.

"Well, if we could have the keys, then," said Justine.

Red Emma fetched them, sleepwalking—two flat, tinny keys on a shower curtain ring. "I really do need to have my fortune told," she said. "I wouldn't want this spread around but I'm considering a change in employment."

"Oh, *I* could help out with that."

"Don't laugh, will you? I'd like to be a mailman. I even passed the tests. Could you really tell me whether that would be a lucky move or not?"

"Of course," said Justine.

Red Emma rang up their bill, which Duncan paid with a BankAmericard so worn it would not emboss properly. Then they filed out, and she stood by the door to watch them go. When Justine passed, Red Emma touched her shoulder. "I'm just so anxious, you see," she said. "I don't sleep good at all. My mind swings back and forth between decisions. Oh, I know it's nothing big. I mean, a mailman, what is that to the world? What's it going to matter a hundred years from now? I don't fool myself it's anything important. Only day after day in this place, the grease causing my hair to flop halfway through the morning and the men all making smart remarks and me just feeding them and feeding them . . . though the pay is good and I really don't know what Uncle Harry would say if I was to quit after all these years."

"Change," said Justine.

"Beg pardon?"

"Change. I don't need cards for that. Take the change. Always change."

"Well—is that my fortune?"

"Yes, it is," said Justine. "Goodbye, Red Emma! See you soon!"

And she was gone, leaving Red Emma to pleat her lower lip with her fingers and ponder beside the plate glass door.

Justine drove the Ford down Main Street with the cat racing back and forth across the rear window ledge, yowling like an old, angry baby while people on the sidewalks stopped and stared. Meg sat with her hands folded; by now she was used to the racket. The grandfather simply shut his hearing aid off and gazed from his bubble of silence at the little wooden Woolworth's, the Texaco, the Amoco, the Arco, a moldering A&P, a neat brick post office with a flag in front. This time Duncan's truck was ahead, and Justine followed him in a right-hand turn down a side street lined with one-story buildings. They passed a drugstore and an electric shop, and then they came to a row of small houses. Duncan parked in front of the first one. Justine pulled in behind him. "Here we are!" she said.

The house was white, worn down to gray. On the porch, square shingled columns rose waist-high and then stopped, giving the overhang a precarious, unreliable look. Although there was no second floor the dormer window of some attic or storage room bulged out of the roof like an eyelid. A snarl of wiry bushes guarded the crawlspace beneath the porch. "Oh, roses!" Justine cried. "Are those roses?" Her grandfather shifted in his seat.

"This house is even worse than the last," said Meg.

"Never mind, here you'll have a room of your own. You won't have to sleep in the living room. Isn't that going to be nice?"

"Yes, Mama," Meg said.

Duncan was already pacing the yard when the others reached him. "I'm going to put a row or two of corn here," he told them. "Out back is too shady but see how much sun we get in front? I'm going to plow up the grass and plant corn and cucumbers. I have this plan for fertilizer, I'm going to buy a blender and grind up all our garbage with a little water. Pay attention, Justine. I want you to save everything, eggshells and orange peels and even bones. The bones we'll pressure-cook first. Have we got a pressure-cooker? We'll make a sort of jelly and spread that around here too."

Meanwhile the cat had streaked under the crawlspace,

where she would stay till the moving was over, and the grand-father was climbing the front steps all hunkered and disapproving, muttering to himself, making an inventory of every splinter and knothole and paint blister, every nail worked loose, windowscreen split, floorboard warped. Meg sat down on the very top step. "I'm cold," she said.

Justine said, "Your father's going to take up farming. Maybe we'll have tomatoes."

"Will we be here to harvest them?" Meg asked nobody.

Justine found the keys in one of her pockets and opened the door. They stepped into a hall smelling of mildew, littered with newspapers and broken cardboard boxes. The kitchen leading off it contained a refrigerator with a motor on top, a dirty gas stove, and a sink on stilts. There was a living room with a boarded-up fireplace. In the back were the bathroom and three bedrooms, all tiny and dark, but Justine swept through flinging up windowshades and stirring the thick, musty air. "Look! Someone left a pair of pliers," she said. "And here's a chair we can use for the porch." She was a pack rat; all of them were. It was a family trait. You could tell that in a flash when they started carrying things in from the truck—the bales of ancient, curly-edged magazines, zipper bags bursting with unfashionable clothes, cardboard boxes marked *Clippings, Used Wrapping Paper, Photos, Empty Bottles*. Duncan and Justine staggered into the grandfather's room carrying a steel filing cabinet from his old office, stuffed with carbon copies of all his personal correspondence for the twenty-three years since his retirement. In one corner of their own room Duncan stacked crates of machine parts and nameless metal objects picked up on walks, which he might someday want to use for some invention. He had cartons of books, most of them second-hand, dealing with things like the development of the quantum theory and the philosophy of Lao-tzu and the tribal life of Ila-speaking Northern Rhodesians. But when all of this clutter had been brought in (and it took the four of them two hours) there was next to nothing left in the truck. Their furniture was barely enough to make the house seem inhabited: three rust-stained mattresses, four kitchen chairs from Goodwill, Great-Grandma's hand-carved rosewood dining table, a sagging sofa and easy chair donated by a neighbor two moves back, and three bureaus of Justine's mother's, their ornate feet and bow fronts self-conscious next to the bedsteads Duncan had constructed out of raw pine boards that gave off a yellow smell. For dishes they had a collection of dimestore plates, some light green, some flowered, some dark brown with white glaze dripped around the edges, and thermal mugs given away free when Esso changed to Exxon. The cutlery with its yellow plastic handles had been salvaged from Aunt Sarah's English picnic basket. There were two saucepans and a skillet. (Justine did not like cooking.) They owned a broom and a sponge mop, but no dustpan, no vacuum cleaner, no squeegee, scrub bucket, or chamois cloth. (Justine did not like cleaning either.) No washing machine or dryer. When all the clothes in the house were dirty the family would lug them to the laundromat. Of course that was not much fun—the four of them struggling with their bulging pillow slips, the grandfather's head ducked way, way low in case of passers-by, all of them a little bedraggled in their very last clean clothes unearthed from the bottom of the drawer or the back of the closet—but wasn't it better than moving those shiny, heavy appliances from place to place? Why, by late afternoon they were completely settled in. There was nothing more to do. It was true that most of the boxes remained to be opened but that was nothing, some were still packed from the *last* move. There was no hurry. Justine was free to stretch out on her mattress, which had the piney-wood smell of home, and work her feet from her shoes and smile at the ceiling while the cat lay on her stomach like a twenty-pound, purring hot water bottle. Duncan could sit on the edge of the bed fooling with a stroboscope he had forgotten he owned. Meg could shut her door and unwrap, from its own special box, from seven layers of tissue paper, her framed photograph of a young man in a clerical robe at least a size too large, which she rewrapped almost immediately and slid to the back of her closet shelf. And in his room across the hall the grandfather could take a photo of his own from his pocket: Caleb Peck in tones of brown, framed

in gold, wearing a hat and tie, his face stark and dignified, playing a violincello while seated in an open stable door twenty feet
off the ground.

3

DUNCAN took a tour of the Blue Bottle Antique Shop with Silas
Amsel, the owner. Since he had already seen it when he applied
for the job, he was not very interested. He ambled along behind
fat, bearded Silas, yawning and drumming his fingers on passing
tabletops. Spider-legged spinet desks, clocks with cherubs and
shepherdesses and Father Time, dusty goblets, mirrors framed in
knobby gold plaster, occasional tables too weak to bear the
weight of a lamp—what was the sense in all this? To tell the
truth, he had never thought about antiques before. He had been
reared in a world where they were taken for granted. No one
ever *bought* them, no one bought anything; the rooms were
crowded with mellowed, well-kept furniture that appeared to
have grown there, and whenever children departed they took
several pieces with them but left the rooms as crowded as ever,
somehow, as if more had sprouted in the night. No, what interested Duncan was the bin of contrivances he had found behind
Silas's counter: rusty cherry pitters, potato quillers, apple corers,
fish scalers, an ingenious spiral cone for separating the white of
an egg from the yolk. Beside the bin was a wicker valise that
opened to make a chair for sitting by the seashore. Where had
all that inventiveness got to, now? How had it faded away?
The bin was marked with a felt-tip pen: *Your choice, $1.* The
valise, which was broken, could be bought for $2.50, if anyone
could find it among the boots and paper bags. When Duncan

took over, he would put the valise in the front window. (He leered suddenly at Silas's broad, ponderous back.) He would polish the utensils and lay them out in rows. He would sell everything humdrum and buy ancient tools at barn auctions and flea markets, until the shop resembled a nineteenth-century inventor's workroom and he could sit inhaling a combination of machine oil and wood and oxidizing iron, his favorite smells.

"Oh, I'm getting old, getting old," said Silas, creaking up the steps at the back of the store to show him where the telephone was. "Be sorry to let loose of the reins but glad of the rest, believe me."

In fact Silas was a good thirty years younger than Grandfather Peck, who could have run the shop with one hand tied behind him, but Duncan was used to this premature aging among people outside the family. Besides, if Silas weren't retiring Duncan would still be looking for a job. He had thought, this time, that he might finally have used up all his mother's relatives. He had wondered if he would ever escape from the health food store, which he had turned into a paying proposition and then, out of boredom, allowed to run down again. Weevils took over the stone-ground wheat and mold got the soy grits and the unsulphured raisins turned to pebbles. He lost his natural gaiety and his recklessness, he fell back on bourbon, solitaire, and a flat-faced silence that not even Justine could penetrate. Was there anything worse than feeling you were *sealed* in a place, to grow old and stale and finally die? His careless bookkeeping and erratic hours, already a matter of principle, became so obvious no employer could overlook them. That was the pattern of Duncan's life—ventures begun light-heartedly, with enthusiasm but only half his attention, the other half devoted to plans for a perpetual motion machine made entirely of screen door springs or a method of breeding stingless honeybees or the entering of a contest, sponsored by an Englishman, for a one-man flying machine no bigger than an armchair. In the last twenty years he had been, among other things, a goat farmer, a photographer, and a cabinetmaker; he had worked in a pet store, a tobacconist's, a record bar, and a gourmet shop; he had taken census, shorn sheep, and fertilized the lawns of a suburban development on a toy tractor. Almost all these jobs had been enjoyable, but only briefly. He began to grow restless. He noticed that he was treading an endless round of days just as his pinched, unimaginative family had done before him. He would start going to work at ten and then eleven, four days a week and then three; and next came the bourbon, the solitaire, the silence in which to reflect upon the bars of his cage. Next another venture. He was his own perpetual motion machine.

Sometimes he worried about Justine. He didn't *want* to be the way he was, uprooting her yearly or even more often, switching Meg to still another school. He knew how the neighbors shook their heads over him. Yet it seemed he suffered from some sort of chronic dissatisfaction which came and went like malaria, and the only way to hold it back was to learn more and more new facts, as if continually surprising his mind. Now peculiar scraps of knowledge were stuck to him like lint from all his jobs. He knew a Toggenburg goat from a Saanen, he could measure a dachshund, by sight alone, for a plaid mackintosh with matching Sherlock Holmes–style hat. He was an authority on the making of yogurt and the application of poisons to broad-leafed weeds during dandelion season. He had also discovered that every shop, even the most unlikely, has a circle of daily customers who become its experts—the elderly gentlemen capping each other's list of imported cheeses, the ladies debating on the use of slippery elm bark, the teenagers intoning the life history of every member of every rock band. At the tobacconist's, college boys could spend hours recalling the time a legendary freshman had found a fully aged and yellowed, hand-carved meerschaum pipe sitting on the top of someone's garbage can. Perched on his stool behind the counter, gloating over the drawings for his pedal-driven flying machine, Duncan absorbed this stray knowledge like sunlight. Never mind that it was useless. And now he was about to find something else to learn, here among these ancient navigating devices and cracked foggy lanterns and ropes of amber beads like half-sucked butter rum balls.

"This is potassium lactate," said Silas, tapping a brown bottle on the telephone table. "We use it to replace the acids in the covers of old leather books."

And he looked surprised at the sudden light that flashed across Duncan's face.

"Now this pad I always keep handy, and the pencil chained. People will call with items to sell, you want to get their addresses. Here, by the way, is a message for you."

He ripped it off the pad. *Habit-Forming Entertainments called, come to lunch first Sun. in Feb.*

"What?" said Duncan.

"He said you would know him. He phoned four times in the last two days. He said if you couldn't make it call back, he's still listed as Exotico."

"Ah," said Duncan, and pocketed the slip. Silas waited but Duncan didn't explain.

"Well, then," Silas said finally, "if you can't think of any questions—but I'll be by, I'll drop by often, of course."

"Of course," said Duncan, and he sighed, but Silas was groaning back down the steps by now and didn't hear him.

Habit-Forming Entertainments, which had been Exotico, Inc., last year and Alonzo's Amazing Amusements the year before that, was located in a cow pasture on the outskirts of Parvis, Maryland. It was a carnival company, of sorts—the kind that is called a forty-miler, although in this case the circuit was considerably wider. It traveled from one tiny town to another, supplying the entertainment for firehouse fairs, church and school bazaars, homecoming celebrations, and the gala openings of new shopping malls. In between trips the entire company lived in trailers in the cow pasture, with a pumpkin-colored tent flying pennants in the middle. They worked year round. Even in the dead of winter, Habit-Forming Entertainments would come trundling across the frost-bitten Maryland countryside to whoever asked for them. They brought mechanical rides, two ponies, a concession stand, a few simple games of chance whenever local law allowed, and five girls to run the games in satin bathing suits with dirty seams. There was also a merry-go-round. It was hard to transport and something was always going wrong with it, the mechanism sticking or the animals toppling over, but Justine preferred it to any other merry-go-round she had ever known. It played only one piece: "The St. James Infirmary Blues." Whenever Justine heard that tune sawing through the air she had to climb on, she didn't care if she *was* too old. She sat astride a laughing white horse, hugging the mane and laughing herself or occasionally crying, because the music was so tinny and sweet and sad and made her nostalgic for times before she was born. And whenever she saw Alonzo Divich, who owned that merry-go-round and all the other equipment, he was whistling "The St. James Infirmary Blues" like a theme song. He said it was the only tune *he* knew, too. He and the merry-go-round: two clumsy, hopeful, cheerful creatures, lumbering along where you would least expect to find them.

He was whistling when Justine and Duncan arrived; they tracked him down by his song. They left the car at the edge of the field and made their way across the frozen stubble toward the trailers, which sat around the tent in a cold, huddled circle like covered wagons braced for Indian attack. In the spring, when the countryside was blooming, this sort of life could seem pleasant, but not today. Today everything was lit with a sickly white winter sun, the inhabitants were shut inside their trailers, the ponies hung their heads. "Oh, the poor things!" Justine cried, and she felt the same when she passed an orange ride all folded on its truckbed like a crumpled baby dinosaur. But the whistling continued, happy as ever, sailing out from behind a plowshed, and when they had rounded the shed there was Alonzo Divich looking untouched by cold or loneliness or time. He was sitting on a boulder braiding rawhide—a large, dark man with a drooping black mustache and drooping eyes. He wore too many colors of clothing, all a little soiled, greasy, strained across the stomach and crotch and under the arms: a rose shirt, a woven Mexican vest, suede dungarees and crumpled boots. When he stood to hug them, he gave off a smell of leather and honey. "Aha!" he said to Justine. "But you haven't changed at all! Even the hat is still the same! Is it rooted there?"

He had no accent—only a curious certainty to his speech. But where did he get his hybrid name, and his coloring, and his flashing gold molars and his habit of hugging other men so un-self-consciously? Justine had asked him outright, once, what nationality he was. "You're the fortune teller, you tell me," he said.

"I read the future, not the past," she told him.

"Well, the past should be easier!"

"It's not. It's far more complicated."

But he had never told her, even so.

He led them to the tent, where folding chairs were grouped around long wheeled conference tables. This was the company's communal hall, although in cold weather it was nearly empty. In one corner a blonde wearing slacks, gilt sandals, and several sweaters was combing out a miniature poodle. Two men in over-alls were seated at a table drinking coffee from green mugs, but they left when Alonzo entered. "Aah, don't go," he said, flop-ping an arm toward their backs. He pulled out chairs at the center table, and seated himself at the head. Almost immediately a dark old lady appeared and spread a tablecloth. Then she brought a bottle and three small glasses, which she set before Alonzo. He filled the glasses exactly to the brim. The old lady reappeared with paper plates, plastic forks, and then trays of rice, hunks of meat in tomato sauce, eggplant, chicken dusted with some peculiar red powder, wrinkled black olives, bowls of beet soup and chopped cucumber in yogurt, great flat disks of bread and pitchers of green Kool-Aid. Steam rose from the plat-ters, and from Alonzo's mouth as he talked in the cold, rubbery-smelling air. "Take some, don't be shy. First Duncan, he's thinner than ever. He's stretching out tall and thin like a dande-lion. How tall are you, Duncan?"

"Six two."

"Double rice for Duncan, Nana!"

The old lady shoveled a mountain onto Duncan's plate.

"Rice prevents heart attacks, stroke, and impotence," said Alonzo.

"It's the thiamine," said Duncan.

"More slivovitz?"

"Oh, I might as well."

Justine ate everything she was given and accepted seconds and thirds, egged on by the approving eye of the old lady who stood behind Alonzo's chair with her hands folded under her apron. Alonzo and Duncan mainly drank, though Alonzo outdistanced Duncan very early and even managed to work in a few slabs of bread stuffed with meat and rice, meanwhile talking steadily. "When I heard you were moving back to Maryland I thought, well then, I can wait. I was contemplating a certain action. But we'll go into that later. I had been thinking, now how will I reach Justine? Then I got your card. It came as a great relief to me."

He leaned back and laced his hands across his stomach, his face a buttery color in the light of the tent. Alonzo was a happy man but forever complaining, as if hoping to fool any jealous gods. Although he loved his carnival business he said that only a fool would stick with it. "Imagine," he always said, "some people suppose this life to be romantic, dancing around the wagons at night. If they were only in my boots! You need to be a mechanic, a lawyer, an accountant. It's all the assembling and disassembling of machinery, and repairs and insurance payments. I'm being robbed by my insurance agency. Disability and liability and major medical and fire and theft and acts of God. Then there is the social security, a headache in itself when you consider all these employees coming and going and the pregnancies and the girls deciding to finish school. And you have to negotiate in every town, some don't allow so much as a ring-the-bottle game, and there's the safety inspectors and the police and the church that wants to put a tray of cupcakes in your hot dog stand . . ."

It was Duncan he talked to; men were best for discussing business. But it was Justine he took away with him at the end of the meal, one large warm thumb and forefinger gripping her upper arm. "May I?" he asked Duncan. "Only long enough to say when I'll become a millionaire."

Duncan said, "Do you still have your mechanic?"

"Lem? Would I be here if I didn't? He's in the purple trailer. He knew you were coming; go right in."

Alonzo walked with his head down, still holding Justine's arm. "You must excuse the state of my place," he said. "I have too many people in it now. My wife has left me but one of her children stayed behind to keep me company. And also Bobby. You've met Bobby, my stepson. Actually my fourth wife's stepson, her ex-husband's boy by a woman from Tampa, Florida. Would you care for Turkish coffee?"

"No, thank you," said Justine, and she stepped inside the little green trailer. Although it was crowded it was neater than her own house, with pots and pans arranged in rows in the tiny kitchen and account books stacked at one end of the corduroy daybed. There was a coffee table that had a stripped look, as if he had just recently cleared it. He smoothed it now with both hands. "For the cards," he said.

"Thank you," said Justine.

She sat down on the daybed. She removed her crumb-littered coat, although even here it was cold. From her carry-all she took the cards in their square of silk.

"Where did you get the silk?" Alonzo asked. (He always did.)

"They came with the cards," she said, unwrapping them. She shuffled them several times, looking off at the blue air outside the trailer window.

"And where did you get the cards?"

"Cut the deck, please."

He cut it. He sat down across from her and looked at her soberly from under curled black brows, as if his future might be read in her face.

Justine first met Alonzo Divich at a church bazaar in 1956, when she was telling fortunes in the Sunday school basement. She was with the white elephants and the potted plants; his carnival was outside. He came in to have his cards read. He was one of those people, she saw, who are addicted to outguessing their futures. Whenever he had an hour to kill, a layover in some town or a lull in his work, he would search out the local seeress. If there were five local seeresses, fine. He would go to all five. He would listen without even breathing. He had heard his fortune, he told Justine, from well over a thousand women, and it had not once been done right. He had not only had his cards read but also his palms, his skull, his moles, his fingernails, his dreams, his handwriting, his tea leaves and coffee grounds. He had been to astrologers and physiognomists, not to mention specialists in bibliomancy, clidomancy, crystal-gazing, and ouija boards. A lady in Montgomery County had set a gamecock to pick corn from a circle of letters; a Georgia woman studied smoke rising from a fire and another dropped melted wax into cold water, forming small nubbly objects that she claimed to be able to interpret. In York County, Pennsylvania, he had had to bake his own barley cakes, which were then broken open and examined under a magnifying glass. And in a marsh near St. Elmo, Alabama, a very old woman had offered to kill a rice rat and study its entrails, but he had felt that such an act might bring bad luck.

He had told Justine all this at once, leaning toward her across the table in her curtained booth while a line of church ladies waited their turns outside. Justine, although she did not know it, wore the tolerant, disillusioned expression of a doctor hearing that his new patient has been to forty other doctors before him, none of them satisfactory. It gave her a look of wisdom. Alonzo decided she was going to turn out to be special. "Lady," he had said, setting his palms on her table, "tell me the answer to my problem. I feel you can."

"What is your problem?"

"Don't you know?"

"How should I?"

"*You're* the fortune teller."

So Justine had to give the speech she had made more often than she could count, and would make many times again, sometimes even to him. "Now I am not a mind reader," she said, "and I have no way at all of guessing what you want to ask, or where you come from or anything else about your past. I read the future. I have a talent for predicting change. If you help me we can search for an answer together; but I'm not going to *outwit* you."

"My problem is this," Alonzo said instantly.

And he sat on a Sunday school chair and took his hat off— a sudden, changeable man, all black and bright and multicolored like a fire that could leap in any direction at any second. "My name is Alonzo Divich," he told her. "I own a carnival business." He jabbed a thumb at the merry-go-round music above them, "The St. James Infirmary Blues" spinning itself out among the cries of children and hot dog vendors, and teenagers clinging to the Tilt-A-Whirl. "I'm divorced, I have this kid. Now I've met a rich widow woman who wants to marry me. She likes the kid, too. She would even live in the trailer. I don't have to change one thing in my life for her. And I'm a marrying fool. I love being married, I tried it twice before. So what's the trouble? The same day we start the talk about a wedding, exact same day, a man I used to know calls and asks me to come and prospect for gold with him beside a lake in Michigan. He says he's onto something. He's going to be a wealthy man, and so am I. But of course there's the kid, and the mortgaged machines, and the woman who doesn't like Michigan. So which do I do?"

Justine was listening with her mouth open. When he finished she said, immediately, "Go look for gold."

"Huh? What about the cards?"

"Oh, the cards," she said.

So she let him cut them and she laid them down, her beautiful cards as limp and greasy as her baby's oilcloth picture books. She chose the simplest formation she knew. She pointed out the meaning while he hung over the table, not breathing: a happy journey, reunion with a friend, a pleasant surprise, and no possibility of money.

"Aha," he said, and she raised her face. "So it's lucky I ran into you. No money!"

"Mr.—"

"Divich. Just call me Alonzo."

"Alonzo, is the money all you're going for?"

"Well, but—"

"Go anyway! Go on! *Don't* just sit around hemming and hawing!"

Then she slapped his money back on his palm, for lack of any better way to show how she felt. And she gathered up her cards without looking at him even though he sat there a minute longer, waiting.

It was four years before she saw Alonzo again. On Independence Day, 1960, she set up a booth at a picnic in Wamburton, Maryland. Nobody there seemed much interested in the future. Finally she repacked her cards and took a walk toward the courthouse, where rides were spinning and balloons were sailing and the merry-go-round was playing "The St. James Infirmary Blues," sending out little shimmering catgut strings that drew her in. She started toward the wooden horses. And there beside the tallest horse was—why, Alonzo Divich!—wiping his face on a red bandanna and quarreling with a mechanic. Only when she came up he turned and stopped in mid-sentence and stared. "You!" he said. He ringed her wrist with his hand and pulled her away, toward a bench where the music was not so loud. She came, holding onto her hat. "Do you know how long I worked to find you?" he shouted.

"Who, me?"

"How often do you move? Are you some sort of forty-miler all your own? First I asked at the church, who was the fortune teller? 'Oh, *Justine*,' they said. Everyone knew you, but they didn't know where you lived. And by the time I found *that* out you had moved but left no forwarding address. Why? Did you owe money? Never mind. I haunted all your lady-friends, I hoped you were a letter writer. But you are not. Then at the tobacconist's where your husband used to work they said—"

"But what did you want me for?" Justine asked.

"To tell my fortune, of course."

"I *told* your fortune."

"Yes, back in nineteen fifty-six. Do you think my life is so steady? *Now* that reading has no bearing at all."

"Oh. Well, no," said Justine, who saw that with him, that would certainly be true. She reached into her bag—at that time a leather pouch gouged by her neighbor's puppy—and pulled out the cards. "And you didn't go look for gold," she said.

"You *do* read the past!"

"Don't be silly. Here you are in Maryland; it's obvious to anyone."

"I didn't, no. I thought about it. Instinct said to follow your advice, but I held back. You know the rest."

"No."

"Yes, you do. I married the widow," he said, "who turned out to be a disappointment. She had no money after all, the kid got on her nerves, what she had wanted all along was to start us a troupe of belly dancers with her as the star. Belly dancers, when half the towns make our game girls wear sweatshirts! I said absolutely not. She left me. I haven't heard from my friend in Michigan but I expect he has a whole sack of gold nuggets by now and meanwhile here I sit, where I was to begin with, only I happen to be married again—oh, you were right! If I had listened to you, think where I might be today!"

"Cut the cards," Justine told him.

"My new wife is pregnant and I have too many kids already," said Alonzo. "She is morning-sick, afternoon-sick, and evening-sick. When I walk into the trailer she throws fruits and vegetables at me. I don't think we are getting along at all. However, that's not my problem, no . . ."

But what his problem *had* been Justine couldn't even remember now. There were so many years in between, so many different formations laid out for him on park benches, tent floors, and trailer furniture. Once he found her he never again lost track of her. He supplied her with change-of-address cards already stamped and filled out, with blanks left for the old address and the new. He adopted her entire family, unfolding for Duncan the mysteries of his diesel engines and his cotton candy machines and the odds on his games of chance, bringing Meg gaudy circus prizes for as long as she was a child, treating the baffled grandfather with elaborate old-world respect and sending Justine a great moldy Smithfield ham every Christmas. He would drive halfway across the state just to ask her a single question, and then overpay her ridiculously when she answered. He mourned her moves to Virginia and Pennsylvania and rejoiced when she was safely back in Maryland. He beat on her front door at unexpected times and when she was not home he threatened to fall apart. "I have to know!" he would cry to Duncan or Meg. "I can't make a move, I am utterly dependent on her!"

Yet the peculiar thing (which Justine had seen too often before to wonder at) was that he very seldom took her advice. Look at all his marriages: seven, at last count. Maybe more. And how many of those had Justine approved? None. He had gone ahead anyway. Later he would come back: "Oh, you were right. I never should have done it. When will I learn?" His wives tended to leave him, taking the children along. Then sooner or later the children drifted back, and there were always a few living in his trailer—sons and stepsons and others whose relationship was not quite clear, even to him. "My wives are gone and I sleep alone but still I have three kids at me night and day, all ages. Next time I will listen to every word you say, I'll follow it to the letter," he said.

He said it now, nearly seventeen years from the day he had first ignored her advice, while Justine laid out the cards on the coffee table in the trailer. "I'm going to do everything you tell me to this time," he said.

"Ha," she said.

She bent closer and peered at the cards. "Money and a jealous woman. You're not getting *married* again."

"No, no." He sighed and stroked his mustache. "Who would marry me? I'm growing old, Justine."

For a second she thought she had heard wrong.

"I'm fifty-two," he said. "Do your cards tell you that?"

It was the only fact he had ever handed her. For some reason it diminished him. Alonzo, possessing an *age?* When she first met him, then, he would have been thirty-five—a young, unsteady number of years for a man, but Alonzo had never been young or unsteady. She raised her eyes and found a sprinkling of white in his hair, and deep grooves extending the droop of his mustache. When he smiled at her, creases rayed out from the corners of his eyes. "Why, Alonzo," she said.

"Yes?"

"Why—"

But she couldn't think what she was trying to say. And Alonzo shot his cuffs impatiently and sat forward on his stool. "Well, never mind *that*," he said. "Get on with my problem."

"Tell me what it is."

"Shall I sell the business to Mrs. Harry Mosely?"

"Who's Mrs. Harry Mosely?"

"What does it matter? A rich lady in Parvis, divorced, wants some kind of business different from all her friends."

"The jealous woman."

"Not of me."

"*Envious* jealous."

"She wears jodhpurs," Alonzo said, and shook his head.

Justine waited.

"Well?" he said.

"Well, what?"

"Do I sell or do I not? I'm asking."

"But you haven't said what the choice is," Justine told him. "What are you selling it *for*? Are you joining another gold rush?"

"No, I thought just something quiet. I have a friend who's in merchandising, he would find me something or other."

"*Merchandising?*"

"What's wrong with that?"

"I'm going to have to study these cards a bit," Justine said, and she bent over them again and rested her forehead on her hand.

"This life is hard, Justine," Alonzo told her. "That tent out there cost five thousand dollars and has a life span of only six years. I pay very high taxes on this pasture but Maryland has gypsy laws so we *have* to live here, it's too expensive to camp around. And occasionally people fail to pay me or the weather keeps the customers away, and a ride rusts to bits at exactly the time I clear the mortgage on it. I have so many people to be responsible for. Also these kids all the time. Can't you understand?"

"Yes, yes."

"Then why are you studying the cards for so long?"

"Because I don't know what to say," she said, and she laid an index finger on the six of hearts and thought a moment. "I see the woman and the money, but everything else is indecisive. No sudden fortune and no disasters. A few petty reverses, a friendship breaking off, but otherwise just—weak."

"*Weak?*" said Alonzo.

She looked directly at him. "Alonzo," she said. "Don't sell your business."

She left it up to him to decide whether it was she or the cards who spoke.

In the late afternoon, when the sun grew warmer, they sat outside on a collapsed sofa and watched two of Alonzo's teenaged boys pitching a baseball back and forth in the long grass behind the trailers. A girl was hanging out diapers, and a man was rotating the tires on his Studebaker. In the field beyond the baseball players, Duncan and Lem were fiddling with a hunk of machinery. Really it was time they started back, but Duncan said this machine was something special. He wanted to invent a ride for it to run. And the sun was warming the top of Justine's head right through her hat, and the dexterous twist of the baseball glove as it rose to meet the ball and the slap of leather on leather lulled her into a trance.

"If I were president, I would not have a personal physician in the White House with me but you, Justine," said Alonzo. "You could read the cards for me every morning before the Cabinet meeting."

She smiled and let her head tip against the back of the sofa.

"Till then, you can join my carnival. *Why* do you always

say no? Coralette, who works the concession stand, she just takes her husband and kids along. They stay in the trailer and read comic books."

"Duncan doesn't like comic books," Justine said.

Out in the field, Duncan raised a sprocket wheel in one gaunt, blackened hand and waved it at her.

"And Meg, she's all grown up? She doesn't come on visits with you now?"

"She doesn't come *anywhere* with us," Justine said sadly. "She studies a lot. She works very hard. She's very conscientious. Other girls wear blue jeans but Meg sews herself these shirtwaist dresses and polishes her shoes every Sunday night and washes her hair every Monday and Thursday. I don't think she approves of us. To tell the truth, Alonzo, I don't believe she thinks much of carnivals either or fortune telling or moving around the way we do. Not that she says so. She's very good about it, really, she's so quiet and she does whatever we tell her to. It kills me to see her bend her head the way she sometimes does."

"Girls are difficult," Alonzo said. "Fortunately I never had many of them."

"I think she's in love with a minister."

"With a what?"

"Well, an *assistant* minister, actually."

"But even so," said Alonzo.

"She went to his church in Semple. She's religious, too. Did I mention that? She went to his young people's group on Sunday evenings. Then they started going out together to lectures and debates and educational slide shows—oh, very proper, but she's only seventeen! And she brought him to our house so we could meet him. It was terrible. We all sat in the living room. Duncan says she has a right to choose whoever she wants but he doesn't think she *chose* this man, she just accepted him. Like a compromise. What else could it be, with a man so meek and puny? He's one of those people with white shiny skin and five o'clock shadow. Duncan says—"

"But after all," said Alonzo, "better that than a motordrome rider. My first wife's girl married a motordrome rider."

"I would prefer a motordrome rider any day," Justine said. Then she sighed. "Oh well, I suppose nobody likes who their children go out with."

"It's true."

"When *I* was courting, my father locked me in my room one time."

"Oh?" said Alonzo. He squinted, following the arc of the baseball floating across the sun.

"I fell in love with my first cousin."

"Oh-ho."

"On top of that, my *shiftless* first cousin. He drank and ran around. For years he had a girlfriend named Glorietta, who always wore red. My aunts and my mother would whisper whenever they mentioned her, even her name. Glorietta de Merino."

"Ah, Glorietta," said Alonzo, and settled back with his face tilted to the sky and his boots stretched out in front of him. "Go on."

"He made terrible grades all through school and dropped out the first year of college. Nobody could ever find him when they wanted him. While *I!* I was an only child. I tried to be as good as possible. Would you believe, until I was twenty years old I had never tasted liverwurst?"

"Liverwurst," said Alonzo, turning it over lazily.

"Because my family didn't happen to eat it. Not that there was anything wrong with it, of course, they just weren't in the habit of ordering it from the market. I didn't know there *was* such a thing as liverwurst! The first time I tasted it I ate a whole pound. But that was later. First I fell in love with my cousin, and went on trips with him and rode in his unsafe car and had to be locked in my room. *Then* I discovered liverwurst."

"But what became of him?" Alonzo asked.

"Who?"

"The first cousin."

"Oh," said Justine. "Why, I married him. Who did you think I was talking about?"

"Duncan?"

"Of *course* Duncan," said Justine, and she sat up again and shaded her eyes. "Cousin Duncan the Bad," she said, and laughed, and even Alonzo, drowsy and heavy in the sun, had to see how happy she looked when she located Duncan's spiky gold head glinting above the weeds.

4

DUNCAN and Justine Peck shared a great-grandfather named Justin Montague Peck, a sharp-eyed, humorless man who became very rich importing coffee, sugar, and guano during the last quarter of the nineteenth century. On any summer day in the 1870's, say, you could find him seated in the old Merchants' Exchange on Gay Street, smoking one of his long black cigars to ward off yellow fever, waiting for news of his ships to be relayed from the lookout tower on Federal Hill. Where he originally came from was uncertain, but the richer he grew the less it mattered. Although he was never welcomed into Baltimore society, which was narrow and ossified even then, he was treated with respect and men often asked his advice on financial issues. Once there was even a short street named after him, but it was changed later on to commemorate a politician.

When Justin Peck was fifty years old, he bought a sycamore-shaded lot in what was then the northern part of town. He built a gaunt house bristling with chimneys and lined with dark, oily wood. He filled it with golden oak furniture and Oriental screens, chandeliers dripping crystal, wine velvet love-seats with buttons and more buttons up and down their backs, heavy paintings leaning out from the walls, curlicued urns, doilies, statuary, bric-a-brac, great globular lamps centered on tasseled scarves, and Persian rugs laid catty-corner and overlapping. Then he married Sarah Cantleigh, the sixteen-year-old daughter of another importer. Nothing is known of their courtship, if there was one, but her wedding portrait still looms in a Baltimore dining room: a child-faced girl with a look of reluctance, of hanging back, which is accentuated by the dress style of the day with its backward-swept lines and the flounce at the rear of the skirt.

In 1880, only nine months after the wedding, Sarah Cantleigh died giving birth to Daniel. In 1881 Justin Peck remarried, this time into stronger stock—a German cutler's daughter named Laura Baum, who rescued Daniel from the old freedwoman who had been tending him. Laura Baum's portrait was never painted, but she lived long enough to be known personally even by Meg, her great-great-step-grandchild. She was a sallow, straight-backed woman who wore her hair in a knot. Although she was twenty when she married, observers said she looked more like forty. But then she looked forty when she died, too, at the age of ninety-seven. And it was clear that she made an excellent mother for little Daniel. She taught him to read and cipher when he was only three years old, and she made certain that his manners were impeccable. When Justin suggested that she stop taking Daniel with her on visits to her father she agreed instantly, even ceasing her own visits although Justin had not asked that of her in so many words. (Her father was very obviously a foreigner, an undignified little man given to practical jokes. His dusty jumbled shop by the harbor was a hangout for seamen and other rough types.) "Always remember, Daniel," she said, straightening his collar, "that you must live up to your family's name." She never explained what she meant by that. Her darkies broke into hissing laughter on the kitchen stairs and asked each other in whispers, "What family? What name? *Peck?*" but she never heard them.

In 1885, Laura had a son of her own. They called him

Caleb. He was blond like his half-brother, but his tilted brown eyes must have snuck in from the Baum side of the family, and he had his Grandpa Baum's delight in noise and crowds. Even as a baby, being wheeled along in his caramel-colored wicker carriage, he would go into fits of glee at the sight of passing strangers. He liked anything musical—church bells, hurdy-gurdies, the chants of the street vendors selling hot crabcakes. When he was a little older he took to the streets himself, riding an iron velocipede with a carpeted seat. He and Daniel were confined to the sidewalk in front of their house, but while Daniel obeyed instructions, leafing through *The Youth's Companion* on the front steps with his chick-yellow head bent low, Caleb would sooner or later be tugged southward by the fire bell or the gathering of a crowd or, of course, the sound of a street musician. He followed the blind harpist and the banjoist, the walking piano that cranked out Italian tunes and the lady who sang "The Pardon Came Too Late." Then someone would think to ask, "Where's Caleb?" His mother came out on the front steps, a fan of creases rising up between her eyebrows. "Daniel, have *you* seen Caleb?" And search parties would have to be sent down all the streets running toward the harbor. Only everybody soon learned: if you wanted to find Caleb, hold still a minute and listen. Whenever you heard distant music somewhere in the town, maybe so faint you thought you imagined it, so thin you blamed the whistling of the streetcar wires, then you could track the sound down and find Caleb straddling his little velocipede, speechless with joy, his appleseed eyes dancing. The maid would touch his sleeve, or Daniel would take his hand, or Laura would grab him by the earlobe, muttering, "*This* is where I find you! Out with a bunch of . . . well, I don't know what your father is going to say. I don't know what he's going to think of you for this."

Only she never told his father. Perhaps she thought that she would be held to blame. Sometimes, from the way she acted, you would think she was afraid of Justin.

On Sundays the Pecks went to church, of course, and on Wednesday evenings Laura had her Ladies' Circle. On holidays there were the formal visitors: Justin's business associates and their wives, along with their starched, ruffled children. But you couldn't say that the Pecks had *friends*, exactly. They képt to themselves. They were suspicious of outsiders. After guests left, the family often remarked on the gentlemen's inferior brand of cigars, the children's poor manners, the wives' regrettable over-use of Pompeiian Bloom rouge. Daniel listened, memorizing their words. Caleb hung out the window to hear an Irish tenor sing "Just a Lock of Hair for Mother."

Daniel was a tall, cool, reflective boy, and from the beginning he planned to study law. Therefore Caleb would take over the importing business. In preparation for this Caleb attended the Salter Academy, walking there daily with his friend Paul and a few of the neighborhood boys. He worked very conscientiously, although sometimes his mother suspected that his heart wasn't in it. Coming home from school he could be waylaid by any passing stranger, he fell willingly into conversation with all sorts of riffraff. He had no discrimination. And he still followed organ grinders. With his pocket money he bought tawdry musical instruments, everything from pennywhistles to a cheap violin sold him by a sailor; he could make music out of anything. He played these instruments not only in his room but outdoors as well, if he wasn't caught and stopped. More than once he was mistakenly showered with coins from someone's window. When Laura heard about it she would grow dark in the face and order him to remember his name. She shut him in the parlor, where he continued to spill out his reckless, made-up tunes on the massive piano draped in fringed silk. Unfortunately the Creole gardener, Lafleur Boudrault, had taught him ragtime. A disreputable, *colored* kind of music. Justin, home in his study doing the accounts, would raise his head to listen for a minute and frown, but then he shrugged it off.

In 1903, Caleb graduated from the Salter Academy. The day after his graduation Justin took him down to his office to show him around. By now, of course, the importing business was very different from what it had been in the '70's. The old full-rigged steamers, which looked like brigantines with smokestacks, had given way to modern ships, and their spectacular journeys to Brazil and Peru and the West Indies had been discontinued in favor of the more profitable coastwise hauls, carrying manufactured goods south and raw materials north. The Merchants' Exchange had been torn down; Caleb would be spending his days in an office above a warehouse, behind a roll-top desk, dealing with ledgers and receipts and bills of lading. Still, it was a fine opportunity for a young man with ambition, Caleb. Caleb?

Caleb turned from the single, sooty window, through which he had been gazing even though it was impossible to see the harbor from there. He said that he would prefer to be a musician.

At first Justin couldn't take it in. He was politely interested. Musician? Whatever for?

Then the situation hit him in the face and he gasped and caved in. He felt for the chair behind him and sat down, preparing bitter, harmful words that would convey all his horror and disgust and contempt. But music was so—no young man would ever seriously—music was for women! For parlors! He felt nauseated by the sight of this boy's intense brown eyes. He could hardly wait to chew him up and spit him out and stamp on what was left.

Instead, all that came from his mouth were strange vowel sounds over which he had no control.

He had to be carried away in his office chair by two men from the warehouse. They laid him in his buggy and folded both arms across his chest, as if he were already dead, and then Caleb drove him home. When Laura came to the door she found Caleb on the topmost step with his father curled in his arms like a baby. But Justin's eyes were two hard, glittering pebbles, and she could feel his rage. "What *happened?*" she asked, and Caleb told her, straight out, while struggling upstairs with his burden to Justin's high carved bed. Laura's face grew as dark as coffee but she said not a word. She had the kitchen maid fetch the doctor from down the street, and she listened stonily to the doctor's diagnosis: apoplexy, brought on by a shock of some sort. He did not hold out much hope for recovery. If Justin lived, he said, one side would likely be paralyzed, although it was too soon to say for certain.

Then Laura went downstairs to the parlor where Caleb stood waiting. "You have killed your half of your father," she said.

On Monday, Caleb started work behind the roll-top desk.

Daniel, meanwhile, had finished his courses at the University in record time and was now preparing himself further by working at the offices of Norris & Wiggen, a fine old respectable law firm. He lived at home and often relieved Laura at his father's sickbed, reading aloud to him from the newspaper or from Laura's enormous Bible. Justin would lie very still with one fist clenched, his flinty blue eyes glaring at the wall. He had not recovered the use of his left side. It was apparent suddenly that he was a very old man, with liver spots across his dry forehead and claws for hands. Half of his face seemed to be melting and running downward. He spoke only with difficulty, and when people misunderstood he would fly into a rage. Because he could not bear to have his weakness observed by the outside world (which would take advantage immediately, he was certain of it), he had determined to stay in his bedroom until he was fully recovered. For he assumed that he was suffering only a brief, treatable illness, his convalescence hampered by a worse-than-useless doctor and a half-wit wife. Therefore he undertook his own cure. He had all the panes in his windows replaced with amethyst glass, which was believed to promote healing. He drank his water from a quassia cup and ordered Laura to send away for various nostrums advertised in the newspaper—celery tonic, pectoral syrup, a revitalizing electric battery worn on a chain around the neck. His only meat was squirrel, easiest on the digestive tract. Yet still he remained flat on his back, whitening and shriveling like a beached fish.

On Friday nights Caleb came and summarized the week's business in a gentle, even voice, directing his statements to the foot of the bed. Justin looked at the wall, pretending not to hear. As a matter of fact it seemed that Caleb was handling everything quite adequately, but it was too late now. The time for that was past, there was no undoing what had been done. Justin went on looking at the wall until Caleb left.

Laura brought out an old busybody she had—a mirror arrangement placed to reflect passers-by on the street below. She thought he might like to keep in touch with things. But when Justin turned his face to the busybody he saw Caleb just descending the front steps, turned faded and remote and long-ago by the blue glass of the windowpanes. He told Laura to take her nonsense elsewhere.

In February, 1904, the Great Fire burned out the heart of Baltimore, sweeping away every tall building in the city and most major businesses, including Justin Peck's. When it was over Justin insisted upon being taken to see the damage for himself. His sons carried him to the buggy and drove him downtown, through the peculiar yellowish light that hung over everything. It was the first trip Justin had made since his illness. From the satisfied look he gave to the rubble and the littered streets and the jagged remains of walls, it seemed that he credited the destruction not to fire but to his own absence. Without him Baltimore had gone up in smoke. Under Caleb's care the warehouse had caved in, the office had disappeared, the roll-top desk had dissolved into ashes. He turned to Daniel with a crooked, bitter smile and waved his good hand to be taken home again.

Now he developed a new obsession: he wanted to leave this combustible city entirely and build further north, way out on Falls Road. He dreamed his room was alight with flames and not a member of his family would come to rescue him. He called in the night for Laura, whose bed he had left some fifteen years ago following her third miscarriage, and he made her sleep by his side with her hand on a brass bell from India. He jarred her awake periodically and sent her out to the hall to sniff for fire. And Caleb, who was working around the clock to rebuild the warehouse, had to come to his father's room every evening and listen to interminable garbled, stammered instructions for the buying of land in Roland Park. Nowadays Caleb always smelled of smoke from the city and he moved in a deep, tired daze. He would rest his cheek against the doorframe and slump until his sooty white shirt appeared to have nothing inside it, while his father wove his tangled mat of words: builders, masons, two fire, two fireproof houses.

Two?

Well, Justin figured Daniel would be marrying Margaret Rose Bell.

Now Margaret Rose Bell was a Washington girl who had come to spend the winter with her cousins, the Edmund Bells. And although it was true that she and Daniel were often seen together, the fact was that she was not yet eighteen years old, and Daniel was still working at Norris & Wiggen. Customarily a man would wait till he was able to buy and furnish a house by himself before he would take a wife.

Yes, but Justin planned to have a great many descendants and he was anxious to get them started.

Land was purchased in Roland Park. Master builders were hired to supervise the construction of two large houses set side by side, with almost no space between them, although great stretches of land lay all about. And meanwhile Margaret Rose was fitted for a complicated ivory satin wedding dress with one hundred and eight pearl buttons running down the back. They were married in the summer. Because the houses were not yet finished Margaret moved into Daniel's boyhood room, where his wooden-wheeled roller skates sat next to his shelf of lawbooks. She was a small, vivid girl who generally wore dresses of soft material like flower petals, and at any moment of the day she could be seen running up and down the stairs, or flinging open windows to watch some excitement in the streets, or darting into Justin's room to see if he needed anything. At the sight of her Justin would begin blinking and nodding in his doddering old man's way, and he would go on nodding and nodding and nodding long after she had kissed the top of his head and left again. Oh, he hadn't been mistaken, Margaret Rose was what this house had needed. And she would be certain to provide descendants. Why, by the fall of 1905, when Justin Peck's golden oak and wine-colored household set off on a caravan of wagons to Roland Park, Margaret Rose was already holding a baby in her lap and expecting another. Things were working out just fine. Everything was going according to plan.

By 1908 they had bought a snorting black Model T Ford with a left-hand steering wheel and splashless flower vases. Each morning the two brothers rode off to work in it—handsome young men in hats and high white collars. Daniel had his own law office now, a walnut-paneled suite of rooms with an oil portrait of his father over the mantel. He was taking on no partners because, he said, he wanted to have his sons for partners, not just anyone. And Caleb had rebuilt his father's warehouse, bigger and better than before. He had a brand new roll-top desk with twice as many cubbyholes.

Whenever Caleb chose to marry, another house would be built beside the first two, but meanwhile he lived at home with his parents. He was a quiet man who became quieter every year. It was a known fact that he drank sometimes, but he never troubled anyone and he never became rowdy or noisy. In fact Margaret Rose said she wished he *would* get noisy, once in a while. She was fond of Caleb. Between them they had a few old jokes, which would cause Margaret to laugh in her low, chuckly way until Caleb, in spite of himself, would let his own mouth turn up shyly at the corners. He would come talk to her in her shady back yard, waiting patiently through all her children's interruptions and requests and minor accidents. And several times she gave evening parties expressly to introduce Caleb to one or another of her pretty cousins. Girls always liked Caleb. But though he might dance with them or take them for a drive, he didn't seem interested in marriage. More often now he stayed home in his room, or he toured the taverns, or he went someplace else, no one knew where. Really, not even Margaret Rose could say for sure what Caleb did with himself.

For Christmas one year, Margaret persuaded Daniel to buy Caleb a Graphophone. She thought it would be the perfect gift for someone so musical. Along with it came disc recordings of Caruso, Arturo Toscanini, and Jan Kubelik on the violin. But these discs affected Caleb the way formal concerts did; he became restless and absent-minded and unhappy. He started pacing across the carpet and up and down the hall and eventually straight through the front door and out of sight, and was not seen again for the remainder of the day. So the Graphophone was never taken up to his bedroom, as Margaret had intended, but drifted into Justin's room instead, where it amused the old man for hours on end. He seemed particularly fond of Caruso. He would order Margaret to stand beside his bed cranking the machine and changing the heavy black discs. Margaret was surprised. If this was the way he felt, why had he forbidden Caleb's music in the house?

For Caleb continued to spend all his money on musical instruments—wooden flutes and harmonicas and cellos and even stringed gourds that only colored people would think of playing. He kept them in his room, but he was not allowed to sound a note on them where Justin could hear. In fact, even the piano was forbidden now, and had been exiled to Daniel's house, where Margaret Rose could tinkle out Czerny without disturbing her father-in-law. If Caleb wanted to make music he had to go far away, usually to the old Samson stable on the other side of a field. He would sit in the loft door blowing whistles or sawing out stringy little street tunes, and only wisps of his music drifted up to the house, never as far as Justin's densely curtained sickroom. Yet Justin always seemed to know when Caleb had been playing, and he would turn his face away irritably when Caleb stopped by later to offer his meticulous, patient account of the previous week's business.

Meanwhile Daniel's house was filling up with children, and his practice was swelling, and he already had it in the back of his mind to become a judge someday while his sons carried on with the law firm. When he came home evenings, and Margaret ran up in her rustling, flowery dress to fling her arms around him, he would be remote and sometimes annoyed. His head was still crowded with torts and claims and statutes. He would set her gently aside and continue toward his study at the rear of the house. So for someone to talk to, Margaret tried giving afternoon tea parties. She invited her cousins and her girlfriends, who came tumbling in crying, "Maggie! Maggie Rose!" and kissing both her cheeks in the new way they had learned from Aunt Alice Bell, who had recently been to Paris. But Daniel said that he was not partial to these affairs. Oh, in the evening maybe, clients or business friends occasionally . . . he didn't want to be unreasonable, he said, but actually he expected his home to be a refuge from the outside world. And nowadays when he came in from a hard day's work he would be sure to find some unknown lady sitting on his leather chair, or a spectacular feather hat on the dining room buffet beneath Sarah Cantleigh's portrait, and once even the brass paperweight moved to the other side of his blotter, when everyone knew that his desk was forbidden territory. Besides, didn't she think she would be better off devoting those hours to her children?

They had six children. In 1905 Justin II was born, in 1906 Sarah, in 1907 Daniel Jr., in 1908 Marcus, in 1909 Laura May, in 1910 Caroline.

In 1911, Margaret Rose left home.

She had wanted to take the children to Washington on the train for her mother's birthday. Daniel didn't think she ought to. After all, she was a Peck now. What did she want with the Bells? Who at any rate were an undisciplined, frivolous, giggling lot. She said she would go anyway. Daniel pointed out that she was her own mistress, certainly, as everyone in his family had noticed more than once, but the children were *his*. And sure enough, there sat Daniel's children in a little bundle staring up at her, all Peck, blue Peck eyes and hair that matched their skin, solemn measuring Peck expressions, not a trace of Margaret Rose. She could go, Daniel said, but she couldn't take the children. And he expected her back on Saturday evening, as there was church to attend Sunday morning.

She went.

Saturday evening Caleb met the train but Margaret was not on it. When Daniel found out he merely pressed his lips together and walked away. Later he was heard telling his mother's servant Sulie to put the children to bed. Apparently no inquiries were going to be made.

On Wednesday Daniel received a letter from Margaret's father. He wrote in brown ink. Everyone knew that ink, because when Margaret's father wrote she would race through the house reading passages to different people and laughing at the funny parts. But Daniel read this letter in silence, and then went up to his room. When he came down again nothing at all was said about it.

In a month the children stopped asking for their mother. The baby stopped crying and the older ones went back to their games and nursery rhymes. Only Caleb seemed to remember Margaret Rose. He went up to Daniel one day and asked him point blank why he didn't go after her. Or Caleb himself would, though Daniel would be better. Daniel looked straight through him. Then Caleb went to Justin, who certainly loved Margaret Rose too and used to wait every day for the fluttering of her petal skirts against the banister. Now Justin merely closed his eyes and pretended not to hear. "But why?" Caleb asked him. "Don't you care? Life is not the same here when Maggie Rose is gone."

In all the accounts of the family history, told by all the aunts and uncles and upstairs maids, that was the only direct quotation of Caleb's that was ever handed down. Two generations later it was to ring in Justine's ears like poetry, taking on more depth and meaning than Caleb had probably intended. But Justin was not moved at all, and he kept his eyes shut very tightly and waited for his son to leave.

Now Laura ran both households, upright and energetic as ever in her ugly brown dresses with her hair screwed back so tightly it stretched her eyes. To the Peck children she was the center of the universe, sometimes the only family member they saw for days. Justin was too old and sick to be bothered, and Daniel hardly ever came home before their bedtime. As for Caleb, he kept to himself. They might catch sight of him striking out across the field toward the Samson stable, the sunlight pale on his Panama hat; or leaving for work in the morning, already tired and beaten-looking; or returning late in the evening with his manner of walking curiously careful. He never played with them. Sometimes on those extra-careful evenings he even got their names confused. He did nothing to earn their attention. So they failed to notice how he appeared to be dimming and wearing through, almost transparent; and how his only friends now were the questionable types in taverns, and how the music from the stable had thinned and shredded until you almost couldn't hear it. Laura noticed. But what could it mean? She pondered over his long, unbreakable silences, the likes of which she had not seen before and would not again until the days of Caleb's great-nephew Duncan, as yet unborn and unthought of. She tried to shame him into more normal behavior. "Where is your common *courtesy?* At least think of the family." But he would only wander off, not hearing, and sometimes he would not reappear for days.

On a Saturday afternoon in the spring of 1912, Daniel was standing at the bay window watching Justin Two ride his bicycle. It was a heavy black iron one, hard for Two to manage, but he had just got the hang of it and he teetered proudly down the driveway. From out of nowhere, Daniel saw a small, clear picture of Caleb on his velocipede merrily pedaling after a flutist on a sidewalk in old Baltimore. The memory was so distinct that he left his house and crossed the yard to his mother's and climbed the stairway to Caleb's room. But Caleb was not there. Nor was he in the kitchen, where he most often ate his meals; nor anywhere else in the house, nor outdoors nor in the stable. And the Ford was parked in the side yard; he wouldn't be downtown. Daniel felt uneasy. He asked the others—the children and Laura. They didn't know. In fact, the last time anyone could remember for sure he had been walking off down the driveway three days earlier, carrying his fiddle. The children saw him go. "Goodbye now," he called to them.

"Goodbye, Uncle Caleb."

But of course that didn't mean a thing, he would surely

have . . . Daniel went to Justin's room. "I can't find Caleb," he said. Justin turned his face away. "Father? I can't—"

A long, glittering tear slid down Justin's stony cheek.

Really, the old man was beginning to let his mind go.

Years later, whenever he was fixing some family event in its proper time slot, Daniel Peck would pause and consider the importance of 1912. Could there be such a thing as an unlucky number? (Justine would look up briefly, but say nothing.) For in 1912 it seemed that the Peck family suddenly cracked and flew apart like an old china teacup. First there was Caleb's disappearance, without a trace except for a bedroom full of hollow, ringing musical instruments and a roll-top desk with an empty whisky bottle in the bottom drawer. So then they had to sell the business, Justin's last link with the outside world. And after that Justin started dying, leaving his family in the same gradual, fading way that Caleb had until it was almost no shock at all to find him lifeless in his bed one morning with his bluish nose pointing heavenward.

In the winter of 1912 there was another envelope from Washington addressed in brown ink. After Daniel read it, he told his children that Margaret Rose had been killed in a fire. They were to pray for her to be forgiven. Now her children wore brown to school and could properly be called poor motherless orphans, although they continued to look surprised whenever some well-meaning lady told them so. They were calm, docile children, a little lacking in imagination but they did well in their lessons. They did not seem to have suffered from all that had happened. Nor did Laura, who continued as spry and capable as ever. Nor Daniel, of course—a man of even temper. Although sometimes, late at night, he would take the Ford and drive aimlessly over the moonlit roads, often ending up in the old section of the city where he had no business any more, and knew no one, and heard nothing but the faint, musical whistling of the streetcar wires in the dark sky overhead.

5

JUSTINE'S CHILDHOOD was dark and velvety and it smelled of dust. There were bearded men under all the furniture, particularly her bed. When her door was shut at night blue worms squiggled through the blackness, but when it was open the knob stuck out exactly like a shotgun barrel sidling through to aim at her head, and she would have to lie motionless for hours pretending to be a wrinkle in the blankets.

In the mornings her father was away, either at the office or out of town, and her mother was in bed with a sick headache, and Justine sat in the living room with the curtains shut so that even to herself she was only a pale glimmer. She was waiting for the maid. First there was the scrabbling of the key in the apartment door and then light, air, motion, the rustle of Claudia's shopping bag and her thin cross mosquito voice. "Now what you doing sitting there? What you up to? What you doing sitting in that chair?" She would yank the curtains open and there was the city of Philadelphia, a wide expanse of blackened brick apartment houses and dying trees in cages and distant factory smokestacks. Then she would dress Justine in a little smocked dress and braid the two skinny braids that she called plaits. "Don't you *go* getting that dress dirty. Don't you *go* messing yourself up, I'll tell Miss Caroline on you." By that time maybe her mother's headache would be lifting, at least enough so that her parched voice could trail out from the bedroom. "Justine? Aren't you even going to say good morning?" Although not an hour ago she had buried her face in the pillow and waved Justine away with one shaky, pearl-studded hand.

Justine's mother wore fluffy nightgowns with eyelet ruffles at the neck. Her hair was the color of Justine's but tightly curled. She was the youngest of Daniel Peck's six children, the baby. Even total strangers could guess that, somehow, from her small, pursed mouth and her habit of ducking her chin when talking to people. Unfortunately she tended to put on weight when unhappy, and she had become a plump, powdery, pouchy woman with her rings permanently embedded in her fingers. Her unhappiness was due to being exiled in Philadelphia. She had never guessed, when agreeing to marry Sam Mayhew, that the Depression would close down the Baltimore branch of his company just six months after the wedding. If she had had any inkling, she said—but she didn't finish the sentence. She just reached for another chocolate, or a petit-four, or one of the pink-frosted cupcakes she grew more and more to resemble.

But Justine loved her mother's soft skin and her puffy bosom and the dimples on the backs of her hands. She liked to huddle beneath the drooping velvet canopy of the bed, which was her mother's real home, surrounded by a circle of chocolate boxes, empty teacups, ladies' magazines, and cream-colored letters from Baltimore. Of course there were days when her mother was up and about, but Justine pictured her only in the dim rosy glow of the bedside lamp. She dwelt on the suspense of entering that room: was she welcome this time, or wasn't she? Some days her mother said, "Oh Justine, can't you let me be?" or wept into her pillow and wouldn't speak at all; but other days she called, "Is that my Justine? Is that my fairy angel? Don't you have one tiny kiss for your poor mama?" And she would sit up and scoop Justine into a spongy, perfumed embrace, depriving her of breathing room for a moment, not that it mattered. Then she flung back the ruffled pink sleeves of her bedjacket and taught Justine the games she had played when *she* was a child—cat's cradle and Miss Fancy's Come to Town and the doodle story, where you drew a map that turned out to be a goose. Or she would have Justine fetch scissors and she would cut, from the Baltimore newspapers, folded stars and paper dolls with pigtails and standing angels made from a circle cleverly slashed here and there as only she knew how. She would tell true stories, better than anything in books: How Uncle Two Scared the Hobo Away, How Grandfather Peck Fooled the Burglar, How the Mayhews' Ugly Dog Buttons Ate My Wedding Dress. She told how Justine was born in Baltimore thanks to split-second timing and not in Philadelphia as everyone had feared. "Well, luckily I had my way," she said. "You know how your daddy is. He didn't understand at all. When you started coming two months early I said, 'Sam, put me on that train,' but he wouldn't do it. I said, 'Sam, what will Father say, he's made all the arrangements at Johns Hopkins!' 'I just hope he didn't lay down a deposit,' your daddy said. So I picked up my suitcase that I had all ready and waiting and I said, 'Listen here, Sam Mayhew . . .' "

At six in the evening Claudia would leave, slamming the door behind her, and Justine's mother would look at the clock and her fingers would fly to her mouth. "How in the world did the time pass?" she would ask, and she would slide to the edge of the bed and feel for her pink satin slippers. "We can't let your daddy catch us lazing about like this." She would put on a navy blue dress with shoulder pads, and cover her rosebud mouth with dark lipstick, turning instantly from pink-and-gold to a heavy, crisply defined stranger like the ones hurrying down the sidewalk five stories below. "Of course my headache hasn't improved one bit," she would say. "I'd go back to bed but your daddy would never understand. He doesn't believe in headaches. He *certainly* doesn't believe in going to bed for them. It just is not his custom, I suppose."

To hear her talk, you would think Sam Mayhew was as different and exotic as an Asian prince, but he was only a small pudgy man with a Baltimore accent.

Then there were days in a row when Justine was not allowed in her mother's room at all, when she would puzzle and puzzle over what magic password had given her entry before. No one could go in but Claudia, carrying the latest string-tied box from the Parisian Pastry Co. Justine was marooned on a scratchy brocade chair in the living room and the bearded men beneath it were only waiting for her to lower one foot so that they could snatch her by the ankle and drag her down. Even Sam Mayhew's homecoming could not rouse his wife from bed. "Oh, go away, Sam, let me be, can't you see a crack is running down in front of my ears?" Sam and Justine ate supper alone, on the gold-rimmed plates that Claudia had laid out in the dining room. "Well, now, Justine, what have you been doing with yourself?" Sam would ask. "Did Claudia take you to the playground? Did you have a nice time on the swings?"

But he would quickly flounder and drown in her blank, astonished stare.

Day after day Justine on her brocade island looked at her mother's old *Books of Knowledge*—tattered maroon volumes with brittle pages, the only things she could reach without setting a foot to the floor. She lost herself in a picture of a train heading through outer space. It had been explained to her that this picture demonstrated the impossibility of man's ever reaching the moon. See how long it would take to cover the distance, even by rail? But to Justine it appeared all too easy, and she felt herself lightening and dwindling and growing dizzy whenever she saw that tiny lone train curving through the endless blackness.

Finally a time would come when she could raise her eyes from a page and find the air parting expectantly to make way for some change; she could always tell when change was coming. And not long afterward the telephone would ring, and Claudia would carry it from the foyer to the bedroom and rouse Justine's mother to shout long distance to Baltimore. "Hello? Oh, Father! Why are you—did Sam tell you to call me? What? Oh, not too well, I'm afraid. I said, not too *well*. Everything just seems to be going wrong, I can't quite . . ."

Justine would listen carefully, trying to discover exactly what had caused her world to collapse. She heard that her mother's nerves were acting up, her headaches were ferocious and no doctor could do a thing, the chandelier had fallen smack out of the ceiling, the landlord was impossible, Claudia showed no respect, there had been a very depressing story in the paper Sunday, Justine was turning sulky, Sam was out of town too much, and really it was entirely the fault of the City of Philadelphia. If he had any feeling, if he cared even a little, she knew it was asking a lot but she wished he would come and straighten things out.

He always came. She was his youngest daughter after all and very far from home, the only one of his children to leave the safety of Roland Park. Which was not to say that he approved of her. Oh, no. As soon as he stepped in the door, late that very night, he was curling his mouth downwards at the welter of pastry boxes and her crumb-littered, used-looking bed, and he was telling her outright that she had grown too fat.

"Yes, Father," Caroline said meekly, and she sat a little straighter and sucked in her stomach.

The next morning, when Justine got up unusually late after an unusually calm, dreamless sleep, she would find the apartment bright with sun and all the curtains open. Claudia was wearing a crisp white scarf and briskly attacking the dust in the cushions. Her mother sat in the dining room fully dressed, eating fresh grapefruit. And in the foyer her grandfather stood at the telephone announcing that he, Judge Peck, would personally drag the landlord through the entire United States judiciary system if that chandelier were not replaced by twelve noon sharp. Then he hung up and cupped Justine's head with his right hand, which was his way of greeting her. He was a bony man in a three-piece pinstriped suit, with fading hair like aged gardenia petals and a gold wafer of a watch that he let her wind. He had brought her a sack of horehound drops. He always did. Justine was certain that no matter what, even if he had rushed here through fires and floods and train wrecks, he would not forget to stop at Lexington Market first for a sack of horehound drops and he would not fail to cup her head in that considering way of his when he had arrived.

Generally during those visits Sam Mayhew would vanish, or if he did come home he wore a gentle, foolish smile and tried to keep out of the way. At any rate, the grandfather was never there for very long. He was a busy man. He came up over the weekend usually, just long enough to get his daughter to her feet again, and he left Sunday evening. Only once did he come on a working day. That was for Justine. She was supposed to be starting kindergarten, the first time she would ever be away from home alone. She refused to go. She wouldn't even get dressed. She became very white and sharp-faced and her mother gave in, sensing that there was no use arguing with her. The next morning when Justine awoke her grandfather Peck was standing by her bed carrying her plaid dress, her ruffled underpants with "Tuesday" embroidered on them and her lace-edged socks. He dressed her very slowly and carefully. Justine would have refused even her grandfather but his hands were so thick and clumsy, untying the bow of her nightgown, and when he stooped to pick up her shoes she could see the pink scalp through his thin pale hair. He even did her braids, though not very well. He even sat across from her and waited with perfect patience while she dawdled over breakfast. Then he helped her with her coat and they left, passing her mother, who wrung her hands in the doorway. They went down streets that were bitterly familiar, where she had shopped with her mother in the dear, safe days before school was ever thought of. At a square brick building her grandfather stopped. He pointed out where Claudia would meet her in the afternoon. He cupped her head briefly and then, after some fumbling and rustling, pushed a sack of horehound drops at her and gave her a little nudge in the direction of the brick building. When she had climbed the steps she looked back and found him still waiting there, squinting against the sunlight. Forever after that, the dark, homely, virtuous taste of horehound drops reminded her of the love and sorrow that ached in the back of her throat on that first day in the outside world.

In summer the leather suitcases would come up in the elevator to be packed, and Justine and her parents would board the evening train to Baltimore. Their arrival was never clear to Justine. She was half asleep, carried off the train and laid in the arms of some white-suited uncle. But when she awoke the next day there she was in Roland Park, all rustling with trees and twittering with birds, in her great-grandmother's white brick house, and if she went to the window she knew that all the houses within her view belonged to Pecks and so did the fleet of shiny black V-8 Fords lining one side of the street, and all the little blond heads dotting the lawn were Peck cousins waiting for her to come out and play.

Her mother would be talking in the dining room, but such a different mother—twinkling and dimpling and telling terrible giggling stories about Philadelphia. Aunts would be grouped around her, drinking their fifth and sixth cups of coffee. Aunt Sarah and Aunt Laura May were spinsters and still lived next door in the grandfather's house along with the bachelor Uncle Dan. Uncle Two's wife Lucy and Uncle Mark's wife Bea were Pecks by marriage only, and lived in the other two houses. They were not as important as the true Peck aunts, but then they *were* the mothers of the cousins. And of course, presiding over everyone was the great-grandma, a tidy, brownish woman. The white rims showing beneath her irises gave her a look of reproach, but as soon as she saw Justine she smiled and the rims disappeared. She offered Justine an enormous Baltimore breakfast—two kinds of meat, three kinds of pastry, and a platter of scrambled eggs —but Justine wasn't hungry. "Naturally," her mother said, laughing her summer laugh, "she's anxious to see her cousins," and she tied Justine's sash and gave her a pat and sent her off.

Justine had six cousins. All of them looked like her and talked like her, all of them knew the story of how Grandfather Peck had fooled the burglar. It was very different from Philadelphia, where her mother, coming to the school play, referred to "that *dark* little boy" and asked, "Who was the child who spoke with such a nasal twang?" With her cousins, there was no need to worry. Baltimore was the only place on earth where Justine would not be going over to the enemy if she agreed to play Prisoner's Base.

Yet even here, wasn't she an outsider of sorts? Her last name was Mayhew. She lived in Philadelphia. She did not always understand her cousins' jokes. And though they drew her into every game, she had the feeling that they were trying to slow down for her in some way. She envied them their quick, bubbling laughter and their golden tans. Occasionally, for one split second, she allowed herself to imagine her parents painlessly dead and some uncle or other adopting her, changing her name to Peck and taking her to live forever in Roland Park with its deep curly shadows and its pools of sunlight.

At such times Aunt Bea, coming out to the front porch to shade her eyes and check the children, would smile and sigh over poor little plain Justine, whose pointed face was wisped with anxiety so that it looked like crazed china or something cobwebbed or netted. And who ran so artificially, so hopefully, at the edge of the other children's games, kicking her heels up too high behind her.

In the evening they all went home. The four houses gave the illusion of belonging to four separate families. But after supper they came out again and sat on Great-Grandma's lawn, the men in their shirtsleeves and the women in fresh print dresses. The children grew overexcited rolling down the slope together. They quarreled and were threatened with an early bedtime, and finally they had to come sit with the grownups until they had calmed down. Sweaty and panting, choking back giggles, itchy from the grass blades that stuck to their skin, they dropped to the ground beside their parents and looked up at the stars while low measured voices murmured all around them. The oldest cousin, Uncle Mark's daughter Esther, held her little brother Richard on her lap and tickled him secretly with a dandelion clock. Nearby, Esther's twin sisters, Alice and Sally, were curled together like puppies with Justine in the middle because she was new and special. And Uncle Two's boys, Claude and Duncan, wrestled without a sound and without a perceptible movement so they wouldn't be caught and sent to bed. Not that the grownups really cared. They were piecing together some memory now, each contributing his own little patch and then sitting back to see how it would turn out. Long after the children had grown calm and loose and dropped off to sleep, one by one, the grownups were still weaving family history in the darkness.

In the winter of 1942, when Justine was nine, her father left for the war. The apartment was dismantled, a moving van came, and Justine and her mother took the train to Baltimore. Her mother cried all the way down. When they arrived she spilled out of the train and into her sisters' arms, still weeping, with her curls plastered to her face and her nose as pink as a rabbit's. Her sisters looked flustered and kept searching their purses for fresh hankies. The situation was new to them; no Peck had ever gone to war. It was believed that old Justin had mysteriously avoided the Civil War altogether, while every member of the family after him had possessed a heart murmur of such obviousness that they had been excused from even the mildest sports, the women cautioned against childbirth and the men saved from combat and long marches and the violence of travel by the unique, hollow stutter in their chests. Which did not prevent them from standing in a semicircle, bright-eyed and healthy and embarrassed, around their baby sister in the railroad station. It was their father who finally took charge. "Come, come," he said, and he herded them out of the station and into the line of Fords at the curb. Justine and her mother rode in his car, at the head of the procession. Justine's mother kept sniffing. Nothing irritated Grandfather Peck more than the sound of someone sniffing. "Look here, Caroline. We people don't *cry*. Get a hold of yourself," he said.

"I can't help it, Father. I just can't help it. I keep thinking of ways I could have been nicer to him. I mean I was never exactly—and I'm just certain he's going to be killed."

"He won't be killed," said Justine.

But nobody was listening.

They settled in Great-Grandma's house, since it had the most room. Justine was entered in the girls' school that Esther and the twins attended. Bit by bit she forgot almost completely the dark, bearded world of Philadelphia, and her mother grew carefree and girlish. Her mother seldom mentioned Sam Mayhew any more but she wrote him dutifully once a week, saying everyone was fine and sent him best regards. Only Justine, looking up sometimes from *The Five Little Peppers* or a game of backgammon, had a sudden picture of Sam Mayhew's sad, kind face and wondered if she had not missed out on something, choosing to be her mother's child alone.

Yet there were her cousins, always embarked on some new

project. Esther wrote plays and her twin sisters shared a single role, speaking in unison. Justine played the princess in Aunt Laura May's blood-red lipstick. Little Richard would take any part you gave him, he was so happy to be included. And Uncle Two's son Claude was fat and studious; he was fine for rainy days, when he told horror stories in a hair-raising whisper in the gloom of the pantry stairwell.

But Duncan Peck was an evil, evil boy, and all his cousins worshipped him.

Duncan was prankish and reckless and wild. He had a habit of disappearing. (Long after she was grown, Justine could still close her eyes and hear his mother calling him—a soft-voiced lady from southern Virginia but my, couldn't she sing out when she had to! "Dun-KUNN? Dun-KUNN?" floated across the twilit lawn, with no more response than a mysterious rustle far away or a gleam of yellow behind the trees, rapidly departing.) While the rest of the cousins seemed content to have only one another for friends, Duncan was always dragging in strangers and the wrong kind of strangers at that, ten-year-old boys with tobacco breath and BB guns and very poor grammar. His cousins took piano lessons and hammered out "Country Gardens" faithfully for one half hour a day, but all Duncan would play was a dented Hohner harmonica—"Chattanooga Choo Choo" complete with whistles and a chucka-chucka and a country-sounding twang that delighted the children and made the grownups flinch. His great-grandma complained that he was impudent and dishonest. It was perfectly obvious that he was lying to any adult who asked him a question, and his lies were extreme, an insult to the intelligence. Also he was accident-prone. To his cousins that was the best part of all. How did he find so many accidents to get into? And such gory ones! He never just broke a bone, no, he had to have the bone sticking *out*, and all his cousins crowding around making sick noises and asking if they could touch it. He was always having a finger dangle by one thread, a concussion that allowed him to talk strangely and draw absolutely perfect freehand circles for one entire day, a purple eye or an artery opened or a tooth knocked horizontal and turning black. And on top of all that, he was never at a loss for something to do. You would never see *him* lolling about the house asking his mother for ideas; he had his own ideas, none of which she approved of. His mind was a flash of light. He knew how to make the electric fan drive Richard's little tin car, he could build traps for animals of all kinds including humans, he had invented a dive-proof kite and a written code that looked like nothing but slants and uprights. Tangled designs for every kind of machine littered his bedroom floor, and he had all those cousins just doting on him and anxious to do the manual labor required. If he had been a cruel boy, or a bully, they never would have felt that way, but he wasn't. At least not to them. It was the grownups he was cruel to.

Justine once saw him hanging from a tree limb, upside down, when the family was out on a picnic. He was safe but Aunt Lucy fretted anyway. "Dun-KUNN? I want you down from there!" she called. All Duncan did was unwrap one leg from the limb. Now he hung precariously, at an impossible angle, with his arms folded. Aunt Lucy rose and began running in ridiculous circles just beneath him, holding out her hands. Duncan grabbed the limb again—was he going to give in? What a disappointment!—but no, he was only readjusting himself so that now he could hang by his feet. All that supported him were his insteps, and it was not the kind of limb you could do that from. He folded his arms again and looked at his mother with a cool, taunting, upside-down stare that gave Justine a sudden chill. Yet wasn't Aunt Lucy laughable—flitting here and there crying, "Oh! Oh!" in a rusty scream. All the cousins had to giggle. Their grandfather set down his deviled egg and rose. "Duncan Peck!" he shouted. "Come down here this *instant!*"

Duncan came down on the top of his head and had to go to the emergency room.

Aunt Lucy, knitting soldiers' socks with her sisters-in-law, wondered and wondered what had made her son turn out this way. She considered all his flaws of character, his disgraceful report cards and the teachers' complaints. (He couldn't spell worth beans, they said, and had never learned that neatness counted. As for his papers, while there was no denying that they were ah, imaginative, at least what parts were readable, his hasty scrawl and his lack of organization and his wild swooping digressions left serious doubts as to his mental stability.) Now, where did all that come from? She reflected on her pregnancy: during her afternoon naps, she and the unborn Duncan had had, why, *battles!* for a comfortable position. Whenever she lay on her back, so the baby rested on the knobs of her spine, he would kick and protest until she gave in and shifted to her side. Of course she had only Claude to compare him with, but she had wondered even at the time: wouldn't the average baby merely have moved to a more comfortable position and let her rest?

The sisters sighed and shook their heads. The cousins, who had been eavesdropping in a row beneath the window, were very interested in pregnancy, but Duncan had a plan to weld all their bicycles together in a gigantic tandem and they couldn't stay to hear more.

When Sam Mayhew returned, his manufacturing company had reopened its Baltimore offices. There was no need to move back to Philadelphia. There was no need even to buy a place of their own, as his wife pointed out. Why bother, when Great-Grandma had three full stories in which she rattled around with no one but old Sulie the maid for company? So they stayed on in the white brick house in Roland Park, and Sam Mayhew rode downtown every day in a V-8 Ford behind his brothers-in-law. The Ford was a homecoming gift from the grandfather, who always had owned Fords and always would. To tell the truth, Sam Mayhew would have preferred a DeSoto. And he would have liked to buy a house in Guilford, which was where his parents lived. Somehow he never got to see his parents any more. But he was not a stubborn man and in the end he agreed to everything, only fading more and more into the background and working longer and longer hours. Once he took a three-day business trip and when he came home, only Sulie noticed he had been away. And *that* was because she had to count out the place settings for dinner every night.

His daughter, Justine, who had been undersized and pathetic when he left, was now a tall narrow beige girl. She had changed into one of those damned Pecks, clannish and secretive with a veiled look in her eyes, some sort of private amusement showing when she watched an outsider. And Sam was an outsider. Not that she was *rude* to him. All the Peck girls had excellent manners. But he knew that he had lost her, all right.

"What do those damned kids do all day? Don't they have any outside friends?" he asked his wife.

"Oh, they're all right. *We* were that way," she said serenely.

And she smiled out across the lawn at her brittle spinster sisters and her stuffy brothers who were all dressed alike, all lawyers as their father had wished them to be, and at the two wives who might have been chosen merely for their ability to be assimilated. Who *were* chosen for that. He looked down suddenly at his own colorless suit, so baggy that it seemed to be uninhabited. Then he sighed and walked away. Nobody noticed him leaving.

None of the girl cousins dated much in high school. At the mixers that were held with the boys' school up the road they were thought to be standoffish. Especially Justine, whose tense, pinched face stopped most of the boys from asking her to dance. Sometimes Sally, the prettier of the twins, might circle the floor with someone, but she tipped her pelvis away stiffly and seemed relieved when the music was over. As for the boy cousins, only Duncan had a steady girlfriend.

Duncan's girlfriend was a dimestore clerk named Glorietta de Merino. In an age when nice girls wore short skirts, Glorietta's swirled just above her ankles. She had a tumbling waterfall of black hair and a beautiful vivid face. There appeared to be sugar crystals on her eyelashes. Her waist was tiny and her breasts precisely cone-shaped, like the radio speakers Duncan was constructing in his basement. Anyone who talked to her appeared to be talking into the speakers—Grandfather Peck included, as Justine noticed when Glorietta came for Sunday dinner. Duncan was the only one who enjoyed that dinner. Even Glorietta must have suspected that things were not going exactly right. For afterwards, she never was seen in any Peck house again. Instead she took up residence in Duncan's car, a forty-dollar 1933 Graham Paige that smelled suspiciously of beer. Whenever the Graham Paige was parked outside, a green blemish in the row of Fords, you could glimpse a flash of Glorietta's red dress through the window. When Duncan taught Justine to drive, Glorietta rode in the back like a lap robe or a Thermos bottle, part of the car. She hummed and popped her chewing gum, ignoring the shrieking gears and the quarrels and near accidents. Later, when Justine had learned the rudiments of driving, Duncan sat in the back as well. Justine could look in the rear view mirror and see his arm cocked carelessly around Glorietta's neck, his face peaceful as he watched the passing scenery. She did not think *she* could ever be so relaxed with someone outside the family.

Once for a school bazaar Justine was asked to run the fortune-telling booth, which she knew nothing about. A very peculiar old biology teacher sent her to a seeress named Olita. "She is *my* fortune teller," she said, as if everyone should have one, "and she'll teach you enough to get by." Duncan and Glorietta drove Justine to a cleaner's in east Baltimore and parked to wait for her. Olita had a room upstairs, behind a plate glass window reading MADAME OLITA, YOUR DESTINY DISCOVERED. Justine began to think this wasn't such a good idea. She turned back toward the car, planning to tell Duncan she had changed her mind, but she found that Duncan was looking squarely at her, half smiling, with a spark in his eyes. It reminded her of the time he had hung from the tree limb. She went on up the stairs.

Madame Olita was a large, sloping woman with a stubby gray haircut, wearing a grandmotherly dress and a cardigan. Her room, which was bare except for two stools and a table, smelled of steam from the cleaner's. Since the biology teacher had called ahead, she already knew what Justine wanted. She had written out a list of things to tell people. "Palms will be simplest," she said. "Palms take much less time than cards, and for a bazaar that's all that counts. Just sound sure of yourself. Take their hands, like so." She reached for Justine's hand and turned it upward, smartly. "Start with the—you could be telling fortunes yourself, if you wanted," she said.

"But I will be," said Justine.

"I mean *seriously* telling fortunes. You have the knack."

"Oh," said Justine. "Well, I don't think I—"

"Do you ever have flashes when you know something is going to happen?"

"No! Really," said Justine. She pulled her hand away.

"All right, all right. Here's the list, then, of the major lines of the palm. Life, mind, heart, fate . . ."

But later, when she had heaved herself up to see Justine to the door, she said, "This is really not a parlor game, you realize."

"No, I'm sure it isn't," Justine said politely.

"*You* know it isn't."

Justine couldn't think what was expected of her. She went on buttoning her coat. Madame Olita leaned forward and jabbed the back of Justine's left hand with one stubby finger. "You have a curved ring of Solomon, a solid line of intuition, and a mystic cross," she said.

"I do?"

"Even one of those denotes a superior fortune teller."

Justine straightened her hat.

"I have a mystic cross too," said Madame Olita, "but I've never found one on anybody else. They are very rare. May I see your right palm, please?"

Justine held it out, unwillingly. Madame Olita's hands felt like warm sandpaper.

"Well?" Justine said finally.

"You are very young," Madame Olita told her.

Justine opened the door to go.

"But you're going to enter into a marriage that will disrupt everything and break your parents' hearts," said Madame Olita, and when Justine spun around Madame Olita gave her a small, yellow smile and lifted a hand in farewell.

Out in the car, Duncan and Glorietta were kissing in broad daylight. "Stop that," Justine said irritably, and Duncan broke away and looked up at her, surprised.

Justine wondered if some aura of Duncan's had rubbed off on her, so that Madame Olita had told the wrong person's fortune.

In the church hall after the sermon one Sunday a boy named Neely Carpenter asked Justine what time it was. "It's approximately twelve thirteen and a half," she told him.

"*Approximately* twelve thirteen and a *half?*"

"My watch says that, you see, but my watch is a little off," said Justine. "It's logical, really." She started laughing. Neely Carpenter, who had always thought of her as a spinster-faced girl, looked surprised for a moment and then asked if she would like a ride home from church.

After that he gave her a ride every Sunday, and he took her to the movies every Saturday night. Justine's mother said she thought that was very sweet. It was the fall of Justine's senior year, after all; she was seventeen. It was about time she had a steady boyfriend. And Neely was a doctor's son recently moved to Roland Park, a serious-looking boy with very straight black hair and excellent manners. "Why don't you invite this Neely boy for Sunday dinner?" Justine's mother asked her.

Sunday dinner was always held at Great-Grandma's house, with four leaves extending the table so that everyone could sit around it. Neely looked a little stunned when he saw how many Pecks there were, but he found a seat between Aunt Sarah and Uncle Dan and did his best to keep his place in the conversation. "Yes, ma'am. No, ma'am," he kept saying. Justine thought he was doing fine. She was proud of her family, too—her aunts in their new rust-colored fall outfits, her handsome cousins, her stately grandfather with his hair turned silvery white and his face puzzled-looking from the effort he had started having to make in order to hear. So she was surprised when later, after Neely had gone home, Duncan said, "You'll never see *him* again."

They were out on Great-Grandma's lawn, where Justine had gone to see Neely off and where Duncan, up to some project or other, was unrolling a gigantic reel of baling wire across the grass. When he raised his head to speak to her Justine was struck by his expression, which was almost the same as his grandfather's. "Why do you say that?" she asked him.

"Nobody takes Sunday dinner with the Pecks and comes back for more."

"Well! Just because *Glorietta!* And besides, you're wrong. He's already asked me to Sue Pope's birthday dance."

"Then he's a fool," said Duncan. "No, I don't mean because of you, Justine. I mean, who would willingly mix with that crowd in the dining room?"

"I would," said Justine. "I thought they were very nice to him."

"Ah, yes! 'Ask if your little friend there would like another potato, Justine.' Little friend! And, 'Tell me, is it true that you go to public school? How *are* the public schools?' And, 'I understand your father is a doctor, um, Reilly. How nice! It's a very rewarding profession, I hear, though a little—mechanical, don't you think? *We* are all lawyers, I suppose you know—' "

"What's wrong with that? They were only showing an interest," Justine said.

"Ho! And then when he asked Great-Grandma if he could help to clear the dishes. *Then* he got it *twice!* 'Oh, my, no, we have a servant, dear.' And, 'Besides,' Aunt Caroline says, 'it's the very best china.' "

"Well?" said Justine. "We do have a servant. And it was the best china."

Duncan stopped unreeling the baling wire. He straightened up and wiped his face on his sleeve. "You really don't see it, do you," he said.

But Justine wouldn't answer. She folded her arms against an autumn wind and looked instead at the four brick houses behind them, where everybody was getting comfortable now with newspapers and needlework and cups of spiced tea. "You know what those houses remind me of?" Duncan said, following her gaze. "Hamsters. Or baby mice, or gerbils. Any of those little animals that cluster in one corner piled on top of each other even when they have a great big cage they are free to spread out in."

"Oh, Duncan," Justine said.

She knew he only talked that way because he was going through a difficult time. Next year he would enter college and he wanted to go to Hopkins instead of the University and study science instead of law. But Grandfather Peck and the uncles kept arguing with him, nagging, pushing him. Of course he could study science, it was a free country, they said, but all the same there was something so *materialistic* about science, whereas law . . . "Peck, Peck, Peck & Peck," said Duncan, referring to the family firm, which was actually called Peck & Sons. "What a perfect name for them." And he would shut himself away in his room, or go riding aimlessly with Glorietta so close beside him that if the Graham Paige were a matchbox (which it almost appeared to be) they would have tipped over long ago.

So Justine didn't worry when he spoke so bitterly. And sure enough, Neely kept on asking her out. He never came to Sunday dinner again but that was because he really had to eat with his *own* family, he said. He did take her to movies and dances and birthday parties. He drove her home the long way around and parked some distance from the Pecks' in order to kiss her good night. He asked if she would like to move to the back seat where they would be more comfortable. "Oh well, oh no—" said Justine, uncertain of the proper answer. She really didn't know what she was supposed to do in this situation. None of her girl cousins could help her, either. All they knew about sex was what Duncan had told them when he was eight; that and the vague, horticultural-sounding information their mothers had given out. So Justine would flutter and debate with herself, but she always ended up saying, "Well actually I'm very comfortable where I am but thank you just the—" Neely, who might have been uncertain too, would look almost relieved. Going home he hummed along with "Good Night, Irene" on the radio. He was starting to talk about their getting married someday, after he was through with medical school. Justine thought he was the best-looking boy in Roland Park and she liked his eyes, which were gray and translucent like quartz, and his quiet, level way of speaking. It was possible that she might even love him, but she didn't know what her mother would say.

By the fall of 1951, Justine had started attending a girls' junior college nearby. She thought she would do English or pre-school education or something. It didn't much matter. Although she had always been a fair student she didn't have any real curiosity and she couldn't think of any career she wanted to aim for. So she and Esther drifted off to college every day in the Ford their grandfather had bought them for commuting, their bright kerchiefs flickering and their hair whipping in the wind. Almost every evening Neely would come over (he was at Hopkins now) to study in the dining room with her. And there were still the Sunday dinners, the cousins alternating with grownups around the table to discourage mischief, and Claude's round face shining with the relief of being home from the University even if just for a day.

But Duncan!

Something came over Duncan that year. No one could quite put a finger on it. He had what he wanted, didn't he? He was studying science at Hopkins, wasn't he? Yet it seemed sometimes that he was more dissatisfied than ever, almost as if he regretted winning. He complained about living at home, which he had to do because Hopkins was so expensive. He said the expense was an excuse; this was just the family's way of punishing him. Punishing! To live at home with your own close family? He was morose and difficult to talk to. He did not appear to have any friends at all, at least none that he would introduce, and Glorietta was no longer to be seen. Well, of course he had always been somewhat of a problem. Surely this was just another of his stages, the aunts told his mother.

But then he started reading Dostoevsky.

Naturally they had all read Dostoevsky—or at least the uncles had, in college. Or *Crime and Punishment*, at any rate. At least in the abridged edition. But this was different. Duncan didn't just *read* Dostoevsky; he sank in, he buried himself in Dostoevsky, he stopped attending classes entirely and stayed in his room devouring obscure novels and diaries none of the rest of the family had heard of. On a soft spring evening, in the midst of a peaceful discussion on the merits of buying a home freezer, Uncle Two's branch of the family might be startled by the crash of enormous footsteps down the stairs and Duncan's wild, wiry figure exploding into the living room to wave a book at them. "Listen! Listen!" and he would read out some passage too loudly and too quickly for them to follow. A jumble of extravagant Russian prose, where emotions were stated outright in a surprising way and a great many extreme adjectives were used and feverish fancies kept darting and flashing. Paragraphs were layered and dense and complicated like chunks of mica. "Did you *hear?*" he shouted. His parents nodded and smiled, their embarrassed expressions giving them the look of sleepers dazzled by bright light. "*Well* then!" he would say, and off he spun, up the stairs. His parents stared at each other. His father went to talk to the grandfather, who understood it no better. "But I thought he was scientific!" he said. "What is he reading for?" And then, "Ah well, never mind. At least it's the classics, they surely can't hurt him."

But that was before Easter Sunday. On Easter Sunday, at the dinner table, the aunts were discussing Mrs. Norman Worth's extensive collection of eggshell miniatures. The uncles were arguing the details of a hypothetical legal problem: If a farmer, while turning on the water to irrigate the fields, accidentally startled another farmer's mule, which, in turn, kicked down the fence enclosing a prize-winning Angus bull, who thereupon . . .

"Neither of these subjects is fit table conversation," Duncan said.

Everybody thought about that for a minute.

"But what's wrong with them, dear?" his mother said finally.

"They're not real."

Great-Grandma, who had lived longest and was hardest to

shock, poured more ice water into her tumbler. "To you they may *not* be," she said, "but I myself find eggshell miniatures fascinating and if I didn't have this tremor I would take them up myself."

"You owe us an apology, Duncan boy," said Uncle Two.

"You owe *me* an apology," said Duncan. "I've spent eighteen years here growing deader and deader, listening to you skate across the surface. Watching you dodge around what matters like painting blue sea around boats, with white spaces left for safety's sake—"

"*What?*"

"Can't you say something that *means* something?" Duncan asked.

"About what?" said his mother.

"I don't care. Anything. Anything but featherstitch and the statute of limitations. Don't you want to get to the bottom of things? Talk about whether there's a God or not."

"But we already know," said his mother.

What was so terrible about that? None of them could see it. But Duncan stood up, as wild-eyed as any Russian, and said, "I'm leaving. I'm going for good."

He slammed out of the dining room. Justine jumped up to follow him, but then she stopped in the doorway, undecided. "*He'll* be back," Uncle Two said comfortably. "It's only growing pains. Ten years from now he'll talk the same as all the rest of us."

"Go after him," the grandfather said.

"What, Father?"

"Well, don't just—*somebody* go. You go, Justine. Go after him, hurry."

Justine went. She flew out the front of Great-Grandma's house and paused, thinking she had already lost him, but then she saw him just coming from Uncle Two's with a cardboard box. He crossed the lawn and heaved the box into the back seat of the Graham Paige. Then he climbed in himself. "Duncan! Wait!" Justine called.

Surprisingly, he waited. She ran up out of breath, clutching her dinner napkin. "Where are you going?" she asked him.

"I'm moving."

"You are?"

She looked at the back seat. It was like him to leave his clothes behind and take his box of tools and scrap metal.

"But Duncan," she said, "what are we going to do without you?"

"You'll manage."

"What if we need you for something? Where will we find you?"

By now other members of the family were straggling onto Great-Grandma's porch. She could tell by the look he flashed over her shoulder. "Bye, Justine," he said. "I've already got a place, beside that bookstore on St. Paul, but don't tell the others."

"But *Duncan*—"

"Bye, Justine."

"Bye, Duncan."

At first the family assumed he would be home in no time. It was only his age. Everybody eighteen expected deep things of people, but it never *lasted*. Yet the days stretched on and there was no word of him. They began to question Justine more closely. "He's all right, he's got a place to stay," was what she had said earlier, but now that wasn't enough. Had he told her where? Because this was not some childhood game any more, surely she was mature enough to realize that. Wasn't she?

But she had promised Duncan.

Aunt Lucy said Justine was cruel and selfish. Justine's mother said there was no call for *that* sort of talk, and then Aunt Lucy broke down and cried. "Now look here. Get a hold of yourself," the grandfather said, which made her turn on him. Why couldn't a person let loose a little, after all? Where was the sin? How come a forty-four-year-old woman didn't have a right to cry in her own house, and state her feelings as she pleased, without a bunch of Pecks crowding around telling her she was not sufficiently dignified, and elegant, and tasteful, and respectable?

"Why, Lucy Hodges!" said Aunt Sarah.

Aunt Lucy gave her a look of pure hatred, there was no other way you could put it.

Justine was miserable. She would much rather tell and be done with it. But even if the grownup rules *were* different, Duncan was still playing by the old ones and he would be furious if she told. She hoped he would come home by himself— "turn himself in" was how she thought of it. Or that Uncle Two, strolling the Hopkins campus with false nonchalance during class break, would run across Duncan on his own. But Duncan didn't come and he wasn't seen on campus, and Uncle Two didn't want to ask at the Dean's office outright and involve other people in family matters. "You owe it to us to tell, Justine," he said. His face was tired and gaunt and there were shadows under his eyes. Aunt Lucy wasn't speaking. Even the cousins looked at Justine with a new edginess. How had she got herself into this? All she wanted was for the family to be happy together. That was the only reason she had run after Duncan in the first place.

She felt like someone who takes a single short step on solid ice and then hears a crack. She was halfway onto a drifting floe, one foot pulling out to sea and the other still on shore.

Then her grandfather said, "Have *you* been to see him?"

"Oh, I don't think he'd like me to, Grandfather."

"Why not? You're his cousin."

"I know."

"Yes, well," her grandfather said, and he pulled at his nose. "Well, never mind that. Go anyway. It's the only way we'll get any peace around here."

"Go visit him?"

"You didn't promise not to do *that*, did you? Go ahead. Don't worry, nobody will follow you."

But Justine half hoped someone *would* follow. Then life could get back to normal.

She knew the address because she had often gone with Duncan to the bookshop he mentioned—a cluttered place with creaky floorboards and great tilting stacks of used technical books. To the left of the shop was a paper sign, orange on black, saying ROOMS. When she opened the door she found narrow wooden steps, and at the top of the steps a dark hall with a toilet at the end. The doors reminded her of school, all thickly painted with scuff-proof brown and marked off with curly metal numbers. But she should have brought a flashlight to read the nameplates by. She moved down the hall very slowly, hunching her shoulders against a feeling of unknown things at the back of her neck, peering at the names scrawled on scraps of ruled paper or adhesive tape: Jones, Brown, Linthicum, T. Jones. No Peck. Only a door to her right with nothing at all, no name in the slot. And that, of course, would be Duncan.

She knocked. When he opened the door she held onto her hat, like someone who has just pressed a fun-house button with no notion of what to expect. But all Duncan said was, "Justine."

"Hello," she said.

"Was there something you wanted?"

"I'm supposed to see if you're all right."

"Well, now you've seen."

"Okay," she said, and turned to go.

"But you might as well come in, I guess. Since you're here."

His room was small and dingy, with stained wallpaper, a flapping torn shade, a speckled mirror, and a metal bed with a sagging mattress. Over in one corner was his cardboard box. He wore the clothes he had left home in, brown suit pants and a white shirt without a tie. He seemed thinner. "It doesn't look as if you're eating right," Justine said.

"Is that what you came to tell me?"

"No."

She sat down very delicately on the edge of the bed. She lifted both hands to her hat, making sure it was perfectly level. For some reason, Duncan smiled.

"Well!" she said finally.

Duncan sat down next to her.

"Your mother is really taking on, Duncan. She's crying where everyone can see her. Your father is—"

"I don't want to hear about that."

"Oh. Well—"

"*I* know what they're doing. I always know, I can tell, I can see as if I'm sitting there. They're talking about someone in the outside world. They're digging the moat a little deeper. They're pointing out all the neighbors' flaws and their slipping dentures and mispronunciations, they're drawing in tighter to keep the enemy out. Why do you think my mother's crying? Because she misses me? Did she say that? Think a minute. Did she? Did any of them? No. They're worried I might be with the wrong kind of people. They're upset to think a Peck is out there in the world someplace. I've lowered the drawbridge."

"Oh *no*, Duncan—" Justine said.

"Everything they do is calculated to keep others at a safe distance. Everything. Look at your hat!"

Justine's hands went up again, uncertainly.

"No, no, it's fine. It's a fine hat," he told her. "But what are you wearing it for?"

"Why, I *always*—"

"Yes, but why? Did you ever take a good look around you? Only old ladies wear hats any more, outside of church. But every woman in our family, even little girls, they all wear hats even if they're just off to the side yard for a breath of air. 'A lady doesn't *go* without a hat, my dear. Only common people.' Common! What's so uncommon about us? We're not famous, we're not society, we haven't been rich since 1930 and we aren't known for brains or beauty. But our ladies wear hats, by God! And we all have perfect manners! We may not ever talk to outsiders about anything more interesting than the weather but at least we do it politely! And we've all been taught that we disapprove of sports cars, golf, women in slacks, chewing gum, the color chartreuse, emotional displays, ranch houses, bridge, mascara, household pets, religious discussions, plastic, politics, nail polish, transparent gems of any color, jewelry shaped like animals, checkered prints . . . we're all told from birth on that no Peck has had a cavity in all recorded history or lost a single tooth; that we're unfailingly punctual even when we're supposed to come late; that we write our bread-and-butter notes no more than an hour after every visit; that we always say 'Baltimore' instead of 'Balmer'; that even when we're wearing our ragged old gardening clothes you can peek down our collars and see 'Brooks Brothers' on the label, and our boots are English and meant for riding though none of us has ever sat on a horse . . ."

He wound down like Great-Grandma's old Graphophone, and slumped forward suddenly with his long hands drooping between his knees.

"But Uncle Two is so *sad,*" said Justine. "He wanders around the Homewood campus all day hoping to—"

"Justine. Will you please get *out?*"

She rose immediately, clutching her little suede purse. But in the doorway Duncan said, "Anyhow, thanks for coming."

"Oh, you're welcome."

"I meant it, Justine. I'm sorry I . . . really, if you wanted to come back sometime I wouldn't mind."

"Well, all right," Justine said.

Then of course when she got home everyone was furious with her, because she hadn't found out one concrete fact. What was he living on? Where was he eating? Was he going to school? Who were his companions?

"I just know he's taken up with some—trash, he does have such peculiar taste in friends," Aunt Lucy said.

And all of them wondered at Justine's sudden look of sorrow.

What Duncan was living on was a pittance paid him by a Hopkins professor. He was double-checking dry facts in a library, and then writing them into the blanks the professor had left in a very long, tedious book on paleobotany. He was eating saltines and peanut butter, washed down with a quart bottle of milk in his room. He had no companions at all, not even Glorietta, with whom he had had a terrible fight several months ago over her habit of saying "between you and I." Eventually he was going to go very far away, perhaps to British Columbia, but at the moment it seemed he just couldn't get up the energy. And no, he was not attending school any more. He was not even reading Dostoevsky, whose writing suddenly appeared to have the squirmy, eye-straining texture of plant cells. As a matter of fact, he thought he might be going crazy. He even *liked* the idea of going crazy. He waited for insanity as if it were some colorful character his parents had always warned him against, but every morning when he woke up his mind was the same efficient piece of machinery it had always been and he felt disappointed.

Several times a week, his cousin Justine would come bringing irritating, endearing gifts—a ridiculous pair of slippers, his striped bedspread from home, once his old blue toothbrush with Ipana caked in the bristles. Whenever he opened the door to her he felt deeply happy to see her thin, sweet face and her streamered hat, but before she had been there five minutes he wanted to throw her out. She had such a gift for saying the wrong thing. "Can I tell the cousins where you are? They want to come too."

"No. God."

"Do you need any money?"

"I can take care of myself, Justine."

"Grandfather gave me some to bring to you."

"Tell him I can take care of myself."

"But I can't give it back to him, Duncan. He was so—he just pushed it into my hand all clumsy and secret. He pretended he wasn't doing anything."

"Change the subject."

"Like in the old days when he gave out horehound drops."

"Justine, I wish you would go now."

She always went. But she always came back, too, and when she stood in his doorway again a few days later he was all the more touched by her stupid, comical persistence. From earliest childhood she had been his favorite cousin—maybe because she was a little more removed, a Mayhew, a Philadelphian, not quite so easy to know. But he was surprised that she would brave his dark stairs and his rudeness. Here she had always seemed so docile! He made a special effort for her, smoothing the spread and offering saltines from his roach-proof tin and suggesting she take her hat off, which of course she would not do. "Justine, I'm glad you came back," he said.

"Why, thank you."

"You may get on my nerves sometimes but at least you show things, you say things outright, you don't feel it's a sin. You were the only one to ask me not to go, the Sunday I left."

"But Grandfather told me to do that," Justine said.

Right away she had managed to get on his nerves again.

She always had an answer. She drove him up a wall. He reached the point where he would turn on her the moment she entered, letting loose a flood of arguments that he had been storing up. "You know what they're like?" (There was no need to say whom he meant.) "You know who they remind me of? People choosing a number on a radio dial. The way they ignore anything that isn't Peck, like flicking past stations that don't concern them, just a split second of jazz or ballgames or revivalist ministers and they wince and move on, and settle finally on the one acceptable station that plays Mantovani. Nothing uncomfortable, nothing extreme, nothing they can't tolerate . . ."

"They tolerated you at that Sunday dinner," Justine said. "Really you were as rude as can be and they tried to see your side of it and act reasonable. Who are you to say they can't talk about eggshells?"

Duncan said, "Nothing outside the family matters. Nobody counts if they're not Pecks. Not even neighbors, not even Sulie. Why, Sulie's been with us since our parents were children, but does anybody know her last name?"

"Boudrault."

"Hmm?"

"She married old Lafleur Boudrault, the gardener."

"Oh, details," said Duncan.

"He died in nineteen forty."

"Little church-lady Emily Post details and nothing underneath. And you're just like them, Justine, you always will be.

Who asked you to come here and clutter up my life?"

But when she was gone, her smell of warm grass hung in the air and the memory of her imperturbable Peck face. At night her chilly little voice ran on and on, arguing, reasoning, imposing logic, even in his dreams. He would wake and punch his flattened pillow and toss beneath the spread that carried her smell too, even from its brief stay in her arms. He wished she were there to argue with; then he wished she were there to apologize to; then he wished she were there to lay her long cool body next to his on the sagging mattress and hold him close all through the deep, steamy Baltimore night.

Justine was not herself; everybody noticed it. Even summer vacation didn't seem to relax her any. She was strange and distant with her family. She began watching her aunts and uncles in a measuring way that made them uncomfortable. "What's the *matter* with her?" her father said once, but his in-laws only smiled blankly; they did not believe in asking too many questions.

It seemed that they accepted Duncan's absence now. Sometimes when Justine came back from visiting him they would forget to ask how he was. Or they would say, "See Duncan, did you?" and go on about their business. Even Aunt Lucy appeared resigned. But one day in August, a particularly hot Saturday morning, Aunt Lucy appeared on Great-Grandma's front steps with a small electric fan. Justine was drying her hair outdoors and reading *Mademoiselle*. "Justine, dear," said Aunt Lucy.

Justine looked up, with her mind still on her magazine. Her aunt wore the expression of a lady heading calm and smiling toward disaster.

"Justine, this is for Duncan," Aunt Lucy said.

"What? Oh, a fan. He could use it."

"Oh, I knew it! I'm so glad I—well, whenever you go to see him, then. Are you going today?"

"Today I'm going on a picnic with Neely. Tomorrow I might, though."

"Don't you think you might stop by this morning? Wouldn't you be able to work it in?"

Aunt Lucy's smile hesitated.

"Of course I could," Justine said, and she took the fan from her aunt's shaky hands.

It was not until she had parked in front of the bookshop that she noticed the little envelope dangling from the fan's grid.

Duncan's room was blasting with heat and he was so hot he seemed to have been oiled. He wore a grayish undershirt. His trousers were creased and limp. "Oh, it's you," was all he said, and then he sat back down on his bed and wiped his face with his balled-up shirt.

"Duncan, I brought you a fan from your mother."

"You've been telling her about my room."

"No, I haven't. She just *guessed* you would need this."

"What's that in the envelope?"

"I don't know."

He broke the string that tied it and pulled out a folded note. First he read it silently and then he groaned and read it aloud.

Dear Duncan,

I am taking the liberty of sending you the fan from my bedroom, now that it is so warm.

Everyone is well although I myself have had a recurrence of those headaches. Just a little tension, the doctor says, so I keep my chin up!

Your father has been working very . . .

"What about the fan from *my* room?" Duncan said. "There is one, you know."

"She gave you her own to show she cares, she didn't know how else to put it," said Justine.

"None of them do. Oh, you can tell who she married into. She's just like all the rest of them now. Too little said and too much communicated, so that if you fight back they can say, 'But why? What did *I* do?' and you won't have any answer. It all takes place in their secret language, they would never say a thing straight out."

"But that's tact. They don't want to embarrass you."

"They don't want to embarrass themselves," Duncan told her.

She said nothing.

"Isn't that right?"

"Probably it is," she said. "But so is the other. There *isn't* any right and wrong. I keep looking at them, trying to decide. Well, everything you say is true but then so is everything I say. And what does it matter, after all? They're your family."

"You know who you sound like? Aunt Sarah, Justine. You're going to grow up an old maid. Or you'll marry a stick like Neely and have him change his name to Peck. I can see it coming. I can see it in that flat straight face of yours, just watch."

But he had gone too far. Even he must have known that. When Justine turned away from him, fumbling for something in her purse, he said, "Anyway!" He jumped up and started pacing the floor. "Well, anyway, tell me all the news," he said.

"Oh . . ."

"Come on!"

"There's nothing much."

"Nothing? Nothing in all those four enormous houses?"

"Well, Aunt Bea has had to get glasses," Justine said.

"Ah."

"She's very shy about them, she wears them on a string tucked inside her blouse. She takes them off between sentences in a newspaper even."

"So Aunt Bea has glasses."

"And Mama's bought a TV."

"A TV. I might have known it would come to that."

"Oh, it's not so bad, Duncan. It's very convenient, don't you think, having a moving talking picture in your home that way? I wonder how they do it."

"Actually it's quite simple," said Duncan. "The *principle's* been around for decades. Have you got a pencil? I'll show you."

"Oh, I wouldn't understand," Justine said.

"Of course you would."

"But I'm not scientific. I don't see how you know those things."

"Those things are nothing," he said, "it's the others I don't get. The ones you take for granted. Like mirrors, for instance," and he stopped his pacing to wave at the mirror on the opposite wall. "I lay awake the other night going crazy over that. I spent hours trying to figure out the laws of reflected images. I couldn't measure the angles of refraction. Do you understand it? Look."

She stood up and looked. She saw herself in the speckled glass, nothing surprising.

"How come it shows my image and not yours?" he asked her. "How come yours and not mine? How come eyes can meet in a mirror when you're not looking at each other in real life? Do you understand the principle?"

In the glass their eyes met, equally blue and distant, as if the mirror were reflecting images already mirrored.

Duncan turned around and set his hands on her shoulders and kissed her on the mouth. He smelled of salt and sunlight. His grip on her was weightless, as if he were holding something back. When she drew away, he let his hands drop to his sides. When she ran out of the room he didn't try to stop her.

Justine wouldn't visit Duncan any more. Her grandfather kept coming around, pressing twenty-dollar bills into her hand, but she didn't know what to tell him and so she took the money in silence. She stuffed it haphazardly into her jewelry box, feeling like a thief even though she never spent it. She quarreled with her mother over a print dress, saying it was old-ladyish, although before she had worn whatever her mother picked out. When school started she studied indifferently and had trouble getting to class on time. Esther had graduated and was teaching nursery school, but now the twins were commuting with Justine and they objected to her late starts. "Is that what you call the point of life?" Justine asked them. "Getting to a class on the dot of nine o'clock?"

The twins looked at each other. Certainly they had never meant to imply that it was the *point* of life, exactly.

On a Saturday night in October, Justine was watching television with Neely in her great-grandma's study. Neely was stroking her neck up and down in a particularly rasping way, but she had been so short-tempered with him lately that she didn't want to protest. Instead she concentrated on the television: a mahogany box with a snowy blue postage stamp in its center, showing a girl who had become engaged due to cleansing her face with cold cream twice a night. She flashed a diamond ring at her girlfriends. "*Your* diamond's going to be *twice* as big," said Neely. "My father's already promised me the money."

"I don't like diamonds," said Justine.

"Why not?"

"I don't like stones that are transparent."

"You don't like *anything* any more, Justine."

On the television, a man held up a watch that would keep running steadily through everything, even a cycle in a washing machine.

"How about me?" Neely asked.

"What?"

"Do you like *me*?"

His finger kept annoying her neck. Justine winced and drew away.

A man in downtown Baltimore was interviewing people coming out of a movie theater. He wanted to see if they had heard of his product, an antibacterial toothpaste. "Goodness, no," said a lady.

"Well, think a minute. Say you have a cold and get over it. You wouldn't want to catch it right back again from your toothbrush, would you?"

"Goodness, no."

He stopped a man in a raincoat.

"Sir? Have you ever thought how risky it is, using the toothbrush you used when you were sick?"

"Why, no, now I never considered that. But you got a point there."

He stopped Duncan.

"Say!" said Neely. "Isn't that your cousin?"

Duncan was wearing some dark shade of jacket that Justine had never seen before. His face was clamped against the cold. There was no one in the world with such a pure, unwavering face. He stooped a little to hear the question, concentrating courteously with his eyes focused on something in the distance. When the man was finished Duncan straightened and thought a moment.

"Actually," he said, "once your body's built up enough resistance to overcome those bacteria in the first place it's very doubtful if—"

The man discontinued the conversation and ran after a fat lady.

Justine went to the front hall for her coat. "Justine?" Neely called. She ignored him. Probably he thought she was out of hearing, maybe gone to the kitchen for soft drinks. At any rate, he didn't call again.

All she told herself was that she owed Duncan a visit. He was her cousin, wasn't he? And she really should give him their grandfather's money. (Which was still crammed in her jewelry box at home.) She had herself convinced. But Duncan must have known exactly how her mind worked, because when he opened the door he stood looking at her for a minute, and then he drew her in and kissed her, and then he said, "Look, I can see the layers sliding across your eyes like shutters until you can properly explain this away." Then he laid her on his bed, with its hollow center that rolled her toward him so that she could feel his warm bones through the thin white fabric of his shirt. He took off her clothes and his. Still she didn't make a single objection, she said none of the things that she had said to Neely. She felt happy and certain, as if everything they did was already familiar. She seemed to be glinting with some secret laughter at this newer, more joyous mischief that they were just inventing, or at Duncan's Puckish face turned suddenly gentle, or at her own self in his mirror eyes, a naked girl wearing a Breton hat.

6

DUNCAN came home in March of 1953. He walked into his great-grandma's dining room one Sunday at dinnertime. "Duncan!" his mother said, half rising. Then, "What on earth is that you're wearing?"

He was wearing a peajacket he had bought from Navy surplus. His hair needed cutting. He had been gone nearly a year and in that time his face had changed in some indefinable way that made him an outsider. The grownups stared and his cousins gave him self-conscious, sidelong glances. All but Justine, who raised her face like a beacon and smiled across the room at him. He smiled back.

"Well, my boy," his grandfather said. "So you're home."

"No," said Duncan, looking at Justine.

But they didn't believe him. "Pull up a chair," his mother said. "Take mine. Get yourself a plate. Have you had one decent meal since you left us?"

"I'm going to get married," Duncan said.

"Married?"

The ghost of Glorietta flashed scarlet through their minds. All the grownups shifted uneasily.

"I'm marrying Justine."

First they thought it was a joke. A tasteless one, but just like him. Then they saw how grave and still the two of them were. "My God," said Justine's mother. She clutched suddenly at a handful of ruffles on her chest. "My God, who would have thought of such a thing?"

Though it seemed to all of them, now, that they should have thought of it long ago. Those visits Justine had paid him! Those trips! Everyone knew she hated traveling as much as any other Peck. Yet day after day this winter she had packed a lunch in Sulie's kitchen and said she wouldn't be home till night. "I'm going on a trip with Duncan. Out to the country somewhere." "Yes, yes, go," they told her. "Keep an eye on him for us." She had cut classes, missed important family gatherings, stopped seeing Neely, grown distant from her cousins—"But it's good she's with Duncan," they told each other. "She's sure to be a good influence on him." How she had deceived them!

Only Sam Mayhew, slow of mind, seemed unable to make the mental leap the Pecks had just accomplished. He looked all around the table, from one person to the other, with his face set to laugh as soon as he saw the joke. "What? What's that?" he said.

The others waved him aside, too busy adjusting to the shock. But Duncan came over and stood squarely in front of him and spoke very quietly, as if to a child.

"Uncle Sam, I'm marrying Justine."

"But—you can't!"

"I'm telling you I am. I'm telling you, not asking you. Nothing is going to make me change my mind."

"You can't."

"Why, it must not even be legal!" said Caroline.

"Yes, it is," Duncan told her.

"*Oh* yes," his grandfather said.

"But—" said Caroline.

"Who's the lawyer here, you or me? Boy's right. It's true. And yes, I know, there's a lot to be said against it. But look at it this way. What nicer girl could he have picked? She's sure to settle him down some. And this way there's no adjustment for them to make, no in-law problems—"

"You ought to be locked up," Sam Mayhew said.

"Sir!" said Grandfather Peck.

"Haven't you heard of inbreeding?"

"Not at the table, Sam."

"Haven't you heard of *genes?*"

"Now, we come of good solid stock," the grandfather said. "No worries there." He picked up the carving knife. "Care for a slice of ham, Duncan boy?"

"He's a blood relative," said Sam Mayhew. "And he's only twenty years old, and he hasn't got a responsible bone in his body. Well, I'm not going to allow it. Justine won't marry Duncan or any other Peck."

"Then we'll elope," Duncan said.

"Elope!" cried Justine's mother. "Oh, anything but that!"

"You are a fool, Caroline," Sam Mayhew said. Then he stood and took Justine by the wrist and pulled her up and toward the door. But she was still calm and so was Duncan. Nothing seemed to disturb them. As Justine passed Duncan he gave her a slow, deep stare that caused the rest of the family to avert their eyes. "*Come*, Justine," her father said. He led her through the living room and up to her bedroom. She went without a protest. He set her in her room and shut her door and locked it, and put the key up on the ledge again before he went back to the others.

In her ruffled rocker, Justine sat and waited. The pointlessness of being locked in her room seemed more comical than annoying, and she was not worried about her family. Hadn't Duncan predicted everything? "Your father's the one who'll be upset. The others will get over it. Anyway, it's always been a bother adapting outside wives. Then your father will give in because he has to. There won't be any problems."

"I know there won't."

"There would be even less if you would just run away with me."

"I want to do this right, I said."

"Does it matter that much? Justine, why does it matter? They're just a bunch of *people*, just some yellow-haired, ordinary people. Why do you have to ask for their approval?"

"Because I love them," Justine said.

He didn't have any answer for that. Love was not a word he used, even to her.

She rocked and gazed at the wintry gray sky, while downstairs the battle went on and on. Great-Grandma soothed everyone, a dry brown thread weaving in and out. She thought this marriage was a wonderful idea; she had never heard of genes. When Sam Mayhew stormed, Grandfather snapped and cut him short. Uncles rumbled and aunts chirped and burbled. And over it all rode Duncan's level voice, sensible and confident. Justine could tell when he began to win. He continued alone, the others fell behind. The worst of the battle was over. All that was left was for the losers to regain face.

Justine felt suddenly stifled and bored. She went into her bathroom for her toothbrush, and took a pack of matches from her bureau drawer. She had not grown up with Duncan for nothing: heating the toothbrush handle very slowly, she pushed it little by little into the lock of her door and then turned it and walked out free. When she re-entered the dining room, they didn't seem surprised to see her. Only Duncan, noticing the toothbrush in her hand, tipped back in his chair and looked amused, but he sobered up when Justine's father rose and came around the table to face her.

"Justine," he said.

"Yes, Daddy."

"It has been pointed out to me that there's nothing I can really do to stop you. All I can hope is that you'll listen to reason. Justine, look. Don't you see why you're doing this? It's merely proximity, the two of you had no one else, *no* one in this family has anyone else. You were thrown too much together, at an age when naturally . . . and you were afraid to turn to some outsider. Admit it. Isn't that correct?"

Justine thought it over. "Well," she said finally, "it does sound correct, yes."

"Well, then."

"But then, *both* sides sound correct. I always agree with who I'm listening to."

He waited, expecting more. All she did was smile. "Aah!" he said suddenly, and turned away, throwing up his hands. "You even *sound* like him. You're a puppet. I've learned something today: set a bad and a good person down together and the bad wins every time. I always wondered."

"Say that again?" said Aunt Lucy. "Is it Duncan you're calling bad?"

"Who else?"

"*Duncan's* not a bad boy."

Even Duncan looked surprised.

"*Justine's* the one who kept the rest of us away from him. *Justine* wouldn't tell his own mother where he was staying! Blame your daughter!"

"Why, Lucy!" Justine's mother said.

Duncan let his chair tip forward. This might turn out to be interesting. But no, they were distracted by a new development: Sam Mayhew buttoning his suit coat. He worked with his elbows out and his clock-shaped face set impassively toward some point above their heads. They knew at once that something important was going on.

"I won't be attending this wedding," he said finally.

"Oh, Sam!" his wife cried.

"And I won't be living here."

"What?"

"I'm moving out to my parents'. I'm going to look for a house in Guilford."

He finished the buttons. He began pulling his shirt cuffs down, neat bands of white above his chubby red hands. "You may come too, of course, Caroline. And Justine if she decides against this marriage. But I warn you: if you come, we will only be visiting your family once a month."

"Once a *month?*"

"The first Sunday of every month, for dinner. We'll go home at three."

"But *Sam—*" his wife said.

"Make your choice, Caroline."

He continued to gaze above her head. Caroline turned to

her family. She was still baby-faced, although the years had worked like gravity pulling on her cheeks. Her weight had settled in upon itself. She looked like a cake that had collapsed. To each brother and sister, to her father and her grandmother, she turned a round lost stare while twisting the pearls on her fingers.

"What's your decision, Caroline?"

"I can't just *leave* them like that."

"All right."

"Sam?" she said.

He walked over to Justine. Duncan rose instantly to his feet. "Justine," Sam Mayhew said, "you have been a disappointing daughter in every way, all your life."

Then Justine rocked back as if she had been hit, but Duncan already stood behind her braced to steady her.

The wedding was to be held in a church. All the family insisted on that. Duncan had not been to church in several years and detested Reverend Didicott, a fat man who came from Aunt Lucy's hometown and had a Southern accent that would surely double the length of the ceremony; but he said he would do whatever Justine wanted. And Justine, half willing anyway, went along with the others, submitting to a long satin dress, Sarah Cantleigh's ivory veil, and a little old lady consultant with an emergency cigar box full of pins, white thread, spirits of ammonia, and a stick of chalk for stains. "Oh, Duncan!" Justine said, as she sped by him on the way to the photographer. "I'm sorry! I know how you must hate this!" But he was surprisingly tolerant. He had agreed to give up his room and move home for the month preceding the wedding; he went without a word to buy a black suit that turned him stern and unfamiliar. During lulls in the excitement, he seemed to be observing Justine very closely. Did he think she would change her mind? Reading *Bride's* magazine, she felt his eyes upon her, weighing her, watching for something. "What is it?" she asked him, but he never would say.

Her mother was everywhere. She bustled and darted, giving commands, trilling out fitting schedules in a voice so gay it seemed about to break off and fly. "Really, no one would guess her husband's left her," Justine told Duncan.

"Don't speak too soon."

"Why?"

"Now she's got the wedding to keep her busy. What about later?"

Later Justine would be far away. One thing Duncan would not agree to was living in Roland Park. Nor even in Baltimore, not even long enough for Justine to finish school. And he would not go back to school himself. So they were renting a little house and a plot of land an hour's drive out in the country, where they used to go on their trips. Duncan planned to start a goat farm. It was what he had always wanted, he said. It was? Justine had never heard him mention it before. But he couldn't go on forever looking up facts for professors; and anyway, he kept losing those jobs, he gave in to a temptation to rewrite their material, making it more colorful, adding his own startling scraps of knowledge and a few untruths. And he and Justine each had a share of old Justin's trust fund. Because of the proliferation of heirs it amounted to almost nothing, but they could manage till the dairy started paying off. "You're strapping yourself in, boy," his grandfather said. "You want an education. And *renting's* no good, it's a shoddy way to do things."

"Sure, Grandfather."

But Duncan went on reading the *Dairy Goat Journal*, rummaging through his shocks of hair as he always did when he was absorbed in something. And a week before the wedding he helped supervise the loading of a Mayflower van containing ancient, massive furniture from the relatives and rolled-up rugs, crates of crystal stemware, gifts of silver and china, linens monogrammed by Aunt Laura May and heavy damask curtains, all meant for their three-room cabin. Justine wasn't entirely sure that everything was suitable, but how else would you furnish a place? She didn't know. Duncan made no comment, only watched without surprise as she directed the movers toward a claw-footed bureau, a tasseled floor lamp, a bedstead with pineapple knobs.

"Prepare your mother, now," he told her. "I mean it. Get her ready for doing without you, because it's going to be a shock for her once it happens."

"I will."

"Prepare *yourself*, Justine."

"Prepare for what?"

"Do you really understand that you'll be leaving here?"

"Of course I do," she said.

Well, naturally she would rather *not* be leaving. It made her sad just to think about it. But nothing mattered as much as the lurch in her stomach when she saw him. When they sat apart in Great-Grandma's study, some inner selves seemed to rise up and meet while their bodies remained seated. In halls and pantries and stairwells, they kissed until they were sick and dizzy. She missed Duncan's room downtown: his jingling bed, the warm pulse in the hollow of his throat, the leathery arch of his right foot curving exactly to the shape of her calf when they fell asleep.

"Still," Duncan said, "I wish I could be sure you know what you're getting into."

At the rehearsal, Esther took the part of the bride for good luck. It was terrible to see her up there so close to Duncan. Her emerald-green sheath showed off her figure, which was better than Justine's. "Tell me," Justine said to Duncan later. "Did you ever think of marrying Esther?"

"No."

"But why me?" she asked.

"Why *me*, for that matter?"

"I don't know," she said.

"Why are you marrying me, Justine?"

"Oh, well, Claude is too fat and Richard's too young."

She didn't understand the strange look he gave her.

On Justine's wedding morning, a pale cool day in April, her mother woke her by pulling open the curtains in her bedroom. "Justine," she said, "listen. Are you awake?"

"Yes."

"I want you to listen a minute."

She was wearing a slithery pink silk dressing gown and already her doll-like face was made up perfectly, her curls precisely flattened. She carried a torn scrap of paper. She sat on Justine's bed and held the paper out to her, smiling a coaxing smile like someone offering medicine. "Your daddy's telephone number," she said.

"My what?"

"Hear what I say, now. I want you to go out in the hall to the phone. I want you to dial this number. It's your grandmother Mayhew's. Ask to speak to your daddy. Say, 'Daddy, today is my wedding day.'"

"Oh, Mama."

"Listen! Say, 'Daddy, this is supposed to be the happiest day of my life. Won't you make it perfect and come give me away?'"

"But I can't talk like that," Justine said.

"Of course you can. And he has that fine suit that's still in the cleaner's bag, I know he took it with him. Why, it wouldn't be any trouble at all! Justine? I beg you, Justine."

"Mama—"

"Please, I've been counting on it. I know it will work. See, I've written the number so neatly? Take it. Take it."

She pressed it into her hands. Justine climbed out of bed, still unwilling.

"Go on, Justine."

In the hall, the telephone sat on a piecrust table. The window above it was partly open, so that Justine in her flimsy cotton nightgown shivered while she dialed.

"Hello," Sam Mayhew said.

She had been expecting her grandmother, a static-voiced old lady she hardly knew. She wasn't prepared for her father yet.

"*Hello,*" he said.

"Daddy?"

There was a pause. Then he said, "Hello, Justine."

"Daddy, I—today is my wedding day."

"Yes, I saw it in the paper."

She was silent. She was taking in his soft, questioning voice, which reminded her of his baffled attempts at conversation long ago in Philadelphia. For the first time she realized that he had actually left. Everything had broken and altered and would not ever be the same.

"Honey," he said. "You can always change your mind."

"No, Daddy, I don't want to change my mind."

"I'm about to buy a house in Guilford. Wouldn't you like that? There's a room for you with blue wallpaper. I know you like blue. You could go away to college, someplace good. Why, you used to be a high-B student! Those Pecks think girls go to college to mark time but—it's not too late. You know that. You can still call it off."

"Daddy, will you come give me away at the wedding?"

"No. I can't lend myself to such a thing."

"I'd really like you to."

"I'm sorry."

Her mother tugged at Justine's nightgown. "Tell about the happiest day of your life!" she hissed.

"Wait—"

"Who's that?" her father asked.

"It's Mama."

"What's she doing there?"

"She says to tell you—"

"Did your mother put you up to this?"

"No, I—she just—"

"Oh," her father said. "I thought it was you that was asking. I wish it had been."

"I *am* asking."

"Justine, I'm not going to come to your wedding. Don't bring it up again. But listen, because these are the last sensible words you'll hear all day, or maybe all the rest of your life: you've got to get out of there."

"*Out*, Daddy . . ."

"You think you *are* getting out, don't you. You're going to farm chickens or something."

"Goats."

"But you're not really leaving at all, and anyway you'll be back within a year."

"But we're going to—"

"I know why you're marrying Duncan. You think I don't. But have you ever asked yourself why Duncan is marrying *you*? Why is he marrying his first cousin?"

"Because we—"

"It's one of two reasons. Either he wants a Peck along to torment, or to lean on. Either he's going to give you hell or else he's knotted tighter to his family than he thinks he is. But whichever, Justine. Whichever. It's not a business you'd care to get involved in."

"I can't talk any more," Justine said.

"What? Hold on there, now—"

But she hung up. Her teeth were chattering. "What happened?" her mother asked. "What *happened*, isn't he coming?"

"No."

"Oh! I see. Well."

"I feel sick."

"That's wedding jitters, it's perfectly natural," her mother said. "Oh, I never should have asked you to call in the first place. It was only for *his* sake."

Then she led Justine back to her room, and covered her with the quilt handstitched by Great-Grandma, and sat with her a while. The quilt gave off a deep, solid warmth. There was a smell of coffee and cinnamon toast floating up from the kitchen, and a soft hymn of Sulie's with a wandering tune. Justine's jaw muscles loosened and she felt herself easing and thawing.

"We're going to do without him just fine," her mother said. "I only wanted to make him think he was a part of things."

Later the minister, Reverend Didicott, told the assistant minister that the Peck–Mayhew wedding was the darnedest business he had ever seen. First of all the way they sat the guests, who were not numerous to begin with: friends clumped in back, and the bride's and groom's joint family up front. There was something dreamlike in the fact that almost everyone in the front section had the same fair, rather expressionless face—over and over again, exactly the same face, distinguished only a little by age or sex. Then the groom, who seemed unsuitably light of heart, followed him around before the ceremony insisting that Christianity was a dying religion. ("It's the only case I know of where *mental* sins count too; it'll never sell," he said. "Take it from me, get out while the getting's good." Right then Reverend Didicott should have refused to marry them, but he couldn't do that to Lucy Hodges Peck, whose family he had known down South.) The bride was given away by her grandfather, an unsmiling man with a mighty snappy way of speaking to people, although so far as was known the bride's father was in excellent health. The groom refused to kiss the bride in public. But the bride's mother was the strangest. Perfectly sedate all through the ceremony, if a little trembly of mouth, gay and flirtatious at the reception afterwards, she chose to fall apart at the going away. Just as the groom was enclosing the bride in his car (which was another whole story, a disgraceful greenish object with a stunted rear end), the mother let out with a scream. "No!" she screamed. "No! How can you just leave me all alone? It's *your* fault your father's gone! How can you drive off like this without a heart?" The bride started to get out but the groom laid a hand on her arm and stopped her, and then they took off in their automobile, which appeared to be led by its nose. The mother threw herself in the grandfather's arms and wept out loud. "We people don't *cry*, Caroline," he said. The most ancient Mrs. Peck of all put on a genteel smile and started humming, and Reverend Didicott looked inside the envelope the groom had given him and found fifty dollars in Confederate money.

Duncan told everyone they would be away on a honeymoon, but they weren't; he just liked to lie. Instead they went straight to the farm. For two weeks they were left to themselves. Duncan worked uninterrupted, settling in eight Toggenburg does and a purebred buck who smelled like a circus, transporting bales of hay and sacks of Purina goat chow, a block of pink salt and a vat of blackstrap molasses he claimed would increase milk production when added to the goats' drinking water. The weather had turned suddenly warm and he went about in his undershirt, whistling "The Wabash Cannonball," while inside their little house Justine threw open all the windows and tied the damask curtains back so they wouldn't hinder the breeze. She had made the place a replica of Great-Grandma's house, if you ignored the green paper walls and the yellowed ceilings. Rugs covered the flowered linoleum, and the four-poster bed hid the fungus growing beneath one window. She fought the foreign smells of kerosene and fatback by hanging Great-Grandma's china pomander ball in the hall. She worked for hours every day constructing meals from Fannie Farmer's cookbook, the one her aunts all used. In the evenings, the two of them sat side by side on the front porch in cane-seated rockers that used to be their grandfather's. They looked out across their scrubby, scraggly land, past the slant-roofed shed where the does stood swaybacked. Like an old country couple they rocked and watched the gravel road, where they might see an occasional pick-up truck bound for the Jordans' farm on the hill or a string of children carrying switches and weedy flowers, dawdling home. Justine thought she would like to stay this way forever: isolated, motionless, barely breathing, cut loose from everyone else. They were like people under glass. They rocked in unison side by side, almost touching but not quite, as if thin wires were stretched between them.

Then the letters started coming. "I keep busy, I go for a lot of walks," her mother said. "Not far, of course. Just up and down your great-grandma's side yard, up and down again." Aunt Lucy said, "We think of you often. Especially Caroline does, you can tell although you know she wouldn't mention it for anything." "Last Sunday," Great-Grandma said, "we laid two places for you supposing you might be back from your honeymoon and would think to come for dinner, as it would do Caroline a world of good, but it seems you couldn't make it."

Justine felt stabbed in the chest. "Dear Mama," she wrote, "I miss you very much. I want to come home for a visit. Duncan says we will just as soon as we can, although of course goats are not something you can just walk off and leave. They have to be milked twice a day and watered, and Duncan has to stay pretty close by anyway because he has put an ad in the paper and soon customers will be coming . . ."

"Dear Ma," Duncan said on a postcard. "High! We're doing fine. Say hello to everybody. Sincerly, Duncan."

The family's ink was black, their envelopes cream. Nearly every morning a cream-colored accordion lay waiting in the mailbox at the end of the driveway. Once Duncan got there before Justine and he scooped the letters out of the box and flung them over his head. "Hoo!" he said, and tipped back his face like a child in a snowstorm while the envelopes tumbled all around him. Justine came running, and bent at the edge of the gravel to gather them up. "Oh, Duncan, I wish you wouldn't do things like this," she told him. "How will I know I've got them all?"

"What does it matter? Each one is just like the next."

It was true. Still she read them closely, often stirring or starting to speak, while Duncan watched her face. Each envelope let out a little gust of Ivory soap, the smell of home. She could imagine the leafy shadows endlessly rearranging themselves outside her bedroom window, and her grandfather's slow, fond smile when he met her at the start of a day. She missed her grandfather very much.

"If you like," Duncan said, "I'll take you this Sunday for dinner. Is that what you want?"

"Yes, it is," she told him.

But somehow they didn't go. Duncan became involved in cleaning the barn, or wiring the new electric fence. Or they simply overslept, waking too slowly with their legs tangled together and their blue eyes opening simultaneously to stare at each other across the pillow, and then the unmilked goats were bleating and there were always so many chores to do. "Maybe next Sunday," Justine would write. When the new sheaf of envelopes arrived she felt chastened and sorry even before she had opened them. But when she took the letters to Duncan out in the barn he only laughed. Like a teacher with a pointer, he would poke a stalk of timothy at stray sentences here and there —reproaches, transparent braveries, phrases with double and triple and quadruple meanings. " 'Of course we're sorry you didn't make it but we understand perfectly, as I had already told your aunts that perhaps we shouldn't expect you.' Ha!" he said.

Justine's face, then, would slowly ease, but she reclaimed the letters and stacked them carefully before she went back to the house.

Then one day a truck rattled up their driveway and a man climbed out, carrying a telephone on the palm of his hand. "Phone," he said, as if Justine should lift the receiver to answer it. But he swung on by her and up the porch steps, with a beltful of tools clanking around his hips. Duncan met him in the doorway. "*We* didn't order that," he said.

"Somebody did."

"Not us."

The man pulled a folded sheet of paper from his pocket and shook it open. "Peck and Sons," he said.

"That's someone else."

"Your name Duncan Peck?"

"Yes."

"This phone is for you, then. Don't complain. Bill goes to Peck and Sons. Wished *I* got presents like that."

"If we had wanted a telephone we would have ordered it on our own," Duncan said.

But Justine said, "Oh, Duncan, it's a *gift!* We can't hurt their feelings."

Duncan studied her a minute. Then he said, "All right."

Now the phone rang once, twice, three times a day even, and Justine would come running in from the fields or the barn to answer it. "Justine," her mother said, "I'm upstairs. I'm standing in the hall here looking into your room and your shelf of dolls along the wall, the Spanish lady with her real lace mantilla that your grandfather gave you in Philadelphia when you were only four, remember? She has the sweetest, saddest face."

"Mama, I'm helping Duncan dehorn a goat."

"Do you remember when Grandfather gave you the Spanish lady? You insisted on taking her to bed with you, though she wasn't a cuddly kind of doll. Your daddy and I came into your room every night after you were asleep and put her up on the bureau again. Oh, you looked so innocent and peaceful! We would stand there a while just watching you. Your daddy didn't have to travel so often then and it seemed we had so much more time together."

"Oh, Mama," Justine would say, "I wish I could be there with you. Don't take on so, please don't cry."

Aunt Sarah called, with Aunt Laura May on the upstairs extension. "She's started staying in bed, Justine, she never gets out of her bathrobe. She has these awful headaches. I called your daddy but I believe that man is possessed. He said he wouldn't come, she should come stay in *his* house and of course that is just not possible, he only has a weekly cleaning lady. Of course she would need more than that, it's all we can do to see to her wants even with Sulie helping out. We're running our feet off."

"We bring all her meals on a tray," Aunt Laura May said.

"We've moved the television up to her bedroom."

"The radio for daytime. *Stella Dallas.*"

Justine said, "We'll come on Sunday."

"Do my ears deceive me?"

"We'll be there around noon," said Justine. "But we can't stay the night, you know, the goats are—"

"The goats, yes."

"Goodbye till then."

She went back out to the field. "Duncan," she said, "I think we'd better go for dinner this Sunday."

"You do, do you."

"It's been six weeks, you know. And they say that Mama is—"

"You don't have to keep harping on it, we'll go."

But in bed that night, when he had just stretched out alongside her and taken her head in his hands, the phone rang again and he said, "Bull's-eye."

"I'll get it," she said.

"Oh, your mother and her X-ray vision. She's worked on this, she's got it timed. She couldn't call when you were just reading *Woman's Day*, no—"

"Let me up, I'll answer," said Justine.

"No, don't. We'll ignore it." But then he said, "How can we ignore a thing like that? Nine rings. Ten."

"I'll only be a minute."

"Eleven," Duncan said. He had laid one arm across her to hold her down but he kept his head raised and his eyes on the black shine of the telephone. "We'll go out and sleep in the field," he told her.

"The *field*, Duncan!"

"Where else? If we answer, she wins. If we lie here and listen she wins. Hear that? Four-letter rings. Come on, Justine."

"Well, just let me get a blanket."

"Here's a blanket."

"I'll need a bathrobe."

"What for?"

"Do you want your pillow?"

"*No* I don't want my pillow."

"And insect repellent."

"Oh, for—"

Then he was off the bed and out of the room. "Duncan?" she said. "Duncan, have you changed your mind?" But before she could follow him he was back, waving the huge iron clippers he used for trimming the goats' hooves. Justine heard a single click. The phone gave a whimper and died.

"Oh, Duncan," Justine said, but she was laughing when she lay back down.

All the next morning the telephone sat silent on the bureau with its comical stub of a tail sticking out. In the afternoon, when they were leaving to do some shopping in town, Duncan locked the front door so that no repairman could come while they were gone. "You *know* the family is going to let them hear about this," he said. "They'll be sending undercover men with their little bags of tools." And sure enough, when they got back there was a card hanging from the doorknob. "What a pity, our telephone representative has been and gone," he said. Still, Justine only laughed.

But in the evening, when they were sitting on the porch, something stopped her rocking. She straightened suddenly and frowned. "Duncan," she said.

"Hmm?"

"I have this funny feeling."

Duncan had been reading a book on how to start a chicken farm, sliding a flashlight down the page because it was already dark. He raised the flashlight now and shone it into her face.

"Something terrible is going on at home," she told him.

"Something terrible's always going on at home."

"I mean it. This is serious. I really mean it."

"What, have you turned psychic?"

"No, but I can tell if there's going to be a *change* of some kind."

He rocked and waited.

"We have to go there," she said.

The flashlight clicked off.

"I'm sorry, Duncan. I'll go alone if you'd rather. But I just feel I—"

"All right, all right."

While she packed an overnight case, he drove up the hill to ask Junior Jordan to tend the goats. They could have done that weeks ago! But then, Justine knew that as well as Duncan. She waited on the porch, clutching her case, shivering a little although the night was warm. When she saw his close-set headlights bobbing toward her, she ran down the steps and opened the car door. "It's all set," Duncan told her. "Climb in."

The car seemed to be drawn down the road by two long yellow cones. Justine was reminded of other trips, before they were married, rushing home to beat a curfew. All through that silent drive she had the feeling that she was some younger, smaller self, anxiously chewing the ribbons of her hat while she wondered if she would be scolded for staying out so late.

In Guilford, at eight o'clock that morning, Sam Mayhew's cleaning lady had found him dead in his kitchen. He was wearing a bathrobe and there was a roll of Tums on the floor beside him. Apparently he had suffered a heart attack. By ten o'clock old Mr. Mayhew had called the Pecks, but at five o'clock that evening Caroline still knew nothing about it. Nobody wanted to tell her. Instead they huddled in small groups downstairs in Great-Grandma's house, whispering bulletins back and forth. "She's in her bed eating the chocolates Marcus brought her." "She's watching a program on flower arranging." "She's trying to get Justine on the telephone again." "Oh, if only we could just never tell her and this would all blow over!"

Then the grandfather arrived from work. He was forcibly retired now but he liked to prowl around his sons' offices, checking up. "What's this?" he said, seeing clusters of women everywhere. When they told him he shook his head sharply, as if getting rid of a fly. "What? But how old was he? Not even out of his forties! And had a *heart* attack? What kind of stock did the man come from, for God's sake?"

Then he went to break the news to Caroline. The others stood around downstairs, pretending to talk but trailing off in the middle of sentences. One by one the uncles came to find out where everybody was, and they had to be told too. Richard arrived with a girlfriend who was asked politely to leave, as there had been an unfortunate occurrence. Aunt Lucy, who had double-dated with Sam and Caroline when they were young, became a little upset and kept hanging onto her husband's arm until Laura May suggested that she fetch her afghan squares to get her mind off things. Then down came the grandfather, sober and dignified, checking his flip-top watch. "Well?" they asked. "How'd she take it?"

"Took it fine."

"What'd she say?"

"Didn't say anything."

"Shall we go up now?"

"Do what you like," he said, and then he went off to his own house, taking Esther with him to fix his supper.

The others tiptoed up the stairs. Caroline was sitting in her bed against stacks of pillows. When they came in she leaned over to lower the volume slightly on the television set. "Caroline, we're so sorry," they said, and Caroline said, "Why, thank you. It's so nice of you to take an interest."

"If there's anything we could be doing now—"

"I can't think of a thing! But I do appreciate your asking."

"Would you like to go over to the funeral home? Of course it's not as if you had still been *together* or anything, I'm not quite sure what is customary in this case but if you feel you—"

"Why, later, perhaps. Not just now."

"It's probably not customary anyway."

"No."

"Well, if you want us, then—"

"Oh, certainly! I'll let you know first thing."

They tiptoed down again. Although they should be going to their homes for supper, they seemed inclined to churn about in Great-Grandma's living room instead. They weren't quite sure just how they should behave. The last death in the family had been in 1912, too long ago for most of them to remember. "Yet after all," Aunt Sarah said finally, "it's not as if Sam Mayhew were really—"

"No. No."

"And after all, he did actually—"

"Oh, he acted like a man possessed."

"Always trying to turn her against us."

"Making *no* effort to understand her."

"And Caroline's so sensitive. It's the way she is."

"Refusing to give his own daughter away."

"But still," said Aunt Lucy, who sometimes grew over-emotional, "Caroline loved him! I know she did, she must have, you could tell she was just torn. And now he's dead. Oh, what will she do now?"

"*Lucy*," her husband said. "About time to feed me my supper, don't you think?"

"Well, all right."

"We'll try to call Justine from our house, Grandma. If the phone's not fixed, I'll drive out there in the morning."

"Oh, think of Justine. How will she ever forgive herself?"

Upstairs, cowboys sang lonesome songs around a campfire and the wind rolled tumbleweed across the desert with a howling sound.

At nine o'clock that evening, Caroline rose up in her pink silk gown and put on her feathered slippers. Before leaving the room she turned off the television set. She descended the stairs, stately and flowing; she crossed the front hall and went out the door. She drifted across the lawn and then onto the road, where she proceeded down the center with her arms out and her steps mincing and careful like a tightrope walker. To the first car that came, she appeared as monstrous and unexpected as a wad of pink bubble gum. The driver gasped and swerved at the last moment. The second driver was harder to surprise. "Do your drinking at *home*, lady!" he shouted out the window, and then he slid smoothly past.

She had to wait for six cars, all told, before she found one that would run her down.

Duncan brought Justine a cup of beef broth and a silver spoon and a linen napkin. He found her sitting in the living room of Great-Grandma's house, all alone, staring into space. "Oh. Thank you," she said. She set the cup on the coffee table.

"I made it myself."

"Thank you."

"Ma said coffee, but coffee has no food value."

She smoothed her dress.

"Broth has protein," Duncan told her. "You can go without protein for months and feel just fine, never notice, but underneath it's doing you harm that can never be repaired. Protein is made up of amino acids, the building blocks of the—"

"Duncan, I can't *believe* you're saying all this."

"I can't either," he told her.

He waited for her to try the broth. She didn't. He squatted beside her. "Justine—" he said.

But no, too late, the aunts had tracked them down again. "Justine? You mustn't sit like this, dear heart—"

They reminded him of ships. They traveled in fleets. Their wide summer skirts billowed and collapsed as they settled all around him, edging him out. But he didn't give in so easily. "We were just talking," he told them.

"She should be in bed."

"What for?"

"She doesn't look at *all* well."

She didn't. Even her hair seemed changed, hanging lank and lifeless around her face. In just four days she had developed a new deep hollow between her collarbones. She was already losing her country tan. If he could just carry her home, to the sunlit fields and their little house with its ridiculous damask curtains! But the aunts rustled and resettled, inching closer. "She ought to be left with us a while, Duncan. She just feels so *sorry*, you see. She's acting just like her poor dear mother did. You can't take her back to sit all alone in the middle of nowhere."

"Alone?"

"She needs looking after."

"*I* look after her," Duncan told them.

"Yes, but—and she could have her old room again, or maybe yours if hers would bring memories. You could go back to your cows or whatever and we would take good—Justine, do you like Duncan's room?"

"Duncan's? Yes."

"There, see?"

"Or she could come to us," Aunt Bea said. "At our house, you see, we have so much excitement, Esther and Richard rushing around and the twins so talkative, she'd just come out of herself in no time."

"Maybe she doesn't want to come out of herself," Duncan said.

"Oh, it helps to have a little company! All those young people making merry. Justine?"

Justine sat like a stone. The old secret, tucked-in smile she used to flash Duncan seemed gone forever. When he rose she didn't even look his way, and it seemed unlikely that she noticed when he left the room.

Now as she cruised through the darkening house she was aware of how everything here was attached to everything else. There was no such thing as a simple, meaningless teacup, even. It was always given by someone dear, commemorating some happy occasion, chipped during some moment of shock, the roses worn transparent by Sulie's scrubbing, a blond stain inside from tea that Sam Mayhew had once drunk, a crack where Caroline, trembling with a headache, had set it down too hard upon the saucer.

She went out the front door that was dented by Justin Peck's invalid's bed in the fall of 1905. She passed her grandfather's front porch, where Maggie Rose stood in the twilight waiting for a Model T. She climbed Uncle Two's front steps, surrounded by ghostly whispers and murmurs of love and scoldings and reproaches and laughter. Upstairs she found Duncan in his room among Erector Set machines he had built when he was twelve, a full-color poster of Princess Pet in the Land of the Ice Cream Star, the Monopoly board in which all seven cousins had played a thirty-eight-hour world series in the spring of 1944. But Duncan—oh, forever in the present!—was whistling "The Wabash Cannonball" and fiddling with a rectangle of lead-colored metal.

She didn't know how he could whistle.

When she came in the room he stopped. "Do you want to lie down?" he asked her. He began clearing his bed of everything on it, a jungle of wires and soldering irons, tubes of flux, glue, and paint. She sat on the edge of the mattress, but she didn't want to stretch out. It was barely eight o'clock. If she slept now she would lie awake for hours later on, as she had last night and the night before.

"Anything you wanted to say?" Duncan asked.

"No."

"I thought you might have come to tell me something."

"No."

"Well." He went back to whatever he was doing, but he didn't whistle any more. "This is a wire-bending jig," he told her.

She didn't comment.

"These pegs can be moved, see? Then you bend the wire around them any way you want. There are all kinds of curves and angles. I could make you a bracelet. Want a bracelet? Or a necklace, if you like."

She laid her fingers across her eyes, cooling them.

"I've got it," he said. "A nose ring. Want a nose ring?"

When she opened her eyes she found a curve of wire nearly touching her nose, giving off a gray smell, sharp at one end. She batted it away. "What are you trying to *do* to me?" she said.

He looked surprised.

"Are you trying to get me angry on purpose?" she asked him.

"Well, not on *purpose*, no—"

"Why are you acting this way?"

"Justine, *I'm* not acting any way."

"How can you play around with little pieces of wire when both my parents are dead, and you're the one that took me far off and cut the telephone cord and laughed at Mama's letters and wouldn't bring me to visit?"

"Justine."

"Daddy *warned* me," she said. "He told me straight out you were marrying me to torment me."

"Oh, did he?"

"Either that, he said, or to lean on me, but I don't picture *that* ever happening."

"Well, he certainly thought of everything, didn't he," Duncan said.

He went back to bending his wire. He adjusted a peg on the jig and turned a right angle.

"I'm sorry," Justine said finally.

"That's all right."

"I just feel so—"

"It's all *right*."

"Duncan, couldn't we just stay here a while?"

He looked up at her.

"We could live in Great-Grandma's house," she said. "Wouldn't that be nice?"

"No, it wouldn't."

"Please?"

"I should have known," he told her. "I didn't really believe you would come away with me in the first place."

"But I feel I'm getting *pulled*. I hate to just go away and leave them. And I can't stay here without you, but you wouldn't say a word against it when they brought it up."

"*I* don't want to pull you, Justine."

"But then they're the only ones doing it, and they'll win."

"Is that the only way you go anywhere? Being pulled?"

She was silent.

"All right," said Duncan. "I'd like you to come with me. It's important. It's more important than they are."

But she went on watching his face.

"Well, how am I supposed to do this?" he asked her. "I was too well trained, I don't feel *comfortable* saying things straight out. They got to me a little too, you know."

"Oh, Duncan," Justine said. "You've said everything straight out since you were four years old and told Aunt Bea she had hair like broccoli."

"No," said Duncan. "I a Peck. I not talk so good but I give swell presents."

Then he handed her his wire, a stick figure wearing Justine's flat hat and triangular dress, looking so straight-backed and light-hearted that even a tribesman in darkest Africa could tell that someone cared for her.

The family lined up to see them off, their faces papery in the morning sun. "I can't believe that you would be going like this," Aunt Lucy said. Justine kissed her. She kissed Aunt Sarah, who said, "Do you think your parents would have understood? Rushing off as if all that mattered was a pack of billy goats?" Justine kissed her way down the entire row, not skipping even Richard, who ducked and blushed, and when she came to her grandfather she hung onto him hard for a moment as if this, not the wedding, were her real leavetaking. "Oh, um, now, Justine," her grandfather said.

"Goodbye, Grandfather."

Duncan opened the car door and she climbed in. The seat covers had a fish-oil smell from the sunlight, and when she leaned out the window to wave the metal was pleasantly hot on her arm. In the trees above them, mockingbirds were singing. Even when the car roared up they didn't hush. "Scientists," said Duncan, "have been investigating the stimuli that cause birds to vocalize in the morning. So far they have determined only one. They sing because they're happy."

DUNCAN bought a dozen copper-colored hens and installed them in a shed he had built himself, complete with a box of oyster shells to assist in egg production and a zinc watering trough in which they all immediately drowned. But the goats flourished, and since only two customers had answered the newspaper ad there were quarts of surplus milk every day. Justine made butter and hand-cranked ice cream. Duncan boiled up kettles of Norwegian cheese. But no sooner had they finished one batch of milk than the goats gave more, and Justine dreamed at night of a white tide rising all around them. "Maybe we should cut down on the blackstrap molasses," she told Duncan.

"Well, I don't know if that would do much good. We seem to have started something we can't stop, here."

In the mornings Justine walked the gravel road with a basket of cheeses, peddling them to the neighbors, who bought them because they had grown to like her. Seeing her trudge up the driveway, in her country-looking hat and her plain cotton dress that was becoming a little faded, Mrs. Jordan would lumber out on her front steps and beam. "Why, it's Justine Peck! How are you, honey?" Justine smiled trustingly, holding out her basket. It was hard for her to ask people to buy things, but she did enjoy the visits. At each house she stopped for a few minutes to sit in the kitchen and talk, and gradually the smells of kerosene and fatback stopped seeming strange to her and she began to feel comfortable with the stooped, prematurely aged women who offered her buttermilk and ginger cake to put some meat on her bones.

Sometimes, though, alone at home, she felt a gust of sorrow blow through her like a wind and she would stop whatever she was doing, hands stilled, face stunned, and gaze into space for several minutes. Once when she was trimming the weeds that drained the fence's current the smell of cut grass swung her back over years and years and she found herself sitting on a twilit lawn, nestled between her parents, listening to the murmur of her family all around her. She dropped the clippers and reached for the nearest object; she gripped the fence until her knuckles turned shiny. The throb of electricity caused a distant, dull ache. Duncan had to pry her fingers loose and say her name several times before she would look up.

They had not been back to Baltimore after that first visit, but she did write home weekly and one or another of the aunts would answer. Occasionally her grandfather composed a solemn, formal, nineteenth-century note saying that everyone was well and sent best regards. If only she could reach out and touch his knobby hand, as if by accident! But all she said in her own letters back was that Duncan was fine, the weather was fine, the goats were doing nicely.

If the sorrow went on too long she drove to Buskville, where she walked the streets for hours. She had been raised to believe that the best cure for grief was shopping, especially for things to wear. But there wasn't that much money and anyway, she discovered she was incapable of purchasing clothes for herself. Putting on a dress that her mother had not picked out was a betrayal. She was reduced to buying little domestic articles in the dimestore: teaballs, lemon reamers, parsley choppers. It seemed very important to have everything that would make her house perfect.

One day in August, having exhausted all the dimestore's possibilities, she walked down a side street and discovered a hand-lettered cardboard sign reading MAGIC MARCIA. LOVE PROBLEMS. ADVICE. She swooped back through time and found herself on Madame Olita's doorstep, Duncan watching her teasingly with one arm hooked around Glorietta de Merino. After a moment she switched her Woolworth's bag to the other hand and rang Magic Marcia's bell.

The woman who answered was thin and dark, with a crimson slash of lipstick. She was not much older than Justine, but there were two little boys with runny noses hanging onto her skirt. Gray straps slid out from her scoop-necked blouse. Justine was sorry she had come, but it was too late to back out.

Then when she was settled at the kitchen table, over the remains of breakfast, it seemed she was expected to ask some specific question. She hadn't known that. "What is it?" the woman asked, flattening Justine's hand like a letter. "Husband? Boyfriend?"

"No, I—just general things, I wanted to know."

The woman sighed. She scratched her head and frowned at Justine's palm. Apparently she saw nothing unusual. "Well," she said finally, "you're going to live a long time, that's for sure."

"Yes," Justine said, bored. Really she had no particular interest in her future, which seemed certain to be happy and uneventful from here on out.

"Good marriage. Probably travel a little. Health is good. Probably have a lot of kids."

"I will?" Justine asked. Duncan didn't seem to want any children. But the woman said, "*Oh* yes."

A question began to tug at the edges of Justine's mind. She stared into space, not listening to the rest of her fortune. "Um, Magic Marcia," she said finally. "Could you tell me something? If your palm predicts a certain future, is there any way you can change it?"

"Huh?"

"If your future is having children, could you deliberately *not* have children? If your future is to cause someone pain, for instance, isn't there some way you could be very careful and *not* cause pain? Can't you escape your fortune?"

"What is written is written," said Magic Marcia, yawning.

"Oh," Justine said.

On Friday she went to Blainestown, having checked the yellow pages beforehand. She climbed the stairs to SERENA, MISSTRESS OF THE OCCULT. This time, she knew exactly what she wanted to ask.

"Could I have avoided my future if my future was to do somebody harm?"

"Man does not avoid the future," Serena said.

On Monday she went back to Blainestown, this time to MADAME AZUKI, ALL QUESTIONS ANSWERED.

"It's in the stars. There is no escape," said Madame Azuki.

"I see."

On Wednesday she went to Baltimore. Duncan was inventing an automatic bean stringer and he only nodded when she told him she would be out for a while. She drove directly to a cluttered section on the east side of town. She found the dry cleaner's, which was exactly the same even to its fly-specked, faded posters showing women in 1940's suits. But Madame Olita's sign on the window above had become a few flecks of paint, and there was a padlock on her door. Justine went into the cleaner's. A large gray man was lining up laundry tags on the counter. "Can you tell me anything about Madame Olita?" she asked him.

"Ah, Madame Olita. She's gone."

"What, is she dead?"

"No, retired. She's not feeling so well, you know? But was she a fortune teller! I don't mind telling you, I used to go to her myself. Okay, so it's mumbo-jumbo. You know why I went? Say you got a problem, some decision to make. You ask your minister. You ask your psychiatrist, psychologist, marriage counselor, lawyer—they all say, 'Well of course I can't decide *for* you and we want to look at all the angles here and I wouldn't want to be responsible for—' They hedge their bets, you see. But not Madame Olita. Not *any* good fortune teller. 'Do X,' they say. 'Forget Y.' 'Stop seeing Z.' It's wonderful, they take full responsibility. What more could we ask?"

"Well, do you know where she is now? Could I just visit her?"

"Sure, she's right down the block. But I don't know how much she's up to. Well, tell her I sent you, Joe sent you. Maybe she could use the company. Five eight three, apartment A."

"Thank you very much," Justine told him.

"Hope you get the answer you want."

She let the door tinkle shut and walked on down the street, passing more cleaners and cut-rate pharmacies and pawnshops. At the end of the block was a large Victorian frame house surrounded by a veranda, and on the veranda sat Madame Olita in a Polynesian wicker chair. Although it was hot, she wore a crocheted shawl. She still had her stubby haircut, but she had lost an enormous amount of weight. Her clothes flopped and her neck was so scrawny that her face appeared to be lunging forward, vulture-like. She looked hollowed out. While Justine climbed the steps she watched without interest, perhaps assuming this was somebody else's visitor. "Hello, Madame Olita," Justine said.

"Hmmm?"

Madame Olita pulled herself together, wrapping the shawl more tightly around her shoulders.

"Joe sent me," Justine said.

"Oh? Joe."

"There's a question I wanted to ask. Would you mind?"

"Well, I'm feeling poorly these days, you see. I don't look into the future much."

"No, it wasn't about the future."

Madame Olita sighed. "Sit down," she said, pointing to the wicker chair beside her. She reached for Justine's hand, as if she hadn't understood.

"But I didn't want—"

Madame Olita bent Justine's palm back and frowned. "Oh, it's you," she said.

Justine felt pleased and shy, as if her unusual lines were her own accomplishment.

"Yes, I see," said Madame Olita, nodding and tapping her teeth with one finger.

"You said my marriage was going to disrupt everything," Justine reminded her.

"Did I."

"You said I would break my parents' hearts. How did you know that?"

"Oh, my dear," said Madame Olita, leaning back suddenly and dropping her hand. "Really, I don't remember. You were young and arrogant, and uncomfortable in my rooms, perhaps I just—"

"But it all came true!"

"Sometimes it does."

"Was that just luck?"

"It may have been. Sometimes it is, sometimes it isn't. Are you asking if I can truly see the future? I can. But more and more it seems to me that people are resisting change, digging in their heels against it. Which does make their futures easy to predict, but why bother? Fortune telling is only good when you forecast a *happening*. It falls flat when you say, 'Never fear, your life will continue in its present course forever . . .' "

She closed her eyes and then opened them and looked puzzled. "But I tend to go on and on," she said. "You had some question you wanted to ask."

Justine sat up straight and placed her hands together. "Madame Olita," she said, "if my fortune was to break my parents' hearts, is it true then that I had no way of avoiding it?"

"Oh, no."

"*No?*"

"Goodness, no. You can change your future. I have seen lines alter in a hand overnight. I have seen cards fall suddenly into places where they refused to appear at any earlier reading."

"I see," said Justine, and then she sank back. It was the first answer that sounded right to her, but now she couldn't think why she had wanted to hear it. She felt limp and drained.

"Otherwise," said Madame Olita, "why take any action at all? No, you can always choose to *some* extent. You can change your future a great deal. Also your past."

"My past?"

"Not what's happened, no," Madame Olita said gently, "but what hold it has on you."

"Oh."

"If you are so interested, I will teach you the art yourself if you like."

"The—oh, well, I—"

"*Cards* would be your skill, I think."

"Thank you anyway," Justine said.

"Never mind. You'll be back. I sit here every day of the week, taking the air. You can always find me. Shut the front gate going out, if you will."

On Monday, Justine told Duncan that she was thinking of becoming a fortune teller. "Oh, really?" he said.

"Aren't you going to laugh?"

"Not yet," he said. "First I have to see how good you are."

So she drove off to Baltimore again, to the white frame house where Madame Olita nodded dimly in her Polynesian chair.

"These are ordinary playing cards," said Madame Olita, but to Justine they looked anything but. They were very old and the back of each was different: antique circus scenes of clowns, trapeze artists, dancing dogs, and bareback riders. "They once belonged to my mother. Who, though you wouldn't believe it to look at me, was a genuine gypsy lady with seven ruffled petticoats and tiny brass cymbals that attached to her fingers for keeping time while she danced. She was raised in an abandoned candy store on Gay Street. Not exactly a painted *wagon*, but still . . . unfortunately she married my father, a high school civics teacher. She left her old life entirely, she cut off her long black hair, she had two daughters whom she sent to Radcliffe. However, I would rather have been raised a gypsy."

She cut the cards. Justine sat across from her with her mouth open.

"It was my plan, after I graduated from Radcliffe, to join a caravan and marry a man with one gold earring. But it didn't work out that way. I looked then more or less as I do today. I never married anyone, let alone a gypsy. So I had to get a job in my father's high school, teaching algebra, but meanwhile I had learned fortune telling from my mother. Dancing I never mastered. I tried, though. My sister was quite good at it. But I bettered her at fortune telling. How I coveted these cards! My mother refused to give them to me. Cards like these are passed on only when the owner is dying, you see, and has no further use for them. Naturally I didn't want my mother to die. But shall I tell you? When she failed to wake from surgery at the age of fifty-seven, the first thing I thought was, 'Now I can have the cards.' I went home and got them out of her wooden chest, then I walked over to the school and resigned my position. I set up shop in east Baltimore, above the cleaner's. I have never laid eyes upon a caravan."

She laid the cards out in concentric circles on a wicker table.

"My sister," she said, "got the cymbals."

Then she frowned and stabbed a card with her forefinger. "But pay attention! These cards are not read like books, you know. They have meanings assigned that you can memorize in half an hour, but ambiguous meanings. The death card, for instance. So *called*. But whose death? The client's, or someone's close to him? And when? Is it real or metaphorical? No, you must think of these cards as tags."

"Tags," Justine said blankly.

"Tags with strings attached, like those surprise boxes at parties. The strings lead into your mind. These cards will pull out what you already know, but have failed to admit or recognize. Which is why palmistry works as well, or tea leaves or the Tarot or crystal balls, although I myself have yet to see a thing in a crystal ball. They all have validity, yes, but only when coupled with your own intuitions. You could take up astrology, even, but I already know: you haven't the scholarly mind for it."

"I prefer cards," said Justine.

"Yes, yes, I know. But pay attention to *everything*. Watch your clients carefully. There will only be two kinds. Most are bored and merely hope to be told that something will happen. A very few lead eventful lives but cannot make decisions, which may be *why* they lead eventful lives; they will ask you to decide."

"Which am I?" said Justine.

"Hmm? I don't know. Maybe neither. You have never asked me to read your fortune, after all."

"Oh. I guess not," Justine said.

"You're still looking backward, anyway," Madame Olita told her.

"No, I'm not!"

"Suit yourself."

After her lessons Justine drove straight home, but threads, strings, *ropes* pulled her in the direction of Roland Park and although she never gave in she had the feeling she was bleeding somewhere inside. "Well, you could go over for lunch," Duncan said, but she thought from the way he spoke that he dreaded her agreeing to it. And she knew that her family would be distressed if they heard about Madame Olita. Then her new accomplishment, which was still as thin and fragile as a freshly hatched egg, would never seem right to her again; that was the way her mind worked. She didn't go.

Did she believe in fortune telling herself? At Madame Olita's she did. She was drawn in, impressed and fascinated by those no-nonsense hands dealing out the future. But then at home she felt compelled to test her faith with Duncan. She laid out her Bicycle playing cards self-consciously in front of him. "Today," she told him, "I learned the formation used by Mademoiselle Le Normand, back in Napoleon's time."

"Le Normand," he said, interested, cataloguing the name in his mind.

"We practiced on Madame Olita's landlady, who is eighty-four years old. I predicted she was going to get married."

He grinned.

"But!" said Justine. "She is! She told me afterward."

"Good for you. Good for *her*."

"Madame Olita says just a little longer and I can set up in business."

"We'll retire and live on your earnings," he said.

She was relieved that he didn't laugh. This was the only special skill she had ever possessed, the only thing she knew that he did not. Once he started memorizing her list of significations, but he got sidetracked while shuffling the cards and worked out a proof for Bernoulli's Law of Averages instead.

There were days when Madame Olita was sharp-tempered and nothing would satisfy her. "Really, Justine, I despair of you!" she said. "Your mind! You have every qualification to be a good fortune teller but you will never be great, you're mentally lazy. You coast along in intuition."

"You said intuition was everything."

"Never! I never said it was *everything*. You have to know

a few facts as well, after all. These cards are like a doctor's instruments. A good doctor has intuition too but he would never throw his instruments away on the strength of it."

"But you said they were just tags, you said—"

"Enough!" And Madame Olita would fling up her hands and then slump in her chair. "You'll spend your life doing readings for housewives and lovesick schoolgirls," she said. "I don't know why I bother."

But other days she was as mild as milk. Then she would tell stories about her clients. "Will I ever forget that first year? All the Negroes came for clues on how to play the numbers. 'Madame Olita I dreamed of handcuffs last night, which is number five nine eight in my Eye of Egypt Dream Book, but also razors, there was a cutting, eight seven three. So which do I play?' 'My dear,' I told them, 'you leave those numbers alone,' and after a while they gave up on me and never came back. But how I tried! I wanted to have some influence, you see, on their lives. I would give them demonstrations of my psychic ability. I would have them choose a card and sight unseen I would tell them what it was."

"I can't do that," Justine said sadly. Duncan had tested her once after reading an article on J. B. Rhine.

"No, I doubt very much that you would be psychic."

"Then how come I can tell the future?"

"People who have led very still lives can often sense change before others can," Madame Olita said.

"My life isn't still," said Justine.

Madame Olita only sighed.

At the last lesson, she gave Justine a test. "It's time for you to read *my* fortune," she said. Justine had been wanting to do that. She settled down happily at the wicker table, while Olita gazed off toward the street. It was one of her irritable days. "Cut the cards," Justine told her, and she said, "Yes, yes, I know," and cut them without looking. Justine chose a very complicated formation. She wanted to do this thoroughly, not missing a thing. She laid each card out with precision, and then sat back and drummed her fingers on her chair arm. After a moment she moved one card a half inch to the left and resettled herself. She frowned. She stopped drumming her fingers.

Madame Olita looked over at her with cool interest. Still Justine didn't speak.

"Never mind," said Madame Olita. "You passed."

Then she became full of bustle, issuing last-minute instructions. "Did I tell you that strangers should pay ahead of time? If they don't like their fortunes they tend to walk out, they'll walk right out on you."

Justine only gathered the cards in silence, one by one.

"Watch where you work, too. Some places have license fees, sometimes hundreds of dollars. It isn't worth it. Are you listening?"

"What?"

"Don't go to Calvert County. Don't go to Cecil County, don't go to Charles."

"But we live on a farm, I'm not going anywhere."

"Ha."

Justine wrapped the cards and set them on the table. She came to stand in front of Madame Olita.

"Be a little mysterious, I didn't tell you *that*," said Madame Olita. "They'll have more faith. Don't let on where you come from or how you learned what you know. Make a point of ignoring personal questions when you're giving a reading. Will you remember all this? What else should you know?"

Then she gave up. "Well, goodbye, Justine," she said.

"Goodbye," said Justine. "Could I come back for a visit?"

"Oh . . . no. No, I'll be going into the hospital for a while, I think. But I wish you luck."

"Thank you," said Justine. She turned to go.

"Oh, and by the way."

Justine turned back. Madame Olita, sagging in her chair, waved one hand toward the cards. "You might as well take those along with you," she said.

When fall came Justine worked up the courage to offer her services at the high school homecoming fair. She donated her fees to the school. After that people began traveling all the way out to the farm, several a week, mostly women, asking if they should get married, or divorced, or sell their land or have a baby or move to California. Justine was astonished. "Duncan," she said, "I don't want to be *responsible* for people. For telling them who to marry and all."

"But I sort of thought you believed in this," Duncan said.

She wound a strand of hair around her finger.

"Well, never mind," he told her. "Just don't say anything that would cause somebody harm. But I don't think people take *bad* advice. They've got intuition too, you know. In fact I'd be surprised if they take any advice at all."

So she continued receiving people in her small, warm kitchen, laying Madame Olita's cards across the surface of Great-Grandma's rosewood table. She became a gatherer of secrets, a keeper of wishes and dreams and plans. Sometimes when people very young or very old came in, full of vague hopes, unable or unwilling to say what they would like to ask, she merely reassured them. But sometimes she was so explicit that her own daring amazed her. "Don't sell any family possessions, particularly jewelry, particularly your mother's," she would say.

"How did *you* know?"

She hadn't known she did know.

Then sometimes people came whose flat, frictionless lives offered Justine no foothold at all, and she slid into whatever general advice came to mind.

"Don't rely too heavily on a man who bites his fingernails."

In the next room, Duncan snorted.

Justine charged three dollars for each reading. They needed it; their milk customers barely paid for the newspaper ad. Juggling the budget to meet the rent, scraping up money from half a dozen sources, Justine had the feeling that she had been through all this years and years ago. Then she remembered: Monopoly. When Duncan had wiped her out and she was selling back hotels and mortgaging her railroads and turning in her get-out-of-jail-free card, all to pay the rent on Boardwalk. Their present problems did not seem much more serious than that. She knew that Duncan would manage.

For Christmas they went home to Baltimore. The family was very cautious and tactful, circling widely around all delicate subjects. It broke Justine's heart to see what an effort they made. She worried about Duncan—would he say something new to hurt them? She went to bed each night exhausted. But Duncan was meticulously polite. He passed around the gifts that Justine had made by hand and he even invited the family to come and visit some Sunday. ("Oh, well, but it's so much more comfortable for you to come here, don't you think?" everybody said.) On the fourth day, when he became very quiet, Justine was quick to agree that they should head back early. She felt sad saying goodbye, particularly to her grandfather, but each time now it seemed a little easier than before.

In February, when money was especially tight, Duncan got a part-time job in town reporting for the Buskville *Bugle*. "But you can't spell!" said Justine.

"Never mind, you can."

For three weeks he ricocheted around the countryside, attending cornerstone layings, turtle derbies, zoning meetings, a Future Farmers contest in parliamentary procedure, a lecture on crop rotation. He enjoyed everything he went to, indiscriminately, and came home full of new scraps of information. "Did you know you can call up earthworms by vibrating a stick in the ground? If you harvest crimson clover too late it will turn into balls in your horses' stomachs. I've learned a quilting pattern from the eighteenth century." But then writing the articles made him irritable. He never did like going at something systematically. He would hand Justine great sheaves of yellow paper all scrawled over and crossed out, with doodles in the margins. When she ran through them with a red pencil, correcting his spelling and slashing through his long digressions, he lost his temper. "Occurrence, o-c-u-r-e-n-c-e," he said. "Why wreck it up adding extra c's and r's?"

"Because that's how it's spelled."

"A waste of letters. This language has no logic to it."

"I can't help that."

"Why'd you cross out my butterfly paragraph?"

"In an article on potato blight?"

"There happened to be a particularly fine great spangled fritillary sitting on the farm agent's shoulder, totally out of season, ignored by everybody, all the way through the lecture. You can't expect me to overlook a thing like that."

And he would type the article complete and hand it in to the office, where any reference to butterflies was immediately deleted.

"They have minds like a snake's intestinal tract," Duncan said.

The fourth week, he attended an amateur musicians' contest. His article that night began very well, describing the contest's history, its sponsors, and the instruments represented. The next paragraph switched suddenly to first person and related his own impromptu entry with a borrowed harmonica, playing "Chattanooga Choo Choo" for which he won fourth prize. In the third paragraph he reflected on the oddity of the word "impromptu," which could easily be mistaken, he said, for the name of some obscure Rumanian composer.

The newspaper editor said that, actually, they didn't need a new reporter as much as they had thought they would.

By March, Duncan was becoming restless. Justine was not sure why. Everything was going well, six does had been dried off in preparation for their kidding in the spring. But Duncan rattled around the house like a bean in a box, staring out one window after another, starting inventions he didn't finish, sending off to the Department of Agriculture for pamphlets on all sorts of impulsive projects: angora rabbits, fruit trees, popcorn. He painted half the kitchen yellow and then quit. He brought home a carload of rhododendron bushes with their roots balled up in burlap and he planted them all around the yard. "But Duncan," Justine said, "do you think this is the proper time?" They were still wearing overcoats to bed; the ground was still cold and gray. "Why do I have to do everything *properly?*" he asked. "Don't worry, I've got a green thumb. A green hand. I'm a whole green *man.*" And sure enough, the rhododendron took heart and started growing. But Duncan went off and forgot all about it; his strange mood hadn't eased in the least. "To tell the truth, Justine," he said, "this winter business is wearing thin. I imagined we'd be sitting by the stove oiling harness leather or something, but we don't *have* any harness leather. Don't you feel tired of it all?"

"No," Justine said.

She watched, frowning, while he measured the kitchen for some shelves. She didn't think he would ever finish them.

In April eight kids were born, all does. "Did you ever see such luck? We've got a whole damn *herd,*" Duncan said. Justine was glad because the bucks would have had to be killed. She spent hours playing with the kids, running across the field so that they would frolic behind her. They kicked up their heels and turned awkward half cartwheels. She set her face next to their muscular little muzzles; their yellow, slashed-looking eyes looked softly back at her. After the first few days they were switched to bottle feedings, and then to milk from a pan, while Justine crouched beside them and stroked their tufted spines. She fed them handfuls of grass to accustom them to solid food, and for most of the day she kept them in her yard. Meanwhile Duncan carried in endless buckets of warm milk, which he filtered and ran through the great silvery separator. There was suddenly a stream of customers with indigestion, allergies, or colicky babies, all desperate for goat milk, and the grocery store in Buskville had shown an interest in carrying Duncan's cheeses. "There," said Justine. "I knew it would work out!"

"Well, yes," Duncan said.

In May, all the kids died in one night from eating rhododendron leaves.

Justine wandered around forlornly for days, mourning as if the kids had been human. But all Duncan would say was, "Isn't it peculiar? You would think if rhododendron was poisonous they'd know it."

"All those lovely little brown soft furry babies," Justine said.

"But then, goats are fairly intelligent. Are intelligence and instinct inversely related?"

"At least we have the nannies still," Justine said. "We don't have to start *completely* over."

"No."

"And there'll always be a new batch next year, and I won't let them in the yard at all."

Duncan picked up her hand. "Justine," he said, "what would you think of getting out of the goat business?"

"What? Oh, Duncan, you can't quit now. Not after one little setback!"

"No, that's not the reason. I've been considering this for some time. I mean, there's no challenge to it any more. Besides, it keeps you tied down, you always have to be around at milking time. It makes me feel *stuck*, I feel so—and I was thinking. You know what I enjoyed most this year? Building that hen house. Putting things together, fixing them up. Now Ma's brother Ed has a sort of cabinetworks down in Virginia, making unfinished furniture and so on. If he could take me in—"

"Virginia? But that's so far. And *I* never knew you wanted to make cabinets."

"Well, I do."

"We're so nice and settled!"

"But I don't like being settled."

"And we would never get back to Baltimore. Duncan, I've already gone far enough, I don't want to go farther. I couldn't stand going farther."

He waited a moment, looking down at her. Then he said, "All right."

They didn't talk about it again.

People came filing through Justine's kitchen for advice on their spring problems: love affairs, unexplainable bouts of wistfulness, sudden waves of grief over people and places they had not even thought they liked. Justine laid her cards on the rosewood table.

"It will work out."

"Just wait through this."

"You will feel better a week from now."

Duncan plodded through carrying buckets full of milk.

He had grown very silent, although if she spoke to him he always answered. He began drinking bourbon at night after supper. He drank from his great-grandfather's crystal stemware. After the second glass his face became radiant and serene and childlike, and he would switch on a lamp in slow motion and start reading paperbacks. The technical books that he usually liked grew a film of dust while he worked his way through a stack of moldy, tattered Westerns the previous tenants had left in the barn. Whenever Justine looked over his shoulder stubbled men were drawling threats and cowboys were reaching for their guns.

"Duncan," Justine said, "wouldn't you like to sit out on the porch with me?"

"Oh, no thank you. Later, maybe."

But later he went to bed, moving dreamily through the house, not asking if she were coming too. She sat alone at the kitchen table and shuffled her cards. Then she laid them in rows, idly, as if she were her own client. She yawned and looked to see what had shaped up.

She saw journeys, upheavals, surprises, new people, luck, crowds, hasty decisions, and unexpected arrivals.

Which meant, of course, that Madame Olita was right: it was not possible to tell your own fortune.

All the same, if she had had a client with these cards! She imagined how she would glance at him, interested for the first time, amazed at his quicksilver life after all the stale ones she had seen up till now. She imagined possessing such a future herself, having to consult the cards every day, so much was going on.

Then it seemed to her that she was not reading her fortune

after all, but accepting little square papers that told her what was expected of her next. She had no choice but to stand up, and gather her cards, and wrap them in their piece of silk before she went to the bedroom to wake Duncan.

This time they moved in a rented truck, which was cheaper than Mayflower. They left behind Justine's beloved goats, Duncan's chewed-looking rhododendron bushes and his empty, echoing, beautifully built hen house. They took most of the Peck furniture as well as ten years' supply of Bag Balm, which turned out to be excellent for chapped hands. And all the way to Virginia, his truck following behind the apple-green Graham Paige, Duncan studied the back of Justine's head and wondered what was going on in her mind. He knew she hated this move. She had joined up with him, he thought, as easily as taking the hand of someone next to her on a sofa. How could she guess that immediately afterward she would be pulled not only off the sofa but also out of the house, out of the city, off to another *state*, even, clinging fast in bewilderment and asking herself what had happened? And now look: she was so bright and reckless, rattling down the highway, he was reminded of her mother's terrible gaiety at the wedding reception. He knew that sooner or later she was going to break down.

Yet in Virginia, in their shallow hot apartment above Uncle Ed Hodges's garage, Justine remained cheerful. She hummed as she settled their belongings in—only, perhaps, taking a little less care this time, leaving the damask curtains unhung and giving Aunt Marybelle, without a thought, the huge walnut breakfront when it wouldn't fit through the apartment door. She located a church bazaar, where she told fortunes, and after that there was a steady trickle of clients. To Duncan they were indistinguishable from her Buskville clients—mostly women, faded housewives and very young girls—and their lives were indistinguishable too, and their futures, which even he could have predicted, but Justine was patient and kind with them and it was plain they all loved her. In the afternoons, if she had no readings, she came to the cabinetworks and watched Duncan build things. At first she was shy among the blunt, sawdusty carpenters, but she warmed up after a while. She made friends with them and told fortunes for their wives and kept their children. Sometimes she even helped out with the work, sitting on a board for someone or sanding down a tabletop. And always she was so joyous. How long could this last?

She said she wanted a baby. Duncan didn't. The idea of a family—a closed circle locking him in, some unlucky child whom *he* would lock in—made him feel desperate. Besides, he was not so sure that it was medically sound. Who knew what might be passed on? He pointed out their heredity: heart murmurs, premature births, their grandfather's deafness.

"But!" Justine said. "Look at our teeth! They're perfect, not a cavity in the lot. Nobody's ever lost one."

"Justine, if I hear one more word about those goddam teeth—"

But in the end he gave in. He agreed to a baby the way Justine, he imagined, had agreed to move to Virginia; he assumed it was necessary for her in some way that he would never understand. And all through her pregnancy he tried to take an interest. He listened to the details of every doctor's appointment, he practiced her breathing exercises with her until he grew light-headed. Twice he drove her to Baltimore for overlong visits with the aunts, who fussed and clucked around her while Duncan skulked nearby with his collar turned up and his hands jammed deep in his pockets. It seemed to him that his part in all this was so *incidental*. But when he steeled himself to suggest that she might want to go to Baltimore for the birth as well, Justine turned a sudden level gaze on him and said, "No, thank you. I'll have it here with you." How did her mind work?

By her seventh month she had started poring over old photographs in the evenings, particularly photographs of her mother. She sat squinting through a magnifying glass, her hard little knot of a stomach straining the faded dress she had worn since she was seventeen. For she hadn't bought any maternity clothes. Was she worried about the expense? In his experience, women *shopped*. He had expected a frilly layette to mount up in some bureau drawer, but the only things she had were what the aunts gave her. All the preparation she had made was to start building a cradle at the cabinetworks. And when he offered to get her a maternity dress himself her eyes spilled over with tears, something that almost never happened. "But I don't *want* anything. Nothing is right. I couldn't stand to buy anything in those stores," she said. Duncan was mystified. He did the only thing he could think of: he went out and bought three yards of flowered material and a Simplicity dress pattern. He assumed there was not much difference between reading a pattern and a blueprint; he could figure it out in no time and run it up on Aunt Marybelle's Singer. But when he got home Justine was in labor, and he had to take her straight to the hospital. It occurred to him during the trip that Justine was going to die. He thought he had known that all his life without admitting it: she would die at an early age because the world was so ironic. The sight of her calm face beside him—she was so *ignorant!*—made him furious. "You are *not* going to leave me with that baby to raise," he told her, and she turned and looked at him gently, from a distance. "No, of course not," she said.

She was right, of course. The birth was easy. Justine didn't die, she didn't come close to dying. He had been angry for nothing, and on top of that he had an eighty-five-cent pattern now which would never be used, because he'd be damned if they would ever go through this again.

Justine wanted to name the baby Margaret Rose, which was fine with him. But he was a little surprised. He had expected to have to argue against Caroline, or Lucy or Laura or Sarah, none of which he could stand. How long had Justine's fancy been taken by her runaway grandmother? Who was never mentioned, not ever, except by Sulie, who had loved Margaret Rose since first arriving to work for the Pecks at age thirteen. Certainly their grandfather never spoke of her. Duncan was curious as to what the old man would say now. Would he object? But no, when he came for a visit and they told him (Justine shouting it fearlessly into his good ear, which was turning bad like the other), he only nodded as if it meant nothing.

Duncan should have guessed. *Justine* knew. In that family wrongdoers vanished without a trace, not even a hole to show where they had been.

They called the baby Meg for short. She was a blond, stocky, serious baby whose silvery eyebrows were quirked in a permanent frown. When she learned to walk, she *trudged;* if she laughed, it was only after a moment of study. Everything she did was laborious, even stringing wooden beads or feeding a doll or lugging around the large cardboard boxes that for several years she insisted on taking wherever she went. It touched Duncan to see her heaving her toys back into the toy chest every evening, unasked. As she grew older, as life became more hurried and scattered, she developed into a housewifely, competent little soul who always knew where things were, and what had been forgotten, and when they were supposed to be somewhere. By the age of six she had her own alarm clock, the only one in the house. For her seventh birthday she asked for a pop-up toaster. (She wanted to make toast like other people, she said, not in the oven.) She fixed her own breakfast, rinsed her own dishes, and hunted her own socks. Every afternoon when school was over she did her entire homework assignment without being told, her soft yellow head bent low, a pencil clutched tight in her fist. She asked to go both to Sunday school and church, neither of which her parents ever attended; she went alone, dressed in clothes from her grandmother, a bonnet and white gloves, clutching a quarter for the collection plate. Saturday afternoons she read her Bible assignment. "Meggie!" Justine would say, swooping down on her. "Come outside! Come play!" But Meg would have to finish and put everything away before she came. Then Justine took her out visiting other children, or hopscotching, or roller skating. If Justine stretched Meg's skates to the largest size she could wear them herself, and she demonstrated all she remembered from the old days. In a strong wind she stood still and was blown backwards, with her skirts pressed wide and flat. She leaned on the air like a figurehead, laughing, but Meg watched dubiously with her thumb in her mouth.

"This is a cricket," Duncan told Meg.

"Ooh."

"Do you want to know how he chirps?"

"No."

"Many people suppose that he does it with his legs but actually—"

Meg looked not at the cricket but at Duncan. Her eyes were transparent, and flat at the bottom.

He had not expected to feel like a father, but he did. Just the curve of her cheek could give him a wrench, or the blue veins inside her wrist or the stolid way she stood watching other children playing. But he was clearer-sighted than Justine, who thought Meg was perfect. He knew, for instance, that although Meg was of normal intelligence she had a mind that plodded and toiled, with narrow borders; that she was fiercely anxious for regularity, permanence, order. It seemed to him that he was the object of an enormous joke: he had feared all the genetic defects but the obvious one, total Peckness. She was more Peck than anybody, more even than stodgy Claude or the soft, placid twins. When she went to Baltimore for a visit she was the darling. There was not one facet of her that was foreign in any way. It was Duncan who was foreign. As she grew older she seemed to realize that, and more and more often the two of them found fault with each other, bickering pointlessly, defending their two worlds. Then Meg, silenced finally by his quicker tongue, would take on a closed, sad look, and he would be reminded of Justine as a child. He remembered how hopefully Justine would follow her cousins, her eyes anxious, her smile hesitant, her dress as carefully kept as when her mother had buttoned it in the morning. He softened, and gently tweaked a sprig of Meg's hair until she gave in and smiled.

But where was the child Justine had been? There was nothing hesitant about her now. She had become fast-moving, kaleidoscopic. There was a sort of dash to everything she did that surprised and fascinated him. When she flew down a street people turned to look after her: an angular, frayed, pretty woman who looked as if she had no idea where she was going.

She still wore the washed-out dresses from her girlhood, their hems adjusted belatedly half a dozen times, either raised to stand out like a spare tire around her knees or lowered and showing all previous levels like lines on ruled paper; and on her feet, Mary Janes with neat little straps; on her head that everlasting Breton, which Duncan had had to replace, twice, when the crown broke through from all the times she had clutched it to her head on her wild, careening journey through life. Her days consisted of a string of unexpected events. Passing a crazy man talking to himself, for instance (whom Duncan pretended not to hear), Justine stopped to answer whatever question he had asked the clouds and ended up involved for years in the man's Houdini-like escapes from asylums. She was the only person Duncan knew who had actually had a baby left on her doorstep. (Later the mother changed her mind, but Justine had been prepared to keep him.) At any moment of the day he might catch sight of her driving seventeen third-graders in a fire engine down Main Street, or picketing a whites-only movie theater with the day's groceries still in her arms, or zipping past his shop window towed by two gigantic St. Bernards when an hour ago she had owned no dogs at all. And she moved so easily from town to town! Oh, at first, of course, she was always a little reluctant. "But I like it here. We were just getting settled." (She could get settled anywhere, he thought, in a cave or a coal mine even; she was like a cat.) "I don't want to leave all our friends," she would say. (*Her* friends, generally; Justine made friends by leaps and bounds while Duncan was more gradual. It seemed he had barely started getting close to people when it was time to leave a place.) "What do we have to go for, Duncan?" But it was plain what they had to go for—there he was, ever grimmer and bleaker, slogging through the days. "Oh, well," she always said in the end. "We'll move. We'll just move, what's wrong with that?" Then the two of them grew light-headed, as if spared from some disaster they had been dreading for weeks. Justine went off too far ahead of time to pack—her favorite occupation, which became easier every year as they left more and more things behind. She had very nearly stopped cooking, stopped cleaning; she had given away her wedding saucepans as if just *being* were enough to take all her time and attention. For dinner she served whatever came to mind, forgetting to eat herself and opening a window instead to beg a street Arab to let Meg have a ride on his horse. "Oh, *Mama*," said Meg, who would not think of riding such an animal and wished that her mother would not embarrass her by hanging out windows. But Duncan drifted on this turbulence happily; during lulls he felt something was missing. When he came home and Justine was out the air seemed empty and dead. He plowed through the rooms calling her name. He went to neighbors. "Is Justine with you? She's not at home, I don't see her anywhere." Until, having tracked her down, he could heave a long sigh and sink onto the nearest flat surface. "I couldn't find you. I didn't know where you were. I didn't know what had happened to you." Then life zoomed into full speed again, the unexpected fluttered all around them like confetti, and Duncan felt peaceful.

Sometimes he remembered that she had not always been this way, though he couldn't put his finger on just when she had changed. Then he wondered if she only *pretended* to be happy, for his sake. Or if she were deliberately cutting across her own grain, like an acrophobe who takes up sky diving. He became suddenly thoughtful, offering her perhaps a visit to Baltimore, although still, after all these years, the mere thought of his family filled him with a contrariness he seemed unable to control. Justine was still very fond of the family. When he pointed out for her the meaning beneath their words, the sharp edge beneath their sweet, trite phrases, Justine pointed out the meaning beneath *that* meaning, and he would have to admit some truth in what she said. She had the pathetic alertness of a child who has had to depend too much on adults; she picked up every inflection, every gesture and untied ribbon and wandering eye, and turned it over and over to study its significance. (Was that how she could read the future? She had foretold Great-Grandma's death, she said, when she noticed her buying all her lotions in very tiny bottles.) So with Justine's words fresh in his mind he would drive to Baltimore feeling charitable and enlightened, though that never lasted past the moment of entering staid chilly Roland Park with its damp trees and gloomy houses and its reluctant maids floating almost motionlessly up the hill from the bus stop, following their slow flat feet while their heads held back. And once they had arrived he kept watching her, trying to see if deep down she hated him for taking her away. But Justine was no different here from any other place. She gave everybody sudden kisses, knocked Aunt Bea's spectacles askew, swooped through the house causing all the fairy lamps and figurines to tremble on the tables, and once at supper she accidentally ate the little glass spoon from her salt dish. All the aunts jumped up and wrung their hands, but Duncan smiled and his forehead smoothed and he rested back upon the white, tumbling waters of life with Justine.

Now the aunts and uncles were old, the grandfather wore a hearing aid, and the cousins (Sally divorced, the rest unmarried, all childless) were developing lines and sags in their curiously innocent faces like aging midgets. The lawns had grown meager and the fleet of Fords was outdated. The only servant was old Sulie, who shuffled around angry about something, as she had been for years, stirring the dust back and forth with a wilted gray rag. Great-Grandma's house was inhabited by Esther and the twins, but Justine was the legal owner. Someday, everyone said, Justine and Duncan would want to come home bringing their sweet Meg, and when they did this house would be ready. Justine only smiled. Of course they would never live there. Yet always in the backs of their minds it waited as a last resort, if all else failed, if they ever were forced to admit defeat. It figured in back-up plans; it moved in on them, inch by inch, whenever money was tight and jobs were scarce, and over the years it had come to contain an imaginary life parallel to their own, advancing when theirs did. They knew what nursery school they would have sent Meg to if they had lived here, and then what grammar school; what pharmacy they would have patronized and where they would have gone for their groceries. Yet only one glance at that house, where it loomed beneath the oaks, was enough to make Duncan grow dark and hollow and he would suddenly lay a hand on Justine's thigh as if she were a square of sunlight on a windowseat, and he just in from the cold.

8

AN INFERIOR CLASS of people tended to travel by bus. Daniel Peck glared at them: three sailors, a colored boy in a crocheted cap, and a sallow, weasely woman with four children whom she kept slapping and pinching. One of the children stuck out his tongue. "Look at there. Did you see that?" Daniel asked his granddaughter.

She glanced up from her magazine.

"Child made a face at me."

She smiled.

"Well, there's nothing funny about it, Justine."

Whatever she said, he didn't quite catch. It bothered him to go motoring with his hearing aid on.

They were returning from Parthenon, Delaware, where finally, after a great deal of tedious correspondence, he had located the youngest son of the past headmaster of Salter Academy. A Mr. Dillard. Mr. Dillard had already informed him by letter that he had never kept in touch with any of his father's students (who were older than he and not likely to be among the living anyway, he said tactlessly), but Daniel Peck knew that memory was not such a well-ordered affair. Sometimes little things could jog it, he knew, sometimes so small a thing as the smell of clover or the sight of a boy wobbling on a bicycle. So he had come in person, bringing his photograph of Caleb and prepared to offer any detail he could think of, a whole wealth of detail flattened and dried in his mind. "He was a tardy boy, always tardy. Perhaps your father mentioned having a student with a tardiness problem. And let's see, he was extremely sociable. Surely if there had ever been a class reunion of any sort he would have attended. Or just come visiting, don't you know. Perhaps come visiting your father years later, he would do that sort of thing. Can you remember such a visitor? Tall boy, blond, this picture doesn't quite show. He had a habit of tilting his head when listening to people. If you were a child he passed on his way to your father's study, for instance, he would most surely have spoken to you. Though he was not a *smiling* person. Did you see him? Do you know?"

But Mr. Dillard did not know. A stooped, red-faced man who wouldn't speak up. There were cartoon fishes all over his bathroom wallpaper. His wife was nice, though. Lovely lady. She offered them homemade butter mints, the first he had tasted in years, and gave Justine the recipe on an index card.

He set his face toward Justine, waiting till she would feel it and raise her head again. "Yes, Grandfather," she said.

"What'd you do with that recipe?"

She looked blank.

"Recipe card Mrs. Dillard gave you."

"Oh!"

"Don't tell me you lost it."

"Oh no. No, I—"

He didn't know the rest of what she said but he could *see* her plainly enough, rummaging through her crushed straw bag and then her dress pockets, one of which was torn halfway off. Gone, then. He would never have those fine butter mints again.

He removed a large leather wallet from the inner breast pocket of his suit coat. He took out a cream-colored envelope and a sheet of stationery. The envelope was already stamped and addressed. He was very well organized. His stepmother had taught him years ago: compose your card of thanks on the carriage ride home. Never allow an hour to elapse before writing a bread-and-butter note. "Then why," Duncan had asked as a child, "don't we write the whole *letter* ahead of time?" But no, that wouldn't do at all. You had to mention something personal that had occurred during the visit, don't you see. As Daniel did now, after frowning a moment at his pen.

Dear Mrs. Dillard,   March 5, 1973
    I write to express my appreciation for your hospitality. Your butter mints were extremely tasty, and it was very kind of you to take the time to see us. We shall remember our visit to you with a great deal of pleasure.

Respectfully,
Daniel J. Peck, Sr.

When he got back to Caro Mill or wherever he would type a copy of this note for his files. He liked to keep a record of all correspondence, particularly that regarding Caleb. His old Underwood typewriter, with its metal keys and high black forehead, was forever set up on the bureau by his bed; his file cabinet was packed solid with letters of inquiry, thank you letters, follow-up letters, for how many years back? How many years?

Well, his stepmother died in 1958. *That* was a hard time. She was the last person on this earth who called him Daniel. He had not realized that until she died. She had journeyed through all his life with him, minus the first few months: seventy-seven years. The only person who remembered his kid soldier doll, and his father's way of widening his eyes when displeased, and the rough warm Belgian blocks that used to pave the streets downtown. She left her house to Justine, and he knew why. (She was uneasy in her mind about that girl, the sweetest of his granddaughters and the most defenseless, dragged from pillar to post by harum-scarum Duncan, whom marriage had not toned down in the least.) But for months after her death Daniel would not enter her house or look at it, and although he allowed Esther and the twins to move in he told them to stay out of her bedroom. He would sort her things later, he said; he was just a little busy right now. He walked around feeling wounded, struck as if for the first time by the fact that the world kept progressing and people aged and died and nothing in life was reversible. Where had it all gone to? Whatever happened to that little brown German step-grandfather he used to have? Or Sarah Cantleigh's family, who cried whenever they saw him, were they all dead by now? Where was that silent, musical brother of his with the tilted head?

But he was a sensible man, and in time he recovered. Then he sent for Sulie with her ring of keys. They went to sort Laura's belongings. "Oh, my soul," Sulie kept saying. "My soul." She had been mad at Laura for decades, but she looked stricken as she gazed around the dark, stale room. Her eyes were triangular and the cords stood out in her neck. She had a wrinkled face like a yellow paper kite. "So this is what it all come to," she said.

"Now if you don't stop that," Daniel told her, "you can just go on back to the kitchen, hear?"

He left the clothes for the women to deal with; that was none of his business. What concerned him were her desk drawers, jewelry boxes, and knick-knack shelves, which held little mementos that should be parceled out among the family. He opened drawers guiltily, shamed by the puffs of lavender scent that rose from everything as if she were still in the room somewhere. "Well, I just don't know," he said to each new object they found, and then when he had laid it aside Sulie would pick it up and say, "Miss *Sarah* always admire this," or "Miss Bea always saying how she wish she had one like it."

"Take it to her then. Fine. Fine," said Daniel.

He kept nothing for himself. Those neat drawers, with everything arranged so precisely and all for nothing, took away his interest in life. And maybe Sulie's, too. At any rate, when he offered her the oval brooch that contained a plait of Laura's mother's hair and had only one little thing wrong with the clasp, Sulie's mouth turned downward. "I don't want it," she said.

"Suit yourself," he told her. Not everyone would put up with Sulie's rudeness the way he did.

In a desk drawer behind a stack of stationery he found an ancient brittle advertisement for Baum's Fine Cutlery. Beneath it, an envelope that looked as if it had been handled a great deal. Inside was a photograph of Caleb playing the cello in a stable loft.

Now, where did that come from?

He had never seen it before, but from the poor focus and the haphazard composition he guessed that it was the work of Margaret Rose that summer she got her Brownie. For a few months she had wandered everywhere, photographing the most unlikely things: Sulie stringing beans, Sarah on her rocking horse, Lafleur Boudrault playing cigar-box guitar and Mark with a mouthful of honeysuckle blossoms. (Daniel had known she was gone for good when he found all her photos of the children missing. But enough of that.) He peered at Caleb's blurred, sharp-featured face. So far as he knew this was the only picture of Caleb in existence. Not counting the one in the album: age two, wearing a ruffled dress and holding an open book he could not possibly have read. And of course all traces of Margaret Rose had been systematically destroyed long ago. Yet in a sense this was a picture of her too, a permanent record of her hasty way of doing things; and her presence could be inferred from the head-on, quizzical look Caleb directed to the camera holder—an expression he reserved for Margaret Rose. Daniel passed a hand over his eyes. "I believe that will be all for today, Sulie," he said.

"What, you quitting?"

"For now."

"Leaving this mess any which old way?"

"*Later* I'll tend to it."

When he left she was poking the piles of belongings with angry, crabbed hands, muttering beneath her breath. He didn't care to hear what she was saying.

Then for several evenings in a row he sat alone in his bedroom studying the photograph, testing the new feeling of sorrow that drove straight through his ribcage. And when that was absorbed (not lessened, just adjusted to) he became, he admitted, a little crazy. He began wondering if this photo didn't have some secret message to it. It was impossible for such an object just to *be*, wasn't it? He studied the angle of Caleb's hat, the set of his cello, the shreds left on the stable wall by some old poster. What was the significance? Meanwhile his bachelor son and his two spinster daughters whispered downstairs, wondering what he could be doing. When Laura May knocked on his door, he jumped and shoved the photo into his pocket. All she found was her father in his easy chair with his arms folded unnaturally across his front.

Then he went to Lucy, who played a little piano still. He pulled her aside one day when she was counting Mason jars in the pantry. "Lucy," he said, "*you* know music."

"Oh, Father Peck, I—"

"Look here. What note is this man playing?"

He showed her the photo. Surprise set little sharp pleats across her forehead. "Why, who—" she said.

"What note is he playing?"

"Oh, well, I don't—actually, it doesn't look to me as if he's playing *any* note."

"What? Speak up."

"Not any note."

"Why, how is that possible? No note at all? I never heard of such a thing."

"It looks to me as if he's just resting his bow on the strings, Father Peck."

"But that would be ridiculous."

"Oh, no, it's really quite—"

"I never heard of such a thing," he said, and then he slammed out of the pantry.

Already he knew he had made a mistake. For Lucy, of course, had to go and tell Two, and Two out of all the family was the most certain to recognize a description of Caleb. Then everybody knew, and everybody asked him what he thought he was up to. Caleb was best forgotten. He was surely dead by now. What did it matter what note he had played on a summer's day in 1910?

When Justine visited home that August, she came to where he sat in his slat chair beneath an oak tree. She kissed his cheek and drew back and looked at him. He could tell she had heard something. They had all been discussing him behind his back. He snorted. "You know, of course, that I am *non compos mentis*," he told her.

She went on studying him, as if she took what he had said seriously. A literal-minded girl, Justine. Always had been.

"Could I see Caleb?" she asked finally.

"Pardon?"

He thought he had heard wrong.

"Your picture of Caleb."

"The others are asking *not* to see it."

"But I don't even know what he looks like," she said.

He frowned at her. Well, no, of course she wouldn't. Probably didn't know much of *anything* about him. Laura never let his name cross her lips; he seldom had himself; and to the others Caleb was nearly forgotten, a distant grownup uncle whom they had never found very interesting.

"Well," Daniel said.

He drew out the photograph, protected now by glass.

"My brother," he said.

"I see," said Justine.

"Generally he did not go about in his shirtsleeves, however."

Justine bent over the photograph. Her lowered eyelids reminded him of wings. "He looks like you," she said.

"But his eyes were brown."

"His face is the same."

"Yes, I know," said Daniel, and he sighed. He took back the picture. "The others, you see, they don't count him any more. To them he's a deserter."

Justine said something he couldn't catch.

"Eh? To me," he said, "he is still a member here. He goes back to nearly as long ago as I can recollect. I just like to think of him, is all. What's wrong with that?"

"Not a thing," Justine said.

"I would give all the remaining years of my life if I could set eyes on him again."

She said something else. He took a swipe at the air, protesting the curtain of muffled sound that separated them.

"If I could just walk to church with him once more," he told her, "only this time, paying closer *attention*, don't you see. If I could pass by the Salter Academy and look in the window and see him wave, or hear him play that foolish messy music of his on the piano in the parlor—if they could just give me back one little scrap of time, that's all I ask!"

"Oh, well," said Justine. "Come around to the front, Grandfather, see how Meg's grown." And then she took him by the hand, so that he had to rise and follow. In a way, he was a little disappointed in Justine. He had thought she might understand his viewpoint, but if she did she didn't let on.

In November of that year, on a cold, waterlogged day, he received an envelope postmarked Honora, Maryland, where Justine was living at the time. There was no letter, only a clipping from the Honora *Herald*, a whole page devoted to education. He was puzzled. Education did not much interest him. But wait: at the bottom was a very old-fashioned photograph of rows and rows of young boys. The caption said:

THE GOOD OLD DAYS
Above, the author's own school, Salter Academy
in Baltimore, around the turn of the century.
Note gaslights along the walls. Author is in
seated row, second from left.

Daniel took off for Honora within the hour, driving his V-8 Ford. He arrived at Justine's house waving the clipping. Justine was in the kitchen reading some lady's future—an occupation he and all the family preferred to ignore. "Never mind that," he told her. " I want to see Ashley Higham."

"Who's Ashley Higham?"

"The man who wrote this piece, of course."

"Oh, then you *do* know him!" Justine said.

"No I don't know him, don't know him from Adam, but it says right here he went to Salter Academy, doesn't it? Says this is him seated, second from left, and not an arm's length away from him is my own brother Caleb, isn't it?"

"Is that right?" said Justine. She set down her cards and got up to have a look. So did the lady, not that it was any of her business.

"Now all I've got to do is find Ashley Higham," Daniel said.

"Oh, well, Grandfather, I don't really know where—"

"*I* know," said the lady.

So it was the lady who led the way to Ashley Higham. And Mr. Higham did, in fact, remember Caleb well, but had not seen him since graduation day in 1903. However, he had a remarkable mind and could reel off the name of every boy, his shaky white index finger slowly traversing the rows of faces. Daniel recorded each name on a sheet of paper. Later he would copy them into a pocket-sized ring notebook that he carried with him everywhere, gradually stuffing it fatter and fatter. For one thing led to another, one man remembered another who had been a friend of Caleb's and *that* man remembered Caleb's elocution teacher, who turned out to be deceased but his grandson in Pennsylvania had saved all his correspondence and from that Daniel found the name of the geography teacher, and so on. His files began filling up. His Ford clocked more miles in a year than it had in all its past life. And bit by bit, as the rest of the family grew more disapproving (first arguing reasonably, then trying to distract him with television and scrapbooks and home-made pie, finally stealing his car keys whenever his back was turned) he began staying for longer periods of time with Justine. Only visiting, of course. It would never do for Caleb to come home unexpectedly and find him vanished without a trace. His house still waited for him in Baltimore, his daughters still kept his room made up. But Justine was the only one who would hop into the car with him at a moment's notice, and go anywhere, and talk to anyone and interpret all the mumbled answers. And when he was discouraged, Justine was the one who bolstered his confidence again.

For he did get discouraged, at first. At first he was in such a hurry. He thought he was right around the corner from success, that was why. Then when he traveled clear across the state to find Caleb's oldest, dearest friend and learned that he had last seen Caleb in 1909, he grew morose and bitter. "I always assumed," he told Justine, "that people keep in touch, that if they lose touch they go back and pick it up again, don't you know. Of course I am more a *family* man myself, family's been my social life. But I would suppose that if you just watched a man's best friend long enough, you would be certain to see the man himself eventually. Well, not Caleb. In fifty years he has not once gone back to pay a call, and his friend has never done a thing about it. What do you make of that?"

Justine said, "Never mind, Grandfather. It will work out." (Was she speaking *professionally?*) And the next morning she was perfectly willing to set off again, cheerful as ever, never losing patience. So there was no need to hurry after all. He began to relax. He began to enjoy the search itself, the endless rattling rides, the motionless blue sky outside the window of his train. (For they had quickly switched to railroad, as his deafness had caused several near accidents and Justine's driving terrified him.) In the old days, merely a business trip to New York had made him feel like a ball of yarn rolling down the road, unwinding his tail of homesickness behind him in a straight line back to Roland Park. But now he learned to concentrate solely on the act of traveling. He liked to imagine that Caleb himself had ridden this very train. He bobbled along on the Southern Railroad Line or the B & O, on dusty plush seats, occasionally stretching his legs on some small-town platform where, perhaps, Caleb had stood before him. And he returned home as confident as when he left, for there was always time to search further, next week or next month or whenever he felt up to it.

If Duncan minded this permanent visit, he never said so. In the beginning Daniel had asked him outright. (Well, as outright as he could get.) "Nowadays, people seem to prefer a minimum of adults in one household, have you noticed?" he had said. But Duncan only smiled. "Some do, some don't," he said. Another of those unexplained remarks of his. He did it on *purpose*. Daniel mulled for several days, and then he went to Justine. "Duncan of course has never kept close family ties," he told her, and waited, trustingly, for her to understand. She did.

"That's true," she said, "but he hasn't said anything so far."

And Daniel was careful to see that he never gave Duncan reason to. He held back from advice (which Lord knows the boy could have used) and praise and criticism. He accepted every change of address without question, although none of them were the least bit necessary. Didn't it occur to Duncan that other people had low periods too, and just sat them out instead of packing up bag and baggage? You endure, you manage to survive, he had never heard of someone so consistently refusing to. But never mind, he didn't say a word. He went uncomplainingly to each new town, he accepted Justine's half-hearted cooking and cleaning, which were, he assumed, the natural result of failing to give a woman any permanence in her life. Why should she bother, in those shabby, limp houses that looked flung down, that seemed to be cowering in expectation of the next disaster? And meanwhile Laura's fine place was sitting empty. (He didn't count Esther and the twins living there, for really they belonged at home with their parents.) But leave it be, leave it be. The only change he made in their lives was to deed his Ford to them once he quit driving. It made him nervous to ride about in the Graham Paige, for which Duncan had to haunt antique shows every time a part wore out. "But I don't like Fords," Duncan said. "I have a deep-seated *hatred* of Fords," and for half a year they had been a two-car family, Justine darting about in the Ford and Duncan in the Graham Paige, whistling cheerfully and looking down from time to time to watch the highway skating along beneath the holes in the floorboards. The engine, he said, was in fine shape, and no doubt it was, for Duncan was an excellent mechanic. But you have to have something to put an engine *in*, not this collection of green metal lace and sprung springs; and on moving day that year, without a word, Duncan had left it sitting in front of the house and driven off in the U-Haul. His grandfather pretended not to notice. He was a tactful man.

He lived in his own tiny, circular world within their larger one. While they moved up and down the eastern seaboard, made their unaccountable decisions, took up their strange acquaintances and then lost them and forgot them, Daniel Peck buttoned his collarless shirt and fastened his pearl-gray suspenders and surveyed his white, impassive face in the bedroom mirror. He wound his gold watch. He tidied his bed. He transformed even his journeys, the most uncertain part of his life, into models of order and routine and predictability. For Justine was always with him, he always had the window seat, she read her *National Geographic*, they carried on their spasmodic, elliptical conversations over the noise of the road. Now they had to ride the buses more and more often, since that was all most towns had these days. They would take long circuitous routes in order to join up someplace, somehow, with a railroad, and even *then* it was usually Amtrak, a garish untrainlike train where nothing went right, where certainly Caleb had never set foot in his life. But still Daniel traveled calm and expressionless, his hands on his knees, a ten-dollar bill pinned inside his undershirt, and his granddaughter's hat brim comfortingly steadfast in the right-hand corner of his vision.

They were drawing close to what's-its-name, Caro Mill. He noticed people rising to put their coats on, and lifting suitcases down from the rack. He noticed within himself a sudden feeling of emptiness. So they were back again, were they? He sighed. Justine looked up again from her magazine.

"We didn't get much done," he told her.

"Why, no."

To her it didn't matter. She thought he felt the same, he had ridden content beside her for so many years now. But lately he had had a sense of impatience, as in the old days when he first began his search. Did that mean he was drawing close to Caleb? Once he almost asked her outright for a reading from her cards—ridiculous business. Of course he had stopped him self in time. Now he stared bleakly out the window at a jumble of service stations and doughnut shops. "So *this* is where we're headed," he said.

"What?"

"It's not much of a place to come back to."

"Oh—" said Justine, and then something else he couldn't catch, but he knew it would be cheerful. Justine did not seem to be easily disappointed. Which was fortunate. Whereas he himself was leaden with disappointment, sinking fast. He felt there was something hopeless about the deep orange sunset glowing beyond an auto junkyard. "Grandfather?" Justine asked, in her most carrying tone. "Are you all right?"

"Yes, certainly."

The bus wheezed past a dismal hotel with tattered window-shades. It stopped in front of the Caro Mill Diner. Place couldn't have a regular terminal, no. Out they had to climb, in the middle of the street. The driver did not so much as give Justine a hand down the steps, or either of the other ladies; Daniel had to do it. He touched his temple for each one in turn as he let go of her arm. "Why, thank you," one lady told him. The other didn't say a word, or else he missed it.

In front of the diner sat the Ford, three feet from a hydrant, battered and dusty and bearing a long new dent in the rear bumper. He studied the damage. In the old days people left notes about such things, giving their names and telephone numbers. Not any more. When he finally climbed into the car he said, "Conscience has vanished."

"Excuse me?"

Justine looked at him, one hand outstretched toward her own door which was flapping open and snarling traffic. "*What's* vanished?"

"Conscience, I said. They dent your bumper and don't even leave a note."

"Perhaps *I*," said Justine, and something else.

"No, if you had done it I would have noticed. Besides, you've *had* this week's accident." His little joke. He laughed, covering his mouth with his fist to turn it into a cough.

Then, *wham!* He was jarred and knocked into the windshield. Aches and pains started up all over, instantly. It seemed that someone had reached down a gigantic hand and flung him like a doll. "Grandfather?" Justine asked. There was a long red welt on the inside of her arm, and a few dots of blood. Just past her, a car had stopped and a man was climbing out. And where the door had been swinging open there was nothing now at all, just clear blank air and then the man's angry face. The man was shouting but all his words were a blur. It didn't matter; Daniel was just relieved to see the cause of his shake-up. Of course, a door torn off! Yet he continued to feel disoriented. When the man had driven away, and Justine stepped out to drag the door to the trunk and heave it in, he was still so dazed that he didn't offer to help. He watched numbly as she slid behind the wheel again. "At least we're well ventilated," she told him. A strange thing to say, or perhaps he had misunderstood. He wished he were home. He raced through the hallways of his mind calling out for Laura, his father, Caleb, Margaret Rose. But really he should never have married Margaret Rose. A shared background was the important thing. If he had not been such a fool for her chuckling laugh and the tender, subtle curve at the small of her back he would have made a more sensible choice, a person he had known all his life. Who was that little girl who used to come visiting with her parents? Melissa, Melinda? But he had wanted someone new and surprising. A terrible mistake. How he hated Margaret Rose! The thought of her made him grind his teeth. He would like to know where she was now so that he could do something dreadful to her, humiliate her in front of all her fancy, tinkling friends. But no, she was dead. He was so disappointed to remember. As usual she had done something first, run ahead of him laughing and looking back at him over her shoulder, and for once he could not refuse to follow.

"Once you're alive, there's no way out but dying," he told Justine.

She looked over at him.

"You've set a thing in motion, you see."

"It's like being pregnant," said Justine. Of course she

couldn't *really* have said that. His ears were bad. His mind was bad. He was going to have to get a hold of himself. He straightened his back and looked out the window, a respectable elderly gentleman admiring the view as they rattled homeward.

Meg Peck and the Reverend Arthur Milsom were sitting in the living room waiting for Meg's parents. Or Arthur was sitting; Meg kept moving around. First she chose the armchair because she wanted to look proper and adult. Then she thought it was more natural to sit next to Arthur on the couch. They were about to ask permission to get married; what would they be doing across the room from each other?

Arthur had on his clerical collar, which wasn't absolutely required but it looked very nice. He was a young, pale, tense man, small but wiry. When he was nervous he cracked his knuckles and his brown eyes grew so dark and sober that he seemed to be glaring. "*Don't* be nervous," Meg told him, sitting back down on the couch. She reached over and took his damp hand.

This visit had been planned for weeks. The first Monday after she turned eighteen, he said, he would come talk to her parents. (Monday was a slow day at the church.) They had worked it out by letter. It was Arthur's feeling that Duncan was the important one, but as Meg pointed out they needed Justine there to smooth things over. For certainly Duncan would be at his sharpest. He didn't like Arthur. (How could anyone not like Arthur?) What they hadn't counted on was Justine's vanishing, taking Grandfather on one of his trips. Now there was no telling when she would be back, and meanwhile Duncan was coming home from work at any minute. They would have to handle him alone after all.

Meg always thought of her parents as Duncan and Justine, although she didn't call them that. It might have been due to the way they acted. They were not very parent-like. She loved them both, but she had developed a permanent inner cringe from wondering how they would embarrass her next. They were so—*extreme*. So irresponsible! They led such angular, slapdash lives, always going off on some tangent, calling over their shoulders for her to come too. And for as long as Meg could remember she had been stumbling after, picking up the trail of cast-off belongings and abandoned projects. All she really wanted was to live like other people. She tried to keep the house neat, like her friends' houses, and to put flowers in the vases and to hide, somehow, whatever tangle of tubes and electrical wires Duncan was working on at the moment. But then it seemed so hopeless when she knew how soon they would be moving on. "We're nomads," Justine told her, "think of it that way"—as if making it sound romantic would help. But there was nothing romantic about this tedious round of utility deposits, rental contracts, high school transcripts and interrupted magazine subscriptions. "He's ruining our *lives!*" she told Justine. Justine looked astonished. "But Meggie darling, *we* can't be the ones to say—" Then Meg's anger would extend to her mother, too, who was so gullible and so quick to give in, and she closed herself up in her room (if they were in a house where she *had* a room) and said no more.

She kept herself occupied with sewing, or pasting pictures in her scrapbook full of model homes—French windows and carpeted kitchens and white velvet couches. She straightened up her closet with all her shoes set side by side and pointing in the same direction. She ironed her own dresses, as she had since she was nine. (Justine thought there was no point to ironing, as long as things were clean.) At the age of ten she had baked her first cake, which everyone admired but no one ate because they were too busy rushing off somewhere; they seemed to live on potato chips from vending machines. Nothing ever worked on a schedule. She was encouraged to bring her friends home at any hour of the day or night. "This family is not a closed unit," Duncan told her—apparently his only rule, if you could call it that. But how could she bring friends when her parents were so certain to make fools of themselves? "Oh, I just love your folks," girls were always saying, little dreaming what agony it would be to have them for their own. For Justine might be found barefoot and waving her dirty playing cards, or sitting at the kitchen

table with three or four unsuitable friends, or racing about looking for her broken straw carry-all in order to go to the diner
whose food she preferred to her own. She had a high-handed,
boisterous way of acting sometimes and she was likely to refer
to Duncan publicly as "Meg's second cousin," her idea of a joke.
And Duncan! Spouting irrelevant, useless facts, thinking out
loud in startling ways, leaving her friends stunned and stupid-
looking. *His* idea of a joke was to hang idiotic newspaper and
ladies' magazine pages all over the house, bearing what he
thought were appropriate messages. On Justine's birthday he
pasted up a bank ad saying WE'RE INCREASING OUR INTEREST,
and after Meg spent too much money on a dress (only because
she wanted to look like the other girls for a change, not all
homemade and tacked together) she found a page Scotch-taped
to her closet door:

HAVE YOU EVER HAD
A BAD TIME IN LEVI'S?

Then she had snatched up the page and stalked in to where
Duncan sat inventing a new keyboard arrangement for the typewriter. "Act your *age!*" she told him. But when he looked up
his face was so surprised and unguarded, and she saw that he
really *was* aging, there were dry lines around his eyes and two
tiny crescents left by his wide, dippy smile. So she laid the paper
down gently, after all, and went away defeated.

Now she sighed, remembering, and Arthur squeezed her
fingers. "In an hour this will all be over," he told her.

"It will never be over."

"I don't understand."

"We're going to be demolished," she said. "I feel it."

But now she had insulted him. He straightened up, which
made him look smaller. He said, "Don't you think I can have a
reasonable discussion with my own girl's parents?"

"Yes but—"

"You forget, I'm a minister. I've convinced families who
swore they'd cut off their daughters without a penny. I've convinced fathers who claimed that—"

"But it wasn't you their daughters were marrying."

"Now don't *worry*. If worst comes to worst we'll just go away quietly and have the ceremony in my own church."

But neither of them wanted that. They wanted everything perfect. Arthur wanted her to be happy, and Meg would only be happy with a white dress that dipped to a point at the waist, Sarah Cantleigh's veil, and a bouquet of baby's breath. She wanted to walk down the aisle of the family's church in Baltimore where her mother had been married; she would like to be guarded by rows and rows of aunts and uncles and second cousins, grave Peck eyes approving her choice. Bridal showers, long-grained rice, Great-Grandma's sixpence in her shoe. Arthur waiting beside the minister, turning his pale, shiny face to watch her procession. Whenever he looked at her, she felt queenly. All right, so he was not a handsome man, but would a handsome man treat her as adoringly as Arthur Milsom did? When they went to lectures she looked at the lecturer and Arthur looked at her. She felt the thin moon of his face turned upon her. He assisted her in and out of cars, through doorways, up the shallowest steps, his hands just barely brushing her. (The aunts would love his manners.) He devoted his entire attention to her, so much so that sometimes, he said, he worried about his jealous God. Nobody had ever, in all her life, felt that way about her before.

A car drove up in front of the house, chugging and grinding familiarly. "There's Mama now!" Meg said. "Look, she beat him home after all." She rose and went out to the porch. Justine was still seated behind the wheel, straight-backed and prim, unguarded by even the vestige of a door. The car looked like a cross-section of something. But, "Certainly makes it easier to get in and out!" she called to Meg, and she waved gaily and stepped onto the sidewalk. "Coming, Grandfather?"

"Mama, I want to talk to you," Meg said.

But then up spoke Dorcas Britt, the lady next door, calling over the hedge in a large, rich voice that seemed to mock Meg's. "Justine, honey! I got to talk to you."

"A man came along doing eighty and flung Grandfather into the windshield," Justine said.

"Mama."

The house was swept suddenly with a variety of colors and shapes—the white, tottering grandfather, Justine flicking back her yellow hair, Dorcas all chartreuse and magenta on red patent-leather spike-heeled sandals. Arthur stood up with his fingers laced in front of him, as he did when greeting church members after the sermon. He wore a determined smile. Meg felt a twist; was she doomed to be embarrassed by *everyone*, all her life, even Arthur? "Mama, Grandfather, you remember Arthur," she said. "Mrs. Britt, this is Arthur, my—Arthur Milsom."

"My baby has been kidnapped," Dorcas told him.

Her baby was nine years old and she was kidnapped regularly, always by her father, who did not have visiting rights, but Arthur didn't know that and he grew white around the lips. "Oh, my heavens!" he cried.

"Arthur. It's all *right*," Meg told him.

"All right?" said Dorcas. "To you, maybe."

"Grandfather was zonked in the forehead," Justine said.

Which caused Arthur to spin next in the grandfather's direction, full of a new supply of horror and sympathy. He hadn't learned yet. Such an expenditure of emotion would drain you in no time, living here. "*Arthur*," Meg said.

"The man was going eighty, at least," said Justine. "How else could he have ripped a door clean off like that?"

"It was already hanging by one hinge, Mama."

" 'You were going eighty,' I told him, but guess what he said? It's against the law to open a car door on the street side. Did you know that? How are we supposed to get into our cars?"

"Perhaps from the sidewalk side," Arthur said carefully.

Justine paused, in the middle of removing her hat, and looked over at him. "Oh. Arthur," she said. "Why, how are you?"

"I'm just *fine*, thank you, Mrs. Peck. How are *you?*"

"And Meg! Meggie, did you find my note? I forgot to tell you I was going off today. Did you have anything to eat when you came home from school?"

She didn't wait for an answer. She kissed Meg on the cheek —a breath of Luden's cough drops. Whenever she kissed people she gave them quick little pats on the shoulder. Meg drew away, trying to regather her dignity. "Mama, when you get a moment," she said.

"But I *have* a moment. All the time in the world. What can I do for you?"

"Don't you have to start supper?"

She meant, Can't you come out in the kitchen and talk without Dorcas? But Justine said, "Oh, I thought we would just have pick-ups tonight." The only one who understood Meg was Dorcas, who drew herself in while remaining, somehow, as billowy and bosomy as a featherbed. A fat blonde with tiny hands and feet. "*You* are not a mother," she said. "You have never had your baby kidnapped. This is not something I can just go home and forget until a more convenient time."

"Perhaps if you called the police," said Arthur.

"Police! Ha!"

"Mama, I want to talk to you a second."

"All right."

"I mean, privately."

"Honey, can't you talk here? Dorcas is a friend, we don't have to be private from *her.*"

"I should say not," said Dorcas.

"Well, I'll wait till Daddy comes home," Meg said.

"Oh, Duncan! Where is he? Shouldn't he be here by now?"

And off she flew to the window, with Dorcas tripping behind her on her ridiculous shoes. "Look here, Justine, you got to help. Won't you lay the cards? I got to know where Ann-Campbell is."

"Oh, well, I'm sure she's all right."

Ann-Campbell would be all right anywhere. Meg pitied her kidnapper. But Justine gave in, soft-hearted as usual. "But maybe just a *quick* reading," she said. And off they went to the kitchen for the cards. Grandfather Peck stood teetering from heel to toe, peering after them. "Are they going to make supper?" he asked Meg.

"They're doing a reading, Grandfather."

"A what?"

"*Reading.*"

"What would they be reading *now?* It's suppertime."

He sat down suddenly in the armchair. There was a long knot growing on his forehead. "Grandfather, you're turning purple," Meg said.

"Ah?"

"Perhaps he needs medical attention," Arthur whispered.

But the grandfather, who could sometimes hear astonishing things, slapped his knee and said, "Nonsense!"

Then there was a blue-and-yellow flash in the door—Duncan, wearing the jeans Mr. Amsel had asked him not to. He sprinted across the hall and into the coat closet. "Daddy?" Meg said.

"Meg, where is that magazine I was reading last night?"

"I don't know."

"Do you have to put everything away all the time?"

"*I* didn't put it anywhere."

"Never mind, I found it."

Off he went again. The door slammed. Arthur began stroking his chin thoughtfully.

"Was that Duncan?" the grandfather asked.

"Yes, Grandfather."

"*You're* a pastor," he told Arthur.

"Assistant pastor, yes sir."

"Here's an idea for a sermon."

"Grandfather."

"All our misery comes from the length of our childhood. Ever thought of that?"

"No, sir, I don't believe I have."

"Look at it this way. Everything arises from boredom, right? Irritation, loneliness, violence, stupidity—all from boredom. Now. Why are we bored? Because the human childhood is so durned lengthy, that's why. Because it takes us so durned long to get grown. Years. Years and years just hanging around waiting. Why, after that just *anything* would be an anticlimax."

"Sugar," Duncan called, crossing the front hall again.

"How's that?"

"Eat more sugar."

"*What'd* he say?"

Duncan stuck his head in the living room door. "Sugar hastens puberty," he said. "All the Eskimos are growing up faster now they've switched to carbohydrates."

Grandfather Peck scratched his head.

"Daddy," said Meg, "we want to talk to you."

"Ah so, Meggie." But then he saw Arthur. "Why, looky there, a man of the cloth."

"Daddy, when Mama gets through—"

"Where *is* your mother?"

"She's reading the cards for Dorcas."

Arthur stood up. Next to Duncan he looked very small and stalwart. "Actually, Mr. Peck," he said, "I feel it would be quite enough just to talk to you."

"Oh, more than enough," said Duncan.

"When I became a man," the grandfather said, "I caught myself thinking, many times, so this is what it's like to be grown up! Plodding back and forth, between work and home. Even being a judge was not what I had hoped. Really you don't make judgments at all; you simply relate what happens today to what has happened yesterday, all the precedents and statutes and amendments. And when you've waded through that, what next? You get old. And you're old for years and years and years. Your hearing goes and your knees go. Some people's teeth go. I myself have kept all my teeth but I wouldn't say it has done much good. After all, whatever I eat I ate a thousand times before. In addition I have become more and more conscious of where the food comes from. Pork tastes like pigs, beef like cows, lamb like sheep's wool, and so forth. Milk chocolate, which I used to consider a treat, nauseates me now. I taste the smell of cow barns."

"I wonder," said Duncan. "If we ran some experiments with *goat's* milk chocolate—"

"The Chinese venerate age. If I were in China people would come to me and say, '*You're* old and wise. What's the meaning of it all?' "

"What *is* the meaning of it all?" Duncan asked.

"I don't know," his grandfather told him.

"Mr. Peck," said Arthur, "I would like to marry your daughter."

The grandfather said, "My daughter?"

But Duncan understood. He gave Arthur a long, clear, untroubled look, as if nothing such a man could say would bother him. Then he said, "She's seventeen."

"Eighteen," said Meg.

"Eighteen? Oh yes."

"And Arthur's twenty-six."

"Well, that's ridiculous," said Duncan. "When you're seventy he'll be seventy-eight."

"So?"

"And you're still in school."

"We're planning a June wedding," said Arthur. "She'll be graduated by then."

"And Daddy, you know I'm not the college type."

"Who is? Who cares about college? Did I ever say I wanted you to go to college? But I didn't say I wanted you to get married right off the bat, either, and go live in Simper, Virginia, sitting in the front pew every Sunday nodding all the flowers off your hat. It's a trap. Do you want to be trapped? I thought you would go off and do something, Meggie, travel somewhere. Leave old Caramel behind if you like, we're not trying to keep you for ourselves. Hitch-hike to California. Take a freight train. Take a *bus*. Learn to surf. Marry somebody unpredictable. Join the Foreign Legion."

"But I can't be that way."

"Try! Anything but this. Just settling for it doesn't matter who, any pale fish in a suit—"

"Mr. Peck," said Arthur, "I understand, of course, that in the heat of the moment—"

"How will you have babies, Reverend Mildew, osmosis?"

"Mama!" Meg called.

"Don't trouble your mother, Meg, I'll see him out myself."

"Unfortunately I am not that easy to discourage," Arthur said.

"That *is* unfortunate." But Duncan was guiding him toward the door anyway, and Arthur was allowing it. "Now," said Duncan, "if by any strange chance Meg still feels the same when she is of a decent age, Reverend, I admit there is nothing I can do about it. Meanwhile, goodbye."

"But I am of age!" Meg said.

The front screen slammed.

Meg looked at her great-grandfather, who smiled a weary smile showing every one of his perfect teeth. She crossed to the kitchen door and opened it.

"Meg," said Dorcas, "your mother's a marvel. My cards say Ann-Campbell is with Joe Pete and I'm to enjoy the rest while she's gone."

"Mama, listen."

Justine looked up. She was seated at the kitchen table, holding both hands rigid. Between each finger were long sprays of raw spaghetti. "Look, Meg!" she said. "I'm learning the I Ching!"

"Is that all you have to do?"

"Well, we should use yarrow stalks but we don't know what they are."

"I just want to tell you this," Meg said. "I blame you as much as him."

"What, Meggie dear?"

"The two of you are as closed as a unit can get, I don't care *what* he says."

"Closed? What?" said Justine, looking bewildered. She

rose, holding out two spaghetti whiskbrooms. "Wait, Meggie darling, I don't—"

But Meg was gone. She ran across the hall and out of the house. There was no sign of Arthur or Duncan in the yard. Only the Ford, melting into the twilight, with a magazine page flapping in the space where the door should have been: WOULDN'T YOU REALLY RATHER HAVE A BUICK?

9

FOR THE POLK VALLEY CHURCH'S April bazaar Justine wore her very best dress—an A-line shift that Duncan had bought her five years ago at a nearly-new sale. She pulled her hair into a sprout on top of her head, covered it over with her hat, and dabbed at her mouth with a pink Tangee lipstick from high school. On her feet she wore her black Mary Janes, on her arm a gypsy bracelet borrowed from the Blue Bottle. Generally speaking, she thought she looked very presentable.

Because the car was in the body shop, Justine had to ask for a lift in Dorcas's baby-blue Cadillac. And Ann-Campbell had to come along, jouncing in the back seat, periodically nosing her sharp little freckled face between the two women to eavesdrop. Justine liked Ann-Campbell. She was certain she was going to lead a very interesting life.

On the way to Polk Valley Dorcas talked about her ex-husband, Joe Pete, whom she had married and divorced three times now. Every time she married him she had a large church wedding all over again, with Ann-Campbell as flower girl in a floor-length organdy dress to cover the scabs, scars, scrapes, bruises, and Band-Aids on her bony knees. Lately relatives had stopped attending, and the gifts had thinned out. "But," said Dorcas, "he's still my first husband, isn't he? I've never been married to anybody else, and neither has he. Why can't I have a wedding like I choose?"

Justine didn't want to think about weddings. They reminded her of Meg. She was worried sick about Meg, who had become very quiet the last few weeks, and whenever she talked it over with Duncan he acted so cross and stubborn that he was no help at all. He said Meg could marry anyone she chose, a Congo chieftain if she cared to, but not a man whose only quality was harmlessness. "Maybe she loves him," Justine said, but doubtfully. She *tried* to believe it. Whenever she saw Arthur she worked at being interested in him. She observed that he was kind-hearted, steady, polite . . . and then her mind would trail off to some other subject and she forgot he was there. She watched Meg, who appeared as placid as ever. But then Meg didn't show emotions, that was all. Of course she loved him or she wouldn't say she wanted to marry him.

Oh, the things she had prepared herself for, when Meg was born! Merely the fact of having a new person in the world implied a stream of unforeseen events endlessly branching and dividing. As Meg grew into her teens Justine was braced for long-haired suitors, LSD, shoplifting, pregnancy, revolutionists, firearms in the closet—anything, for her daughter's sake she could deal with anything! She just hadn't expected Arthur Milsom, exactly.

"Thursday night Joe Pete calls up. 'Will you be at home a while?' Where would I go to? On no alimony at all and six months behind in child support. And Joe Pete's a rich man, Britt Texaco. 'Joe Pete,' I told him, I said, 'all in the world that's left for me to do tonight is read my November seventy-two *Modern Movies*,' and he says, 'Fine, for I'm bringing back your daughter and you owe me forty-eight ninety-five for my new emerald rug which she dribble-bleached with a gallon of Clorox. I won't charge for the Clorox,' he says. 'Well and good,' I tell him, 'you can take that up with the FBI when they haul you in for kidnap.' *I'm* no fool."

"When he brought me back he stayed all night," said Ann-Campbell.

"It's his English Leather aftershave," said Dorcas.

Justine laughed.

The church parking lot was packed with cars, flashing the afternoon sunlight off their chrome, and ladies were swarming in the front yard and spilling down the hill as far as the cemetery. "I want to get a hot dog," Ann-Campbell said, "and you owe me a balloon from that time at the shopping center, and I need a caramel apple. If they have cotton candy, can I have some? If they're selling lemon sticks—"

"Ann-Campbell, you promised me you would act nice now if I let you stay out of school today."

"In school we do this math," Ann-Campbell told Justine.

"*Oh* yes," said Justine, who had disliked math.

"If five mothers are fighting over ten blond wigs, how many does each of them get? They want me to say two, but how can I be sure? Maybe one wig's ugly and nobody takes it. Maybe one mother's stronger than the rest and she gets five. Or one's got a head that's too big for the—"

"Ann-Campbell Britt, you are sending a shooting sharp pain right down between my shoulder blades," her mother told her.

If Justine had had to choose what child would most likely be Duncan's in all the world, she would have said Ann-Campbell. Never Meg.

The bazaar was in the church basement, down a flight of linoleum steps. It took Justine's eyes a minute to get used to the dimness. Then she saw rows of booths covered with crêpe paper, and more ladies bustling around in pantsuits and varnished hairdos. Justine hated pantsuits. Whenever she saw one she had an urge to tell the owner some scandalous fortune, loudly enough to be heard everywhere: "The father of your next-to-last baby has run off with a cigar-smoking redhead."

But she kept her bright smile and waited, clutching her bag, until the woman in charge noticed she was there. Mrs. Edge's pantsuit was pale aqua, Justine's least favorite color. Oh, but she would have to get over this mood she was in. She widened her smile another inch. "I'm Justine Peck," she said. "I promised to come tell fortunes."

"Mrs. Peck? Why, I thought you would be darker. We've heard such amazing things about you, dear. Now *somewhere*, let me see now . . ."

Mrs. Edge led the way toward a card table. It was covered with a white cloth to which stars and crescent moons had been pinned. Justine followed and behind her came Dorcas, wobbling on her spike heels and humming. There was no telling where Ann-Campbell had got to.

"Now dear, this is your cashbox. I've laid a few dollar bills in for change. Is there anything else you'll be wanting? I do hope you won't be chilly. Perhaps you should have brought a wrap."

"Oh no, I'll be fine," said Justine, who was always burning up.

"Why! Here's Mrs. Linthicum, our pastor's wife. Mrs. Peck here is just a *wizard* telling fortunes, Mrs. L."

"Oh, then you can start on me," Mrs. Linthicum said. *She* was wearing a dress, and a little brown mushroom of a hat. She was a tall wispy woman with freckles seeping through her pink face powder. When she sat down in the folding chair she arranged herself so graciously, smoothing her skirt beneath her and then patting her bosom as if to make certain it was there, that Justine felt an unexplainable rush of sorrow. She reached over without planning to and touched Mrs. Linthicum's freckled hand. "Oh, is it the *left* palm you read?" asked Mrs. Linthicum.

"No, no, I don't read palms," said Justine, withdrawing her hand.

But she could easily have read that one, with its lengthwise groove and the worn wedding ring no wider than a thread.

She took out her cards and unwrapped them. "Why, how fascinating," said Mrs. Linthicum.

"Is there anything in particular you want to know?" Justine asked.

"Oh, nothing I can think of."

Dorcas leaned closer, giving off waves of Tabu, while Justine laid the cards down very, very gently. Madame Olita used to snap them down, but that was before they had started falling apart. When these went, where would she get more? She gazed into space, considering.

"I'm not afraid to hear, if it's bad," said Mrs. Linthicum.

Justine pulled her eyes back to the cards. "Oh, it's not bad, not at all," she said. "You're going to do just fine."

"I am?"

"You'll continue to have money worries, but not serious ones. You shouldn't be so concerned about your children. They will turn out all right. No trips in sight. No illness. You have true friends and a loving husband."

"Well, of course," said Mrs. Linthicum.

"All in all it's a very good life," Justine said. She cleared her throat and steadied her voice. "Anybody would be happy to have a formation like this one."

"Why, thank you very much," said Mrs. Linthicum. Then when the silence had stretched on a while she gave a little laugh and rose to pay her fee, pressing Justine's palm briefly with her cool, wilted fingers. When she left, Justine gazed after her for so long that Dorcas waggled a hand in front of her face and said, "You in there?"

Then others came, woman after woman, giggling a little in front of their friends. "No tall dark strangers? No ocean trips?" Several young girls filed through, a little boy in a baseball suit, a man in platform heels, an old lady. Justine tried to pin her mind to what she was doing. This was how she attracted future clients, after all. "You will have a minor car accident," she told one girl, relieved to see something concrete.

"Even if I drive slower?"

"No, maybe not."

"Then what's the point of all this?"

"I don't know."

"To warn you to *start* driving slower, Miss!" Dorcas cried. "Honestly, Justine! Where are you today?"

Oh, beautiful Dorcas, with her watery silk dress showing dimpled knees and her jangling bracelets and creamy throat! *Her* fortune altered from week to week. Which gave Justine a greater likelihood of error, but at least she enjoyed doing it.

During a lull they captured Ann-Campbell, who was winning too many prizes anyway tossing nickels into ashtrays, and Justine read her cards. Ann-Campbell leaned over her with a cone of cotton candy, smelling of burnt sugar and money. "You'll have to travel your whole life long to use up all the travel cards I'm seeing," Justine told her.

"*I* know that."

Then Dorcas, who had learned palmistry in high school, examined Ann-Campbell's little square hand—a mass of warts and deep, soiled lines. "I find travel too," she said, "but I don't know, Ann-Campbell gets carsick. Let me see yours, Justine."

Justine turned her palm up. Secretly she had become as addicted to the future as Alonzo Divich, now that life moved so quickly.

"Oh, talk about *travel!*" said Dorcas.

"What do you see?"

"Lots of trips. Oh, well, there's much too much to read here. You have an indecisive nature, there are lots of . . . but I'm not too sure what *this* means. And then a frequent change in surroundings and tendency to—"

"But is it a *good* palm?"

"I'm telling you, Justine! Of course it is, it's just full of things."

"No, I mean—"

Dorcas raised her head.

"Oh well, it doesn't matter," Justine told her finally.

She never did say what she had meant. She sat silent, frowning at the cracked square of silk in her lap, while beside her Ann-Campbell started firmly, grimly patting her arm with the hand that wasn't holding the cotton candy.

Duncan looked up from polishing a Cinderella pastry cutter and found Justine staring at him through the plate glass window, directly beneath his hand-lettered sign, ANTIC TOOLS WANTED. She was wearing her fanciest church bazaar outfit and there was a chain of safety pins dangling from the tip of her left breast. When he waved she waved back, but she kept on standing there. He rose and came close to the glass, popping his mouth like a goldfish. She smiled. "Come *in!*" he shouted.

So she came, leaving the door swinging open behind her. "I was just passing," she told him.

"You want to hear about my movie?"

"Yes."

"I'm going to buy a camera and walk around filming to one side of things, wherever the action isn't. Say there's a touchdown at a football game, I'll narrow in on one straggling player at the other end of the field. If I see a purse-snatcher I'll find someone reading a newspaper just to the right of the victim."

"What's the point?" Justine asked.

"Point? It'll be the first realistic movie ever made. In true life you're *never* focused on where the action is. Or not so often. Not so finely." He stopped and looked at her. "Point?" he said. "You don't usually ask me that."

"Duncan, I wish I knew what we should be doing about Meg."

"Oh. School called. She cut all her afternoon classes, they said. Is she sick?"

"Why, I don't know. I haven't been home."

"Every day this week she's had a headache."

"See there? No wonder I worry," Justine said. "I ought to go look in on her." But instead she sat down on a knobby piano stool he had been trying to get rid of for months. "I am forty and one-third years old," she said.

Duncan blew on the pastry cutter and started polishing it again.

"Doesn't it seem to you that things are going by very fast?"

"I have always thought everything moved too slowly," he said. "But I know I'm in the minority."

"How did we *get* here?"

But when Duncan looked up, she had her eyes fixed on the opposite wall as if she didn't want an answer.

He set down his work and rose to walk around the shop, passing his rows of polished tools and utensils. They did his heart good. He ignored what Silas had brought in from his tours of the auction sales—the china and scrolled furniture, which he allowed to pile up in dim corners. He paused beside a nineteenth-century pressure scale and laid his hand upon it gradually, delighting in its intricate, precise design. Behind him he heard the familiar *plop, plop* of Justine's cards. What would she be asking, all alone? But when he turned he saw that she was laying the cards absent-mindedly, the way another person might doodle or chew a pencil. Her eyes were on something far away; she smoothed each card blindly as she set it on the sewing chest beside her.

While he watched, she frowned and collected her thoughts. She looked down at what she had laid out. "Why, Duncan," she said.

"What is it?"

"Why—"

"What is it, Justine?"

"Never mind, don't worry. Don't worry."

"Who says I'm worried?"

But she was already out the door, running down the street with her hat streamers fluttering. It was the first time Duncan had ever known her to leave her cards behind.

Daniel Peck was on the front porch, rearranging a sheaf of correspondence, when Justine came dashing up the walk between the rows of sprouting vegetables. She looked wild-eyed and flustered, but then she often did. "Grandfather," she called, "have you seen Meg?"

He tried to think.

"*Meg.*"

"Well, now I wonder where she could be," he said.

"What time is it?"

He fumbled in his pocket and hauled out lengths of gold chain hand over hand, raising his eyebrows when his fingers met up with a watch. "Ah! Five twelve," he said.

She spun past him, into the house, clattering the screen door behind her. He felt the noise rather than heard it. He felt his bones jar. Then there was peace, and he returned to a letter dated April 10, 1973. He squinted in the twilight at a ragged blue script.

Dear Mr. Peck:

In response to your query of March 17, I am sorry to say that I do not recall my grandmother's ever mentioning a Caleb Peck or, for that matter, any other young man she used to dance with. I was not aware that she danced. However my cousin Amabel Perce (Mrs. John M.) of Duluth, Minnesota may know more. I myself was never at all close to my grandmother and am certainly not the one to . . .

He sighed. Long white fingers entered his vision, fluttering another letter on top of the first.

Dear Mama,

I have gone to be married in Arthur's church. We will be living with Arthur's mother. Don't worry about me, I'll finish school in Semple. I will keep in touch.

Love,
Meg

"Eh? What's this?" he asked Justine.

She merely lifted an arm and dropped it, as if she couldn't speak.

"Why," he said, "*I* didn't know it was proper for ministers to elope."

Justine went down the porch steps, back through the vegetables toward the street, drifting along slower than he had seen her in years.

"Justine? Wasn't that fellow a minister?"

She didn't answer. In the end he simply filed the letter away among his other correspondence and went on with what he had been doing before.

10

By May the whole front yard was a tangle of cucumber vines and little green stalks of corn. Neighbors began knocking on the door. "Justine, of course it's your lawn to plant as you please although frankly it seems . . . but never mind, what is that smell? What we want to know is, that *smell!*"

"Oh, just things from the blender."

"The—? When you turn down this street it's the first thing you notice. It smells like a zoo. A city dump. A *slaughter*house."

"I'll mention it to Duncan," Justine said. But her face was lit up and her eyes all curly, she was so happy to see somebody. She would reach out to touch visitors on the wrist or shoulder, drawing them in. "Since you're here, why don't you stay?"

"Oh, well . . ."

"We can sit out back. You won't smell a thing."

"Oh, well, maybe for a minute."

"I'll make you lemonade, or coffee. Anything. What would you like?"

The fact was, Justine hated to be alone. She had felt so restless and unhappy lately, wandering from room to room, try-ing to start up conversations with her grandfather when he was too busy with his own thoughts to answer. "Grandfather, isn't there any place you'd like to go?"

"How's that?"

"Do you want to *go* somewhere, I said."

"No, no."

She sank back and twisted a piece of her hair. It was impos-sible to drive off on her own; a car was so private. Like a sealed black box. She would end up speeding just to get her isolation over with, or she would run a stop sign because even horns and curses were better than silence. So instead of driving she walked to Duncan's shop, missing no opportunity to speak to passers-by. "Hello, Mr. Hill, did you get the money I said you would?

Where's *Mrs.* Hill? Wait, Red Emma, I'll walk along with you,"
and she would run to catch up and travel three blocks out of her
way, pausing at each house while Red Emma delivered the mail.
She parted from people with difficulty, dragging it out, loitering
on the sidewalk fiddling with a button and finding new things to
say to them. She dreaded walking even half a block with only
her own thoughts for company. And when finally she arrived at
the Blue Bottle she would be full of pent-up words that exploded from her before she was fully in the door. "Duncan, Red
Emma told me . . . Bertha Millar asked . . . oh, Duncan, I
just had a thought, can we borrow a wayward girl from the
police station?"

"A *what's* that?"

"Surely they must have some, wouldn't you think? We
could leave our name and the next time the police arrest somebody they could bring her to us. I mean the house seems so—"

"Well now, wait a minute."

But she would be off to something new, picking up merchandise and putting it down. "Oh look, a locket like Aunt Bea's
almost. And Aunt Sarah's dinner ring but the stone's a different
color. Isn't it funny they call these antiques? They're only what
our aunts wear every day of their lives. What's this thing, Duncan?"

"A Victorian slide pendant," Duncan said glumly. "If you
ask me, it's junk. All this stuff is junk. Yesterday Silas brought
in a whole carton full, he'd been to some flea market. 'Here, take
this,' he said, 'and get rid of that mess on the table, it doesn't
look nice.' Do you know what he called *mess?* A genuine
chromatrope I bought from old Mrs. Milhauser, and a Boston
bathing pan with a pump that still works . . . where is it now?
I wanted to show you. He dumped it in some corner or other.
He doesn't like tools and things with moving parts, he says they
clutter the shop. We spend all our time shifting each other's
merchandise into hiding places and out again, in and out. Look
at that chair! He likes it. He wants me to ask a hundred and
fifty dollars for it."

Justine looked at a chair with a curved spine that was all

pointed leaves and flowers and little sharp berries. On one of its finials Duncan had impaled a liniment ad. "I've a good mind to quit this job," he said, but she didn't bother answering that. He would never quit in the middle of a fight.

She wanted him to come with her somewhere. "Maybe we could take a trip," she told him.

"All right."

"Just spur of the moment."

"All right."

"We might even stop and see Meg."

But then his face grew cold and stubborn. "Not a chance. Not until we're asked, Justine."

"But she *said*. She said in her letters."

" 'We'll have you over sometime soon,' is what she said. Pay attention."

He knew Meg's letters by heart, the same as Justine. It was all an act, his unconcern. ("Duncan," she had told him, "Meg has gone to marry Alfred, I mean Arthur," and he had grown motionless for one split second before continuing to close up shop.) "As long as we don't come for a meal," she said now, "why do we have to wait to be invited?"

"We're not going till we are, I tell you."

"Oh, that's ridiculous. She's our *daughter*."

"So what?"

"Remember when she was colicky, all those evenings you walked up and down with Meggie on your shoulder? You sang 'Blues in the Night.' Her head was straight up and wobbling, her forehead would get all wrinkled from trying not to miss a word."

"Merely singing 'Blues in the Night' to someone does not obligate me to pay them an uninvited visit seventeen years later."

"Eighteen," said Justine.

"Eighteen."

"You used to take her to the circus when she was too little to hold down a spring-up seat. For three straight hours you leaned on it for her so she wouldn't pop right up again."

"There was an intermission."

"Even so."

"Merely leaning on a spring-up seat for someone—"

"And she's not just *someone*. She's not just any old person that you would treat so formally the minute she hurt your feelings."

"Who's hurt?" Duncan said.

"Look at Grandfather. Do you know what I found him doing the other day? He was at the kitchen table all hunched over with his head in his hands. I thought something was wrong. Then he sat up and I saw he'd been studying this world map in the Hammond atlas. Not Maryland, not the United States, the *world*, Duncan. That's how far he let Caleb run before he would go after him. Are we going to do that too?"

"We're never going to forget that man, are we," Duncan said. "The one that got away." He set down a crimping iron. "However, we're wandering off the subject here. Meg has not vanished. We know exactly where she is. She writes us a letter once a week. All I'm saying is don't repeat history, give her a little breathing space. Let her ask us first."

"Oh, there's always some excuse."

"I'm just telling you what I think."

"Do you wish I hadn't come after *you*, when you left home?"

"No."

"Well, I wish it sometimes, Duncan Peck."

"No doubt you do," said Duncan.

"And if you ever walk off again, you realize I won't follow. I'll have them declare you legally dead, I'll remarry right away."

"Of course," he said serenely.

There was no way to win a fight with that man.

She stormed out of the shop and then stood on the sidewalk, wondering what to do with herself. Everything seemed irritating. The sunlight was too sharp for her eyes. The traffic was too noisy, a swarm of gigantic glaring station wagons. She hated the way the women drivers were poised at the Main Street traffic light, all lifting their arms simultaneously to orchestrate their hairdos. She turned in the other direction, toward home, which was not where she wanted to be but she couldn't think of any place else.

In the kitchen, her grandfather was washing the dishes. Periodically he had these spells of trying to make the house look cared for. He wore around his waist a striped linen dishtowel with an enormous charred hole in its center. He bent over the sink, unaware of Justine's presence, doggedly scrubbing a saucepan with a piece of dried gourd that Duncan had grown two years ago after reading about its scouring properties. The gourd looked like a chunk of hardened beige seaweed. From time to time he stopped scrubbing and examined it, frowning, as if he found it difficult to believe. Then he rinsed the saucepan and plodded over to the table with it, head bowed, shoulders hunched. "Hello, Grandfather," Justine said. "Grandfather?"

He started and looked up. "Eh?"

"You don't have to wash the dishes."

"I'd like to know what we'd eat off tonight if I didn't."

"We could always go to the diner," Justine said.

"Ha."

He dried the saucepan on a corner of his apron. Then he set it on a stack of meticulously cleaned, polished plates and trudged back to the sink. He was so stooped that, from behind, his head seemed to disappear. All Justine saw was his rounded shoulders, the elastic X of his suspenders in the hollow of his spine, and his trousers draped and formless as if he had no seat. Nowadays, everywhere Justine looked she found something to make her sad.

She would have liked to write Meg another letter, but she had sent one just this morning. So she went instead to Meg's bedroom, to open her closet and stare at the row of shirtdresses that seemed to be leading a gentle muted life of their own. Someday soon, Meg said in her letters, she would stop by for the rest of her things or her parents could bring them when they came to visit. But Justine felt comforted by what was left behind and she would be sorry to see the room stripped. She took a deep breath of Meg's clean smell: Ivory soap and fresh-ironed fabric. She stroked the collar of the nearest dress, with its precise topstitching, and then she lifted the cover of the sewing machine to admire Meg's mastery of such a complex, wheeled invention. She would have opened bureau drawers, but Meg was particular about her privacy.

When Meg was a baby, Justine had realized for the first time that it was possible to die. She had felt suddenly fragile under the responsibility of staying alive to raise her daughter. (In those days, she expected to do it perfectly; she thought no one else could manage.) She developed a fear of fire that was so unfounded she couldn't even tell Duncan because of course he would laugh at her. Over and over again she imagined the salty smell of smoke in the air, or a flickering red glow reflected on the wall. If Duncan were home he could get them out of anything, but what if it happened in the daytime while he was at work? By herself she was so young and skinny and incompetent. Then gradually, she developed an escape plan. They were living in Uncle Ed Hodges's garage apartment at the time. If fire broke out she could snatch up the baby, climb out on the kitchen window ledge, and make a long, desperate leap to the roof of Uncle Ed's back porch. Once she had pictured all this she relaxed, and eventually she forgot her fear completely. It was not till years later, returning to Uncle Ed's for a visit, that she saw that such a leap would have been insane. It was not only too far, it was also upward. She would have had to soar through the air like some surrealistic figure in a painting by Chagall, feet set neatly together and arms primly clasping the baby. But in those days, she might have managed anything. She was so necessary. Even when Meg had left infancy, given up first Justine's breast and then her lap and finally gone to play in other rooms altogether, Justine had to *be* there. She had to be the feeder, the fixer, the sounding board for an endless stream of announcements. "Mama my dress is dirty, Sammy hit me, the violets are out. Mama there's a spider in my chocolate milk, a moth in my bath, a ladybug on the windowscreen. My stomach aches. My mosquito bites itch. Janie has a hamster, Edwin's in the asparagus, I broke the handle off my teapot, Melissa has a music box you can watch right through the glass." Justine nodded, barely listening; the only answer required was, "Yes, dear." Then Meg was satisfied, as if things came into existence only when she was certain her mother knew about them. And now what? Justine had raised her daughter without dying after all; she was freed from her fears. But at night she woke up shaky and sad, and she pressed her face against Duncan's chest and said, "I'm not necessary any more."

"To me you are," he said.

He didn't see what she meant. He hadn't had that feeling of being essential to Meg in the first place; he couldn't know how it felt to lose it.

She wandered to other rooms, to hers and Duncan's with its unmade bed and scattered clothing, to the hall where she tripped over a stack of lumber. Everything looked dusty and stale. She hung out the living room window to be revived by Ann-Campbell, who was taunting a playmate among the cucumber vines:

> Little boy your teeth are green
> And your tongue it is rotting away.
> Better gargle with some gasoline,
> Brush with Comet and vomit today.

She returned to the kitchen, feeling more cheerful. "Grandfather, let's take a trip," she said.

"A what?"

"A trip."

"But we don't have any leads right now, Justine."

"Why wait for leads? Oh, why won't anyone *do* anything? Are we just going to sit here? Am I going to get rooted to the living room couch?"

Her grandfather watched her, with his eyes wide and blank and his hands endlessly drying an Exxon coffee mug on the corner of his apron.

Justine took her grandfather to an afternoon concert in Palmfield, although she did not like classical music and her grandfather couldn't hear it. The two of them sat rigid in their seats, directing unblinking blue stares toward the outline of a set of car keys in the violin soloist's trouser pocket. Then they went home by bus with Justine as dissatisfied as ever, bored and melancholy. Each time strangers rose to leave she mourned them. Who knew in what way they might have affected her life?

She took Duncan, her grandfather, and Ann-Campbell Britt to the funeral of a chihuahua belonging to an old lady client. "*What* is this? *Where* are we going?" her grandfather kept asking. "Don't worry, just come," said Justine. "Why do you care? Just grab up your hearing aid and come, Grandfather. If you want things to happen you have to run a few blind errands, you know." So he came, grumbling, and they sat on folding chairs in a cow pasture that had recently been turned into a pets' memorial garden. "The casket cost one hundred and forty-five dollars," Justine whispered to Duncan. "It's all metal. But they could have settled for wood: thirty-two ninety-eight. Mrs. Bazley told me. She selected the hymns herself. The minister is fully ordained."

"Oh, excellent," said Duncan, "I wonder if he needs an assistant," and after the service he went up and offered Arthur Milsom's address to the minister. But Grandfather Peck wandered among the wreaths and urns looking baffled. Why had he been brought here? Justine could no longer tell him. She rode home beside Duncan without a word, swinging one foot and rapidly chewing coffee beans that she had taken to keeping in a tin container at the bottom of her bag.

On Sundays she drove her grandfather to Plankhurst for Quaker meeting, which used to be something she tried to get out of because she didn't like sitting still so long. Now she would go anywhere. Grandfather Peck was not, of course, a Quaker and had no intention of becoming one, but he resented regular church services because he claimed the minister wouldn't speak up. It made him feel left out, he said. Even the Quakers would sometimes take it into their heads to rise and mumble, perversely keeping their faces turned away so that he couldn't read their lips. Then he whispered, "What? What?"—a harsh sound sawing through the air. He made Justine write everything down for him on a 3 × 5 memo pad he kept in his breast pocket. Justine would click the retractable point of his ballpoint pen in and out, in and out, waiting for a five-minute speech to be over, and then she wrote, "He says that God must have made even Nixon," or "Peace is not possible as long as neighbors can still argue over a lawn mower."

"*That* took him five minutes?"

"Ssh."

"But what was he up there working his mouth all that time for?"

"Ssh, Grandfather. Later."

"You must have left something out," he told her.

She would hand back his pen and pad, and sigh, and check the Seth Thomas clock on the mantel and run her eyes once more down the rows of straight-backed radiant adults and fidgety children lining the wooden benches. After twenty minutes the children were excused, rising like chirping, squeaking mice to follow the pied piper First-Day School teacher out of the room, breaking into a storm of whistles and shouts and stamping feet before the door was properly shut again. She should have gone with them, she always thought. The silence that followed was deep enough to drown in. She would plow desperately through her straw bag, rustling and jingling, coming up finally with her tin container of coffee beans. When she bit into them, she filled the meetinghouse with the smell of breakfast.

Once her grandfather wrote on the pad himself, several lines of hurried spiky handwriting that he passed to her. "Read this out when no one else is talking," he whispered. She struggled to her feet, hanging onto her hat. Anything to break the silence. "My grandfather wants me to read this," she said. " 'I used to think that heaven was—palatable? Palatial. I was told it had pearly gates and was paved with gold. But now I hope they are wrong about that. I would prefer to find that heaven was a small town with a bandstand in the park and a great many trees, and I would know everybody in it and none of them would ever die or move away or age or alter.' "

She sat down and gave him back the memo pad. She took the top off her coffee beans but then she put it on again, and kept the container cupped in her hands while she gazed steadily out the window into the sunlit trees.

One afternoon toward the end of May the doorbell rang and Justine, flying to answer it, found Alonzo Divich standing on the porch. Although it was hot he wore a very woolly sheepskin vest. He carried a cowboy hat, swinging by a soiled string. "Alonzo!" Justine said.

"I was afraid you might have moved," he told her.

"Oh no. Come in."

He followed her into the hall, shaking the floor with each step. Grandfather Peck was on the living room couch writing a letter to his daughters. "Don't get up," Alonzo called to him, although the grandfather was still firmly seated, giving him that stare of shocked disbelief he always wore for Alonzo. "How's the heart, eh?" Alonzo asked. "How's the heart?"

"Hearth?"

"Nothing's wrong with his heart," said Justine. "Come into the kitchen, Alonzo, if you want your cards read. You know I can't do it right with Grandfather watching."

While she cleared the remains of breakfast from the table, Alonzo wandered around the kitchen examining things and whistling. "Your calendar is two months ahead," he told Justine.

"Is it?"

"Most people's would be behind."

"Yes, well."

She went to the living room for her carry-all. When she returned Alonzo was standing at the open refrigerator, looking into a bowl of moldy strawberries. "How is my friend Duncan?" he asked her.

"He's fine."

"Maybe I'll drop by and see him. Is Meg out of school yet?"

"She's married."

"Married."

"She eloped with that minister."

"I'm sorry, Justine."

He shut the refrigerator and sat down at the table to watch her shuffle the cards. He looked tired and hot, and the grooves alongside his mustache were silvered with sweat. A disk with Arabic lettering gleamed in the opening of his shirt. Last time it had been a turquoise cross. She didn't ask why; he wouldn't have answered. "Alonzo," was all she said, "you have no idea how it gladdens my heart to see you. Cut, please." He cut the cards. She laid them out, one by one. Then she looked up. "Well?" she asked.

Alonzo said, "You realize, last time I took your advice."

"You did?"

"When you told me not to sell the business."

"Oh yes. Well, I should hope so," said Justine.

"It was the first time you ever said to keep on with something I was already doing."

She stopped swinging her foot.

"But I was tempted to disobey you anyway," he told her. "I admit. I went to see my friend, the one in merchandising. He has these clients, you understand, department stores and such, they come to him for ideas on . . . but anyway. I said I might join up with him. 'Oh, fine,' he tells me. But then he starts suggesting I wear a different style of clothes. Well, that I can follow. I am practical, I know how the world works. But he doesn't see, he's still trying to convince me. 'Face it, Alonzo,' he says, 'we all have to give in in little ways. Look at *me*. I'm a tall man,' he says. And he is, a fine tall man. 'Well,' he says, 'when important clients come, know what I do? I try to stay seated as much as possible, and if I stand I kind of squinch down. I don't *stoop*,' he says, 'that's too obvious. Just bend at the knees a little. Understand, it's not something I think of so consciously. But you can see a client, important fellow like that, he wouldn't feel right if I was to tower over him. You got to keep a watch for such things, Alonzo.' "

He shook his head, and pulled his great silver belt buckle around to where it wouldn't cut into his stomach so.

"Justine," he said, "do you know that I have never before done what you told me to do?"

"I'm not surprised," she said.

"I mean it. You're always right, but only because I go against instructions and things turn out badly just the way you said they would. Now I discover things turn out badly anyhow. Is that your secret? I've found it, ha? You give people advice they'll be sure not to follow. Right?"

She laughed. "No, Alonzo," she said. "And I'm glad you didn't sell the carnival. *Whatever's* gone wrong."

"My mechanic's been arrested."

"Lem?"

"He robbed a bank in nineteen sixty-nine. They *say*."

"Oh, I see."

"Now, here's what I want to know. Is he coming back, or not? I mean if he's coming soon I'll hold the machines together somehow and wait it out, but if he's guilty, on the other hand—"

"Well, I don't think I'm supposed to say if someone's *guilty* or not."

"Look here! What do I care about guilt? All they lost was two hundred dollars, let him keep it. Besides a little matter of a shooting. I want to know about my *business*. I want to know if I should just give up, because to tell the truth this fellow Lem was a man I relied on. He saw to everything. Now, merchandising is out but there is always something else, and the jodhpur lady still wants my carnival. Shall I sell, after all? Is the man gone forever?"

Justine frowned at a card.

"You see what I've fallen to," Alonzo said. "I used to ask about beautiful women. Now it's financial matters."

"Well, Lem is not coming back," said Justine.

"I knew it."

"But you shouldn't sell the carnival."

"How can you keep saying such a stupid thing?"

"Don't argue with me, argue with the cards. Have you ever seen anything like it? I've turned up every jack in the deck, you'll have all the mechanics you want."

"Oh, of course," Alonzo said. "One after the other. The first one drinks, the second leaves with my ponies—"

"And look at the women! Look, Alonzo, you're not paying attention. See? Here you are, the king of hearts. And here's the queen of hearts, the queen of clubs, the queen of diamonds . . ."

Alonzo sat forward, peering at the cards, resting his hand upon his knees.

"Here is the good luck card, the card of friendship, the celebration card . . ."

"All right, all *right!*" Alonzo said.

She sat back and smiled at him.

"Oh, Justine," he told her sadly, "sometimes I think I would like to go live in a cabin in the woods, all alone. I'd take a lifetime supply of slivovitz, my accordion, plenty of food, perhaps some books. Do you know I've never read an entire book? Just the good parts. I think about hibernating like a bear, just eating and drinking and sleeping. No tax, insurance, electric bills, alimony, repairs or repainting or Rustoleum, no women to mess up my life, no one shooting bank guards, no children. Then here you come galloping along in your terrible hat and your two sharp hipbones like pebbles in your pockets and you tell me all these things I may expect, a life full of surprises. How can I refuse? I feel curious all over again, I like to know what will happen next."

And he shook his head, stroking downward on his mustache, but he did not look so tired as when he had arrived. All his tiredness seemed to have passed to Justine, who sat slumped in her chair with her hands limp on the cards.

Duncan and Justine were on the front steps, watching the fireflies spark all around them. "Today I sold an antique garden engine," Duncan said.

"What's a garden engine?"

"It's this big wheeled thing to spray water on your flowers. What a relief! I bought it with my own money in a moment of weakness. I kept it sitting in the back room; I had to open the double doors to get it in and then I was afraid it would go right through the floorboards. A man named Newton Norton bought it. He's just started reconstructing this old-time farmhouse out in the country."

"Well, that's nice," said Justine.

"He also bought some fuller's shears, and all my carpentry tools."

"That's nice."

He looked over at her.

"When I went into Meg's room," she said, "and found her note telling me she'd gone, I never read anything that hurt so. But then I looked up, and there I was reflected in the window that was just starting to go dark outside. There were these deep black shadows in my eyes and cheekbones. I thought, 'My, don't I look interesting? Like someone who has had something *dramatic* happen.' I thought that!"

She laid her face against Duncan's sleeve. Duncan put his arm around her and pulled her closer, but he didn't say anything.

11

LUCY PECK had to ride in the suicide seat, beside her husband Two, who was driving. Laura May and Sarah got to sit in back. Lucy had to put up with the hot air rushing in Two's open window and Mantovani playing much too loudly on the radio. She had to say what roads to take when she couldn't even *fold* a map right, much less read it. "Now the next thing is you're going to turn left, about a quarter-inch after Seven Stone Road. Or, I don't know. What would a little bitty broken blue line seem to mean?" Her husband set his front teeth together very,

very delicately, not a good sign at all. A bumble bee flew in past his nose, causing Lucy to cry out and fling her road map into the air. And meanwhile there sat Laura May and Sarah, protected by layered hats with brown veils, contemplating two separate views peacefully like children being taken for a drive.

It was the sixth of June and they were on their way to Caro Mill, Maryland, to celebrate their father's ninety-third birthday. Unfortunately his birthday fell on a Wednesday this year, which meant that no one who worked could come along. And Bea was confined to her bed with lower back pain. It was up to them: Lucy and the maiden aunts, and Two, who was now retired. Between them they had loaded the car with presents and fruit, a Thermos of Sanka, Laura May's needlework, Sarah's knitting, insect repellent, sunscreen, Bufferin, Gelusil, a Triple-A tour guide, a can of Fix-a-Flat, a fire extinguisher, six emergency flares, and a white banner reading SEND HELP. They had had the Texaco man check the gas, oil, water, brake fluid, transmission fluid, tire pressure, and windshield cleaner. Then Two nosed the car out into traffic and they were on their way, with enough horns honking behind them to remind Lucy of an orchestra tuning up. Young people nowadays were so impatient. Luckily Two was not a man who could be fussed, and he went on driving at his same stately tempo. In his old age he had shrunk somewhat, and was made to seem even smaller by his habit of tipping his head back as he peered through the windshield. His eyes were narrow blue hyphens. His mouth was pulled downward by two ropes in his neck. When he decided to turn left from the right-hand lane he signaled imperiously out the window, still facing front, maintaining his cool Apache profile for Lucy to marvel at while behind them more horns honked. "Kindly check the odometer, Lucy," was all he said. "I would be interested in knowing our mileage on this trip."

"Yes, dear."

Once they hit the open road they were dazzled by too much sunshine and too wide an expanse of fields. It was some time since they had been in the country. (One year ago today, to be exact.) Lucy longed for her wing chair in which she could sit encircled, almost, with the wings working like a mule's blinders to confine her gaze to the latest historical romance. The upholstery was embroidered in satin-stitch, which she loved to stroke absently as she read. Then in the back yard her Sea Foam roses were just opening; there were going to be more this year than ever before and she was missing one entire day's worth. And it was so much cooler and greener at home, so shadowy, so thickly treed that when you spoke outdoors your voice came echoing back, clear and close, as if reflected from a vaulted green ceiling not far above your head. Here the sun turned everything pale. Pinkish barns sped past and bleached gray road-banks, and beige creeks spanned by wooden bridges like dried-up, whitening bones. Lucy turned and sought out her sisters-in-law—a double pair of webbed eyes reluctantly drawn to hers. "Really, traveling makes me sad," Lucy told them. But they didn't answer (Lucy always said such *personal* things), so she faced front again.

At Plankhurst there was a very confusing crossroads and she sent Two thirteen miles out of the way before the mistake was realized. "Oh, I'm just so—I just can't tell you how badly I feel about this," she said. Two grunted. In the back seat her sisters-in-law gave her disappointed looks that made her want to cry. "I just seem to do everything wrong," she said. Nobody denied it.

Two hours out of Baltimore they began to encounter signs for Caro Mill, although still it seemed they were in the depths of the country. The only buildings were farmhouses, widely scattered, and occasionally a little grocery store patched with soft drink ads. Then they swooped over a hill and there was the town all spread out before them, a clutter of untidy buildings. They had traveled this Main Street annually for years, although each time in a different location. They had passed this very Woolworth's, diner, pizza parlor, fabric store displaying dingy bolts of cloth turning gray along the creases. Still, Lucy sat up straighter and began perking the lace at the neck of her dress. Two pressed his thin white hair flat against his head, and in back there were rustles and whispers. "Oh, I do hope Father likes the—" "Remind me to ask Father if he wouldn't care to—" But Duncan was the one Lucy thought of, not her father-in-law at all. It was for Duncan she had bought this hat (only wouldn't he think the wooden cherries were—old-ladyish, maybe?) and put on these coins of rouge and her eighteen-hour girdle and the Sunday pearls. (Only come to think of it, hadn't he always laughed at the family's fondness for pearls?) She twisted her rings. "Perhaps he won't be home," she said.

"Who?" Two asked, although of course he knew.

"It *is* a working day. Though Justine said he comes home for lunch. But perhaps he won't. I mean, one time—"

One time when they visited he had gone fishing with a friend. A *plumber* or something. Another time he had wandered around the house all afternoon wearing earphones on a very long cord, following a baseball game. You could only grasp the depth of the insult when you remembered that Duncan did not like sports and would prefer to do almost anything but listen to a game. "*One* time—" she said, but Two's voice cracked across hers like a whip.

"Leave it," he said. "What'd you do with Justine's letter?"

"Letter?"

"Her *letter*, Lucy. Telling us how to get to their house."

"Oh. Oh, why I—"

She remembered suddenly that she had left the letter at home on the dining room buffet, but she didn't want to say so. "Why, *someplace* here," she said, riffling through her pocketbook. Two let out a long puff of air. He slowed and beckoned from the window, startling a fat lady standing on the median line. "Pardon me," he said. "We are looking for Watchmaker Street. For twenty-one Watchmaker Street."

"Oh, *Justine*," the lady said.

Everyone flinched. Justine's name was always bandied about so. Like common property.

"Why, you just turn left at the next light," she said, "go two blocks and turn left again. That's Watchmaker Street."

"Thank you."

He rolled the window all the way up.

Now they were silent, concentrating on the view, wondering what sort of house they were headed for. Hoping, just this once, for something really fine. But no. Of course: there it was, a flimsy, no-account little place. Tacked to the screen was what appeared to be a magazine ad for traveler's checks. YOU ARE FAR, FAR FROM HOME, it said, IN UNFAMILIAR TERRITORY . . . But then out flew Justine, barefoot, glowing, in a dress with a lopsided hem. "Uncle Two!" she cried. "Aunt Lucy! You got here!" She hugged them—some of them twice over. She called for her grandfather, who naturally couldn't hear. She showed Laura May and Sarah up the rickety steps and into the house to find him, and then she ran out again to help Two and Lucy unload the trunk. "Duncan will be here in a minute," she said. "He's coming for lunch. Oh look! This is Aunt Bea's gift, I know the wrapping. Will you look at that bow?" But then she dropped it. Fortunately it was not breakable. Lucy had often wondered: was accident-proneness *catching?* Justine had been such a careful little girl. "I wrote and asked Meg to come too but they're having final exams," Justine said. "It seems to me these birthday parties get smaller every year. She sent her love to all of you."

"Oh, bless her heart," Lucy said. "Well, some of these things are her wedding presents. Did we tell you we're giving her your great-grandma's silver?"

Not a one of them was tactless enough to comment on Meg's manner of marrying.

"Now," said Two. "Tell me straight. How's Duncan's business going?"

"Oh, fine, Uncle Two. Just fine."

"What is it again? Jewelry?"

But then Grandfather Peck came down the steps, bending in an odd flimsy way at the knees, and he had to be greeted and fussed over. Lucy kissed his bristly white cheek, Two shook his hand. "Happy birthday!" Lucy shouted.

"How's the what?"

"Happy birthday!"

He looked at her for a moment, considering. "Oh, very well, thank you," he said finally.

"You don't have to shout, Aunt Lucy," Justine told her. "Only narrow *in*. You know what I mean?"

"Oh yes," said Lucy, although she didn't. They went through this on every visit.

Once they were inside the house, there was the usual difficulty in knowing what to say about it. Certainly *some* comment seemed called for. But the rooms were small and dark. The windows were curtained only by great tangles of plants all merging and mingling and sending long runners clear across the floor. There were not nearly enough places to sit. In one of the little back bedrooms, Lucy was horrified to glimpse an absolutely bare, rust-stained mattress, striped blue and white. It reminded her of the time her church group had toured a flophouse for their social service project. "Justine, dear heart," she said, "have we interrupted your bedmaking?"

"My what? Oh no, I'm going to run the sheets down to the laundromat this evening."

"Perhaps I could help you put the fresh ones on."

"But I don't have any others," Justine said.

Lucy sat down very suddenly on a chrome-legged chair that had been dragged out of the kitchen.

Grandfather Peck never would open his presents until after lunch. He had them taken to the table, and meanwhile he and Two settled themselves in the living room and discussed business affairs. Since both of them were retired, it was a vague, wistful, second-hand sort of discussion. "Dan I believe is very much involved with that Kingham matter," Two said. "*You* remember Kingham."

"Oh yes. What was that again?"

"Well, let's see, I'm not quite . . . but he says it's moving just fine."

"Fine, is it."

Perhaps Two should not have retired just yet. But he would feel better when his brothers joined him—Dan in two years, Marcus the year after that. (Sixty-eight was the age they had agreed upon.) Then Claude and Richard could run things on their own. There was no point in working yourself straight into the grave. Still, Two seemed bored and listless as he sat sunk in a corner of the threadbare couch. His father nodded opposite him. His father was so aged that he had reached a saturation point; no new wrinkles had been added in years. He looked not much different from the way he had at seventy. Not much different from Two, as a matter of fact. They might have been brothers. This was how they all ended up, then: arriving at some sort of barrier and sitting down to wait for death, joined eventually by others who had started out later. In the end, the quarter-century that divided their generations amounted to nothing and was swept away. Lucy passed a hand over her own wispy, corrugated forehead. She looked at Two, a handsome man whom she had determined to call Justin back when they were courting, but finally she had given in and called him what his family did. They won, as they always had. Everything was leveled, there were no extremes of joy or sorrow any more but only habit, routine, ancient family names and rites and customs, slow careful old people moving cautiously around furniture that had sat in the same positions for fifty years.

But just as she felt herself sinking into a marsh of despair, she heard Duncan's light quick step across the porch. She saw him fling the screen door open—such a tall boy, or man rather, with his eyes lit from within and that awning of fair hair flopping over his high, pure, untouched forehead. She rose and smoothed her skirt down and held her purse more tightly to her stomach. "Duncan, darling," she said. His kiss was as hurried as ever, brief and light as a raindrop, but she felt her heart floating softly upward and she was certain that this time everything was going to go wonderfully.

For lunch Justine served baked ham, potatoes, and snap beans. Everyone was pleasantly surprised. "Why, Justine," said Two, "this is excellent. This ham is very tasty."

"Oh, Grandfather did that."

"Hmm?"

They stared at her. She seemed perfectly serious. Her grandfather was absorbed in salting his beans and could not be contacted.

For dessert they had a layer cake with nine large candles on it and three small ones. Lucy watched closely while it was sliced. "Is it a mix, dear?" she asked.

"Oh, no."

"You made it from scratch?"

"Grandfather made it."

This time, he looked up. He gave them a shy, crooked smile and then lowered his white eyelashes. "Why, Father Peck!" Lucy said.

"I did the ham too," he said. "She tell you that?"

"Yes, she did."

"Also the potatoes. I baked them first, you see, then scooped them out . . . found it in Fannie Farmer. Some people call them potato boats."

Two looked at his watch.

"The cake is what is known as a war cake," said the grandfather. "It makes do with considerably less butter and eggs than we would normally use, you see. After all, we're living in reduced circumstances."

He seemed to savor the last two words: reduced circumstances. Lucy thought they sounded smugly technical, like devaluated currency or municipal bonds. For a very brief moment she wondered if he didn't almost *enjoy* this life– these dismal houses, weird friends, separations from the family, this moving about and fortune telling. If he weren't almost proud of the queer situations he found himself in. But then Sarah said, "Remember Grandma's orange peel cake?" and his face became suddenly thin and lost.

"Oh. Oh yes," he said.

"She used to mix it secretly in the pantry. Remember? She said she would give the recipe to Sulie but Sulie says she never did. Although of course we can't be too sure of that."

"I wonder what was in it," Justine said dreamily, and she paused so long with her knife in mid-air that Two grew impatient.

"*Come* on," he said. He looked at his watch again. "It's one thirty-two. Do you always have dinner so late?"

"Mostly we don't have dinner at all," Justine said.

"I ask because last year we ate around noon. Dessert was served shortly before one."

"Was it?"

"The year *before* that, we ate even earlier."

"Did we?"

"Is this a new hobby of yours?" Duncan asked Two. "Are you planning to graph us?"

"To—no. No, it's just a little matter of timing, you understand. I thought the presents would be opened by one o'clock. Maybe we could do them before dessert."

"But I had counted on enjoying my cake," the grandfather said.

He and Two stared at each other, a pair of old, cross men. "This is a matter of timing, Father," Two told him.

"Of what?"

"*Timing!*"

"Speak up."

Two groaned.

"The worst of it is," Lucy whispered to Justine, "now Two is growing a teensy bit deaf himself."

"I most certainly am *not*," Two said.

"Sorry, dear."

Two picked up a small flat package. "From Sarah," he said. "Happy birthday."

Two's father took the package and turned it over. How many times had Lucy watched him painfully untie a bow, peel off the Scotch tape, remove the paper and fold it carefully for future use before he would look to see what he had been given? Year after year he received this cascade of shirts and socks and monogrammed handkerchiefs, all in glossy white boxes and handsome paper, tied with loopy satin bows. To each gift he said, "Why, thank you. Thank you very much," after which he replaced it in its box. Probably none of these things would ever be used. Except, of course, Justine's: a crumpled white sack of horehound drops that honestly seemed to delight him, although that had been her gift for as long as anyone could remember. "Can you figure it out?" he said. "Stuff's practically impossible to find any more but every year she manages. Expensive, too. *Justine* makes do with Luden's cough drops but I fail to see the resemblance myself." He popped a lozenge in his mouth and passed the sack around. Only Justine took one. Nobody else could stand them. "Last chance till next year," he told Lucy, flooding her with his pharmaceutical breath. Lucy shook her head.

Duncan of course gave nothing at all, and would never allow Justine to pencil his name beside hers on the sack of horehound drops. He didn't believe in celebrating birthdays. He would give presents any time, to anyone, sudden surprising *touching* presents, but not when the rules said he was supposed to. And this year there was no gift from Meg either. Lucy was watching. Not so much as a tie clasp or a bureau top organizer. She felt a brief surge of wicked joy: now Duncan himself knew the pain of having an ungrateful child. Perhaps he had thought, when Meg eloped, So this is what it feels like! This is what my parents have had to put up with all my life! But then she was ashamed of herself, and she felt truly sorry that her granddaughter had somehow forgotten such an important occasion.

Next to last came Laura May's gift: needlework, as usual. This year a family tree, embroidered on natural linen with a wooden frame. "Why, thank you," said her father. "Thank you very much." But instead of setting it back down, he held it in both hands and looked at it for a long, silent moment. A diamond shape, that was what it was. Lucy had never noticed before. Justin alone began it and Meg alone ended it. In between there was a sudden glorious spread of children, but what had they come to? Nothing. Claude, Esther, the twins, and Richard stood alone, unmarried, without descendants. (Laura May had tactfully left off all record of Sally's divorce and Richard's annulment.) Only Duncan on the far left, son of the oldest child, and Justine on the far right, daughter of the youngest child, were connected by a V-shaped line that spilled out their single offspring at the bottom of the diamond. There was no room for anyone below Meg's name. Lucy shook her head. "But," said Justine, "maybe Meg will have six children and things will start all over again!"

Maybe so. Lucy pictured the diamond shape endlessly repeated, like the design on the border of a blanket. But the thought failed to cheer her up.

Then came the last gift, the largest, a gigantic cube two feet square. The card was the largest too. It had to be. *Birthday greetings and many happy returns from your sons Justin II, Daniel Jr., and Marcus.*

"*Well* now," said Grandfather Peck.

Two began chuckling. The wrapping was a joke.

First the striped paper, then a large white box. A slightly smaller box inside, then fleur-de-lis paper covering another box, then another, another . . .

Grandfather Peck grew bewildered. Mountains of ribbon and tissue rose around him. "What's all this?" he kept asking. "What's . . . I don't understand."

"Keep going," Two said.

He and his brothers had spent an entire evening working on the wrapping. Ordinarily they were not humorous men, but while fitting cartons inside cartons on Lucy's dining room table they had chortled like schoolboys, and Lucy had had to smile. She smiled now, seeing Two's face all squeezed together to keep the laughter in. "Go on, go on," he kept saying.

A hatbox, containing a shoebox, containing a stationery box, containing a playing card box, containing a matchbox. And finally the gift itself, wrapped in white paper. Two was laughing so hard that the corners of his eyes were damp. "It's a joke," he explained to Duncan. "See?"

"Typical," said Duncan.

"No, see? They did it at this office party, when Dan's secretary got married. They wrapped a little tiny present in a great big box, funniest thing you ever saw."

"It would be funnier if they had wrapped a great big present in a little *tiny* box," said Duncan.

"No, see—"

Grandfather Peck removed the Scotch tape from the minute rectangle of paper. He opened the paper carefully, but for once did not fold it and set it aside. Perhaps because it was too small. Perhaps because he was too shocked: his present was a single calling card.

" 'Worth and Everjohn, Inc.,' " he read out. " 'Your Local Domestic Investigating Agency. 19 Main Street, Caro Mill, Maryland. Why Stay in Doubt? Call Us and Find Out. All Reports in Strictest . . .' " He looked up at Two. "I don't quite understand," he said.

But instead of answering Two rose and left the room. They heard him open the front screen door. "All right now!" he shouted.

The man he brought back with him looked like Abe Lincoln, even to the narrow border of beard along his jawline. He wore a black suit, a very starched white shirt, and a string tie. Probably he was in his thirties, but his weary, hungry expression made him seem older. Runlets of sweat streaked his temples. There was a pulse in the hollow of one cheek. "Sorry to have kept you out there so long," Two was saying. "I know you must be hot."

"Oh, I didn't have nothing else to do."

"Father, this is Mr. Eli Everjohn," Two said.

Mr. Everjohn held out his hand, which seemed to have an unusual number of bones in it. Grandfather Peck peered into his face. "I don't understand," he said.

"Your birthday present, Father."

"Oh, naturally," Duncan said to no one. "I'm surprised they didn't gift-wrap the man himself."

"Well, they thought of it," Lucy told him.

"Father, Mr. Everjohn's a detective," said Two.

"Yes?"

"He tracks people down."

"Yes, of course," said Grandfather Peck. He waited patiently, ready to smile as soon as he saw the point.

"He's going to track Uncle Caleb for you."

"How's that?"

"See, Dan and Mark and I pooled together and hired him. We thought, why not get this thing settled? I mean determine, once and for all, that Uncle Caleb is . . . I mean *you're* not getting anywhere, Father. Now we'll spare no expense. We've picked a man who's located here so that you can keep tabs, help out in any way that's needed, and no matter how long it takes we're prepared to foot the bill. Understand? That's our little gift to you. Happy birthday."

His father stared at him.

"Didn't you hear?" Two asked.

"But I don't . . ."

Mr. Everjohn's hand remained outstretched, motionless. You would think that he went through this every day.

"I don't believe I require any assistance, thank you just the same," Grandfather Peck told him.

"But Father! It's your birthday present."

"Then it's his to refuse," Duncan said.

"Stay out of this, Duncan."

Duncan rose and came around the table. He shook Mr. Everjohn's hand. "I believe," he said, "that my grandfather likes to track his own people."

"Certainly, for fifteen *years!*" Two shouted.

But he was not a shouting man. Even his sisters, fluttering their hands toward their ears, couldn't hold it against him. This was all Duncan's doing, some germ he spread. "Two, dear," Lucy told him, and right away he lowered his voice.

"Oh," he said, "don't think I don't know why you've let him live here, Duncan. You *like* to see this happening, your grandfather chasing rainbows on the Greyhound bus line. But consider him, for once. At the present rate, how long will it be before he's successful?"

"Forever, probably," Duncan said. "But at least he's happier than most other Pecks I know."

Everyone looked at the grandfather. He stared blandly back, not giving away a thing.

"And I doubt if success is what we want here," said Duncan. "What would you do with Caleb now? Where would you fit him in? In the end you'd just have to let him run on, like a fox after a foxhunt."

"Oh, was he a sportsman?" Mr. Everjohn asked.

"What? I don't know. No."

"Of course not," said Two.

Mr. Everjohn took a spiral notebook from his shirt pocket. He uncapped a Bic pen and wrote something down. In the sudden silence Justine said, "Maybe you'd like a seat."

"What for?" Duncan asked. "He's not staying."

And his grandfather said, "Yes, actually *Justine* and I—"

"That's just what we're trying to spare you," Two told him. "These endless, fruitless searches, wandering about the country like a pair of—let a professional do it." He turned to Duncan. "As for what to do with Caleb," he said, speaking very low and fast, "I seriously doubt that that problem will arise. If you follow me."

"What, do you imagine he's dead?"

Two gave his father a sidelong glance.

"You can't stand to think he's alive and well and staying away on *purpose*," Duncan said. "Can you? But he's a Peck and he's not even ninety, barely in his prime. I'll bet you a bottle of bourbon he's sitting in an old folks' home this very minute watching *The Dating Game*."

Grandfather Peck slammed a hand down on the table. Everybody stared.

"I've stood a lot from you, Duncan," he said, "but not this. *I do not have a brother in an old folks' home.*"

If he had spoken to Lucy that way she would have crumbled and died, but Duncan only raised his eyebrows. (And though she blushed for him, she felt a little thrill that nothing these Pecks could do would ever really touch him.)

"Mr. Everjohn," said the grandfather, "I'll tell you all I know, and then you get to work. I am not a drinking man but I want to collect a bottle of bourbon from my grandson here."

Then he stood up and led Mr. Everjohn to the living room. Two went with them but the others stayed in the kitchen, gazing down at their slices of cake, which no one had the appetite for. Lucy tore her napkin to shreds and wondered where the Gelusil was. Sarah fanned herself with a sheaf of folded wrapping paper. Justine was chewing on a birthday candle and Laura May had picked up the family tree to admire her own embroidery. Only Duncan, circling the table aimlessly, seemed to have any energy left. He whistled something unfamiliar. He touched a strand of Justine's hair as he passed. He looked over Laura May's shoulder at the family tree. "Has it occurred to you," he asked her, "that someone somewhere may still be searching for Justin?"

By four o'clock Two still hadn't made a move to go. And he was the one who hated night driving! He said he had to get everything straight with the detective first. Lucy could tell he was beginning to regret his choice, not that there *was* much choice in a town like Caro Mill. This Mr. Everjohn was turning out to be a little peculiar. The more peculiar he got the grimmer Two's face grew, and the gayer Duncan's. Justine became downright hospitable and offered Mr. Everjohn root beer and birthday cake. By now they were all in the living room, the aunts in a row on the couch and the others in kitchen chairs, having been lured there one after another by the goings-on. Grandfather Peck was giving Mr. Everjohn the names of every classmate Uncle Caleb had ever had. Every teacher, friend, and business associate. Where did he get them all? Then Uncle Caleb's church, school, barber, tailor, doctor, tavern . . . she had never known a Peck to frequent a tavern. But Mr. Everjohn did not look surprised. He continued filling his spiral notebook, scribbling away at unexpected moments for unexplainable lengths of time. He requested and pocketed the grandfather's treasured photo, saying he would have a copy made, but why, when it was half a century out of date? He listened to a recital of the entire attendance sheet of a vacation Bible school that had opened, and closed forever, in the summer of 1893. Whole strings of names were allowed to slip by, but then he would pounce on one and fill two pages. What was he writing? Lucy sat up very straight, but she couldn't see into his lap.

Now another peculiar thing was, how a man of business could spare so many hours. Naturally a detective was not like a *lawyer* or anything, but still you would think he had appointments and commitments. Mr. Everjohn seemed ready to give the Pecks the rest of his life. He sat without fidgeting, keeping his sharp knees clamped together and his elbows close to his body. One trouser leg was rucked up to show a shin like a stick of timber. He wrote with his pen held so awkwardly that it made Lucy's hand ache. When he asked questions, they were always the least likely. For instance, he wanted to know Uncle Caleb's smoking habits, the name of his childhood nursemaid, his mother's birthday, and his preference in shoes. He asked about Laura's reading matter and Justin's will, about religious beliefs and shipping schedules. The stranger the questions, the more excited Grandfather Peck became. It was like going to the doctor for a headache and having him examine your toenails. What un-dreamed-of things he must know! Even when Mr. Everjohn asked about Margaret Rose, Grandfather Peck barely flinched. "Of course, that's something I never think about," he said. "I've forgotten her entirely."

"Ah," said Mr. Everjohn. When he opened his mouth like that, his face became impossibly long and his cheeks sank in.

"Anyway, she left before Caleb did," said the grandfather.

"Now where was it she went to?"

You could have heard a pin drop.

"Washington," said the grandfather.

"Oh yes."

"She got a job. But she died."

"What kind of job?"

"There's not much point in going into this," the grandfather said.

"I got to know anyway, Mr. Peck."

"Uh, she laundered money."

"Money."

"She worked for the U.S. Treasury. She washed old bills."

Mr. Everjohn's deep, bruised-looking eyes searched mournfully around the room.

"It's perfectly possible," Duncan told him. "They used to wash them and coat them with rosin. For crispness. In the past they weren't so quick to throw things away. They had a machine that—"

"I see," said Mr. Everjohn. "Cause of death?"

"Boardinghouse fire," said Grandfather Peck.

"She live in a boardinghouse?"

"Her parents wouldn't *let* her stay with them, you see. In those days women were expected to be better behaved. They tried to make her come back to Baltimore. Her father wrote and told me."

"Now. You sure she really died."

"They buried her, didn't they?"

"I was thinking maybe that was where your brother went to: Washington. Maybe the *two* of them. You ever consider that?"

Lucy had. But Grandfather Peck was merely impatient. "If he were such a scoundrel, why would I be looking for him?" he asked.

"*Oh* yes," said Mr. Everjohn, and he seemed perfectly satisfied. He slipped the notebook and pencil back into his pocket. "Well, I think I got something here to start on."

"We certainly appreciate your making a housecall, Mr. Everjohn," Two said.

"Why, that's all right."

"I never expected to take so much of your time, but of course I am fully prepared to—"

"Think nothing of it," Mr. Everjohn said. "To be honest,

this town don't keep a man very busy." He felt beneath his chair for his hat and then rose, unfolding foot by foot. With a hat on he looked more like Lincoln than ever. The crown was even slightly squared, the brim oddly curved. "There's so little call for us, me and my partner have to shadow each other's wives for practice," he said.

"Really," said Two.

"Women's lives are right dull, I've found. My partner's wife goes to one store for toothpaste and another for mouthwash, just to get herself two outings."

"Well, I know you have to be getting back," said Two.

"Now *my* wife takes *lessons*. She will sign up for anything. You wouldn't believe the places Joe has got to follow her to."

"May I expect your bill on a monthly basis?"

"Pet grooming. Exotic dance. Kung-fu. Stretch-'n-Sew."

"Oh, Eli!" cried Justine, making one of her shocking leaps to a first-name friendship. "Won't you take your wife a piece of birthday cake?"

"She's on this diet," Mr. Everjohn said gloomily. "She goes to Weight Watchers and Slenderella, and every Thursday from two to four she's got her this class in low-carbohydrate food preparation." He shook Justine's hand too hard. "I'll keep in touch," he told her.

"Well, drop in any time. Grandfather will want to hear."

"And thank you again for your patience," Two said.

But the minute Mr. Everjohn was out the door, Two collapsed in his chair. "I knew we should have used a Baltimore man," he told Lucy.

"Well, there, dear."

"I must have the names of twenty good detectives back home. But no, Marcus said it had to be a Caro Mill fellow. That way Father could handle things, he said. Otherwise *we'd* be the ones to—"

"Well, I thought he was very nice," Justine said, returning from the front door.

"If you children would live in a civilized area, Justine—"

"Caro Mill is civilized."

Two turned to Duncan, who was playing with what looked to be an auto part over by the window. "You need to come back to Baltimore, boy," he said. "What's stopping you? Jobs? You know there's lots to do in a law office that wouldn't take a degree. Your cousins could fix you up. Quick mind like yours, there's *lots* to—"

"Thanks anyway," Duncan said.

"Do Justine good. See there? She's looking a little tired."

Lucy glanced over at her. Why, she was. It was true. Now that she was not running or laughing or talking too much, her face seemed strained and pale. Blame Meg, that's who. Children! She shifted her gaze to Duncan, an aging little boy. Secretly her favorite son, and she had always imagined what a fine man he would be once he was grown and mellowed. But that had never happened. He was preserved forever as he had been at ten, reckless and inconsiderate, not kind at all, not ever willing to make allowance for other people's weaknesses. He had needed a good strong wife to settle him down and round his sharp edges, but he hadn't got one. Only Justine. Was Justine the way she was *deliberately?* Had she just flat out decided one day that she would refuse to take responsibility, that Duncan could go caroming straight to hell taking wife and daughter along before she would say a word? Something made Lucy speak up suddenly, when she hadn't even known she was going to. "Oh," she said, "if only poor dear Caroline could have been with us today!"

The look Duncan gave her was as cold and hard as glass, but Lucy felt her little triumph warming all her bones when she saw how still Justine grew.

By the time they were back in the car it was very nearly twilight. Even so, Lucy took the preaddressed envelope out of her purse and unfolded a sheet of stationery and wrote, as Two had taught her to:

Dear Justine,   June 6, 1973
    Thank you so much for the lovely time! As always you made a perfectly charming hostess, and the War Cake was

delicious. We shall remember our visit with a great deal of pleasure.

> Love,
> Aunt Lucy

She placed the note in the envelope and sealed it. "Whenever you notice a mailbox, Two . . ." she said, but then she trailed off, bleakly tapping the letter against her purse. Two moved his lips as he drove. In back, Laura May and Sarah sat side by side beneath veiled brown hats and looked out the windows at their separate views.

12

Now JUSTINE and her grandfather had no place to go. At first they hardly noticed; they traveled less during the summer months anyway. But as June dragged on, hot and humid, and then July took over, Justine grew unhappier. She didn't have enough to do with herself. There was some troubled feeling gnawing at the back of her mind. Uneasiness drove her into quarreling with Duncan, snapping at her grandfather, telling skimpy, half-hearted fortunes for her clients. She spoke with an unplaceable foreign accent for days at a time. She insulted Dorcas. The cat moved out of the house and into the crawlspace behind the rose bushes. Her grandfather sat on the porch, unusually still, with his face slack and vacant.

"Look, Grandfather," Justine said, "isn't there someone you would like to look up? How about that man in Delaware? Maybe he's remembered something new."

"It wouldn't be any use," her grandfather said.

"Well, I don't see why not."

"That detective fellow didn't even take his name down. Took hardly *any* of those names. Seemed to think they would serve no purpose whatsoever."

"Oh, what does *he* know," Justine said.

She had begun to resent Eli's odd, probing questions and the mysterious silence that followed all answers. After each of his visits she felt tampered with. He had a way of arriving when no one was home and settling himself to wait on the front porch. When she and her grandfather returned he would loom up, tall and black as a raven, with his squared-off hat centered over his chest. "Eli!" she always cried, but her heart grew thick, as if preparing against invasion. And her grandfather, who made a point of remembering every passing name, said, "Mr.—ah," and stood scowling down at his shoes like a forgetful schoolboy. But Eli was humble and awkward, and he began by discussing something harmless—his shadowing practice, his wife's calligraphy lessons. After all, he was in no hurry. Then Justine warmed to him all over again, to his absurd fringe of a beard as precise as the brush on a typewriter eraser and his preposterously long, multiple-jointed fingers fumbling at his hat; and her grandfather relaxed enough to grow politely bored. "Come inside, Eli," Justine would say. "I'll make you some iced tea." But at that very moment his face would narrow, his fingers would grow still. "What all were the records your family owned?" he might ask.

"What?"

"*Recordings.* For that old-timey phonograph."

She had to turn to her grandfather, who scuffed the porch floorboards petulantly. "Caruso, I remember," he said finally. "Other things. Red Label discs."

"Oh yes. Red Seal."

"In the beginning they were called Red Label."

"Ah," said Eli.

"Don't you know *anything?*"

"But what besides Caruso? Any more?"

"I don't recall."

"It's something I got to find out," said Eli, but he wouldn't say why. "Well, I reckon I'll just have to go to Baltimore again. You've kept them, now."

"We've kept everything," said Grandfather Peck. And when he went inside he would slam the screen door. Yet it was plain that Eli's questions intrigued him. For the remainder of the day he would be thinking hard, frowning until his eyebrows met. "Can you tell me why he would ask such a thing? What has he got up his sleeve? That fellow must know something we just have no idea of, Justine."

But for the grandfather, after all, finding Caleb was the only goal. For Justine the point of the search had been the trips themselves, and now she felt bereft and useless. She wandered from room to room, absently carrying her straw bag around with her as if she were a visitor, long after her grandfather had settled himself in the armchair to plan what he would say first when he and Caleb met.

Meanwhile Duncan was selling antique tools by the dozen, by the gross, faster than he could stock them. Why did things always work out this way? Newton Norton, the man who had bought the garden engine, was reconstructing his ancient farm down to the last pitchfork in the barn. He haunted the Blue Bottle, seizing on old rusty pliers and milking lanterns, blacksmith's implements, kitchen utensils. "If you could see Silas's face!" Duncan told Justine. "Sometimes Newton Norton has to call for a truck just to take his purchases home."

"He must be crazy," said Justine. "What if he has to move someday?"

They were on the front porch, Duncan sitting on a stool while Justine gave him a haircut with the kitchen shears. His hair was thick and straight, audible when it fell. She cut it in layers down the back like a shingled roof, and then when she combed it the layers sifted magically together and evened out. She combed again, floating off into a trance among the shimmering yellow ribbons. She cut another inch off. "Maybe I should have been a barber," she said.

"Let's not get carried away here," Duncan told her.

By now it was August and their corn was so tall it blocked their view of the street. Cars swished by unseen, almost unheard. (Duncan was interested in the effect of greenery upon the decibel count.) People walking past were no more than disembodied voices.

"Hello!" they called, apparently taking it on faith that someone was there to answer. "Well, hi!" said Justine. She waved her flashing shears in the air. Duncan didn't look up. He had his mind on other things.

"I told Silas, 'See there?' He wouldn't let me buy that old sewing machine of Mrs. Farnsworth's, now he's sorry. Newton Norton tracked it down himself and gave her twice what it was worth. But you know Silas. 'Yes,' he said, 'but once he's got this farm of his set up, what then? Hmm?' Well, yesterday Newton Norton opened his place to the public, a fully working nineteenth-century farm. Admission two dollars. Fifty cents for children. *Plus*. Cooking lessons. A six-week course in old-time American cooking. You learn in this kitchen that has a wood stove and a fireplace big enough to roast an ox. You make cabbage custard and codfish cakes—well, to tell the truth, none of it sounded edible. But *somebody* must like it. All this morning women were coming in asking for sausage guns. Bird's-eye maple sauerkraut mashers. They snatched up these hand-cranked machines that I hadn't even quite figured out yet, things to pare cucumbers and strip corncobs and peel potatoes. By noon I'd sold every utensil in the place."

"Think of that! You're a success," said Justine, trimming around his ears.

"That's what they call it."

But he spoke through a yawn, and then sneezed when a snippet of hair landed on his nose. His face glinted all over with stray blond sparks. He didn't *look* like a success.

On the fourth Sunday in August, the three of them drove to Semple to visit Meg. They were supposed to go earlier but always at the last minute Duncan claimed that something had come up. He had to attend an auction, or a special flea market, now that Silas was urging him to buy more tools. Yet he returned without any tools whatsoever—only, once, a carton of rusty Prince Albert tobacco tins. "These are antiques?" Justine asked. "Imagine, they used to be garbage. I used to see them in the weeds along Roland Avenue. But where are the tools? What about the kitchen utensils?"

"None of them appealed to me," said Duncan. "Only Prince Albert."

"In the end, the silliest things get valuable. We shouldn't throw *anything* out."

"It doesn't seem to me that we do," said Duncan.

Now he wanted to cancel the trip yet another time (he said there was a Tailgate Treasures near Washington) but Justine had caught on to him. "It's not possible," she said. "You know how long we waited for Meg to invite us. Now we've put her off twice. What will she think?"

"Maybe just you and Grandfather could go. I could go to Washington alone."

"What on, bicycle?"

"I could borrow Silas's station wagon," he said.

"Besides, I don't want to go just with Grandfather. I'd really like you with me this time."

"Maybe in the fall, when things are quieter."

"I don't understand you, Duncan," Justine told him. "What is it you have against this visit?"

But then he grew touchy. He always did object to the way she dragged his secret feelings into the open.

Still, on the fourth Sunday in August there he was, maybe a little grimmer than usual but resigned to the trip, heading the Ford along a gritty two-lane highway toward Semple with Justine sitting beside him and Grandfather Peck next to the window. On the rear seat was a stack of Meg's summer dresses and a paper bag containing a dozen ears of corn. ("But the corn will be wasted," Duncan said. "Reverend Mildew will try to eat it with a knife and fork.") Meg's other belongings—her set of Nancy Drew mysteries and her pennants and bottles of cologne

—remained in her room. Duncan had thought they should bring everything in one fell swoop but Justine preferred not to. "All she asked for were her summer dresses," she said. "Maybe she doesn't have space yet for the rest."

Duncan, who never dragged anyone's secret feelings into the open if he could possibly help it, merely nodded and let her have her way.

They reached the outskirts of Semple at two in the afternoon. *Welcome to Semple, Va.*, "*Prettiest Little Town in the South,*" the sign said, looming above a stack of pine boards weathering in a lumberyard. They bounced over railroad tracks, past rusty, gaping boxcars. "Now *there* was a town," said Grandfather Peck. "Had its own train."

"Only freight trains, Grandfather," Justine said.

"Pardon? Freight? Didn't we go to Nashville once from here?"

"That was from Fredericksburg. Three years back."

"Oh yes."

"Here we had to take a bus to Richmond and *then* catch a train."

"Nashville was where that boy played the banjo," said her grandfather. "His great-uncle taught Caleb how to work a stringed instrument when they were both fourteen."

"That's the place," Justine said.

He slumped, as if the conversation had taken everything out of him.

On Main Street Justine saw someone she knew—old Miss Wheeler, who used to ask the cards whether she should put her father in a nursing home—and she wanted to stop and speak to her, but Duncan wouldn't hear of it. "I'd like to get this over with, Justine," he said. Going back to places always did make him cross. When they passed the Wayfarer's Diner and then the Whole Self Health Food Store, whose tattered awning and baggy screens leapt out like familiar faces, Justine could feel the edginess in the skin of his arm. "Never mind, we're only visiting," she told him. But she had trespassed again and he drew himself in, moving slightly away from her so that their arms no longer touched and there was a sudden coolness along her left thigh.

Arthur Milsom's church was a large brick building on the other side of town. Justine had never attended it, but of course Meg had pointed it out to her—she remembered how the steeple had seemed sharper than necessary, barbed with some glittery metal at the tip. The rectory was brick also, but the house of the assistant pastor, next door to the rectory, was a small white cottage without trees or shrubs, set on a square of artificial-looking grass. There was a bald picture window with a double-globed, rosebud-painted lamp centered in it, and beside the front walk a hitching post in the shape of a small boy with a newly whitened face and black hands. Duncan stopped to study it, but Justine took her grandfather by the elbow and hurried him up the steps. "*Where* is this?" he asked her.

"This is Meg's, Grandfather. We're visiting Meg."

"Yes, yes, but—" And he revolved slowly, staring all about him. Justine pressed the doorbell, which was centered in a brass cross with scalloped edges. From somewhere far away she heard a whole melody ringing out in slow, measured, golden tones. Then the door opened and there was Meg, thinner and more poised, with longer hair. "Hello, Mama," she said. She kissed Justine's cheek, and then her great-grandfather's. When Duncan had turned from the hitching post and climbed the steps she kissed his cheek as well. "Hello, Daddy," she said.

"Well, Meggums."

"I thought you might change your mind and not come."

"Would I do a thing like that?"

She didn't smile.

She led them across sculptured blue carpeting into the living room, where Christ gazed out of gilt frames on every wall. Most of the furniture seemed to come in twos—two identical tables flanking the sofa, two beaded lamps, two ice-blue satin easy chairs with skirted ottomans. On the spinet piano in the corner there were two framed photographs, one of Arthur in a clerical robe and the other of Meg with some sort of shiny drapery across her bare shoulders—but so retouched, so flawlessly complexioned, her hair so lacquered, that it took Justine a moment to recognize her. Besides, what right did some unknown woman have to set Meg's photo in her living room? Justine picked it up and studied it. Meg said, "Oh, that's my— that's just the picture we put in the paper when we—" She snatched the photo away and set it down. "I'll get Mother Milsom," she said.

Justine sought out Duncan, who was slouched on the sofa leafing through a *Lady's Circle*. His feet, in enormous grease-spattered desert boots, were resting on the coffee table. "Duncan!" she said, slapping his knee. He looked up and then moved his feet carefully, picking his way between china rabbits and birds, candles shaped like angels, a nativity scene in a seashell and a green glass shoe full of sourballs. Justine let out a long breath and settled down beside him. Across the room, her grandfather paced the carpet with his hands clasped behind his back. He did not like to sit when he would have to struggle up again so soon for the entrance of a lady. He paused before first one Christ and then another, peering closely at a series of melancholy brown eyes and lily-white necks. "Religious art in the *living* room?" he said.

"Ssh," Justine told him.

"But I was always taught that that was in poor taste," he said. "Unless it was an original."

"Grandfather."

She looked at the door where Meg had disappeared. There was no telling how much could be heard. "Grandfather," she said, "wouldn't you like to—"

"They've got him in the dining room too," said Duncan, peering through the other doorway. "Praying in the garden."

"Oh, Duncan, what do you care? When did you ever give a thought to interior decorating?"

He frowned at her. "So you're going to take their side," he said.

"I didn't know there were sides."

"How's that?" asked her grandfather.

"Duncan thinks I'm defecting."

"Hmm?"

"*Defecting.*"

"Nonsense," said her grandfather. "You're as smart as anybody."

Duncan laughed. Justine turned on him. "Duncan," she said, "I certainly hope you're not going to go into one of your silly fits here. Duncan, I mean this. For Meg's sake, now, can't we just try to—"

But then whispery footsteps crossed the carpet, and a lady in white entered the room with Meg just behind her. "Mother Milsom, I'd like you to meet my mother," Meg said. "And my father, and my great-grandfather Peck." Meg's face was stern and her forehead was tweaked together in the center; she was warning her family not to disgrace her. So Duncan rose to his full height, keeping one thumb in his magazine, while the grandfather touched his temple and Justine stood up and held out her hand. Mrs. Milsom's fingers felt like damp spaghetti. She was a long, wilted lady with light-brown hair parted in the center and crimped tight to her head, a pale tragic face, eyes as black and precisely lidded as a playing-card queen's. Her dress, which was made of something crêpey, hung limp over her flat chest, billowed hollowly at the waist and wrists, and dripped in layers to her skinny sharp legs. She wore pointed silver pumps from the Sixties. When she smiled her eyes remained wide and lusterless, as if she were keeping in mind some secret sorrow. "So finally we meet," she said.

"We would have come before but Duncan was buying Prince Albert tins," Justine told her. Nervousness always did make her talk too much.

"*I* understand. Won't you be seated? Margaret, darling, would you care to serve the iced tea?"

Meg looked at her mother. Then she left the room. Mrs. Milsom floated slowly downward into one of the satin chairs, parts of her appearing to settle whole minutes after other parts. She laid her hands delicately together. "Arthur I hope will be joining us shortly," she said. "At the moment he's napping."

"Arthur naps?" said Duncan.

"It's a fourth Sunday. His day to preach. Preaching takes so much out of him. Naturally we had been hoping that you would be here in time to hear his sermon, but apparently things did not fall out that way." She gave Justine a deep, mournful look.

"Oh well—" said Justine. They would have come for the sermon, even Duncan—anything for Meg—but Meg had specifically told them not to arrive till after lunch.

"Generally on fourth Sundays he awakes with a headache," said Mrs. Milsom, "and sustains it during the entire service and even afterward, until he admits that I am right and takes to his bed. He suffers real pain. This is not some ordinary headache."

"Maybe he should switch to *fifth* Sundays," Duncan said. "Sixth, even."

Justine shot him a look.

"Where's the minister?" asked Grandfather Peck, settling creakily into an armchair.

"*Grandfather*, turn on your—"

"Arthur is napping, Mr. Peck," said Mrs. Milsom. Her voice was thinned to just the right pitch. "I know all about the deaf," she told Justine. "My father was afflicted. In his later years he would go so far as to sing the 'Doxology' while his congregation was on 'Bringing in the Sheaves.' "

"Oh, your father was a minister too," Justine said.

"Oh yes. *Oh* yes. All my family."

"And your husband?"

"No, ah—he was in construction."

"I see."

"But *my* family, now they have been clergy for a great many years. I myself am a healer."

"Is that right?" said Duncan. He stopped rolling up his magazine. "You heal by faith?"

"I certainly do."

She smiled at him, her eyes like black pools. Then Meg came tinkling and clinking through the doorway with a tray, and Justine tensed because she herself, of course, would have spilled ice cubes into Mrs. Milsom's snowy lap or tripped over the veins in the carpet. She forgot that Meg was as graceful and confident as her maiden aunts. The tray paused at each person, dipping neatly, holding steady. Mrs. Milsom watched its progress with her lower lip caught between her teeth. She was tense too, as if Meg were *her* daughter. It wasn't fair. She had no right. Justine snatched a tumbler off the tray and a disk of tea flew onto the sofa cushion, but Duncan instantly covered it with his *Lady's Circle.* "Mama. It's sweetened," Meg whispered.

"What?" Justine said aloud.

"It's *sweetened.*"

"The tea is sweetened," said Mrs. Milsom. "Thank you, Margaret. Won't you take some yourself?"

"I was thinking I might go see if Arthur's awake."

"Oh no, dear, I wouldn't do that just yet."

"He did say to wake him when they came."

"If we do he'll have his head till tomorrow, believe me," said Mrs. Milsom. "I know him." She smiled and patted the arm of her chair. "Come sit with us a while."

So Meg came to perch at Mrs. Milsom's side, and Justine averted her eyes and concentrated on her tea. It was a fact that the only thing she couldn't stand was sweetened tea. It made her gag. She would feel sick and heavy for the rest of the day. Still she drank it, searching with her tongue for the nearest ice cube to dilute the sugary taste. Duncan, who didn't care one way or the other, finished his own drink in one breath and set the glass down upon the polished table. "Well," he said. "So you've got your diploma, Meggie."

She nodded. Her hair touched her collar, a little less neat than it used to be. Maybe she was trying to look older.

"So what next?" Duncan asked her.

"Oh, I don't know."

"Going to get some kind of a job?"

"Mr. Peck," said Mrs. Milsom, "being a minister's wife *is* a job."

Duncan looked over at her. Justine grew worried, but in the end all he said was, "I meant, *besides* that."

"Oh, there's nothing besides that. Believe me, I know. I'm a minister's daughter. And I've been standing behind Arthur all this time filling in until he found himself a wife: attending teas and sewing circles, helping at bazaars, fixing casseroles—"

"Meggie, your mother must know people," Duncan said. "All sorts of people with jobs to offer, I'm sure of it. How about Pooch Sims? The veterinarian." He turned to Justine. "*She* could use someone."

"Oh, Mr. Peck," said Mrs. Milsom. She laughed and her ice cubes rattled. "Margaret wouldn't want to do that."

Everyone looked at Meg. She stared down into her glass.

"Would you, Meg?" Duncan asked.

"No," said Meg, "I guess I wouldn't."

"Well, then, what?"

"Oh, I don't know, Daddy. Mother Milsom's right, I do have a lot to do already. I've taken over the nursery at church and I have so many calls to pay and everything."

Justine's teeth seemed to be growing fur, and still she hadn't made a dent in her drink. She longed for something sour or salty. She had a craving for pickles, lemon rind, a potato chip even. But Mrs. Milsom gazed at her so reproachfully that she raised the glass and took another swallow.

"Mainly of course the minister's wife is a *buffer*," said Mrs. Milsom. "She filters his calls, tries to handle the little things that so clutter his day—oh, Margaret can tell you. We've been teaching her all about it. Arthur is not terribly strong, you see. He's allergic to so much. And he has these headaches."

"But I thought you were a healer," Duncan said.

"A healer, yes! I have a little group that meets on Sunday evenings. Anyone can come. I inherited the gift from my father, who once gave sight to a blind man."

"But your father was deaf."

"He still had the *gift*, Mr. Peck."

"I meant—"

"Of course the gift must be kept alive by prayer and faith, it has to be nurtured along. That's what I tell Arthur. I feel that Arthur very definitely has the gift. I am working with him on it now. So far there has seemed to be some—I don't know, some sort of *resistance*, I'm just not—but we're working, I'm sure we'll get there."

"How about Grandfather here?" Duncan asked. "*He* could use some help."

She hesitated.

"Think you could just clap a couple of hands on his ears to oblige us?"

"Well, I'm not—is it nerve deafness, or what?"

"Oh, if faith only heals certain *kinds*," said Duncan.

Both Meg and Justine stirred, uneasily. Duncan gave them a wide, innocent smile that did not reassure them. "But never mind," he said, "my real interest was headaches."

"Headaches, Mr. Peck? Do you suffer from headaches?"

"No, your son does."

"My son."

"Arthur."

"Oh, *Arthur*," she said blankly.

"Didn't you say that Arthur got headaches?"

"Why, yes."

Duncan looked at her for a moment, honestly puzzled. "But then," he said, "why can't you heal him?"

Mrs. Milsom clasped her hands tightly. Her mouth became blurred and her eyes filled with what must surely be black tears; but no, when they spilled over they were clear and they made white tracks down her hollow white cheeks.

"Oh, Duncan," Justine said. But what had he done, after all? Nobody understood, except perhaps Meg, who quickly buried her nose in her tea glass. Then Mrs. Milsom straightened and darted an index finger beneath each eye, quick as a frog's tongue. "Well!" she said. "Haven't we had nice weather for August?"

"It's been very nice," Duncan told her gently. And he must have been planning to stay that way to the end, sober and courteous; he would never willingly hurt anybody. Except that Justine chose that moment to reach toward the green glass shoe on the coffee table—sourballs! right under her nose!—and choose a lemony yellow globe and pop it into her mouth, where she instantly discovered that she had eaten a marble. While everyone watched in silence she plucked it out delicately between thumb and forefinger and replaced it, only a little shinier than before, in the green glass shoe. "*I* thought we could have used more rain," she told the ring of faces.

Duncan made a peculiar sound. So he *was* going to have a silly fit after all. Justine had to sit as straight as a statue, dignified enough for the two of them, while at intervals Duncan steamed and chortled like an electric percolator on the couch beside her.

When Arthur was up (pale and rumpled, inadequate-looking in a short-sleeved Hawaiian shirt) they moved out to the back yard to admire Mrs. Milsom's flowerbeds, then over to the church to see the new red carpet just recently installed in the aisles. They tiptoed through the vaulted, echoing nave with their faces very serious. They were all particularly careful of one another, if you didn't count Duncan's pinching Justine when he didn't know Mrs. Milsom was looking. They were so appreciative, so soft-voiced and attentive, that by the time they had assembled beside the Ford to say their goodbyes everyone was exhausted. But Mrs. Milsom held out both hands bravely for the sack of sun-baked corn, and Arthur insisted on taking the entire burden of wedding silver from the trunk. He staggered off, stringy-armed, sway-backed beneath his load. Meg remained beside the car with her pile of shirtwaist dresses. "Well," said Justine, "I suppose we'll be seeing you soon." She felt bruised by disappointment. She had imagined that this visit might, in some way, wrap things up—that whatever had gone wrong in their family might finally be straightened out, or at least understood; and that having seen Meg settled and happy she could let her go at last. She had supposed that care and responsibility could be shucked like old skin, leaving her cool and smooth and lightweight. But Meg's face was screwed so tight it made her ache, and she would never be free of Meg's old, anxious eyes. "Meggie, is there anything you need?" she asked. "I mean, if you think of something, anything at all—"

"I'm sorry about the tea," Meg said.

"Tea?"

"I told her you didn't drink it sweetened."

"Oh, that's all right, honey."

"She was making it after lunch and I said, 'Don't put sugar in it, Mama likes hers with just lemon.' But she said, 'Oh, everybody likes their tea with sugar, it's so refreshing.' I said, 'But—' "

"Meg, I don't care," said Justine.

"I said I would mix a separate glass then," Meg told Duncan, "but she doesn't really like me in her kitchen."

Duncan studied her. Grandfather Peck stroked his chin.

"She does everything, even makes our bed up. She says I don't know hospital corners. You never taught me about hospital corners, Mama."

"I'm sorry, honey."

"I wanted to have you for lunch today, I said I would cook it myself. You know I can cook. Simple things, at least. Fannie Farmer. But she said it wasn't possible because her group was coming over for supper, these people in her healing group. She had to have the kitchen to herself. The people in her healing group are all old and strange, they have chronic illnesses and they think she helps, and then sometimes they bring her someone new and they all pray together holding hands."

"Does it work?" Justine asked.

"What? No. I don't know. I thought when I got married we would be so—regular. I thought finally we—I didn't know all this would be going on. When I met her she was like anybody else. Except for wearing white. She did wear white all the time. But I didn't know then about this healing. She wants Arthur to learn healing too and she even wanted to look at *my* hands, she wondered if I have the gift."

"Do you?" Justine asked.

"Mama! I wouldn't go along with a thing like that."

"Well, I don't know, at least it would be a new experience."

"I don't want new experiences, I want a normal happy life. But Arthur just won't stand up to her, really he—and now she wants him to develop his gift because hers is going. She thinks it's because of her age. At the meetings they pray and cry, you can hear them everywhere in the house. She reminds God of what she used to accomplish: once she stopped a man in the middle of a heart attack."

"She did?"

"She says she has so much left to do, she should be allowed to keep her gift. She says it's unjust. There are people sick just everywhere, she says, and blind and crippled and suffering pain, and here she is powerless and she can't even stop her own son's headaches any more. She goes on and on about it, calling out so everyone can hear: just because a little time has passed, she says, *that*'s no reason to let her dwindle down this way."

"Well, I should say not," said Justine.

Meg paused and gave her a look. "Are you listening?" she asked.

"Certainly I'm listening."

"I live among *crazy* people!"

"You should leave," Duncan told her.

"Oh, Duncan," said Justine. She turned to Meg. "Meggie darling, maybe you could just—or look at it this way. Imagine you were handed a stack of instructions. Things that you should undertake. Blind errands, peculiar invitations . . . things you're supposed to go through, and come out different on the other side. Living with a faith healer. *I* never got to live with a faith healer."

"That's what you're going to tell your daughter?" Duncan said. "Just accept whatever comes along? Endure? Adapt?"

"Well—"

"And how would people end up if they all did that?"

Justine hesitated.

"Never mind, Mama," Meg told her. "I didn't mean to mention it, anyway."

So Justine got into the car, but untidily and with backward glances because so much seemed still unsettled. The troubled feeling was nagging at her mind again. She couldn't quite put her finger on it. She felt as if she had mislaid an object somewhere, something important that would thread through all her thoughts until she found it. But she sat forward briskly and called out the window, "Meggie darling!"

"What is it?"

"If you do have to do bazaar work, you know, if you need any help, I'll be happy to drive down any time and tell fortunes."

"Thank you, Mama."

"You know I have a lot of steady clients here."

"Well, that's very nice of you, Mama," Meg said. But Justine could tell that she had made a mistake. She should have offered something plainer and sturdier—anything but more gifts from heaven.

By the time they reached Caro Mill it was night, and the streets had a dismal abandoned look. The only place open was the diner, eerily lit and vacant except for Black Emma swabbing the counter. "Maybe we could stop for coffee," said Justine. But the car slid by, and neither Duncan nor her grandfather answered. (They had not spoken all the way home, either one of them. Only Justine had chattered on and on until she wondered herself when she would shut up.) "Duncan?" she said. "Couldn't we stop for coffee?"

"We have coffee at home."

"I don't want to go home," she said. "I have this peculiar feeling. I wouldn't mind staying the *night* somewhere, even. Duncan?"

But he said, "*Endure*," and turned sharply down Watchmaker Street. She blinked and looked at him.

In front of their house, when the engine had died and the headlights had faded, the three of them sat motionless for a moment gazing through the windshield, as if being borne along on some darker, more silent journey. Then Justine touched her grandfather's arm. "Here we are," she said.

"Eh?"

He stumbled out, latching the door inconclusively behind him, and Justine slid after Duncan out the driver's side. They went single file up the walk between looming rustling cornstalks. At the porch, they stopped short. A shadow unfolded itself from the steps. "Eli!" Justine said.

"Eh?" said her grandfather.

And Duncan said, "Well, Eli. What have you found for us?"

"Caleb Peck," said Eli.

13

ELI EVERJOHN drank his coffee white, preferred Jane Parker angel food cake to taco chips, and was perfectly comfortable sitting on a chrome-legged chair in the kitchen. He had to make all that clear before they would let him get on with his report. "Listen here," he kept saying. "Listen. It struck me right off—" But Justine would interrupt to ask, couldn't she take his hat? wouldn't he be cooler in his shirtsleeves? And old Mr. Peck trudged around and around him, thinking hard, occasionally offering interruptions of his own. "I believe I ought to fetch my notebook, Justine."

"Yes, Grandfather, I would do that."

"I believe that windowscreen is torn. Where else would these mosquitoes be coming from?"

"I'll find the swatter."

"Oh, leave it, leave it. Mr. Everjohn here has something he wants to say to us."

But when Eli took a breath Justine halted him. "Wait, I've been wanting something sour all *day*. Don't start without me."

"*Justine—*" Duncan said.

Eli Everjohn was a patient man. (In his business, he had to be.) Still, he had been dreaming of this moment for a good long time now. He had come over on a Sunday evening expressly to bring this news, which he thought might cause him to burst if he left it till Monday: in just under three months, he had accomplished what a whole family could not do in sixty-one years. He had performed a spectacular piece of deduction, and now he wanted to tell about it in his own slantwise, gradual way so that everyone could admire how one clue had built upon another, one path led to the next, with sudden inspired leaps of the imagination to bridge them. True detective work was an art. *Finding* was an art. He was grateful to the Peck family for handing him this assignment. (How could he ever again settle for guarding anniversary gifts or pretending to read *Newsweek* in front of beauty parlors?) So he cleared his throat, and pushed his coffee cup a certain distance away, and plaited his long fingers on the table before him and began as he had planned. "It struck me right off," he said, "that there was one thing the same in all accounts of Caleb Peck."

"You'll have to speak up," said the old man.

"Oh. Sorry. It *struck* me—"

"Justine, I think my battery's going."

"Will you let the man *speak?*" Duncan said.

So that Eli, with the last of his patience worn away, ended up blurting it out after all and ruining the moment he had planned for so long. "Mr. Caleb Peck," he said, "is in Box Hill, Louisiana, alive and well."

It had struck Eli right off that there was one thing the same in all accounts of Caleb Peck: he was a musical man. To his family that was only a detail, like the color of his eyes or his tendency to wear a Panama hat just a little past the season. But to Caleb, wasn't it more? Eli pondered, sifting what he had heard and endlessly rearranging it. He traveled a few blind alleys. He scanned the alumni lists of several well-known music schools, including Baltimore's Peabody Institute. He checked the family's old phonograph records for performers whom Caleb might have been moved to seek out. He inquired as to Caleb's piano teacher —someone young and pretty, maybe? Someone inspirational, to teach him those Czerny exercises he found crumbling away on top of the piano in old Mr. Peck's Baltimore parlor? But no, the Czerny was Margaret Rose's, said Mr. Peck. Caleb had not liked Czerny. He was not, to tell the truth, very fond of the classical mode. And he had never had a music teacher of any kind. Only little Billy Pope passing on his fiddle lessons, and a leatherbound book telling how to play the woodwinds (which in those days were really made of wood—see the ebony flute in Caleb's old bedroom?) and for the piano, Lafleur Boudrault, who taught him ragtime.

Was this Lafleur Boudrault young and pretty, by any chance?

But Lafleur Boudrault was the Creole gardener, not pretty at all—a scar down one cheek and a permanent wink. Long dead now. Survived by his wife Sulie. He wouldn't have helped out anyway: a cross-grained sort.

Eli traveled once again to Baltimore and sought out Sulie, who was moving a dustcloth around and around the attic. Nowadays all she did was dust. She would not give up her cloth, which had to be pried from her fingers in her sleep as you would pry a pet blanket from a child in order to wash it. And what she dusted was not helpful at all—never the furniture, which Lord knows could *use* a dusting, all those bulbs and scallops and crevices; but only the hidden places that didn't count, the undersides of drawers and the backs of picture frames and now these trunks and cartons in the attic, which she had been on for weeks and weeks. They couldn't get her to stop. They wanted to pension her off; didn't she have family somewhere? They were almost certain there had been a daughter. But Sulie only laughed her cracked, rapid laugh and said, "*Now* you wants to do it.

Now you wants." Oh, she was mad, no question about it. But Eli needed Caleb's contemporaries and there were not all that many to pick and choose from. He climbed the narrow, hollow, pine-smelling steps to Laura's attic, submerging first his head and then his shoulders and then his wool-wrapped body in a heat so intense that it seemed to be liquid, and at the last he was merely floating upward in a throbbing dull haze. He swam between crazed china hurricane lamps and slanted portraits, across rugs rolled and stacked like logs, toward the spindly figure briskly polishing an empty Pears soap box down where the dusty light fingered its way through the louvers. "Mrs. Sulie Boudrault?" he asked, and without looking up she nodded and hummed and went on polishing.

"Widow of Lafleur Boudrault?"

She nodded.

"You wouldn't happen to know where Mr. Caleb Peck has got to."

Then she stopped polishing.

"Well, I thought they wouldn't never ask," she said.

She settled him on a china barrel, and she herself sat on a stack of *St. Nicholas* magazines with her dustcloth clutched daintily in her lap. She was a very small woman with stretched-looking skin and yellow eyes. Her manner of speaking was clear and reasonable, and her story proceeded in a well-ordered way. No wonder: she had had over half a century in which to arrange it.

"When first Mr. Caleb had left us," she said, "I told Lafleur, 'Lafleur, what do I say?' For I known where he had went to yet I would hate to give him away. 'Lafleur, do I lie?' 'That ain't never going to come up,' he say. 'Them folks don't think you know *nothing*.' Well, I was certain he was wrong. I waited for old Mrs. Laura to fix me with her little eyes. She the one to watch for. Mr. Justin the First couldn't do nothing, maybe wouldn't have anyhow, but he had that Mrs. Laura so scared she would do it for him and more besides. She was one scared lady, and it had turned her mean and spiteful. Watch out for Mrs. Laura, I told myself, and so I watch and waited and plan how to answer what she ask. But she never do. Never once. Never even, 'Sulie, do you recollect if you served Mr. Caleb breakfast that day?' Never a word."

Sulie set her skirt out all about her—a long draggled white eyelet affair that hit halfway down her skinny calves, with ankle-high copper-toed work shoes swinging below them. After thinking a moment, she dug down into her pocket and came up with a handful of Oreos, mashed and limp. "Have you a cookie," she said.

"Thank you," said Eli.

"She never ask. Nor none of the others. Took me some time to see they never would. 'Why, looky there!' I say to Lafleur at last, and he say, 'Told you so. They don't reckon just old us would know *nothing*,' he say. So my eyes was opened. That was how. I made up my mind I wouldn't tell till they say straight out, 'Sulie, do you know?' And Mrs. Laura I wouldn't give the time of *day* even. I never did. She live forty-six years after Mr. Caleb had went and I never spoken to her once, but I don't fool myself she realize that. 'Sulie is getting so *sullen*,' was what she say. Even that tooken her five or so years to notice good."

Eli finished the Oreo and dusted off his hands. From his pocket he took a spiral notebook and a Bic pen. He opened to a blank page.

"Now," said Sulie.

She stood up, as if to recite.

"Mr. Caleb was a musical man," she said.

"I had heard he was."

"He like *most* music, but colored best. He like ragtime and he copied everything Lafleur do on the piano. He like stories about them musicians in New Orleans, which is where Lafleur come from. Lafleur had got his self in a speck of trouble down there and couldn't go back, but he would tell about the piano players in Storyville and what all went on. Understand this was back *long* time ago. Didn't many people know about such things.

"Then times got hard and Miss Maggie Rose left us. I had

to move on over to Mr. Daniel's house and tend the babies. I was not but in my teens then. I had just did get married to old Lafleur. I didn't know much but I saw how Mr. Caleb was mighty quiet and maybe took a tad more to drink than was needed. But I never thought he'd leave. One night he come down cellar to our bedroom, me and Lafleur's. Knocks on our door. 'Lafleur,' he say, 'this fellow down at the tavern is talking about a trip to New Orleans.'

" 'Is that so,' say Lafleur.

" 'Wants me to go along.'

" 'That so.'

" 'Well, I'm thinking of doing it.'

" 'Why, sure,' Lafleur tell him.

" 'Permanent,' Mr. Caleb say. 'Unannounced.'

"But still, you see, we didn't have no notion he was serious.

"He ask Lafleur was there someplace to go, to stay a whiles. Lafleur mention this white folks' boardinghouse over near where his sister live at. Mr. Caleb wroten it down on a piece of paper and fold it careful and left. We didn't think a thing more about it. Come morning he arrive for breakfast, sometime he would do that. Eat in Mr. Daniel's kitchen. 'Fix me a lot now, Sulie,' he say. 'Can't travel far on an empty stomach.' Well, I thought he meant travel to *town*. I fix him hotcakes. I set out his breakfast and when he had done finished he thank me politely and left. I never did see him again."

She considered her fingernails, ridged and yellowed like old piano keys.

"Could I have that boardinghouse address?" Eli asked her.

"Yes, why surely," she said, and she gave it to him, slowly and clearly, having saved it up on purpose all these years, and he wrote it in his notebook. Then she faded off, so that Eli thought she had forgotten him. He rose with care and tiptoed to the attic steps. He had already dipped one ankle into the coolness below when she called him. "Mr. Whoever-you-are!"

"Ma'am?"

"When you tell how you found him," she said, "make certain you put in that Sulie known the answer all along."

So now he had an address, but it was sixty-one years old. He knew he couldn't expect too much. He caught a plane to New Orleans that night. He took a cab to where a boardinghouse had stood in the spring of 1912. All he saw was a supermarket, lit inside with ghostly blue night lights, hulking on an asphalt parking lot.

"I reckon there's no sense hanging around," he told the cab driver.

Eli registered at a small hotel from which immediately, despite the hour, he called every Peck in the telephone book. No one had an ancestor named Caleb. He went to bed and slept a sound, dreamless sleep. On the following day, he set out walking. He picked his way past suspicious-looking hidden court-yards and lacy balconies, secret fountains splashing, leprous scaly stucco, monstrous greenery and live oaks dripping beards of moss, through surprising pockets of light where the air seemed to lie like colored veils. In various echoing buildings, archives both official and unofficial, he wandered gloomily with his hands in his pockets peering at yellowed sheet music, clippings, menus, and sporting-house directories under glass, as well as cases full of dented trumpets and valve trombones that appeared to have come from the dimestore. In the evenings he attended night-clubs, where, wincing against the clatter of brass and drums, he sidled between the tables to stare at the curling photographs on the walls and the programs once handed out during Fourth of July celebrations. There was no Caleb Peck. There was never that stiff, old-fashioned white man's face or Panama hat.

Eli's wife called, sounding lank and dragged out with the heat. "But it's hotter here," he told her. "And you ought to see the bugs." She didn't care; she wanted him home. What was he doing there, anyhow?

"I'll be back in another week," he told her. "In a week I'm going to have this thing wrapped up."

It was August eighteenth. Although he did not have a single new clue, he was beginning to feel excited.

Now he started shadowing the gaudy, sunglassed tourists, who seemed to know something he did not. They were always in possession of secret addresses: the lodgings of palsied old sax-hornists, clarinetists, past employees of the Streckfus Excursion Lines and granddaughters of Buddy Bolden's girlfriends. (Who was Buddy Bolden?) Eli slipped in behind them through narrow doors, into dingy parlors or taverns or bedrooms. Sometimes he was ushered out again. Sometimes he would pass unnoticed. Then he introduced questions of his own, all of them out of place:

"You wouldn't know a jazz *cellist*, by some chance."

"Any good musicians out of Baltimore?"

"Whereabouts were you in the spring of nineteen twelve?"

Ancient, dusty eyes peered back at him, but never ancient enough. "Nineteen twelve? What kind of memory do you think I got, boy?"

By imperceptible degrees the Pecks had altered Eli. He had begun to ignore the passage of time, as if it were somehow *common*. He felt irritated that ordinary people could not do the same.

Days were tiresome, yes, and hard on the feet, but nights were worse. The string of clubs, bars, cafés, dance halls, and strip joints went on forever, and all the music sounded the same to him: badly organized. Eli slipped into a place and out again, into the next. He ducked away at any mention of cover charge, waved off waiters and hostesses. When pressed, he ordered Dr. Pepper; mostly he left before things had gone that far. The scent of success discouraged him. He wanted failure, spooky little hole-in-the-wall cafés. For surely, he was thinking now, Caleb himself was a failure. Whatever he had ended up doing, it had not left any mark upon this town.

He entered bars that smelled of mildewed wood, that had names like The High Note or Sportin' Life, where a few musicians played raggedly and without much interest. A black man sang above a guitar:

My train done left, Lord, done left me by the track,
My train done left, Lord, done left me by the track.
Tell the folks in Whisky Alley
I ain't never coming back . . .

Eli shook his head. He slid past a drunkard and returned to the sidewalk, where he milled among the tourists in a greasy, neon-lit, garlic-smelling night.

The following morning, he was up unusually early. He ate breakfast in a coffee shop near where he had been the night before, and he strolled past the same bars, but they were closed now. Farther down, an aproned man was sweeping the entrance of a strip joint that looked cheerful and homely by daylight. "Tell me," Eli said to him. "You know that little old bar back there? Easy Livin'?"

The man squinted. "What about it?"

"You know what time it opens?"

"Most likely not till evening," said the man. "You got a wait, fellow."

"Well, thank you," Eli said.

This morning he did not delve any further into the archives of jazz. He bought a paper and read it in a park. He had a second cup of coffee and a glazed doughnut. Then when the movies opened, he toured the city catching Jimmy Stewart films. Eli very much admired Jimmy Stewart.

At six o'clock he had a plate of scrambled eggs in a diner, followed by another cup of coffee and apple pie à la mode. Then he set off toward Easy Livin'—on foot, since it wasn't far. He took his time. He nodded soberly as he walked and he looked about him with a well-meaning expression such as Jimmy Stewart might have worn. When he reached his destination, he straightened his string tie before stepping through the battered door.

Easy Livin' was dark even now, when it was barely twilight. There was a bar with a brass rail, a few scarred tables, and at the end of the room a raw wooden platform for the entertainers. At the moment, there were no other customers. Only a boy behind the bar, and on the platform the black man who had sung the night before. He was squatting to hitch up some sort of electrical wire. He didn't even look around when Eli came up behind him.

"Say," said Eli. "Could I ask about a song?"

The singer grunted and then rose, brushing off his dungarees. He said, "This here is not one of them jazz joints, baby. Go on up the street."

"Last *night* you were singing," Eli said.

"Only the blues."

"Ah," said Eli, who did not see the difference. He pondered a moment. The singer looked down at him with his hands on his hips. "Well," Eli said, "you were singing this here song I was wondering about."

"Which."

"Song about a train."

"*All* songs got trains," the singer said patiently.

"Song about Whisky Alley."

"Mm-*hmm*."

"You recall it?" Eli asked.

"I sung it, didn't I?"

"You know who wrote it?"

"Now how would I know that?" the singer said, but then, all of a sudden: "Stringtail Man."

"Who?"

"The Stringtail Man."

"Well, who was that?"

"*I* don't know. White fellow."

"But he's got to have a name," Eli said.

"Naw. Not that I ever knew of. White fellow with a fiddle."

"A fiddle," said Eli. "Well—I mean, ain't that a little peculiar for jazz?"

"Blues," said the singer.

"Blues, then."

"Now I don't know a thing more than what I told you," said the singer. But he hunkered down, anyway, getting closer to Eli's level. "This fellow was *away* back, long before my time. He was lead man for White-Eye, old colored guitar man that used to play the streets. Now White-Eye was blind and the fiddler would lead him around. But whenever he fiddled, looked like the music just got *into* him somewhat and he would commence to dancing. Old White-Eye would hear the notes hopping to one side and then to the other and sometimes roaming off entirely if the music was fast and the fiddler dancing fast to match. So White-Eye hitched his self to the fiddler's belt by means of a string, which is how we come by the Stringtail Man. *Anybody* roundabouts can tell you *that* much."

"I see," said Eli.

"How come you to ask?"

"Well, there used to be this tavern in Baltimore, Maryland, called Whisky Alley," Eli said. "Close by the waterfront."

"So?"

"You don't recollect where this Stringtail fellow was *from*, by any chance."

"Naw."

"Well, how about White-Eye?"

"Him neither."

"No, his name. Didn't he have a name?"

"White-Eye. White-Eye. White-Eye—Ramford!" said the singer, snapping his fingers. "Didn't know I could do it."

"I'm very much obliged," Eli said. He dug down in his trousers pocket. "Can I buy you a Dr. Pepper?"

The singer looked at him for a moment. "Naw, baby," he said finally.

"Well, thanks, then."

"Nothing to it."

By noon the following day, Eli had contacted every Ramford in the telephone book. He had located White-Eye Ramford's great-granddaughter, a waitress; from there he had gone to see a Mrs. Clarine Ramford Tucker, who was residing in the Lydia Lockford Nursing Home for the Colored and Indigent; and from there to a Baptist cemetery in a swampy-smelling section outside the city. The sight of Abel Ramford's crumbling headstone, a small Gothic arch over a sunken grave obviously neglected for years, smothered by Queen Anne's lace and chicory, brought Eli up short, and for a long time he stood silent with his hat in his hands, wondering if this were the end of his road. Then he took heart and went to see the caretaker. He learned that Mr. Ramford's site had no visitors at all, so far as was known; but that every year on All Saints' Day a bouquet of white carnations was brought by Altona Florists, a very high-class flower shop with lavender delivery trucks.

And Altona Florists said yes, they did have a standing order for that date: a dozen white carnations delivered to this little colored cemetery way the hell and gone; and the bill was sent to Box Hill, Louisiana, to a Mr. Caleb Peck.

That was Saturday, August twenty-fifth. It had taken Eli exactly eighty-one days to complete his search.

Because he had been warned not to approach Caleb in person ("I want to do that much myself," Mr. Peck had said), Eli came home without that final satisfaction. But it was almost enough just to tell his story in Justine's kitchen and watch the old man's astonishment. "What? What?" he said, even when he had clearly heard. He started circling the table again, kneading his hands as if they were cold. "I don't understand."

"He's in Louisiana, Grandfather."

"But—we never did go anywhere near there. Did we, Justine?"

"We didn't know."

"We never thought of it," said Mr. Peck. "Louisiana is one you forget when you're trying to name all the states in the Union. What would he be doing there?"

"Eli says—"

"I always suspected that Sulie was no durn good."

"Now Grandfather, you didn't either, you know how you used to rely on her."

"She took advantage," he said. "Why, if we somehow missed asking her—and I don't believe for a minute that we did—it was an oversight. Just chance! How long are we going to be held accountable for every little slip and error?" He frowned at Eli. "And you say Caleb is a—"

"Fiddler."

"I don't understand."

"*Fiddler*."

"Yes, but I don't—" He turned to Justine. "That doesn't make sense," he told her.

"You always did say he was a musical man," she said.

"It's the wrong Caleb."

"No sir!" said Eli, lifting his head sharply. "No indeed, Mr. Peck."

"Bound to be.."

"Would I come to you if I wasn't sure yet?" Eli fumbled in his breast pocket, brought out his notebook, and turned the curly, gray-rimmed pages. "Here. I checked this man out, listen here. Caleb Justin Peck, born February fourteenth, eighteen eighty-five, Baltimore, Maryland. Who else could it be?"

"How'd you learn all that? I told you not to go near him."

"I called and spoke to a nurse at the Home."

"Home?"

Eli flipped back one page in his notebook. "Evergreen County Home for the Elderly, two fourteen Hamilton Street, Box Hill, Louisiana."

Mr. Peck felt behind him for a chair and sat down very slowly.

"If you say a word," Justine whispered to Duncan, "I'll kill you. I'll kill you."

"I wasn't going to say anything."

Eli looked from one face to the other, confused.

"But of course he's not *in* the Home," said Mr. Peck.

"Why, yes."

"He just lives nearby. Or visits some acquaintance there."

"He's a resident."

"He is?"

"Room nineteen."

Mr. Peck rubbed his chin.

"I'm sorry," said Eli, although previously he hadn't felt one way or the other about it.

"My brother is in a Home."

"Well now, I'm sure it's—"

"My own brother in a Home." His eyes flashed suddenly over to Duncan, spiky blue eyes like burs. "You will want your bottle of bourbon or whatever."

"Forget it," said Duncan. He looked somehow tired, not himself at all.

"Why!" said Mr. Peck. "Why, Caleb must be *old!*"

Nobody spoke.

Mr. Peck thought a moment. "He is eighty-eight years old," he said at last.

Telling the news was not as much fun as Eli had expected it would be.

14

21 Watchmaker Street
Caro Mill, Maryland
August 27, 1973

Dear Caleb,
    I take pen in hand to

21 Watchmaker Street
Caro Mill, Maryland
August 27, 1973

Dear Caleb,
    When I heard you were alive, Caleb, my heart

21 Watchmaker Street
Caro Mill, Maryland
August 27, 1973

Dear Caleb,

This is your brother writing. My name, in the very likely event that you have forgotten, is

21 Watchmaker Street
Caro Mill, Maryland
August 27, 1973

Dear Caleb,

I take pen in hand to express my hope that you are in good health and spirits.

Originally I had planned to visit unannounced, extending personally an invitation to stay with us here in Caro Mill. However my grandson reminded me that perhaps you had no wish to see your family again. I told him that of course this would not be the case. Is it?

A great deal of water has flowed under the bridge. Altogether now I have seven grandchildren and one great-grandchild. I regret to inform you that both of our parents passed on some time ago, as well as the baby, Caroline. My sons and two grandsons are running the firm etc.—but it is difficult to impart all this via the post. I am hoping that soon we shall be speaking face to face instead.

My grandchildren Duncan and Justine, who live at the above address and with whom I often visit, second my invitation and look forward to making your acquaintance. Should you find yourself short of cash at the moment I would be willing to provide the airplane ticket. I understand that one may fly from New Orleans, journeying from Box Hill by Greyhound bus which if I am correct is the only recourse in those parts.

I have flown by airplane myself on several occasions. Airplanes are now quite a common occurrence and what the Ford has developed into will be difficult for you to believe.

Of course it is no disgrace to find oneself residing in a

Home, if alternatives are lacking and one's family has all passed on. In your case I do not know about the alternatives, but I do know that your family *has not all passed on.* They are mostly alive and would never consider allowing one of their number to enter a Home for any reason whatsoever. You must surely have guessed this and yet, by some manner of logic which utterly confounds me, chose not to call upon your own flesh and blood in an hour of need.

But we will let bygones be bygones.

But in what way did the family ever injure you? If our father was, perhaps, overmuch involved in business, our mother a trifle strict, was that so important that you must ruin your life for it and then, having completed the ruin, fail to turn to us for aid?

But there is no point in dwelling upon such things.

I neglected to mention that I was made a Judge, though now of course retired. It is my understanding that you entered the musical world in some capacity, which is not quite clear to me though I hope to hear more about it when we meet.

My grandson says that you have a right to be left alone, and that surely you would have contacted us long ago if you had any desire to see us. Of course it is not my intention to intrude where I am not wanted.

You could have sent us a telegram collect from anywhere in the country and we would have come immediately, yet you chose not to. This to me, Caleb, speaks of some *spitefulness,* for surely you knew that it would pain us to think of a Peck in any such Institution. You were always contrary, even as a child, and caused our mother much worry, due to your stubborn nature which, as I gather, you never managed to overcome.

But enough of that. It is all over now.

My grandson says that your whereabouts is your own secret, to keep or not as you see fit, and consequently I must not let the rest of the family know without your permission. He has instructed the friend who found you not to notify my sons until you allow it. He says we had no right to run you to the ground this way. I told my grandson that I did not believe you would view it in such a light. Surely you understand that my only desire was to see you once more and perhaps have a little talk, not about anything in particular, which there never seemed to be enough time for back in 1912.

To tell the truth, Caleb, it appears that my ties to the present have weakened. I cannot feel that what happens today is of any real importance to me. I am not overly connected to my own descendants, not even to my granddaughter. She means well of course but is so different from me and so unlike my earlier recollections of her, perhaps I would not know her if I came upon her unexpectedly in the street. Consequently it is my hope that you will answer this letter, and that you and I may soon meet to talk over those years which once seemed so long ago but now appear clearer than they were even while we lived them.

I remain

Your brother,
Daniel J. Peck, Sr.

15

JUSTINE stood on her front walk, ignoring a shower that was more mist than rain, talking to Red Emma. "Say you mailed a letter August twenty-seventh," she said. "Or *I* don't know, it was afternoon; maybe it went out the twenty-eighth. No, because he sent it direct from the post office. He has stopped trusting the corner boxes ever since they changed to red and blue. Say you mailed a letter August twenty-seventh, and it was going to a little town in Louisiana. How long would it take?"

"Airmail?" asked Red Emma.

"He doesn't trust airmail."

"He doesn't trust *anything!*"

"There've been so many plane crashes lately."

"Well, I would give it three days," said Red Emma. "And considering he didn't mail early in the day and it's going to a little town, make it four."

"So it got there August thirtieth," Justine said.

Red Emma nodded. Tiny droplets clung to her curls like the dew on a cobweb, and her face was shiny and her mail pouch was growing speckled.

"Then how long back again?" Justine asked. "Four more?"

"I would say so."

"Plus a day in between for the answer to be written."

"Well, if it would *take* a whole day."

"September fourth," said Justine. "A week ago. I don't think Grandfather can stand to wait much longer."

"Really he ought to develop some other interest," Red Emma told her. "Join the Golden Age Club."

"Oh, I don't think he'd like it."

"But he would be so popular! With his fine head of hair and all his teeth."

"Maybe so," said Justine, "but I don't picture it."

She waved goodbye and went back to the house with her mail—a sample packet of salad dressing mix and a postcard from Meg. "Here," she said to Duncan. He was playing solitaire on the living room floor. When she tossed him the postcard he picked it up and squinted at the picture, which showed thousands of people stretched out nearly naked on a strip of sand. He turned the card over. " 'Dear Mama and Daddy and Grandfather,' " he read. " 'Here we are with the Young Marrieds Fellowship having just a wonderful time and wish you were . . . ' " He passed the card to his grandfather, who was sitting on the couch doing nothing at all.

"What's this?" said his grandfather.

"Card from Meg."

"Oh, I see."

He set the card very carefully on the couch beside him and went back to staring into space.

"Grandfather, would you like to play cribbage?" Justine asked him.

"Cribbage? No."

"It's just as well, you always forget the rules," Duncan told her.

"Would you like a game of chess, Grandfather?"

He looked at her blankly.

"Or a trip in the car. You don't want to just *sit*."

"Why not?" he asked her.

Duncan laughed.

"It isn't funny," Justine told him. "Oh, when is this rain going to stop?" She swept tangles of plant vines aside in order to peer through the window. "I wish we had somewhere to go. I wish we could just get in the car and drive, or catch a train somewhere."

"You know," her grandfather said, "my feelings won't be hurt at all if he doesn't ever answer."

Justine turned to look at him.

"Anyhow, what was I thinking of? It would be so tiring, having to bring him up to date on all that's happened. Too much has gone on. I might not know him. He might not know *me*. I might look old to him. Now I recall we were often short-tempered. Why, we couldn't sit and talk five minutes without one or the other of us losing patience! And he never showed much interest in the children. And I wouldn't know *what* to say about his music and all. Then look at that place he's living in. Who knows what goes on there? Probably they have this schedule of activities, and special shelves to put your pajamas on and rules and medication and refreshment hours and seating arrangements that I would just have no inkling of. We have nothing in common. Know what I dreamed last night? No, maybe *two* nights ago. I dreamed that I saw Caleb driving down the street. Looking fine, just as fine as always. But his car! Peculiar little foreign station wagon, with a pinchy face and windows too big for it like one of those durned chihuahua dogs you see around. 'Caleb!' I called to him, 'what are you *doing* driving that thing?' and all he did was turn and wave. You would think that he belonged in it."

"Grandfather, it will work out," Justine told him. "All week I've had this feeling of change coming. He's going to write any day now. We'll send him a plane ticket and settle him in Meg's old room."

"Then what?"

"What?"

"*Then* what, I said. Then what will we do? 'Oh, it will work out, it will work out.' You're always so blasted cheerful, Justine. But where is your common sense?"

"Why, Grandfather—"

"Sometimes it gets too much for me," he told Duncan. "*You* expect me to have the patience of a saint."

"Not at all," Duncan said.

"You think I shouldn't say how I feel. Underneath, you think that."

"Do what you like, I don't care."

"In my childhood I was trained to hold things in, you see. But I thought I was holding them until a certain *time*. I assumed that someday, somewhere, I would again be given the opportunity to spend all that saved-up feeling. When will that be?"

Nobody answered. Justine stayed braced against the windowframe, Duncan lowered a three of spades and stared at him. Finally their grandfather rose and went off to his room, leaning on each piece of furniture as he passed it.

At noon Justine had to eat lunch alone. Duncan had left for the shop and her grandfather, when she knocked on his door, said that he was busy. From the sudden squawk of metal on metal she guessed that he was rearranging his filing cabinet. "But maybe you could just come out and have some coffee," she called.

"Eh?"

"You could keep me company."

"How's that?"

She gave up and went back to the kitchen. She opened a

bottle of pickled onions and set it on the table, went to the drawer for a fork, and then suddenly straightened and frowned. This premonition of hers was pressing now against her temples and the small of her back. She returned to her grandfather's room and knocked again. "I was wondering," she called. "Would you like a cup of tea, instead?"

"Justine."

"I asked if—"

"Justine, I don't feel so well."

She opened the door instantly. Her grandfather sat on his bed holding a sheaf of papers. His face was white and slick and the papers were trembling. "What is it?" she asked.

He passed a hand across his eyes. "I was standing over there, you see," he said, "just rearranging my files a bit. I was just *standing* there when I felt so—"

He trailed off and looked at the shaking papers.

"Lie down," Justine told him. When he didn't seem to hear she touched his shoulder, pushing him gently backward until he gave in. She bent to scoop his feet up and set them on the bed. Now he lay half on his side, half on his back, breathing a little too quickly. "Are you sick to your stomach?" she asked him.

He nodded.

"*Oh,* then. Probably just . . . are you dizzy?"

He nodded.

"Well . . . but your chest doesn't hurt."

He nodded again.

"Does it? Say something."

"Yes."

"I see," Justine said.

She thought a moment. Then she went to the open window and leaned out. Next door, Ann-Campbell stood in a wading pool wearing bikini underpants, tilting her face into the rain and singing,

We are fine mermaids of high pedigree,
We eat baby sharks and we pee in the sea . . .

"Ann-Campbell!" Justine called. "Go get your mother. Hurry. I want her to call the ambulance in Plankhurst."

Ann-Campbell broke off her song.

"Hurry, Ann-Campbell! Tell her to call Duncan too. My grandfather's having a heart attack."

Ann-Campbell darted off, all flashing angles and freckles and patches of peeled skin. Justine turned back to her grandfather. "A what?" he said, bewildered. "Having a what?"

"Well, maybé not."

He pressed a hand to his chest.

"Is there anything I can get you?" she asked him. "Do you want a drink of water? Or—I don't know, maybe you aren't supposed to. Just lie still, Grandfather."

He did not look capable of doing anything else. He seemed to be flattened, sinking into his mattress. Nevertheless, his neck was tightly strung as if he were determined to keep his head just slightly off the pillow; it was not dignified to be seen in a horizontal position. Perhaps he even wished she would leave him in privacy, but she couldn't. She paced around and around the tiny room, willing into him all her strength and her burning, aimless energy. She kept being drawn to the window, which opened onto the side yard and would not have shown her the ambulance even if it could come so soon. "Oh, I wish Caro Mill had a hospital of its own!" she cried.

"I would never agree to a hospital," her grandfather said. He closed his eyes.

Then the screen door slammed and Justine could breathe again. "Duncan?" she called. "Is that you?"

But it was only Dorcas, clattering across the floor on her spike-heeled sandals. She stuck her bubbly head in the door and rounded her eyes at Grandfather Peck, who pretended to be asleep. "Justine honey, I called right away," she said. "They're sending an ambulance. Now I'm going to stand on the corner and wave it down."

"And Duncan? Did you call Duncan?" Justine asked.

Dorcas was already leaving, but her voice floated back. "He's coming too, he'll be here in a minute."

Justine went back to the bed and sat down on the edge of it. She laid a hand on her grandfather's cold, damp forehead. His eyes flew open and he gave her a look she had not seen him wear before: he seemed to be asking something from her. "What is it?" she said.

"Justine, I—there seems to be a considerable amount of pain starting up."

"Oh, where is Duncan?"

"I believe that I'm having a heart attack."

She picked up both his hands, which passed on their shakiness to her. His eyes withdrew and he thought something over in the gray of the ceiling. "Well," he said finally, "I had certainly hoped for more than *this* out of life."

"Don't talk!" she told him. She jumped up and ran to the window again. "Oh, where is—"

Then something made her turn, some sound much smaller than a click, and she saw that her grandfather had let his head rest at last and his hands were still and his face was calm and dead.

While she waited for Duncan she went into the living room, but it made her sad to abandon her grandfather and she returned to the bedroom. Even now, after all, there was that pinstriped collarless shirt and the silvery slant of hair, those perfect teeth glinting between the thin Peck lips, the waxy gray cord of his hearing aid and the deep-socketed eyes, closed but still leaking their blueness into the white of the lids. There was more to him than soul; there was this body, which would have looked different worn by any other man. She memorized the single stark line running alongside each corner of his mouth, drawn by pride and firmness of purpose. She willed his gnarled hands to press into hers, one more time, a bitter oval of horehound, but she did not reach out to touch him. He was too much present still, and would not have approved. Instead she slightly altered the position of his pillow, causing his head to lie straighter; and when the movement set up a rustling of papers she pulled from beneath his shoulder the sheaf of letters he had held, his carbon copies on onionskin. Their new creases and the blurred gray softness of the type made them seem to have come from someone already long dead and forgotten. "Dear Caleb," she read, from the top page. "I take pen in hand to express my hope that . . ." Her eyes slid down, line by line. When she reached the end of the letter she lowered it and stared at her grandfather's closed, set face.

"Justine!" Duncan called.

She spun around.

"Justine? Dorcas says—"

He stopped in the doorway, and then walked in and picked up his grandfather's wrist. "Well," he said after a moment, and when he set the wrist back down he was so gentle that there was no sound at all. Then he came to stand in front of Justine. "I'm sorry," he told her.

She held the letter out to him, and he took it from her to read it. First he sighed, then he smiled; then he stopped reading and looked over at her.

"Oh, Duncan," Justine said, "how could he write such a thing?"

But when he reached for her, she dodged his hands and went to the opposite side of the room.

16

Down the curved, gleaming staircase (which in her girlhood she used to descend holding onto her chest, to prevent exercising off what little she had), across the porch where her great-grandmother had often sat listing the three permissible excuses for typing a note of condolence (paralytic stroke, severed tendons, and amputation) Justine moved dimly beside her husband, wearing the suit she had worn to her mother's funeral and clutching one frayed white glove. (She had not been able to find the other.) She entered her uncle Mark's car; she rode through Roland Park, alighted in front of the church, and climbed the steps leaning backward slightly as if she feared what she would find inside. But inside there was only a density of carpet and shadowy pastel light from the windows, and up front an anonymous coffin. Then a cemetery as flat and well mown as a golf course, rows upon rows of glazed granite headstones including PECK Justin Montague, PECK Laura Baum, MAYHEW Caroline Peck and finally an admirably well cut rectangular ditch beside which the coffin lay like something forgotten, abandoned at the brink, while more words were said. Afterwards the family went home to receive their callers, who had been streaming in for the past two days and continued even now that it was over—elderly gentlemen, ladies in hats and gloves and veils and crocheted shawls in spite of the heat. "My," they said to Justine, "are *you* that little girl of Caroline's? But you used to be so—well, you certainly have—now, this is your husband, isn't it? *Him* I recognize."

Him they recognized. From her new distance Justine turned and looked at him, at his boyish pointy chin and his gawky way of standing, twining one leg about the other and rocking slightly with his hands in his back pockets so that his elbows jutted out to spear passers-by. The upturned corners of his mouth made him appear to be smiling mysteriously, teasingly, and perhaps he was. "Why, Duncan!" said Justine, dropping her glove. "You haven't changed a bit!"

An old lady mumbled, embarrassed at her mistake. Plainly these two were not married and perhaps not even related, in spite of the resemblance. Then Duncan stooped for the glove and handed it formally to Justine, and Justine turned and went off alone.

Not only had Duncan remained the same but so had her aunts and uncles, solidified in their flowery dresses and summer suits, and her cluster of cousins passing trays of tea cakes as they had when they were children. Only Justine stood swaybacked, chewing the empty finger of her glove, in a distant corner of the room.

"You were that little girl who used to be so sweet," a spindled-shanked lady told her. "And still are, I'm sure. You used to bring me little handfuls of flowers. You would never stay and talk because you were too shy."

Justine removed the glove from her mouth and gave her a sweet, shy smile, but the lady was not deceived and moved on immediately.

When the guests were gone Duncan escaped to bed, but the rest of the family had a light supper in the kitchen, working around Sulie, who was dusting the pipes under the sink. They laid out memories of Grandfather Peck, one by one. Aunt Lucy cried a little. Aunt Sarah became irritable and informed Justine that there was no call to wear a hat in her own family's house. "Oh, I'm sorry," said Justine, removing it. Then she didn't know what to do with it. She balanced it on her lap, leaving her sandwich untouched. She was feeling very tired. Really she would have liked to go off to sleep. But she stayed on, and by the time the aunts and uncles had risen to go she had her second wind and remained in the kitchen with the cousins, who discussed memories of their own. *They* remembered their grandfather's expression at that picnic for which Duncan had made him a Noxzema and olive sandwich, and first they sputtered into their iced tea and then laughed outright. Justine looked around at each blond, lit-up face, remembering times when she had been a member here. When she and the girls were eleven and twelve and thirteen, what on earth had they all found so funny that it made them laugh until they squeaked?

Esther was now the supervisor of a nursery school. Alice was a librarian, while Sally, the prettier twin, had returned from her month-long marriage a little less outgoing than she used to be and now taught piano in the privacy of Great-Grandma's house, on a modern blond upright that looked peculiar in the wine-colored parlor. Richard had a high-rise apartment downtown, and Claude lived over the garage behind Uncle Two's and spent all his money on steel engravings that nobody liked. New little lines were pricked in all their faces and their hair was dryer and duller, their hands growing freckles; but still they were the same. Only Justine was different, and when she tried to talk to them she had the sense of swimming hard against a strong current. Frustration made her clumsy, and she spilled a glass of ice cubes into Claude's lap but everyone said it didn't matter a bit.

Upstairs, in her old pink-and-white bedroom, she undressed in the dark so as not to wake Duncan and lay down beside him. It was going to be one of those nights when she couldn't sleep. She felt a familiar alertness in her legs, as if she were tightrope-walking on a rubber band. Voices swam in and out of her hearing: Duncan at twelve, explaining shotgun poker; Richard asking if he could come too; Aunt Bea naming all the wedding gifts she had received in the summer of 1930; and her grandfather calling, "Wait for me, Justine! There's no need to rush so." But she had rushed anyway. She had been so quick and brash, so loud, so impatient, which must explain that constant look of puzzlement he had worn in his later years; for where was the old slow, tender Justine?

"Wait for me," she heard Meg say, and she clearly saw Meg's five-year-old face, apple-round, rosy with heat, in the shadows of a spiral staircase in a lighthouse on the New Jersey coastline. They had stopped there on the way back from an unsuccessful job interview. (Justine had always wanted to live in a lighthouse.) Justine had climbed up and up, tumbling over her feet in her haste to see what was at the top, while Meg trudged panting behind. There were two hundred and seventy-eight steps, a sign outside had said. But when Justine reached the top, she found the catwalk enclosed in clear plastic, which clouded the view. The only room was a small dark alcove in which a uniformed park guard sat tipping his chair, reading a paperback Mickey Spillane. So she didn't want to live there after all. She descended more slowly, still breathless from her upward run, and on the next to the last flight she found Meg sobbing on a windowsill while Duncan tried to comfort her. "Oh, *honey!*"

Justine cried. "I forgot all about you!" But had that taught her anything? She had only speeded up with every year, gathering momentum. Racing toward some undefined future and letting the past roll up behind her, swooping Meg along under one arm but neglecting to listen to her or to ask if she wanted this trip at all. So Meg grew up alone, self-reared, and left home alone for a sad stunted life she had not really wanted; and Grandfather Peck became ever more lost and bewildered stumbling through a series of paper shanties. And Justine awoke one day to wonder how it had happened: what she had mislaid was Justine herself.

But Duncan, who had changed her whole life and taken all her past away from her, slept on as cool as ever, and on the crown of his head was the same little sprig of a cowlick he had had when he was four.

In the morning everyone suggested they stay a while, but Duncan said he was anxious to get going. He barely tolerated the lengthy discussion on traffic conditions, alternate routes, and whether or not to take a Thermos. He acted jittery and exasperated during the loading of the car trunk, while the uncles were padding more of Meg's wedding presents with the flowered sheets that Aunt Lucy had insisted they accept. ("I can't forget that bare mattress in your little home," she had said, shuddering. "*Nobody* just washes their linens and puts them right back on. You give them a rest in a cupboard first, which increases their life span by sixty-six percent.") Then there were the ritual cold drinks out on the porch, with Duncan finishing first and nervously rattling his ice cubes while waiting for Justine. Justine took extra long, to make up for him. She kept gazing around her at her family. "If only you could have got in touch with Meg!" Aunt Sarah told her.

"We'll call and break the news as soon as she gets back from the beach."

"She'll feel terrible, missing the funeral."

There was a quavering in the air, thin sad thoughts hovering among them. Uncle Two cleared his throat sharply. "Well!"

he said. "I never asked how the health food business was going."

"Antiques," Duncan said.

"Antiques, then."

"It's okay." He looked off across the lawn and tapped his glass. "Justine, we have to get started if we want to beat the heat."

"Oh. All right," she said. But she would rather have stayed. It gave her a tearing feeling to have to rise and kiss each soft, kind face in turn.

The family descended the steps with elaborate care, proving their reluctance to say goodbye—except for Duncan, of course, who danced down the walk ahead of them tossing and catching a spangle of car keys. "Duncan, boy," said Uncle Mark, "if your grandfather left any unpaid bills, now, medical expenses and so on—"

"I'll let you know."

"And I suppose I'd better write those detective fellows, tell them to close their case." He opened the car door for Justine. "Durned people have been spending money like water anyway," he told her. "I'm glad to be shed of them."

Justine threw Duncan a glance, but he wouldn't meet it. He had made her promise to keep Caleb's secret forever, unless he changed his mind and wrote. So all she could say to her uncle was, "I'll tell Eli myself, if you like."

"His latest expenditures are downright *bizarre*," her uncle said. "Why would he want to bribe a florist?"

"I'll take care of it."

She climbed into the car, and Duncan started the motor. "Finally," he muttered. Then they were off, zooming down the road scattering a cloud of maple-seed propellers while Justine leaned out the window to wave. Aunt Lucy shouted something. "What?" Justine called. Aunt Lucy shouted again.

"Duncan, stop," said Justine. "Your mother's trying to tell us something."

Duncan slammed on the brakes. The car whined into reverse. "What?" Justine called.

"I said, *Don't forget to rest your linens!*"

Duncan clapped a hand to his head, but Justine only nodded and called, "Thank you, Aunt Lucy," and blew her a kiss, and then more kisses for all the others, until Duncan jerked the car into forward again and bore her away.

17

DUNCAN had been playing solitaire for months now, but nobody guessed it had been that long because at first he had kept it a secret. At first he always did. Like an alcoholic hiding his bottle while everyone else drinks in public, he had stashed decks of cards in out-of-the-way places and he played in uncomfortable and poorly lit corners. At the smallest sound he was ready to scoop his game together and look up with an innocent face and a smile. (He did not like to be caught depending on things.) But gradually, drugged with patience and canfield and accordion, he forgot his surroundings and forgot to hide the cards, then failed to notice when someone came upon him, then finally wandered into the living room absent-mindedly and laid out his game in the center of the floor where everyone had to stumble over the great spread V of his legs. He played throughout meals, visits, family quarrels, and his grandfather's wake. He returned from Baltimore carrying a suitcase in which a single deck of cards had scattered itself through everything—interleaving with the pleats of Justine's funeral skirt and standing upright among the bristles of her hairbrush. But he didn't bother collecting them. He took instead a double deck that had been waiting all this time behind a begonia pot, and he settled himself on the floor and laid out a hand of spider, which was his favorite, most absorbing game, requiring hours and days of deliberation and strategy and intricate plotting. He kept losing and laying out new set-ups. Justine wandered through the rooms still wearing her hat.

At the Blue Bottle, when he went, he played on a scarred wooden desk behind the counter. He swept away stacks of bills, circulars, and correspondence, clearing the large space that spider required. When the bell tinkled over the door he didn't hear. If he had to answer a question or ring up a purchase he was annoyed, and showed it. Couldn't they see he was busy? By now he despised antiques. He despised the people who collected them—artificial-looking ladies who had, no doubt, thirty years ago thrown away the identical beechwood rolling pins that they were now rebuying at such exorbitant prices. And to make it worse, Silas Amsel had become a nuisance. Once the shop had proved a success, he *expected* things of Duncan. He was always waiting to hear good news. Duncan couldn't stand to have things expected of him. Gradually he sold less and less, bought fewer tools, behaved more rudely toward the customers. Silas began to complain. He mentioned trivial lapses: the few times Duncan had forgotten to lock up, and the mornings he was slightly late. There was a misplaced bronze he claimed had been stolen. (As if anyone would bother stealing an object so ugly, or so heavy.) There were little spats and insults every time Silas came to the shop. And he came more and more often, and stayed longer, and meddled more. He would start grumbling even before he was fully inside. He would stand in the doorway, shaking his head. Duncan pretended not to see him. (Sometimes he *really* didn't see him.) He remained seated, pondering over a vast network of playing cards, one finger hooked in a bottle of Old Crow. He felt the air turning gluey with the weight of other people's disapproval, suspicions, hopes, preconceived notions. Only Justine allowed him to go unclassified.

Justine trailed through the shop and out again with the crumpled streamers of her hat fluttering indecisively.

"I'll be finished in a minute," he called, and she said, "Hmm?" and returned, vaguely. She did not shut doors behind her; so for her the antique sleighbell was forever still, a fact he appreciated. She lacked finality. She was the other shoe which never dropped. He looked up from his cards and sent her a smile so deep and sudden that it would surely have wiped all the forlornness off her face if she had seen it, but she didn't. She was studying a chipped paperweight. She looked lost. Nowadays all she would talk about was her grandfather, his wishes she had not granted and gifts she had not thanked him for. She did not mention Caleb. Duncan waited for her to, but she didn't. Now it was October and if she were disappointed, leafing through the mail every morning with her listless, uncertain fingers, she didn't show it. She merely returned to the same old subject: she unwrapped the past endlessly, untying the ribbons, removing the tissue, untying more ribbons. "Do you remember when he took us on the train? I don't know where to. He took all us children, it was some kind of outing. Some patriotic occasion of some sort. I believe he was sorry before we'd even left the depot but it was too late to back out and he didn't want—"

Duncan couldn't remember. He suspected that he had been left at home. But he didn't say so to Justine. He watched her turning the crystal paperweight, and peering into it, and then raising her eyes to examine without interest her own reflection in an ormolu mirror. "Look at me," she said, "I'm one of those eccentric old ladies you see on the street, with a beat-up hat and a shopping bag."

But to him she was an awkward girl-cousin wearing very long shoes, and the comical up-dip at the ends of her hair was enough to make him leave his cards and come set a kiss on her cool cheek.

"You might find me going through a trash basket," she said, still to the mirror. She ignored his kiss.

"Maybe we should take a trip," Duncan told her. "Somewhere we've never been."

"Children would make bets on what I carry in my string bag."

But her bag was straw, not string, and he *knew* what she carried. Coffee beans, and salty things to nibble on, and the future wrapped in a square of rotting silk. Hadn't she always? She turned from the mirror, as if guessing his thoughts, and opened the bag to show him. He saw neither food nor cards but only sheaves of yellowed photographs belonging to her grandfather. Aunts and uncles standing around in the ocean, by waterfalls, beside new cars; cousins holding up fish and diplomas and Bible-study trophies; Grandfather Peck carefully posed, 8 x 10, behind an enormous empty desk, beneath a parade of *Maryland Digest*s and *ALR* volumes; somebody's bride; somebody's baby; Duncan laughing; Great-Grandma guarding her soul against theft by camera; more uncles; more aunts at someone's garden party, clustered together with their faces frozen in surprise. (They would run to a mirror just beforehand and then run back, level, bearing their chosen expressions as carefully as jellies on a platter.) Justine snapped her bag shut again. She gave him a long measuring stare that turned him cold. "That's what I carry," she said, "but don't tell the children."

Then she walked out. The bell quivered but kept silent. Duncan thought of going after her—asking at least where she was headed, or whether she would be there to fill the house for him when he got home. Or most important: what he had done to make her look at him that way. The way other people had looked at him all his life. All his life they had marked him as thoughtless and mischievous, wicked even; yet he had continued to feel that somehow, underneath, he was a good man. With Justine, he *was* a good man. Had she changed her mind about him? He didn't want to know. He didn't want to ask, and have to hear her answer. In the end all he did was return to his game of solitaire.

In an airport waiting room, at eleven thirty in the morning, Justine sat in a vinyl chair with her straw bag balanced on her knees. She was watching a group of students on standby. The regular passengers had already filed through, and now an official took a stack of blue tickets from his podium and began calling out each standby's name. They cheered and came forward, one by one. They accepted their tickets like Oscars, smiling at the official and then waving triumphantly to their friends, who clapped. Justine clapped too. "Mr. Flagg!" the official called.

"Mr. Brant!" Mr. Flagg beamed. Mr. Brant kissed his ticket. "Mrs. Peck!" And though Justine had no one with her, she was so carried away by all the gaiety that she beamed too, and turned back to bow to the empty row of chairs before she headed through the gate marked *New Orleans*.

18

AT NIGHT, in his narrow white cot, with old men wheezing and snoring all around him, he lay flat on his back and smiled at the ceiling and hummed "Broken Yo-Yo" till the matron came and shut him up. "Just *what* do you think you're doing?" He didn't answer, but the humming stopped. A fellow at the end of the row called out for a bedpan. The matron left, on dull rubbery heels. The fellow went on calling for a while but without much interest, and eventually he fell silent and merely squeaked from time to time. Caleb continued smiling at the ceiling. What no one guessed was that "Broken Yo-Yo" was still tumbling note on note inside his head.

From four a.m. till five he slept, dreaming first of a cobbled street down which he ran, more agile than he had been in years; then of fields of black-eyed Susans; then of grim machinery grinding and crumpling his hands. He awoke massaging his fingers. The ache was always worse in the early morning hours. He lay watching the darkness lift, the ceiling whiten, the sky outside the one gigantic window grow opaque. The tossing forms around him stilled, signifying wakefulness, although none of them spoke. This was the hour when old men gave in to insomnia, which had been tracking them down all night. They would rather not admit their defeat. They lay gritting their gums together, tensed as if on guard, betraying themselves only by a dry cough or the occasional sandpapery sound of one foot rubbing against the other. Caleb was stillest of all, but now "Stone Pony Blues" was spinning between his ears.

At six o'clock the matron came to snap on a switch. Long after she had gone, fluorescent tubes were fluttering and pausing and collecting themselves to fill the room with glare. The sky appeared to darken again. Morning came later now; it was fall. In December he would have been here seven years and he knew every shadow and slant of light, all the sounds of night and morning and mealtimes, which he tabulated with a sense of contentment.

Those who could manage for themselves began to struggle out of bed and into their bathrobes. Caleb's bathrobe was a rubberized raincoat, whose belt he tied clumsily without moving his fingers. He had asked Roy's wife Luray for a real bathrobe this coming Christmas and he was fairly certain she would bring him one. He slipped his feet into paper scuffs and went off across the hall to the toilets. Already a line had formed. While he waited he hummed. The old men went on discussing their constipation, indigestion, leg cramps, and backaches. They were used to his humming.

For breakfast there were grits, shredded wheat biscuits, and coffee. The men sat on long wooden benches, eating from tin plates with compartments. The women sat on the other side of the dining hall. They could have mingled with the men if they wished but they didn't, perhaps preferring not to be seen in their flowered dusters, with their veiny white legs poking out and their scalps showing through the thin strands of hair. Caleb, however, bowed and smiled in their direction before taking his place on a bench.

After breakfast they went to the social room. Some watched television, most just stared into space. Those who were crippled were wheeled in and parked like grocery carts. A gin rummy game started up in one corner but lapsed, with the players merely holding their cards and sitting vacantly as if frozen. A man with a cane told another man how his son had done him out of a house and five acres. Caleb himself did not have anyone to talk to at the moment. His only friend had died in August. Jesse Dole, a horn player who had been recorded several times in the days when you blew into a large black morning glory and it came out of another morning glory in someone's parlor. They used to sit in this very spot between the radiator and the Formica coffee table, arguing the fine points of their different styles of music. Then one night Jesse died and they collected him in his bedsheet and swung him onto a stretcher, leaving Caleb to spend his days all alone with the vinyl chair beside him empty. The others thought he was a little odd. They didn't have much to do with him. But Caleb was accustomed to making friends with anyone, and he knew that sooner or later he would find somebody or somebody would find him, maybe some new man coming in with new stories to tell. Till then, Caleb sat tranquilly in the social room with his knotty hands resting on his knees and his eyes fixed upon the green linoleum floor. For lack of anything else he had begun thinking back on his memories, which wasn't like him. He had never been a man to dwell on the past. Leaving places, he forgot them, always looking ahead to the next; but he had supposed that someday he would have the time to sit down and take a look at where he had been and this must be it.

New Orleans in the early part of the century: jitney dances at the Okeh Pavilion and the faint strains of quadrilles, schottisches, and polkas, and musical beggars one to a block playing anything that made a fine noise. White-Eye Ramford bowling along the sidewalk with his buckle-kneed gait, plucking notes like little golden fruits and singing and stumbling so you thought he was drunk, till you saw his flickering black paper eyelids and the blind, seeking roll of his head. He had lost his sight at twelve or maybe twenty, his stories differed; and by the time he reached middle age he should have learned how to navigate but he hadn't. He was hopeless. A plump, clumsy, hopeless man with a mild face, wincing when he stumbled and then moving on, resigned, plucking more notes from his cracked guitar. He wore a ragged white carnation in his buttonhole, and a derby on his head. It was the fall of 1914. Caleb was on his way home from the sugar refinery and he stopped and stared. Then he followed behind. Till the blind man called, "Who that?" and Caleb melted into a doorway. The next day, the same street, Caleb brought along his fiddle. When he heard the guitar he started playing. High haunting notes wailed and rose, commenting on the tune, climbing behind it. He had known immediately what this sort of music required. The guitar readjusted, making way for the fiddle, and the two of them continued down the street. Someone dropped a coin into a lard bucket hanging from the guitarist's belt. "Thank you," said Caleb, always well mannered. The guitarist spun around. "*White* man?" he cried. Caleb was so pleased at his surprise that he hardly noticed he was left standing foolishly alone. He was certain (because he wanted it so much) that the two of them would meet again, and that he would go on playing his fiddle behind the cracked guitar until he was accepted. Or tolerated, at least. Or recognized to be unavoidable.

In 1912 or 1913 you could run into Caleb Peck in just about any sporting house or dance hall in the city, always propped against the piano or the edge of the bandstand, puzzled and wistful, worn down from his menial daytime job, hoping to be allowed to fill in for some musician, though no one was that eager to have him. After all he did not play any brass, and most had no use for a fiddle. As for piano, he was a musical Rip Van Winkle. He had learned from a man who left New Orleans in the nineteenth century, when jazz was still spelled with two s's. So in 1912 and 1913 Caleb merely hung around the edges of places, with a thin strained face from so much listening, from absorbing so much, from trying to understand. But in 1914 he discovered the blues, which he understood instantly without the slightest effort, and for the next twenty years you could find him in the same small area of the Vieux Carré, linked to a blind man by a length of twine and playing a fiddle above a slippery song.

While he stared now at the streaks of detergent on the

green linoleum, he could hear White-Eye's loopy thin voice and the twang he made sliding a bottleneck down the strings of his guitar. He sang "Careless Love" and "Mr. Crump." He sang what Caleb made up—"Shut House" and "Whisky Alley" and "Cane Sugar Blues." Then "The Stringtail Blues," which some people credited to Caleb too but it was plainly White-Eye's, telling how a blind man felt leaning on other people. Caleb's fiddle shimmered and lilted, the guitar notes thrummed beneath it. Caleb had turned shabby, and not quite clean. It took money to be clean. He was surprised sometimes when he caught sight of himself in a window: that lanky man in a grimy frayed suit. Often he bore welts from the bedbugs in his rooming house, where he continued to live alone, unmarried, year after year. He had a great many friends but they were mostly transients, disappearing unexpectedly and resurfacing sometimes months later and sometimes never. Only White-Eye was permanent. Yet you could not say that they were friends, at least not in any visible way. They hardly talked at all. They never discussed their personal affairs. But some people noticed how their two stringed instruments spoke together continuously like old relations recollecting and nodding and agreeing, and how when Caleb and White-Eye parted for the night they stood silent a moment, as if wishing for something more to say, before turning and shambling off in their separate directions. At night White-Eye went to a wife he never named and an unkown number of descendants. Caleb went to work as watchman in a coffee warehouse; otherwise he would have starved. (He took no more than a deceptive jingle of coins from the lard bucket.) For twenty years he existed on four hours of sleep a night. He did it for the sake of a single body of music: those peculiarly prideful songs celebrating depression, a state he had once known very well. He could no longer imagine any other kind of life. If you asked where he came from, or who his family was, he would answer readily but without real thought. He never pictured the city he named or the people. His mind veered away from them, somehow. He preferred the present. He was happy where he was.

The other street musicians dwindled to a handful, and

Storyville was closed and the jazz players went off to Chicago or the excursion boats or the artificial bands hired by debutantes' mothers. But White-Eye and the Stringtail Man continued, supporting themselves more or less even through the Crash in 1929. They had become a fixture. Though not famous, they were familiar; and the poorest people were willing to give up a coin in order to keep the world from changing any more than it already had.

In 1934, on a Monday morning very early in the year, Caleb set out searching as he always did for the first faint sound of White-Eye's guitar. (Their meetings were never prearranged. You would never suppose, at the close of a day, that they were planning to see each other tomorrow.) But he had not gone two blocks when a brown woman wearing a shawl came up and touched the scroll of his fiddle, and told him White-Eye was dead. She was his widow. On the very morning of the wake she had taken the trouble to locate Caleb and break the news and invite him to the funeral—a fact that he appreciated, though all he did was nod. Then he went home and sat for a long time on his bed. He wouldn't answer when his landlady called him. But he did attend the funeral the following afternoon and even accompanied the family to the cemetery, a remote little field outside the city. He stood at the edge of the swampy grave between two tea-colored girls who stared at him and giggled. Throughout the ceremony he kept brushing his hair off his forehead with the back of his hand. He was, by then, nearly fifty years old. It was the first time he had stopped to realize that.

Now Caleb traveled the streets alone. Since he had never been a singer he merely fiddled. (No one guessed that White-Eye's voice still rang inside his head.) The solitary strains of his music had a curious trick of blending with street sounds—with the voices of black women passing by or the hum of trolley lines or a huckster's call. First you heard nothing; then you wondered; then the music separated itself and soared away and you stood stock still with your mouth open. But when people offered him a coin, moved by what they thought they might have heard, they found no tin cup to drop it in. They tucked it

into his pockets instead. At night Caleb would find all his pockets lumpy and heavy and sometimes even a crumpled paper bill
stuck into his belt. He could not always remember where it had
come from. He merely piled it on top of his bureau. But as the
months passed the dazed feeling left him, and one noon when
he was sitting in a café eating red beans and rice he looked up
at the waitress pouring coffee and realized that life was still
going on.

He stayed in New Orleans two more years, and might have
stayed forever if he had not fallen in with a pair of cornetists
who talked him into taking a trip to Peacham. Peacham was a
small, pretty town just to the north, still suffering like anyplace
else from hard times and unemployment. But the mayor had hit
upon a solution: he planned to make it a resort. (Nobody
thought to ask him who would have the money to go there.) He
published a three-color brochure claiming that Peacham had all
the advantages of New Orleans with none of the crowds or city
soot: fine food, lively bars, two full-sized nightclubs rocking
with jazz, and musicians on every street corner. Then he set to
work importing busloads of chefs, waitresses, and bartenders, as
well as players of every known musical instrument. (In all the
native population there were only three pianists—classical—and
the minister's daughter, who played the harp.) References were
unnecessary. So were auditions. In a creaky wooden hotel on
the wrong side of town musicians were stacked on top of one
another like crated chickens, venturing out each morning to
look picturesque on designated corners. But there was no one to
drop money in their cups. The only visitors to Peacham were
the same as always—aging citizens' grown sons and daughters,
come to spend a duty week in their parents' homes. One by one
the new employees lost hope and left, claiming they had never
thought it would work anyhow. Only Caleb stayed. He had
landed there more or less by accident, reluctant to leave New
Orleans, but as it turned out he happened to like Peacham just
fine. He figured he could enjoy himself there as well as anyplace else.

Now he worked days as janitor for an elementary school,

and in the evenings he played his fiddle on the corner he had been assigned. He ate his meals at Sam's Café, where a large red kind-faced waitress gave him double helpings of everything because she thought he was too skinny. This woman's name was Bess. She lived just behind the café with her two-year-old boy. It was her opinion that Caleb's hotel charged too much for his room, and bit by bit she persuaded him to move in with her instead. It wasn't hard. (He was so agreeable.) Before he knew it he found himself settled in her kerosene-lit shack, in her brown metal bed, beneath her thin puckered quilt, which smelled faintly of bacon grease. If she was, perhaps, not the one he would have chosen out of all the women in the world, at least she was cheerful and easy-going. Sometimes he even considered marrying her, in order to give her son Roy a last name, but they were already so comfortable together that he never got around to it.

By 1942 Bess had saved enough money to buy a café of her own in Box Hill, a town some twenty miles away. Caleb wasn't sure he wanted to go; he liked it where he was. But Bess had her mind made up and so he followed, amiably enough, lugging his fiddle and his pennywhistle and a flute and a change of clothes. This time he took a job as short-order cook in Bess's café. He found a park to do his fiddling in, a new crowd of children and courting couples to hear him in the evenings. Only nowadays more and more of the men wore uniforms, and the girls' clothes too were uniform-like—square-shouldered, economical of fabric—and he wondered sometimes, playing his same old music, whether people could really understand it any more. In his head, White-Eye Ramford still sang of despair and jealousy and cruel women and other rich, wasteful things. The couples who listened seemed too efficient for all that.

There was some trouble with Caleb's fingers—a little stiffness in the mornings. His bow hand could not get going at all if the weather was damp. And by now his hair was nearly white and his whiskers grew out silver whenever he went unshaven. On several occasions he was startled to find his father's face gazing at him from mirrors. Only his father, of course, would not have worn a dirty Panama hat, especially in the house, or a bibbed white apron stained with catsup or trousers fastened with a safety pin.

Bess's café was close to the freight tracks, between a seed store and a liquor store. There were some tough-looking men in those parts, but nothing that Bess couldn't handle. Or so she said. Till one evening in March of 1948 when two customers started arguing over a mule and one drew a gun and shot Bess through the heart by accident. Caleb was fiddling at the time. When he returned, he thought he had walked into a movie. These milling policemen, detectives, and ambulance attendants, this woman on the floor with a purple stain down her front, surely had nothing to do with the real world. In fact he had trouble believing she was dead, and never properly mourned her except in pieces—her good-natured smile, her warm hands, her stolid fat legs in white stockings, all of which occurred to him in unexpected flashes for many years afterward.

Of course now Caleb was free to go anywhere, but he had the responsibility of Bess's boy Roy, who was only thirteen or fourteen at the time. And besides, he liked Box Hill. He enjoyed his work as short-order cook, frying up masses of hash browns and lace-edged eggs in record time, and since the café now belonged to Roy what else could they do but stay on?

Year by year the café became more weathered, the sign saying "Bess's Place" flaked and buckled. Roy grew into a stooped, skinny young man with an anxious look to him. They took turns minding the business. Evenings Caleb could still go out and fiddle "Stack O'Lee" and "Jogo Blues." But his hands were knotted tighter and tighter now, and there were days when he had to leave the fiddle in its case. Then even the penny-whistle was beyond him; there was no way to tamp the airholes properly when his fingers stayed stiff and clenched. So he set about relearning the harmonica, which he had last played as a very young man. The warm metal in his hands and the smell of spit-dampened wood reminded him of home. He paused and looked out across the counter. Where were they all now? Dead?

He wiped the harmonica on his trousers and went back to his song.

Roy said they needed a waitress. This was in 1963 or so. They had the same small group of customers they always had, railroad workers mostly and old men from the rooming houses nearby. Caleb couldn't see that they had any sudden need for a waitress. But Roy went and got one anyhow, and once he had then Caleb understood. This was a pretty little blond girl, name of Luray Spivey. Before six weeks had passed she was Mrs. Roy Pickett and there was a jukebox in the corner playing rock-and-roll, not to mention all the changes in the apartment upstairs, where he and Roy had lived alone for so many years. She covered the walls of Roy's bedroom with pictures of movie stars torn out of magazines, mainly Troy Donahue and Bobby Darin. She brightened the living room with curtains, cushions, plastic carnations and seashells. She followed Caleb around picking up his soiled clothes with little housewifely noises that amused him. "Hoo-*ee!*" she would say, holding an undershirt by the tips of her fingers. But she wasn't the kind to run a man down. She knew when to stop housekeeping, too, and sit with Roy and Caleb and a six-pack of beer in front of the second-hand television she had talked Roy into buying for her. In the café she cheered everybody up, with her little pert jokes and the way she would toss her head and the flippy short white skirt that spun around her when she moved off to the grill with an order. All the customers enjoyed having her around.

Then the twins were born, in the fall of 1964. Well, of course life is hard with twins; you can't expect a woman to be as easy-going as ever. Plus there was the financial angle. Certainly people require more money once they start having children. Luray was just *frazzled* with money worries, you could see it. She wanted so many things for her babies. She was always after Roy to take a second job, maybe driving a cab. "How we going to even eat?" she would ask him, standing there scared and fierce in her seersucker duster. (Once she had ordered her clothes off the back pages of movie magazines, all these sequined low-necked dresses and push-up bras.) So Roy took a job with the Prompt Taxi Company from six to twelve every night and Caleb ran the café alone. Not that he minded. There wasn't much business anyway and he had just about given up his evening fiddling now that the park was gone and his hands were so stubborn and contrary. (Besides, sometimes lately when he played he had the feeling that people thought of him as a—character, really. Someone colorful. He had never meant to be that, he only wanted to make a little music.) So he would putter around the café fixing special dishes and talking to the customers, most of whom were friends, and after the plates were rinsed he might pull out his harmonica and settle himself on a stool at the counter and give them a tune or two. "Pig Meat Papa" he played, and "Broke and Hungry Blues" and "Nobody Knows You When You're Down and Out." The old men listened and nodded heavily and, "Now that is so," they said when he was done—a much finer audience than any courting couple. Till Luray came down from upstairs with her hair in curlers and her duster clutched around her. "What all is going on here? Caleb, you have woken both babies when I had just slaved my butt off putting them down. What is everybody sitting here for? Shoo now! Shoo!" As if they were taking up seats that someone else wanted, when it was clear no more customers were coming; and anyway, they were having fun. There was no point to hurrying off when you were having fun.

Then Luray got back in her transparent white uniform and said she saw that she would have to start waiting tables again; men customers would leave her tips that they wouldn't leave Caleb. "Well, naturally," Caleb said. "They're personal friends, they wouldn't want to embarrass me." "It don't embarrass *me*," said Luray, tossing her head. She would open the stair door, listening for the babies. Caleb worried about her leaving them alone but she said they would be fine. She was saving up to buy them an electric bottle sterilizer. Caleb didn't think a sterilizer was all that necessary but he could see that, to Luray, there was always the chance that some single magic object might be the one to guarantee that her babies would live happily forever; and maybe the sterilizer was that object. So he was not surprised when after the sterilizer was bought she started saving up for a double stroller, and after that a pair of collapsible canvas carbeds although they didn't own a car. And he didn't hold it against her when she started criticizing his work, although certainly there were times when she got him down. "What do I see you doing here? How come you to be using pure cream? What you got in mind for all them eggs?"

The fact was that Caleb was pretty much a custom chef by now. He had known his few patrons a very long time, and since he was not a man who easily showed his liking for people he chose to cook them their favorite foods instead—the comfort foods that every man turns to when he is feeling low. For Jim Bolt it was hot milk and whisky; for old Emmett Gray, fried garden-fresh tomatoes with just a sprinkle of sugar; and Mr. Ebsen the freight agent liked home-baked bread. The narrow aluminum shelves behind the counter, meant to hold only dry cereals, potato chips, and Hostess cream-filled cupcakes, were a jumble of condiments in Mason jars and Twinings tea from England, Scotch oatmeal tins, Old Bay crab spice, and Major Grey chutney. The café appeared, in fact, to be a kitchen in the home of a very large family. It had looked that way for years, but this was the first time Luray noticed. "What kind of a business *is* this?" she asked. "Do you want to send us all to the poorhouse? Here am I with these two growing babies and lying awake at night just wondering will we manage and there you are cooking up French omelettes and rice pudding, things not even on the menu and I don't even want to know how much you're charging for them . . ."

Luray took over his job, whipping an apron around her little tiny waist. She acted as if she thought Caleb had grown weak in the head. She sent him up to tend the babies. Caleb had never been good with children. The sight of them made him wretched; he was so sorry for humans in the state of childhood that he couldn't stand to be near them. When one of the babies cried his insides knotted up and he felt bleak and hopeless. So he tended them as if from a distance, holding himself aloof, and as soon as it was naptime he hurried downstairs to socialize with the customers. He sat turning on a stool, talking and laughing, a little silly with relief, plunking down money from his own pocket to pay for a cup of coffee so Luray wouldn't send him off. He would fish out his harmonica with stiff, thickened fingers and give the men "Shut House" or "Whisky Alley." Till Luray stopped in front of him with her hands on her hips and her head cocked. "Hear that? Hear what I hear? Hear them babies crying?" Then Caleb put away his harmonica and went back upstairs on slow, heavy feet.

In the fall of 1966, Luray found out she was pregnant again. She was not very happy about it. Money seemed scarcer than ever, the twins were getting to be a handful, and already the apartment was cramped. Caleb slept on the couch now, and the babies were in his old room. When he got up in the night he stumbled over blocks and wheeled toys and cold soggy diapers all the way to the bathroom, where likely as not Luray had shut herself in ahead of him. "Go away!" she would shout. "Go back to bed, you old skunk!"

One morning she went out all dressed up, leaving Roy to tend the café and Caleb to mind the babies. When she came back she told Caleb she had found him a place to move into. "Oh! Well," Caleb said.

He had thought a couple of times himself about moving, but not so concretely. And then there was the money. "This café just can't *support* two apartments, Luray," he said.

"It's not an apartment."

"Oh, a room? Well, fine, that'll be—"

"This is a place the county helps out with."

Then she flashed Roy a sudden look, and Roy hung his head in that bashful way he had and his face got red. But still Caleb didn't understand.

He understood only when they deposited him in the gray brick building with the concrete yard, with attendants squeaking in their rubber-soled shoes down the corridors. "But—Luray?" he said. Roy wandered off and looked at a bulletin board. The back of his neck was splotchy. Only Luray was willing to face Caleb. "Now you know they'll take good care of you," she told him. "Well, after all. It's not like you were any real relation or anything." She was balancing a baby on each arm, standing sway-backed against their weight—a thin, enormously pregnant woman with washed-out hair and cloudy skin. What could he say to her? There was no way he could even be angry, she was so dismal and pathetic. "Well," he said. "Never mind."

Though later, when the nurse told him he couldn't keep his harmonica here, he did feel one flash of rage that shook him from head to foot, and he wondered if he would be able to stand it after all.

Now he had to hum to make his music. Unfortunately he had a rather flat, toneless voice, and a tendency to hit the notes smack dab instead of slithering around on them as White-Eye Ramford used to. Still, it was better than nothing. And as time went by he made a few acquaintances, discovered a dogwood tree in the concrete yard, and began to enjoy the steady rhythm of bed, meals, social hour, nap. He had always liked to think that he could get along anywhere. Also he did have visitors. Some of these old men had no one. He had Roy and Luray coming by once a month or more with their four little tow-headed boys—Roy as young as ever, somehow, Luray dried and hollowed out. But she was very kind now. When the clock struck four and the matron shooed them from the visitors' parlor Luray would reach forward to touch Caleb's hand, or sometimes peck his cheek. "Now we'll be coming back, you hear?" she said. She always said, "Don't see us out, you sit right where you're at and stay comfortable." But he came anyway, out the steel door and across the concrete yard, to where the gate would clang shut in his face. He would wave through the grille, and Luray would tell her boys to wave back. And maybe halfway up the street, heading toward the bus stop, she would turn to smile and her chin would lift just as it used to, as if she were letting him know that underneath, she was still that sweet perky Luray Spivey and she felt just as bewildered as he did by the way things had worked out.

In his patched vinyl chair in the social room he hummed

old snatches of song, joyous mournful chants for St. Louis and East St. Louis, Memphis and Beale Street, Pratt City and Parchman Farm. But it was a fact that he never hummed the "Stringtail Blues" at all, though White-Eye Ramford sang it continually in the echoing streets of his mind:

> Once I walk proud, once I prance up and down,
> Now I holds to a string and they leads me around . . .

The morning the letter came he had been sitting like this in the social room. He remembered that when the attendant tossed the envelope into his lap he had expected a good half hour, perhaps, of studying pictures of floral arrangements. (Altona Florists were his only correspondents.) Bouquets named "Remembrance," "Friendly Thoughts," and "Elegance," which you could send clear across the continent without ever setting foot in a shop. But when he ripped open the envelope what he found instead was a typewritten letter of some sort. He checked the outside address. Mr. Caleb Peck, yes. All the postmark said was "U.S. Postal Service Md." Whatever had happened to postmarks?

Maryland.

He shook the letter open. "Dear Caleb," he read. He skipped to the signature. "Your brother, Daniel J. Peck, Sr." A stone seemed to drop on his chest. But he was glad, of course, that his brother was still alive. He remembered Daniel with affection, and there were certain flashing images that could touch him even now, if he allowed them to—Daniel's yellow head bent over a schoolbook; the brave, scared look he sometimes gave his father; the embarrassed pride on his face when Maggie Rose came down the aisle in her wedding dress. Yet Caleb shrank in his vinyl chair, and glanced about the room as if checking for intruders. Then he read the rest of the letter.

It seemed that Daniel was inviting him to pay a visit. He was asking him to come to a place called Caro Mill. Caleb had never heard of Caro Mill. He found it difficult to imagine his brother anywhere but Baltimore. And when he pictured accepting the invitation he pictured Baltimore still, even with this letter before him—a streetcar rattling toward the sandy, shaded roads of Roland Park, a house with cloth dolls and hobbyhorses scattered across the lawn. Daniel descending the steps to welcome him, smiling with those clear, level eyes that tended to squint a little as if dazzled by their own blueness. Caleb smiled back, nodding gently. Then he started and returned to the letter.

He learned that his parents were dead, which of course he had assumed for many years. (Yet still he was stunned.) And the baby, Caroline, whom he had forgotten all about. But where was Maggie Rose, had she ever returned? Daniel neglected to say. Caleb raised his eyes and saw her small, dear, laughing face beneath a ribboned hat. But she would be an old lady now. She had grandchildren. Her sons were lawyers, her husband a judge. It was 1973.

Yet the language in this letter came from an earlier age, and the stiff, self-conscious voice of the young Daniel Peck rang clearly in Caleb's ears. All the old burdens were dropped upon him: reproaches, forgiveness, reproaches again. An endless advancing and retreating and readvancing against which no counterattack was possible. "You must surely have guessed . . ." "But we will let bygones be bygones." But, "You were always contrary, even as a child, and caused our mother much . . ." Then Caleb reached the final paragraph, skimming rather than reading (so that none of it should really soak in). "To tell the truth, Caleb," his brother said, and held out his hand and stood waiting. As in the old days, when after weeks of distance he would climb all the steps to Caleb's room simply to invite him for a walk; or some other member of the family would, for they were all alike, all advancing and retreating too, and Caleb had spent far too many years belatedly summoning up his defenses only to have them washed away by some loving touch on his shoulder, some words in that secret language which, perhaps, all families had, but this was the only one Caleb had ever been able to understand. He was angry and then regretful; he rebelled against them all, their niggling, narrow ways, but then some homeliness in the turned-down corners of their mouths would pull at him; then he reached out, and was drowned in their airless warmth and burdened with reminders of all the ways he had disappointed them.

So he asked an attendant for writing paper, chafing and excited for the three hours it took her to bring it, but once it came the stony feeling weighed him down again and he found it impossible to form the proper words. Besides, his hands ached. His fingers would not grasp the pencil firmly. He folded the blank page and stuffed it in his pocket, where Daniel's letter was. Days passed. Weeks passed. For a while his family infiltrated every thought he had, but eventually they faded, returning only occasionally when he put on the coat that served as bathrobe and a rustle in the pocket cast a brief shadow over his morning.

For lunch there was chicken à la king on toast. After lunch came naptime. Wheelchair patients were laid out like strips of bacon on their beds, but most of the others—rebelling in little ways—wandered in the aisles or stood at the window or sat upright in bed in nests of thin, patched blankets. Caleb himself lay down but did not sleep. He was mentally playing the fiddle. Anyone watching closely could have seen the fingers of his left hand twitch from time to time or his lips just faintly move, uttering no sound. He was playing the "Georgia Crawl" and every note was coming just the way he wanted.

After naps they were supposed to stay in the social room till supper. Caleb, however, wandered out into the yard, and since he always went to the same place nobody tried to stop him. He sat on a bench beneath the little dogwood tree growing from a circle in the concrete. Its upper branches were dry and bare. Lower down, a few red leaves shook in a cold wind. Caleb turned up the collar of his raincoat and huddled into himself. Before long it would be winter and they wouldn't let him come here any more. By next spring the tree might have died. He was not much of a nature lover, but the thought of sitting in utter blankness, unsheltered by even this cluster of dry twigs, made him feel exposed. He glanced around, suddenly wary. All he saw was a woman in a flat hat picking her way across the concrete.

Now visiting hours were well under way and outsiders would be everywhere, their unexpected colors turning the Home drabber than its residents had realized. Perhaps this one was lost. She moved toward him as if fording a river full of slippery stones. Her straw-colored hair, hanging gracelessly to her shoulders, made him think of the very young girls of his youth, but when she came closer he saw that she was middle-aged. She looked directly at him with a peculiarly searching expression. She held out her hand. "Caleb Peck?" she asked.

"Why, yes."

He took the hand, although she was a stranger. He would go along with anything; he always had.

"I am Justine Peck."

"Oh?"

He looked at her more closely, past the helter-skelter hat and the aging clothes to her sandy face, sharp nose, blue eyes. He would know her anywhere, he thought. (But he hadn't.) A sad kind of shock went through him. He continued holding onto her bony hand.

"I am Daniel Peck's granddaughter."

"Oh yes. His granddaughter."

"Whom he didn't feel connected to," she said.

"Yes, I seem to remember . . ."

He let go of her hand to reach toward his pocket, the one that rustled.

"I have bad news," he heard.

His—niece? Great-niece. Sat beside him on the bench, light as a bird. He knew what she was going to say. "Daniel is dead," he told her. How could he have awakened this morning so contented, not guessing what had happened?

"He had a heart attack," she said.

He felt cheated and bitter. A deep pain began flowering

inside him. His hand continued automatically to his pocket, found the letter and pulled it out. "But I hadn't yet answered," he said. "*Eventually* I was going to."

"Well, of course."

Which was not what he had been afraid she would say.

He opened out the letter, blinking through a mist, and smoothed it on the bench between them. Daniel's typing was conscientious and stalwart and pathetic. This wasn't fair; it was like having him die twice. "It isn't fair," he told Justine.

"It's not. It's not at all."

She sat watching a pigeon while Caleb reread the letter. The margins wobbled and shimmered. Now everything came clear to him. He saw kinder, gentler meanings in Daniel's words; the other meanings were no longer there. He understood the effort involved, the hesitations, searches for the proper phrase, false beginnings tossed in wastebaskets.

"I should have written," he told Justine.

She went on watching the pigeon.

"It always seemed to work out with them that I didn't do what I should have. Did do what I shouldn't have."

Her gaze shifted to him, transparent blue eyes whose familiarity continued to confuse him.

"How did he find me?" he asked her. Before, he had barely wondered.

"A detective did it," said Justine, "but we'd been hunting for years."

"I thought they would just forget about me."

She started to say something, and stopped. Then she said, "I used to read the cards for you."

"The—?"

"Fortune-telling cards."

"Oh yes," he said.

"I asked, would Grandfather ever locate you? The cards said yes. However there was always room for error, because Grandfather didn't cut the cards himself. He wouldn't have approved. I never thought of asking would he actually *see* you."

Caleb folded the letter and put it back in his pocket. He was not sure what they were talking about.

"Uncle Caleb," said Justine, "will you come home with me?"

"Oh well I—that's very kind of you."

"You know we'd love to have you. Duncan and I. Duncan is another grandchild, I married him. You'd like him."

"Married him, did you," said Caleb, unsurprised. He sniffed, and then blotted both eyes on the sleeve of his raincoat. "*Well* now," he said. "Whose little girl are you?"

"Caroline's."

"Caroline's? I thought she was the baby, I thought she died."

"Only after she grew up," said Justine. "Duncan is Uncle Two's."

"Two's? Oh, Justin Two."

He contemplated the pigeon, whose feathers reminded him of a changeable taffeta dress that Maggie Rose had once worn. Justin Two was the most demanding of all her children, he seemed to remember; the loudest and the shrillest, the most likely to interrupt a conversation. "Tell me," he said, "is he still the same?"

"Yes," said Justine, as if she knew what he meant.

He laughed.

Justine said, "Listen. You can't stay here! I went to that office in there to ask for you and they said, 'He's out by the tree, but you've only got twenty minutes. Then visiting hours will be over,' they said. I said, 'But I've been traveling since yesterday! I am his great-niece Justine Peck and I've come all the way from Caro Mill, Maryland. I *have* to spend more than twenty *minutes!*' 'Sorry, Miss,' they said, 'rules are rules.' You can't stay in a place like this!"

"It's true," said Caleb, "they do like rules."

"Will you come? We could leave this evening."

"Oh, well you see they'd never let me do it," Caleb said. "No. You weren't the person who signed me in here, they'd never just let me . . . or if they did, there'd be so much paperwork. It would take some arranging. Perhaps several weeks before they would allow me to—"

"*Allow* you?" Justine said. "What, are you in prison?"

Caleb blinked and looked around him.

"Never mind, just come," said Justine. "You already have your coat on. There's nothing you want from inside, is there? We can go over the wall in back, where it's lowest. They won't even see us leave."

"You mean—*escape?*" said Caleb.

"Won't you just come away with me?"

People had been saying that to him all his life. He had still not learned to turn them down.

19

EVERY NOW AND THEN Justine would catch a glimpse of Caleb— as he passed a doorway, or skimmed in and out of view in front windows while walking the porch—and she would mistake him for Grandfather Peck and her heart would leap. She had never managed to believe that some people truly will not be seen again. Look, there was that jutting head, the glint of silver hair, the long nose pinched white at the tip! But then she would notice his eyes. The shock of brown eyes in her grandfather's face. Or she would call and he would answer instantly, wincing if she spoke to him too loudly, which she was always doing, out of habit. Or his clothes gave him away—her grandfather's, yes, but on Caleb they looked scruffy and poorly cut. She sank back, wherever she was, and Duncan looked at her curiously but said nothing.

Duncan was playing Battue now, moving yellow plastic

disks among a triangle of pegs. For him it appeared to be another game of solitaire, not a puzzle; he had solved the puzzle
years ago. The disks clicked steadily like the beads of an abacus
or a rosary, their rhythm dictated by the churning of private
thoughts. What were Duncan's private thoughts? He wouldn't
say. He kept the bourbon bottle beside him, always nearly
empty, it seemed, its cheap wavery glass perfectly clear down to
the inch or so of yellow in the bottom. Occasionally he smoked
a doll-sized metal pipe containing foul-smelling leaves and seeds
and stems. Then he would grow dreamy and whimsical, although the leaves were so old now (having been stored nearly
forever in an oregano bottle in the kitchen) that Justine suspected they had lost all their potency. He suggested unusual
projects—for instance, planting the little round seeds on some
village green. "Once a year we could have a new ritual, the
Burning of the Green. All the villagers could sit around breathing the smoke and getting happy on a specified day." Justine
looked sideways at Caleb to see if he were shocked. He didn't
seem to be. He was not above accepting a slug or two of bourbon himself (those rigid, grandfatherly lips poised at the rim of
a bottle!) and perhaps would have tried the pipe as well, if
smoke did not make him cough. Nevertheless, Justine continually felt the need to tell him, "You mustn't think Duncan's always like this."

"He's not?" said Caleb.

"No, really he's just—it will pass."

Then she wondered why she bothered explaining, for Caleb
only looked disappointed. He had some sort of expectation of
them that Justine couldn't understand. On the trip, for instance,
his moods had kept shifting until she hadn't known what to
think of him. First he was elated, almost all the way to New
Orleans. It was her favorite view of Caleb so far: his face alight,
looking much like Duncan's, just as she had always known it
would. He was tense with excitement and his hands moved rapidly as he spoke. (Yet Justine had been taught that a Peck does
not gesticulate.) He told her his whole life, everything that had
happened to him since leaving Baltimore—*buckets* of life, tor-

rents of names and places, snatches of song broken off and sentences left unfinished. She had the feeling that he had been saving it up for sixty years, until he could locate a family member. But then when he had finished and she questioned him on the fine points—"Whatever happened to the friend you went to New Orleans with?" "What sort of man was White-Eye Ramford?" "Did you ever think of coming home?"—he became morose and short of words. "I don't know. I don't know," he muttered. Thinking to cheer him up, she said, "When we get to New Orleans we'll buy you some shoes. You can't get on a plane in paper slippers." But if anything, that only deepened his gloom. He looked out the window, his thumb and middle finger steadily stroking the corners of his mouth in a way that made her uncomfortable. But of course: he was mourning his brother. She should have thought. No doubt he had only been making an effort for her sake, earlier, and it had worn him out. So she let him sit in silence, and when they reached New Orleans she didn't mention his shoes again. He did, though. He became suddenly brisk. "Say now!" he said. "Weren't we going to change out of these paper scuffs? We can't go back to the family looking unkempt."

"Well, if you want to," Justine said carefully.

"Unfortunately I am out of funds at the moment but—"

"Oh, I'll take care of that."

In that respect, at least, he showed his background. He did not make any sort of unseemly fuss over financial matters.

They had to stay overnight in a very poor hotel, for which Justine was apologetic, but Caleb didn't seem to mind. He retired early after eating a large quantity of salad; fresh fruits and vegetables were some sort of obsession with him. When he waved good night in the corridor he looked just fine, but the next morning on the plane he was up and down, up and down. Talkative, then moody. Mostly moody. He asked her unlikely questions. "How many ships do you have?"

"Ships? What?"

"Do you own or lease them now?"

"*Ships!* Oh," said Justine. "We're not importers any more."

"You're not?"

"The family sold it all."

"Why! When did they do that?"

"Right after you left," said Justine.

Then he sank into himself again, and hardly spoke until they had landed and caught the two connecting buses to Caro Mill. When she led him up Watchmaker Street she felt she was *laboring* with him, he looked so dismal. But at her front walk he stopped short. "Here?" he said. "Is this where you live?"

For the first time she noticed how unsteady the house appeared, how the screens bagged and the steps buckled. She wondered what that rusty motor was doing on the porch. "Yes, it is," she said.

She felt him staring at her. She focused on the tips of her shoes.

"This is your *house?*"

"Yes."

"And what is this yellow stuff in the yard?"

"Why, cornstalks."

"I mean—*eating* corn?"

"Well, Duncan wanted to grow some, you see, and he said the back didn't get enough sun. He said we could grind up the garbage for fertilizer and spread it on the—"

She felt herself growing desperate, trying to convince him that really their life was perfectly logical. But she shouldn't have bothered. For when finally she raised her eyes (just a glance at his face to see how she was doing) she found the corners of his mouth perked upwards like Duncan's, his expression bright and merry again. He was back to being cheerful. And he remained cheerful ever after, growing more light-hearted day by day. He fit right in. She couldn't understand him.

Sometimes Duncan let the Battue disks fall silent a moment while he read the newspapers. Help Wanted, of course. "Look, Justine, someone in Virginia wants a zoo keeper."

"You've never been a zoo keeper, Duncan."

"Right."

"I mean you don't know the first thing about it."

"Right."

"You have a job. Duncan, you *have* a job, and you should have been there three hours ago."

Then he would rise, steady on his feet but a little slow, his face luminous and calm and angelic as only bourbon could make it, and he would very, very carefully button himself into his jacket. "If you really want to know," he said (but speaking in Caleb's general direction), "I don't believe in people sacrificing themselves for the sake of other people."

"But neither do I, Duncan," she said.

He didn't have any answer for that.

So he would give a little salute to Caleb, and turn up his collar as if facing winter winds before he set off for the antique shop. Where there would be no customers anyway, now that opening hours were so uncertain. Where antiques lay in a jumble, dusty and neglected, and half the lightbulbs were out and the window was patched with adhesive tape. Look at this very newspaper column, spindled now on a Battue peg: WANTED *antique shop mgr. must be reliable apply Silas Amsel Box 46 Caro Mill.* But Justine was firm and cool and deliberate. Like her grandfather, she stiffened her pointy chin and set her head at a commanding angle. "It's time we learned to stay in one place," she told Duncan every night when he came home.

"Whatever you say, Justine."

There was something underneath, some considerateness in his voice that made her turn on him. "Don't you think so?" she asked him.

"Whatever you say."

"Not what *I* say. Don't you think so yourself? We've been moving around forever."

"That's very true," he said.

"Why do you keep agreeing with me? Do you feel you have to humor me in some way?"

"No, no."

But he did. She knew he did. It was because of her fetching Caleb. Wasn't it? Duncan seemed to think she had gone crazy, or senile—or who knows?—running off like that to get Caleb. (She had assumed he would understand. She had called the antique shop from Box Hill: "I'll be away overnight, I think, Duncan, I don't think I can find a plane out of New Orleans till tomorrow." "New Orleans? Is that where you are? I thought you had left me," he said. "I went home for lunch and you weren't there." She said, "*I* wouldn't leave you"—forgetting altogether that up till that afternoon she had been seriously considering it. She was so excited about meeting Caleb. And it was so good to hear Duncan's voice on the telephone. It had completely slipped her mind how angry she was with him.) When she came back from New Orleans, Duncan gave Caleb a long look and then shook his hand. But the look he gave Justine was longer—a gentle, sad, *pitying* look, which she was going to remember till the end of her days. What could he be pitying her for? He didn't even know that she had done all this illegally, so to speak. Yet during supper that night he had been so soft-voiced and solicitous, as if she were sick. When really there was nothing more natural than having your great-uncle come to stay with you.

Not that Duncan minded having Caleb. He got along with him very well. Better than Justine herself did, in fact. They had long discussions on jazz and blues and Creole food. Duncan would ask about Lafleur Boudrault, and Whisky Alley, and musical funerals and old-time cathouses, about which (Justine was surprised to hear) Caleb seemed to know everything. Caleb played Duncan's harmonica, drawing forth from it such beautiful, disreputable sounds that Justine stood motionless and open-mouthed. *This* was her great-*uncle?*

But he didn't like to be called Great-Uncle, or even Uncle. Perhaps he had been without relatives too long for such titles to sit easy on him. "Just 'Caleb' will do," he said. And there had been so many difficulties in the way of his paying the rest of the family a visit. He was too tired from the trip; he was just getting used to Caro Mill; his arthritis was acting up. Thanksgiving would be better, he said. They could arrive unannounced and take the family by surprise. "Thanksgiving!" said Justine. It was barely November. Was it fair to keep everyone in the dark for so long? She was all for going this Sunday, perhaps, for Sunday dinner at Uncle Two's. But Caleb refused, offering a dozen shiftless excuses. ("I'm scared I wouldn't know anybody's name," he said.) Justine sighed. She had to admit there were times when Caleb disappointed her.

No, more than that. Tell the truth. There were times when she almost disliked him.

He had gone so far afield, it seemed. He had journeyed such a distance from his family. Now it appeared that the return trip was not that easy, maybe even impossible. He had a hundred habits and qualities that the Pecks would not have tolerated, skills they neither possessed nor wanted, bits of knowledge they would not know existed. Often he said things that horrified her. "Maybe," he said, "we could just *never* let the family know, have you thought of that?"

"Why, Caleb!"

"I mean—Justine, I'm happy here with you and Duncan. Why go anywhere else? It would be like meeting strangers."

"That's ridiculous! It's ridiculous."

"I don't have anything in common with them, Justine."

"How can you say such a thing?"

"Do you think a one of them would recognize me?"

No. Not a one of them. Deep down, she knew it, and he and she would stare at each other in absolute agreement even while she continued to protest.

Sometimes she shut herself in her room and pulled out Caleb's old photo, which she had taken from her grandfather's pocket after he died. She studied it as if it could be read, not merely looked at. The gleam of Caleb's Panama, the set of his shoulders, the perfect crispness of his tie. Nowadays he did not even wear a tie. His old jauntiness had become, somehow, *boldness;* his speech had a sharp, unpleasant tang. There was something spineless and lackadaisical in the way he walked. And she could not help noticing that still, wearing Daniel's clothes and Duncan's aftershave, he had the musty cabbage smell of a public institution.

Well, after all, he had been away so long.

Yes, but he had gone by degrees, traveling only where led, merely proving himself adaptable, endlessly adaptable.

As Justine herself had.

Then a trembling would rise from the soles of her feet, turn her stomach queasy, pass through the hollow of her chest to beat in her throat like a second heart. She stuffed the snapshot beneath a stack of magazines and hurried out to join the others.

In the afternoons, with Duncan asleep on the floor beside his disks, Justine brought Caleb up to date on the family. Even though he seemed not to care, she sat at the table earnestly filling him with history. She was amazed at how little time it took to tell—all those events unfolding over months and years, summed up now in minutes. "Richard did get married but it was annulled, the girl's father had it annulled because she was under age, and since then he's lived downtown in a—"

"Now, which was Richard?"

"Why, Uncle Mark's son," she said.

When she told how her mother died she spoke without inflection, as if hoping he wouldn't catch it, but of course he did. He made no comment. When she talked about fortune telling he only looked interested. What did he really think? She imagined that he was about to define her; that at last, after clearing his throat, he would sum her up, announce where she had been heading all her life. She tensed expectantly whenever she caught him looking around the house, or glancing at her clothes, or staring at some toothless woman in socks and Wedgies who came to have her cards read. Surely he was judging their life, whose skimpiness she had just begun to realize. Any moment now he would give his verdict. But he never did. She kept trying to explain herself, even so. "You see we have always just— Duncan has kept wanting us to move around," she told him.

"Is that right," said Caleb.

"He likes to travel."

"But he hasn't traveled *far*."

"What?" She searched her memory for other family news,

meanwhile absently cracking a coffee bean with her teeth. "Now Aunt Lucy, she always says—"

"Lucy? I didn't remember Daniel had a Lucy."

"Lucy is Two's wife, Caleb. I told you that."

"Ah yes." He nodded. "It must be hard trying to keep all this straight."

"I don't have to *try*. They're family. Now, what was I telling you about Aunt Lucy?"

"You said—who did you say she was?"

So that she grew exasperated. "Don't you have any *memory?*" she asked him. "Don't you feel any connection at all?"

"Memory, yes. Connection, no."

She believed him. At night, tossing in her bed, she told Duncan, "We might as well have picked a stranger off the streets."

"What makes you think so?"

"He's not connected, he says. He *admits* it. That scroungy old man—if he had written a letter when he should have I bet Grandfather would be alive today. He doesn't have a trace of the family left in him and he tells me so as if he's proud of it. He doesn't have a trace."

"He does, though."

"What are you talking about?"

"Oh, use your head, Justine. Who do you know who acts more like a Peck? Consider that he has remained alone his whole life long, never let in anybody who wasn't a blood relative. Never got close to White-Eye, never married that waitress, never was a father to Roy. Can't you read between the lines? Look at what Luray said: it's not as if he were a real relation. You say the Pecks haven't left a trace?"

"You don't know the first thing about it," Justine said. "Of course he didn't get close to White-Eye. He was careful and respectful. He had *tact*." And she would flounce over on her side away from him, preparing for another night of insomnia.

Then the next afternoon, facing Caleb, who wore his brother's pinstriped shirt, she was full of new hope and energy. "I think you're going to like my cousin Claude," she told him.

"Oh yes?"

"He collects engravings. He's the only one besides you who's interested in the arts."

But, "I believe I'll make coffee out of some of those beans, Justine," he said. Then she would notice how metallic his eyes were, and how there was something raw and uncared-for about his skin, which was stretched too tightly across the bridge of his nose.

He had taken over the kitchen by now, as if he guessed how she felt about cooking. (The first supper she served him was hot dogs scorched in a skillet.) He prepared every meal so seriously and so tenderly that it tasted like a gift. "Eat it all," he told them at suppertime. "If you don't finish it, how can I make more? I want to get started on something new." He would hum as he worked, clattering pots, cursing the scarcity of equipment. "But that's all right, I can make do with anything. Put me in the pokiest diner and I will cook you up a seven-course meal. Why did I ever retire? I let Luray talk me into it. Here I've been thinking I had no means of support, but I do! I'm going to get a job and contribute to the household, I have it all worked out."

But even Duncan looked doubtful when he heard that. "Well, look," he said. "I wouldn't want to discourage you, but *age* might stand in your way, don't you think?"

"Never mind my age," said Caleb. "Oh, for the quality places, yes. But there is always some little café by the tracks or the water where they don't give a hang, and that's where I'll ask."

"Well, at least why don't you wait a little. If we move or anything, you don't want to go through a whole new job application."

"But we're not moving," said Justine.

"Oh, no hurry," Caleb said. "I play it by ear. I wait to see what falls out and who is going in what direction. I always have." He smiled. "It's funny," he said, "I'd forgotten the taste of garlic. Can you beat that? It's peculiar how you associate some foods with people. Or times you used to have, or places . . . Bess always liked garlic-buttered popcorn. The two of us must have eaten bushels of it. Now you could bring me some and I don't know, it would taste so *unfamiliar* somehow. I suppose everybody's like that. Best friend I ever had liked Blue Peter sardines on saltine crackers, but maybe if I were to track him down today I'd find he doesn't even remember them any more."

Duncan listened so hard he forgot to eat. Justine slid a salt shaker back and forth. Why did Caleb have to talk about food all the time? No one else in the family did. All they asked was that their meals be nourishing, and not too unusual in taste. They tended to like white things, foods baked in cream sauce. They would have been horrified by the peppery shrimp casserole that Caleb had served tonight. "Listen!" Justine said suddenly. "How can we be sure you're Caleb Peck?"

Both men stared.

"How do we know you're not some impostor?"

"Justine," said Duncan.

She ignored him. She was watching Caleb. "But who else would bother?" Caleb asked her.

"You're not like them in any way."

Caleb shrugged. (A foreign gesture.) "For that matter," he said, "how do I know *you're* a Peck?"

"We're not even sure that Eli's honest," Justine said. "Maybe he just picked up some stranger and coached him. Maybe the two of you framed this whole story together. After all, there must be money involved. Caleb's share of the will must have been drawing interest for sixty years."

"Caleb didn't *have* any share of the will," Duncan told her. "Justine, I wish you would—"

But Caleb only nodded, sober and proud somehow, as if he were receiving compliments.

In the night there was a pounding on the door, and shouting and the beam of headlights across the bedroom ceiling. Justine, wide awake as usual, crawled over Duncan and threw a bathrobe around her shoulders. "Just a minute," she called. Duncan stirred and then sat up. From Caleb's room came the rustle of bedclothes. Justine ran through the hallway, breathless and shivering. Someone had died. Something was wrong with Meg. She had never realized how many possibilities there were for disaster, or how calm and joyous her life had been until this moment.

But it was only Tucker Dawcett, whose wife had her fortune told weekly to see if he were faithful and never believed it when the answer was yes. Tucker was just a sweet skinny man with buck teeth. He jogged in a sweatsuit every morning and worked as a, let's see—

Policeman.

Her teeth started chattering again.

Tucker coughed, and then showed her his identification in a plastic envelope. (Why on earth?) For all she knew it was his YMCA card. "Oh. Tucker," she said.

"Could I speak with you a moment, Justine?"

From the hall doorway, Duncan said, "Do you know what time it is?"

"Police business," said Tucker.

Duncan came up behind Justine without a sound.

"Now I have to ask you folks this question," Tucker said. "Are you all related to a Mr. Caleb Peck?"

"You get us up at one a.m. to ask us that?" Duncan said.

"Now I know, I know how trying this must be," Tucker told him. Through the screen his face looked grainy; out of tiredness or embarrassment he kept his eyes down. "Fact is I was sacked out at home myself. Doug Tilghman called from the station asking me to run this little errand. I wanted to wait till morning but he said we would look pretty silly if Louisiana called back in a couple hours and we hadn't done a thing."

"Louisiana?" said Duncan.

"See they got this lady down there claiming a Mr. Caleb Peck has been kidnapped."

Duncan looked at Justine.

"Seems like he was in a home of some sort. This lady, Mrs. Luray Pickett, went to visit him last Sunday and found he'd disappeared. Home hadn't noticed. Seems somebody at the office remembered a Justine Peck come from Caro Mill to visit him, and he was never seen again."

"So?" said Duncan.

"Well, I believe that would be kidnapping, or stealing at least. See, the man was institutionalized. He didn't have no right to be leaving of his own free will. Or would it be aiding and abetting? Well, look. *I* don't care about it. Let an old fellow go where he wants, I always say. But Doug Tilghman said I had to just ask, because some lady somewhere is fit to be tied. Mrs. Luray Pickett. I said, 'Look, Doug, can't this wait till morning? I mean what will the Pecks think of us for this?' I said, and he said, 'Tell them I'm just as sorry as I can be but these policemen in Louisiana have this lady name of Mrs. Luray Pickett who is kicking up a storm, calling them and visiting, asking why they're not doing more. She says she put the man in a Home herself and saw to his every need, never let a month go by without . . . and here he has been removed and not so much as a by-your-leave. She says if anybody thought she wasn't taking proper care they could just come to her in person, there was no need to steal the man, and she will thank the police to get him replaced or she'll know the reason why. And also—' Well, and it's true there's not many Justine Pecks. I mean the *name* is odd. And especially from Caro Mill. Of course you do have that old man staying with you now . . ."

"Tucker," said Duncan, "don't you know that all our family is from Baltimore?"

"That's true, they are."

"And have you ever heard either one of us mention a relative in Louisiana?"

"Well, not directly," said Tucker.

"So," said Duncan.

"Well, I knew there was nothing to it," Tucker told him. "Sorry to have woken you folks up." And for the first time he raised his eyes to meet theirs. "I'll tell the wife I saw you," he said. "Night, now."

"Night," said Duncan.

He turned on the porch light and shut the door. Justine

waited, but he didn't say a word. Maybe he was angry. She should have told him from the beginning. Only at the beginning he had been so odd, and after that it was never the proper moment. Now what? Would he make her send Caleb back again? Then it occurred to her that all this time Caleb must have been listening, bolt upright in bed, terrified they would give him away. "That poor old man!" she said, and slid past Duncan to open Caleb's door.

He was gone.

His bed was unmade, and his pajamas lay at the foot. His rubberized raincoat no longer hung from the closet door. Duncan's harmonica was missing from the bureau. And the window was wide open, empty and black, the paper shade lisping in the wind. "Duncan!" Justine called. "Hurry, we have to find him!"

She already had one leg over the windowsill before he stopped her. He took hold of her arm and said, "Let him get a little head start again first, Justine."

20

DUNCAN sat on the floor with a twelve-hundred-piece jigsaw puzzle, "Sunset in the Rockies." He had found all the straight edges and constructed the frame; but now he was simply moving pieces around, picking one up and tapping it against his teeth while he stared into space, setting it down, picking up another, turning several over to expose their gray cardboard backs. He considered turning the whole puzzle over and doing it all in gray.

He considered moving Justine back to Baltimore.

"Is that what you want?" he asked her when she came through wearing her hat.

She looked startled. "What?"

"I asked if you wanted to move to Baltimore."

"Baltimore?"

"Baltimore, *Maryland*, Justine."

She stared at him.

"We'll live in Great-Grandma's house. *Your* house," he told her. "I'll find some kind of busywork with Peck and Sons. You know Dad's always said I could."

"You mean, stay forever?"

"No reason not to."

"Never again move?"

"Not unless you liked."

She thought a while, biting her lip.

"But you might not be happy there," she told him finally.

Which was her way of saying yes. He felt the answer settling on him by degrees, like a large heavy blanket drifting down. He was done for. Yet at the same time he had a sense of relief, almost. What else would you call this sudden giddiness? The other shoe had fallen. He nearly laughed.

Underneath, he must have known all through their marriage that this was where they were headed.

Justine fit books into cardboard boxes. Then machine parts. Duncan let his jigsaw puzzle dissolve and scatter while he took up a new kind of solitaire. Lately he had become talkative and fanciful, almost silly; he was emerging from his silence. But the bourbon and the solitaire remained, because he had lost his job by now and if he didn't look occupied in some way Justine would ask him to help her. That was one thing he could not do. He would feel like a child repacking his pathetic provisions— blanket, alarm clock, teddy bear—after half a night of running away. Or like some sea animal, declawed and deformed by battle, scuttling back to his shell with whatever scraps of himself he could salvage. He remained on the floor, pretending to be deep in his game. Meanwhile his mind had sprung awake again and was playing games of its own. He composed a list of all his favorite words, aloud. "Luncheon. Reality. Silver salver. Ippolitov-Ivanov." Justine sat back and wiped her hair off her forehead.

"Sometimes I wonder why we travel with so much *stuff*," she told him.

One of the puzzling things about Justine was that she always seemed to be shaking lately, and it hadn't stopped when he decided to move her to Baltimore. The streamers of her hat trembled gently, and whenever she drank coffee (which was the only thing she would touch) she spilled it. She reminded him of a fragile tree full of birds. But what could he do that he hadn't already done? He tried diverting her thoughts. "Justine," he said. "You know? In twenty years I firmly believe we will be traveling instantaneously by transposition of matter. You get in this glass box, see, if you want to go to, say, Omaha, and someone in Omaha gets in *another* glass box—"

"I travel fast enough as it is," said Justine, "and way too far."

"You haven't traveled so far," Duncan said. "Then bulletin boards would spring up everywhere: 'Gentleman from Detroit wishes to go to Pittsburgh; does anyone in Pittsburgh wish to go to Detroit?' There would be new hope for the unemployed. Bums could make money being transposed to Cincinnati when someone in Cincinnati wanted to get out. You go to a park bench. 'Look, fellow,' you say—"

"But it would always be me who ended up accepting," said Justine. She rose, and for no apparent reason examined her face in the speckled metal switchplate on the wall. "I can turn into anyone. That's my curse."

Her curse was her ability to see all sides of every question, but that wasn't something Duncan wanted changed and so he didn't mention it. Finally Justine turned away and bent to pack another box.

She was fitting some things of Meg's in now. Each object she handled very gently and lovingly, taking much longer than necessary. She rolled a stray belt meant for a dress Meg might not even be wearing any more, and she tucked it in beside a mildewed high school almanac. She took the lid off a tin of pebbles that Meg had collected on a Virginia beach in the summer of 1965, and she held each pebble up to the light and smoothed it with her fingers before replacing it.

At mealtimes, if he remembered, Duncan made sandwiches and poured two glasses of milk. But Justine seemed to have given up on eating. She didn't even go to the diner; she didn't go anywhere. When he urged her she would take one bite of her sandwich and then set it down. "Come on. Eat," he told her. Though he could see that it wasn't possible. He could tell from the way she chewed; her mouth was too dry, or too small, or something. Never mind, she would eat when she got to Baltimore. Aunts would take her in hand. He thought of the aunts for the first time with gratitude, imagining how they would relieve him of Justine's dull white face and her limpness. Then he caught himself and looked away from her eyes, which were fixed on him too steadily.

He could always leave her, of course. He could settle her in Baltimore and then go off again on his own. But he knew that he wouldn't. If he didn't have Justine he wouldn't even know how to see things, what to look at; nothing would exist for him if he couldn't tell Justine about it. The first flat-brimmed hat in a department store window would break him. He would be unable to last the night without her rustling, burning wakefulness guarding his sleep. So he put away all thoughts of leaving, and he wrote the letter to Peck & Sons asking for work. But when the answer came, he didn't want to open it. He stuffed it in his pocket, angry already at the phrases he knew it would contain. Finally Justine found it, and opened it for him. "Well? What does it say?" he asked.

"Oh . . . they'll get you something."

"But what does it *say*? Are they glad I'm finally listening to reason? Do they say they always knew we would end up coming home?"

"No, they don't mention it," Justine said.

He snatched the letter away from her—his Uncle Mark's signature beneath a secretary's crisp black typing. Probably, his uncle said, there would be some employment for him although it was hard to say what, on such short notice. And no, the firm had no need of a fix-it man, what kind of a question was that? And of course it was true that Great-Grandma's house was legally Justine's, although really the family had been the ones to see to its maintenance all these years and Esther and the twins were so accustomed to living there . . .

All in all, Duncan thought the letter sounded disconcerted. As if secretly the family had *enjoyed* having the two of them ricocheting around somewhere. He had not expected that. Nor had he expected to feel so offended, once he found it out.

But the wheels were set in motion, anyway, and now they gave notice to the landlord and made arrangements with the movers. ("I'm not hiring a U-Haul," Duncan said. "I don't have Grandfather." But really he was just indulging in his new policy of floating to places. He pictured the Mayflower men hauling out the living room rug by its corners while he remained seated on it, steadily playing forty thieves.) They notified the electric company and the water department, breaking off ties, unplugging all their cords to Caro Mill and reeling them in. They wrote a letter to Meg giving their new address. ("Although," Justine said, "there is no way we can ever let Caleb know . . .") Nowadays when Duncan passed the Blue Bottle he saw an unfamiliar young man established behind the counter, picking his fingernails and gazing idly out the reglazed window with its display of gilded china teacups.

At Thanksgiving they stayed home, since they would be going to Baltimore anyway in another few days. They ate dinner on the living room floor: a combination pizza that Duncan had bought from a takeout place. "Really you shouldn't have," Justine said. She meant because of the cost; their money was nearly gone. They were living on BankAmericard. "But it wasn't expensive," said Duncan, "and I thought you *liked* combination pizzas. I told them to put extra anchovies on. Why aren't you eating?"

She took a bite. She didn't seem to be tasting it.

"Isn't it good?"

"If Caleb were here we'd be taking him to the family today," she said.

"If he were here, yes."

"And they wouldn't have liked him."

He leaned forward and tapped her plate. "Eat," he told her.

The morning after Thanksgiving Dorcas came to have her cards read. She was considering marrying a moviehouse owner named Willis Ralph McGee. "How do you like the name Dorcas McGee?" she asked Duncan.

Behind her, Ann-Campbell said, "It stinks."

"Who asked you?"

Now that it was cold Dorcas wore a car coat heaped with blond fake fur, but her feet were still in spike-heeled sandals. Blood-red toenails glinted beneath nylon, overrun the next moment by the last of Duncan's forty cards. She moved her toes a fraction of an inch away. "You said I would meet somebody soon, Justine, and so I did," she said. "Now I want to know what kind of husband he would make."

"Lousy," said Ann-Campbell.

"Will you hush that?"

"My daddy, Joe Pete Britt, is not ever going to stand for this," said Ann-Campbell. "Here, Justine, I brung in your mail. There's a bill from Howard pharmacy, a Korvette ad—"

"Just *give* it to her, Ann-Campbell."

Justine set down a roll of binder's twine and took the letters. "Well, here is something from Mayflower," she said. "I just hope they're not putting off the moving date."

"I hope they *do!*" said Dorcas. "Just years and years."

"Here's something from—who do we know in Wyoming?"

Justine tore the envelope open. Duncan laid down a nine of clubs, which Dorcas immediately stepped on. "Now I don't want to hurry you or anything," Dorcas said, "but me and Ann-Campbell are going out to Woolworth's for a hot fudge sundae and we were just stopping by *briefly* to get my fortune told."

"You prick a balloon," Ann-Campbell told Duncan, "and see what number is wrote on it. That's the price of your hot fudge sundae. Could be a nickel. Could be a penny."

"Is that so," said Duncan. "Would you move your foot a little, Dorcas?"

"Could be forty-nine cents," said Dorcas. "It always has been."

"Well!" said Justine.

They all looked up at her, but it seemed she was reading a letter. She would read for a moment and then look up, then start reading it all over again. "What is it?" Duncan asked her.

"Well, it's a—"

He waited, but she went back to the letter.

"Reason I'm in a hurry is that tonight we have this special date," Dorcas said. "I have a feeling he's going to propose. Now I don't want to answer without knowing what the cards say, do I?"

"Certainly not," said Duncan.

"Justine? If you don't want to do it all you have to do is tell me."

"Look at this, Duncan," Justine said.

He took the letter, a cream-colored sheet crumpled and gray around the edges.

November 20, 1973

Dear Justine,

I want to apologize for taking so long to write, but circumstances prevented me up until now.

It was very kind of you to invite me to stay with you. The frankfurters you cooked were delicious, and I shall remember my visit with a great deal of pleasure for a long time to come.

Love,
Caleb Peck

Duncan laughed—a single, sharp sound. He handed the letter back.

"It's a thank you note," said Justine.

"That's right."

"A bread-and-butter note."

"That's what they call them."

"I just want to ask you one thing," Dorcas said. "And I want an honest answer. Hear? Now Justine, you have been putting me off all morning and it's not the first time. Other people have noticed too. Nowadays you just *drift* the cards down like your heart's not in it. Anything anybody asks you definite, should they do it or should they not, you don't want to reply. You just shuck it off, like. Well, what I want to know is, do you not really care to read the future any more? Are you trying to phase it out? Because all you got to do is say the word, Justine. Not to keep on going with your mind on something else the way you have been lately."

"What?" said Justine.

Dorcas looked over at Duncan.

"Oh, your *fortune*," Justine said.

"That's right."

"Well, let me find my . . ."

She fetched the straw carry-all, unwrapped the cards from their square of silk.

"My great-uncle Caleb wrote a thank you note," she told Dorcas.

"Now isn't that nice."

"Thanking us for his visit."

"You can always tell good upbringing, is what *I* say," said Dorcas, but her eyes were on the cards, which Justine was gently shuffling over and over again. "Aren't you going to want a table to lay those out on? Or you're just going to go on shuffling evermore."

"*Oh* yes," said Justine. And they went off to the kitchen, leaving Ann-Campbell behind. Ann-Campbell squatted next to Duncan. "Will Justine let Mama say yes to Mr. McGee?" she asked him.

"I don't know."

"Will she tell her to marry daddy again, Joe Pete Britt?"

"Tune in next week and find out," said Duncan.

"Huh?"

"Nothing." He tipped back his head for a swallow of bourbon.

"Who is this great-uncle Caleb man?"

"That old guy we had around for a while," Duncan said. "Who is either very dumb or very very smart, it's hard to tell which."

"If she marries Mr. McGee I might just come along to Baltimore with you all," said Ann-Campbell, edging closer. "I think that might be what's going to happen. Justine will tell her to go ahead."

"Justine won't tell her *anything*, don't worry," Duncan said. "She hardly opens her mouth any more."

But just then he heard her laugh, a clear light sound that startled him, and he looked up from his cards and met Ann-Campbell's speckled green eyes fixed thoughtfully upon him.

After lunch Justine worked in the yard a while, pulling up yellowed cornstalks. She returned with her face pink. Starchy-smelling air trailed behind her. "Feel," she said, and laid her stinging hands on Duncan's cheek. He drew back. "Doesn't it make you want to get outdoors?" she asked him.

"Not exactly."

"Aren't you tired of sitting here?"

She spun away from him and went off toward the kitchen. A minute later he heard her running water in the sink, clattering dishes, but she must have grown tired of that, because very soon she was back in the living room. She stood at the window a moment, and then took a second pack of cards from the sill and settled down on the floor with them, not far from where Duncan sat playing forty thieves. He could hear her murmuring to herself as she laid them out. ". . . the queen of change, beside the king. The wish card, the journey card . . . why so many journeys? Look how far the loved ones are! This is the card for journeys beyond other journeys, I've never had that one before. The card for, what was it?"

She fell silent. Duncan looked up to find her chewing a thumbnail and staring into space.

Shortly afterward she left, sliding into an old lumberjacket that used to be Duncan's. She didn't say where she was going. Duncan heard the Ford start up, a burry sound in the frozen air. First he was pleased, but then he wondered if she would keep her mind sufficiently on her driving. He noticed how empty the house felt. There was a strong wind blowing up from the north, whistling through all the cracks. The sky was white, and the room seemed lit by a bleak cold glare that hurt Duncan's eyes. Everywhere he looked there was something dismal to see: packing cases, dry dead plants on the windowsill, a sprawl of tomato-stained pizza wrappings from the day before. He rose and went to the bedroom. He was only planning to rest; he lay on the unmade bed with one arm across his eyes and thought about the turn his life was taking. But then he fell asleep and dreamed about antiques—jewelry that came in clusters and jungles of carved chair legs. Even in his sleep it was impossible to find any space that was pure and simple and clean of line.

When he woke it was dark. Justine was still not back. He got up and felt his way to the kitchen, where he turned on the light and made himself a peanut butter sandwich. The cat watched him from the stovetop. "So this is what it's like to be grown up!" Duncan told her. She blinked and looked away, offended. He took his sandwich into the living room and settled down again beside his unfinished game. It was clear he was not going to win. Still, he shifted cards doggedly and pondered a choice of moves, munching meanwhile on his sandwich. There was nothing else to do.

Then the Ford drove up, and a minute later Justine's quick footsteps crossed the porch. When she opened the door he kept his eyes on the cards; she would never guess how glad he was to see her. "We're out of peanut butter," was all he said.

"Oh, are we?"

He moved a deuce.

"I think I'm losing," he said.

"Never mind." She came to kneel in front of him, a flash of red plaid, and scooped his cards up. Some were left on the rug and some flew out of her hands. "Well, wait a minute," Duncan said.

"Shall I tell your fortune?"

She had never told his fortune in all his life. He stared at her. But Justine only smiled—bright-eyed, out of breath, her hat a little crooked—and began laying cards in a disorderly row that she didn't even glance at. "You are about to alter your entire way of life," she said, smacking down some jack or king. She was watching Duncan's face.

"Yes, well," said Duncan, reaching for his bottle.

"You are going to become a fix-it man for a carnival."

He set the bottle down.

"Your wife will be their fortune teller. You'll have a purple trailer in Parvis, Maryland, and live happily ever after. How do you like me so far?"

"You're crazy," he said, but he was smiling, and he didn't even protest when Justine spilled all the rest of his bourbon while leaning over the cards to give him a kiss.

21

ON MOVING DAY they got a late start, which was fine because there wasn't that much to move. They were taking only their books and clothes, plus Duncan's spare parts and inventions, packed in a little orange U-Haul van. They were leaving everything else behind. Furniture would be supplied in the trailer. Built in. Justine liked the idea of having everything built in. She enjoyed telling people they were traveling light, and would have thrown away even some things they needed if Duncan hadn't stopped her.

It was a clear, frosty morning in December, with a sky as blue as opals and a pale sun. Some of the neighbors had come to see them off. Dorcas Britt and her husband Joe Pete, and Ann-Campbell with Justine's cat struggling in her arms. Red Emma, Black Emma, old Mrs. Hewitt and her poodle. Maureen Worth from across the street, still in her bathrobe, and Mrs. Tucker Dawcett, who stood a little apart and looked sad and wistful, as if she expected even now to be handed news of her husband's unfaithfulness like a parting gift. Justine went from one to another, setting her face against theirs and giving them little pats and making promises. "Of course we'll be back. You know we will." Duncan was rearranging boxes in the U-Haul, and from time to time he cursed and stopped to rub his hands together. Red Emma threw him a dark, sullen look that he failed to see. "You tell him to bring you on weekends, hear?" she said. "Don't you let him just keep carting you off every which way." She kissed Justine's cheek. Mrs. Hewitt hugged her. "Oh, it just seems like people are always *going*, leaving, moving on . . ."

"But it's not far," said Justine. "And you can all come visit."

"In a trailer? In a cow pasture?" Dorcas said.

"You're going to love it," Justine told her. "*We're* going to love it. Oh, I can feel good luck in my bones, I know when we're doing something right. Besides, next month it will be nineteen seventy-four. Add all the digits and you get twenty-one, add those and you come up with three. Our lucky number. Did you ever see a clearer sign?"

Someone pushed a pot of ivy into her arms. Then a rubber plant. She was carrying so much they had to open the car door for her and help her settle things in. "Just put them anywhere," she said. "The front seat is fine." The front seat was already full of food for the trip—Fritos, Cheez Doodles, salt herring and

coffee beans and a box of Luden's. This year she was the only
person in the car. Though next year, who could tell? She took
the cat from Ann-Campbell, and then once the cat was in she
had to get in herself and slam the door, fast, and roll down the
window no more than a slit. "Ask Duncan if he's ready to
start," she said. The clanging of the tailgate was her answer.
"Well, I guess I'll be saying goodbye then." For the first time
her voice was sad, and appeared to drift out too slowly on the
mist of her breath. "We don't want to hit the rush hour." She
stuck a cold silver key in the ignition and kneaded her fingers.
Hanging from the gearshift knob was a National Safety Council
ad torn out of a magazine: cupids with black straps slanted
across their chests, I LOVE YOU, WEAR YOUR SEAT BELT. She
turned and looked at the cat, who glared at her from behind a
begonia plant. "Well, then," she said, and roared the engine up
and left, waving her hand out the slit in the window.

Behind her the U-Haul's engine started too, and the crowd
of neighbors moved over to Duncan. "Have a good trip!"
"Drive safely, hear?" The truck rolled off. "Oh, aren't you
ashamed," Red Emma called suddenly, "taking her away from
us like this?" But Duncan only waved. He must not have heard.
Or else he was too intent on catching up with Justine, who by
now was only a puff of smoke in the distance.

Anne Tyler
Celestial Navigation £2.95

When his mother dies, Jeremy Pauling is left in sole charge of her
dilapidated boarding-house. But Jeremy is a bachelor recluse, almost
unable to deal with the outside world – and his only passion is making
sculptures out of odds and ends. Then Mary Tell, his new lodger, arrives to
offer a challenge he cannot really cope with ...

'Miss Tyler has created two characters at once entirely original and entirely
convincing. Hers is a quiet but immensely strong novel, to admire and
treasure' SUNDAY TELEGRAPH

'Her fiction is filled with displaced persons who persist stubbornly in their
own destinies. They are "oddballs", visionaries, lonely souls, but she has a
way of transcribing their peculiarities with such loving wholeness that
when we examine them we keep finding more and more pieces of
ourselves' NEW YORK TIMES

'A must for readers who appreciate the quality novel'
PUBLISHERS WEEKLY

'She writes with virtuosity and perfect confidence, insight and compassion
... a rich, revelatory novel' THE TIMES

Simone Signoret
Adieu Volodia £3.95

Spanning the years 1919 to 1945, this vivid and moving saga of love and
war – by France's most celebrated actress – tells the story of two Jewish
families who have fled persecution to settle in Paris shortly after the
Russian Revolution. They work in the garment industry, speak Yiddish, and
have nightmares, but never speak of the past. They are determined that
their children shall grow up free, and French.

The life the children become caught up in is the exotic, make-believe world
of theatre and costume design and the excitement of the growing film
industry. But as the shadow of Fascism falls over Europe and war looms,
their hard-won freedom becomes threatened by ominous echoes from their
parents' past.

'Sometimes as brutal as Goya, often as lyrical and glowing as Monet, as
clear, precise and immaculately constructed as a Canaletto, as vivid and
ablaze with colour and light as Bonnard, *Adieu Volodia* is, indeed,
monumental' DIRK BOGARDE

'Subtle, comic . . . brilliant' THE GUARDIAN

'A powerful and moving story' THE LISTENER

'A tour de force . . . urgency, tension and humour permeate the novel which
pulsates with a vibrancy emanating all too naturally from one who lived
and loved in a France transfixed by Hitler's men' JEWISH CHRONICLE

Joyce Carol Oates
Marya: A Life £3.50

From the author of *Solstice*, this is the most personal, and perhaps the most fascinating, of Joyce Carol Oates's many varied novels. Marya's greatest wish is to blend in with others, but even at high school this seems impossible: too bright, her teachers tell her; singled out, her priest maintains; too sharp for her own good, says the aunt who brings her up. Through university, graduate-school love affairs and career, an outwardly conventional path hides a turmoil of self-doubt and a nature that is sometimes maddening, sometimes pitiable and sometimes heroic.

'A fine, sustained success; bleak as its heroine, vivid as the world she passes through unseeing, taut as the strands of net Marya weaves around herself' BERNARD LEVIN, THE SUNDAY TIMES

'*Marya* is a complex and subtle novel. The author has an exceptional gift for physical description, for establishing place as well as character, so that by the end the reader feels he has experienced not only Marya's life, but a piece of America as well' SELINA HASTINGS, THE DAILY TELEGRAPH

'Joyce Carol Oates has invented more than a character – Marya is someone one knows, a difficult, vulnerable, brilliantly mixed-up mess' OPTIONS

Colleen McCullough
Tim £2.95

Tim was twenty-five. He had the body of a Greek god, but his mind was the mind of a child. Mary was over forty, a cultured career woman living alone. They met by chance in the backwater of a Sydney street. And from that moment a powerful magnetism drew them together. First as friends. Then as much, much more . . .

Tim is a unique love. It stands as the starting point in the career of Colleen McCullough, now the internationally acclaimed author of *The Thorn Birds*, *An Indecent Obsession* and *A Creed for the Third Millenium*. Inspired, moving and vividly real, it is a story that only she could have written.

'Explores unplumbed areas of sensibility with a delightful freshness' THE NEW YORK TIMES

'A sensitive and wholly believable novel which tugs at the heartstrings without waxing sentimental' AUSTRALIAN WOMEN'S WEEKLY

'Accomplished, sensitive and wise . . . a love story with a difference' PUBLISHERS' WEEKLY

Grace Ingoldby
Last Dance With You £2.95

Witty, skilful and sparkling with originality, *Last Dance With You*
generously fulfils the promise of Grace Ingoldby's acclaimed first novel,
Across the Water.

Difficult and impulsive to the bitter end, Richard Francis Fox leaves home
at the age of eighty-two to drown himself in the oily and quite
unspectacular waters off the Isle of Wight. The suicide of this once-
eminent man creates a hideous gap in the lives of his dwindled entourage
left stranded at The Round House in Wiltshire: Joyce, his elderly secretary,
Ralph, who lives on Fox charity in the family cottage; and Peter, his forty-
year-old son, who returns for the funeral and, despite his better instincts,
finds himself staying on.

Last Dance With You describes Peter's year at The Round House following
his father's death – among people who have all seen better days and who
cling with desperate obstinacy to carefully edited memories. Here
conversation has reached the point of inconsequential small talk; here, in
the circular rooms and passageways, the dead apparently hold sway.
Dominant women both dead and alive exacerbate Peter's state of shock
and loneliness until he can only describe himself as 'emotionally
incontinent' or 'technically dead'. Unease is heightened by the arrival of
Kate, his father's young protegée, and Nicola, who eagerly and efficiently
sets herself to tackle the muddle his father has left behind. Shunted out of
the spotlight, Peter struggles to regain his sense of humour and
perspective, to make sense of both his father's life and his own, and to
throw off the black dog of the past.

'Grace Ingoldby's style is sharp and ironic, but she looks at the futility of
the games people play with compassion as well as wit'
DAILY TELEGRAPH

'If Peter learns anything about his father, it's that he went to his death
irascible, opinionated, fully himself. Grace Ingoldby is a shrewd and stylish
analyst of emotion' OBSERVER

'An assured book, strong and sensitive and deeply moving'
COSMOPOLITAN

Elaine Dundy
The Dud Avocado £2.95

'American girls are just like avocados . . . a hard centre with the tender meat all wrapped up in a shiny casing . . . so green, so eternally green . . .'

Into the joyful Paris of the 1950s sweeps Sally Jay Gorce, a young American woman of good family and wayward inclinations. Her girlhood ambitions to be a bullfighter and jazz singer have been frustrated by her uncomprehending parents. But now she is free for the first time in the city of *cabaret* and the *avant garde* to pursue a career on the stage. But all of France is a stage for Sally, the scourge of all Americans-in-Paris, as tough as she is sweet, as formidable as she is alluring . . .

'Scandalous and entertaining . . . both funny and true' THE STANDARD

'A champagne cocktail . . . rich, invigorating, and deceptively simple to the taste . . . One falls for Sally Jay from a great height from the first sentence' OBSERVER

'As delightful and delicate an examination of how it is to be twenty and in love and in Paris as I've ever read' THE SUNDAY TIMES

'The writing, like Sally Jay herself, has high spirits and is laced with astringencies a class and a half above the wise-crack' THE TIMES

Lisa St Aubin de Terán
Black Idol £3.99

On the afternoon of 10 December 1929 the notorious American poet and publisher Harry Crosby borrowed a friend's New York apartment to entertain his mistress. The full story of what happened at the Hotel des Artistes remains a mystery which *Black Idol* explores with extraordinary imaginative power.

Through the voice of Harry's mistress, Josephine Rotch Bigelow, we follow the story of Harry's life and of his violent and obsessional affair with the girl from Back Bay, Boston. Her tempestuous monologue, passionate and bitter by turn, plunges us into the poet's Boston childhood and his horrific experiences during the First World War; it tells of the rebellious and exotic lifestyles which took him from Boston to Paris and the Middle East, and of his literary friendships, as founder of the Black Sun Press, with Hemingway and Hart Crane. Josephine is by no means his first lover. Having read his diaries, she confronts Harry with his countless other obsessive and fantastic affairs.

The setting is the reckless Twenties world of Cole Porter and black silk stockings, opium—Harry's black idol—and orgies, as disturbing as it is compelling. *Black Idol* has the absorbing, exotic richness of Lisa St Aubin de Terán's earlier novels. With its subtle reworking of historical fact it is both unusual and haunting.

All Pan books are available at your local bookshop or newsagent, or can be ordered direct from the publisher. Indicate the number of copies required and fill in the form below.

Send to: **CS Department, Pan Books Ltd., P.O. Box 40,
              Basingstoke, Hants.   RG21 2YT.**

or phone: 0256 469551 (Ansaphone), quoting title, author
              and Credit Card number.

Please enclose a remittance* to the value of the cover price plus: 60p for the first book plus 30p per copy for each additional book ordered to a maximum charge of £2.40 to cover postage and packing.

*Payment may be made in sterling by UK personal cheque, postal order, sterling draft or international money order, made payable to Pan Books Ltd.

Alternatively by Barclaycard/Access:

Card No. | | | | | | | | | | | | | | | | | | |

_____

                    Signature:

Applicable only in the UK and Republic of Ireland.

While every effort is made to keep prices low, it is sometimes necessary to increase prices at short notice. Pan Books reserve the right to show on covers and charge new retail prices which may differ from those advertised in the text or elsewhere.

NAME AND ADDRESS IN BLOCK LETTERS PLEASE:

....

Name ————————————————————————————

Address ———————————————————————————

_____

_____

_____

                                                            3/87